# SCHOOL OF CORRUPTION/SEXUAL REVENGE

## ALSO BY RAY GORDON

*Sex Practice*
*House of Lust*
*Addicted*
*The Uninhibited*
*The Degenerates*
*Red Hot*
*Depravicus*
*Schoolgirl Lust*
*Hot Sheets*
*The Splits*
*Sexual Service*
*Lust Quest*
*Dangerous and Dark Desires*
*Sextro*

# School of Corruption/ Sexual Revenge

RAY GORDON

BLUE MOON BOOKS
NEW YORK

*School of Corruption / Sexual Revenge*

*School of Corruption* copyright © 2002 by Ray Gordon
*Sexual Revenge* copyright © 2003 by Ray Gordon

Published by
Blue Moon Books
An Imprint of Avalon Publishing Group Incorporated
245 West 17th Street, 11th floor
New York, NY 10011-5300

First Blue Moon Books Edition 2004

School of Corruption was originally published in the U.K. in 2002 by
Hodder and Stoughton, a division of Hodder Headline.
Sexual Revenge was originally published in the U.K. in 2003 by Hodder
and Stoughton, a division of Hodder Headline.

All rights reserved. No part of this book may be reproduced or transmitted
in any form without written permission from the publisher, except by
reviewers who may quote brief excerpts in connection with a review.

ISBN 1-56201-436-6

9 8 7 6 5 4 3 2 1

Printed in Canada
Distributed by Publishers Group West

# School of Corruption

# I

Spadger Heath Sixth Form College huddled behind an engineering works amid acres of tower blocks and run-down terraced houses. The nineteen-fifties building, with its cracked windows and peeling paint wasn't what Christina had envisaged, but this was her first job after qualifying as an English teacher and she was determined to make the best of it. A year or two at Spadger Heath and she'd move on, perhaps secure a post at a private school. But now she had her first day to get through.

Standing behind her desk at the front of the class, Christina gazed at the sea of expectant faces. Although she'd excelled herself during her training, nothing could have prepared her for her first day at Spadger Heath. Recalling the advice she'd been given, she leaned on her desk, clutching its sides to steady her trembling hands as her lecturer's words came to mind. *You must remain calm. At least be seen to be strong even if you're falling apart inside. Don't let them get to you. There will be pupils who dislike you, and pupils you despise. Come across as friendly, but with an air of authority.*

'Good morning,' she said, her mouth dry, her voice croaky. 'I'm Christina Shaw, your new English teacher.'

'Are you sure?' a lad called from the back of the class.

'I'm positive,' she chuckled amid a roar of laughter. 'And who might you be?'

'I might be anyone,' he replied.

'His name's David Brown,' a petite blonde called.

'Obviously it's going to take me a while to get to know your names,' Christina said, sitting at her desk as her trembling legs sagged beneath her. 'I'd like you to take some paper and write your names down. Place them on your desks so that I can see them from here and I'll do my best to get to know you all before the day's out.'

*So far so good*, Christina thought, glancing at her watch. It was going to be a long day, but she felt positive, if a bit panicky. Watching the teenagers scribbling at their desks, she was looking forward to the evening. Her flatmate, Alison, had suggested that they find a local pub and celebrate Christina's first day at Spadger Heath College. Alison had come to London to find work and had bumped into Christina at a letting agency. The girls had got on well and had decided to share the only property the agency had within their price range. It was a small two-bedroom flat above a Chinese takeaway, but it had been recently decorated and was clean.

'OK.' Christina smiled, glancing at the sheets of paper propped up on her pupils' desks. 'Let's start with you, Carole,' she said, gazing at a dark-haired girl at the front of the class. 'Tell me a little about yourself.'

'I'm seventeen, I hate school, and I want to be a model,' the girl replied morosely.

'She's a lesbian,' a boy guffawed.

'Fuck off, Smith,' the girl returned.

'Er . . . You want to be a model?' Christina cut in, trying to show an interest.

'Me dad wants me to work in the box factory with me mum,' she sighed. 'But I want to get out of this dump and be a model. I know I can do it.'

'I'm sure you can. OK, Jerry, tell me about yourself,' Christina said, smiling at the boy next to Carole.

'Ain't nothin' to tell,' he murmured.

'Oh, come on. What are your interests?'

'Ain't got none.'

'All right, we'll come back to you in a minute. Brian, you're next.'

'I want to be a pimp,' the boy told Christina. 'It's good money, a good life.'

'It's also illegal, Brian.'

'Everything he does is illegal,' Carole giggled.

'Yeah, but I've got money. You work for me, and you'll have money.'

'Yeah, go on, Caz,' David Brown laughed from the back of the class. 'Work for Brian as a prostitute. You might as well, seeing as you're a whore anyway.'

'That'll do, David,' Christina broke in.

'She *is* a whore,' he persisted. 'Everyone's fucked her.'

'Shut your fucking mouth, Brown,' Carole yelled.

'I'll bet Jones hasn't fucked her,' a ginger-haired lad chortled. 'He prefers blokes' arseholes.'

'Let's move on,' Christina said firmly, thinking it best to ignore the expletives for a while.

'Have you got a fella, Mrs?' Brown asked.

'Er . . . no, not at the moment,' she replied. 'So, who's next? John Whiting. Tell me about yourself.'

'I'm into Trance music, I work in a pub . . .'

'You work in a pub?' Christina breathed surprisedly, her blue eyes narrowing as she frowned.

'Yeah, the Steampacket – down by the station.'

'And 'e don't give us no free drinks,' someone complained.

'I'm going to the dentist,' Brown announced, leaving his desk and walking to the door.

'Do you have an appointment . . .' Christina began as he left the classroom and closed the door.

'He's going to meet Delainy,' a girl called out.

'Who's Delainy?'

'Keep your mouth shut, Burrows,' a boy hissed.

'It might be best if you write about yourselves,' Christina said, glancing at her watch again. 'Take your time, and write as much as you can about your likes and dislikes, your interests and aspirations.'

'Our what?' someone asked.

'Your dreams, your ambitions. Leave your papers on my desk before you go to break.'

Christina made it through to the first break and flopped into an old armchair in the empty staffroom. She'd not yet exerted her authority over the students, she reflected. The foul language, the lewd comments . . . It was best to allow the teenagers some leeway. Her plan was to mould them over time. After all, she was the newcomer and she would have to be accepted by her students before she could begin to lay down the law. Mentally exhausted, she focused her thoughts on the evening. The prospect of going out for a drink with Alison would get her through the day.

'Carter,' a man in his mid-forties said, walking into the room and sitting next to Christina. 'Geography.'

'Pleased to meet you.' Christina smiled, shaking his hand. 'Er . . . Christina Shaw, English.'

'Yes, I know. So, how's it going?'

'Not too bad. I'm trying to get to know the students before I . . .'

'You'll never get to know the little bastards,' he

laughed, sitting down beside her. 'You don't *want* to get to know them.'

'They *are* people,' Christina said. 'No matter what sort of upbringing they've had, they are people who deserve a chance to—'

'How old are you?'

'Twenty-four.'

'Fresh out of training, keen, eager . . . I know the type. They're little shits, Christina. No-hopers, losers, scum.'

'I'll form my own opinion once I get to know them a little better,' she replied, surprised by his attitude.

'I'm sure you will. That's Rogers,' he said as a tall, thin man wandered into the staffroom. 'Science.'

'Oh, right.'

'He's a psychological mess. The little shits broke him down.'

'Why does he stay?'

'What else can he do? There's no other work around here.'

'He could go to another school.'

'He'd never get a job at another school. He's a ruined man. If you want my advice, get out of here now. I'm not being sexist, but a young woman like you doesn't stand a chance in hell in a dump like this.'

'I'm determined to give it my best,' Christina said. 'These kids deserve—'

'Kids?' he laughed. 'They became adults years ago. They're streetwise, and you'll never change them. I can tell you that at least one girl in your class is on the game, another makes blue movies, a group of lads . . .'

'If I could get to know them, understand them . . .'

'Understand pond life? Get out of here while you can.'

Returning to the classroom, Christina gazed at the

words scrawled on the blackboard. 'Do you suck cock and swallow spunk?' she read, shaking her head as she grabbed the rubber. Cleaning the board, she knew that they were going to do their best to grind her down, but she wasn't going to allow that to happen. Turning, she looked at the sheets of paper on her desk. *They have hopes and dreams*, she mused, reading one girl's neat handwriting. *I want to get out of this area and make something of myself.*

Hearing a noise coming from the stockroom, Christina listened at the door. Someone was in there, she knew as she turned the handle and inched the door open. A tall, good-looking lad was going through some papers, searching the shelves for something. Wishing she'd taken the headmaster's advice and kept the stockroom locked, she found that she couldn't recall the lad's name.

'What are you doing?' she asked, entering the room.

'Nothing,' he answered, grinning. 'What are *you* doing?'

'You shouldn't be in here. What's your name?'

'Doogan, Barry Doogan.'

'OK, Barry, I think you'd better put those papers down and leave.'

'You're not bad-looking,' he said, stroking her long blonde hair. 'Fancy coming out for a drink sometime?'

'Barry, please put those papers . . .'

'You've got a good body on you. Nice curves, nice tits.'

'That's enough, Barry,' she said firmly, backing off towards the door as she realized that she could be in danger.

'What's the matter? I'll bet you like a bit of rough. Do you think I'm a bit of rough?'

'Do you want me to get the headmaster? Unless you leave here now—'

'You asked us to tell you about ourselves. Now you tell me about yourself.'

'I will, once you leave the stockroom.'

'Don't tell me what to do, Mrs,' he said, walking past her and closing the door. 'Experienced, are you? The young tarts don't know what they're doing, but I'll bet you know exactly what to do.'

Backing against the wall as he reached out and squeezed the firm mounds of her breasts through her blouse, Christina tried to push him away. He was strong, his large hands clutching her wrists as he pushed his crotch hard against her lower stomach, sandwiching her between his obvious erection and the wall. Cold fear gripping her, unable to speak, she tried to kick out but couldn't move.

'I like you,' he said, his face close to hers. 'I'll bet you're a good fuck. I'll tell you what I'll do. I run things around here, ask anyone. You keep me happy, and I'll make sure that—'

'Get off me!' she finally screamed.

'I like a fighter,' he laughed, releasing her.

'I'll report this to—'

'You do that, and I'll make your life a misery. You said you hadn't got a bloke, a man friend. You must miss a length of cock. I'll bet you're gagging for it. Think about it, Mrs. I run things around here, remember that.'

As Doogan left the room, Christina slid down the wall and sat on the floor. Her heart racing, her hands trembling, she'd not expected anything like this. The expletives, the lewd comments . . . She could have dealt with that. But not . . . Finally hauling herself up and wiping her tear-stained cheeks, she left the stockroom and grabbed her bag from the locked drawer of her desk.

Taking the papers from her desk, she stuffed them into her bag, walked briskly along the corridor and fled the building. She'd failed, she knew as made her way through the narrow streets to her flat. Perhaps Carter had been right. They were little shits, bastards, scum.

Home at last, Christina wished that Alison was there. She was out job-hunting, had three interviews to attend and probably wouldn't be back until late afternoon. Filling the kettle for coffee, her breathing slowing as she calmed down, she took a mug from the cupboard. She couldn't go back to the college, she knew. She'd find another job, ask Alison what was on offer locally – if anything. As a last resort, she could go back to her parents' house in Hertfordshire.

Her father had wanted her to join the family firm of accountants, but Christina had set her heart on teaching. He'd said that she wouldn't last five minutes in London, which had fired her determination to make a go of it. He was right, she reflected. Not even managing to get through the morning, she had failed miserably. Pouring her coffee, she sat at the kitchen table and hung her head.

Recalling the young man's words, she sighed. *You must miss a length of cock. I'll bet you're gagging for it.* Her one and only boyfriend worked for her father. He was an up-and-coming accountant from a good family, the sort of man her father would have liked Christina to marry. Life could have been easy, she mused. Working for her father, a company car, good money . . . Had she agreed to marry Charles, she'd have lived the good life. Holidays abroad, money . . .

'Fuck Charles,' she breathed, surprised by her choice of words. With good looks and a brilliant future ahead of him, Charles would make a fine husband for someone.

But not for Christina. He was haughty, staid. Never doing anything on the spur of the moment, his idea of fun was a picnic down by the river. Christina would have enjoyed the picnics, but Charles had always invited his friends along. They'd talk shop and drink too much wine and Christina would have to drive them home.

Christina recalled their lovemaking. The act was cold, wooden, performed in silence. Charles would breathe deeply, grunt and pump his sperm into her vagina before rolling off her naked body and going to sleep. Did she miss a length of cock, as Barry had crudely put it? Finishing her coffee, she pushed all thoughts of Charles out of her mind and pulled the papers from her bag. Some of the pupils' work was appalling: the spelling was atrocious and the grammar non-existent.

'I'm sixteen and pregnant,' she read. There was no name on the paper. 'I don't know who the father is.' Taking another paper, she sighed. 'I want to learn to play the piano but we haven't got any money.' Placing the papers on the table, Christina wandered though the hall into the lounge and gazed out of the window at the busy street. A scruffy man was sitting on the pavement opposite, drinking white cider from a bottle. *No-hopers, losers, scum.*

'What are you doing here?' Alison asked as she breezed into the room and tossed her long black hair over her shoulder.

'I . . . I have a free period,' Christina said, smiling.

'Guess what? I've got a job,' the other girl trilled.

'Oh, that *is* good news. Tell me about it.'

'Assistant to the receptionist at a local doctor's surgery. The receptionist is leaving in a couple of months and, hopefully, I'll take her place.'

'I'm pleased for you, Alison,' Christina said warmly.

'So, how's *your* day been so far? Are you all right? You're not your usual bubbly self.'

'I've had a hard morning,' Christina confessed. 'The students are difficult, to say the least.'

'But you expected that.'

'I didn't expect the girls to tell the boys to fuck off.'

'This is London, Christina, a run-down part of London. You must have realized that . . .'

'One boy got me in the stockroom. Boy? What am I saying? He's a six-foot young adult. He pushed himself against me, squeezed my breasts and . . .'

'God. What did you do?'

'What *could* I do?'

'Go to the headmaster.'

'And have that yob make my life a misery? I walked out.'

'What? You can't do that.'

'I've done it.'

'Go back, Christina. For God's sake, are you going to allow one boy to destroy your career?'

'I don't know.'

'Go back. You know what'll happen if you don't.'

'I'll get the sack.'

'Yes, but worse than that. You father will laugh at you.'

Alison was right, she knew. If she walked out on her first day, her father would laugh at her and she'd never get another teaching job. Congratulating Alison on her job, she grabbed her bag and walked back to the college. No, she wasn't going to allow one boy to destroy her career. Boy? That was a joke. They were all adults. Taking a deep breath, Christina walked through the gates, half expecting the headmaster to be waiting for her. Funnily enough, no one had missed her, and she walked into the classroom with her head held high.

'OK,' she shouted above the bedlam. 'Settle down, please.' Glancing at the blackboard, she found herself gazing at a colour picture of an erect penis rising above a huge scrotum. 'The erect penis,' she said loudly. A hush fell over the room as dozens of eyes gazed at her expectantly. 'I don't know who drew this, but it's not bad. Presumably, these white squiggles represent the sperm issuing from the . . . Can anyone tell me the correct name for this part?' she asked, pointing to the neatly coloured purple glans.

'That's the knob,' a boy laughed.

'I said the *correct* name. Come on, surely someone knows?'

'Purple-headed warrior,' another boy called out.

'It's the glans,' she enlightened them, writing the word on the board. 'The plural, anyone?'

'Glanses?' a girl suggested.

'Glandes,' Christina corrected her, writing the word on the board. 'As you're all so interested in the penis, I wonder whether anyone can tell me where the seminal fluid is produced in the body? I'm not talking about the sperm, but the liquid containing the sperm.'

'Bollocks,' a lad chuckled.

'No, Jackson, you're wrong.'

'He ain't,' another boy called. 'Spunk comes from your bollocks.'

'Sperm is produced in the testicles. The whitish liquid is produced in the prostate gland. It seems that the boys know nothing about their own bodies,' she smiled.

'We know about girls' cunts,' someone yelled out, laughing coarsely.

'Do you? Do you really, Davis?'

'I never said it,' he complained.

'Yes, you did. OK, let's see just how much you know about girls. Where and what is the hymen?'

'Well . . . It's, er . . .'

'I know,' a lad said eagerly, raising his hand.

'I'm asking Davis. All right, here's another one for you, Davis. In the female, what is the prepuce?'

'I . . . I dunno,' he murmured.

'For someone who professes to know all about the female pudenda, you appear to know nothing at all.'

'Yes, I do,' he retorted. 'Just because I don't know your fancy words . . .'

'All right, I'll keep it simple. You've heard of the cervix?'

'Yeah, I have,' he replied triumphantly. 'It's where birds get cancer.'

'That's right, Davis, well done. So, where is the cervix?'

'Well, in tits. Cervix cancer in breasts and that.'

'The cervix, Davis, is located at the far end of the vaginal canal. I suggest that you read up on female anatomy before going out with girls. Right, let's move on. I noticed some books on punctuation in the stockroom,' she said, moving to the door. 'I'll pass them round and we'll begin with the basics.'

In the stockroom, Christina felt rather pleased with herself as she sorted through the pile of books. She'd certainly shot Davis down in flames, and very much doubted that he'd give her any more trouble. Barry Doogan had kept quiet, she reflected, making a mental note to thank Alison for her support and encouragement. Once she'd asserted her authority, shown that she was in charge, she was sure that the students would settle down and she could get somewhere.

'Oh, you can pass these round,' she said as Barry walked into the stockroom.

'You made Davis look like a prat,' he whispered angrily, his dark eyes staring hard at her.

'If Davis looked like a prat, then it was his own doing,' she responded.

'I've already told you, Mrs. *I* run things around here.'

'No, Barry, you don't. You might run things out of school but, in class, I—'

'Think you're clever with your big words, don't you?'

'Big words?'

'This pudenda thing or whatever it is. Round here, cocks are cocks and cunts are cunts, OK?'

'Do you know where the word "cunt" originates?' she asked.

'No, and I don't care. But I do know that you've got a cunt. And I'd like to see it.'

'Get back to your desk,' Christina hissed through gritted teeth.

'Would you like this shoved up your cunt?' Barry sniggered, unzipping his trousers and pulling his flaccid penis out. 'You make prats out of my mates, and I'll shove this down your throat.'

'Put that pathetic thing away,' she murmured.

'OK, teacher, let's go back to class. I'll show you who how I can fuck things up for you.'

As he left the room, Christina grabbed the pile of books and tried to compose herself. She knew that she mustn't appear ruffled, she mustn't allow them to get to her. Barry Doogan was trouble, she reflected. The ringleader, he was going to have to be tamed before she could make any progress with the others. He certainly had a big penis, she found herself thinking as she returned to the classroom and dumped the books on Carole's desk. Even flaccid, the thing was huge. Asking Carole to pass the books round, she did her best not to catch Barry's gaze. Cleaning the blackboard, her breathing slowing, she finally turned and faced the class.

'OK,' she said. 'Open the books at the section headed "commas", please. You'll see from the first example how, when used incorrectly, commas completely change the meaning of the sentence. John was sick, and tired of working.'

'Aren't we all,' Barry laughed.

'Now look at the second sentence. John was sick and tired of working. You'll notice that the comma in the first sentence—'

'This is kids' stuff,' a pretty auburn-haired girl complained. 'We did this in junior school.'

'Er . . . Janice,' Christina said, reading the girl's name. 'I'm trying to establish how much you've learned. I realize that this will be kids' stuff to some of you, but please bear with me.'

'I'd rather go back to talking about cunts,' Barry chortled, the class roaring with laughter as he lit a cigarette.

'Please don't smoke in the classroom,' Christina snapped.

'Tight, hot, wet cunts oozing with spunk.'

'I shall go to the headmaster and have you removed from my class,' she said, leaving the room and slamming the door shut.

Making her way to the headmaster's study, Christina knew that Barry Doogan had to be dealt with if she was going to make any progress. *Don't let them get to you. There will be pupils who dislike you, and pupils you despise.* Again recalling her lecturer's words, she was determined not to be beaten by one student.

'Ah, Miss Shaw,' the headmaster murmured as she knocked and entered. 'I was about to send for you.'

'Oh?' she said, closing the door.

'I've had a complaint. Barry Doogan came to see me earlier.'

'A complaint? But I've come to see you about *him*, Mr Wright. He's been—'

'This is a serious matter, Miss Shaw. Please, sit down.'

'Barry Doogan is . . .' she began, sitting opposite the balding man.

'Miss Shaw, I realize that this is your first day at Spadger Heath and that things can't be easy for you. Doogan said that you grabbed him in the stockroom.'

'*I* grabbed *him*?' she gasped.

'His crotch, Miss Shaw.'

'But he—'

'Whether you grabbed him or not isn't the issue. The point is that a complaint has been made against a member of my staff.'

'So the fact that he pulled his penis out in the stockroom is neither here nor there?'

'I know Doogan of old, Miss Shaw. I know his tricks. And I don't believe for one minute that you did anything of the sort. But do be aware that complaints of this nature can be very dangerous, very damaging to the college.'

'So what do you suggest I do the next time he shows me his penis?'

'Never get yourself into a situation where you are alone with a student. I would have thought that was obvious.'

'He was going through papers in the stockroom during break.'

'Why wasn't the stockroom locked, Miss Shaw?'

'Well, I . . .'

'You'd better get back to your class.'

Leaving the study, Christina couldn't believe the man's attitude. Doogan had pressed himself against her, pulled his penis out, and had then made a complaint about her? Returning to her class, she felt anger welling from the pit of her stomach as Doogan folded his arms, reclining in his chair and grinning triumphantly. This was war, she thought, doing her best not to show her rage. Ordering the class to read up on the use of commas, she called Doogan to the front of the class. Slouching, he mooched up to her desk and grinned.

'I want a word with you,' she said, walking into the stockroom.

'Yeah?' he chuckled, following her and closing the door. 'Old man Wright give you a bollocking, then?'

'You seem to think that you're some kind of bigwig,' she said, looking him up and down. 'You're a silly little schoolboy, Doogan.'

'You want to watch your mouth, Mrs,' he murmured, unzipping his trousers and taking his penis out. 'As I said, I'll shove this down your throat.'

'Look at it,' she laughed, gazing at his flaccid penis. 'Is that it? Is that the best you can do?'

'I've never had any complaints.'

'This is supposed to shock me, is it? You pull your cock out and think that I'll faint?'

'As I said, you watch your mouth or I'll—'

'Shove it down my throat? I doubt that it would reach the back of my mouth, let alone—'

'Don't push your luck, teacher,' he hissed, thrusting his hand up her skirt and clutching the swell of her panties.

Christina knew that she'd pushed her luck too far as he yanked her panties to one side and massaged the swell of her fleshy pussy lips. This was tantamount to rape, but no one would believe her story. The headmaster would probably sack her if she ran to him crying rape. After all, he had the reputation of the college to think about. *Some reputation*, she reflected, Doogan's crude words about her wet cunt battering her racked mind. She knew that she had to put a stop to Doogan or leave her job. Pushing him away, she forced a laugh as she again looked down at his flaccid penis.

'So this is your manhood?' she asked sarcastically, taking his fleshy shaft in her hand. 'Come on, then. Stiffen up and show me how big a man you really are.'

'What are you doing?' he asked, confusion reflected in his dark eyes as she ran her hand up and down his inflating shaft.

'You mean to say that a girl's never done this to you?' she asked, laughing softly. 'The big man, Barry Doogan, is a virgin?'

'No, no, I meant . . .'

'Come on, Barry, get it out of your system,' she breathed, wanking his solid cock faster. 'Come on, shoot your sperm.'

Breathing deeply, his legs sagging, Doogan gasped as his sperm shot from his throbbing knob. Christina moved to one wide, aiming his spunk away from her skirt as the white liquid splattered over the tiled floor.

She felt her stomach somersault as she wanked his solid shaft, gazing at the sheer size of his erection as she brought out his spunk and drained his full balls. The creamy liquid running down her hand, her clitoris swelling as she thought of his rock-hard shaft thrusting deep into the tight sheath of her vagina, she finally let go of his penis and wiped her hand on the side of a cardboard box.

'I hope that will shut you up for a while,' she said, leaving the young man shuddering in the aftermath of his orgasm as she returned to her class. Sitting at her desk, her gaze darting between her students as they stared at her, she wished that she'd never taken Doogan into the stockroom. It had been a grave mistake, she knew. She was sure that he wouldn't go running to the headmaster, but he would probably be back for another hand job. If word got out . . . She tried not to think of the consequences as she watched him returning to his desk, a huge grin on his face.

The rest of the day passed pretty much without incident, and Christina was pleased to get home. Keeping her guilty secret from Alison, she cooked a stir-fry for dinner and they broke open a bottle of red wine. Alison was full of life, chatting about her new job, but Christina was quiet and withdrawn. Doogan would probably tell his friends about what had happened in the stockroom. Christina could only hope that they wouldn't believe him, thinking that he was mouthing off to look big in front of his mates.

'You didn't tell me what you did about that lad in the stockroom,' Alison said as she washed up the dinner plates.

'Barry Doogan,' Christina murmured. 'I . . . I put him straight. Told him that there'd be trouble unless he behaved himself.'

'Good for you. Shall we find a local pub, then?'
'Yes,' Christina replied abstractedly.
'There's one down the road. I saw it today when I was job-hunting. It's The Steampacket, by the station. They have live music and—'
'Let's find somewhere quiet,' Christina broke in. 'Somewhere to sit quietly and chat.'
'Whatever. There's a pub round the corner at the end of the road. The Hen and Chicken or something. It looked quiet enough when I passed it earlier.'
'That'll do,' Christina said and smiled. 'It's been a long day, a noisy day. I need to sit quietly and relax.'
'Right, I'll get changed and then we'll go.'
Christina wandered into the lounge as Alison went to her room to change. Riddled with guilt as she pictured Doogan's rock-hard penis in her hand, his sperm shooting from his throbbing knob and splattering the tiled floor, she wondered what day two at Spadger Heath College would bring. Doogan would want his cock appeased again, she was sure. *Come across as friendly, but with an air of authority*, she mused, recalling again her lecturer's words. *Intimate, but with an air of authority?* she speculated.
'Ready?' Alison asked, appearing in the lounge doorway wearing a white blouse and red miniskirt.
'Ready,' Christina answered cheerfully, taking her bag from the sofa.
'I've been looking forward to this all day,' the dark-haired girl said as they left the flat and walked down the busy road. 'I've got a job and you got through your first day. Now we can relax and down a few vodkas.'
Entering the pub, Christina glanced at the half-dozen customers dotted around the bar. Much to her relief,

none of her students were there. The pub was traditional – no music, no entertainment. Not the sort of place where youngsters would gather. Thinking that the pub would become her regular haunt, Christina ordered the drinks and sat on a bar stool. Alison began chatting about London, hoping she'd meet a young man and fall in love. That was the last thing Christina wanted. Away from her parents, she was looking forward to her freedom, doing what she wanted when she wanted without having to answer to anyone.

'I haven't had sex for months,' Alison giggled as the vodka began to take effect. 'I haven't even laid *eyes* on a dick, let alone my hands.'

'Neither have I,' Christina said, forcing a smile as she again recalled Doogan's solid penis in her grip.

'Met anyone you fancy at the college?'

'No, no. They're too old for me.'

'The teachers might be too old but what about the students?'

'The students?'

'They're – what – seventeen, eighteen?'

'Yes, they are, but . . .'

'We're in our early twenties, so they're not *that* much younger than us. Some of the girls I've seen look at least twenty. What are the fellas like?'

'Alison, I've not looked at them in that way. They're my students.'

'I know, but one of them must have caught your eye. Imagine having an affair with a student. God, that's the sort of thing you read about in the papers.'

'Yes, well . . . No one's going to read about *me* in the papers.'

'Oh, I forgot to tell you. A man called for you. Charles.'

'Oh, God. I'll bet my father gave him the number. What did he want?'

'He wants you to call him.'

'Did he say what about?'

'Nope. Who is he?'

'My ex-boyfriend. I'll ring him later.'

'He sounded very posh.'

'He *is* very posh. That's the trouble with him, among other things.'

'He wouldn't fit in around here, then?'

'No way. Let's have another drink.'

'My turn.' Alison smiled, opening her bag. 'Same again?'

'Please.'

Wandering over to a table, Christina sat down and gazed out of the window. Charles wouldn't fit in at all, she thought. He'd be horrified if he knew that Christina was sitting in a smoke-filled pub, knocking back vodka. And if he discovered that she'd wanked a student to orgasm in the stockroom . . . But Charles was no longer part of her life. At least, he wasn't supposed to be.

'Here's to day two at your job,' Alison beamed, placing Christina's drink on the table and sitting down. 'Cheers.'

'Cheers.' Christina grinned back at her flatmate and raised her glass.

'And let's hope that Doogan or whatever his name is leaves you alone now that you've put him in his place.'

'Yes, let's hope.'

# 2

Christina had taken a shower and had had her breakfast by seven-thirty. Wandering around the flat, feeling a little panicky, she tried to plan her day. Now that Doogan was under control, she might be able to assess the students and discover the extent of their education. *If* Doogan was under control. Wondering whether to divide the students into groups, dependent on their ability, she looked up as Alison peered round the lounge door.

'Morning, Alison,' she greeted her flatmate. 'You're bright and early.'

'I don't start work until next week but I don't want to slip into the habit of getting up late,' the other girl said. 'You've finished in the bathroom?'

'Yes, it's all yours.'

'A coffee wouldn't go amiss.'

'All right. You take a shower and I'll make you a cup of coffee.'

Alison was OK, Christina thought happily as she filled the kettle. Despite initial concerns, the flat-share was working out extremely well. Pouring the coffee, Christina glanced at the kitchen clock. She didn't have to leave for another hour and so she decided to ring her mother. She should have phoned the previous evening but by the time she'd got home it had been too late. Praying that her mother wouldn't talk about Charles, she grabbed the wall phone and punched in the number. The woman was pleased to hear from her, asking why she'd not rung before and how her first day had been.

'I couldn't ring last night,' Christina said apologetically. 'But my first day went very well.'

'What are the children like?' she asked.

'Children?' Christina laughed. 'Mother, they're young adults.'

'Of course, it's a sixth-form college, isn't it? Will you be coming home at the weekend?'

'If I can. I'll have to see how things go.'

'Have you phoned Charles yet?'

'No, no, I haven't,' Christina sighed, raising her eyebrows as Alison wandered into the kitchen naked.

'You should have called him, Christina.'

'Yes, I . . . Why, mother? Why should I have called Charles?'

'Because he'd like to know how you're getting on. He must miss you terribly.'

'We've split up, mother. We're no longer . . .'

'It's such a shame, Christina. Your father was hoping that you'd—'

'Look, I have to go,' Christina said, gazing at the firm mounds of Alison's breasts, her sex crack clearly visible through her sparse pubic curls. 'I'll call you this evening.'

'All right, dear. Do call Charles.'

'Yes, yes – I will.'

Hanging up, Christina tried to avert her gaze as Alison sipped her coffee. The girl seemed oblivious to her own nakedness, wandering around the kitchen displaying everything she had. She was extremely attractive, Christina observed, eyeing the violin curves of Alison's young body. She'd never seen another girl naked before, and began to realize what a sheltered life she'd led. Trying not to look as if she was staring, she eyed Alison's long black hair cascading over her shoulders, the brown teats of her young breasts pointing to the ceiling . . . Gazing out of the window, Christina dragged her thoughts away from the girl's beauty and remarked on the hot weather as the sun shone in a clear blue sky.

'I don't know what I'm going to do today,' Alison said. 'It's a shame we haven't got a garden. I could have sunbathed, got myself a nice tan.'

'You've already got a tan,' Christina murmured, turning and staring at the girl's naked body again.

'I went to Cyprus a few months ago. The trouble is, the tan's wearing off.'

'Aren't you going to put something on?' Christina asked, her gaze riveted on the girl's elongated nipples rising alluringly from the dark discs of her areolae.

'Oh, sorry . . . I'm used to wandering around like this. If it's a problem—'

'No, no – I don't mind.'

'There was a garden at my last flat. It was completely private, no one overlooking the patio or the lawn. I spent most of my time in a bikini – or naked.'

'It would be nice to have a garden,' Christina said, finishing her coffee. 'That's one thing I miss about my parents' house. Still, you never know. We might move on to better things once we've got some money coming in.'

'God knows what sort of rent they'd want for a flat with a garden,' Alison sighed. 'Right, I'm going to get dressed. I might go for a walk later, get to know the area.'

'I'll leave you to get on,' Christina said, glancing at the

other girl's full sex lips. 'I know it's rather early, but I think I'll go to the college. I'll see you this evening.'

'OK. I hope you have a good day.'

'Fingers crossed.'

'Don't let that Doogan lad get to you.'

'No, I won't. I'll see you later.'

Grabbing her bag, Christina left the flat and walked the short distance to the college. What plans had Doogan in mind? she wondered, musing on what the day might bring. Bringing out his sperm had certainly quietened him down, but it was hardly the way for a teacher to behave. Doogan would want more, she knew as she passed through the gates of the college. He'd try to get her into the stockroom, haul his solid penis out and . . . She dared not take her involvement with the lad any further. Wanking him had been a grave mistake, so she intended to put the incident behind her and move on.

Dumping her bag on her desk, she looked around the deserted classroom. She could be happy at Spadger Heath, she reflected. If only she could settle in and establish herself, gain a little respect from the students, she'd enjoy the work. Smiling, she realized that the day would come when she'd look back on her time at Spadger Heath College and laugh. The months passed so quickly, she mused. Before she knew it, she'd have been at the college for a year, two years . . . Things were going to work out well, she concluded. The flat was all right for the time being, she got on well with Alison . . .

'You're an early bird,' Carter chuckled as he appeared in the doorway. 'You must be keen.'

'I am,' Christina replied. 'My first day went well, and I'm looking forward to the challenges today brings.'

'Challenges?' he snorted. 'That's one way to put it. Any trouble from Brown or Doogan yet?'

'Brown disappeared yesterday morning and Doogan . . . well, he's OK.'

'Doogan's OK?' Caster laughed disbelievingly. 'If he hasn't started on you yet . . . Christ, he must have taken a shine to you.'

'We get on,' she said softly.

'You must have a magic touch.'

'A magic touch,' she echoed, recalling her hand running up and down the solid shaft of Doogan's penis. 'Maybe I have.'

'You'll have to let me in on your secret. Well, I'd best prepare for the arrival of the scum. See you at break.'

*A magic touch?* she mused, recalling again wanking Doogan's huge cock to orgasm, his sperm running over her hand, splattering on the floor. *If Carter knew*, she reflected fearfully, imagining her name splashed across the front pages of the Sunday tabloids. But no one would ever discover her sordid secret, she thought. Even if Doogan took it upon himself to spread the dirty word, no one would believe him. His friends would laugh at him if he said that the teacher had wanked him. They'd think that he was trying to show off.

Walking into the stockroom, Christina sorted through the books, trying to bring some semblance of order to the mess. The stockroom was a shambles, with boxes full of old newspapers and other rubbish lining the shelves. Reckoning that the previous teacher had had no interest in the job, she placed the books into neat piles and began to stack the boxes of rubbish on the floor.

'Ah, Little Miss Hand Job,' Brown chortled, leaning in the doorway.

'Good morning, David.' Christina smiled back, dreading to think what he meant.

'I hear you're pretty good with your hands,' he said, walking into the room.

'With my hands?' she murmured, realizing that Doogan had opened his mouth. 'What *are* you talking about?'

'Baz Doogan. You tossed him off in here.'

'I did *what*?' she gasped, forcing a laugh. 'He's been dreaming.'

'That's what he reckons.'

'He's having you on, David. Would you mind taking those boxes out, please?'

'He told me that you—'

'David, I don't know what Barry has been telling you. And I don't think I want to know.'

'Oh, come on. Give me a quicky, like you did . . .'

'I'm sorry, David, but I have no idea what you're talking about. I suggest you go back to Barry and ask him—'

'He told me what you did to him. Baz doesn't lie.'

'I'm not saying that he's lying. He's joking, David, winding you up.'

'Ah, Miss Shaw,' the headmaster said gruffly. 'Brown, what are you up to? What are you doing in here?'

'Taking these out,' the youth mumbled, grabbing the boxes from the floor and leaving the room.

'Miss Shaw, there have been some changes to the timetable. There's a copy for you.'

'Oh, thank you,' she said, smiling and taking the papers.

'How are you getting on?'

'Fine, fine. I'm just sorting out . . .'

'As I said yesterday, don't put yourself in a position where you're alone with a male student.'

'No, I was—'

'And keep this room locked when you're not around.'

Wandering into the classroom as the man left, Christina sighed. He was hardly the sort of headmaster one could approach, she reflected. Carter would have made a better head than Mr Wright. At least his timely entrance had saved her from Brown's sexual demands. Wondering what Doogan had said as Brown walked towards her, she knew that she was going to have to nip this in the bud. First Doogan, then Brown, then . . . This was going to have to stop, and stop now.

'I want what you gave Baz,' Brown said.

'David, I've already told you that I . . .'

'OK, if that's the way you want it. Don't expect things to be quiet in class today.'

'Oh, I see,' she laughed. '*Now* I get the picture.'

'Good. In that case . . .'

'You're a virgin, too?'

'*What?*' he breathed, his dark eyes frowning. 'I'm not a bloody—'

'Look, we'll talk about this later. The others will be here at any minute.'

'Talk about what?'

'Your virginity, David.'

'No, you don't understand.'

'I understand only too well. We'll have a chat during break.'

As the students began filing into the room, Brown mooched towards his desk and sat down. Christina knew that she had one hell of a problem on her hands. She should never have appeased Doogan's lusting penis, but she couldn't turn the clock back. What was done was done.

Strangely, Brown didn't disrupt the lesson as he'd threatened. Christina put it down to his confusion. He was probably waiting for the outcome of their forthcoming chat during break before carrying out his threat to disrupt the class. What Christina was going to say to him, she had no idea. Doogan was a fool, she reflected. To open his mouth like . . . One thing was for sure. He'd ruined his chances of any further sexual contact with her. Would she have appeased his cock again had he not blabbed to Brown? Christina dreaded to think.

Barry Doogan didn't turn up for class, which Christina thought was probably a blessing. The morning going fairly well with only a few minor disruptions and she thought that she might be winning. Carole had taken an interest in the lesson, much to Christina's surprise, and Davis hadn't dared to comment on penises or vaginas. As the students left the classroom for break, Christina kept her eye on Brown. He was hovering by his desk, obviously waiting until the others had gone before making a move.

'So,' he said, walking up to Christina's desk. 'What's this chat about?'

'I would have thought that you'd have a girlfriend,' Christina said.

'I've had a few,' he responded.

'So why do you want me?'

'I don't want you. What I said was that I want you to give me what you gave Baz.'

'Barry and I had a long chat. He was worried about girls and . . . I don't know what he told you, David.'

'He said that you'd tossed him off.'

'He's winding you up, like I said. We talked about relationships. He has a problem, which I'm not prepared to tell you about.'

'Baz has got a problem?' he echoed, puzzlement mirrored in his wide eyes.

'What's *your* problem, David?'

'I haven't got any problems.'

'Then why do you want me to masturbate you?'

'I . . . well, because . . . Why the hell do you think?'

'I really don't know. Unless you want me to teach you, that is.'

'Look, don't mess me about. You wanked Baz. He told me in secret.'

'In confidence.'

'What?'

'Go on, David.'

'I want the same. If you don't, then I'll tell everyone what Baz told me.'

Biting her lip, Christina wasn't sure what to do. She'd already made the mistake of wanking Barry to orgasm. To appease David's cock by bringing out his sperm wasn't going to help the situation. If anything, wanking another student would only make matters worse. Or would it? Gazing into the lad's dark eyes as she pondered on her next move, she felt her stomach somersault, her clitoris inflate. He *was* good-looking, she mused, realizing that she was setting out on a dangerous road as she glanced down at the crotch of his tight trousers. Recalling Doogan's words about a bit of rough and missing a length of cock, she realized that her arousal was soaring.

Having spent too long with Charles, she felt that she needed to catch up, to make up for lost time. This was an ideal opportunity, she reflected, her blue-eyed gaze fixed on David's bulging crotch. Not only could she gain a little sexual experience, but she'd be able to control the ringleaders. Once Brown and Doogan were beholden to her, she'd have no trouble controlling the rest of the class. But was this the right way to exert her authority over the ringleaders? There was no *other* way, she knew as she walked slowly towards the stockroom with David in tow. It was this, or walk out on her job.

*Shit*, she thought, her conscience nagging her as David followed her into the stockroom and closed the door behind him. Turning to face David, she wished that she'd dumped Charles long ago and gone out with several men. Having endured sex with Charles, she was still as inexperienced as a virgin. Charles and his fumbling and grunting had taught her nothing. *A bit of rough?* she mused, feeling a wetness between the full lips of her vagina. She'd never really had a proper length of cock. Was that what she wanted now? Was this to control the ringleaders, or satisfy her craving for sex?

'Well,' David breathed, grinning as he unzipped his trousers and hauled his erect penis out.

'Yes,' Christina murmured abstractedly, gazing at the lad's purple knob as he fully retracted his foreskin.

'Want to suck it?'

*Suck it?* She'd never taken a penis into her wet mouth. Sex with Charles had consisted of the missionary position, vaginal penetration, humping and grunting and sperming. Dropping to her knees, she gazed longingly at the youth's glistening purple glans, the small sperm-slit. As he eased his full balls out through his zip, she gazed at his veined shaft. He was so big, she thought. Charles's prick was nothing in comparison – she couldn't believe the sheer girth of David's huge organ.

Moving her head forward, Christina parted her succulent lips. This was wrong, she knew as she took the ripe plum of his twitching cock into her hot mouth and licked his sperm-slit. Savouring the salty taste of his swollen glans, she closed her eyes and breathed deeply through her nose. This was wrong, word would get out, there'd be trouble . . . Trouble or not, she had succumbed to her latent desires. She sucked and mouthed on the huge glans, taking the solid shaft in her small hand and beginning her wanking motions as David gasped in the grip of his male pleasure.

She needed sex as much as any other woman, she knew as she waited in anticipation for his sperm to gush and fill her mouth. After three years with Charles, her one and only boyfriend . . . Did Alison suck men's cocks? she found herself wondering as she wanked David's rockhard shaft faster in her desperation to taste his sperm. Her thoughts drifted, lurched. She couldn't stay on at Spadger Heath now, she reflected. Wanking Barry and now sucking David . . . She'd have no authority over the students now that she'd behaved no better than a common whore. And they'd have no respect for her.

'God,' David breathed, his cock twitching as he pumped out his creamy sperm and filled his teacher's mouth. Christina savoured the warm liquid, running her tongue over his throbbing glans as her mouth filled and overflowed. Finally swallowing her prize, she wanked his cock shaft faster, draining his heaving balls as he towered above her. On and on his flow of semen gushed, flooding her tongue, filling her cheeks as she did her best to drink from his fountainhead.

'You're good,' the lad gasped as his flow finally stemmed.

'Thank you,' Christina murmured, slipping his salivated glans out of her mouth and lapping up the last of the sperm oozing from his slit.

'You've obviously sucked a few cocks in your time.'

'Quite a few,' she said, wondering why she was lying. What was she trying to prove?

'You're the sort of teacher we need,' he laughed.

'Are you going to be the sort of student I need?' She smiled, rising to her feet. 'Or are you going to disrupt the lessons and—'

'Not me,' he said, zipping his trousers. 'I like you, and I reckon we'll get on well.'

'I certainly hope so, David. If we work together rather than against each other, I'm sure we can make our days pleasant.'

'You've made *my* day,' he laughed.

'And I'll make your day again, if you deserve it. Mess me about, and you'll not find yourself in the stockroom with me again.'

'I wouldn't mess you about. Baz Doogan . . . Did you . . .'

'That's my business, David. And what *we* did is *our* business. I don't want you telling the others about it, do you understand?'

'Of course.'

'One word about this to anyone, and you can forget any future . . . As I said, you won't find yourself in here with me again. Right, I have things to do. You've got geography after break, haven't you?'

'Yes.'

'OK, off you go.'

As he left, Christina licked her sperm-glossed lips, her stomach somersaulting as her expectant clitoris swelled and her juices of desire flowed into the tight crotch of her cotton panties. Confusion swamping her mind as she made her way to the staffroom, she tried to come to terms with her guilt. Was it guilt or triumph? she wondered. She'd tamed the ringleaders, and yet ... She didn't know what to think. She'd brought off two students in as many days. What the hell would day three bring? Trying to clear her mind of images of David's purple knob pumping sperm into her mouth, she sat in the armchair next to Carter.

'All right?' he asked, smiling.

'Yes, fine,' Christina replied.

'Still no problems?'

'No, not really. One or two disruptions but, apart from that, things are great.'

'I don't know how you do it,' he sighed. 'You carry on for three months, and you'll hold the record.'

'The record?'

'As form teacher. The one before you lasted just short of three months. Of course, you have a long way to go yet.'

'Yes, yes, I have,' she murmured abstractedly, the taste of sperm lingering on her tongue.

*Three months?* she wondered. How many cocks would she have sucked and wanked by the time she held the record? This was so far removed from her parents' house and her life in a leafy country village. She'd visited London several times but had never seen the run-down areas, let alone been part of the community. It was a different world, she reflected. Only sixty miles by car, but it seemed like a thousand miles away from the world she'd grown up in.

Carter mumbled something about a geography lesson and the 'little shits' as he left the room. He had the wrong attitude, Christina thought as she poured herself a cup of coffee. But did she have the right one? she mused, returning to her armchair. More than an English teacher, she knew that, to an extent, she had to become part of the class, one of the students. They weren't interested in geography. What did they care which city was the capital of America? What did they care about punctuation or grammar? One of them worked in a pub during the evenings. Was he really bothered about geography or English? But Christina hoped that she could at least try to give them some sort of start in life. Perhaps she could open their eyes to . . . Hadn't Brown and Doogan opened *her* eyes? She had as much to learn as the students, if not more.

'No class, Miss Shaw?' the head murmured as he entered the staffroom.

'I have a free period,' she replied. 'I'm going to take a look around the college.'

'You seem to be settling in quite well.'

'Yes, I am. I'm enjoying the challenge.'

'Let's hope you continue to do so.'

'Thank you.'

Heading for her classroom, Christina felt positive. The situation with Doogan and Brown wasn't ideal, but at least she had some sort of control over them. She also had some sort of sex life, which pleased her. Wanking and sucking the boys brought her pleasure, she had to admit. Noticing a young girl sitting at the back of the room, Christina closed the door and walked over to her. It was Bryony Philips, an attractive blonde who'd kept herself to herself during lessons. Her head hung low, she hadn't appeared to notice Christina.

'Are you all right?' Christina asked the girl

'Oh, I didn't see you come in,' Bryony said, looking up in surprise and giving a slight smile. 'Yes, I'm OK. Just feeling a little down, that's all.'

'Anything I can do to help?'

'Well, I . . . Actually, you might be able to help me.'

'Go on,' Christina said, pulling out a chair and sitting down opposite the girl.

'I was hoping you'd come back. I've been waiting for you.'

'Oh?'

'I feel that I might be able to talk to you. It's my . . . my breasts.'

'Your breasts?' Christina echoed, involuntarily looking down at the girl's partially open blouse. 'What's wrong with your breasts?'

'They're very small,' the girl confessed.

'I wouldn't worry about that.' Christina smiled. 'You're young. They've plenty of time to develop.'

'Yes, but . . . I'll show you what I mean,' Bryony said, unbuttoning her blouse.

'Bryony, there's no need to . . .'

'I have to show you,' the girl persisted. 'I can't ask my mum about it. You're the only one I can turn to.'

'It's one thing talking your problems over with me, but quite another to show me your breasts. I don't need to see them, Bryony.'

'I only want your opinion, Miss. As I said, I can't ask my mum because . . . well, I just can't.'

'All right, you'd better come into the stockroom,' Christina suggested, getting up. 'Just in case someone walks in and gets the wrong idea.'

As Bryony followed her to the stockroom, Christina felt pleased that the girl had been able to come to her with her problems. But she also wondered why she wanted to expose her young breasts. This was all part of the job, Christina thought, closing the door. Bryony had been unable to go to her mother for help and advice and had turned to her teacher. There was obviously some trust developing, she thought happily. Watching the girl open her blouse and lift the silk cups of her bra away from the petite mounds of her breasts, Christina was almost mesmerized as she gazed at the brown teats of Bryony's elongated nipples.

'There's nothing wrong with you,' she said, smiling reassuringly.

'But they're so small,' Bryony sighed.

'I had the same problem . . . Not problem. "Concern" would be a better word. When I was your age I used to wonder why my breasts were so small.'

'Touch them,' the girl said, moving closer to Christina. 'They don't feel right, somehow.'

'Bryony, I . . .' Christina stammered, realizing that she'd been gripped by an overwhelming sudden desire to reach out, feel the girl's small breasts and stroke the brown protrusions of her sensitive nipples.

'Squeeze them and tell me if you think they're all right.'

Reaching out, Christina tentatively squeezed the girl's left breast. The petite mound was firm, the skin unblemished and smooth in youth. Her fingertips brushing against the girl's milk teat, she felt her stomach somersault. Was Bryony leading her on? she wondered, circling the darkening disc of her areola with her fingertip. Was this a dare? Or was the girl genuinely concerned about her small breasts? Brown or Doogan might have put her up to this, Christina reflected, squeezing and kneading both breasts.

'There's nothing wrong with you,' Christina finally said, lowering her hands.

'If you say so,' the girl sighed.

'I *do* say so,' Christina said softly, her gaze transfixed on her student's ripening nipples. 'Bryony, has anyone said anything about me?'

'Said anything?' Bryony echoed, cupping the mounds of her breasts in her bra and buttoning her blouse. 'Said what?'

'Brown or Doogan . . . Have they said anything?'

'No, nothing. Miss, would you look at my . . . you know, down there?'

'Bryony, I think this has gone far enough,' Christina said firmly, aware of an unfamiliar yearning to gaze at the girl's young pussy. 'You'd better go to your next class.'

'It's just that I . . .'

'Just that you what? Look, there's nothing wrong with you.'

'You're the only one I can talk to, Miss.'

'Talking is one thing, but showing me your—'

'You won't help me, then?'

'All right,' Christina conceded, realizing that this really was going too far. 'Show me what the problem is.'

As Bryony lifted her skirt up over her stomach and tugged her panties down her firm thighs, Christina was sure that the girl was leading her on. The boys had put her up to this, she knew as she gazed in awe at the fleshy cushions of her student's hairless pussy lips. Her pink inner labia protruding invitingly from her tightly closed sex crack, she parted her feet and lifted her skirt higher. Unsure what to do, Christina couldn't drag her stare away from the perfectly formed lips of Bryony's young pussy. Her heart racing, her breathing quickening, she stepped back and turned her head away.

'That's enough,' she said. 'I know what you're up to and . . .'

'Up to?' the girl breathed, cocking her head to one side. 'What do you mean?'

'Bryony, schoolgirls don't show their breasts to their teachers. Or pull their knickers down in front of them.'

'But, Miss . . .'

'But nothing. Go to your next lesson, please.'

'I have a small lump just inside me. I thought . . .'

'A lump? Are you sure?'

'Yes, Miss.'

'Then, you must go to your doctor.'

'I can't. He . . . he's a strange man. Whenever I go to see him, he examines me down there. No matter what's wrong with me, he . . .'

'You should report him, Bryony.'

'What's the point? No one would believe me. I was hoping you'd feel me and . . . Please, Miss. I can't ask my mother.'

'All right,' Christina sighed, reckoning that the girl was genuinely worried. 'This is unethical, to say the least, but I'll . . . Just quickly, all right?'

'All right.'

Kneeling, Christina parted the hairless lips of Bryony's vulva and slipped her finger into the tight, wet sheath of her student's teenage pussy. She could feel nothing out of the ordinary as she massaged the hot walls of the girl's pussy. Pushing her finger into her tight sex shaft, she gazed at her clitoris emerging from beneath pinken hood. This was another mistake, she knew as Bryony began to breathe deeply, heavily. Unethical, dangerous . . . But Christina's main concern was her own rising arousal, the unfamiliar thoughts surfacing from the murky depths of her mind as she massaged the young girl's inner flesh.

Slipping a second finger into Bryony's tightening vaginal sheath, Christina began to tremble. Her mind thronging with uncharacteristic thoughts as the girl parted her feet further, she knew that she was teetering on the edge of committing a lesbian act. Examining the girl was one thing, but massaging deep inside her pussy, gazing at her ripening clitoris, imagining sucking and tonguing her there . . . *God, no*, she thought, licking her succulent lips. Taking a deep breath, Christina slipped her wet fingers out of the girl's snug quim and stood up before she went too far.

'There doesn't seem to be anything wrong,' she said softly, aware of the girl's juices of arousal running down her sticky fingers.

'I hope you're right,' Bryony mumbled.

'Sort your clothes out and go to your next class.'

'Yes, Miss.'

Watching the girl leave, Christina raised her hand and gazed at the girl-juice glistening on her fingers. Had the boys put Bryony up to this? If Christina had been set up . . . Sure that the girl was honest, she left the stockroom and wiped her hand on a tissue. The experience had unnerved her, she knew as she pictured the young girl's hairless vaginal lips and recalled the inner heat of her young body. 'God,' she breathed, realizing suddenly that Bryony had shaved. Holding her hand to her mouth, she was sure that Bryony had been conning her. Displaying her young breasts, dropping her panties and exposing the shaved lips of her vagina . . . Why had the girl shaved her vulval flesh?

Despite feeling that she'd been taken for a ride, Christina had to admit that she'd enjoyed the experience. In a way, she was hoping that the girl would come to her again, allow her to finger her tight pussy and... Shaking her head, Christina tried to push all thoughts of the girl's beautiful young body from her mind. It was bad enough that she'd wanked Doogan and sucked Brown, let alone fingered a young student's pussy. Eyeing Alison's naked body that morning had roused *something* within the dark depths of her mind, but she wasn't sure exactly what latent desires lurked deep within her subconscious.

Her thoughts focusing on lesbianism, she bit her lip as she recalled a girlfriend she'd had at school. She'd been blonde, young and extremely attractive. Christina had fallen for her, had a crush on her, but nothing had come of it other than one stolen kiss. She recalled locking her lips to her friend's mouth, tasting her saliva, breathing in the scent of her hair. But that was normal, she tried to convince herself. It wasn't unheard of for young schoolgirls to become close, intimate, during their growing.

'Sorry, Miss,' Bryony said as she entered the classroom. 'I thought I'd better explain.'

'Explain what?'

'There's nothing wrong with me,' she confessed, hanging her head.

'I realized that, Bryony. So what's this all about?'

'I . . . I like you,' the girl admitted.

'Bryony, I know what it's like to be your age. Your feelings are confused, you—'

'I'm not confused. I know what I feel, what I think.'

'Yes, but you can't . . .'

'Did you like what you did to me?'

'I . . . Bryony, whether I liked it or not . . . Look, I

examined you because I thought there was something wrong with you. There was no other reason.'

'Oh, right.'

'Have you been out with boys yet?'

'No, I haven't.'

'You'll sort your feelings out once you've got a boyfriend. In the meantime, try not to think about . . . well, you know.'

Watching Bryony walk away, Christina knew exactly how the girl felt. What worried her was that she was beginning to feel the same. Sighing, she tried again to push all thoughts of the girl's young body from her mind. This was ridiculous, she reflected. Doogan, Brown – and now Bryony. Living with her parents in a country house, Christina had never mixed much with teenagers before, and she thought briefly that the attraction was innocent enough. But she was kidding herself, she knew. The excitement, the danger . . . The feel of Doogan's solid cock in her hand, his sperm running over her hand . . . Brown's knob in her mouth, pumping sperm over her tongue . . .

'Shit,' Christina breathed, banging her fist on her desk. Unsure of her feelings as she again pictured Alison's naked body, imagined Bryony standing naked before her, she knew that she had to pull herself together. Her first two days at Spadger Heath had been a total disaster. If she were found out, she'd be in real trouble. But she had only been trying to fit in with the students, to get them to accept her and . . . 'That's not the way to do it,' she sighed, walking to the window and looking out across the car park to the engineering works. Cursing her stupidity, she decided to put an end to the ridiculous games she'd started. Doogan and Brown were just going to have to accept her without the wanking and sucking. Bryony would just have to . . .

'Miss,' Bryony said softly as she approached from behind.

'What is it now?' Christina snapped. 'I'm sorry, I didn't mean to be angry. What is it?'

'Would you mind if I came to your flat this evening?'

'My . . . Yes, Bryony, I *would* mind. I'm your teacher, for God's sake.'

'I know where you live.'

'How?'

'I followed you home.'

'Christ, this is getting out of hand. Go away, Bryony. Please go away and leave me alone.'

Somehow managing to get through the rest of the day, Christina knew that she couldn't stay on at Spadger Heath. She'd made a complete mess of her first two days, and realized now that she had no choice but to leave her job. She'd meant well, she reflected. Trying to get on with the students, trying to . . . Grabbing her bag after the class had left, she avoided Bryony and headed home. Perhaps she'd be able to talk to Alison, she mused. Get her flatmate's advice and . . . and what? 'What's done is done,' she breathed as she neared the flat. 'I've fucked up big time.'

# 3

Reading the note that Alison had left, Christina felt despondent. Her flatmate had gone to visit her parents and wouldn't be back until late, at least midnight. Although she didn't feel like eating, Christina did her best to force down a tin of soup and two slices of bread. She'd been looking forward to the evening, talking her problems over with Alison. Now she had nothing but an empty flat and several boring hours ahead of her.

Switching the TV on, she flicked through the channels and turned it off. She slipped a CD into the hi-fi and mooched around the room before flopping onto the sofa. Normally, she'd have busied herself with something, but her mind was brimming with thoughts of the stockroom. Unconsciously slipping her hand between her thighs as she pictured Bryony's naked pussy lips, she massaged the swell of her moist panties. Her hand slipping in around the edge of the flimsy undergarment, she parted her thighs wider and toyed with the petals of her wet inner lips. Breathing deeply as she pulled and twisted her inner labia, she again pictured Bryony's hairless sex slit.

Telling herself that her thoughts about the girl were uncharacteristic, Christina knew that she wasn't a latent lesbian. It had been a long time since she'd had a fulfilling sexual relationship, she reflected as her clitoris swelled. Thinking back, she realized that her relationship with Charles could hardly be described even as sexual, let alone fulfilling. In fact, Christina had *never* had a fulfilling sexual relationship, and she put that down as the reason for her unusual feelings about Bryony.

Massaging the solid nub of her clitoris, Christina closed her eyes and sank into a warm pool of satisfaction. She'd never masturbated regularly. Apart from rubbing her clitoris during her younger years, her only self-induced orgasms had been when Charles had swiftly pumped his sperm into her vagina, withdrawn from her unsatisfied quim and left her in desperate need of sexual relief. Had *Bryony* left her craving sexual relief? she pondered, picturing again the fleshy swell of the girl's hairless vulval lips. Christina knew instinctively that Bryony wouldn't give up. The girl obviously had a powerful crush on her teacher, and would pursue her quest for love until . . . *Love?* Christina mused, her clitoris ripening beneath her caressing fingertip. She'd not found love with Charles. Would she ever find love? she wondered. Then the doorbell rang.

Leaping to her feet and adjusting her skirt, she had a nagging feeling that it was Bryony. She'd been wondering whether the girl would turn up. Wondering or hoping? If it *was* Bryony, then she'd talk to her, she decided, walking to the door. Talk over her problems, try to get the girl to see sense. Opening the door, she gazed at Bryony, her long blonde hair, her tight T-shirt and red miniskirt. She looked older out of her college uniform – mature, sensual, alluring . . .

'I thought you might come round,' she said softly. 'You'd better come in.'

'I wasn't going to,' Bryony said as Christina closed the

door behind her. 'I waited outside for ages. I wasn't going to—'

'Come into the lounge and sit down,' Christina interrupted the girl. 'I need to ask you something.'

'Oh?' the girl murmured, sitting on the sofa as Christina stood with her back to the window.

'Why have you shaved, Bryony?'

'I . . . I don't know.'

'You don't know?' Christina chuckled. 'You mean, it was an accident?'

'No, no, I . . . I prefer it that way.'

'I see. Tell me about yourself, Bryony. You've said that you can't go to your doctor, you can't talk to your mother . . . What about your father?'

'He went off with some young girl,' she sighed. 'My mother's always drunk. The house is a tip, there's never any food . . .'

'Do you have brothers or sisters?'

'No, I don't. It's just me and mum.'

'Mum and me,' Christina corrected her, wishing she hadn't.

'Mum's always on the gin. She never does housework or cooking. No wonder my dad went off.'

'What do you do during the evenings? Have you any interests?'

'I sit in my room. It's the only tidy place in the house. There's no television so . . . We do have a telly, but the aerial blew down and mum can't afford to get it fixed.'

'Bryony, I think it would be an idea if you joined a club. Say, tennis or swimming. Something to give you an interest and get you out of the house.'

'I like swimming, but we haven't got any money. What

money we get from the social, mum spends on drink. It's nice here. I wish I had a flat.'

'It's above a Chinese takeaway, Bryony. It's hardly nice.'

'Compared with my house, this is brilliant.'

'Would you like some tea or coffee?'

'Tea, please. No sugar.'

'Switch the TV on. There might be something you can watch while I make the tea.'

Filling the kettle, Christina felt sorry for Bryony. The girl didn't have a proper home, a loving mother, meals waiting for her . . . She probably did her own washing and ironing, cooked her own meals if there was any food in the house. But that wasn't Christina's problem. In a run-down area of London, this was to be expected. There again, Christina realized that not all mothers drank gin. There was no excuse for wasting money on alcohol, and no need to live in a hovel. Pouring the tea, Christina knew that she could only help Bryony by giving her advice. She couldn't help financially, but she could befriend the girl and help her as best she could by advising her.

'No, Bryony,' she gasped as she took the teas into the lounge. 'Please, put your clothes on.'

'But I thought . . .' the girl began, standing naked by the sofa.

'For God's sake. What the hell do you think you're doing?'

'But, Miss . . .'

'You come round here when I specifically told you not to, you string me a load of lies about your mother and your home . . . And now you're naked in my lounge. Get dressed and get out of my flat.'

Watching as the girl picked up her panties from the sofa, Christina scrutinized the violin curves of her naked body. She was young and attractive, her beautiful body not yet fully developed. Her breasts were pointed, not fully rounded, her nipples elongated out of proportion to her firm mounds. Eyeing the hairless crack of Bryony's pussy, Christina felt her clitoris swell as her juices of desire seeped into her tight panties. Unable to finish masturbating, she was already in a high state of arousal. Gazing at Bryony's delicious body was too much for her to bear. If she just touched her, caressed her, stroked her . . . But this was wrong, she decided as the girl tugged her panties up her long, shapely legs.

Placing the teas on the small table by the TV, Christina focused on the girl's young breasts, the sensitive buds of her ripening milk teats. Bryony was innocent, she concluded. Although the girl had stripped naked, she probably didn't know right from wrong. Perhaps she was trying to find love, and thought that this was the best way to do it. She might have seen her father chasing after a young girl, and thought as a result that sex was the way to get what she wanted. Her upbringing was at fault. Bryony was innocent.

'I'm sorry, Miss,' she sighed, picking up her bra from the sofa. 'I thought . . .'

'I know what you thought, Bryony.' Christina smiled. 'You want to be loved, don't you?'

'I've never been loved.'

'I can't love you, Bryony. You do understand that, don't you?'

'No, I don't. You said in class that you haven't got a boyfriend. I thought that you might be lonely, like I am.'

'I do get lonely at times. Tell me, why do you believe

that sex is a means to forming a relationship? We could have become friends without having . . . It's lesbian sex, Bryony. That's what you're offering me. Lesbian sex.'

'I've never liked boys. When you smiled at me in class, I thought—'

'Smiled at you? Bryony, my smiling at a girl isn't a signal. It doesn't mean to say that I want lesbian sex just because I smile at you.'

'OK, so I got the wrong message. I'm sorry.'

'No, no, don't be sorry. It's not your fault.'

'I just want to be held.'

'Put your bra down,' Christina said softly. 'Move your clothes and sit on the sofa.'

Joining the girl as she did what she'd been told, Christina felt her stomach somersault, her clitoris swelling as she reached out and stroked Bryony's thigh. This was very wrong, she knew, but . . . but what? she wondered. The girl wanted to be held, loved. Was that so very wrong? Christina needed love and physical contact. After Charles, she needed to find . . . she needed to find a man to share her life with, not to embark on a lesbian relationship with one of her students. But if she only saw Bryony once a week, perhaps invited her round once a week for . . . She was trying to convince herself that having sex with the girl was acceptable.

'I can't have a relationship with you,' she said softly, her fingers dangerously near to the girl's hairless vulva.

'It's just nice to have someone sit with me and touch me,' Bryony murmured, parting her young thighs and reclining on the sofa.

'I'll sit with you and touch you. But you must understand that we can't go further than that.'

'Yes, I understand. That's nice. I like you stroking me.

My mother has never held me, loved me. It's nice, being loved.'

This wasn't love, Christina thought, her fingers caressing the smooth flesh just above the girl's sex crack. This was fulfilling a need. Whose need? she wondered. Bryony craved love and physical attention. What did *she* crave? Alone in her bed at night, alone with her naked body, her clitoris . . . What did she crave? Her fingertip hovering at the top of Bryony's vaginal slit, only half an inch from her clitoris, Christina knew that she was weakening in her soaring arousal. She dared not masturbate the girl, she knew as she gazed longingly at her erect nipples rising alluringly from the darkening discs of her areolae. If she massaged her clitoris, took her to orgasm, the girl would want to reciprocate and . . .

'That's nice,' Bryony murmured dreamily as Christina's fingertip brushed the sensitive tip of her solid clitoris. 'No one's ever touched me there.'

'Do you masturbate?' Christina asked.

'Yes, most nights. It's all I have. It's the only way I have of escaping my horrible life.'

'Life needn't be horrible.'

'It needn't be, but it is.'

Deciding to bring the girl her much-needed pleasure, Christina massaged the nub of her ripe clitoris. *Just this once*, she thought, vowing never to touch Bryony again. With Alison usually around in the evenings, she knew that she'd not have much opportunity to masturbate the naked girl. Temptation wouldn't raise its ugly head, she wouldn't have to fight her inner desires. And if Alison happened to be out . . . Christina wouldn't answer the door. The stockroom would remain locked, out of bounds to all students, particularly Doogan and Brown. And Bryony.

Massaging the girl's clitoris faster, Christina leaned forward, her mouth dangerously close to the young beauty's nipple. Fighting temptation, she expertly masturbated the girl, desperately trying not to suck the teat of her barely developed breast into her wet mouth. Bryony was close to her climax, Christina knew as she began her gasping and writhing. Sucking on her ripe nipple would add to her pleasure, take her to her goal and . . .

'God,' Christina breathed, taking the elongated protrusion into her hot mouth and sucking hard. She'd fought her inner battle and lost. Now she'd set out on an unknown road, begun an uncertain journey to . . . She dreaded to think where her journey was taking her. This wasn't love, she tried to convince herself as she mouthed and suckled at the girl's breast. This was cold comfort, a means to an end, giving physical pleasure for the sake of pleasure. A hundred questions battered Christina's mind as Bryony teetered on the verge of her orgasm. Why had she been so weak? Why couldn't she have fought her inner desires? Why did she *have* such desires?

'Oh, oh,' Bryony gasped as she arched her back and flung her legs wide apart. She was there, Christina knew as she felt the girl's rock-hard clitoris pulsating beneath her vibrating fingertip. Her naked body shaking violently, Bryony squirmed and writhed, crying out as her obvious pleasure gripped her very soul. Christina had never touched another girl sexually, let alone witnessed one in the grip of a massive orgasm. Sucking and biting Bryony's nipple, she slowed her masturbating rhythm as the girl shuddered and fell limp. Twitching, her naked body glowing, she finally let out a long sigh of pleasure as she relaxed in the aftermath of her orgasm.

Slipping the girl's nipple out of her mouth, Christina looked down at Bryony's inflamed vulval flesh, the pouting wet lips of her hairless pussy. She was tempted to lick her there, taste her teenage juices of arousal and suck another orgasm out of her detumescing clitoris. Bryony lay still, her eyes closed, her legs parted as she recovered from her lesbian pleasure. Gazing at the girl, the smooth flesh of her youthful body, Christina tried desperately to drag her gaze away from the beautiful sight of her yawning sex crack, the opaque liquid clinging to the pink wings of her inner labia.

'Rest your head on the arm of the sofa,' she said, stroking the girl's long blonde hair. Leaving one foot on the floor, Bryony lifted her leg and placed her other foot behind Christina, resting her head on the sofa arm. Her thighs parted wide, her vulval crack gaping, she closed her eyes again and relaxed. Christina leaned forward, her mouth close to the girl's hairless pussy. This was wrong, she kept telling herself. To lick a young girl's pussy, to lap up her vaginal cream and . . .

Rising to her feet, Christina paced the lounge floor. Glancing at her naked student every now and then, she clenched her fists as she tried to fight temptation. More than temptation, she felt that she was fighting for her femininity, her womanhood. She wasn't a lesbian, and vowed not to succumb to the young girl's naked body, the wet slit of her teenage pussy. To lick the girl there would be . . . It would be wonderful, she knew. To run her tongue up and down her sex crack, tasting her, teasing out her clitoris, sucking her . . .

'Shit,' Christina whispered, gazing at the sleeping beauty's swollen pussy lips. This was a fight she knew she was going to lose unless . . . *Why doesn't Alison come home?* she thought, hoping for something or someone to take temptation away from her. *Why did Bryony have to come round? Why did she strip? Why can't I control myself?* 'Shit.' *Am I a lesbian?* Dashing into the kitchen as the phone rang, she was relieved to hear Alison's voice.

'Are you coming home yet?' she asked hopefully.

'No, that's why I'm calling. I knew I was going to be late, but it looks as though I might stay overnight.'

'Overnight?' Christina breathed, disappointedly. 'Alison, you don't have to stay . . .'

'I haven't seen my parents for a while. You know what it's like.'

'I suppose so.'

'You'll be all right on your own, won't you?'

'I'm not— yes, yes I'll be fine.'

'OK, I'll see you tomorrow.'

'Yes, tomorrow.'

That was all she needed, Christina thought, standing in the lounge doorway and staring longingly at Bryony's naked body. She felt that she was climbing the walls, craving a drug. She'd never smoked, but now she had some idea of what it must be like to crave for a cigarette. How long should she allow the girl to sleep on the sofa? Bryony's mother would wonder where . . . No. Her mother was probably drunk, sprawled across a sofa in a state of semi-consciousness. Christina decided to talk to Bryony. She'd wake her and get her to dress. Bryony needed to talk. They both needed to talk.

'Bryony,' she said, kneeling on the floor by the sofa. 'Bryony, wake up.' The girl stirred, breathing deeply as Christina focused on her naked body. Her long blonde hair cascading over her fresh face like a curtain of gold silk, the teenager looked like an angel. The wet crack of her exquisite vagina glistening in the light, she was a temptress, impossible to refuse. Moving her head forward, Christina kissed the girl's naked mons, breathing in her female scent, trying again to fight her inner desires.

'Just this once,' she whispered, pushing her tongue out and tasting the creamy valley of her girl-sex. Trembling, Christina repeatedly swept her tongue up the young beauty's vaginal crack, lapping up her teenage juices of arousal, savouring the aphrodisiacal taste of her young pussy. Parting the fleshy pads of Bryony's outer sex lips, Christina slipped her tongue into her vaginal hole, licking and tasting her there as her own juices of arousal seeped between the inner wings of her labia. *Just this once*, she thought, parting the girl's love lips further, exposing the pinken nubble of her ripe clitoris. Licking her there, teasing her solid pleasure bud, she locked her lips to the girl's wet flesh and sucked hard on her inflated clitoris.

Bryony stirred again, her breathing fast and shallow as she responded to the lesbian licking. This was the girl's own fault, Christina mused. Had she not persisted, had she not stripped and offered her young body for lesbian sex . . . Schoolteachers were supposed to be in control, Christina knew. They were supposed to teach their students right from wrong, to help them grow up and develop into decent people. What had she done to help the girl? she wondered. Masturbated her, sucked and bitten her nipple, tongued her vagina, licked her sweet clitoris . . .

'That's nice,' Bryony murmured dreamily. 'I like feeling your tongue there.' Reaching down, Bryony pulled her sex lips wide apart, stretching the fleshy cushions and exposing the intimate folds of her wet valley. Her clitoris fully emerging from beneath its pink bonnet, she trembled as Christina sucked and licked her sensitive pleasure spot. The girl suddenly shuddered, her naked body shaking violently as she cried out and gripped Christina's head. Grinding her open cunt flesh hard against her teacher's mouth, she let out her orgasmic juices as her clitoris exploded.

Drowning in the young girl's cuntal juices, barely able to breathe, Christina sucked and mouthed on her pulsating clitoris, lost in her sexual delirium as Bryony screamed out in the grip of her illicit lesbian pleasure. The smooth flesh of the girl's wet vulva pressed hard against her face, she sustained her student's orgasm, licking and mouthing, sucking and slurping. Never had Christina known that such pleasure was obtainable from lesbian oral sex. Drinking from the teenager's cunt, swallowing her fresh orgasmic juices, she swept her tongue up and down her valley, repeatedly caressing her pulsating clitoris, taking the girl ever higher to her sexual heaven.

'No more,' Bryony finally gasped, her inner thighs crushing Christina's head as she convulsed wildly. Sucking out the girl's creamy offering, Christina drank from her hot cunt, swallowing her flowing juices until she'd drained her sex sheath and the girl pushed her away. Licking her lips, she sat back on her heels and gazed at the rubicund cushions of Bryony's inflamed outer labia, the engorged petals of her inner lips.

Guilt consuming her, she watched the girl shuddering as she recovered from her lesbian-induced orgasm. Christina should never have succumbed to her vulgar desires, she knew. She'd behaved immorally, taught the young girl things she was far too young to know. Christina should have known nothing about lesbian oral sex. *What have I done?* she thought guiltily, watching the smooth plateau of the girl's stomach rising and falling as she recovered from her orgasm. *What the hell have I done?*

'You'd better get dressed and go home,' she said as Bryony hauled her naked body up from the sofa.

'What about you?' the girl asked, her pretty face framed by her sex-matted blonde hair, her succulent lips furling into a smile.

'Me?' Christina said. 'What do you mean?'

'What about . . . You know what I mean.'

'I . . . Oh, I see.'

'Aren't you going to let me love you?'

Her mind racing with a thousand thoughts, Christina bit her lip. Alison would be out all night. This was an opportunity to experience another girl's intimate attention. Did she want to feel another girl's tongue lapping between the full lips of her vagina? Charles had never licked her there – his lovemaking consisted of his penis thrusting into her vagina, sperming over her cervix. Just that. Christina was torn so many ways, riddled with guilt. How could she ever face Bryony in class, knowing that she'd licked and sucked the girl's clitoris to orgasm? If she were now to allow the girl to reciprocate . . .

'Well?' Bryony smiled. 'Don't you want to be loved?'

'It's not that I don't want to,' Christina sighed, pacing the floor in her confusion. 'It's wrong, Bryony. What I did to you was wrong, and if I allow you to—'

'Haven't you ever done anything that was wrong?' the girl asked. 'Anyway, who says it's wrong to love each other?'

'Loving each other is . . . Love should be between a man and a woman, Bryony.'

'Why?'

'Well, because . . . That's just the way it is. Yes, I would like physical attention. I don't have a boyfriend and I do get lonely.'

'If you want me to stop, then I will,' the girl said, her full lips curving in a lascivious grin.

Slipping off the sofa, Bryony stood in front of Christina and unbuttoned her blouse. Christina raised her hands to stop the girl, but hesitated. Looking down, she watched Bryony part the silk material, revealing her full bra. Her heart racing, she thought again that this was wrong as Bryony lifted the cups of Christina's bra away from her firm breasts. Given their freedom, her nipples elongated, standing proud from the chocolate-brown discs of her areolae. Was this what she wanted? she wondered again as Bryony leaned forward and sucked her nipple into her wet mouth. The heavenly sensations transmitting deep into her breast as the girl sucked and tongued her ripening milk teat, she let out a rush of breath.

'Bryony,' she murmured as the girl moved her attention to her other breast, sucking and nibbling her brown teat. She could feel the girl's hands sliding down her hips, her fingers slipping between the top of her skirt and her naked flesh. Her breathing unsteady, Christina stood motionless as her skirt slipped down her thighs, the material tumbling around her ankles and settling on the carpet. Kneeling, Bryony pressed her face into the warm swell of Christina's panties, breathing in her girl-scent, kissing and loving her there.

'Bryony, no,' Christina gasped as she felt her panties

being pulled down to reveal the sparse blonde down covering the gentle rise of her mons, the fleshy cushions of her outer labia. Quivering, Christina looked down at her naked student, the sheen of her blonde hair as she moved forward, her eager mouth close to her teacher's pussy lips. Christina held her breath, waiting in anticipation as she felt the girl's hot breath on the most intimate part of her trembling body. Did she want another girl's tongue there, licking her sex valley, stiffening the pink bud of her clitoris?

Naked apart from her bra rucked above her full breasts, Christina looked around the room. This was her home, she reflected. The photographs of her parents on the mantelpiece, the flowers in the vase that Alison had bought to brighten up the room. Standing naked in front of her naked student, waiting for the feel of the girl's wet tongue licking her sex slit . . . This was wrong, so very wrong. She should never have answered the door to Bryony. She should never have comforted her, stroked the naked flesh of her thigh, massaged her clitoris to orgasm, sucked and licked her pussy . . . No one would know, Christina consoled herself as Bryony parted the fleshy lips of her vulva with her slender fingers. No one, not even Alison, would discover the sordid truth. Christina had had sex with a young female student, Christina had abused her position of trust and tongued a young girl's pussy, Christina had . . . In her weakness, her yearning to be comforted, Christina had fallen prey to her inner desires. Was that a crime?

'Please,' Christina whispered, looking down at Bryony's full lips as the young student examined the intimate folds nestling within her teacher's girl crack. 'Bryony, I don't think . . .' Closing her eyes and breathing heavily,

Christina shuddered as the girl's tongue ran up the full length of her wet vaginal valley. 'God,' she murmured, her clitoris emerging from its hide as if it was actively seeking the caress of the girl's tongue. The sensations driving her wild, Christina felt her trembling legs sagging beneath her as Bryony parted her teacher's pussy lips further and drove her tongue deep into Christina's drenched sex sheath.

Tossing her head back, Christina clutched Bryony's head as her tongue snaked inside the wet sheath of her tightening pussy. Bryony's hot breath, her wet tongue, her nose pressing hard against Christina's solid clitoris . . . Christina had never known such immense pleasure. If only her nagging conscience would free her, she knew that she'd sink into the warm pool of lesbian love and give herself completely to her young student. But the nagging persisted. Where would this intimate relationship lead her? What would Bryony's mother say if she discovered that her daughter's teacher was having a lesbian affair with her darling girl? What if Alison walked into the room?

'Sit on the sofa,' Bryony said, her pussy-wet face looking up at her teacher.

'Bryony,' Christina began as she moved to the sofa and perched her buttocks on the edge of the cushion. 'Bryony, I don't—'

'Shush. Lie back and open your legs,' Bryony said huskily, settling between Christina's feet. 'Let me love you properly.'

Her head back, her eyes closed, her thighs wide, Christina shuddered as Bryony locked her succulent lips to the bared flesh of her teacher's gaping vaginal valley. The girl's mouth hard against Christina's pubic bone, she sucked hard on her erect clitoris, the pressure bringing out the full length of her pleasure bud. Gasping, Christina tossed her head from side to side as the beautiful sensations built. No man could have done this, she reflected. Only a girl knew how to pleasure another girl.

Christina's orgasm came quickly, her pulsating clitoris erupting with pleasure, her womb rhythmically contracting, her juices of lesbian desire gushing from the spasming sheath of her vagina. Riding the crest of her climax, her naked body shaking violently, she clutched Bryony's head, grinding the flesh of her open pussy hard against the girl's face as she drifted through clouds of sexual pleasure, floating on a sea of lesbian sex. Again and again her clitoris erupted, her orgasm peaking, rocking her very soul until she thought she'd pass out with the intense pleasure her naked body was bringing her.

'Enough,' she finally managed to gasp. Bryony knew exactly what to do as her teacher's orgasm began to wane. Licking gently, sucking, mouthing, tonguing, she brought Christina slowly down from her sexual heaven. Her limbs twitching, her trembling body convulsing, Christina lay gasping for breath as her young student brought out the last ripples of pure sexual bliss from her subsiding clitoris. Her eyes rolling, she was unable to focus on the girl as she sat back on her heels and licked her cunny-creamed lips. Christina tried to speak, but the words wouldn't come. She tried to sit upright, but her naked body wouldn't respond.

'Are you all right?' Bryony asked.

'Yes, yes,' Christina finally breathed. 'God, yes.'

'Would you like me to shave you?'

'What? No, no, I . . . Bryony, you'd better go home now.'

'Home?' the girl echoed, her angelic face reflecting an inner sadness.

'Your mother will wonder where you are.'

'My mother never wonders where I am. She doesn't care where I am. She'll be drunk, anyway.'

'Yes, but . . . Bryony, I need time to think, time alone.'

'Think about what?'

'Us . . . me . . . I don't know.'

'What's the matter?'

'Everything's the matter.'

'Haven't I pleased you? I thought I'd loved you properly.'

'Yes, yes, you have. For God's sake. Can't you see that this is wrong? I'm your teacher, you're a girl and . . . You should be loving boys, Bryony. And so should I. Men, I mean. God, I don't know what I'm trying to say. You're what, eighteen?'

'No, no. I'm only—'

'I don't want to know. You're the student and I'm the teacher. This shouldn't be happening between us. Apart from that, we're both females. And then there's your age. Everything about us is wrong, Bryony.'

'I don't see what's wrong,' the girl sighed.

'No, I don't think you do. You're like a flower, Bryony. Fresh, beautiful . . . but not fully bloomed. You need to develop and—'

'You're talking about my breasts, aren't you?'

'No, no, of course not. I'm trying to say that you're too young.'

'You want someone older?'

'God, Bryony. Why don't you understand? Yes, someone older. But a man.'

'Oh.'

'I'm sorry, but we can't take this any further. Please don't come here again.'

'All right, if that's what you want.'

'It is. I'm sorry, Bryony.'

Watching the girl dress, Christina felt her stomach churning. This wasn't what she'd wanted at all. But she knew that she had to end the affair before it became a full-blown lesbian relationship. *Another grave mistake*, she reflected, folding her arms to conceal the erect nipples of her full breasts. Now she had not only Brown and Doogan to face in class, but Bryony as well. *Authority and respect?* she mused as Bryony finished dressing. Again believing that her only option was to leave Spadger Heath College, she smiled as Bryony walked to the lounge door.

'You do understand, don't you?' she said.

'No, I don't,' Bryony sighed, her head hung low, her golden locks falling over her pretty face. 'I'll never understand why two people can't love each other when they both know that they want to. If you were hungry and there was a plate of food in front of you, you'd eat it. Why deny yourself what you know you want and need? Goodbye, Miss.'

Hearing the front door slam shut, Christina sighed. Bryony was right, she reflected. But society wouldn't allow it. The rules and conventions of society had to be observed. Thinking again that, if no one knew of her illicit relationship with the girl, there'd be no harm in carrying on, she left the sofa and went to the front door to call her back. Hesitating, she mooched into the kitchen and filled the kettle. Never before had she known such a battle to rage in her mind. Right, wrong, society . . . Her head aching, she poured herself a cup of coffee and wandered into her room.

Lying on her bed, Christina stared at the cracks in the ceiling. Wondering what Bryony was thinking, she recalled the young girl's tongue lapping between her pussy lips, her hot mouth sucking an orgasm out of her pulsating clitoris. 'No,' she breathed, wondering about seeing the girl again. She closed her eyes as sleep engulfed her and her coffee went cold while she dreamed her lesbian dreams.

# 4

Walking to the college, Christina knew that she was going to have to be strong. Avoiding Bryony's longing gaze wasn't going to be easy, but she had to compose herself and try to put the beautiful lesbian experience behind her. She would have loved to invite Bryony to her flat, strip her exquisitely young beauty and love her again, but . . . Love? Christina knew that there was a world of difference between love and lust. Or was there? Love, lust, hate. Such emotions were so complex that it was difficult to understand them, let alone differentiate between them. All Christina could do was try to forget about Bryony and return to normality.

Deciding to keep the stockroom locked, she was pleased that she'd worn a long skirt and high-necked blouse. Concealing her curves and mounds with drab clothes, she might not attract attention from certain randy students. Wandering into the classroom, she dumped her bag on the desk and sighed. This wasn't going to be a good day. She'd not planned her lesson, not slept well, and had missed breakfast. To make matters worse, images of Bryony's hairless pussy lips continually loomed in her racked mind. At least she had the afternoon free, giving her a chance to catch up on some sleep.

'Good morning, Brian,' Christina said cheerily, looking up as the would-be pimp walked into the classroom. 'You're bright and early.'

'Yeah,' he murmured, brushing his long hair away from his face. 'I've been hearing things about you.'

'Hearing things?' she echoed fearfully, her stomach churning. If this was about her escapades in the stockroom . . . She really didn't need this. 'You've heard nothing bad, I hope?'

'That depends, doesn't it?'

'Depends on what?'

'What you reckon is bad.'

'Why don't you just say what you want to say, Brian? It's rather early in the day to play games with words.'

'I thought we'd go into the stockroom and discuss my proposition,' he said, grinning.

'Proposition? Brian, you're not making any sense. What do you want to go into the stockroom for? Is there some thing you need? Some paper or . . .'

'There's something I need, all right,' he sniggered. 'I need you to give me a wank.'

'I *beg* your pardon?' Christina gasped, feigning shock. 'How dare you—'

'You can cut out the acting. Why don't you go to the old man and tell him that I've been a naughty boy?'

'I will, don't you worry. I'll go and see Mr Wright and—'

'And tell him that you wanked Baz Doogan?'

'Brian, I suggest you go and sit down. I think it best that I forget what you just said.'

'*You* might forget it, but other people won't when I tell them that you wanked Baz in the stockroom.'

'Are you threatening me?'

'Yes, I am. All I want is a quick wank. The others will be here soon. You've got about five minutes to decide.'

Biting her lip, Christina leaned on her desk and hung her head. The situation was crazy, she reflected, her breathing unsteady. Her third day at Spadger Heath was going to be the third day of a continuing nightmare. Doogan had obviously opened his mouth, probably boasting to half the school about Miss Shaw wanking him off in the stockroom. There was a choice, Christina decided. She could confine her stockroom masturbation sessions to the three lads on the condition that they tell no one. Or she could end it there and then and take the inevitable flak. The second option wasn't really viable, she concluded. The flak would become a full-scale blitz, not least from the headmaster. She'd already told the first two lads not to open their mouths. *Boys will be boys*, she reflected uneasily. If she complied with Brian's wish, he'd only go boasting to his friends.

'How many people has Doogan lied to?' she asked. 'He's told you some cock and bull story about me, obviously to make himself look big. How many other people has he told?'

'I don't think he's told anyone else. When he told me last night, he said that I was to keep my mouth shut. So what's it to be?'

'Barry and I have what I thought was a secret. Seeing as he's told you . . . If I let you in on our game, you must promise me that you'll tell no one.'

'Yeah, of course,' he said, leering.

'I mean it, Brian. One word to anyone, and that's it.'

'Yeah, yeah, OK.'

'Come into the stockroom, Brian.'

Taking the key from her bag and unlocking the door, Christina glanced at her watch. She had fifteen minutes or so before the others arrived. *Time enough to make another fatal mistake*, she mused, leading the boy into the room and closing the door. Having a supply of fresh teenager cock to play with pleased her, but the attendant dangers worried her. It didn't matter what the boys thought of her. A tart, a slag, a whore . . . But it was imperative that word of her indecent behaviour didn't get out. Too many students knew of her stockroom exploits as it was and, if the other teachers got wind of her sexual activities, she'd not only be out of a job but disgraced.

Scrutinizing Brian as he waited patiently for her intimate attention, she had a feeling of power over him. The students had thought that they'd had power over their new teacher, but the tables were turning. Their taunts and jibes were becoming less and there'd been little or no swearing. Perhaps this was the answer, she concluded. Come to an agreement with the ringleaders, wank their eager cocks regularly to keep their hormones under control . . .

'Well?' she said, looking down at Brian's crotch. 'Aren't you going to get it out?'

'Yes,' he murmured – almost sheepishly – as he tugged his zip down.

'You're not shy, are you?'

'No, no,' he replied, hauling his stiffening penis out of his trousers.

'Remember, one word of this to anyone and you'll get no more.'

'I know that.'

Taking the fleshy shaft of Brian's cock in her hand, Christina rolled his foreskin back and forth over his swollen knob with her thumb. A pang of arousal jolting her contracting womb, she realized that she enjoyed appeasing the boys' cocks as much as they enjoyed her intimate attention. What was Charles doing for sexual relief? she wondered. She thought once more about her life at home with her parents. Living in comparative luxury with no money worries had been fine, but she now realized how sheltered her life had been. She was hardly living a sheltered life now, she reflected. This was the third boy she'd wanked either by hand or mouth since starting at Spadger Heath College, not to mention her lesbian encounter with Bryony.

Watching Brian's purple knob appear and disappear as she rolled his foreskin back and forth, Christina thought about kneeling and taking his ripe plum into her thirsty mouth. Brown had enjoyed her mouthing and sucking, and Doogan had that pleasure to look forward to. Or did he? It was one thing being known for her illicit wanking, but quite another to be named a cocksucker. Eyeing again Brian's swollen knob, his spermslit, she felt her knees bending. She was weakening in her arousal, she knew as she licked her full lips. Weakening in her arousal, and plunging ever deeper into her stupidity.

Again, she tried to justify her actions to herself. Wanking the three boys obviously wasn't the way most teachers behaved, but was it really that bad? They enjoyed it, she was beginning to love it, and she could get on with her lessons uninterrupted. Although she'd planned to talk to Alison about her problems, she now thought it best not to mention anything. Her thinking was changing. What she'd initially looked upon as a problem was now becoming most pleasurable. Wanking the teenagers to orgasm, bringing out their fresh spunk . . . Was that a problem? Only if word got round, she mused again. Keep this secret, and she'd not only enjoy the lads' solid cocks but she'd keep her job.

As Brian gasped, his young body trembling, Christina watched his spunk jetting from his twitching knob-head. Splattering over the floor, the white liquid flowed in torrents from his orgasming cock, and she began to wish that she'd engulfed his purple glans in her mouth and swallowed his sex juices. *Maybe next time*, she reflected, her clitoris rousing, emerging from beneath its pinken hood. Sperm running over her hand, she brought out the last of the lad's pleasure and released his young cock. His face flushed, his legs sagging, he shuddered as he leaned against the wall to steady himself.

*Number three*, Christina reflected, lapping up the sperm from her hand as Brian watched in amazement. Cleaning her fingers, the taste of sperm lingering on her tongue, she opened the door and ordered him out of the room. Obediently following her instructions, he sat at his desk as she closed the stockroom door and turned the key. *Stockroom?* she mused. *Sex room, more like*. Pleased to think that she only had to get through the morning, she sorted through her papers as the students filed into the classroom. An afternoon off, relaxing at home, was just what she needed.

'Is it all right if I come round this evening?' Bryony asked as she approached Christina's desk.

'No,' Christina said firmly, gazing into the girl's sparkling eyes. 'Go to your desk and sit down, please.'

'How can you be like this after—'

'Do as you're told, Bryony.'

'You'll be sorry,' the girl snapped, mooching across the room to her desk.

Sighing, Christina hoped that this particular student

wasn't going to cause problems. She knew only too well that, at Bryony's tender age, the girl's hormones would be running wild and she might do something stupid Bryony obviously believed that she was in love. Hormones, love, lust . . . They were lethal ingredients that could easily explode into a very dangerous situation. Christina did her best to get through the morning, despite one or two disruptions from a couple of boys who weren't under her control – yet.

Checking Bryony's address before she left the college, Christina decided to visit the girl's mother. She wasn't sure what she was going to say, but she wanted to get an idea of Bryony's home life, perhaps get a chance to look around. The girl might well have been lying, making out that she lived in a hell-hole to gain some sympathy. Perhaps her mother was really a loving woman who kept the home nice and cooked decent meals for her daughter. Knocking on the front door, Christina's first impression wasn't favourable. The small front garden was a mass of weeds and rubbish and the front window had been broken and boarded up.

'Yes?' a scruffy middle-aged woman asked as she opened the door.

'Hello,' Christina smiled. 'I'm Bryony's teacher and—'

'You'd better come in,' the woman snapped, walking down the hall. 'What's the little slut done now?'

'Oh, she hasn't done anything,' Christina said, closing the door and following the woman into the front room. 'I just thought that . . .'

Her words tailing off as she looked around the room and breathed in the unmistakable smell of alcohol fumes, Christina shook her head. The place really was a tip.

Clothes and newspapers strewn everywhere, empty gin bottles littering every available shelf – she realized that Bryony had been telling the truth. Although Christina felt sorry for the girl, she knew that she couldn't invite her to her flat and befriend her. Befriend her? Bryony didn't want friendship, she wanted lesbian sex. Declining the offer of a seat as the girl's mother pushed a pile of clothes off the armchair, Christina asked her whether she was managing to cope with her daughter.

'Cope with her?' she scoffed. 'There's no *coping* with the little slut. She does nothing around the house, nothing to help me. All she does is sit in her room.'

'May I see her room?' Christina asked.

'See what you like. It's top of the stairs, on the right.'

Climbing the stairs, Christina didn't know why she'd gone to the house. She'd gain nothing by speaking to her mother, or by looking at Bryony's room. Opening the door, she gazed at the neatly made bed, a row of books lined up on a shelf above a small desk. Bryony was obviously doing her best to lead a normal life, Christina mused. Albeit under extremely difficult circumstances. Opening the bedside table drawer, she knew that she shouldn't be rummaging through the girl's things. It was just that she wanted to know more about Bryony, what sort of person she was.

Christina frowned as she pulled out a small vibrator. The pink shaft was encrusted with dried vaginal juice, and she imagined the girl lying in her bed taking herself to massive orgasms. Switching the device on, she smiled as it buzzed softly in her hand. Bryony shaved her pussy, used a vibrator . . . *Hormones running amok*, Christina told herself, slipping the vibrator back into the drawer. Leaving the room, she closed the door and went downstairs to the lounge.

'She keeps her bedroom nice,' she said, gazing at the woman sprawled across the sofa. 'Does she have a boyfriend?'

'God knows what she gets up to. I never know whether she's in or out, let alone screwing boys. Knowing that little slut, she's probably—'

'Why do you call her a slut?'

'Her father went off with a girl not much older than Bryony. All teenage girls are sluts.'

'Well, I'll be going,' Christina said, forcing a smile. 'I'll tell her you called.'

'Yes, please do that. Goodbye.'

Leaving the house, Christina realized that Bryony needed some help. Her mother's attitude towards young girls was understandable, but why had her father walked out? There were two sides to every story, Christina reflected, wondering what Charles was doing. Walking the short distance to her flat, she knew that it would be a mistake to invite Bryony there. But she felt that she had to do something. Perhaps, the next time Alison was out for the evening, she'd ask the girl to call round for a chat. *Only a chat*, she vowed, dumping her bag on the hall table.

Filling the kettle, she didn't realize that Alison was in until the girl appeared in the kitchen doorway dressed only in her bra and panties. Scrutinizing the mounds of her breasts, her nipples pushing against the thin silk cups, Christina felt her womb contract. She had to drag her gaze away from her flatmate's curvaceous young body, she knew as she offered her a cup of coffee. Lesbian sex with Bryony was one thing, but to . . .

'How long have you been back?' Christina asked, spooning coffee into two cups.

'About an hour,' Alison replied. 'I didn't expect you home.'

'I have the afternoon off.'

'The afternoon off? I thought teachers worked long hours.'

'They do. Although I'm not at the college right now, I'm still supposed to be preparing lessons. How are your parents?'

'They're OK. We . . . we had a long chat. My mother and I don't agree on certain issues.'

'Oh?'

'She can't accept me, the way I am. Anyway, what did you get up to last night?'

'Oh, er . . . Nothing, really. I stayed in and relaxed.'

'Who was your visitor?'

'Visitor?' Christina echoed, wondering whether Alison knew about Bryony. 'I didn't have a visitor.'

'I found a pair of panties in the lounge. They were tucked beneath the sofa.'

'Oh, they're mine,' Christina said, averting her gaze as Alison stared hard at her.

'Your name's B. Johnson, is it?'

'Er . . . I don't understand.'

'It's all right, you don't have to tell me what you get up to.'

'I haven't been up to anything, Alison. OK, so one of my students came to see me. I wasn't going to mention it since it's not allowed. The college don't like—'

'Not allowed? You think I'd tell them?'

'No, no. It's just that . . . Bryony is a mixed-up girl.'

'And a lesbian?'

'Yes. No . . . I mean . . .'

'Christina, my mother can't accept me because I'm a lesbian.'

'Oh, er . . . Right.'

'Are you?'

'No, no, I . . . Look, we need to talk. Let's take our coffee into the lounge.'

Walking through the hall, Christina wondered why she wasn't shocked by the girl's revelation. *Alison, a lesbian? I'm living with a lesbian*, she thought, wondering whether that would change things. She knew that she was going to have to put her cards on the table. Alison had admitted that she was a lesbian, and Christina felt that she owed it to the other girl to be honest. How was it possible to be honest, though? she mused. She didn't know whether she was a lesbian or not, so honesty didn't come into it. Sitting in the armchair as Alison reclined on the sofa, she recalled her flatmate's words. *I haven't even laid eyes on a dick, let alone my hands*. Wondering why the girl had said that, she assumed that she was trying to conceal her lesbianism by making out that she fancied men.

'So you don't want to lay your hands on a dick, then?' Christina asked.

'My hands . . . Oh, you mean what I said in the pub the other night. I didn't know your thoughts or feelings on the matter. We were getting on very well. Sharing the flat was working out well and I didn't want to ruin everything.'

'Have you got a girlfriend?'

'No, no. I did have but . . . That finished months ago. So, tell me about this Bryony girl.'

'There's nothing to tell, really,' Christina sighed.

'Nothing to tell?' Alison giggled. 'I find her panties

beneath the sofa, and you say there's nothing to tell? How long has this been going on?'

'It hasn't. God, this is only my third day at the college. She came here once, and that was last night. I left her in here and, when I got back, she'd stripped off.'

'And?'

'And . . . and we . . . you know?'

'Yes, I think I do. How old is she?'

'Eighteen, I think. Look, Alison, it was a one-off. I'm not a lesbian. At least, I don't think I am.'

'I remember going through that stage. I was fourteen when I got friendly with a girl in my class at school. We went for a walk in the park and ended up in the woods. At first, we were only mucking about, experimenting sexually. We talked about masturbation and one thing led to another. We were together, as a couple, for about a year. I learned a lot about myself during that time. I discovered that I wasn't interested in the boys and . . . I finally let myself go, found my own path. I'd been fighting my feelings, my desires. Once I stopped fighting, I began to enjoy my sexuality. So, you're not interested in the teenage hulks in your class?'

'That's just it,' Christina sighed. 'I've . . . I've been with three boys since I started at the college.'

'Been with . . . ?'

'No, no. I mean . . . I masturbated them. In fact, I sucked one of them off. God, you must think me awful.'

'Not at all. My only concern would be the scandal if it came to light.'

'I've thought about that. In fact, that's *all* I've thought about. I'm in a mess, aren't I?'

'No, I don't think so. What did you feel after you'd been with Bryony?'

'I don't know. That's the problem, I don't know.'

'I'll tell you what I did. I was only fourteen, of course. But I met this girl again, and we masturbated each other again. I still wasn't sure what I was or what I wanted so I saw her again. That time, we went further. You know, licking and sucking each other to orgasm. I think it must have been after that third time that I made my mind up. We'd been naked in the woods, kissing, licking, mouthing . . . Once I'd let myself go and got into it, I realized that I'd never known anything like it. As I said, we were together for a year or so. If I were you, I'd see this Bryony again and—'

'There are complications, Alison. Her mother, her home life . . . There are far too many complications. Apart from that, she's too young.'

'In that case, discover your true sexual identity by going with an older girl.'

Averting her gaze, Christina wondered whether Alison was suggesting that she have a sexual relationship with *her*. The girl was quite attractive, Christina thought. But to have sex with her . . . Everything would change, she reflected. They'd be in each other's beds, they'd no longer enjoy the privacy of their own rooms . . . Christina had made enough mistakes for one week. To embark on a sexual relationship with Alison would only add to the mess.

'Tell me what you think,' Alison said, rising to her feet and unhooking her bra. Her full breasts tumbling from the silk cups, her nipples stiffening pertly in the relatively cool air of the lounge, she tossed the garment over the back of the chair as Christina gazed open-mouthed at her. Slipping her thumbs between the tight elastic of her panties and her shapely hips, Alison began to pull the garment down. The top of her sex crack came into view and she lowered her panties further, revealing the full length of her creamy pinken slit to Christina's wide-eyed stare.

'"Well?' Alison smiled.

'I've seen you naked before,' Christina replied, focusing on the girl's ruby inner lips peeping from her sex crack.

'You've *seen* but you haven't *touched*,' Alison said huskily, walking across the room and standing in front of Christina. 'Go on, touch me.'

Reaching out, Christina stroked the soft swell of her flatmate's vaginal lips, her fingertip tentatively brushing the sensitive petals of her inner labia. She tried to fight her inner desire, the overwhelming feeling to move forward and lick the creamy valley of the other girl's pussy. Taking Alison's fleshy outer lips between her fingers and thumbs, she peeled the soft sex pads apart, exposing the wet inner flesh of her sex valley. Examining the girl there, she focused on her ripening clitoris. The pink budling emerging from beneath its fleshy hood, swelling as her arousal heightened, Alison let out a rush of breath as Christina stretched her outer labia further apart, opening her vulval cleft as wide as she could without causing pain.

'Feel inside me,' Alison breathed, looking down at her open vaginal valley. Stroking the pink funnel of flesh surrounding the entrance to her friend's sex sheath, Christina slipped her finger deep into the fiery heat of her wet duct. Massaging the fleshy walls of her vagina, caressing her urethral opening, she twisted and bent her finger, sending the girl into raptures of sexual pleasure. Alison's legs sagged beneath her trembling body as she clung to Christina's head to support herself while the girl drove a second finger into the tightening duct of her sex-drenched pussy.

Having wanked Brian and brought out his sperm that morning, Christina couldn't believe that she now had two fingers embedded deep within the wet sheath of her flatmate's tight pussy. There was going to be no end to her sexual encounters, she knew as she turned her thoughts to Bryony. The girl was so young, fresh, curvaceous, alluring . . . Imagining her lying in her bed with her legs wide apart, the buzzing tip of her vibrator pressed against the solid nub of her clitoris, Christina felt a quiver run through her young womb.

Was it possible to fall in love with another girl? she wondered, easing a third finger into Alison's tightening vaginal duct. Christina had never known love, and was now beginning to believe that love, lust and sex were one and the same. Licking and masturbating a girl to orgasm wasn't love, she reflected. And yet it hadn't been purely cold sex with Bryony. There had been something else in their caressing, their licking – but what? Love was indefinable, she concluded, slipping her creamy-wet fingers out of Alison's hot vaginal duct.

Moving forward, Christina parted the other girl's fleshy love lips and pressed her mouth hard against the glistening pink flesh surrounding her erect clitoris. Alison gasped and shuddered as Christina's tongue repeatedly swept over the sensitive tip of her pleasure nodule. Placing one foot on the sofa, she thrust her hips forward, grinding her cunt flesh hard against Christina's hot mouth, sighing in her ecstasy as her immensely responsive clitoris transmitted ripples of pure sexual pleasure deep into her trembling womb.

'Enjoying yourself?' Alison asked, looking down at Christina. Nodding her head, Christina sucked on the girl's solid clitoris and slipped three fingers deep into the spasming sheath of her tight vagina. More than merely enjoying herself, she was loving with a passion every instant of sucking and fingering her friend's pussy. Managing to force all four fingers deep into the stretched sheath of Alison's vagina, she kneaded her inner flesh. Sucking and licking her swollen clitoris, she knew that her lesbian flatmate was nearing her orgasm as she let out whimpers of satisfaction.

'Oh, God,' Alison murmured, clutching Christina's head as her clitoris exploded in orgasm. Her ejaculatory juices streaming down Christina's hand, she shuddered violently as her lesbian-induced pleasure peaked. 'God, my beautiful cunt,' she whimpered, the crude word surprising Christina and, at the same time, sending her own arousal through the roof. Sustaining the girl's orgasm, Christina repeatedly thrust her fingers deep into the wet heat of her vagina and mouthed and sucked on her pulsating clitoris. Breathing in her girl-scent, savouring the taste of her clitoris, Christina knew that this was only the beginning of the lesbian affair. They'd be having sex at every opportunity now, enjoying each other's naked bodies, loving and licking, sucking and mouthing . . .

'That's enough,' Alison finally gasped, her curvaceous young body crumpling to the floor as Christina's wet fingers left the tight sheath of the girl's inflamed pussy. Lying on the carpet with her limbs spread, Alison's naked body convulsed and twitched as she recovered from her girl-induced climax. Christina watched her flatmate's juices of arousal trickling from her rubicund sex crack, the creamy fluid running down between her rounded buttocks and pooling on the floor.

Would Alison reciprocate? she wondered, recalling Bryony's tongue lapping between her vaginal lips. Gazing at Alison's pretty mouth, her full red lips, Christina wasn't sure whether she wanted to experience lesbian sex with two girls in two days. *Three lads and two girls in three days?* she reflected, her clitoris swelling in expectation. She recalled her flatmate's words. *I'd been fighting my feelings, my desires. Once I stopped fighting, I began to enjoy my sexuality.* Realizing that she had to give herself a chance to discover her true sexual identity, she decided to offer her young body to Alison for lesbian sex.

'I enjoyed that,' she said, looking down at Alison as her naked body stopped writhing. Alison stretched languorously before adopting a cross-legged sitting position on the floor.

'And so did I,' Alison giggled, her sparkling eyes gazing longingly up at Christina. 'There are things I could teach you,' she murmured. 'Things that . . . I think it would be best to take you slowly along the path to true lesbian sex.'

'And how do you intend to do that?' Christina asked, her stomach somersaulting.

'Slip your panties off, lie back on the sofa with your legs open – and I'll show you.'

Lifting her superbly rounded buttocks clear of the sofa, Christina pulled her panties off and reclined, her thighs parted. As Alison settled at her feet and pulled her skirt up over her stomach, she imagined Charles walking in and discovering the shocking truth. Charles would be horrified – he'd call her a filthy slut, a whore. Wondering whether to tell him that she'd found true love with another girl, Christina let out a rush of breath as Alison parted the swollen lips of her vagina and teased the nub of her erect clitoris with the tip of her wet tongue.

Alison knew exactly what to do, Christina thought as the girl's tongue lightly brushed the tip of her sensitive clitoris again. She could feel her juices of lesbian arousal seeping between the engorged wings of her inner vaginal lips, trickling down to the sensitive brown tissue surrounding her bottom-hole. Gasping as her flatmate ran her fingertip over the funnel of pink flesh surrounding the gaping entrance to her contracting vaginal canal, expertly teasing her there, Christina closed her eyes and let herself go.

'That's it,' Alison murmured, her wet tongue caressing the tip of Christina's solid clitoris. 'Relax completely. Close your eyes and let me take you to your sexual heaven.' Her firm young breasts and stomach quivering with nervous desire, Christina parted her thighs as widely as she could, offering the most intimate sexual centre of her beautiful body to her lesbian friend. She could hear the slurping sounds of sex as Alison's tongue worked around the wet portal to her drenched pussy. Lapping up her cunt milk, the girl slipped her tongue into Christina's hot sex shaft, teasing her inner flesh, working on her sensitive urethral opening. To Christina's surprise, Alison moved down, her wet tongue delving between the firm orbs of Christina's buttocks, as if trying to gain access to the tightly closed ring of her anus.

'It's all right,' Alison reassured her student of lesbian sex. 'Move forward on the sofa so your bum is over the edge of the cushion.' Complying, Christina slid down the sofa, the small of her back resting on the edge of the cushion, her thighs still parted wide. She could feel

Alison's wet tongue delving into her anal valley, the girl's saliva mingling with her own juices of sex as she parted the warm globes of her bottom. Gasping, Christina reached beneath her young body and yanked her buttocks wide apart as her flatmate's tongue teased her brown ring, tasting and wetting her there.

'God,' she breathed as the tip of Alison's tongue slipped into her anal hole. 'Alison, I . . . Oh, God. This isn't right.' Ignoring her, Alison continued her anal French kissing, pushing her wet tongue deeper into Christina's tight rectum. Writhing and squirming on the sofa as the new and exciting sensations permeated her very being, Christina yanked the rounded cheeks of her buttocks further apart, offering the open hole of her anus to her lesbian friend.

*If Charles could see me now*, she thought, imagining the young man's face as he witnessed the crude lesbian anilingus. Had Charles paid Christina's young body this kind of attention, had he taken her to these amazing sexual heights . . . But he hadn't. Charles had only driven his solid cock into Christina's vagina and spunked her cervix, never giving a thought to her feminine needs, to her true pleasure. Charles had lost, Christina reflected, her young body quivering as Alison licked the creamy-wet walls of her tightening vagina. His pompous attitude, his seeming obliviousness to Christina's feminine desires . . . No doubt he'd find a girl who would be willing to lie back and allow him to satisfy his cock once a week. But he'd never experience the crudities of sex, the blissful sensations of anilingus. Charles had lost.

Her body jolting as Alison thrust a finger deep into the hot tube of her rectum, Christina could hardly believe the wondrous sensations produced by the crude act. She could feel the delicate tissue of her anus gripping the girl's pistoning finger, the secret nerve endings tingling as her young womb rhythmically contracted and her juices of desire gushed from the gaping entrance of her tight pussy. Alison was good, she mused as the girl thrust at least two fingers into the wet heat of Christina's vaginal sheath, massaging the thin membrane dividing her sex ducts with her double pistoning.

Christina let out whimpers of sexual bliss as her young friend sucked her ripe clitoris into her hot mouth and swept her tongue over its sensitive tip. Her body glowing, alive with the thrill of crude sex, Christina threw her head back, her eyes rolling, her nostrils flaring as Alison held her on the verge of orgasm. Teetering of the brink of ecstasy, the walls of convention crumbling, she finally accepted that she was bisexual if not a full-blown lesbian. Imagining a boy's cock sperming in her mouth, the creamy liquid overflowing and dribbling down her chin as she drank from the throbbing knob, she cried out as her orgasm erupted within the pulsating nubble of her solid clitoris.

'More, more,' she gasped, her young body shaking violently, her juices of Sapphic arousal streaming from her contracting vagina and flooding over Alison's hand as she repeatedly thrust her fingers in and out of Christina's inflamed sex holes. Convulsing wildly, Christina screamed out as her pleasure ripped through her nervous system, gripping her very soul. If this was taking her slowly along the path to true lesbian sex, then what other sexual delights would she encounter during her journey, she wondered. If this was just the beginning of the road to lesbian fulfilment, then what unimaginable ecstasy lay in wait at the end?

'All right?' Alison asked as Christina's orgasm began to wane.

'Yes, yes,' she breathed, her naked thighs twitching uncontrollably. 'God, I've never—'

'Just relax,' Alison murmured, slowing her double finger-thrusting. 'Come down slowly. This evening, I'll take you higher. This evening, I'll love you like you've never been loved before.'

'Yes, yes,' Christina breathed again, her mind spinning in her sexual delirium.

Her flatmate's fingers finally sliding out of her inflamed sex sheaths, Christina lay quivering on the sofa in the aftermath of her girl-induced pleasure. Her thoughts drifting, she pictured Bryony's hairless vulval lips, the young girl's clitoris pulsating in orgasm. Images of teenage boys' swollen knobs spunking in her mouth loomed in her racked mind, heavy balls, solid penile shafts, fleshy cunt labia, the unfurling petals of inner lips dripping with girl-cum . . .

Sleep creeping up on her as Alison took the quilt from her bed and covered her sated body, Christina felt warm, satisfied, fulfilled, loved. Everything was working out well, she reflected. Her first three days at the college, her flatmate . . . Nothing would go wrong. The boys were happy, Alison was happy, Bryony . . . Bryony would be all right. Christina would take the girl slowly along the path to true lesbian sex. Everything was going to be all right. Wasn't it?

# 5

Christina woke to find herself alone in the flat. She felt hot and sticky around her vulval area. Her sex juices partially dried on her smooth thighs, her sparse pubic curls matted on her Venus mound, she took a shower before making herself a cup of coffee. As she sat at the kitchen table, wondering where Alison had got to, she pondered on the forthcoming evening. Alcohol would loosen her up, she mused, deciding to get in some vodka for the hours of lesbian lust ahead. Did she need to loosen up? She'd done pretty well with Alison. Letting go, relaxing, offering her young body to the girl for crude sex . . . Vodka would wipe out any remaining inhibitions, she decided, wondering whether she should tongue Alison's bottom-hole.

Anilingus would be interesting. Licking and sucking a girl's anus, tasting her there, tonguing inside the tight tube of her rectum . . . There was nothing more intimate, she concluded. From straight sex with Charles to lesbian sex *and* crude anal tonguing . . . there was nothing more perverse. Or was there? Christina had never given a second thought to her bottom-hole. Charles had probably thought that it hadn't existed, using only her vagina to satisfy his cock. What would Alison's anus taste like?

The notion sending quivers through her young womb, Christina began to wonder whether she was in some way abnormal. Her overwhelming desire to commit anilingus on another girl wasn't normal, surely? She knew nothing about other girls' sex lives, but she couldn't imagine any of her friends licking each other's anuses. But as long as the crude act was committed in the privacy of her flat, no one would think badly of her, she decided, her pink tongue licking her succulent lips as she imagined tasting Alison's anal portal. Would Bryony enjoy anilingus?

As the evening drew near, Christina slipped out to the local off-licence and bought two bottles of vodka and some orange juice. The scene was set, she mused, slipping a CD into the hi-fi and placing the drinks and glasses on the lounge table. All set for an evening of crude lesbian lust. Wearing a short red skirt and white blouse, with no panties or bra underneath these revealing outer garments, she felt her clitoris swell as she waited for Alison to return. Again wondering where the girl had got to, she poured herself a vodka and orange and sat on the sofa. Sipping her drink, the alcohol quickly taking effect, the soft music drifting lazily around the room, her juices of desire flowing between her engorged love lips . . . All she needed now was her lesbian lover.

'She's probably in the lounge,' Alison said, closing the front door. Wondering who the girl had brought back to the flat, Christina felt her stomach churning. This was supposed to be *their* evening, an evening of love, lust, crude sex. Alison must have bumped into a friend. Perhaps it was a fleeting visit, a quick cup of coffee and a look around the flat before leaving. Perhaps the evening was about to be ruined. As the lounge door opened and Alison appeared, Christina looked up.

'Guess who I found hovering outside?' Alison said, her pretty face beaming.

'Found outside?' Christina murmured, frowning. 'I don't know.'

'Hello,' Bryony said softly, following Alison into the room.

'Bryony, I . . .'

'I said that she could join us,' Alison announced, licking her succulent lips provocatively.

'Is that all right?' Bryony asked. 'I mean, you don't mind?'

'No, I . . . I suppose it's all right.'

Bryony sat on the sofa next to Christina, her short skirt revealing her naked thighs as she leaned back. Was she wearing panties? Had she used her vibrator? Christina wondered whether Alison had a threesome in mind, three-way lesbian sex. Not sure whether she wanted to be part of any such games, Christina wondered what to do. This wasn't how it was meant to be. Sex with her flatmate and one of her students? This wasn't what she'd envisaged. Besides, Bryony was too young for such things. Watching Alison pour a glass of vodka and orange and pass it to the younger girl, Christina knew that this could easily get out of hand. Bryony was naive, gullible, and probably easily led. If the girl drank too much and Alison suggested three-way sex . . .

'This is cosy,' Alison said, smiling at Christina. 'Bryony, why don't you go into the bathroom and get ready?'

'Get ready?' the girl echoed questioningly.

'Aren't you going to slip out of your clothes?'

'Oh, er . . . yes, all right,' she replied, leaving the sofa. Knocking back her drink, she placed her glass on the table and moved to the door. 'I won't be a minute.'

'Alison,' Christina whispered as the door closed. 'I don't think this is a good idea.'

'I think it's a *great* idea,' the other girl retorted. 'She wants sex. And who better than us to—'

'I was trying to break off my relationship with her – such as it is,' Christina added hastily. 'She's too young, for starters. She's a student of mine, she believes that she's in love with me . . .'

'Too young, my tongue-hungry arse. Let yourself go, Christina. Just relax and enjoy the evening. I have an idea. Bryony can be our sex slave.'

'*What?*'

'We'll tell her what to do, instruct her in the ways of—'

'Alison . . .'

'Shush, I think she's coming back.'

As the younger girl walked into the room, Christina gazed longingly at the violin curves of her teenage body, the petite mounds of her breasts, the hairless lips of her vulva. She was beautiful, eager, willing . . . But surely it wouldn't be a good idea to use her as a sex slave. Christina realized that she didn't know Alison at all. Although the girl had seemed fairly quiet and reserved at first, she obviously had hidden erotic fantasies. How deep did her sexual desires run? Christina wondered. Suggesting that they should use Bryony as a sex slave wasn't what Christina had expected of her flatmate. There again, she'd not thought that Alison was a lesbian before they'd licked and . . . But then, wasn't Christina herself a lesbian?

'You have a lovely body,' Alison said, refilling the younger girl's glass. 'There, drink that.'

'Thanks,' Bryony murmured, taking her drink. 'I didn't know that you lived with another girl,' she said, looking at Christina.

'Yes, er, er . . . we share the flat.'

Sitting in the armchair and scrutinizing Bryony's curves and crevices, Alison licked her full red lips. 'Why don't you come and stand over here?' she asked. 'I'd like to take a closer look at you.'

Following Alison's instructions, Bryony stood in front of her and allowed her to stroke the petite mounds of her mammary spheres, the fleshy swell of her hairless vaginal lips. Christina watched Alison's hands wandering over the girl's naked body, running over her hips, cupping the firm moons of her buttocks. Christina had to admit that the sight aroused her, but she was still in two minds about allowing her young student to be used like this.

'Turn round and bend over,' Alison ordered the girl. Christina gazed in awe as Bryony leaned over and touched the floor, her naked buttocks projected, the gully of her bottom unashamedly displayed. Parting the full moons of her firm young arse, Alison moved forward on the chair and swept her tongue up and down the girl's anal valley, obviously delighting in the crude act, the bitter-sweet taste of her anus, as she fervently slurped and mouthed between Bryony's bum cheeks.

Her stomach somersaulting, Christina wondered whether she was jealous as she heard the young student's gasps of lesbian pleasure and watched her naked body trembling. Then, recalling Alison's words, she decided to let go and enjoy herself as she settled on the floor beside Bryony. Parting the fleshy swell of the girl's naked vaginal lips, she thrust three fingers deep into her tightening pussy and massaged her creamy inner flesh as Alison licked her sensitive anal ring with her wet tongue. Bryony shuddered, letting out whimpers of pleasure as both holes were expertly stimulated. Perhaps the evening wasn't going to be so bad after all, Christina mused, her fingers squelching the girl's pussy juices.

'You've been a naughty little girl,' Alison hissed, slapping Bryony's rounded buttocks with her palm.

'Ouch,' Bryony cried as the next slap resounded around the room and her naked body jolted.

'A *very* naughty little girl.'

Christina watched as Alison spanked the girl's firm anal orbs, wondering whether her flatmate was in control of her senses as she giggled wickedly. Bryony let out a yelp with every slap on her naked bottom, her young body trembling uncontrollably as Christina slipped her fingers out of her vaginal sheath. This wasn't right, Christina thought, watching Alison stand up. Holding the girl still with one hand and spanking her bum cheeks as hard as she could with the other, she seemed to be delighting in her dominant role. Was this what she'd had in mind for Christina? Had she gazed at Christina's bottom billowing her short skirt and imagined spanking her there?

'Alison,' Christina murmured. 'I don't think—'

'She's our sex slave,' the girl interrupted, grinning. 'Sex slaves should be taught their place.'

'Please, that's enough,' Bryony whimpered, struggling to stand up.

'I've barely started,' Alison chuckled, repeatedly spanking the girl's reddening bottom orbs. 'You *do* want to be our friend, don't you, Bryony?'

'Yes, but . . .'

'In that case, you'll do as you're told.'

Sitting on her heels, Christina watched the gruelling spanking, sure that Bryony could escape Alison's grip if she really wanted to. This wasn't lesbian sex, she reflected. Where was the pleasure, the loving caress of female fingertips, the gentle massaging? Confused, Christina imagined having her own buttocks spanked by Alison. Would she derive pleasure or pain from the cruel act? she pondered. Or both? Although whimpering and putting up what in any case looked like a perfunctory struggle, Bryony seemed to be enjoying the experience. But Alison shouldn't have exploited the fact that Bryony was young and lonely and needed friends.

'Are you going to behave yourself now?' Alison asked the trembling girl.

'Yes, yes, I will,' Bryony whimpered.

'You may stand up now and undress me.'

'All right.'

'All right, *mistress*.'

'All right, mistress.'

Christina was learning, she knew as she watched Bryony unbuttoning Alison's blouse. The girl's buttocks glowing a fire-red, her juices of lesbian desire running in rivers down her inner thighs, she slipped the blouse over her mistress's shoulders and unhooked her bra. Bryony was obviously enjoying playing the role of a slave. Perhaps she'd done this before? Christina reflected. She was into vibrators, and might well have a girlfriend she shared her young body with. Perhaps they regularly spanked each other. Gazing at Alison's stiffening nipples, the darkening discs of her areolae as their slave removed her clothing, Christina wondered whether spanking was something she wanted to learn about. Spanking, pain, pleasure ... Alison would probably be into bondage next, Christina mused as she climbed to her feet. If she wasn't already.

Pouring herself a large vodka and orange as Bryony

tugged Alison's skirt down to her ankles, Christina settled on the sofa to watch the lesbian show. She wasn't sure whether she wanted to join in, deciding to let the girls get on with it and perhaps make up a threesome later in the evening. Feeling left out, she watched Bryony tug Alison's panties down to her ankles. Bryony was supposed to have been Christina's friend, her secret lesbian lover, but now . . .

'I need a tongue bath,' Alison said, kneeling on the floor and resting her head on the armchair cushion. 'Lick my bottom, slave.'

'Yes, mistress,' Bryony replied, settling obediently on the floor behind Alison.

Kneeling between Alison's spread legs Bryony parted the girl's naked anal orbs and exposed the brown ring of her tightly closed anus. Watching with bated breath, Christina felt her clitoris inflate as Bryony moved forward, her pink tongue emerging between her full lips. Tentatively licking Alison's brown anal tissue, she began slurping fervently at the girl's bottom-hole. Obviously savouring the taste of her mistress's most private orifice, she yanked her anal cheeks wider apart and moaned softly through her nose.

Christina felt a pang of jealousy as she recalled Bryony's first visit to the flat and pictured her naked body, her petite breasts. Her breasts were barely formed, the small mounds cone-shaped, the areolae appearing to be pulled out by the elongated nipples. Christina pondered on the situation once more as Bryony followed Alison's orders and pushed her tongue deep into her rectal duct. This wasn't how it was supposed to be. Bryony was very young – she needed nurturing, loving. Again, Christina felt left out. But there was nothing she could do other than join the girls in their illicit lesbian pleasure.

'Finger my arsehole,' Alison murmured, her naked body trembling as she projected her buttocks further. Her crude words sending Christina's own arousal sky-high, Alison moaned softly as Bryony pushed the tip of her fingers past her yielding anal sphincter muscles. 'Come and join us,' Alison said, turning her head and gazing at Christina. Leaving the sofa, Christina settled on the floor and held Alison's rounded buttocks wide apart as Bryony drove her finger deep into the girl's tight rectal tube.

Christina had never seen the crude act of anal fingering. Gazing at Alison's delicate brown tissue stretched tautly around Bryony's finger, she pulled her flatmate's firm buttocks wider apart, allowing the girl better access to her mistress's anal canal. Following Alison's instructions, Bryony managed to force a second finger into her dilating anus. To her horror, Christina was overwhelmed by a compelling need to commit vulgar sexual acts on her flatmate. She imagined forcing a candle deep into the girl's rectal sheath, pushing a plastic deodorant bottle into her anal canal and abusing her. *Is this normal?* she wondered, grinning as Bryony managed to drive a third finger into Alison's anal tight duct.

Far removed from her life with her parents in a beautiful country house, Christina was discovering a new world. A world of impoverishment in a run-down part of London, a world of crude lesbian sex. More than a culture shock, this was something that Christina had never envisaged. She'd thought that she'd be teaching her students English, not the fine art of masturbation, blow jobs and lesbian sex. She'd imagined meeting a nice young man, perhaps embarking on a relationship leading to . . . It didn't matter what she'd expected, she realized that she was now part of that new world.

Leaning over, Christina licked Alison's naked buttocks, keeping her eye on the girl's painfully stretched anal ring as Bryony fingered her bottom-hole. Did she want to lick Alison there? Did she want to taste her anus, savour the bitter-sweet flavour of her most private hole? As Bryony withdrew her fingers in readiness to thrust into her mistress again, Christina licked Alison's taut anal tissue. Lapping fervently too at Bryony's fingers, her taste buds alive, she closed her eyes and lost herself in her sexual delirium.

It was the sheer crudity of the act that drove her on, sent her arousal soaring – she knew that as she tongued Alison's dark anal eye. As Bryony slipped her fingers out of the girl's anal duct, Christina pushed her tongue into Alison's bottom-hole and locked her lips to her brown tissue. Sucking hard, licking deep inside her rectal sheath, she thought that she could plunge no deeper into the mire of lewdness. Her nose pressed hard against her flatmate's bared anal gully, she breathed in her rectal scent. There was nothing more decadent, more debased, she reflected, forcing her wet tongue deeper into Alison's delicious rectum.

'Bryony, go to my room and look in the dressing-table drawer,' Alison breathed, her firm buttocks twitching. 'You'll find my vibrator there. I want it up my arse.'

Licking her lips, Christina sat up and watched Bryony leave the room. Both girls had vibrators, she mused, wondering why she'd never owned one. She'd missed out, she knew as her thoughts turned to Charles. Oral sex, anal fingering, clitoral vibrating . . . She'd led the life of a nun. As Bryony returned, clutching a huge vibrator, Christina was sure that Alison's rectum would never accommodate the massive pink shaft. Passing the device to Christina, Bryony yanked Alison's rounded bum cheeks wide apart, exposing the salivated brown ring of her tight anus.

'Do it,' Alison murmured, wiggling her hips as she made herself comfortable. Pressing the rounded tip of the vibrator hard against the girl's anal tissue, Christina pushed and twisted the shaft. Amazed as the plastic phallus drove into the girl, her delicate anal tissue dilating as the tapered shaft sank deep into her rectal canal, Christina switched the device on. Shaking violently, Alison let out cries of sheer sexual bliss as the pink shaft drove deeper into her hot bowels, transmitting its electrifying vibrations into her contracting womb.

Withdrawing the buzzing vibrator until only the tip remained in Alison's rectum, Christina licked the pink shaft. Salivating the hot phallus, lubricating the vibrating rod, she drove the device deep into the girl's trembling body. Alison's bottom bucked as Christina pistoned her arsehole, repeatedly thrusting the vibrator into her hot bowels. Lying on her back, Bryony positioned her head between Alison's splayed thighs and lapped at her dripping vaginal crack. The young student knew exactly what to do, Christina observed, realizing that her pupil might not be as naive as she'd at first thought.

Watching the girl's tongue driving deep into Alison's vaginal sheath, Christina continued to pump her flatmate's rectal tube with the buzzing vibrator. The thrusting phallus taking the girl closer to her orgasm as Bryony tongued and sucked her vaginal opening, Alison cried out again in the grip of her lesbian pleasure. She was about to come, Christina knew as she watched the girl's creamy juices of desire gushing from her gaping vaginal entrance and flooding Bryony's face.

'Yes,' Alison cried, her orgasm exploding, her naked body shaking fiercely. The sound of Bryony's tongue lapping and slurping at the girl's cream-drenched vaginal entrance sent Christina into a sexual near-frenzy as she pistoned Alison's inflamed anal duct with the vibrator. This wasn't love, she thought. This was hard, raw, cold sex. The kind of sex she was rapidly becoming used to. *Who needs love?* she reflected, slapping Alison's twitching buttocks as hard as she could.

Sinking her teeth into one of her flatmate's naked buttocks, Christina continued to piston Alison's anal canal with the vibrator as Bryony sustained her multiple orgasm with her tonguing and mouthing. The idea of using Bryony as a sex slave was beginning to appeal to Christina. She imagined moving the girl into the flat, having her cook and clean and satisfy the needs of her mistresses' clitorises. There'd be no need for the slave to go to college, either. With somewhere to live and work to do, she could put the college and her drunken mother behind her. Realizing that she was fantasizing, Christina slowed her rectal pistoning as Alison's orgasm began to wane. Watching Bryony mouthing and sucking between Alison's inflamed vaginal lips, she leaped to her feet and dashed into the kitchen as the phone rang.

'Hello,' she said, pressing the receiver to her ear.

'Hello, Miss Shaw,' a male voice murmured. 'You have something I want.'

'I'm sorry? Who is this?'

'A work colleague. I've discovered your little secret, Miss Shaw.'

'My secret? I don't know what you're talking about.'

'The things you get up to in the stockroom. I have a proposition.'

'I have no idea what you're talking about,' Christina said softly, her heart racing, her mind spinning. 'Who are you?'

'A fellow teacher. Unless you want me to go to the head, or the newspapers, I suggest you do as I ask.'

'Newspapers? Look, I . . .'

'Don't play games with me, Miss Shaw. Meet me at the college in fifteen minutes. I'll be waiting in your classroom.'

'The college is closed. Besides, I—'

'The caretaker will be there, and *you*'d better be there.'

As the man hung up, Christina bit her lip. This was serious, she knew as she grabbed her bag from the hall table. She'd not recognized the man's voice, but she hadn't met all the teachers yet. Deciding to say nothing to Alison and Bryony as she left the flat, she knew that she had to put a stop to this before it properly started. One of the boys had obviously been blabbing, she mused. She'd taken a huge risk in trusting stupid teenage boys. And now it looked as though she had a serious problem on her hands. Walking down the street, the cool evening air wafting up her short skirt, she realized that she wasn't wearing a bra or panties.

'Shit,' she cursed, walking through the college gates to the main building. Alison had taken over with Bryony, and now some teacher or other was trying to get in on the act. This wasn't at all what she'd expected, and she began to wonder again whether she should leave the college. At least Charles hadn't turned up uninvited, she thought. Her parents would be coming up to see the flat at some stage. If they brought Charles along . . . well, she'd deal with that if and when it happened.

Waiting in her classroom, her hands trembling, Christina tried to devise a plan. Whoever her would-be blackmailer was obviously knew what she did in the stockroom, so there was no point in denying it. And it was pretty obvious what he wanted in return for his silence. But she wasn't going to engage in a sexual relationship with one of the teachers, particularly an enforced sexual relationship. The three lads and Bryony were more than enough, let alone a member of staff demanding that she wank his cock and bring out his sperm. And then there was Alison, she reflected. This wasn't how it was supposed to have been.

'I'm pleased that you decided to meet me,' a balding man said, grinning as he wandered into the classroom. 'Ponting,' he said, holding his hand out. 'Don Ponting, physical education.'

'What's all this about?' Christina asked, declining to shake his hand.

'You wouldn't be here if you didn't know what it was about,' he chuckled. 'You've proved your guilt by turning up. Shall we go into the stockroom?'

'Look, you've obviously discovered that I'm having a relationship with one of my students. I know it's wrong, but he is eighteen and—'

'Only one student, Miss Shaw?'

'What are you implying?'

'I'm not implying anything, I'm stating facts. You're having sex with at least three male students.'

'I am *not*,' she retorted angrily, wondering which of the teenagers had blabbed.

'Let's be sensible about this,' Ponting said softly. 'When you arrived on Monday, I looked at you and thought, now there's a nice piece of fresh meat.'

'Fresh meat?' Christina gasped indignantly. 'How dare you . . .'

'Nice breasts, shapely hips . . . and then I discover that you're rather generous with your young body. All I want is what you gave the students. If not, then I'll just have to—'

'You think you can blackmail me?'

'Blackmail is an ugly word, Miss Shaw. Let's just say that I want to join your gang of lads. I want to be part of the games, that's all. Shall we go into the stockroom now?'

Ponting was a nasty little man, Christina concluded, gazing at his crisp white shirt and tie. Whatever he was, he was deadly serious, and she didn't want any trouble. *This could be a real turn for the worse*, she reflected. Embarking on this particular road to inevitable disaster was like cutting her own throat. But what choice did she have? She either risked Ponting running to the head and shouting his mouth off, or she . . . wanked him in the stockroom? Reckoning him to be in his mid-forties, she looked him up and down. He was clean enough, smartly dressed, but he was also a bastard.

'Come on, Miss Shaw,' he said irritably. 'We haven't got all day.'

'Are you married?' she asked him.

'Married? Oh, I see. You're thinking of telling my wife. No, no, I'm not married. Sorry to disappoint you.'

'It doesn't disappoint me. And it doesn't surprise me.'

'Shall we get on with it?' he sighed, walking towards the stockroom.

'I've left the key at home,' she said triumphantly. 'Sorry to disappoint *you*.'

'In that case, we'll do it here,' he grinned, returning to her desk and unzipping his trousers.

Christina watched as he pulled out his erect penis and

fully retracted his foreskin. He was no better than the teenagers, she thought, wondering how they were supposed to learn anything from an idiot like Ponting. Thanking God that he knew nothing about her relationship with Bryony, she couldn't believe his audacity as he eased his heavy balls out of his trousers and thrust his hips forward. The purple head of his cock pressed against her miniskirt and he squeezed the mounds of her firm breasts.

'Take a good look at my cock,' he sniggered. 'You should think yourself lucky, Miss Shaw. Many a woman would give her right arm to have my cock up her. Look at the size of it, the sheer length.'

'I can't believe what I'm hearing,' she sighed. 'Many a woman would give her right arm for that? You live in a dream world, Ponting.'

'Just get on with it,' he hissed.

Grabbing the fleshy shaft of his cock, Christina rolled Ponting's foreskin back and forth over his swollen knob. He wasn't badly endowed, she observed, imagining him wanking as he thought about the teenage girls at the college. *Fresh meat*? she thought, again unable to believe the man's audacity. Deciding to annoy him, she held his penis by the root, neglecting the bulbous knob of his solid shaft as she wanked him slowly.

'Do it properly,' he breathed.

'It's not that easy,' she said crossly.

'What do you mean?'

'Well, you haven't got much to get hold of, have you?' She laughed sarcastically. 'The boys are far bigger.'

'Shut up and suck it,' he hissed.

'Suck *that*? You must be joking.'

'You'd better . . .'

'Listen to me, Pointing. You're a nasty little man with a small cock. I'll wank you, and that's all.'

Obviously deciding to take what was on offer, Pointing let out a rush of breath as Christina wanked the solid shaft of his cock. His eyes rolling, his breathing fast and shallow as she rolled his foreskin back and forth over his purple glans, Christina realized that he'd soon shoot his spunk over the stockroom floor. Slowing her masturbating rhythm, she decided to rile him again. But, grabbing her hand, he wanked his cock faster with it, his body shaking as he let out a long low moan of pleasure. His sperm jetting from his cock-slit, splattering Christina's skirt as he pressed himself against her, he grabbed her beautifully rounded buttocks and held her crotch tight against his erect penis as his full balls drained. Christina gave a helpless cry of disgust as she felt his stiff prick pulsing against her skirt-covered pubic mound, discharging its slippery load in spurt after spurt.

'You're a sad bastard,' she spat, looking down at her skirt as she finally managed to pull away.

'You can keep your spermed skirt under your pillow and lick it when you think of me,' he grinned, a long strand of spunk hanging from his glistening knob. 'Why don't you suck my knob clean?'

'You could have had *this*,' she said, lifting her skirt and displaying her naked vulval slit to his wide eyes. 'If you hadn't been such a fool, you could have had anything you'd wanted.'

'I will, Miss Shaw. I'll have your cunt – *and* your arse. When I'm ready, that is.'

'You'll have nothing,' she hissed, tugging her skirt down and doing her best to wipe off the spunk.

'I'll meet you after class tomorrow,' he said, zipping

his trousers. 'Make sure you have the key to the stockroom because I'm going to fuck your sweet little cunt.'

'Get out,' she breathed. 'Just get out.'

As Ponting left the room, Christina sat at her desk and hung her head. She should have denied all knowledge of the teenagers and the stockroom, made out that someone had been winding him up. The evil little man would be back for more, she knew. If he started blabbing to the other teachers . . . What was done was done, she reflected sadly, wondering what Alison and Bryony were up to. Looking at the empty desks, she wondered whether she'd be in class tomorrow. The way things were going, it might be best if she went back to her parents' house and forgot about the college. Her father would laugh, she thought. He'd tell her that she should stay with Charles and take a job with his company.

'I'm not going back,' she sighed, banging her clenched fist on the desk.

'You all right, Miss?' an ageing man asked, standing in the doorway. 'I'm Thompson, the caretaker.'

'Oh, er . . . yes, I'm fine,' Christina said, smiling at the man.

'I'll be locking up soon.'

'I came back for some papers. Sorry if I've kept you.'

'No, not at all. You're new here, aren't you?'

'Yes, I am. Shaw, Christina Shaw.'

'How are you coping with the rabble?'

'Oh, not too bad at all. It'll take me a while to settle in, but I'm enjoying the work.'

'Teachers come and go so fast that I can't keep up with it. Anyway, when you're ready.'

'Yes, of course.'

Leaving the classroom, Christina decided not to go

straight back to the flat. It was a lovely evening. As the sun sank below the chimneys of the engineering works, she walked to the common and sat on a bench to think. Recalling her parents' garden as she looked at the trees around the edge of the common, she wondered whether she'd ever be a city girl. Perhaps a rural school would have been better, she reflected. Younger pupils keen to learn, decent teachers . . . The money would be less, but the rents would be cheaper. She'd be able to afford a flat on her own. Things weren't working out in London. Even Alison hadn't turned out to be . . . Alison couldn't help the way she was, Christina thought, wondering again what she was doing with Bryony. Besides, Christina herself wasn't exactly free of blame.

There was one way to leave the college without her father laughing at her, she concluded. Apply for a job at a school in a village or small town. *It wouldn't be admitting defeat*, she tried to convince herself. Leave the college, London, the flat, Alison, Bryony . . . That had to be the answer.

# 6

'Christina, you didn't say you were coming,' her mother exclaimed, beaming.

'A surprise visit,' Christina said, dumping her bag on the kitchen table. 'How are you?'

'Fine, fine. Don't you have classes today?'

'I . . . I have the day off,' Christina lied. 'I woke up early and Alison had gone out so I thought I'd come and see you.'

'I'm pleased you did. You've just missed your father. He's gone to the office.'

'Oh, not to worry.'

'You'll see him this evening. If you're staying, of course.'

'I won't be able to stay all day, I'm afraid.'

'That's a shame. He'd have loved to have seen you, dear. Sit yourself down and I'll make some tea. So, how's the job? Tell me all about it.'

Sitting at the table, Christina wasn't sure that she still had a job after lying to the head about being ill. He'd complained that they were short-staffed and that there was no one to take her class. He'd also reminded her that this was her first week and taking a day off wasn't going to look good on her record. Christina had snapped at him, telling him that she hadn't been able to plan her illness to fit in with the college's timetable. He'd said that he wanted a talk with her, which she'd thought had sounded ominous. She was to be in his study at eight-thirty the following morning to discuss her progress at the college.

'Well?' her mother said, pouring the tea. 'How are you getting on? What's your flatmate like? Do you like the other teachers? And have you phoned Charles yet?'

'Alison's OK,' Christina replied, recalling licking and fingering the girl to orgasm. 'She's . . . she's great. The other teachers are all right, not that I've met them all yet.'

'And Charles?' the woman persisted. 'He's been expecting you to call.'

'Mother, Charles and I . . . We're no longer together.'

'Yes, but he's such a nice young man. I'm sure the two of you will be walking down the aisle before long.'

'How can we walk down the aisle and get married if we're not together any more?'

'You have your tea and I'll ring your father. He might be able to get away from the office for a while. I know he'd love to see you.'

Christina left the table and wandered through the back door into the garden as her mother lifted the phone. She didn't really want to see her father. She was in a mess, and he'd realize that something was wrong. And she certainly didn't intend to contact Charles. She began to wish that she'd gone to the college instead of taking the day off to visit her mother. But she'd got to the point where she couldn't face the students, Bryony or Alison. Let alone Ponting. Alison had been in bed by the time she'd got back to the flat last night. She'd been sleeping that morning, and Christina had made her escape to avoid explaining where she'd been all evening. Looking around the garden, the summer sun warming her, she realized that she felt homesick.

'Your father will be here soon,' her mother announced, stepping out onto the patio with Christina's tea. 'He's bringing Charles with him.'

'Oh,' Christina sighed. 'Mother, I . . .'

'You don't seem too pleased, dear.'

'I don't want to see Charles. We're no longer together. Why can't you understand that?'

'It's only because you've moved to London. You and Charles will always be together. Your father says that—'

'With respect, what father thinks can't change my feelings. Charles and I just aren't suited.'

'Yes, but . . .'

'I wouldn't be happy with Charles. You do want me to be happy, don't you?'

'Of course, dear. Now, when Charles gets here . . .'

Christina scrutinized her mother as she rambled on about Charles and her father. It was sad, Christina reflected, gazing at the woman's blonde hair. She was only in her early forties and far from unattractive. But she'd been oppressed by her husband. He ruled the roost, said how things were going to be, laid down the law. She'd wanted to take up painting, but he'd not thought it a good idea. She'd tried to become involved in the local church, but he'd denounced religion and wouldn't allow her to go near the place.

Christina's father meant well, but he tended to bully people. Charles was very much like him, Christina reflected. That was probably why the two men got on so well together. It was a shame that her father hadn't had a son, she mused. Particularly a son like Charles. There again, her father treated Charles like a son. They were always together. In the office, on the golf course . . .

'Don't you agree, dear?' Christina's mother asked.

'What? Oh, er . . . Sorry, I was daydreaming.'

'I was saying that Charles—'

'I really miss this garden,' Christina cut in, trying to change the subject. 'Living in a flat might be all right in the winter, but not in the summer. I remember spending weekends sunbathing out here. The birds singing, no traffic noise or diesel fumes . . .'

'Perhaps you'll find a flat with a garden.'

'Yes, but the rents are very high.'

'Your father was saying that, if you make a go of it at the college . . . You won't tell him that I said anything, will you?'

'No, of course not. What did he say?'

'He was talking about rented accommodation and how much it was costing you. He might buy a flat in London. You could live there and . . .'

'I thought he was totally against my teaching? Especially in London.'

'Yes, but . . . He said that if that's what you really want to do, and you make a go of it, then he'll buy a flat.'

'What if I decided to move to another college?'

'He'd sell the flat. He says that you can't go wrong buying property.'

'That's not strictly true. There again, knowing father, he'll come out of it with a massive profit'

'Ah, that'll be him,' her mother said, leaving Christina on the patio with her tea.

She could hear Charles talking to her mother. Her father's bellowing voice resounding around the house, Christina wrung her hands nervously. She shouldn't feel this way, she knew. But her father was a formidable man. *He should have been a headmaster*, she thought, imagining him wielding a bamboo cane in the study of an independent school for boys. The male voices growing louder, Christina took a deep breath as Charles stepped onto the patio. Her parents had obviously decided to give them some time together. No. Her father had decided.

'Christina,' Charles said, grinning from ear to ear. 'How are you?'

'Hello, Charles,' she murmured, forcing a smile. 'I'm fine. And you?'

'Busy, busy,' he replied, brushing his dark hair away from his forehead. 'How's the teaching game?'

'I'm loving every minute of it,' she said, eyeing his pinstriped suit and imagining him as a teacher.

'Oh, that's a shame. I was rather hoping that you'd give it up.'

'Give up teaching? Why would I do that?'

'Well, because . . . Christina, you have everything you need here. Working for your father, you'd find that—'

'Sitting in a stuffy office, working for my father? That's having everything, is it?'

'And me. You'd be with me, Christina. What is there to do in a flat during the evenings?'

'There's never a dull moment, I can assure you. Alison, she's my flatmate. We go out, meet people and—'

'Meet people? Christina, the sort of people living in that area are hardly the type . . .'

'I'm not looking to meet a certain type of person, Charles,' she broke in, doing her best not to let the man annoy her. 'I'm meeting people, real people with interesting lives.'

'Interesting lives?' he echoed mockingly. 'What, you mean factory workers and . . .'

'You drive a car, don't you?'

'Of course. What's that got to do with it?'

'It was built in a factory, Charles. It was built by people.'

'Yes, but . . . I mean, they're hardly the type of people you'd socialize with.'

'Why's that?'

'Well, because . . . They're just not. They drink pints of beer in seedy pubs and go to football matches . . .'

'I met a chap who works for an engineering firm the other day. He drinks gin and tonic and enjoys cricket.'

'You know what I mean, Christina. So, who is this chap? Where did you meet him?'

Christina thought for a moment and then grinned at Charles. 'I met him in the local bingo hall,' she finally announced.

'The bingo hall?' he laughed. 'You go to bingo?'

'Yes. It's great fun. I won ten pounds the other night.'

'Christina, bingo is for the—'

'The what, Charles? The lower classes?'

'Well, yes.'

'Christina, darling,' her father said, stepping onto the patio and hugging her. 'How are you?'

'Hello, father. I'm fine.'

'It's good to see you, darling. I was saying to your mother that it can't be easy for you, living in a ghetto.'

'A ghetto?' she laughed, realizing how alike her father and Charles were. 'I have a lovely flat. It's not in a ghetto.'

'Yes, but it's amid slums. So, when are you going to forget about this teaching nonsense and come home?'

'Christina was saying that she goes to bingo,' Charles broke in.

'Bingo?' her father chuckled. 'She's pulling your leg, old boy. No daughter of mine would be seen dead playing bingo. Now, Christina. Miss Stapleton is leaving the company. She's been my personal secretary for God only knows how many years. How would you like the job?'

'Father, I already have a job.'

'I'm talking about a real job, darling.'

'Shall we talk about it later?' Christina's mother suggested. 'I expect Charles and Christina have things to discuss.'

As her parents went back into the house, Christina felt her stomach sink. They didn't want to believe that she'd finished with Charles. They were burying their heads in the sand. Talking about walking down the aisle, planning for the future . . . And as for working as her father's personal secretary . . . There was no point in trying to argue. In time, her parents would realize that she wasn't going to be with Charles, let alone marry him.

'I thought you were going to ring me?' Charles said, plunging his hands into his trouser pockets.

'Did I say I would?' she asked, frowning.

'No, but . . . well, I thought you'd give me a call to let me know how you were.'

'Let's walk down the garden, Charles. It's a beautiful day.'

The more Christina listened to Charles and her father, the more determined she became to break free from all they stood for, all they represented. She loved her father very much, but that didn't mean to say that she had to be entwined in his life. Charles was simply trying to be like her father. He agreed with everything the man said, jumped to attention whenever he clicked his fingers . . . Charles wasn't consciously trying to be like him, he just *was* like him. The way he thrust his hands into his pockets, the way he walked . . . Charles could have easily been her father's son. Wondering whether she could get Charles to back off, somehow change his mind about her, Christina decided to shock him. She waited until they were out of sight of the house before turning to face him.

'Ever had a blow job?' she asked him unashamedly.

'Christina,' he gasped. 'I can see that London hasn't done you any good at all.'

'It's a simple enough question. And London has nothing to do with it. Has a girl ever sucked your cock?'

'Good grief. What your father would say, I really don't—'

'I'm asking *you*, Charles. Not my father.'

'Very well, then. To answer your question. No, a girl has never done that. For one thing, I've never known the type of girl who'd even dream of doing such a thing.'

'What's wrong with oral sex?'

'It's just not . . .'

'Would you like *me* to suck your cock?' she giggled.

'Christina,' he whispered through gritted teeth as she tugged his zip down. 'What the hell do you think you're doing?'

'Pulling your cock out,' she chuckled. 'Would you like me to wank you?'

'No, I mean . . . Not here, for God's sake.'

'Let me wank you, Charles. I want to watch your spunk shooting out of your knob.'

'Christina, please . . .'

Dropping to her knees, Christina sucked the man's purple knob-plum into her hot mouth and ran her tongue over its silky-smooth surface. He gasped, looking down at her in disbelief as she took his ripe glans to the back of her throat and sank her teeth gently into the fleshy shaft of his twitching penis. Wondering what he was thinking as she sucked and mouthed on his salty knob, she reckoned that he must have been sucked off before. He must have known some girl or other who'd been into oral sex. There again, knowing Charles . . .

'Christina,' he murmured, clutching her head as his orgasm approached. 'Christina, for God's sake . . .' Ignoring him, she imagined her father witnessing the crude act. The man would go mad and probably sack Charles. Wondering whether her father had ever come in a woman's mouth, she looked up at Charles as she tongued his sperm-slit. He was enjoying her intimate attention, and she reckoned again that a girl had sucked him and swallowed his sperm. Why he seemed to think that oral sex was disgusting, she had no idea. There was something wrong with him, she concluded. All normal men loved having their knobs sucked by pretty girls.

His sperm jetting into her gobbling mouth, bathing her tongue, filling her cheeks, Charles stifled his moans of pleasure as he rocked his hips. Christina gobbled on his throbbing glans, running her tongue around his cockhead's rim, tonguing his slit, sustaining his orgasm as she kneeled in front of him. Drinking from his pulsating knob, she dragged his heavy balls out of his trousers and cupped them in the palm of her hand. Swallowing hard, maintaining his sperm flow by wanking his solid cock and running her tongue around his swollen knob, she drank from his fountainhead until she'd drained his balls.

Lapping up the spilled spunk from his deflating shaft,

she licked Charles's rolling balls, delighting in his gasped protests as he towered over her. Why he was protesting, she couldn't imagine. Did he wank? she wondered, repeatedly running her spermed tongue up his shaft to his glistening knob. Did he imagine crude sexual acts as he wanked his rock-hard cock and brought out his spunk? The next time he masturbated, he'd imagine his cock in Christina's mouth, his sperm jetting to the back of her throat.

'God,' Charles breathed, moving back and zipping up his trousers. 'Who on earth taught you to . . . What *have* you been up to in London?'

'Up to?' Christina echoed, deliberately allowing his sperm to dribble down her chin as she stood in front of him. 'What do you mean?'

'Wipe your face, for Christ's sake,' he whispered.

'You taste nice,' she giggled, licking her sperm-glossed lips. 'I love the taste of fresh spunk.'

'Christina, I don't know what you've been doing in London. In fact, I dread to think. But you've changed.'

'For the better?'

'Yes . . . No, I mean . . . What on earth possessed you to behave like a . . . a common whore?'

'Your cock possessed me. Didn't you enjoy fucking my mouth?'

'Good grief. You've obviously done that before. You're not the sort of girl I thought you were, Christina.'

'Don't pretend that you didn't enjoy it, Charles,' she retorted angrily. 'I can't abide hypocrisy. There's nothing men like more than fucking girls' mouths and you know it.'

'Why are you talking like this?' he asked her, his dark eyes peering closely at her. 'I've never heard you swear before, let alone . . . let alone behave the way you did just now.'

'Behave the way I did? Oral sex is *fun*, Charles. Most people enjoy oral sex. Had our sex life been a little more exciting, we'd have still been together.'

'We *are* together, aren't we?' he asked pathetically.

'You just called me a whore.'

'No, I meant that you'd behaved—'

'What you did or didn't mean doesn't matter. It's over, Charles.'

'If it's over, then why did you just . . . you know.'

'Because I enjoy doing that.'

'Oh, so it doesn't matter who the man is?'

'Of course it matters.'

'What're your criteria? You have to have some liking for the man? Or perhaps it's just—'

'My flatmate Alison is a lesbian,' Christina announced proudly.

'A lesbian? Well, at least you're safe enough living with the likes of her,' he scoffed.

'Am I?'

'Christina,' her mother called from the house. 'I've made some more tea.'

'All right, mother.' She turned to Charles. 'We'd better go back.'

'What did you mean about your flatmate? You *are* safe with her, aren't you?'

'She plays bingo, so I doubt it.'

Walking back to the house with Charles in tow, Christina felt good. She'd made some sort of stand, at long last. She'd also made several decisions. She wasn't going to work for her father, she wasn't going to move back home, and she wasn't going to spend the rest of her life with Charles. And it wouldn't be a good idea to live in a flat owned by her father. She didn't want to be beholden to the man. This was her life and she was going to live it her way. Sitting on the patio as her mother brought out the tea on a tray, she felt confident for the first time in her life. Even the likes of that little creep Ponting weren't going to get to her now.

'This is like old times,' Christina's mother said. 'I wish you'd come home, dear.'

'She won't listen to me,' Charles sighed. 'She should forget this teaching nonsense and take up her father's offer. London's doing her no good at all.'

'You see?' her father interjected as he stepped onto the patio and plunged his hands into his trouser pockets. 'Charles knows what he's talking about, Christina. He knows what's best for you.'

'Does he, father?' she asked, frowning. 'Does he really?'

'You mark my words, young lady. You won't find a better man than Charles.'

'Actually, I've made a new friend in London.'

'Oh?'

'You'd like him, father. His name's . . . Barry, Barry Doogan.'

'And what does he do?'

'He's . . . he's something in the City.'

'Doogan,' her father murmured pensively. 'I can't say that I know of that name in the City.'

'What do you mean by a new *friend*?' Charles asked, suspicion reflected in his frowning expression.

'Just that. We're becoming good friends.'

'What does he do, exactly?' her father persisted.

'He's a stockbroker,' she lied, watching Charles for a reaction.

'How old is he, dear?' her mother asked.

'Thirty-two. He has a lovely flat in Highgate.'

'Was he the one who taught you?' Charles murmured, glaring at Christina.

'Yes, yes, he was.'

'Taught you what, dear? Don't let your tea go cold.'

'No, I won't. I was telling Charles that I've been learning how to roll my Rs. It's all to do with how you use your tongue. It's silly, really.'

'Ridiculous, if you ask me,' Charles mumbled. 'Er . . . hadn't we better be getting back to the office, Mr Shaw?'

'Yes, we had. So, this Doogan fellow. What's his father do?'

'He's something to do with the Diplomatic Corps. I'm not sure what, exactly. He travels around the world most of the time. You'll have to meet him. He's a lovely man, father.'

'Yes, I will. Right, we'd better be going. It's nice to have seen you, darling.'

'And you, father. Goodbye, Charles.'

'Goodbye, Christina.'

Concealing a grin as the men went into the house, Christina felt smug. She'd been ruled by Charles for too long. Had she stayed with him, married him, she'd have ended up like her mother. *Barry Doogan a stockbroker?* she giggled inwardly, sipping her tea. Wondering what the lad would become, she pictured him in a suit, crisp white shirt and tie. *Given a decent education he might have made it*, she reflected. It was all right for the likes of Charles. Money, a private education, university . . . Charles was a pompous git, she mused. At least Barry Doogan was genuine, down-to-earth. And he enjoyed the baser side of sex.

Wandering down the garden, Christina pondered on the idea of her father buying a flat in London. The rent she was paying now was horrendous, even though she was going halves with Alison. A decent home was important, she mused. After a long day at the college, it would be nice to have a garden to relax in, perhaps have some friends round for a barbecue. But she realized again that she would be indebted for ever to her father. Her thoughts turning to Ponting, she sighed. He was going to become a real problem, she reflected. Ponting had to be dealt with if she was going to stay on at the college. Deciding to return to London, she went back into the house to find her mother.

'I have to go,' she said, watching the woman preparing sandwiches in the kitchen.

'I was just making some lunch,' her mother sighed. 'Can't you stay for a while longer?'

'No, I have to get back. I'll be down to see you again.'

'All right, dear. It's been nice having you here, even thought it wasn't for long. Do you want a lift to the station?'

'It's all right, I'll walk,' Christina replied, taking her bag from the table as she followed her mother through the hall. 'It's not far and it's a lovely day.'

'I'll ring you this evening.'

'All right, mother. You take care of yourself.'

'And you, dear.'

Sitting on the almost empty train, Christina wondered what to do about Ponting. She wouldn't mind masturbating him to orgasm now and then, as long as he didn't demand more of her. Realizing that he'd demand far more than a quick wank in the stockroom, she thought about getting Doogan to help her. If he had a word with

Ponting, told him to back off, threatened him . . . But that might lead to all sorts of trouble. She'd just have to deal with Ponting herself. Smiling, she pictured the man's solid cock in her hand, his spunk jetting from his throbbing knob. Wanking a cock and bringing out the sperm wasn't at all unpleasant, she reflected. Quite the opposite, in fact. Would Ponting enjoy mouth-fucking her? There was definitely something wrong with Charles, she concluded.

Watching a young man as he got in at the next station and sat opposite her, Christina stared at the bulging crotch of his tight jeans. Since starting at the college, sex was constantly on her mind, and she found herself wondering whether all men wanked. Did the young man run his hand up and down the rock-hard shaft of his cock and shoot his spunk over the floor? Reckoning him to be in his mid-teens, she reclined in her seat and parted her thighs just enough to expose the triangular patch of her tight panties. After only a few seconds, his gaze was locked between her legs, his expression a mixture of surprise and delight as he adjusted the crotch of his trousers.

The next time he wanked, he'd remember her, picture the bulging patch of tight material covering her full sex lips. Would he like to spunk over her breasts? Christina wondered, imagining his white rain showering her naked body. She was becoming hooked on wanking men to the point where it might become an obsession. The feel of a solid penis in her hand, rolling the foreskin back and forth over the swollen glans, watching the spunk jetting from the slit . . . Wondering whether her mother wanked her father's cock, she couldn't picture the act. *They must have fucked at least once to have had me*, she thought, trying to imagine her father spunking over her mother's cervix.

Catching the young man's gaze, she knew what he wanted. She knew what *she* wanted. Was his cock big? she wondered, her young womb contracting, her juices of lust wetting her panties. Would he allow her to give him a quick wank on the train? It occurred to her that she'd wanked several cocks since starting at the college, but had not had one pistoning the tight sheath of her hot pussy. Perhaps the young man would enjoy slipping the length of his penis deep into her tight vagina and sperming her.

Parting her thighs further, her stomach somersaulting, she was gripped by an overwhelming desire to behave like a common slut. *A common whore?* she mused, recalling Charles's cruel words. By opening her legs to a stranger, perhaps she was making a stand against her father and what he stood for. It would be exciting to behave like a common whore, she mused, licking her lips provocatively as she gazed at the young man. Perhaps she was trying to prove something.

She had about ten minutes before the train pulled in at her station. Her heart banging hard against her chest, she knew that she couldn't let this opportunity pass her by. If she didn't act now, she might regret it for ever. Wondering whether she'd feel guilty if she allowed him to fuck her, she realized that no one would ever know of her sordid act. Again recalling the words of the pompous Charles, she wondered what her criteria were. The man wasn't bad-looking, his jeans were bulging with his obvious arousal . . . That was good enough, she concluded.

'Why don't you get your cock out?' she asked him,

pulling the tight material of her panties to one side and exposing the swell of her fleshy vaginal lips to his wide-eyed stare. 'Kneel on the floor and push your cock into my hot cunt.'

Saying nothing, the stunned man slipped off his seat and kneeled on the floor. Unzipping his jeans, he hauled his solid penis out and gripped it by the base as Christina slid her buttocks forward on her seat and opened her legs wide. Keeping her panties pulled to one side, she watched the young man pull his foreskin back and slip his purple knob between the pinken wings of her splayed inner lips. She needed this, she knew as his rock-hard shaft glided deep into her cream-drenched sex duct. The last man she'd allowed to impale her on his penis had been Charles, and that had been some time ago.

'You're amazing,' the young teenager breathed, eyeing the outer lips of Christina's pussy stretched tautly around the wide root of his cock as he fully impaled her. 'I've never met anyone like you.'

'And you're not likely to again,' Christina murmured, pulling her panties still further to one side as he began his fucking motions.

'I don't even know your name.'

'You don't have to know my name,' she giggled. 'All you have to do is fuck me.'

Her own crude words delighting her, Christina imagined Charles witnessing her wanton act of decadence, listening to her vulgar language as a complete stranger fucked her tight cunt. He'd go mad, call her every name under the sun. Her father would be none too pleased, either. This was debauchery at its lowest, she mused, listening to the squelching sounds of her copious vaginal juices as the young man repeatedly drove his solid cock deep into her sex-wet pussy. Meeting a total stranger on a train, opening her legs and allowing him to fuck her . . . This was sexual gratification at its highest.

Watching the young man's pussy-slimed shaft repeatedly thrusting deep into her cunny, Christina felt her clitoris swelling, her young womb contracting. She was going to come, she knew as the train rocked and lurched. The man's swollen knob battering her ripe cervix, her lower stomach rising and falling as he thrust into her pussy, she closed her eyes as he gasped and flooded her vaginal canal with his creamy sperm. Her own climax erupting within the pulsating nub of her clitoris, she threw her head back and let out a moan of pleasure.

Her young body shaking fiercely, her juices of lust gushing from the bloated entrance to her spasming pussy, Christina repeatedly pushed her hips forward to meet the young man's thrusts. Again and again his throbbing knob buffeted her ripe cervix, his copious flow of creamy sperm filling her vaginal cavity as his heavy balls drained. Her vaginal muscles spasming, gripping his cock shaft like a velvet-jawed vice, she thought it strange that she'd never see the young man again. *Ships passing*, she reflected as her orgasm peaked, sending electrifying shock waves of sex through her contracting womb.

'God, you're good,' the young man gasped, repeatedly thrusting the shaft of his penis deep into her convulsing cunt with a vengeance. 'Hot, tight, wet . . .' Grinning, Christina drifted in her sexual delirium, her young body shaking violently, her mind blown away on a cloud on lust. Her pleasure finally beginning to leave her trembling body, her head lolling from side to side, she realized that the train was slowing down as the young man made his last thrusts. She had a couple of minutes before arriving at her station, time enough to cover her sperm-oozing vaginal crack with her panties and adjust her clothing.

Watching the man's deflating penis sliding out of her inflamed vagina, Christina leaned forward as he stood up. Taking his sperm-glistening cock into her mouth, she cleansed him, sucking out the remnants of his orgasmic cream as he towered over her, trembling in the aftermath of his fucking. She could taste her vaginal juices as she rolled her tongue around his purple knob. *The taste of sex*, she mused, sucking hard and running her hand up his shaft to squeeze out the last of his sperm.

'I'd like to see you again,' he said, zipping his trousers as she slipped his cock out of her spunked mouth.

'We'll never meet again,' Christina murmured, licking her spermed lips as she looked up at him.

'Why not? After what we just did . . . I mean . . .'

'Ships passing in the night,' she said, concealing her spunked pussy slit under her tight panties.

'We can pass again, can't we? I'm Rob, by the way.'

'And I'm the Devil's daughter,' Christina giggled, leaving her seat as the train stopped at the station.

'Please . . . Don't go without even—'

Walking along the platform with her bag slung over her shoulder, Christina smiled at the young man peering out of the window as the train pulled away. *The Devil's daughter?* she mused. Perhaps she was right. Her tight panties filling with a cocktail of sperm and girl-juice as she moved, she wondered how many more strangers she'd allow to fuck her. Sucking and wanking the students was nothing in comparison to screwing a stranger on the train, she reflected. Tossing off Ponting was insignificant. *The Devil's daughter?* Feeling more confident, she finally reached the flat and let herself in.

# 7

'Where have you been?' Alison asked almost accusingly, emerging from her room.

'To see my parents,' Christina replied. She dropped her bag on the kitchen table and filled the kettle. 'How did you get on with Bryony last night?'

'It was great. Do you know, she licked me until . . . Where did you go? I heard the phone ring and then the front door close.'

'I had to go over to the college.'

'What, at night?'

'There was a problem about some exam papers.'

'You had to go there at night? I don't know what the time was but it must have been at least—'

'It was important, Alison. The exams are coming up and . . . Anyway, I was up early this morning and decided to go and see my parents.'

'Why aren't you at work?'

'Why all these questions, Alison? I have the day off. Unofficially, that is.'

'I'm sorry. I was worried, that's all. You disappeared last night, you were up and gone first thing this morning . . . By the way, the college rang.'

'Oh, God. Who was it?'

'It was Mr Wright. I didn't know what to say. As far as

I was aware, you'd gone to work. If you're going to take a day off, you should at least tell me.'

'So, what did you say?'

'I could tell by his tone that he was in a bad mood. I guessed that you were skiving off so I said that you were sleeping because you were ill. Luckily, I got it right.'

'Thanks. How long did Bryony stay?'

'Not long. I think she was hoping that you'd come back. She's got the hots for you, Christina.'

'I know. That's why I was trying to break off with her. When you invited her in, I . . .'

'I guessed who she was when I saw her hanging around outside. She was looking up at the window, obviously hoping to see you.'

'She's going to become a nuisance. In fact, she already *is* a nuisance.'

'I feel sorry for her.'

'So do I. Her mother's a drunk, her home is a slum . . . But that's not my problem.'

'She could move in with us.'

'Alison, I really don't think . . .'

'Why not?'

'To be honest, the thought crossed my mind too. The thing is, we've only got two bedrooms.'

'She could spend a night in your bed and the next in mine. She could swap beds every night.'

'That wouldn't work. She'd have to have her own room.'

'I don't see why. She could clean the flat, do the washing and ironing . . . It might work out extremely well.'

Pondering on the idea as she made the coffee, Christina was sure that Bryony would jump at the chance to move in. And she doubted that the girl's mother would object. But this wasn't how it was supposed to have been, she reflected. Since starting at the college, everything had been turned upside down. Wanking the lads in the stockroom, having sex with young Bryony, Alison turning out to be a lesbian . . . At least Charles had finally got the message. Gazing at Alison's stiff nipples clearly defined by her tight T-shirt, the band of flesh just above her short skirt, Christina was aware of her vaginal muscles tightening. She could feel again that her panties were full of sperm and girl-juice. Would Alison enjoy drinking from her sex-flooded pussy? she wondered. Her clitoris swelling as she imagined the other girl's tongue delving into her sex-drenched vagina, she wondered whether her flatmate would realize that she was lapping up sperm.

This was no time for sex, Christina thought, sipping her coffee as she gazed at the neat indent of Alison's navel. Trying to drag her thoughts away from lesbian sex, she wondered whether to ring the headmaster. It might be an idea to let him know that she was feeling better and would be in tomorrow morning. He was a miserable man, she mused, wondering whether he was married and trying to picture him with his solid cock shafting a wet pussy. Her panties soaked with sperm, the creamy liquid trickling down her inner thighs, she decided to take a shower before doing anything.

'Want me to soap you?' Alison asked, following Christina into the bathroom.

'No, thanks,' Christina murmured, knowing full well that she'd succumb to her lesbian desires if Alison ran her hands all over her naked body. 'I'm just having a quick shower since I have things to do.'

'At least allow me to undress you,' the girl breathed,

dropping to her knees and tugging Christina's skirt down.

'Alison, I . . .'

'What's the matter?'

'Nothing.'

Stepping out of her skirt, Christina watched as Alison pulled the fuck-wet panties down and gazed longingly at the sex-sticky crack of Christina's vagina. Would the girl lap up her juices? Christina wondered. Would she realize, Christina asked herself again, that she was drinking sperm as she pressed her full lips to her vaginal entrance and sucked and tongued her there? Christina shuddered as Alison's tongue ran up and down her spunk-dripping sex slit. Peeling her fleshy outer lips apart, Alison lapped at the pink flesh surrounding her vaginal entrance, drinking the heady blend of girl-juice and sperm from the hot sheath of her tightening pussy. She obviously didn't realize what the creamy liquid was, probably thinking that Christina was simply extremely wet in her lesbian arousal.

'I love your cunt,' Alison murmured, her wet tongue snaking inside Christina's hot pussy, licking the cream-coated walls of her vaginal canal. 'You have a beautiful cunt.' The crude word excited Christina and she parted her feet wide and projected her hips, allowing her lesbian lover deeper access to her hot sex duct. The thought of Alison lapping up the young man's sperm from her hot vagina sent an electrifying quiver through Christina's womb. She could hear the slurping sounds of oral sex, feel the girl's saliva running down her inner thighs. The girl's wet tongue sweeping over the sensitive nub of her clitoris, Christina shuddered as she realized that her young cunt was fast beginning to rule her head.

'Say "cunt" again,' she breathed, her ripening clitoris pulsating.

'Cunt,' Alison murmured. 'I love your hot cunt. Do you want me to tongue your arse?'

'Yes, yes – tongue my arse,' Christina replied eagerly.

'Turn round and bend over the bath and I'll tongue-fuck your sweet arsehole.'

Taking her position as she pondered on the crude words, Christina let out a low moan of sexual satisfaction as her flatmate parted the firm orbs of her buttocks and ran her wet tongue over the delicate brown tissue surrounding her private hole. Shuddering, Christina felt the girl's tongue delving into her anus, wetting her there, teasing her secret nerve endings of illicit pleasure. Her feet wide apart, she leaned further over the bath and projected her pert buttocks as Alison slipped a wet finger past the tight ring of her anus.

'Is that nice?' Alison asked, massaging the hot walls of Christina's rectal duct.

'God, yes,' Christina murmured, gyrating her hips as the incredibly arousing sensations rippled through her young womb.

'Has anyone ever finger-fucked your beautiful arse?'

'No, never.'

'You like me talking dirty, don't you?'

'Yes, yes,' Christina breathed shakily. 'I love your dirty words.'

'You have a tight cunt and a beautiful arse. Do you want my tongue up your arse again?'

'Yes, yes.'

'Licking deep inside your hot arse?'

'God, yes.'

'Reach behind your back and open your arsehole for me and I'll tongue-fuck your rectum.'

Parting her buttocks to the extreme, fully opening the brown entrance to her hot rectal tube, Christina felt a quiver run through her pelvis as Alison's tongue drove deep into her anal canal. She could feel her flatmate's tongue inside her, wetting her, licking and teasing the sensitive walls of her rectum. The girl's full lips pressed hard against her anal opening as she tongued deep inside her anal duct, never had Christina known that such incredible pleasure could be had from such a decadent act. Christina knew now that she had two sex holes, two lust sheaths. She had more than just her vaginal canal. Had Charles pleasured her like this, tongue-fucked her tight arsehole . . . But Charles was no longer a feature of her life. Her neglected clitoris painfully solid, she moaned softly as her lesbian lover massaged her rectal sheath, sending electrifying tremors of crude sex through her naked body. She'd never really needed Charles, she realized.

'Are you ready for two fingers?' Alison asked unashamedly.

'Yes, two fingers,' Christina replied eagerly, holding her rounded buttocks wide apart.

'First one, then two . . . We'll see how many fingers you can take.'

Shuddering as Alison forced a second finger deep into the hot duct of her rectum, Christina let out a gasp of pleasure. The brown ring of her anal eye dilating, the tight tube of her arse stretching as Alison flexed her fingers, Christina felt dizzy in the grip of her new-found decadence. She'd never dreamed of opening her vagina to another girl, let alone her bottom-hole. To hold her anus wide open and offer her rectal sheath to a lesbian's tongue and fingers was debased in the extreme, so obscene that the very notion of the act sent her arousal sky-high.

'Three fingers,' Alison announced gleefully.

'Yes, yes,' Christina breathed.

'OK, are you ready?'

'Just do it.'

'Anything you say.'

Grimacing as Alison pushed the tip of her third finger past her already stretched anal ring, Christina held her breath. The mixture of pain and pleasure driving her wild as the girl's finger began to slide into her inflamed anal sheath, she finally let out a rush of breath. Alison's three fingers completely impaling her, massaging deep inside her trembling body, she was sure that she could take no more as the girl pushed and twisted her hand, trying to force all four fingers into her arse.

'No,' she breathed, the delicate tissue of her anus dilating to capacity. 'Alison, I . . .'

'Relax,' the girl said, licking the rounded cheeks of Christina's buttocks. 'You're all tensed up. Just relax and I'll fist your beautiful arse.'

'Fist?' Christina gasped surprisedly. 'For God's sake—'

'It's OK, I've done this before. Just relax.'

Doing her best to relax her muscles as her lesbian lover managed to drive four fingers into her inflamed anal canal, Christina knew that she'd never be able to accommodate the girl's whole fist. There *were* limits, she reflected, trying to picture the brown tissue of her anus stretched painfully around Alison's wrist. It just wasn't possible to take a complete fist up her arse, she was sure.

Squeezing her eyes shut as her flatmate again pushed and twisted her hand, Christina sensed that the girl was obviously determined to sink her fist deep into Christina's anal passage.

'Lubrication,' Alison murmured, grabbing a shampoo bottle from the shelf. Christina could feel the cooling liquid running down the splayed gully of her buttocks, oiling her painfully stretched anal tissue. Alison continued to twist and push her hand, her fingers slipping slowly into Christina's bottom-hole as the girl's brown ring yielded. Christina couldn't believe that her lesbian lover had succeeded in her illicit mission when she announced that her entire fist was embedded in Christina's rectal canal. Twisting her fist, Alison massaged the inner core of Christina's naked body. The shampoo lubricating the crude coupling, lather emerging from her bloated rectal duct and running down her thighs, Christina rocked back and forth with the anal pistoning. To her surprise, the sensation wasn't one of pain, but a pleasurable bloating feeling deep within her pelvis.

'I told you that I'd do it,' Alison trilled victoriously, the sucking sound of the shampoo resounding around the bathroom.

'God,' Christina breathed shakily. 'I can't believe it.'

'You should see your bum. Your arsehole is tight around my wrist. Does it feel nice?'

'Yes, yes, it does. It's incredible to think that—'

'Don't think about the physiology,' the other girl laughed. 'You just concentrate on your clitty. I'm going to bring you off.'

Reaching between Christina's thighs with her free hand, Alison parted the trembling girl's fleshy love lips and began to massage the swollen nubble of her sensitive clitoris. Christina shuddered, her naked body alive with sensations of crude sex as her rectal muscles tightened around her lover's clenched fist. Her juices of desire streaming from the gaping entrance to her neglected vagina, she leaned on the side of the bath to steady herself as the incredible sensations permeated her very being. Her clitoris painfully solid, her flatmate's fist driving deep into the dank heat of her bowels, she shook uncontrollably in her debauched act.

Wishing that Bryony was helping Alison to pleasure her naked body, Christina wondered whether the young student would call round that evening. Perhaps she'd enjoy an anal fisting, she thought as her vaginal muscles spasmed, squeezing out her copious juices of lesbian lust. Would the girl enjoy a double sex-fisting? Her teenage cunt bloated by Alison's clenched fist, her rectal cavern stretched to accommodate Christina's fist . . . Young Bryony was in for the time of her life the next time she called at the flat.

Shuddering with her building pleasure, Christina whimpered in her lesbian desire as her partner in lust continued to massage the swollen nodule of her painfully hard cumbud and fist-fuck the hot duct of her rectum. Her whimpers growing louder, her womb rhythmically contracting, she leaned further over the side of the bath as her vagina tightened, spewing out its creamy sex juices. Her clitoris close to orgasm, her inflamed rectal sheath gripping Alison's pistoning fist, Christina breathed heavily as she teetered on the brink of her climax.

'I'm going to shave you,' Alison announced, her fist twisting deep within Christina's inflamed rectal tube. Saying nothing, Christina pictured Bryony's hairless vulval flesh, the smooth love lips of her naked pussy. Wondering whether to allow Alison to strip her pubic hair from her cunt lips and Venus mound, she realized that she'd travelled so far down the path of crude sex that whatever she did now wouldn't really make any difference. Wanking the students in the stockroom, sucking off Charles in the garden, licking and fingering Bryony's teenage pussy, fucking a stranger on a train, and now allowing Alison to fist-fuck her tight arse . . . Shaving would be the least of the decadent sexual acts that she'd committed.

'Yes,' Christina cried, her orgasm exploding within the solid tip of her palpitating clitoris. Increasing her anal-fisting rhythm, Alison fervently massaged Christina's orgasming clitoris, taking her to heights of sexual ecstasy she'd never known before. Her pelvic cavity bloated to the extreme, she felt that her entire body was inflating as her flatmate repeatedly thrust her clenched fist deep into the hot depths of her bowels. Her orgasmic juices streaming from the dilated opening of her vagina, running in rivers of cum-milk down her inner thighs, she realized that her bladder was about to drain as her orgasm peaked.

As the sound of liquid splashing onto the floor between her feet rang loudly in her ears, Christina felt no shame. In her mind, this was just part of her ever-deepening decadence. The profane act added to her sense of debauchery, heightening her illicit pleasure. She could feel Alison's head between her legs, her tongue running up her inner thighs, lapping up the stream of golden liquid coursing down her smooth flesh. Slurping at her drenched pubic hair, lapping up the golden offering, Alison continued her rectal fisting, her clitoral massaging, sustaining her lesbian lover's multiple orgasm until the girl could barely stand on her sagging legs.

'You dirty little cow,' Alison giggled, her tongue running over Christina's wet vulval lips as the flow of golden liquid began to slow. 'I'll thrash you before I shave your sweet cunt.'

'God,' Christina breathed shakily, her pleasure beginning to recede. 'That's enough. I can't take any more.'

'Of course you can,' the insistent lesbian returned, twisting her fist and pistoning the girl's rectum. 'You're going to have to take a lot more than this.'

Finally crumpling over the side of the bath, Christina's naked body convulsed wildly as Alison withdrew her fist from the burning sheath of her abused rectum. Christina felt as though her bottom-hole was gaping, sagging open at least three inches, as she quivered and breathed heavily in the aftermath of her incredibly decadent experience. Wondering whether the inflamed ring of her anus would ever recover, she clung to the basin and finally managed to climb to her feet.

'No more,' she breathed, her glazed eyes staring at the razor and shaving foam in Alison's hand. 'I need to rest. I'm going to lie down.'

'Yes, you lie on your bed and rest. I'll shave you while you relax.'

'Alison, I . . .'

'Come on, go to your room. I'll look after you.'

Staggering to her room with Alison in tow, Christina collapsed onto her bed and lay on her back. She was in no fit state to protest as she heard a hissing sound and then felt cooling foam smothering the sex-wet flesh of her crimsoned vulva. Almost delirious in the aftermath of her massive orgasm, her naked body exhausted, she closed her eyes and drifted in a sleeplike state as her flatmate massaged the white foam into her mons, the fleshy swell of her love lips. She felt the razor running over her vulval flesh as Alison worked between her thighs, stripping away her pubic curls, taking her back to prepubescence. Was this what she wanted?

Christina recalled her younger days of sexual discovery, the dreamy nights of toying with her naked love lips, tentatively running her fingertip up and down the wet valley of her pink pussy. She'd discovered the delights her clitoris had to offer quite by accident when playing in the garden one afternoon. She'd been straddling a low wall, her legs open wide, her panties pressing against the rough brickwork. Rocking to and fro, she'd felt unfamiliar sensations emanating from within the moist valley between her firm pussy lips. The feeling was pleasant, nothing more. Until she decided to experiment.

Out of sight of the house, she'd slipped her panties off and sat on the wall again. The rough bricks scraping and grazing her hairless sex cushions as she'd writhed and squirmed, she'd been surprised by the new pleasures her young body was bringing her. Looking down, she'd investigated between her legs, her fingers probing within her pink crack, rubbing the hard spot there. She'd often examined herself after that day, but had never achieved an orgasm until she'd been lying in the bath one evening.

Rubbing between the rise of her firm sex lips, massaging the hard nodule nestling within the top of her girl-slit, she'd found that her pleasure had built. The more she'd massaged her solid sex spot, the greater her pleasure had become until she'd achieved her pioneering orgasm. Shuddering in the bath, the water lapping at her swollen pussy lips, she'd continued to rub her clitoris, sustaining her orgasm as she'd whimpered and cried out in the grips of her self-loving.

Her mother had opened the door and walked in when she'd heard the whimpers. Christina had said that she'd been singing, but her mother had noticed the girl's flushed face, the sparkle in her blue eyes. The woman must have known that Christina had discovered her clitoris, but had said nothing. Perhaps she had masturbated in the bath when she'd been young. Christina had thought it unlikely, but she often wondered whether her mother massaged between her sex lips. Had she sucked the sperm from an orgasming knob and swallowed the male cream of orgasm? Probably not.

'Almost done,' Alison said, taking a tissue from the dressing table and wiping away the foam and pubic curls from Christina's vaginal lips. 'Oh, yes,' she trilled excitedly. 'You look just like a little schoolgirl. I'll get a flannel from the bathroom and clean you up before giving your beautiful cunt a good licking-out.'

As the girl left the room, Christina managed to lift her head and gaze at Alison's handiwork. Her pubic curls had gone and her pussy lips were smooth, the gentle rise of her mons pale in its blatant nakedness. Christina recalled again her younger years before her pubic hair had sprouted. The firm lips of her vulva had been soft to the touch, smooth in her tender years. Stroking the outer lips of her pussy as she recalled her early days of masturbation, she decided that she was pleased with the result of Alison's work. What would Charles think?

'Like it?' the girl asked as she breezed back into the room, holding a wet flannel.

'Yes, I think I do,' Christina replied, resting her head on the bed again. 'It's taken years off me.'

'Years off your pussy, at least,' Alison chuckled, sitting on the edge of the bed and cleansing Christina's vaginal hillocks with the warm flannel. 'What do you want first? A good cunt-licking or a thrashing?'

'I don't want a thrashing,' Christina murmured, her head lolling from side to side. 'God, I feel knackered.'

'You'll soon recover. How does your bum-hole feel?'

'Damned sore. It feels as if it's hanging wide open.'

'Good – that's what I like to hear. Right, I'll go and get my leather belt and bring a warm glow to your buttocks.'

'Alison, I . . .'

Sighing as the girl left, Christina told herself that she wasn't going to allow her to thrash her with a leather belt. A mild spanking was one thing, but a severe whipping . . . Were there no limits to her flatmate's debauchery? She lifted her head again and gazed at her hairless pussy lips. Fisting, shaving . . . There *were* no limits, she concluded, deciding to take a shower and wash away the girl-cum and urine from her naked body. Propping herself up on her elbows, she was about to swing her feet off the bed when Alison appeared in the doorway, wielding a leather belt.

'I don't want a thrashing,' Christina said firmly as the girl crossed the room and rolled her onto her stomach. 'Alison, if you—'

'Of course you want a thrashing,' she giggled, bringing the belt down across Christina's rounded buttocks with a loud crack.

'Alison! For God's sake, I—'

'And another one,' Alison shrieked gleefully, the belt landing squarely across the tensed orbs of Christina's naked bottom.

Squeezing her eyes shut, Christina buried her face in

the pillow as the girl repeatedly lashed the burning globes of her stinging buttocks with the leather belt. She could have easily clambered off the bed and put a stop to the gruelling punishment, but the notion of a thrashing intrigued her. As her buttocks grew numb, the pain turning to pleasure, she recalled reading about spanking and bondage in a women's magazine. She'd been surprised by the number of women who'd admitted to having their naked bodies bound with rope and their bottoms spanked until they'd glowed a fire-red. They'd enjoyed the degradation, the enforced spanking of their naked bottoms, and the crude act had become part of their sex lives. Now Christina was beginning to understand why.

Listening to the crack of the belt each time it swished through the air and lashed her fiery bottom cheeks, she heard Alison chuckling softly. The girl was obviously in her element, Christina concluded as her naked bottom bucked beneath the leather belt. There certainly was far more to Alison than met the eye, she mused, her juices of arousal seeping between the hairless lips of her vulva. When she'd first met the girl in the letting agency, she'd had no idea that she was a lesbian, let alone a sex-crazed nymphomaniac. Had Alison guessed that Christina would offer her naked body in the name of lesbian lust?

'Turn over,' Alison told Christina.

'I was enjoying that,' Christina said, rolling onto her back. 'Why do you want me to . . . Argh!' she cried as the leather belt swished through the air and bit into the firm flesh of her young breasts. 'Alison! Please—'

'Relax,' the girl laughed, bringing the belt down across the elongated teats of her erect nipples. 'I'll thrash your little pink pussy next.'

'You won't,' Christina protested, grabbing the belt. 'I didn't mind you thrashing my bum, but you're not going to—'

'At least try it,' Alison cut in. 'I love having my tits whipped, and my cunt. I'll be gentle, OK?'

'No, it's *not* OK,' Christina retorted. 'What the hell do you think I am?'

'A girl who enjoys lesbian sex. A girl who enjoyed an arse-fisting, a bum-thrashing, a . . .'

'All right,' Christina finally conceded, releasing the belt as she realized that she'd probably enjoy the illicit act. 'But you must do it gently.'

'Gently it is.'

Her arms by her sides, Christina allowed her flatmate to whip the firm mounds of her young breasts softly. The leather belt repeatedly slapping the brown teats of her sensitive nipples, darkening the discs of her areolae, she decided that she quite liked the unfamiliar sensations. Never had she dreamed that she'd allow anyone to whip her young breasts, let alone another girl. She was learning, she reflected, her nipples becoming puffy as her breasts warmed beneath the lashing belt. Learning about her young body, other girls' bodies, their teenage breasts and juicy pussies. Becoming keener to learn more, to experience the baser side of sex, she spread her limbs, offering her nakedness to her lesbian lover.

As the leather belt struck her swollen vaginal lips, she let out a yelp and jumped. But, knowing that she could halt the moderate lashing at any time, she was able to relax and enjoy the new pleasures her lesbian lover was bringing her. As she listened to the soft sound of the belt slapping her swollen sex cushions, the wings of her inner lips emerging as if to meet the rough leather strap, she parted her thighs wider. The sensations were strange, she mused as her inner lips protruded fully from her opening sex crack and swelled beneath the lashing of the belt. Slightly painful but most pleasurable, she found that the whipping of her hairless vulval flesh was sending her libido sky-high. She wanted Alison to lash her pussy harder but, to her surprise, she was somewhat embarrassed and decided not to ask the girl.

'All right?' Alison asked, smiling, her lust-sparkling eyes peering at Christina.

'Yes, very much so,' Christina replied, returning her smile.

'A little harder?'

'Well, I . . . OK, but not too hard.'

The leather belt biting harder into the soft pads of her vaginal lips as Alison added a little severity to the lashing, Christina tensed her naked body and dug her fingernails into the quilt. Again, she found that she was enjoying the combination of sexual pain and pleasure. She already knew the feeling of a wet tongue running up and down her vaginal slit, her clitoris pulsating in orgasm, a penis shafting the tight sheath of her pussy. But the leather belt was bringing her new and strangely stimulating sensations.

Her pussy lips reddening, her clitoris solid, she could feel her milky juices of desire trickling from her vaginal opening and running down between her thrashed buttocks to soothe the sensitive tissue of her inflamed anus. Again and again the leather belt whipped her burning vulval flesh, each lash becoming progressively harder as Alison chuckled wickedly in the grips of her debauchery. Christina didn't want to halt the punishment until she was sure that she could take no more. Her naked body rigid, she endured the beautiful vulval whipping until her puffy vaginal lips became painfully swollen. Lifting her head and gazing at her abused vulva, her pretty face grimacing, she finally ordered Alison to stop the thrashing.

'Oh, I was just getting into it,' the girl murmured despondently, lowering the belt to her side.

'God, that was . . .'

'Amazing?'

'Yes, yes, it was. I've never known anything like it. You've obviously been into this sort of thing before.'

'Let's just say that I have a little experience in bondage and spanking. Talking of which, how about bondage? Would you like to try it?'

'Er . . . no, I don't think so,' Christina replied softly. 'I'm absolutely knackered. I think I'll sleep for a while.'

'Go on, you'll love it. I'll tell you what I'll do. I'll tie you to the bed with headscarves. Just loosely knotted around your wrists and ankles and tied to the legs of the bed. I have some long scarfs that I used to use for—'

'Not now, Alison,' Christina sighed. 'Maybe another time.'

'You are an old stick-in-the-mud, Christina. Why don't you let yourself go and have some fun?'

'Haven't I already done that? I've let you shave me, I've—'

'I'll go and get the scarfs.'

Sighing again as Alison went to her room, Christina really didn't want to be tied down. Exhausted, she'd had more than enough sex for one day. Besides, she had to phone the headmaster and let him know that she'd be in the following morning. The thought of returning to the college worrying her, she wondered how far Ponting would demand that she go in return for his silence. Had he mentioned his blackmail threats to his friends, she wondered. If he was in with some of the other male teachers and had told them about Christina's illicit exploits, they might demand that she should wank or suck their cocks, too.

Wondering where it would all end as Alison returned and secured her ankles to the bed legs with the headscarves, Christina thought again about the incredible changes she'd been through since starting at the college. Her whole life turned upside down, her sexual identity in turmoil... She stretched her arms out and allowed the other girl to run the headscarves from her wrists to the bed legs. Her limps spread, she watched her friend settle on the bed between her thighs. The girl's tongue running up and down her opening sex slit, Christina let out a sigh of pleasure as her clitoris immediately responded to the lesbian attention. Did she want this to end?

'You taste nice,' Alison murmured, pressing her succulent lips hard against the pink funnel of wet flesh around Christina's vaginal entrance. 'I love drinking from your cunt. Make some more milk for me.' Relaxing as the girl's tongue slipped deep into the hot shaft of her tight cunt, Christina closed her eyes and revelled in the delicious sensations of lesbian oral sex. This was sheer sexual bliss, she thought, her clitoris swelling, her milky juices of desire flowing from her inner nectaries. Listening to Alison slurping and drinking from her sex-drenched cunt, she felt her womb contract, her nipples stiffen as her arousal lifted her higher, closer to her sexual heaven.

'Shit,' Alison breathed as someone hammered on the door. The bell rang too as she leaped off the bed and released Christina. 'I think I know who it is,' she said, wiping the girl-cum from her mouth with the back of her hand.

'Who?' Christina asked, grabbing some clothes from the wardrobe and hurriedly dressing. 'What's the panic?'

'Look, you stay in your room and I'll get rid of them. Or I'll try to. Just stay in here, OK?'

'If you say so.'

'I do say so. This could be trouble,' she murmured, walking to the door. 'Big trouble.'

# 8

'Settle down, please,' Christina said, watching a paper dart fly across the classroom. 'I'd like you to take out your books and begin your essays on . . .' Christina's words tailing off as the door opened, she gazed at the headmaster. 'I was just . . .' she began, realizing too late that she should have been in his office at eight-thirty that morning.

'My study, Miss Shaw. Now, please,' he snapped.

'Yes, yes, of course. Er . . . While I'm gone,' she said, turning to her sniggering class. 'While I'm gone, you can begin your essays.'

Leaving the room, Christina was fuming as she followed the head to his study. To snap at her like that in front of her class was outrageous. The man obviously had no idea of etiquette. Her hands trembling as she closed the study door behind her, she was about to yell at the man but managed to restrain herself. After all, she had taken a day off and then not turned up at his study that morning. Deciding that they were both in the wrong, she calmed herself as she sat in front of the head at his desk.

'I'm not at all happy, Miss Shaw,' he began, his beady eyes peering intently at her.

'I'm sorry about this morning. I was—'

'I'm not talking about this morning,' he cut in rudely. 'You were ill yesterday?'

'Yes, yes, I was. I think it must have been a stomach bug.'

'Then why were you seen entering the railway station?'

'The railway . . . I went to see my doctor. I've only recently moved here and my doctor's surgery is in—'

'You were seen entering the station at the very time I rang you. Your flatmate, or whoever she is, said that you were ill in bed.'

'Yes, yes, that's right. I decided to go and see my doctor and left the flat without telling her. She was in the bathroom and I . . .'

'I'm not interested in the movements of your flatmate, Miss Shaw. But I *am* interested in your sexual activities.'

'My sexual activities?' Christina gasped. 'If you're talking about my private life, then that's my business.'

'I'm talking about your sexual activities during the working day, Miss Shaw. Your sexual activities *here* – in the college.'

'*What*? Look, I don't know what this is all about, but I can assure you that . . .'

'It's about your sexual activities in your stockroom. Mr Ponting has informed me that—'

'Mr Ponting?' she echoed.

'Our physical education master.'

'I haven't met him.'

'Haven't you?'

'I've never heard of him, Mr Wright. Bear in mind that I only started here on Monday. I've not had a chance to meet the other teachers yet. I did get chatting to Mr Carter the other day. But he's the only other teacher I've met.'

'This is all rather odd, Miss Shaw,' the head murmured, rubbing his lined forehead as he stared at her.

'Mr Ponting told me that he'd met you in your classroom and you revealed to him your sexual activities with your students in the stockroom.'

'What?'

'He also told me that you suggested that he join you in the stockroom for . . . He said that you offered to have sex with him, Miss Shaw.'

'*I* offered to have sex with *him*? Good God. This is unbelievable. I've never met the man, let alone offered to have sex with him.'

'This really is most confusing. Don Ponting has been with us for eight years. I know him well and I can't believe that he's . . .'

'Lying?'

'Don Ponting isn't a liar, Miss Shaw.'

'I'm not suggesting that he's lying, Mr Wright. All I can think is that he's mistaken.'

'He'd hardly be mistaken about something of this nature.'

'In that case, he *is* lying. Although I can't for the life of me think why. If you recall, there was an accusation made the other day by one of the students.'

'Yes, but this is . . .'

'This is the same thing. There seems to be a conspiracy against me, Mr Wright.'

'I wouldn't go as far as to say that.'

'Wouldn't you? Mr Ponting doesn't even know me. He might have seen me around the college, but we've never spoken, let alone . . . My God. To say that I offered to have sex with him is . . .'

'I think I'd better get him in here and we'll thrash this out.'

'Yes, I think you better had.'

Wringing her hands as the headmaster lifted the phone and asked someone to send Don Ponting to his study, Christina reckoned that she wouldn't have too much trouble in dealing with this. If she stuck to her story, said that she'd never met Ponting, there'd be no proving otherwise. Whatever happened, she thought Ponting was a first-rate bastard. She'd wanked his cock and brought out his spunk, and he'd dropped her in the shit in return. Ponting was going to have to be dealt with, and Christina reckoned that she knew exactly how to do it.

'Ah, Don,' the head said, smiling at the man as he knocked and entered the study. 'There seems to be some confusion over—'

'There's no confusion,' Christina broke in, standing up and facing Ponting. 'I've never met this man.'

'We met in your classroom,' Ponting returned. 'You said that . . .'

'I'm sorry, Mr Ponting. I've not met any of the teachers yet. I only started at the college on Monday and—'

'She's lying,' the man said. 'I went to her classroom to introduce myself and she . . . I've already told you what she suggested.'

'This is most confusing,' the head sighed.

'I agree,' Christina said. 'I can't think why Mr Ponting believes that he's met me. Are you sure you're not muddling me up with . . .'

'You know damn well that we met,' the man cut in angrily. 'You've been molesting the students in your stockroom. You've had sex with—'

'That's quite an accusation,' Christina gasped. 'I hope, for your sake, that you can substantiate your outrageous statement.'

'Can you?' the head asked.

'I can't prove it,' Ponting replied.

'You'll be hearing from my solicitor,' Christina warned him.

'Er . . . Miss Shaw,' the head said, offering her a smile. 'There's obviously been a mistake. I really don't think we need go to solicitors.' Turning to Ponting, he raised his eyebrows and pursed his lips. 'We don't want to get involved with solicitors, do we?' he asked.

'Well, I . . .' Ponting murmured, obviously realizing that his plan had failed miserably. 'No, I suppose not.'

'Good, good. Let's put this behind us and move on. Is that all right with you, Miss Shaw?'

'It is this time. But if there's one more allegation from Mr Ponting, I shall go straight to my solicitor. And the local paper.'

'The local . . .' the head stammered. 'Yes, well . . . That's the end of the matter.'

Leaving the study, Christina felt triumphant as she walked down the corridor. But she also felt anger welling from the pit of her stomach. Why had Ponting tried to cause trouble, she wondered. He'd got what he'd wanted by threatening her and she'd have wanked him again had he not . . . Hearing him mumbling something behind her, she stopped and turned. He was a nasty piece of work, she mused, eyeing him up and down. But she'd beaten him. This time, at least.

'Think you're clever, don't you?' he sniggered.

'Why did you do it?' she asked. 'Why did you go running to Wright after I'd—'

'To make sure that you do exactly what I tell you when I tell you.'

'What are you talking about?'

'Sex, Miss Shaw. I want full-blown sex with you.'

'You might have got it if you hadn't thrown the shit at the fan.'

'I *will* get it. Of that, I can assure you.'

'You thrive on trouble, don't you? I know your type, Ponting. You're sexually inadequate. You're a weak little man who can't have a proper relationship with a woman so you have to get off on some power thing to—'

'I saw you yesterday,' he interrupted her, his face grinning. 'I had the day off and happened to see you walking to the station.'

'And?'

'I followed you.'

'You really are a sad little man, aren't you?'

'Call me what you like, it doesn't bother me. I want sex with you, and I'm going to get it. If I don't, then you'll find yourself out of a job.'

'And you'll find yourself—'

'Don't threaten me, Miss Shaw. I have far more on you than you realize.'

'Such as?'

'Your relationship with Bryony.'

Watching him walk off down the corridor, Christina felt her stomach churn. Her hands were trembling. He couldn't have known about Bryony, she was sure. There again, he must have known something, otherwise he wouldn't have mentioned her name. Wondering whether the girl had said anything to anyone, she returned to her class and sat at her desk. The students were unusually quiet, which she found odd. Did they know something, she wondered as they got on with their work. Trying not to catch Bryony's gaze, she managed to get through the lesson until the bell rang.

'Don't run,' she yelled as the students left the room. Bryony hung back, obviously wanting to talk to Christina. To be seen alone with the girl would lead to trouble, Christina knew as the others left. If Ponting happened to walk past . . . This was ridiculous, she decided. If she couldn't talk to one of her students without having to worry about Ponting causing trouble . . .

'What is it, Bryony?' she asked as the girl hovered by her desk.

'About the other night,' the girl began sheepishly.

'What about it?'

'You went out and I—'

'Bryony, I'm very busy. Please, get to the point.'

'I need to see you regularly,' the girl confessed. 'I think about you all the time. I've been dreaming about you and . . .'

'Bryony, this has got to stop,' Christina sighed, gazing longingly at the girl's teenage breasts beneath her tight blouse. 'There's already been a lot of trouble because . . . Have you told anyone about . . . about us?'

'No, I haven't.'

'Are you sure? I mean, have you mentioned it to anyone in the college?'

'Honestly, I've not said anything. May I come and see you this evening?'

'Bryony . . . Look, someone's been causing trouble. Word has got out that we . . . I don't know what's been said but people are beginning to talk about us.'

'Don't you want me?'

'It's not a question of whether or not I want you. Don't you understand? I'm your teacher, for God's sake. This sort of thing is not only frowned upon but . . . Christ,

Bryony. We're the same sex. Having an affair with a male student would be bad enough, but to . . .'

'I love licking you, tasting you. All I want is to be with you, have sex with you.'

Biting her lip, Christina gazed into the girl's wide eyes. The situation was extremely dangerous, but Christina couldn't help her feelings, her inner desires. She wanted the girl, she knew as she gazed again at the tight material of her blouse following the contours of her developing young breasts. Wondering whether Ponting had seen Bryony outside the flat and was putting two and two together, Christina knew that she had to see the girl again.

'I have a free period,' she said, glancing at the wall clock.

'So have I,' Bryony murmured.

'We need to talk, but not here.'

'What about the common?' the girl asked eagerly, expectation reflected in her sparkling eyes. 'I could meet you on the common. It's behind the—'

'I know where it is. All right, I'll meet you there. But only to talk, Bryony. You *do* understand that, don't you?'

'Yes, yes, I do. I'll go now.'

'I'll leave in about ten minutes.'

'I'll see you by the pond.'

Christina instinctively knew that this was going to be her biggest mistake yet. She also knew that she was going to do far more than simply talk to Bryony. It was impossible to deny her feelings for the girl, her lust for her curvaceous body. Leaving the college, she felt her clitoris swell in expectation of lesbian sex. She was weak, she knew as she approached the common. Weak in her lust for lesbian sex, weak in her craving for a teenage girl's naked body.

The common was deserted, but Christina repeatedly turned her head to make sure that she wasn't being followed. As she walked across the grass towards the pond, she imagined Ponting following her, spying on her. The man knew nothing of her relationship with Bryony, she was sure as she saw the girl hovering by the pond. He might have seen them talking, or seen the girl entering the flat, but that proved nothing. Ponting was shooting in the dark, grabbing at straws in an effort to force Christina to commit crude sexual acts with him. Ponting was a bastard, and he'd pay dearly for his threats.

'So,' Christina said, smiling as she stood in front of Bryony. 'I think we need to talk.'

'Yes, we do,' the girl agreed, unbuttoning the top of her blouse. 'It's very hot today.'

'We're here to *talk*, Bryony,' Christina said, trying to convince herself rather than the girl as she gazed at the shallow ravine of her student's cleavage between her barely developed breasts. 'If we're to see each other, we're going to have to be very careful.'

'Let's go into the woods,' Bryony suggested. 'People might notice us, here in the open.'

'All right,' Christina replied, walking towards the trees. 'Bryony, what happened at my flat the other night was . . . Well, it wasn't right. Alison should never have—'

'You enjoyed it, didn't you?'

'Yes, yes, I did. Mind you, most of the action was between you and Alison.'

'That's because you went out. I was waiting for you to come back. If you had, we could have loved.'

'Yes, we could have. Look, if we're going to see each

other, then we must keep Alison out of it. She's . . . she's a strange girl, to say the least. Her idea of sex involves bondage and whipping.'

'I like that sort of thing,' Bryony confessed as they walked into the woods. 'I love being spanked.'

'Bryony, we're not here to . . . Christ, it's no good.'

'What isn't?'

'It's no good trying to deny my feelings. I want you, Bryony. It's wrong, it's unethical, it's . . . God, how I want you.'

'You can have me,' the girl said, her pretty face beaming as she slipped her blouse over her shoulders. 'Will you spank me?' she asked, wandering along a narrow path into a clearing.

'Yes, yes, I'll spank you,' Christina murmured, eyeing the girl's small bra. 'Take your clothes off and I'll spank you.'

Sitting on the grass as the younger girl slipped her skirt down her slender legs, Christina wondered why she was unable to control her sexual desires. She even found herself thinking about Ponting's cock, remembering wanking him off and watching his spunk shoot from his throbbing knob. Ponting was a bastard, but he had a cock. Imagining the man driving his solid penis deep into the wet heat of her pussy, she felt her womb contract, her juices of lust seeping between the engorged lips of her hairless vulva.

'I shaved again this morning,' Bryony announced, displaying the firm lips of her vagina as she stepped out of her panties and stood naked in front of Christina.

'You have a beautiful cunt,' Christina murmured, recalling Alison's arousing words.

'I like you talking like that,' Bryony giggled. 'Say

something else. Tell me about my cunt, what you'd like to do to my cunt.'

'Bryony, you're too young for this sort of thing.'

'Too young? But isn't that how you like me? You like young girls, don't you?'

'No, no, I . . .'

'I know what you like. You like the thought of young girls' cunts. You like cunts without hair, young cunts with—'

'Stop it, Bryony,' Christina broke in, guilt swamping her as she realized that the girl was right.

'It's all right, I do understand. Do you think I'm naughty?'

'Yes, very.'

'Then you'd better spank me.'

'Not with that,' Christina gasped as the girl snapped a branch off a nearby bush. 'Bryony, that'll hurt you and . . .'

'That's what I want.'

'If you're sure.'

'Yes, I am.'

Taking the branch as the girl got down on all fours and stuck out the rounded cheeks of her naked buttocks, Christina couldn't believe that this was happening. Reckoning the bush was actually a small bay tree, she looked at the branch and felt the sharp edges of the leaves. She was going to have to be careful, she knew as she gazed longingly at Bryony's firm bottom. The rough branch with its projecting twigs could easily damage the hitherto unblemished flesh of the girl's buttocks. She was going to have to be gentle in her thrashing, gentle in her lesbian loving.

'Do it,' Bryony said impatiently, her pretty face

pressed against the grass, her knees parted wide. Kneeling by the girl's side and raising the branch above her head, Christina felt her stomach somersault as she focused on her young student's hairless pussy lips bulging invitingly between her slender thighs. This was wrong, she knew. She shouldn't be in the woods with one of her young students. She should have fought her inner desires, taken control of her craving for lesbian lust. Was Bryony right, she wondered. Did the thought of young girls excite her? Was she into young teenage girls? If she was, then . . . There was no if about it, Christina knew as she watched the opaque liquid of lust trickling between Bryony's naked love lips. Young schoolgirls were extremely arousing, she reflected. Young, fresh, firm, virginal . . . This was a new and potentially dangerous discovery.

'Do it,' Bryony said again, obviously thirsting for the feel of the branch against her pert buttocks. Bringing the branch down, Christina watched the girl's buttocks tense as the rough leaves bit into her pale flesh. Raising the branch above her head again, she brought it down across the girl's twitching bottom with a loud crack. Bryony's naked body jolted, her juices of lust streaming from the opening entrance to her young vagina and streaming down her inner thighs. Again, Christina lashed her naked buttocks to the accompaniment of the girl's whimpers of debased pleasure.

Recalling Alison thrashing the firm globes of Christina's buttocks with the leather belt, Christina had considerable understanding of the pleasure to be derived from the debauched act. Bryony was obviously revelling in the thrashing as the branch repeatedly bit into her crimsoning flesh. Her sighs and whimpers growing louder, her juices of sex streaming from the entrance to her lust sheath, she began to tremble as Christina thrashed the glowing flesh of her naked bottom harder.

'Talk dirty,' the girl said shakily, her bum cheeks turning a fire-red beneath the rough branch. 'Do it harder and talk dirty to me.'

'You're a naughty girl,' Christina said, wondering whether to let go of her inhibitions and allow her true thoughts and feelings to show. 'You're a very naughty girl and . . . I love your little cunt. I love your hard young tits, your sweet bumhole. Your cunt is beautiful. I'm going to lick your cunt, suck out your sex cream, bite your hairless lips, eat you, tongue-fuck you, lick your bottom and—'

'Yes, yes,' Bryony gasped as Christina thrashed the burning flesh of her fiery buttocks harder. 'Talk really dirty to me.'

'I'm going to fuck your tight cunt with my fist,' Christina said, wondering where her crude words were coming from. 'I'm going to lick your arse out and then bum-fuck you with my fist.'

'Piss on me,' Bryony cried. 'Tell me that you want to piss all over my cunt.'

Continuing the gruelling thrashing, Christina thought about the girl's vulgar words, the decadence of the crude act she'd suggested. Recalling her bladder draining as Alison had fisted her rectal canal, she realized again that she had some understanding of the darker side of sex, the immense pleasure that could be had from such debased sexual acts. But where were her thoughts coming from, she wondered. Obviously from the murky depths of her mind – but how did they get there?

Living a sheltered life with her parents, enduring straight sex with Charles, Christina hadn't even dreamed that one day she'd be involved in a debased lesbian relationship, let alone be thrashing a young girl's naked bottom. To think about urinating . . . Wondering whether all girls harboured such wanton thoughts, she continued the naked-buttock thrashing until Bryony rolled onto her side and lay gasping on the grass. Her legs open, her head tossing from side to side, she was obviously lost in her sexual delirium.

'Are you all right?' Christina asked her, eyeing the elongated teats of her nipples rising alluringly from her pert breasts. 'Bryony, are you OK?'

'Yes, yes,' the girl breathed, opening her eyes and smiling. 'Fist me now. Fist my cunt and make me come.'

'I don't think . . .' Christina began, wondering whether the girl could take it. 'Bryony, I think you need to rest before—'

'No, no. I don't need to rest. I want you to fist my cunt. Use me and abuse me, do anything and everything to me. Please, you must use my body.'

'Why are you like this?' Christina asked, shaking her head. 'You're far too young to . . .'

'I'm the way I am, OK? *Why* I'm like this doesn't matter. Fist my cunt, hurt me, abuse me.'

'I'm not going to hurt you,' Christina returned, her blue eyes clouding as she frowned. 'Thrashing you was bad enough, but . . . I'll fist you, OK?'

'Yes, yes.'

Parting Bryony's swollen vaginal lips, opening the sex-drenched entrance to her teenage cunt, Christina slipped three fingers into her tight pleasure duct. Stirring the cream within her hot cunt, Christina lubricated her fingers, wondering whether the girl's young vagina could accommodate her fist. Bryony was a sex-crazed nymphomaniac, she mused, recalling when she'd been the girl's age. Christina had masturbated, but had never thought of having a fist forced into her vaginal canal. She'd never dreamed of fingering her bottom-hole, having her naked buttocks thrashed or . . .

'Keep going,' Bryony gasped as Christina's fingers slipped deeper into her hot pussy sheath. 'Go on, it's all right. Push your fist right up my cunt.' Watching the girl's hairless outer lips stretching tautly around her knuckles, Christina managed to ease half her hand into her teenage pussy. Her solid clitoris forced out from beneath its pinken hood, her inner lips stretching like pink elastic, Bryony opened her legs to the extreme. To her surprise, Christina watched her fist sink into the girl's pelvic cavity as if it had been sucked in. The girl's swollen and inflamed love lips hugging her slender wrist, Christina felt the inner heat of her young body as Bryony's cunt tightened around her fist.

'OK?' she asked, gazing in awe at the lewd sight.

'Yes, yes,' Bryony replied, her eyes rolling, her breathing fast and shallow. 'Fist me and bite my tits,' she said, her head lolling from side to side. 'Fist me hard and bite my nipples hard.'

Leaning over the girl's trembling body, Christina sank her teeth gently into the brown protrusion of her erect nipple and sucked hard on her darkening areola. Bryony gasped, her naked body shaking violently as Christina began pistoning her young cunt with her clenched fist. She was far too young for this sort of thing, Christina reflected again as she bit harder into the girl's swelling nipple. She should have been going to clubs and discos, meeting boys of her own age. She should have been experimenting sexually with boys, discovering her clitoris, the delights of the penis.

But everyone was different, Christina concluded as she listened to the arousing sound of her fist squelching the girl's lubricious sex juices. Bryony had had a difficult life so far. Her mother was a drunkard, her father had run off with a young tart, she lived in a slum . . . Perhaps she'd found some solace in the perverted use of her young body. Perhaps she'd grown to believe that you only got pleasure from sex if pain was involved. Christina doubted that the girl could understand a loving relationship. Sex, in her mind, seemed to be a punishing and torturous act where her young body was subjected to pain and abuse. Was there anything wrong with that? Christina wondered, sucking harder on Bryony's erect nipple as she twisted her fist deep within her bloated vaginal cavern. As long as Bryony was happy . . . But she wasn't, was she?

Bryony was in desperate need of a relationship, and was obviously looking to Christina to fulfil her desires. Christina was enjoying the crude sex, although the acts Bryony had demanded she commit worried her. Moving to the girl's other nipple, she sank her teeth into her areola and sucked hard on the sensitive protrusion of her milk teat. Bryony squirmed and writhed, letting out gasps and whimpers of exquisite pleasure as she neared her girl-induced climax. Wondering about the young girl's previous sexual experiences, Christina imagined her having sex with other girls from the college. It was unlikely that she'd had a string of girlfriends, but she was certainly experienced in the baser acts of sex.

'I'm coming,' Bryony cried, gyrating her shapely hips as her vaginal muscles tightened around Christina's pistoning fist. 'God, my cunt. I'm . . . I'm coming.' Writhing on the grass as her orgasm erupted within her pulsating clitoris, she screamed out her immense pleasure. 'Bite me harder,' she gasped, clutching Christina's head and forcing her mouth harder against the firm mound of her young breast. 'Fist-fuck my cunt. Bite my tit harder. Fuck my beautiful cunt.'

Doing her best to comply with the girl's perverted demands, Christina wondered whether she'd enjoy a pussy-thrashing. Recalling the leather belt lashing her own naked cunny lips, she eyed the branch lying on the ground and imagined lashing the girl's shaved vulva. Knowing Bryony, she'd delight in the decadent act, Christina was sure as she sustained her massive orgasm with her thrusting fist. If Bryony were to move into the flat, there'd be non-stop crude sex, Christina knew. Would that be such a bad thing, she wondered, sinking her teeth into the shuddering girl's areola. Shaving, fisting, bondage and whipping . . . Having Bryony at the flat could prove to be very rewarding. There again, in view of Ponting's comments, having Bryony move in wouldn't be such a good idea.

The only way Christina would be able to have a relationship with the girl would be to keep it secret. Even telling Alison would be out of the question. The girl might let something slip and . . . It was a great shame that people didn't mind their own business, Christina reflected as Bryony began to come down from her mind-blowing orgasm. Too many people knew too much. Too many people were watching, prying.

'God, that was incredible,' Bryony gasped. 'I want you to piss all over my cunt now.'

'No, Bryony,' Christina returned. 'There are limits and I really don't think—'

'Why not?' the girl asked disappointedly. 'What's wrong with pissing on me?'

'What's *wrong* with it? What's *right* about it? I think we've already gone far enough. Too far, in fact.'

'Gone too far? What do you mean?'

'Sex should be . . . Oh, I don't know,' Christina sighed, wondering which of them was right. Perhaps Bryony's perception of sex was right, she mused, massaging the girl's inner vaginal flesh with her clenched fist. 'Bryony, thrashing you with the branch and fisting you—'

'Was beautiful,' the girl said, her pretty face beaming. 'I don't see why what we do should matter, whatever it is. If we enjoy it, then why not do it?'

Sliding her cunny-wet fist out of the trembling girl's inflamed vagina, Christina reflected on Bryony's words. *If we enjoy it, then why not do it?* Was that the way to look at it, she wondered, her fist leaving the girl's abused body with a loud sucking sound. That might be the way to look at it, but would *Christina* enjoy urinating over the girl's naked vulval crack? There *were* limits, she mused, wondering why. Who laid out the rules? Who set out the way things should be? Society?

'We'd better be getting back,' Christina said, rising to her feet.

'Not yet,' Bryony sighed. 'My next class isn't until after lunch. There's no hurry.'

'Bryony, I have things to do. As it is, I took the day off yesterday. Mr Wright isn't too pleased with me, so—'

'He's never pleased with anyone. Apart from Ponting, of course.'

'Ponting?'

'They're good friends.'

'I thought as much,' Christina murmured, settling down beside Bryony again. 'What's Ponting like?'

'He's a pig,' the girl breathed. 'No one likes him. His wife is—'

'His *wife*?' Christina cut in. 'You mean, he's married?'

'He'd have to be to have a wife, wouldn't he?'

'Yes, no, I mean . . .'

'Yes, he's married. His wife works for the council. I think she's a council planner or something.'

'That's interesting,' Christina murmured pensively. 'Bryony, I have an idea in mind. You say that you don't like Ponting?'

'I hate him.'

'Good, good. How about helping me to get him sacked?'

'Sacked? Yes, I'd be all for it but . . . How?'

'I have a plan. Look, I have to get back now. I'll talk to you this evening, OK?'

'You want me to come to your flat?'

'Well, I . . . I suppose you'll have to. I'll explain why later, but I want you to go in the back way. There's a fire escape leading down to an alley. I'll leave the window open and . . .'

'You want me to climb in through a window?' Bryony asked, grabbing her school clothes and getting dressed.

'Yes. I'll tell you why later. I reckon that, between us, we can be rid of Ponting once and for all.'

'I certainly hope so. Do you know, he tried to look at me in the changing room the other week. And another time I caught him sniffing a pair of knickers in the changing rooms.'

'That's excellent,' Christina giggled.

'What's excellent about it? He's a dirty old man.'

'All will be revealed later, my little angel. Now, I really must be going.'

'OK, I'll see you this evening.'

'Right you are.'

Leaving the clearing, Christina couldn't stop grinning. Ponting was married, a sniffer of schoolgirls' panties, a sad pervert, a blackmailer . . . Her plan was going to work, she knew as she walked back to the college. With Bryony's help, Mr Ponting was going to have to face not only the prospect of being sacked from his job but divorce.

# 9

'Oh, hello,' Christina said, leaning on the phone-box door as a woman answered at the other end of the line. 'Is Don there, please?'

'Don?' the woman echoed. 'I'm afraid he's out. May I take a message?'

'Yes, thanks. This is Sally. I can't make it for our usual drink but—'

'Your usual drink? I'm sorry, but I think you must have the wrong number.'

'Oh,' Christina breathed. 'I must have misdialled. I wanted to speak to Don Ponting.'

'Er . . . in that case, you do have the right number. Who did you say you were?'

'My name's Sally. We usually meet for a drink and then go out but I can't make it tonight.'

'Did he give you this number?'

'No, he didn't. Actually, I got it from the college. I'm a student there. You must be Don's mother. He's told me quite a lot about you.'

'His mother? Er . . . yes, that's right. So, how long have you known Don?'

'Oh, we've been going out together for about three months now. He obviously wants to keep it quiet, seeing as I'm a student. But we're very serious about each other. Has he not mentioned me to you?'

'Yes, yes, he has. How old are you?'

'Only sixteen. I know about the age difference but we're in love. Don reckons that age doesn't matter.'

'Yes, I'm sure he does.'

'Well, I'm sorry to have troubled you. I hope we meet before long.'

'Oh, we will. I can assure you of that.'

'Sorry again for disturbing you. Goodbye.'

Leaving the phone box, Christina ran back to the flat and raced up the stairs. With stage one of her plan completed, she took a bottle of wine from the fridge and grabbed a glass. Bryony was due in about half an hour, giving Alison plenty of time to finish her make-up before going out for the evening. Christina hadn't mentioned Bryony's visit in case Alison decided to stay in and join the sexy fun. Fortunately, she'd decided to go and see a band playing at the local pub.

'Oh, you're back,' Alison said, appearing in the kitchen doorway. 'Did you make your phone call?'

'Yes, I did. And it worked perfectly.'

'Tell me about it later. I want to get a good seat at the pub. If I turn up late, I'll end up standing for the entire evening.'

'When are you going to tell me about that man who called last night?'

'It's nothing, Christina. Just some man I used to know, that's all.'

'You seemed pretty worried about it.'

'Did I? Oh well, there's nothing to worry about. God, look at the time. I'd better go.'

'OK. Have a good time.'

'Are you sure you won't come with me?'

'I can't, Alison. I have so much work to do that I'm just going to have to stay in.'

'Right. Well, don't work too hard. I should be home about midnight.'

'OK, see you later.'

The scene set, Christina opened the wine and filled her glass. Bryony's visit would be fruitful, she was sure as she imagined Ponting getting home to his questioning wife. He was going to have a hell of a job explaining things to her. And once the woman had heard that her husband had been caught in the woods with young Bryony and with his trousers down, all hell would break loose. That was, of course, if Bryony agreed to take part in the plot. Christina was pretty sure that she could rely on the girl. After all, she hated Ponting and would obviously be only too pleased to see the back of him.

Bryony arrived via the back window at seven and wandered into the lounge to find Christina. The girl was wearing a short red skirt, red shoes and a white blouse. She looked far younger than her years, giving Christina another idea. If it got around that Ponting had been screwing an under-age girl, he'd be hung, drawn and quartered. But, before making any further plans, Christina had to get Bryony's agreement.

'You look lovely,' Christina said, rising to her feet and pouring the girl a glass of wine.

'Thanks. It wasn't easy climbing through the window in this skirt. My mum said that I look like a whore, dressed like this.'

'You look beautiful, Bryony. There's your drink. Now, sit down and I'll tell you about my plan.'

'By the way, I . . . I don't know how to tell you this.'

'What? What is it?'

'Doogan and Brown followed me. They saw me climb through the window.'

'Ah, right. Er . . . not to worry. I don't think they'll come knocking at my door.'

'They said that they . . . The thing is . . .'

'Come on, tell me.'

'They said that they'll come round later for sex.'

'Did they, now? We'll see about that. Don't worry about the likes of Doogan and Brown. I'll deal with them if I have to. OK, so here's this plan of mine: the idea is that Ponting is caught in the woods with you.'

'Having sex with me?'

'No, you won't have to go that far. All we need is for someone to stumble across you and let the cat out of the bag.'

'I'll say that he raped me,' the girl suggested.

'No, we don't need to go down that road. It'll be enough for Ponting to be caught with a young female student. He'll be suspended from the college, and his wife will leave him. That's a pretty good plan, don't you agree?'

'Yes, but who's going to catch us in the woods? Whoever it is might not want to get involved once things start getting—'

'Our witness will want to get involved, all right. The reason being that our witness will be Ponting's wife.'

'God, That'll cause trouble.'

'Exactly. When Mrs Ponting discovers you naked in the woods and her husband with his cock out . . .'

'Won't I be in trouble?'

'Hardly. You're old enough to have sex, aren't you? Besides, Ponting lured you into the woods. He said that he'd make sure that you'd get bad exam results if you didn't go to the woods and have sex with him. OK, do you want to play your part?'

'Yes, yes, of course. It'll be fun.'

'That's one way to look at it,' Christina giggled. 'However, this isn't a game. We're going to have to get it right first time. There'll be no rehearsals, Bryony. And do bear in mind that if his wife doesn't turn up for any reason . . . Actually, that won't be a problem. I'll be on hand to rescue you if things start to go too far.'

'That'll be Doogan and Brown,' Bryony sighed as the doorbell rang.

'OK, I'll go and talk to them. You wait there. Help yourself to the wine.'

Bounding down the stairs, Christina hoped that Alison hadn't come back for some reason. Realizing that the girl would use her key, she reckoned that Bryony was right and Doogan and Brown had come round to try their luck. Opening the door, she gazed at the lads, eyeing the tight crotches of their jeans as they stood on the step, grinning. Doogan spoke first, suggesting that they join Christina and Bryony for a few beers.

'I don't have any beers,' Christina replied.

'We do,' Brown said, holding up two carrier bags.

'I'm helping Bryony with her college work.'

'Does she normally climb in through the window in a skirt that's not worth wearing?' Doogan asked.

'You're fucking her, aren't you?' Brown chortled.

'For you information, Brown, I do not have a penis.'

'No, but you've got a tongue and fingers.'

'For God's sake. What is it with you two?'

'Sex,' Doogan replied. 'You like a length of cock, don't you?'

Looking down at the lad's crotch again, Christina felt

her young womb contract, the lips of her vulva swell. With Alison out of the way for the evening, it might be worth inviting the young studs in for a few drinks, Christina mused. She was feeling somewhat thirsty, but not for wine or beer. The thought of fresh spunk playing on her mind, rousing her taste buds, she wondered whether to invite the lads in for an hour or so. Bryony would be none too pleased, she knew. But there was time enough to drain the lads' balls and still enjoy an evening of lesbian sex before Alison rolled in at midnight.

'You may come in for a while,' she conceded. 'Only an hour, no more.'

'We don't take *that* long,' Doogan sniggered.

'No, that's the trouble with teenage boys,' Christina riposted.

'No, I meant—'

'I know what you meant. Come on up, and close the door behind you.'

Leading the way, Christina walked into the lounge and smiled at Bryony. The girl had heard Christina's conversation with the boys and was gazing, almost expectantly, at the door. She seemed to conceal a smile as they walked into the room and grinned at her. Had this been Bryony's idea? Christina wondered, sipping her wine as the lads swigged lager from their cans. Perhaps the girl wanted to experience a length of cock, as Doogan had so tastefully put it.

'Well,' Christina said, refilling her glass. 'This is cosy.'

'I can come back later if—' Bryony began.

'No, no,' Christina interrupted her. 'I think you might learn something if you stay.'

'I'll teach her,' Doogan chuckled.

'Doogan, you couldn't teach your grandmother to suck cock,' Christina retorted.

'Hey, you're OK,' Brown laughed. 'You're cool.'

'I'm red-hot, Brown. Now, why don't you lads strip off while I sit next to Bryony and watch?'

'Strip off?' Doogan echoed, his deep-set eyes darkening as he frowned.

'I thought you might want to show off. All you two think about is sex, so let's have a good look at your equipment.'

Nudging Bryony as she sat down next to her, Christina watched the lads pull their T-shirts over their heads and unbuckle their belts. She had them just where she wanted them, she knew as they tugged their jeans down. This might have been unethical, she mused as they pulled their boxer shorts down, their erect cocks catapulting to attention. It might have been immoral, wrong . . . But, whatever it was, she reckoned that she was now in complete control of her class. And, having made a fool of Ponting, the future was looking better than ever.

'Do we get to fuck the tart?' Brown asked, grinning at Bryony.

'If you carry on like that, Brown, you'll end up having to wank,' Christina returned. 'What do you think, Bryony?'

'I . . . I don't know,' the girl replied sheepishly.

'I'm talking about their cocks. What do you think about their cocks?'

'Oh, I see. They're all right, I suppose. I've never—'

'It's all right, you don't have to mention that. Why don't you take a look at one? Grab one and feel it.'

'OK.'

'Choose one. Which one would you like?'

'I'll have . . . er . . . Doogan.'

'You heard the girl, Doogan. Come and stand over here and let her examine your cock.'

Grinning, Doogan stood in front of Bryony with the opening of his foreskin only inches from her fresh face. Taking his weapon by the root, she squeezed it as if testing its rigidity before moving her hand up his erect shaft and fully retracting his foreskin. Christina watched the girl examine Doogan's purple knob, wondering whether she'd take it into her hot mouth and suck it. This wasn't how she'd expected the evening to turn out, she thought as Bryony moved her head forward and pushed her tongue out. Would the girl take the purple knob into her mouth and explore the sperm-slit with her tongue? Christina would have preferred her to use her tongue to caress Christina's clitoris to orgasm, but there would be plenty of time later for lesbian sex.

Brown took the liberty of standing in front of Christina and offering his erect cock to her mouth as she turned and looked up at him. Taking his fleshy shaft in her hand, she pulled his foreskin back. She was aware of Bryony watching her as she parted her full lips. Perhaps the girl was waiting for Christina to take the lead and would suck Doogan's swollen knob once Christina had taken Brown's plum into her wet mouth. Deciding to drain the lads' balls and get them out of the flat, Christina engulfed the young man's glans between her succulent wet lips and tongued his sperm-slit.

'Go on, then,' Doogan said, looking down at Bryony as she hesitated, holding his purple knob an inch or so away from her pretty mouth. 'Do what the teacher lady is doing.' Moving forward, Bryony slipped the lad's swollen glans between her full lips and teased the silky-smooth surface with her wet tongue. Doogan gasped, his naked body visibly shaking as Bryony explored his rounded cock-head with her pink tongue. Tasting the salty knob, she moved her hand slowly up and down his twitching shaft, watching Christina from the corner of her eye as if seeking her approval.

Winking at the girl, Christina cupped Brown's heavy balls in the palm of her free hand, kneading the lad's sperm-spheres, adding to his pleasure as he breathed heavily in his soaring arousal. Copying her mentor, Bryony took Doogan's ball sac in her hand, feeling the two eggs through the fleshy bag, learning about male anatomy as she quickened her wanking motions. Would the girl swallow Doogan's sperm? Christina wondered. Or would she move back, spit his knob out of her mouth at the first taste of his salty spunk and leave him to wank?

Gobbling on Brown's solid plum, Christina kept her eye on Bryony. What was the girl thinking, she wondered. Taking her first cock into her wet mouth, licking the swollen glans, running her tongue around the salty rim . . . Would this change her sexual preference? Would she now take an interest in boys, decide that sucking cocks was far more satisfying than licking pussies? Christina realized that she was feeling a little jealous as she watched the girl's full lips rolling back and forth along the teenager's solid penile shaft.

'Wait,' Christina said, moving her head back and slipping Brown's swollen glans out of her mouth. 'Bryony, I want to see you take both knobs into your mouth.'

'But that's not possible,' the girl replied.

'It *is* possible. Just do as I say, all right?'

'All right.'

'Go on, Brown. Go and join Doogan.'

Standing beside his friend, Brown offered his purple plum to Bryony's open mouth alongside Doogan's twitching glans. The girl obediently took both knobs into her mouth, her full lips stretched tautly around the rims of their helmets as she cupped the two pairs of balls in her small hands. The lewd sight sending ripples of sex through Christina's young womb, she looked up at the lads. Noticing the sheer pleasure apparent in their expressions as the girl mouthed and tongued their solid knobs, Christina hoped that they'd pump out their sperm simultaneously.

'Use your tongue, Bryony,' she instructed her young student. Nodding her head, the girl slurped and sucked on the bulbous sex globes, obviously realizing that her mouth would soon flood with fresh sperm. The lads' gasps resounding around the room, Christina knew that they were about to shoot their spunk to the back of the girl's throat and drain their full balls. Clutching Bryony's head, she was determined that the girl wouldn't escape the gush of spunk. The boys' shafts rigid, their balls rolling, they let out low moans of debased pleasure as their sperm pumps activated.

Clutching Bryony's head, forcing her to drink the fresh cream from the twitching cocks, Christina watched the white liquid spill from her bloated mouth and dribble down her chin. The orgasmic fluid pouring from Bryony's mouth and splattering her red skirt as the boys pumped out their sperm, Christina ordered her pupil to swallow. The girl did her best, repeatedly gulping down the gushing spunk as her cheeks filled and her pretty mouth overflowed. Christina could hear her swallowing, drinking from the orgasming fountainheads as the boys shuddered and let out rushes of breath.

'Good girl,' Christina finally praised her student as the spent knobs slipped out of her sperm-flooded mouth. 'Did you enjoy that?'

'Yes, I think . . . I think so,' the girl spluttered, wiping her mouth with the back of her hand.

'I know I did,' Doogan chortled, his snakelike penis hanging down over his hairy ball sac.

'That goes without saying,' Christina said brusquely. 'And now, Bryony, I think you should experience a penis inside your pussy.'

'If you say so,' the girl replied, her pink tongue licking her sperm-glossed lips.

'I do say so. Slip your panties off. That's it. Now lie back on the sofa with your bum over the edge of the cushion and open your legs wide.'

'Like this?' Bryony murmured, kicking her moist panties aside and taking her position.

'Yes, like that. Now, you two, which of you is going to . . .' Shaking her head as she eyed their flaccid cocks, Christina sighed. 'Is that the best you can do?' she asked.

'Give us a minute,' Brown returned. 'We're not bloody supermen.'

'You can say that again. I don't know, I really don't. You have a beautiful young girl offering you her shaved pussy, and your cocks look like dead slugs.'

'We've just done her mouth,' Brown moaned. 'What the hell do you expect?'

'Too much, obviously. You're going to have to do better than this. All this talk about girls, and you can only come once? Real studs, I must say.'

'OK, OK,' Doogan said, wanking his stiffening shaft. 'There, you see?'

'It's a start,' Christina murmured. 'OK, Doogan, it looks as if you're about ready so you go first.'

Christina could hardly believe how much things had changed as Doogan kneeled on the floor between Bryony's parted feet. Again, she recalled her experiences since she'd started at the college. It was incredible to think that she'd had so many sexual partners, male and female, within such a short space of time. It was as if she'd suddenly woken up to her sexuality after years of dormancy and was now making up for lost time. Sperm swallowing, cunny drinking, anal fisting . . . Was there anything she'd not experienced during her first week at the college?

'Ouch,' Bryony moaned as Doogan pushed his solid cock deep into the tight sheath of her vagina.

'You're at the wrong angle, Bryony,' Christina said. 'Swivel your hips so that . . . That's it. Good girl.'

'God, she's fucking tight,' Doogan gasped, gazing at the girl's swollen outer lips hugging the root of his penis as he fully impaled her on his solid rod.

'There's no need to be crude,' Christina snapped.

'Crude?' Brown chortled, gazing at the lewd coupling. 'He's got his cock stuffed up the tart's cunt, and you reckon he's crude because he says she's fucking tight?'

'You know what I mean, Brown,' Christina sighed, lifting her buttocks clear of the sofa and slipping her panties off. 'By the look of your cock, you're finally ready to do something useful with it,' she said, reclining on the sofa.

Her rounded buttocks over the edge of the cushion, she ordered the lad to copy his friend by kneeling between her feet and slipping his solid cock deep into the wet sheath of her cunt. Brown didn't hesitate. Taking his penis by the root, he guided his purple knob between the splayed wings of Christina's inner lips and drove the entire length of his rock-hard rod deep into her trembling body. Christina breathed heavily as she watched him withdraw his pussy-slimed shaft and drive into her again. Her love lips rolling back and forth along his sex-glistening member, she could feel the swollen bulb of his knob repeatedly battering her ripe cervix as he quickened his fucking motions. The sofa rocking as the boys found their rhythm, their cocks fucking the girls' cunts to the accompaniment of gasps of pleasure, Christina grabbed Bryony's hand as if to guide her through her first crude pussy-fucking.

'All right?' she asked, turning her head and smiling at the flushed-faced girl.

'Oh, yes,' she breathed, her eyes rolling, her lips furling into a wicked grin. 'I think I'm going to come.'

'Just relax and let yourself go. Feel the spunk filling you, your pussy tightening, your clitoris—'

'Oh, oh,' Bryony gasped, her young body shaking uncontrollably as she neared her climax. 'Oh, I think . . . I . . . I'm coming.'

'Fuck her, Doogan,' Christina cried, her own orgasm about to explode within her solid clitoris. 'Spunk her, for God's sake.'

'I am, I am,' the lad breathed, his face grimacing as he pumped out his sperm.

Christina could feel Brown's sperm gushing deep into her cunt as he too reached his shuddering climax. Gripping Bryony's hand, Christina watched the lad's sperm-wet shaft gliding in and out of her cunt, the dripping petals of her inner lips rolling back and forth along the sticky sex rod. She was in her element, she knew as

Bryony let out a cry of sexual satisfaction, her orgasm obviously peaking as her young stud fucked her senseless.

The boys were OK, Christina mused, gazing in turn at their grimacing faces. They'd obviously lost their virginity some time ago, but they were still learning. Bryony experiencing her pioneering fuck, the boys furthering their sex education, Christina was also learning more of the baser side of sex. But there was one thing she'd not yet experienced, something that had been playing on her mind since her debased sex session with Alison. One sexual act that she'd thought about trying, but hadn't had the opportunity, let alone the nerve, to attempt.

Her immense pleasure beginning to recede, Christina watched Bryony's flushed face, her gasping mouth, her wide eyes, as the girl was obviously in the grips of a multiple orgasm. Bryony's young body twitched and convulsed, her cunt spewing out a blend of sperm and girl-cum as Doogan, apparently proving that he was a stud by fucking her with a vengeance, repeatedly rammed into her. The squelching sounds of crude fucking resounded around the room and he appeared to have amazing staying power.

To Christina's disappointment, Brown withdrew his deflating cock from the spasming sheath of her pussy and sat back on his heels as his friend continued with his forbidden fucking. Realizing that she'd got the wrong lad, Christina was at least pleased for Bryony. The girl letting out a scream as her orgasm gripped her, she tossed her head from side to side as she drifted in her sexual delirium. She was bound to prefer cock to pussies now, Christina reflected sadly, her own clitoris in dire need of attention.

'Come on, Brown,' she hissed. 'You can't leave me like this. Lick my clit and suck your spunk out of my cunt.' Moving forward, the boy parted Christina's hairless love lips and pressed his mouth hard against the pink flesh surrounding her solid clitoris. Sucking and licking, he slipped two fingers deep into the spermed sheath of her hot cunt and massaged her inner flesh as she writhed and gasped on the sofa in her sexual ecstasy. Again, Bryony cried out in her coming as Doogan amazed everyone by continuing to shaft her tight cunt with his rock-hard cock. Doogan was a lad worth knowing, Christina thought, looking down as Brown slipped his fingers out of her cunt and began sucking out his sperm. Doogan was the fucker, and Brown the sucker, she concluded.

Again pondering on the illicit act she'd been thinking about, Christina reckoned that this might be the opportunity she'd been waiting for. The lads had drained their balls twice but Doogan, at least, should be able to muster up another erection and squeeze out a little more sperm. As Brown concentrated on her solid clitoris, Christina wondered whether his cock was stiffening again. Determined to experience the crudest sex yet, she pushed him away and looked down at his penis.

'That'll do,' she said, eyeing the solid organ. 'Can you manage it again?'

'You bet,' he replied, grinning as he grabbed his sex rod by the base. 'I'll fill your tight cunt again, no worries.'

'I'm not talking about my cunt,' Christina breathed huskily.

'A mouth-fuck?' Brown asked.

'An *arse*-fuck,' Christina replied, her crude words sending an electrifying quiver through her young womb.

'You mean . . .' Bryony gasped as Doogan slipped his deflating cock out of her well-spunked pussy.

'Yes, I mean an arse-fuck,' Christina giggled. 'Why not?'

'Yeah, why not?' Brown said. 'I'll go for it.'

'Fucking hell,' Doogan murmured. 'You're some teacher lady.'

'I don't think *lady* is an appropriate word,' Christina said, kneeling on the floor and resting her head on the sofa cushion. 'OK, Brown, do your stuff.'

As Brown scooped up the girl-cream and sperm from her gaping pussy-hole and lubricated the delicate tissue surrounding the entrance to her rectal duct, Christina reached behind her back and yanked the firm cheeks of her bottom wide apart. Her brown hole gaping, inviting the lad's swollen knob, she waited in anticipation as he smeared a good helping of cream between her splayed bum cheeks again. She'd had no trouble accommodating Alison's fist, and knew very well that the boy's cock would glide with ease deep into her hot rectum. It was the very thought of the illicit act that sent quivers of sex all through her young body.

Gasping as she felt Brown's huge plum pressing against the sensitive tissue of her anus, she recalled Alison's words and did her best to relax her muscles. Doogan and Bryony watched with bated breath as Brown's sex globe slipped past her anal sphincter muscles and drove slowly into the tight sheath of her arse. Christina shuddered, her breathing deep and ragged as she felt the teenager's cock-head sink deeper into the very core of her young body. This was it, her fantasy come true, she mused as she stretched her bum cheeks wider apart to allow the intruding member deeper penetration into the dank heat of her bowels.

The lad's balls pressing hard against the swollen lips of her hairless vulva, Christina released her buttocks and slipped her hands between Bryony's parted thighs. Driving two fingers deep into the heat of the young girl's cunt, she felt dizzy in her sexual frenzy. She craved anything and everything depraved, her thoughts lurching from one obscene act to another as Brown began his anal-fucking motions. Her trembling body rocking, her face buried in the sofa cushion, she revelled in the sensations of the boy's rock-hard cock gliding in and out of her tightening rectal tube. This really was sexual heaven, she reflected, massaging Bryony's inner vaginal flesh as her own lust duct rhythmically contracted and spewed out its contents of sperm and girl-cream. Wondering whether she should have asked Alison to stay and join in the debauchery, she shuddered as Brown grabbed her shapely hips and quickened his anal fucking.

'Here it comes,' the lad breathed, his lower stomach slapping Christina's naked buttocks, his swinging balls repeatedly slapping the hairless cushions of her inflamed love lips. Christina could feel his sperm pumping deep into her fiery arse duct, lubricating his throbbing knob as it glided back and forth along her contracting rectal tube. Imagining sucking the sperm out of Doogan's knob as Brown fucked the tight duct of her arse, Christina slipped her fingers out of Bryony's vaginal sheath and shuddered her last shudder as Brown withdrew his spent cock from the burning depths of her bowels.

'That was amazing,' the lad breathed, watching his sperm oozing from the dilated eye of Christina's anus.

'It certainly was,' Christina replied shakily. 'We must do that again.'

'I'll do it,' Doogan rejoined.

'Give me a minute to rest and then . . .'

'When we needed to rest you said—'

'I know, I know. All right, do it.'

Squeezing her eyes shut as she felt the bulbous knob of Doogan's cock slip past her well-oiled anal sphincter muscles, Christina wondered how much more debased sex she could take. Her bowels already brimming with spunk, she quivered uncontrollably as she thought about taking another load deep into her tight arse. She could certainly take Doogan, she reflected, imagining several more lads queuing up to fuck her arsehole. If Ponting knew of her lewd behaviour, he'd no doubt offer her anything to sink his solid cock deep into her hot arse and fuck her there.

'Christ, your arse feels good,' Doogan breathed, withdrawing his solid cock and ramming his knob-head deep into her bowels. Quivering, Christina felt as if her pelvic cavity was being pumped up as the lad repeatedly drove his swollen glans deep into the heat of her sperm-brimming bowels. Her thoughts turning to the planned downfall of Ponting, she listened to the squelching sound of Brown's sperm as Doogan pistoned her tightening rectal duct. If the man's wife caught him with his cock embedded deep within young Bryony's arsehole, she'd scream blue murder.

Bryony was going to have to experience anal sex, Christina decided as Doogan gasped, his cock shaft swelling as his sperm gushed from his throbbing knob and filled her bowels. Anal sex in the woods with Ponting? Why not? As Doogan satisfied his carnal cravings, Christina wondered how to lure Mrs Ponting to the woods to witness her husband's vulgar act of infidelity,

An anonymous phone call? Ponting would realize that he'd been set up, but what the hell?

'Can I do that tart Bryony's arse?' Brown asked as Doogan slowed his anal-fucking rhythm.

'*May* I do that tart's arse?' Christina corrected him.

'Can, may . . . I just want to fuck her arse.'

'No, you may not,' Christina said, her young body shuddering as Doogan's cock shaft withdrew slowly from the inflamed tube of her rectum. Dragging her trembling body up, she flopped onto the sofa beside Bryony. 'Dress now,' she ordered the teenage lads. 'It's time you were going.'

They didn't complain as they donned their clothes. They'd had a damned good time, Christina reflected, deciding to order Bryony to suck the boys' sperm out of her anal duct once they were alone. They had nothing to complain about. Doogan talked about the weekend as they finished dressing. Asking Christina whether they could call round for a Saturday-morning sex session, he moved to the door.

'Is that OK?' he said, his dark eyes gleaming.

'No,' Christina replied. 'I'm away for the weekend.'

'Where are you going?' Bryony asked.

'I'll tell you later. By the way, Doogan, I need you to do something for me.'

'Anything.'

'And you, Brown. I want to run a tight ship at the college. I want our class to be an example to the entire college. Well behaved, hard-working . . .'

'What's that got to do with us?' Brown asked.

'You're the ringleaders. Get our class into shape, and I'll make it worth your while. Do you understand what I'm saying?'

'Yes,' Doogan murmured. 'We control the class, knock them into shape, and we get sex in return.'

'That sums it up very well, Doogan. I don't want any trouble. I want our class to be a shining example to the college. Homework not only done but handed in on time, no absenteeism, respect for the teachers . . . In return, you two will have more sex than you can cope with. Right, off you go and I'll see you both on Monday morning.'

'OK, teacher lady,' Doogan chortled. 'Thanks for having us.'

'I'm not going to answer that.'

As they left the flat, Christina refilled the glasses with wine and retook her seat next to Bryony. She wondered how Alison was enjoying the live music at the pub. Wishing that she'd rented a flat on her own, she recalled her father's idea of buying a flat in London. Bryony would make an ideal flatmate, she reflected. Into anything and everything, the girl would be a good companion, a housemaid, a sex slave . . . But, at this stage, it was only a dream, Christina knew. The phone rang. Grabbing the receiver, she winked at Bryony and told her that they had an evening of lesbian sex to look forward to.

'Hello,' she said, pressing the receiver to her ear.

'Is that you, Shaw?' a man asked rudely.

'Pardon?'

'This is Don Ponting. What the hell do you think you're playing at by ringing my wife and—'

'I have no idea what you're talking about,' Christina replied, her pretty face beaming. 'I didn't even know you were married.'

'I know your game, you slag. You won't get away with this, I hope you realize that.'

'Get away with what? Look, I don't take kindly to people phoning me with threats. If you have a problem with your wife, then that's your problem.'

Slamming the phone down, Christina knew that she was going to have to put her plan into action. Smiling at Bryony as the girl asked what the trouble was, she ordered the girl to dress. There was time enough for lesbian sex later. For now, the downfall of Ponting took priority. Saturday morning? She recalled Doogan's words. What better time to lure Ponting to the woods with Bryony as bait? One phone call to the man's wife, and she was bound to walk to the common and investigate.

# 10

Bryony's phone call to Ponting went as planned. Fortunately, the man had not only answered the phone but had fallen for the girl's lies. Bryony had asked him to meet her on the common as she had some information about Miss Shaw. Suspicious at first, Ponting had finally agreed to meet her when she'd said that the woman was not only making her life hell but was sexually abusing a dozen or more students.

'OK,' Christina said as they left the phone box. 'You look great in that short skirt. You'll have no trouble luring Ponting into the woods.'

'Will I have to strip off?' the girl asked as they walked to the common.

'I reckon so. Don't worry, though,' Christina said, flashing the girl a reassuring smile. 'We have half an hour before he's due to arrive. I'll make sure that his wife turns up before things go too far. Besides, I'll be lurking in the bushes so, if Ponting does come on strong, I'll be there to help you.'

Reaching the common, the girls headed for the woods and finalized their plans. Watching Bryony sitting on a log, Christina did her best to drag her gaze away from the triangular patch of red material bulging between her student's inner thighs. Gazing at the girl's long blonde hair framing her fresh face, she knew that she had to keep her mind on the plan. There was time for sex, she mused, checking her watch. Biting her lip as she felt her clitoris swell, her juices of lesbian desire seeping between the swelling lips of her vulva, she turned her thoughts to Ponting.

'OK,' she said. 'Ponting will meet you by the pond. You'll bring him here to this clearing where I'll be hiding in the bushes. I've got my mobile phone so I'll ring his wife the minute I hear you approaching. It'll only take her about ten minutes to get here, giving you time enough to—'

'What if she's not in?' Bryony asked, cocking her head to one side.

'I've done my homework,' Christina replied triumphantly. 'More than my homework, I rang her this morning.'

'You rang her?'

'I said that I was from the Post Office and that we had a special delivery. She said she'd be in all morning.'

'She believed that?' the girl asked, frowning as she looked up at Christina.

'Whether she believed it or not doesn't matter. She said that she'd be in all morning. Don't worry, nothing will go wrong.'

'So I start talking to Ponting about you, tell him that you're making my life at the college hell, and . . .'

'He'll be staring at your breasts and thighs. Make sure that your blouse is open and, if you can, sit on the bench and expose your panties. You're very young and very beautiful, Bryony. There's no way that sad old pervert will be able to resist you.'

'OK, so I suggest we take a walk and I lead him into the woods.'

'That's right. From there, you shouldn't have any problems. Ponting will make the first move, I'm sure of that. When his wife arrives, grab your clothes and run. Right, you'd better go and wait by the pond. Good luck.'

'Thanks,' the girl said, offering Christina a smile. 'You *will* be here, won't you?'

'Yes, hiding in the bushes. Off you go. And don't worry.'

As the girl left the clearing, Christina decided to wait behind the bushes at the edge of the woods. She'd have a good view of the common from there, and have enough time to get back to the clearing once Bryony led Ponting towards the trees. Taking up her position, she watched the girl hanging around by the pond. There was no sign of their victim, but it was a little early. Praying that the man would turn up, she checked her mobile phone. The battery was fully charged, the woman's number in the memory . . . Nothing could go wrong – could it?

Grinning with relief as she noticed Ponting walking across the common towards Bryony, Christina ducked behind the bushes. The man started talking to the girl as she sat on the bench. His thoughts would turn to sex the minute he glimpsed the tight material of her red panties hugging her bulging sex lips. Ponting was walking into a trap, Christina reflected. But the trap was his own weakness. He wouldn't be able to fight his inner desires, she knew. Not that he'd want to fight them. As they headed towards the trees, Christina raced along the path to the clearing and settled down behind the bushes there.

Punching the buttons on her mobile phone, she waited for the woman to answer. 'Come on, come on,' she breathed as she heard Bryony and Ponting approaching. 'Ah, Mrs Ponting?' she asked as the woman answered.

'Yes.'

'Go to the common. I think you'll find your husband in the woods with a young student from the college.'

'What? Who is this?'

'Someone who doesn't like adultery, Mrs Ponting. If I were you, I'd hurry up. You'll find them in the woods just beyond the pond.'

'But . . .'

Switching her phone off, Christina felt her sex juices seeping into her tight panties as she imagined Ponting shafting Bryony's tight pussy. But it wouldn't get that far, she was sure. By the time Bryony was naked and Ponting had his erect cock out, the man's wife would appear. It would be up to Bryony to spread the news of Ponting's despicable behaviour around the college Christina would tell the headmaster that the girl had come to her in a flood of tears and . . .

'Do you often come here?' Ponting asked, following Bryony into the clearing.

'Yes, I like it here,' she replied, sitting on the log with her thighs parted.

'Miss Shaw has been making your life hell, then?'

'She always picks on me,' Bryony sighed, hanging her head. 'She's been having sex with several students and she . . . I just want to see the back of her.'

'So do I,' Ponting admitted. 'She's nothing but trouble. Tell me, why did you ring me about Miss Shaw?'

'Well, because . . .'

'It seems rather odd that you should phone me. You could have gone to—'

'The truth is . . . I . . . I like you,' Bryony murmured.

'You like me? What do you mean by that?'

'I've often seen you around the college and . . . Will you think me awful if I say that I like older men?'

'No, not at all,' Ponting replied, his narrow lips furling into a grin as he eyed the girl's tight panties. 'We should get to know each other a little better, Bryony. I must admit that I've always had my eye on you. You're a very attractive young girl. But I'm not convinced.'

'Not convinced? What do you mean?'

'A girl rang my wife yesterday, saying that she was having an affair with me.'

'Really? Who was she?'

'I don't know, but she was obviously out to cause trouble. When you rang and suggested that I should meet you on the common, I began to wonder. You must agree that it's rather odd. A girl ringing my wife yesterday and then you ringing and asking to meet here on the common? Coincidence, or—'

'I know nothing about a girl ringing your wife. I wanted to talk to you about Miss Shaw.'

*Come on, Bryony*, Christina urged the girl mentally. Time was running out fast, Christina knew. If Mrs Ponting arrived and Bryony was fully clothed, the plan would have failed miserably. Christina hadn't reckoned that Ponting would become suspicious. She'd thought that, with one glimpse of Bryony's tight panties, he wouldn't hesitate to make a move. Breathing a sigh of relief, Christina smiled as Bryony parted her thighs further and told Ponting that she'd always fancied him.

'Do you normally sit like that?' Ponting asked, his wide eyes focused on the tight material concealing the girl's full love lips.

'No,' she replied sheepishly. 'I just thought that . . .'

'What are you offering me?' he asked, the crotch of his trousers bulging.

'What do you think?' Bryony giggled impishly. 'Don't you want me?'

'I'm still not convinced,' he murmured, much to Christina's annoyance.

'Perhaps this will convince you,' Bryony said, standing and tugging her short skirt down.

Ponting watched as the girl slipped her blouse off and unhooked her bra. Tugging her panties down her slender legs, she stood naked in front of the man and asked him to slip his trousers off. He hesitated, checking his watch and looking around the clearing as she ran her hands over the mounds of her small breasts. Christina reckoned that he might have guessed that this was a set-up. A naked teenage girl with a hairless pussy blatantly offering him sex and he was hesitating? His wife would arrive at any minute, and Christina was sure that her plan had gone terribly wrong. Unless Bryony unzipped his trousers and pulled his cock out . . .

'Would you like me to suck your cock?' Bryony asked, kneeling in front of Ponting.

'Now *that* sounds like a good idea,' he replied, unbuckling his belt and dropping his trousers.

'Mmm, you're big,' she breathed, running her fingers up and down the length of his solid penis. 'Take your trousers off, and your shirt. If we're going to have sex, then we should both be naked.'

'You're quite a girl,' Ponting chortled, removing his shirt and stepping out of his trousers and shoes. 'Let's see you suck my knob, then,' he said, retracting his foreskin fully.

Relaxing as Bryony took his swollen glans into her wet

mouth, Christina checked her watch. Ponting's wife should have arrived by now, she thought, hoping that the second part of her plan wasn't going to fail. Ponting obviously wanting more than a blow job, he slipped his cock out of the girl's mouth and ordered her to get on all fours. Complying, she looked towards the bushes as the man kneeled behind her and parted the firm orbs of her buttocks. She was going to have to endure a fucking, Christina decided, praying again for the man's wife to appear.

'You're a tight-cunted little whore,' Ponting gasped, driving the entire length of his rock-hard penis deep into Bryony's vaginal duct. 'I'm going to fill your dirty little cunt with sperm and then I'll fuck your arsehole.' Remaining silent, Bryony rocked back and forth, meeting the man's penile thrusts as Christina watched the lewd scene with bated breath. Her arousal soaring, Christina wished that she could join in the debauchery. Her clitoris solid between her engorged vaginal lips, she slipped her hand down the front of her wet panties and massaged her pleasure spot.

'No,' Bryony whimpered as Ponting slipped his cunny-wet cock out of her well-juiced cunt and forced his purple knob into her anal hole.

'Shut up, you dirty little whore,' Ponting returned, driving the full length of his cock deep into the girl's arse. 'You lure me here and strip off . . . Don't start complaining.'

Biting her lip as she listened to Bryony's whimpers, Christina wasn't sure what to do. By the look of it, the man's wife wasn't going to turn up. This was all she needed, she thought apprehensively as Ponting began spanking Bryony's naked buttocks with the palm of his hand. Repeatedly ramming his purple knob deep into her bowels, he spanked her harder. Her whimpers obviously driving him on, he thrashed her rounded bottom cheeks until her pale flesh glowed a fire-red. Christina was going to have to put a halt to the abuse, she knew. About to leap out from the bushes, she thought that she heard twigs cracking underfoot.

'My God!' Mrs Ponting cried as she entered the clearing and stared open-mouthed at the lewd scene. 'Don, what on earth—'

'Helen,' Ponting gasped, yanking his cock out of Bryony's inflamed bottom-hole, his spunk shooting over the girl's burning buttocks. 'Helen, come back!'

As the woman hurried back to the common, Ponting sat back on his heels and glared at Bryony as she grabbed her clothes and clambered to her feet. He must have realized that he'd been set up, Christina thought as Bryony tugged her panties up her long legs. What he'd do now, she had no idea. Grabbing his shirt, he stood up with his limp penis snaking over his spunk-dripping balls and took hold of Bryony's arm.

'Clever,' he hissed. 'Very clever. But it won't work.'

'What do you mean?' Bryony asked, feigning innocence.

'That bitch Shaw put you up to this, didn't she?'

'Put me up to what? Who was that woman?'

'My wife. I thought it was odd when you rang me this morning. All this rubbish about Shaw making your life a misery. You get on very well with her, don't you? Intimately, in fact.'

'No, I don't,' Bryony said, pulling away from the man. 'I told you, I can't stand her.'

'So, the plan was to have my wife arrive and witness

my adultery. Which she did, so the plan worked. Miss Shaw is clever,' he breathed. 'Very clever.'

Wondering what Ponting's next move would be, Christina remained in her hiding place. His marriage was over, she was sure of that. His marriage in ruins, his job finished, Ponting was getting all he deserved. Bryony had done well, Christina reflected. The girl had had to endure the bastard's cock up her arse, but the plan couldn't have worked out better. Wondering why Ponting wasn't dressing, Christina cocked her head and listened as she heard twigs cracking underfoot again. Had the man's wife returned to have a go at him? she wondered.

'As I said, Miss Shaw has been very clever,' Ponting hissed, snatching Bryony's skirt away from her as she picked it up.

'But not clever enough,' Mrs Ponting said, grinning as she walked back into the clearing.

'But . . .' Bryony gasped, frowning at the woman. 'I . . . I don't understand!'

'No, you wouldn't,' Ponting chuckled. 'Will you explain?' he asked, turning to his wife.

'I'd be delighted,' she replied, standing in front of the quaking girl. 'You see, Bryony, my husband and I have what some would call an unorthodox marriage. We enjoy sex, but not only with each other. Don brings men home for me and I bring women home for him. We were hoping that something like this would happen because, apart from enjoying other men, I also enjoy young girls.'

Christina could hardly believe what she was hearing as the woman told Bryony of her lesbian exploits with the many young college girls her husband had brought home. Don Ponting and his wife were not going to be easy to deal with. Wondering what to do, Christina thought about emerging from her hiding place and confronting the couple. But what could she say? Her plan in ruins, she watched the woman squeeze Bryony's firm breasts. The girl was about to be subjected to a session of lesbian abuse, and there was nothing Christina could do about it.

'You obviously hoped to break up our marriage,' Ponting said, glaring at Bryony. 'But I reckon that there was more.'

'Your job,' his wife murmured. 'She planned to have you sacked.'

'That's a thought. But how? No one would believe her story . . . Wait a minute. Where's Miss Shaw?'

'I . . . I don't know,' Bryony stammered.

'Someone would have to witness this,' he murmured pensively. 'Shaw may be lurking somewhere close by.'

'I doubt it,' his wife said, pulling and twisting Bryony's erect nipples. 'Let's not worry about her. It's this little beauty I'm interested in.'

Tearing the girl's panties from her young body, Ponting's wife gazed longingly at her hairless sex crack, the engorged wings of her inner lips protruding from her valley of desire. Mrs Ponting was in her forties, not unattractive, and was dressed in a shortish skirt and white blouse. Christina watched as she kneeled on the ground and kissed the gentle rise of Bryony's mons. She didn't look like a lesbian, Christina mused. And she certainly didn't look like the sort of woman who'd force a young girl into crude lesbian sex.

Watching Bryony obediently follow the woman's instructions, turning and bending over to touch her toes, Christina frowned as Ponting lay on the ground with his thighs between her parted feet. Realizing what the lewd couple were up to as the man ordered Bryony to suck his cock, she watched with bated breath as the man's wife parted the young girl's buttocks and licked her exposed anal inlet. Christina's clitoris swelled, her juices of lust seeping into the tight material of her panties as she watched the woman tonguing Bryony's inflamed bottom hole. Sucking on the man's swollen knob, her hands resting on the ground, the girl shuddered as her arousal obviously heightened.

'You taste beautiful,' Mrs Ponting murmured, slipping her hand between Bryony's thighs and sinking several fingers deep into her vaginal sheath. 'You'll enjoy having my husband's cock up your bottom again before we've finished with you.'

Again, Christina wondered whether to emerge from her hiding place and confront the wicked pair. Ponting thrust his hips, his buttocks repeatedly leaving the ground as he mouth-fucked Bryony. Was she enjoying herself? Christina wondered, the slurping sound of the woman's anal tonguing filling her ears. Bryony could have made a run for it, she reflected. Or she could have called Christina for help. Perhaps there was more to the young girl than Christina had realized. She'd certainly enjoyed sucking and fucking the young lads, and she'd not really protested when Ponting had forced his solid penis deep into her rectal duct.

'She's been whipped,' Mrs Ponting said, moving her head back and gazing at the girl's weal-lined anal globes.

'I noticed that,' Ponting gasped, repeatedly driving his purple glans to the back of Bryony's throat.

'She's a slut, that's for sure,' the woman murmured, snapping a branch off a nearby bush. 'And sluts should be severely thrashed.'

Standing by the girl's side, Mrs Ponting brought the branch down across the firm orbs of Bryony's naked bottom with a deafening crack. Bryony's young body jolting, she moaned through her nose as Ponting continued his crude mouth-fucking and the branch repeatedly lashed her anal spheres. Christina again wondered whether to leap out from the bushes and halt the abuse as Bryony let out a shriek but, to her horror, Christina realized that the lewd sight was sending her own libido soaring sky-high. Biting her lip as Ponting drove his cock-head deep into the young girl's mouth again, she knew that she should do something to help her friend, but . . . Something was surfacing from the dark depths of her mind, she sensed as she watched the gruelling thrashing. Something sinister, almost evil.

Hoping that the lashing would continue until Bryony begged for mercy, Christina realized that a darker side of her being was emerging. In just one week, she'd changed from a sexually inexperienced young lady with hopes for a teaching career to a bisexual nymphomaniac. Why? Had wanking the boys to orgasm in the stockroom changed her? Had the sight of Bryony's teenage breasts and shaved pussy transformed her? Reckoning that her inner desires had always been there, lurking in the murky depths of her subconscious, Christina began to wonder about her true character.

Recalling a dream she'd often had during her early teens about a young girl tied down to a table with her legs parted as far as they'd go, the hairless lips of her pussy spread wide, she began to wonder whether she'd always been sexually deviant. Her years with Charles had probably suppressed her inner desires, her true character only emerging now that she was free and living in London.

The thought worrying her, she watched the gruelling buttock-thrashing and listened to the sound of the branch swishing and thwacking as Ponting gasped and filled Bryony's gobbling mouth with his spunk.

Her hand down the front of her soaked panties again, Christina massaged the solid protrusion of her ripe clitoris, stifling her gasps of sexual pleasure as the merciless thrashing continued. Running her finger down her wet valley of desire, following the curvature of her pubic bone, she drove her finger up, across the small spot of her urethral opening and into the wet heat of her tightening vaginal canal. Massaging her hot inner flesh, she parted her knees, opening the very centre of her trembling body as her clitoris swelled and pulsated. She was going to come, she knew as her womb trembled and contracted. Listening to Bryony's screams echoing through the trees, she rubbed her G-spot faster, her pistoning hand massaging the sensitive tip of her solid clitoris.

'God,' she breathed, her head hanging, her long blonde hair falling in a curtain of gold silk over her flushed face as her orgasm erupted and shook the very core of her young body. Shaking uncontrollably, she was thankful for Bryony's screams as her gasps grew louder in her self-loving. Her orgasm peaking as she listened to the sound to the branch cracking across the teenage girl's crimsoned buttocks, she felt her panties filling with her copious juices of lust. On and on her pleasure rolled through her trembling body as Ponting clambered to his feet and grabbed his victim, forcing her to remain in the degrading position and take the unrelenting buttock-whipping.

As her pleasure began to wane, Christina knew that Bryony wasn't going to thank her for leaving her to her fate. What did the future hold now, she wondered, caressing the wet walls of her vagina, sending ripples of sex throughout her quivering body. Would Bryony turn her back on Christina? What would the Pontings do now? They might lure Bryony to their house for regular sessions of debauched sex. At least Alison wasn't involved, Christina thought thankfully, slipping her cunny-wet hand out of her soaked panties.

'That'll do for the time being,' Mrs Ponting said, dropping the branch onto the ground as her husband released the whimpering girl. 'I think the time has come for you to pleasure me,' she chuckled, lifting her skirt and tugging her wet panties down. 'Kneel in front of your mistress,' she ordered Bryony. 'Kneel in front of me and lick me.'

Complying, with some rough urging from Ponting, Bryony pushed her pretty face hard against the woman's hair-covered vulva. The woman reached down and peeled apart the fleshy lips of her pussy, and Bryony was forced to lick the wet flesh within her gaping valley. Clutching her head, Ponting wanked his cock, his swollen knob rubbing against the girl's blonde hair as he gasped in his debauchery. His wife gave out moans of girl-induced pleasure as Bryony's tongue worked around the solid protrusion of her sensitive clitoris and she began to tremble as her climax neared.

Christina watched Ponting's purple globe repeatedly appear and disappear as he ran his hand up and down the length of his granite-hard penis. Gasps of sexual pleasure resounded around the woods as she slipped her hand down the front of her sopping-wet panties and again located the nubble of her erect clitoris. She needed to come again, she knew as she encircled her swollen cumbud with her wet fingertip. Reaching behind her back with her free hand, her finger slipping between her firm buttocks, she teased the eye of her sensitive anus as Mrs Ponting's whimpers of lust grew louder.

Christina couldn't help herself as she drove her finger past her brown ring and deep into the heat of her rectum. Her debauched act sending delightful quivers of crude sex deep into her young pelvis, she caressed her solid clitoris faster, doing her best to stifle her gasps as her debased pleasure built and rocked the very core of her young body. Driving a second finger deep into the tight duct of her rectum, she massaged her stretched inner flesh, the sensations transmitting deep into her bowels as her clitoris swelled painfully beneath her caressing fingertip.

'Yes,' Ponting's wife cried as her orgasm erupted within her palpitating clitoris. Christina watched as Ponting's knob swelled and his sperm shot from his slit, splattering Bryony's golden hair. Her own orgasm peaking, Christina forced a third finger past her defeated anal-sphincter muscles and deep into her inflamed rectal sheath. She needed a cock shafting the tight tube of her vagina, a throbbing knob pumping sperm into her thirsty mouth as a third organ fucked the inflamed canal of her rectum. Again wondering whether to join the debauchery, she trembled as her pleasure finally began to recede.

Stilling her fingers deep within her rectal duct, Christina slowed her clitoral masturbating to a gentle rhythm, bringing out the last tremors of sex from her abused body as the last of Ponting's sperm rained over Bryony's blonde hair. His wife staggering back as her orgasm began to subside, she stood with her panties around her ankles, her skirt rucked up around her stomach, her sex-matted pubic curls blatantly displayed. Gazing at Bryony's pussy-wet face, Christina slipped her fingers out of her rectum and shuddered in the aftermath of her self-induced coming.

This hadn't been what she'd envisaged at all, she reflected, licking her juice-glistening fingers as she waited for the Pontings to make their next move. Watching Ponting tug his trousers up his legs, she was thankful that the debauchery was over. How she was going to face the man at the college on Monday, she had no idea. He knew that she'd set him up, and would no doubt retaliate in some way.

'I'll be seeing you at the college,' Ponting said, gazing into Bryony's blue eyes.

'And I'll be seeing you at our house,' the woman rejoined. 'My husband will tell you when to call. If you don't turn up, you'll find that your life at the college will be as miserable as sin.'

'Bear in mind that I'm well in with the headmaster,' Ponting sniggered. 'One or two lies to him, and you'll find yourself thrown out. Do you understand?'

'Yes,' Bryony murmured, her head hung low, sperm running down strands of her blonde hair.

'We have a special room,' the woman chuckled. 'A room where we entertain young girls. My husband has set up a table with handcuffs and . . . You'll enjoy visiting our sex room, Bryony. In fact, I think I'd like you to visit us this evening. Yes, about seven o'clock. Do you know where we live?'

'Yes, but . . .' Bryony began.

'Seven o'clock,' Ponting snapped, grabbing the girl's arm. 'If you don't turn up, then you'll be very, very sorry.'

As the evil pair left the clearing, Bryony looked towards the bushes where Christina was hiding. The plan hadn't only failed, Christina mused as she emerged from the bushes, but Bryony was now in a dire situation. If the girl didn't turn up that evening, there was no doubt that Ponting would be true to his word and have her expelled from the college. Wondering what to say as she stood in front of the naked girl, Christina offered her a slight smile.

'I'm sorry,' she murmured. 'I didn't think it would turn out like this.'

'It's not your fault,' Bryony replied.

'No, but I still feel guilty. What the hell we do now, I really don't know.'

'I'll have to go,' Bryony murmured. 'If I don't, then . . .'

'Before you give in, let's think about this. It's a long time until this evening arrives. We have time to think of something. For starters, if they have a special room, a sex den or whatever, we might be able to expose their activities.'

'Is it illegal?' Bryony asked, wiping the sperm from her hair. 'Surely there's nothing unlawful about having a sex den.'

'It depends what you do in that sex den,' Christina replied. 'You're right, there's nothing illegal about owning handcuffs and whips or what-have-you. But if Ponting is luring young college girls into the den and . . .'

'They're old enough,' Bryony cut in, picking up her skirt from the ground. 'God, my bum's really sore. It's up to the girls, isn't it?'

'Not if Ponting is threatening them the way he threatened you. If he's telling them that they'll fail their exams or find themselves expelled . . . We're going to have to look at this from a different angle.'

Watching Bryony dress, Christina thought about the coming evening. The girl would have to visit the evil pair, she knew. She could think of no way to deal with the likes of Ponting and his wife. Wandering through the woods with the girl in tow, Christina checked her watch as they emerged from the trees and headed across the common. Feeling somewhat responsible for Bryony, she wondered whether she should suggest that the girl move into the flat. That wouldn't put a stop to Ponting's threats and abuse, but at least Christina could keep an eye on her.

'So what shall I do?' Bryony asked as they stopped by the pond.

'I don't know yet,' Christina replied, sitting on the bench.

'Can't you do something to Ponting at the college?'

'What do you mean, *do something*?'

'Get him into trouble.'

'He's well in with the head, Bryony.'

'Yes, but what's to stop you ringing the head and pretending to be an irate parent? You could complain and—'

'I've got it,' Christina cut in, looking up at the girl's pretty face lit by the sun. 'If I can get Doogan and Brown to . . . No, it won't work.'

'What were you going to say?'

'I was wondering whether Doogan and Brown could get their hands on Ponting's reports. His register, sports line-up, teams, class reports . . .'

'What good would that do?'

'If he was seen to be shoddy, losing papers, getting

football matches wrong, the teams turning up at the wrong venues ... The trouble is that it would take too long. It might be weeks before the head started to realize that Ponting was getting into a mess.'

'What if I started spreading rumours about him?'

'What sort of rumours?'

'Well, I could say that he's been seen with boys in the changing rooms. You know, gay stuff.'

'That's a good idea, Bryony. But, again, it would take a long time.'

'OK, how about this? I go to his house this evening and you have the place raided.'

'Raided? No, no, I don't think so. Unless ... Yes, that's it. Doogan and Brown turn up at his house. They find the front door open and then discover you in the sex den with Ponting and his wife ...'

'But the front door won't be open.'

'Oh, yes, it will. I'll make sure of that. They could go there in connection with some football match or whatever.'

'I'm not going,' Bryony suddenly announced. 'I'm not going to get mixed up in all this.'

'But you *are* mixed up in it,' Christina retorted. 'He'll make your life hell at the college unless you go to his place.'

'No, he won't. He won't be able to do anything to me.'

'Why? What are you talking about?'

'I'm not going back to college. I hate it and, what with all this, I might as well leave.'

'Well, that's one way around the problem, but ... Bryony, what will you do?'

'I want to leave home. I've wanted to leave for a long time. I don't like my home, I don't like college ... I'll get a job and find a flat somewhere.'

'OK, instead of going to Ponting's house at seven, come and see me. I have a proposition for you, Bryony.'

'OK,' the girl said, a smile on her pretty face as if she'd guessed what Christina's idea was. 'I'd better be going. I'll see you this evening.'

'Yes. I'll look forward to it.'

Watching the girl walk off across the common, Christina knew that she'd be doing the right thing by suggesting that she should move into the flat. Alison had been all for it, so there wouldn't be a problem there. Ponting would still have to be dealt with, but at least Bryony would be safe. Closing her eyes as she reclined on the bench and relaxed beneath the sun, Christina was looking forward to the evening. And to Monday morning when Ponting would discover that he could no longer threaten his latest recruit.

# 11

'I've changed my mind,' Alison said firmly.

'But it was your idea,' Christina retorted, pacing the lounge floor. 'I've invited her round to tell her that she can move in with us. What's changed your mind?'

'Oh, I don't know. She'll get under our feet. As you said, she'd need a room of her own. I know that I said she could bed-hop between us, but it wouldn't work. You said yourself that it wouldn't work.'

'I know I did. It's just that . . . OK, not to worry. So, did you have a good time last night?'

'Yes, the band were really good. What did you get up to? Anything interesting?'

'Er . . . no, I just caught up with my work. Will you be in this evening?'

'Why? Is it that you want the girl to yourself?'

'No, of course not. I need to talk to her, that's all. I think she's guessed that I'm going to ask her to move in.'

'I wasn't going to mention this yet, but . . . I might be moving out.'

'Oh?'

'I was waiting to see how things developed between us. I'm also waiting to hear about a job I've applied for at a hotel. I'd be living in, so . . . well, I'd be a damned sight better off financially. I'd have a room, food, drinks . . . The trouble is, what will you do without my half of the rent?'

'God only knows. Bryony reckons that she's going to leave college and get a job, so I suppose we could manage.'

'I don't even know whether I've got the job yet. I was feeling really bad about letting you down, but if Bryony moves in . . .'

'When will you hear?'

'Monday, I hope. If I pay my share of the rent up to the end of the month, that'll give Bryony time to find a job before the rent's due again. Want some coffee?'

'Mmm, please.'

Flopping onto the sofa, Christina realized again that nothing was turning out as she'd thought it would. This was a bombshell that she didn't need. There was no way she could pay all the rent on her income and, unless Bryony found herself a job, they'd be out of the flat. Even if the girl did find a job, they might not get on, living together. Wondering whether to leave the flat and go back to her parents' house, Christina began to feel despondent. The time had come for a major rethink, she decided, grabbing the ringing phone.

'How are you, dear?' her mother asked.

'Oh, I'm fine. I was going to ring you this evening.'

'We were hoping you'd be down to see us as it's the weekend.'

'Yes, I . . . I'm hoping to make it tomorrow.'

'Only there's something we have to talk about.'

'Oh? What's that?'

'Someone from your college rang your father. He said that—'

'Wait a minute. Who was it? Who rang? And when?'

'About half an hour ago. It was a Mr Ponting.'

'God,' Christina breathed, her stomach sinking. 'What did he want?'

'We're very worried about you, dear.'

'Yes, but what did Ponting say?'

'We can't talk about it on the phone. When you come down tomorrow . . .'

'Mother, at least give me a clue as to what this is about.'

'Mr Ponting was saying that you've been mixing with certain people. He was concerned, Christina. He said that you're sleeping with anyone and everyone and . . .'

'And you believe him?'

'Well, we—'

'Mother, Ponting is a liar and a troublemaker. The reason he's saying these things is because he asked me out and I said no. He has a reputation at the college. He hounds the young girls, he threatens—'

'Have you told the headmaster about him?'

'I'm about to do that. I was hoping that he'd back off, but he's obviously got psychological problems and . . . Look, we'll talk about this tomorrow.'

'All right, dear. As long as you're not getting into trouble and . . .'

'I can assure you, mother, there are no problems here. Ponting's a sick man. Just ignore whatever he's been saying.'

'That should put your father's mind at rest. You know how he worries about you.'

'Yes, I know. Look, I'll be down in the morning.'

'All right. And you'll stay for lunch?'

'Yes, yes, I will.'

'All right. We'll see you tomorrow.'

'OK. Goodbye, mother.'

As she replaced the receiver, Christina was fuming. Her heart racing, she knew that Ponting wasn't going to leave her alone. This had become a personal battle, and one that was going to be very difficult, if not impossible, to win. Was this how things were in London? she mused as Alison brought the coffees in and placed the cups on the low table. Sex, blackmail, lies, deception . . . After living in the country where everyone knew everyone else and things were quiet, Christina didn't think that she'd ever fit in with the city. Recalling the local school, she could have got a job there but there'd have been no future. Spadger Heath College, so she'd believed, would provide a stepping stone to bigger and better things.

'Who was that?' Alison asked.

'My mother. She wants me to visit tomorrow. I might do more than visit. I might go back permanently.'

'God, Christina. This is because of me, isn't it?'

'No, no.'

'Yes, it is. I feel really guilty now. I was already feeling bad, but—'

'Alison, this is *not* because of you. I've been thinking about going home for some time now. You might have swayed my decision, but I'm not giving up everything here simply because you might be moving out. There must be plenty of people looking for flat-shares. Bryony aside, I'm sure I wouldn't have a problem finding someone.'

'Why's she leaving college?'

'It's not just the college. She wants to leave home.'

'From what you've said about her mother, I'm not surprised. Anyway, you were asking whether I'm going out this evening. I was going to stay in but as you—'

'Alison, don't let me push you out. If you want to stay in, then . . .'

'You need to talk to Bryony. I'll go to the pub. There's another band on tonight.'

'If you're sure.'

'Of course I'm sure. Besides, I love the music, the atmosphere. What will you do if you go home? Your parents live in the country, don't they?'

'Yes, they do.'

'What will you do for work?'

'I don't know. I'm not even sure yet that I'm going home. I've completed my first week at the college, apart from the day I took off. It's not been easy, but I managed to get through the week. If I stay in London, I'm sure that things will work out.'

'So what's the problem?'

'It's the way of life here. The people here are different. Bear in mind that I'm a country girl. When I landed myself the job at the college, I had the idea that I'd be teaching English and—'

'You are, aren't you?'

'Yes, but I didn't expect . . . I don't know what I expected. I thought I'd enjoy the lessons, setting work for the students, getting to know them . . .'

'You've got to know them, all right,' Alison giggled. 'Intimately, I'd say.'

'Exactly. That's just the point, Alison. I never dreamed that I'd be having sex with my female flatmate, let alone the students. And as for having sex with a young female student . . .'

'You know what your problem is? You worry too much. Sex is sex, Christina. Why dwell on things? We had sex and it was great. I don't spend all my time going over the implications of lesbian sex, wondering whether it's right or wrong, analysing things, feeling guilty . . .'

'That's because you're different.'

'We're the same, Christina. The only difference is that you think too much. As I've said many times before, relax and let yourself go. Right, I'm going to take a shower before I go to the pub.'

She was right, Christina thought as Alison left the room. There was no point in analysing things, worrying about right or wrong. But Christina couldn't help the way she was. Wanking the students in the stockroom, lesbian sex with Alison and Bryony, wanking Ponting and watching his sperm shoot from his throbbing knob, taking cocks up her arse . . . Every lewd act she'd committed played on her mind, and she couldn't help that. Alison was free of guilt, getting on with her life and enjoying crude sex without worrying.

Pacing the lounge floor, Christina thought about her father. If she gave up teaching and went home, he'd harp on about her working for him. He'd also say, *I told you so.* Charles would . . . There was no way Christina was going to work at the same company as Charles. There was only one thing for it, she decided. She was going to have to stay on at the flat and carry on teaching. Evaluating the situation, she reckoned that, apart from Ponting, she had no insurmountable problems.

'I'll see you later,' Alison said, popping her head round the lounge door. 'I hope your chat with Bryony goes all right.'

'Yes, I'm sure it will,' Christina said, putting a smile on her pretty face. 'I'll probably still be up when you get back.'

'Great. We'll have a coffee and you can tell me how you got on.'

Checking her watch as Alison bounded down the

stairs, Christina sighed. 'Fifteen minutes,' she breathed, pacing the floor again. Ponting would be checking his watch, she mused, imagining the man and his wife preparing their sex den for Bryony's visit. The man would have a shock when he discovered that Bryony had left the college. He'd obviously go all out to get at Christina, but she was beginning to formulate a plan. If Brown and Doogan did their bit in return for crude sex and enabled Christina to run the best class in the college, old man Wright would have nothing but praise for her. Ponting's lies wouldn't sit too well with the head, particularly if Christina spread a few lies and rumours concerning the PE master.

The doorbell rang at seven o'clock and Christina bounded down the stairs. Still not sure what to say to Bryony, she wondered whether to allow the girl to share her room until Alison moved out. *If* the other girl moved out, that was. Opening the door, she frowned. Bryony was standing on the step, holding a large black bag. Had she brought her things round thinking that she was moving in? Christina invited her in anyway. Dumping her bag in the lounge, Bryony smiled at Christina.

'So,' Christina said, eyeing the bag. 'Would you like a drink?'

'Vodka, if you have any.'

'I think there's some left,' Christina said, grabbing two glasses from the kitchen. 'Do you want tonic or orange with it?' she called.

'Anything.'

Returning to the lounge with the drinks, Christina passed the girl a glass. 'Here's to your new life away from the college,' she said, raising her glass.

Sipping her drink, Christina gazed at Bryony's slender

legs, the gentle rise of her teenage breasts beneath her tight T-shirt, her stiff nipples clearly defined by the thin material. Her long blonde hair cascading over her shoulders, she was extremely attractive. And very young, Christina thought, wondering whether to ask what was in the bag. Perhaps the girl was too young to share the flat, she reflected. There again, living with a woman who was drunk most of the time, Bryony was no doubt used to fending for herself. Washing, ironing, cooking . . . Bryony had to do everything not only for herself but also for her drunken mother.

'Is Alison out?' Bryony asked, sitting on the sofa.

'Yes, she's gone to the pub,' Christina replied, glimpsing the triangular patch of the girl's red panties.

'You said that you had a proposition for me.'

'Er . . . yes, that's right. Actually, things have changed since I said that. You see . . .'

'I've told my mother that I'm moving out.'

'Why did you tell her that? I mean, have you found somewhere to live?'

'Well, I thought . . .'

'Bryony, we don't have a spare room here.'

'I know, but I could share with you. Just until I find a flat.'

'Alison might be moving out before long. If she does, then you can have her room. What about money, Bryony? I can't pay the rent on my own, not on my meagre income.'

'I've got a job.'

'Already? That was quick.'

'Having decided to leave college, I spent the afternoon looking for work. I start on Monday.'

'Where?'

'A massage parlour.'

'Bryony . . . A massage parlour? For God's sake. You do know what happens in those places, don't you?'

'Of course, I do. I don't mind wanking off old men. I start on two hundred a week.'

'At least you'll be able to pay your half of the rent. But I don't like it, Bryony. The thought of you working in a place like that . . .'

'It won't be for ever. I'm not going to make a career out of it.'

'No, but you get used to that sort of money and you'll find that you won't be able to do anything else.'

'I thought you'd be pleased.'

'I am pleased that you've found work, but . . . As long as it's only for a while. While you're working there, use the opportunity to look for something better.'

'One girl I was talking to said that she earns around five hundred a week.'

'That doesn't surprise me. It's prostitution, Bryony.'

'I'll only be wanking old men.'

'Yes, to begin with. Then you'll want more money and move on to—'

'Aren't *you* prostituting yourself?'

'How do you mean?'

'Don't you remember your words? *In return, you two will have more sex than you can cope with*. That's what you said to Doogan and Brown. You offered them sex to help you control the class.'

'That's different, Bryony. OK, I suppose it's not different but . . .'

'It's exactly the same. They do something for you and in return you have sex with them. I wank off old men and in return I get paid.'

'All right, all right. So, what's in the bag? Your things?'

'Some of my clothes, yes. I'll have to make several trips to get the rest of my stuff.'

'God knows where you're going to put everything. My room's fairly big but . . . I expect we'll be able to sort something out.'

'I'll leave my bag here and go and get some more.'

'All right. What Alison will say, I really don't know. Anyway, let me worry about that.'

'OK, I'll see you again in about half an hour.'

Tidying her room, Christina made some space in the wardrobe for Bryony's clothes. Fortunately, she had a double bed so sleeping wouldn't be a problem – she hoped. Alison wasn't going to be happy but, if Bryony didn't disturb her by getting in the way too much, things should work out. At least Bryony was well away from Ponting now, Christina reflected, dreading the thought of visiting her parents. What Ponting had said, she dared not even hazard a guess. The man was out to cause trouble, that was for sure.

Dashing into the kitchen as the phone rang, Christina hoped that it wasn't her mother again. This was all getting too much, she thought, lifting the receiver. What with Ponting somehow discovering her parents' phone number and causing trouble, Bryony turning up with her things, Alison changing her mind about the girl moving in and—

'Miss Shaw?' a male voice asked.

'Yes,' Christina replied, not recognizing it.

'Mr Wright here. I'm sorry to have to call you at home but I need to speak to you concerning a matter of some gravity.'

'Oh, er . . . yes, of course.'

'It's in connection with certain allegations.'

'Allegations?' Christina echoed, raising her gaze to the ceiling. 'What allegations?'

'Mr Ponting called me and . . . Look, I'd rather not discuss this over the telephone. Are you busy this evening?'

'Er . . . no, not really.'

'May I call round? If it's convenient, that is.'

'Yes, that's a good idea, Mr Wright. I think we should sort this out once and for all.'

'Good, good. Say, half an hour?'

'Yes, that's fine.'

'As I said, I'm sorry to have to call you like this. It's just that the allegations are . . . This is a somewhat delicate matter.'

'I'm sure it is.'

'I'll see you soon.'

'Yes, Mr Wright. Goodbye.'

Slamming the phone down, Christina knew that Ponting had been trying to cause trouble again. Unless she dealt with the man, she was going to be out of a job, she knew. She poured herself a large vodka. Pacing the lounge floor, her stomach knotted, she was fuming. When Bryony arrived with two bulging plastic bags and announced that she was going to make another trip, Christina told her not to return for at least an hour. The girl frowned, cocking her head to one side as she asked what was wrong. Christina lied to her, saying that the landlord was due to call and she didn't want to have to explain who Bryony was.

As the girl left, Christina wondered what Ponting had said to Wright. Whatever he'd said, it was bound to involve sex, she thought. He must have worked out that Bryony not turning up at his house had something to do with Christina and now he was out to cause her more trouble. As the doorbell rang, Christina bounded down the stairs and brushed her long blonde hair back with her fingers. Taking a deep breath, she opened the door and smiled at the headmaster.

'Come up,' she invited him, closing the door as he stepped into the hall.

'Thank you,' he said, following her up the stairs to the lounge. 'I'm sorry to have to call like this.'

'It's not a problem,' Christina breathed. 'In fact, I'm rather pleased that you're here.'

'Oh?'

'This thing with Mr Ponting is going too far. He's been phoning me, ringing my doorbell, following me . . .'

'Oh, I didn't realize that.'

'So what's the allegation? Oh, please sit down.'

'Thank you.'

'Would you like a drink?'

'Er . . . well . . .'

'Tea, coffee? Or I have some beers in the fridge.'

'A beer would be rather nice, thank you.'

'What's Mr Ponting been saying this time?' Christina called from the kitchen. 'More lies, I suppose,' she said, returning and passing the man a can of lager.

'Thank you. This is rather difficult, Miss Shaw.'

'Just say it.'

'All right. Mr Ponting told me that you were in the woods on the common with a young female student.'

'Yes, that's right.'

'You don't deny it?'

'No, of course not. I bumped into Bryony Philips on

the common and she was telling me about fungi. She's into nature – plants and the like. Anyway, we went into the woods and she pointed out some rather interesting mushrooms.'

'I see. The thing is, Mr Ponting said that he happened to see you . . . He said that you were having sex with the girl.'

'Having sex?' Christina laughed. 'Hardly, Mr Wright. Bryony and I were looking at fungi. I think you'll agree that there's nothing further removed from sex than gazing at fungi.'

'Er . . . yes, yes, of course. The point is that Mr Ponting was out walking with his wife. They both saw you having sex in the woods with Bryony, Miss Shaw. Now, Mrs Ponting is a well-respected woman and I—'

'When was this?' Christina asked.

'Today. This morning, in fact.'

'No, no. I was with Bryony on the common yesterday. I had a free period and decided to get some air . . . I've been nowhere near the common today.'

'May I ask where you were this morning?'

'Of course. I woke at seven, met Bryony at the station at eight, and we took the train to Hertfordshire to visit my parents.'

'Oh, I see. Tell me, why did you take Bryony with you?'

'Because she wanted to meet a friend of mine who's heavily into botany.'

'I'm sorry to have to ask you this, but . . . Would your parents confirm your visit?'

'Of course they would, Mr Wright. Bryony spent an hour or so taking my mother around the garden pointing out various types of fungi. My parents have a country house with a large garden. Ideal for fungi, according to Bryony. What I'd like to know is why Mr Ponting is saying these terrible things about me. And Bryony, for goodness' sake.'

'Yes, that's what I'd like to know,' the man murmured pensively, swigging lager from his can.

'Have there been rumours like this before? I mean, has anyone ever said anything about Mr Ponting?'

'Why do you ask?'

'Because I heard something . . . I shouldn't tell tales out of school, but I heard that there have been rumours about Mr Ponting in the past.'

'I'm not at liberty to go into the details but, yes, there have been one or two allegations made against Mr Ponting. What I intend to do is write to your parents for confirmation of your visit, if that's all right with you?'

'Of course. You'd best write to my mother as my father's away on business most of the time.'

'I'm sorry to have to do this.'

'Not at all, Mr Wright. I can see that you're in a difficult position. To be honest, I'd do the same. Would you like another beer?'

'Oh, well . . . If you're sure.'

'Of course I'm sure.'

Wandering into the kitchen, Christina decided to take Bryony to her parents' house the following day. Her mother would write back to the head saying that the visit was on the Sunday, but that didn't really matter. Christina would tell Wright that her mother had mixed the days up and get around the problem that way. Taking a beer from the fridge, she realized that she should make the most of Wright's visit. If she could get to know him, gain his confidence, she'd be in with a better chance of winning the battle against Ponting. Returning to the lounge, she popped the can of lager and passed it to Wright.

'It's a good job I walked here,' he said, swigging from the can.

'You don't live far, then?'

'About half a mile away. To be honest, it's nice to get out for a change. Stuck at home by myself at weekends isn't much fun.'

'Oh, you're not married?'

'No, no. I was, many years ago. Things didn't work out, I'm afraid.'

'I'm sorry to hear that.'

Eyeing the crotch of his trousers, Christina knew of one way to get well in with Wright. But, if she made a move and it went terribly wrong, she'd have blown everything. This was going to have to be played very carefully, she knew as the head rambled on about his lonely evenings and weekends. Deciding to begin by sitting opposite the man and *inadvertently* allowing him a glimpse of her tight panties, she took her drink from the table and sat with her thighs parted slightly.

Nodding and smiling where appropriate, Christina made out that she was listening to his every word as he talked about the college. Parting her thighs a little further, she was pleased that she'd worn a short skirt – but was Wright going to notice that her wares were on display? He seemed so wrapped up in the college, so concerned with the years he'd spent there as head, that she doubted he'd bat an eyelid even if he were to glimpse the tight material of her panties hugging her full love lips. Beginning to wonder whether he was gay, she knocked back her drink and was about to go to the kitchen to refill her glass when she noticed Wright's wide-eyed gaze transfixed between her shapely thighs.

Asking about the history of the college, Christina allowed her thighs to part further as she lay back in the armchair. Wright fidgeted on the sofa, adjusting the crotch of his trousers as his arousal heightened. Christina knew that if she could get his cock out and bring him some pleasure she'd not only be well in with the man but might even gain some control over him. This was the ultimate in using her femininity to gain power, she reflected. She almost had her class under control by using sex and now . . . But, she wondered, was this right? Recalling Alison's words, she realized that she was worrying again, analysing the situation, when all she needed to do was relax and enjoy herself.

'Are you, er . . .' Wright murmured hesitantly. 'Are you seeing anyone? A boyfriend, I mean.'

'No, no,' Christina replied, smiling at the man and licking her full lips provocatively. 'I did have a boyfriend but, when I moved here, we split up. How about you? Any special lady friend?'

'Oh, no,' he laughed. 'I'm too old. Well, I'm only in my fifties but . . . Not getting out a great deal, I don't have the opportunity to meet anyone. I don't think I'd marry again. Having said that, it would be nice to have a lady friend.'

'That's how I feel. A friend, someone to go out with now and then, but no ties. What about sex? I mean . . . sorry, I shouldn't be asking you about sex.'

'Ah, sex,' he sighed, swigging from his can again. 'To be honest, it's been so long that I can't remember.'

'There must be times when you . . . well, you know?'

'Oh, yes, there are plenty of times when I think about sex. You're young – it must be difficult for you at times?'

'It's very difficult. I tend to throw myself into my work, which helps. That's one reason why I thought Mr Ponting's accusations were so odd. I haven't even got a boyfriend, let alone . . . I'm pretty sure that he was mistaken about me. I reckon he's mixing me up with someone else.'

'Oh no, he was positive that it was you in the woods with Bryony.'

'Well, that's most strange,' Christina sighed, wondering where to take it from here. 'Obviously, I won't mention it to Bryony. If she thinks that Mr Ponting has been suggesting that she's having a lesbian relationship with me . . . The poor girl would fall apart.'

'Well, I certainly won't tell her. And I'll have a word with Mr Ponting. I don't want him saying anything to the girl.'

Watching the man finish his lager, Christina went to the kitchen and took another can from the fridge. Reckoning that he wasn't used to drinking, she knew that the alcohol would soon loosen him up as she passed him the can and refilled her glass with vodka and tonic. The man was in dire need of sex, that was obvious. But Christina didn't want to bolster Ponting's allegations by coming across as a wanton whore. If Wright made the first move, she reflected, sitting in the armchair and sipping her drink . . . There was little chance of that, she concluded, again displaying the tight crotch of her moistening panties to his bug-eyed stare.

As Wright dragged his gaze away from Christina's bulging panties and looked out of the window, she pulled the tight material to one side just enough to expose the hairless lip of her vulva. That was as far as she could go without appearing to be a common slut, she knew as the man turned his head and said something about the nice weather. Replying to his comment, Christina watched his expression as he focused on the swell of her exposed labial cushion. His eyes widening, he again adjusted the crotch of his trousers and fidgeted on the sofa.

This was taking too long, Christina thought, glancing at her watch. Bryony would be back with more of her things before long, destroying any chance of Christina having sex with Wright. Tossing caution to the wind, she decided to make the first move. Her fingers running up and down her inner thigh, dangerously close to her bulging outer lips, she let out a sigh of pleasure. Wright finished his can of lager and averted his gaze as his obvious embarrassment got the better of him. But Christina wasn't going to allow this opportunity to pass her by.

'Why don't you come over here?' she asked. 'Kneel on the floor and touch me.'

'Well, I . . .' Wright stammered, sliding off the sofa and walking towards the girl.

'All this talk about sex has turned me on. You're a very attractive man, Mr Wright. We're both lonely so why don't we enjoy each other's company?'

'Yes, of course,' he murmured, dropping to his knees and gazing longingly at her exposed swollen outer lips. 'Why don't we?'

Closing her eyes as the man kissed the smooth flesh of her inner thighs, Christina pulled her panties to one side and exposed the full length of her drenched sex crack. Wright didn't hesitate, pressing his mouth hard against the firm lips of her vagina and licking the creamy-wet valley of her pussy. Gasping, Christina shuddered as he parted her swollen love lips and repeatedly swept his tongue over the sensitive tip of her solid clitoris. She'd got Wright exactly where she'd wanted him, she reflected as he drove a finger deep into the hugging sheath of her sex-juiced cunt. Never again would he call her to his study and accuse her of having sex with the students. The only time he'd call her to his study would be when he wanted her young body, when he craved the tight duct of her hot cunt.

'Fuck me,' Christina murmured, her clitoris near to orgasm beneath the man's snaking tongue. 'I want you to fuck me really hard.' Remaining silent, Wright hauled out his erect penis and drove his solid knob between the splayed petals of her inner labia. Christina shuddered, moving her buttocks forward on the chair as the man's huge cock glided deep into the tight duct of her vagina until his bulbous glans pressed against the soft firmness of her ripe cervix.

Withdrawing his cunny-slimed sex rod, he drove into her again, the squelching juices of her pussy spraying from her bloated vaginal entrance and splattering her inner thighs with every forceful thrust of his massive cock. He was quite a man, Christina mused, her vaginal muscles spasming, tightening around his pistoning shaft. She'd soon have him eating out of her hand, she knew as his gasps grew louder. He might have been her boss, but now she'd call the shots. Taking time off wouldn't be a problem, Ponting wouldn't pose a threat . . .

'God, I'm there already,' he breathed, his swinging balls draining as his spunk shot from his throbbing knob and filled Christina's rhythmically contracting cunt. Again and again he drove his orgasming cock-head deep into her young body, his low moans of male pleasure reverberating around the room as he fucked her with a vengeance. Wondering how long it had been since he'd last sunk his knob into a tight cunt, Christina knew that this would be the first of many illicit fucking sessions with the sex-starved man. So much for writing to her mother, she mused. That would hardly be necessary now that Wright was her partner in lust. Grunting as he rocked his hips, sperm jetting from his knob-slit and filling the inflamed sheath of her vagina, he finally slowed his fucking rhythm.

'I'm sorry,' he breathed, stilling his deflating cock within her vaginal sheath.

'Why are you sorry?' she asked.

'I was too quick for you. You didn't . . . you didn't have time to come.'

'Don't worry,' Christina chuckled. 'We'll have plenty of opportunities to . . .'

'You mean, we'll do this again?' he asked surprisedly.

'Of course we shall. If you want to, that is?'

'Oh, yes. Yes, we'll definitely do this again. And next time . . .'

'Next time, I'll come,' she giggled as he slipped his flaccid cock shaft out of her sperm-drenched vaginal cavern. 'Next time, we'll spend an hour or more having sex. Will you still be writing to my mother?' she asked as he staggered to his feet and zipped his trousers.

'No, I don't think so. It seems to me that Don Ponting is trying to cause trouble.'

'It looks that way,' Christina said, concealing her spermed sex crack with her wet panties. 'But why would he want to do that?'

'Perhaps he was hoping to get what you just gave me.'

'Maybe. Look, I have a friend calling round this evening, so . . .'

'I have to be going anyway. Oh, there's my home phone number,' he said, passing her a card. 'Right, I'll see you on Monday.'

'Yes, of course.'

'Er . . . feel free to come to my study. If you want to chat or whatever.'

'Thanks, I will. Look, I'm sorry to hurry you.'

'No, no, it's all right. I'll see myself out.'

'OK, Mr . . . I can hardly call you Mr Wright now that we've—'

'Ian, Ian Wright. It's Christina, isn't it?'

'Yes. OK, Ian. Until Monday.'

'OK. And, thanks for . . . for everything.'

'You're more than welcome to everything I have.'

Christina couldn't stop grinning as she listened to the man walking down the stairs. Hearing the front door close, she leaped out of her chair and punched the air with her fist. She felt as though all her problems had been solved – albeit by prostituting herself. Again recalling Alison's words, she tried not to worry about her wanton whoredom or to analyse what she'd done. There was still one problem to be faced, she reflected. Alison hadn't wanted Bryony to move in. But that was a minor worry, she decided, topping up her glass with neat vodka. Ponting could go fuck himself, she thought happily. And Alison would be OK, she was sure. Now Christina could really start living – and fucking.

# 12

Waking beside Bryony on Sunday morning. Christina leaped out of bed and went into Alison's room. The girl still hadn't come home, and Christina could only assume that she'd met someone in the pub and gone back to their place. Returning to her room, she gazed at Bryony's pretty face as she slept. She looked so young and innocent with her eyes closed, her long lashes fluttering and her blonde hair fanned out across the pillow. Young – but not so innocent.

Hoping that she had made the right decision by allowing the girl to move in, Christina looked around the room. There were several plastic sacks full of Bryony's clothes and bits and pieces that would have to be sorted out. But there was all day to deal with that, she thought, suddenly remembering that she'd promised to visit her mother. While walking into the kitchen and filling the kettle, Christina wondered whether to take Bryony with her or not. It wouldn't be easy explaining Bryony to her parents, but she didn't want to leave the girl alone in the flat all day. Particularly since Alison would return at some stage and wonder why Bryony had moved in. The phone rang. Grabbing it before it woke Bryony, Christina grinned as she heard Ponting's voice.

'I just thought I'd remind you that it's Monday

tomorrow,' he said. 'We all hate Monday mornings, but not as much as you're going to.'

'And why's that, Mr Ponting?' she asked.

'There's still one way open to you, Miss Shaw. If you want to hang on to your job, then you'll meet me later this morning – on the common – and have sex with me.'

'All right,' she sighed. 'You win, Mr Ponting. I'm desperate to keep my job and I'm willing to do whatever you want.'

'Good, good,' he chuckled. 'I thought you'd see sense before it was too late and you lost your job. OK, it's now eight-thirty. I'll meet you on the common by the woods at ten.'

'I'll be there.'

'Excellent, Miss Shaw. I reckon that we're going to get along very well together. See you soon.'

'Yes. Goodbye.'

Replacing the receiver, Christina rubbed her chin thoughtfully. This could prove to be yet another break of the type that she needed, she mused, pouring herself a cup of coffee. A wicked plan coming into her mind as she sat at the table and toyed with her teaspoon, she decided to take a quick shower before dressing in a short skirt and loose-fitting blouse. She'd meet Ponting on the common, and allow him to lead her into the woods. But he wouldn't be leading her along the path to sex. He'd be following a path to his own come-uppance. Eyeing Wright's card on the table, she grabbed the phone and punched the buttons.

'Hello, Ian,' she said as the man answered.

'Oh, Christina. You're up bright and early.'

'Sorry if it's too early.'

'No, no, not at all.'

'I've just had a call from Mr Ponting.'

'Oh?'

'He wants me to meet him on the common at ten . . . ten-fifteen.'

'Why?'

'He didn't say. But, in view of his dreadful allegations, I thought I'd better let you know.'

'Yes, yes, I see. This is most odd. Will you go?'

'Well, I'm not sure. After all he's said, I don't think it would be wise.'

'I'll tell you what we'll do. You go along at ten-fifteen, and I'll be there. Out of sight, of course.'

'That's very good of you, Ian I must say that I'm very worried.'

'You must be. I'll be there, you can rely on me.'

'Thank you, Ian. And thank you for last night. It was truly wonderful.'

'Thank *you*, Christina.'

This was going to be very interesting, Christina thought happily as she downed her coffee and took a shower. If things worked out, the headmaster would arrive to find Ponting completely naked and Christina in a state of shock. Dressed and ready to go, she checked her watch. Nine-thirty, time enough to get there before Ponting. Checking on the sleeping Bryony, she kissed the girl's cheek before leaving the flat.

The common was deserted, and Christina reckoned that everyone was having a Sunday morning lie-in. She headed for the pond. She was going to have to get the timing right, she knew as she sat on the bench and gazed at the rippling water glistening beneath the summer sun. It wouldn't be too difficult to get Ponting to strip naked, but the head was going to have to turn up before

Christina herself was forced to strip. Trying to think positively, Christina repeatedly checked her watch and scanned the common for signs of life.

'It'll be all right,' she breathed, praying that Ponting wouldn't bring his wife along. That would really cock things up, she reflected, imagining the woman demanding lesbian sex. Finally noticing Ponting heading towards her, she left the bench and waited by the entrance to the woods. Doing her best to formulate her plan, she smiled as the man approached. This was the opportunity she'd been waiting for, and she prayed for nothing to go wrong as she felt her stomach churning. Dressed in tight blue jeans and an open-neck shirt, Ponting grinned as he reached Christina and stood in front of her. At least he was alone, she thought, licking her full lips provocatively as she asked him whether his balls were full.

'They certainly are,' Ponting replied surprisedly, his face lighting up as he eyed the deep ravine of her cleavage. 'You're looking forward to this, aren't you?' he asked.

'Oh, yes,' she giggled, keeping an eye out for the head. 'Very much so.'

'Why the change of tune? I didn't think—'

'I need my job. Besides, I love sex. Having sex in return for keeping my job sounds like a pretty good deal to me.'

'Well, this is a turn-up for the books. I must say that I thought you were going to be difficult about this.'

'Oh no, no. You see, I had to be sure about you before doing this sort of thing. I loved wanking you off at the college, and I wanted to go a lot further.'

'Really?'

'I've been thinking about you, wanking your cock. You're big – very big. In fact, I've thought of nothing else recently.'

'Well, I don't know what to say.'

'I had to be sure that you were OK before going any further. I have to admit that I didn't like your threats, but . . . well, I suppose that was the only way you'd thought you'd get your hands inside my panties. You only had to ask, and I'd have opened my legs as wide as I could for you.'

'Right. In that case, shall we go into the woods?'

'Yes, why not?' Christina replied, noticing Wright approaching in the distance. 'Before we do, tell me what you like.'

'What I like? Well, anal sex is one of my little fetishes. Are you into that?'

'God, very much so. You may think this is silly, but I like playing games.'

'What sort of games?'

'I used to play this with my boyfriend. You go into the woods and strip off. I'll follow in a couple of minutes and you leap out of the bushes. I have to pretend that I don't know you and—'

'Yes, I'm with you,' Ponting said, his face beaming.

'I know it sounds silly, but . . .'

'Not at all. I'll have to introduce you to my wife. You'd get on well with her.'

'I'm sure I would. OK, ready when you are.'

'Just give me a couple of minutes.'

Watching the man enter the woods, Christina knew that this was going to work. Ponting allowed his cock to rule his head, that was his problem. Falling for a trick like that, he obviously only had one thing in mind. Crude sex.

As Wright edged his way around the bushes by the pond, Christina waved, beckoning him to follow before she entered the woods. This was perfect, she mused, stealthily making her way along the narrow path into the trees. Unless Ponting had some sort of trick up his sleeve, this was going to be the man's downfall.

Christina had only gone twenty yards or so when Ponting leaped out of the undergrowth and blocked her way. His penis was solidly erect, his foreskin fully retracted, his purple knob pointing to the sky. Eyeing his heavy balls, she thought what a shame it was that she wasn't even going to have time to suck his cock and savour the salty taste of his glans. His glistening weapon-head looked most inviting, she mused, her mouth watering as she licked her succulent lips. As he ran his hand up and down his solid shaft, she reached out and brushed the globe of his knob with her fingertip. She was desperate to take him into her mouth and suck the fresh spunk from his throbbing knob. But she wasn't going to allow her weakness to become her undoing.

'And where are you off to, little girl?' Ponting asked, playing the game admirably.

'I was . . . Please, I have to . . .' Christina stammered, hearing a twig crack somewhere behind her. 'I was just walking home through the woods.'

'You'd like to suck my cock, wouldn't you?'

'No, please . . .'

'I'm sure you'd like to suck my cock and drink my sperm. Would you like me to push my huge cock right up your tight little cunt and fuck you?'

'No, please,' she whimpered, aware of Wright close behind her. 'Keep away from me!' she cried. 'You vile man! Get away from me!'

'What's the matter?' Ponting asked, his beady eyes narrowing still further as Christina backed away.

'You vile man!' Christina cried again. 'You tricked me into coming here and—'

'What the . . .' Wright gasped, appearing on the scene. 'My God, man. What the hell . . .'

'Oh, Mr Wright,' Christina sobbed, throwing her arms around his neck and clinging to him as Ponting dived back into the bushes. 'I'm so glad you're here.'

'What happened?'

'He said that he'd found some fungi for Bryony and . . . he disappeared and then leaped out at me with no clothes on.'

'All right, all right. Calm yourself. Let's get out of here. I'll deal with Ponting on Monday morning.'

'I know you don't want any trouble at the college, but the man should be imprisoned for attempted rape.'

'That would be difficult to prove, Christina. But I will sack him, I promise you. Now, are you sure you're OK?'

'Yes, I think so. I've never been so frightened in my life. I should never have agreed to meet the pervert. I might have guessed that he'd planned something like this. If I'd been alone—'

'Well, you weren't. Thank God you'd had the sense to call me.'

Walking across the common to the pond, Christina did her best to suppress the grin on her face. Ponting sacked? This called for a party, she decided. Reaching the edge of the common and walking along the quiet street with Wright, she turned her thoughts to visiting her parents. She wished that she had the day free to help Bryony sort her things out – and also to do some explaining to Alison. But she'd promised her mother and couldn't let her down. Saying goodbye to Wright as they reached her flat, she arranged to see him that evening for a walk on the common. She hadn't had the pleasure of sucking his purple knob to orgasm yet, but that was soon to change, she decided.

'Let's go,' she said, finding Bryony munching toast in the kitchen.

'Go? Go where?'

'To visit my parents. Is Alison back yet?'

'No, she's not. Where have you been?'

'For a walk on the common. We'll sort your things out later.'

'I've done it,' the girl said, a smile on her pretty face. 'I've hung my clothes up and put everything away. Want some coffee?'

'Yes, please. OK, we'll go to my parents' house for lunch. It'll save us cooking and keep my mother happy, if nothing else.'

Sitting at the table, Christina watched Bryony pour the coffee. The girl's skirt was far too short, almost revealing the swell of her panties. She had a beautiful young body, Christina mused, glimpsing her red panties as she bent over to take the milk from the fridge. Working in a massage parlour, she'd be groped and abused by dirty old men. The thought of ageing men fingering Bryony's teenage pussy as she wanked their cocks and brought out their sperm displeased Christina. Bryony was young and fresh, and shouldn't have to have her beautiful body sullied by perverts. But what choice was there? The girl had to work to pay her share of the rent.

Answering the ringing phone as Bryony placed the coffee cups on the table, Christina wasn't surprised to hear Ponting's voice. Ranting and raving, spitting out his threats, he was understandably unhappy with Christina. She listened for a while, delighting in the man's predicament as Bryony gestured silently that she was going to get her bag from the bedroom. Finally interrupting Ponting, Christina made out that she had had no idea that Wright was going to be walking on the common.

'You lying bitch,' Ponting hissed. 'You planned the whole fucking thing.'

'I was looking forward to having sex with you,' she said softly. 'Why would I arrange for Wright to mess things up?'

'You know what'll happen now, don't you? I'll be chucked out of the college.'

'I doubt that it'll come to that.'

'Of course it'll come to that, for fuck's sake. You set me up good and proper.'

'The head told me that he often walks on the common on Sunday mornings.'

'I heard what you were saying to him, you fucking bitch. Making out that you were terrified and—'

'All right, so I set you up. What the hell did you expect me to do? You and your lesbian wife abusing young Bryony in the woods . . .'

'You can talk. I know exactly what *you* get up to.'

'And you rang my mother with your crap. Yes, you will be chucked out of the college. You deserve it, that's all I can say.'

'I'll tell you this, Miss Shaw. I won't go away. I might not be at the college, but I'll always be around. I'll have you for this, believe you me.'

As Ponting hung up, Christina bit her lip. She didn't want to be looking over her shoulder every time she went out. There again, what could the man do? But he was crazy, and crazy people did crazy things, she knew. Finishing her coffee as Bryony appeared in the doorway, Christina grabbed her bag and left the flat with the girl. Walking to the station, Christina found herself glancing over her shoulder every few minutes, looking at the drivers as cars passed. This was ridiculous, she knew. There was nothing Ponting could do to her.

During the train journey, Christina told Bryony about Charles. The girl laughed when she heard what a pompous git he was and burst into a fit of giggles when Christina said that she'd sucked his cock in the garden. It was a shame that the girl couldn't meet Charles, Christina reflected. There again, he was that well in with her father that he might turn up at the house and join them for Sunday lunch. What with Bryony's short skirt and revealing blouse ... Christina was having wicked thoughts, imagining Bryony in the garden with Charles, sucking the sperm from his throbbing knob. If Charles did turn up, the day might prove to be very interesting.

Arriving at her parents' house, Christina introduced Bryony as one of her students. Her mother didn't appear to be too pleased, but welcomed the girl and offered her a cup of tea. Christina guessed that it was Bryony's short skirt that her mother disapproved of rather than anything else. She should have made the girl wear something more suitable, but it was too late now. Leaving Bryony on the patio with her tea, Christina followed her mother into the house as the woman frowned and beckoned her.

'What is it?' she asked once they'd reached the kitchen.
'Is that girl your lover?' her mother asked directly.
'What?' Christina giggled. 'My—'
'That man who rang said that you were having an affair with a young girl, a student.'

'Mother, that man who rang is being sacked.'
'Oh?'
'He's been lying about everyone, causing trouble at the college and . . . My lover? How on earth could you believe a thing like that?'
'Well, I . . . He described her, went into great detail.'
'You didn't tell me that.'
'No, not over the phone. He said that you'd been having an affair with the girl and you'd been . . .'
'Been what?'
'Spanking her naked bottom in the stockroom.'
'God, as if I'd do such a thing. He's been telling the headmaster that the science teacher has been abusing young lads.'
'Goodness me,' the older woman gasped.
'None of it's true. He's getting the sack tomorrow, so we can forget about him. Bryony is in my class at the college. Her home life is very difficult so, to give her a break, I suggested that she come here with me. I should have phoned and told you, I suppose. But it was a last-minute decision. You don't mind, do you?'
'No, not now that you've explained things. I'm sorry, dear. I didn't think that you were like that. It's just that . . . Oh, I don't know. What with that man ringing and the things Charles has been saying, I just thought—'
'Charles? What's he been saying?'
'He's not said anything to your father, but . . . He came round the other day and had a long chat with me.'
'About me, presumably?'
'Yes. He seems to think that you're mixing with the wrong type of people. When he told me that you have a man friend – a man in his sixties . . .'
'What? This is crazy. Yes, I do have a male friend. I

told you about him when I was last here. His name's Barry Doogan.'

'Charles has been up to London, dear. He's seen your flat, and the college.'

'When was this?'

'I don't know. The other day, I think. He was going to ring your doorbell and . . . Christina, he saw several middle-aged men leaving your flat.'

'Middle-aged men?'

'He made some enquiries locally and . . . well, it seems that your flat is a brothel.'

'This is bloody stupid,' Christina spat. 'I'm sorry, I know I shouldn't have sworn. Charles obviously went to the wrong place.'

'He saw you, dear. He saw you leaving the flat.'

'Several middle-aged men? No one's been to see us. Apart from Bryony and a couple of the other students. Does Charles know that I'll be here today?'

'No, not unless your father's told him. They're playing golf, so Charles might come back with your father.'

'I hope he does because I want to ask him about this. My flat, a brothel? That's ludicrous.'

Christina was becoming increasingly incensed by the allegations and accusations made against her. Charles was obviously lying to cause trouble. Unless the middle-aged men had been to see Alison. No, she'd have mentioned it. It was jealousy, she concluded, following her mother out to the patio. Ponting was jealous because she was young and attractive and had wanked off a few lads. He'd wanted her, wanted to have sex with her, and she'd turned him down. Charles was jealous because Christina was making a new life for herself in London and meeting interesting people.

'This is a lovely garden,' Bryony said, looking up from her seat at the table. 'May I have a look round?'

'Of course,' Christina's mother replied. 'Bryony, it's . . . it's lovely to meet you.'

'I'll show you round,' Christina said. 'We might find some fungi.'

'Fungi?' Bryony echoed, her blue eyes narrowing in puzzlement as she stood up.

'I'll explain later. Come on.'

Walking to the end of the garden, Christina sat on the bench beneath the willow tree and asked Bryony to join her. It *was* a lovely garden, and Christina missed it very much. But she'd left home now and was forging a new life. *A new life?* she reflected. Sex and more sex, that was her life. But was it, she wondered. She was doing well at the college, had a nice enough flat . . . There was nothing wrong with being a nymphomaniac, she thought, eyeing Bryony's naked thighs.

'I wish I lived somewhere like this,' Bryony sighed. 'London stinks.'

'No, it doesn't,' Christina laughed. 'There's the common with the pond and the woods, there's the park . . .'

'And diesel fumes and too many people.'

'Why not move away, then? I mean, if you hate it that much, get out into the country.'

'What would I do in the country? Where would I work? On a farm?'

'You might enjoy that. In fact, *I* might even enjoy working on a farm.'

'Mucking out horses and milking cows?' Bryony giggled.

'Why not? Think about it. Your job involves milking old men.'

'That's awful. God, put like that it sounds as if—'

'Seriously, I think things are going to turn out all right. If Alison moves out, you can have her room. Things at the college will be different now. I'll tell you all about that later. So, everything's OK.'

'I suppose I'd better let the college know that I'm not going back.'

'I'll deal with that, don't worry.'

Hearing her father's voice, Christina took a deep breath. Charles would have told him about the middle-aged men and the flat being a brothel, she was sure. Hopefully, her mother would put him right, stopping him from launching an all-out attack on Christina's London lifestyle. Her stomach churning as she heard Charles laughing, she decided to confront him. Ponting's lies were bad enough. To think that Charles was running to her mother with *his* crap was infuriating.

'Ah, Christina,' Charles said as he approached. 'And you must be Bryony.'

'Hello,' Bryony said softly, smiling at the man.

'Good morning. Charles,' Christina murmured coldly. 'I hear that you've been to London.'

'Er . . . yes, that's right.'

'I'm going to look around the garden again,' Bryony said, obviously aware of an atmosphere as she wandered off.

'I hear that you've been telling my mother that I'm a prostitute and that I'm running a brothel,' Christina said once Bryony was out of earshot.

'I didn't say that you were a prostitute,' he retorted indignantly.

'You said that my flat is a brothel, Charles. Prostitutes work in brothels, don't they?'

'Well yes, but . . .'

'Did it not occur to you that the men you saw leaving my flat might have been to see Alison?'

'You were there, Christina. I saw you about half an hour later.'

'I was *not* there, Charles. These men, whoever they are, must have been to see Alison. They might have been members of her family. Why you have to jump to the conclusion that they're clients, I really don't know.'

'I didn't say that they were clients.'

'What you did or didn't say doesn't matter. It's what you implied to my mother that pisses me off. And what's all this about a man friend of mine? You told my mother that I was with a man in his sixties.'

'I saw you walking down the street with a man who must have been in his sixties if he was a day.'

'So you immediately thought that I was sleeping with him, fucking him and sucking spunk out of his knob?'

'Christina . . . For God's sake.'

'I don't even know who this man is, Charles. I might have been walking with one of the other teachers. It could have been anyone. Why go running to my mother with your ridiculous tales?'

'I'm sorry, Christina. I worry about you, you know that. Anyway, why have you brought that young girl with you? God, she must be about fourteen. What's going on there?'

'*What's going on there?* What the hell do you mean by that?'

'I—'

'For God's sake, Charles. Are you now thinking that I'm having an affair with an under-age girl?'

'No, I meant . . . It just seems odd that you should be going around with a girl who's obviously—'

'Too young to fuck?'

'Christina, I do wish you'd stop using foul words. They're not necessary. As a teacher of English, you should know better.'

'I don't know which is worse, Charles. My foul words or your foul mind. First you go around saying that I'm screwing a man in his sixties, and then you say that I'm having lesbian sex with an under-age girl. I'd rather say *fuck* and *cunt* than fill my mind with disgusting thoughts about illegal sexual acts with young girls.'

'We're not getting on too well, are we?' Charles sighed.

'No, we're not. How do you expect us to get on well when you go running to my mother and worrying her with all your crap? What I do in London is my business. Even if I was into prostitution and running a brothel, it would have nothing to do with you.'

'I realize that, Christina. Oh, here comes your friend.'

'Well, Bryony?' Christina asked, smiling at the girl. 'What do you think of the garden?'

'It's lovely,' she replied, sitting next to Christina on the bench. 'I've never seen such a big garden.'

'I must go to the loo,' Christina said, rising to her feet and winking at the girl. 'You stay and talk to Charles.' Looking down at Bryony's thighs, Christina winked again and nodded her head. 'I must also ring Alison. You two can get to know each other while I'm gone.'

Stopping once she was out of sight, Christina peered through a bush and watched Charles. He was standing in front of Bryony, his gaze fixed unblinkingly on the triangular red patch of her panties as she parted her thighs. She was an obedient girl, Christina mused. Parting her thighs further, Bryony had obviously understood Christina's winking and nodding and knew exactly what to do. But what would Charles do, Christina wondered. He thought, wrongly, that the girl was no more than fourteen years old. Would he make a move towards her?

'Christina said that we should get to know each other,' Charles said, grinning at the girl. 'I'd like to get to know you a *lot* better, Bryony.'

'Would you?' Bryony asked, parting her thighs even further, the narrow strip of her panties barely wide enough to conceal the hairless lips of her pussy. 'That sounds interesting.'

'It could be. You're a very attractive young girl. Do you usually sit like that?'

'Only when I'm with older men,' she giggled. 'But when I'm with a really good-looking man like you I sit like *this*.'

Christina stifled a giggle as Bryony tugged the tight material of her red panties to one side and blatantly displayed the shaved lips of her teenage pussy. Charles stared in disbelief as she spread her thighs as wide as she could, her vaginal lips parting to reveal the intricate inner folds of her sex valley to his wide eyes. Bryony was great fun, Christina thought happily as the girl stretched the lips of her vulva wide apart, exposing the creamy-wet entrance to her cunt. The girl was going to make an excellent flatmate, she reflected, wondering what Charles would do.

'Well,' Charles breathed, the crotch of his trousers bulging as he stared at the girl's open sex hole. 'I must say that I've never seen a young girl sitting like that before. How old . . . no, I'd better not ask.'

'I'm fourteen,' Bryony lied, counting the fingers that Christina held up in quick succession as the older girl peered over the top of the bush behind Charles.

'Christ,' Charles gasped. 'Fourteen? I don't think—'

'Aren't you going to touch me?' Bryony asked, licking her succulent lips provocatively as she lay back on the bench with her firm bottom over its edge.

'Yes,' Charles replied unhesitatingly, kneeling in front of her and driving a finger deep into the hot sheath of her young pussy.

'If you're quick, you'll have time to fuck me before Christina gets back.'

'God, I . . .' Charles stammered, slipping a second finger into her contracting vagina. 'I really don't think . . .'

'Don't you want to fuck my little cunt?' Bryony sighed.

'Yes, but . . .'

'I'd love to feel your hard cock sliding deep into my wet cunt. And your sperm filling me.'

Withdrawing his cunny-dripping fingers, Charles unzipped his trousers and pulled his solid cock out. He was a bloody hypocrite, Christina mused, watching him stab at the girl's open lust hole with his purple knob. He'd made out that he was some sort of high and mighty man of great morality – and now he was forcing his cock into the wet cunt of a girl he believed to be only fourteen! Watching his rock-hard shaft sink deeper into her young body, Christina was in two minds as to whether or not to leap out of the bushes and confront him. He wasn't going to get away with his hypocrisy, that was for sure.

'God, you're tight,' Charles breathed, fully impaling the trembling girl on his lust staff.

'So I should be,' Bryony giggled. 'I'm only *just* fourteen.'

'Only just . . . Bloody hell.'

'Fuck me really hard, Charles. Fuck me really hard and fill my tight cunt with spunk.'

Repeatedly ramming his swollen knob deep into the young girl's hot cunt, Charles let out moans and gasps of debased pleasure. Groping at her blouse, he slipped his hand inside and squeezed the firmness of her teenage breasts as he fucked her with a vengeance. Leaning forward, he locked his lips to her full mouth, his tongue meeting hers as he rocked his hips and lost himself in the grip of what he mistakenly imagined to be his illicit sexual act. Christina waited, biding her time as her ex-boyfriend committed the vulgar act. Slipping her hand down the front of her wet panties, she massaged the solid nubble of her erect clitoris, the arousing scene sending ripples of pleasure through her contracting womb as her clitoris responded to her intimate caress.

'Coming,' Charles announced, gasping. The girl's young body flopped back and forth like a rag doll as he repeatedly rammed his throbbing knob deep into her tightening cunt and filled her with his gushing sperm. Again and again he drove his purple glans into the fiery heat of her teenage cunt, his balls draining as the squelching and gasping sounds of furtive sex sounded through the garden. Christina stifled her own gasps of sexual satisfaction as her clitoris erupted in orgasm, her curvaceous body shaking violently as Charles made his last penile thrusts into the sex-dizzy younger girl.

Finally coming down from her sexual heaven, Christina sucked her vaginal cream from her sticky fingers and adjusted her clothing. Charles was breathing heavily, his body collapsed over Bryony, his penis embedded deep within her spunked vaginal cavern as he recovered from his forbidden fucking. The time was right, Christina mused, checking her clothing before emerging from her hiding place and standing behind Charles. Once again, hypocrisy was about to be exposed.

'My God,' Christina gasped, holding her hand to her mouth.

'Oh, er . . .' Charles stammered, moving back and slipping his cunny-wet cock out of Bryony's sperm-flooded cunt. 'Christina, I . . .'

'Don't say anything, Charles. I was thinking that we might get back together but . . . Just don't ever speak to me again.'

'Christina, you don't understand,' he whined, rising to his feet and zipping his trousers. 'That young tart made me—'

'She *made* you fuck her?' Christina laughed bitterly. 'She's thirteen years old, Charles.'

'Thirteen?' he breathed, his face reddening. 'But I thought she was at least—'

'*Nearly* fourteen,' Bryony said, concealing the sperm-wet crack of her pussy with her tight panties.

'You'd better leave,' Christina sobbed, wiping her eyes. 'Just leave.'

'Yes, yes, of course,' Charles murmured, walking towards the house.

'That's that bastard dealt with,' Christina giggled once he was out of earshot. 'And now, young lady, I'd better deal with you most severely.'

Kneeling in front of Bryony, Christina pulled the girl's soaked panties aside and pressed her mouth to her gaping vaginal entrance. Sucking out the sperm and girl-cum, she swallowed the heady blend of sex as Bryony trembled and writhed on the bench. The day couldn't have turned out better, Christina reflected, drinking from the brimming sheath of the young lesbian's hot cunt. They could now look forward to lunch – without Charles – and then spend the afternoon relaxing beneath the sun in the garden.

Monday was going to be another interesting day, Christina knew as she drained the girl's hot cunt. Ponting sacked, giving the headmaster a quick blow job in his study . . . She might even wank off Doogan and Brown, she reflected. If they had the class under control, she might even allow them to fuck her tight bottom-hole. Monday morning was going to be most interesting. But she still had Alison to face. And Ponting's threats to worry about.

# 13

'This morning, we're going to look at spoken English,' Christina said, standing behind her desk as the headmaster appeared in the doorway.

'Excuse me, Miss,' Brown said, rising to his feet. 'The essay—'

'I'm sorry to interrupt the lesson,' Wright said, obviously stunned by the control Christina seemed to have over her class.

'I'm sorry, sir,' Brown said, retaking his seat.

'No, no, not at all, Brown. Might I have a quick word, Miss Shaw?'

'Yes, of course,' Christina replied, walking to the door. 'I'll be five minutes,' she said to the class. 'Presumably you all managed to complete your essays over the weekend?'

'Yes, Miss,' the students replied in unison.

'All right, read through them and then place them on my desk.'

Following the head to his study, Christina realized that Brown and Doogan had kept their word and had ordered their fellow students to behave. What the lads had threatened the class with, Christina dreaded to think. But whatever it was had worked, which was all that mattered. Closing the door behind her as she followed Wright into the study, she wondered whether he'd spoken to Ponting yet. If the man had dared to show his face at the college, that was.

'Your class are remarkably well behaved,' Wright said, perching himself on the edge of his desk. 'Never in all my years at this college have I know such obedience, such good behaviour. You'll have to tell me how you did it, let me in on your secret.'

'It's just a matter of handling them properly,' Christina said, imagining handling the lads' cocks in return for their efforts. 'One or two of the boys were pretty hard to handle at first, but I soon softened them up.'

'It's truly remarkable, Christina. I congratulate you.'

'Thank you.'

'Now, I want to talk to you about Mr Ponting.'

'Have you spoken to him yet? I haven't seen him around this morning.'

'No, you won't be seeing him at the college again. He rang in first thing with his resignation. Which I immediately accepted, of course. I know that you will think that I'm putting the college first, but . . . I don't believe it's necessary to take any further action, do you?'

'No, I don't. We'd gain nothing by taking this any further. As long as Mr Ponting has gone, that's fine by me.'

'Good, good. So, I now have the job of finding another sports master. Er . . . Christina?'

'Yes?'

'About the weekend. I enjoyed . . . er . . . I enjoyed your company very much. I hope we can see each other again.'

'Of course we will, Ian. There's nothing I'd like more.'

'I was hoping you'd say that. If you're free during break, come and join me for a coffee.'

'Thanks, I'd love to. Well, I'd better be getting back to my class.'

'Right you are.'

Leaving the study, Christina grinned as she walked along the corridor. Ponting had resigned, Christina herself was well in with the headmaster, the students were models of good behaviour, Bryony . . . Wondering how the girl was getting on at the massage parlour, Christina decided to tell the head, when she joined him for coffee later that morning, that the girl had left the college. Everything was going so well, Christina reflected. Too well, perhaps? Returning to her class, she was amazed to find a neat pile of completed essays on her desk. This was far too good to be true, she thought, beginning the lesson on spoken English.

As the class filed out of the room at break time, Christina noticed one student hanging back. It was Simpson, a good-looking lad who had pretty much kept himself to himself during lessons. Reckoning that he was trying to pluck up the courage to talk to her as she went through the motions of sorting out his books, Christina wandered over to his desk and asked whether he was enjoying college.

'Sort of,' he replied. 'But I'm not happy with Doogan's threats.'

'Threats?' Christina echoed, feigning puzzlement.

'We behave in class, or we get it on the way home.'

'I see. Don't you *want* to behave in class?'

'It's not that. It's . . . I know what you're up to.'

'Up to?'

'It's not right, what you're doing.'

'Simpson, I'm not doing anything other than teaching English.'

'I know what you do in the stockroom. It's not right, Miss. It's not moral or ethical.'

'What do I do in the stockroom?' Christina asked, realizing that she could have a problem on her hands.

'You know what you do. I don't like it, Miss. You might think me old-fashioned or whatever, but I'm wondering whether to report it.'

'Report what?' Christina asked, sure now that she was facing a major problem.

'It's not right to—'

'To do *this*?' she whispered huskily, massaging the boy's penis through his trousers.

'Yes, no . . . I mean . . .'

'Don't you like it, Simpson?'

'No, I . . .'

'That's nice, isn't it? I can feel you stiffening. You like me stiffening you like this, don't you?'

'This isn't . . .'

'Isn't right? Tell me what's wrong with it. Now you're really stiff. I can feel you, your hardness. Would you like me to stop?'

'Yes, no . . . Someone might come in.'

'No, they won't,' she breathed, unzipping his trousers and pulling his solid penis out. 'That's what you want, isn't it?' she asked, rolling his foreskin back and forth over the swollen globe of his cock. 'No, don't pull away. Let me massage you, Simpson. Allow me to relax you, take all your worries and tension away.'

Watching the lad's eyes roll as she ran her hand up and down the length of his twitching cock, Christina knew that she'd solved yet another problem. This was easy, she reflected. To control teenage boys, all she needed to do was massage their young cocks and bring out their sperm. Wondering whether to kneel down and take the lad's purple globe into her wet mouth, she glanced at the door. It was too risky, she decided, wanking the lad faster. Beginning to gasp, his knees sagging, Christina knew that he'd soon be shooting his sperm all over the floor.

'You like me wanking your cock, don't you?' she asked.

'Yes, yes,' he breathed.

'You'd like me to wank you every day, wouldn't you?'

'I . . . I'm coming.'

'I want your sperm to run all over my hand. Then I'll lap it up, swallow your spunk. You'd love to feel your knob in my mouth, wouldn't you?'

'God, yes. I—'

Kneeling, Christina couldn't help herself as she retracted his foreskin fully and sucked his salty knob deep into her hot mouth. Simpson gasped, whimpering and trembling as he clung to her head and filled her pretty mouth with his gushing spunk. Hauling his heavy balls out of his trousers, Christina massaged the fleshy bag of his scrotum and kneaded his sperm eggs as he gasped in his mouth-fucking. Gobbling and sucking on his orgasming knob, Christina drank from his teenage fountainhead. Wondering whether he'd ever slipped his cock into a girl's mouth and spunked down her throat, she imagined him wanking. He'd think about fucking her hot mouth every time he wanked from now on. He'd picture his purple knob between her full lips, her tongue teasing his sperm-slit as she swallowed his orgasmic offering.

Finally slipping Simpson's spent penis out of her sperm-flooded mouth, Christina stood in front of him and grinned. White liquid dribbling down her chin, she moved forward, locked her glossed lips to his and pushed her tongue deep into his mouth. To her surprise, his cock stiffened again, his solid shaft pressing hard against her lower stomach as he tasted his spunk on her tongue. This was the beauty of young lads, she reflected, grabbing his hard penile shaft. They could come again and again.

'Are you all right now?' she asked, moving back and smiling at him.

'Yes, yes, I . . .' he stammered as she wanked his solid shaft.

'There's no time to wank you again,' she said, reluctantly releasing his cock. 'Tomorrow, I'll let you mouth-fuck me.'

'What about . . .'

'You want to fuck my tight cunt?'

'God, yes.'

'OK, tomorrow you can fuck me properly. Now, you'd better get going.'

As the boy zipped up his trousers and left the classroom, Christina licked her spermed lips. Her clitoris in dire need of appeasing, she checked her watch before making her way to the head's study. Wishing she'd got the lad to slip his hand down the front of her wet panties and massage the solid nub of her pleasure spot to orgasm, she wondered whether the head would oblige her by masturbating her. He'd enjoyed locking his mouth to her vulval flesh, sucking and licking her swollen clitoris. He might enjoy a quick vaginal slurp during break.

Walking to the head's study, the crotch of her tight panties soaking up her copious vaginal juices, Christina wondered how many more students she'd have to satisfy sexually to keep them under control. Did it really matter? She pondered: even if it reached the stage where she was regularly wanking every lad in her class, she didn't see that there'd be a problem. Far from it, in fact. The feel of a solid teenage cock in her hand and sperm running over her fingers was hardly a *problem*.

'Ah, Christina,' the head said, standing and smiling as she knocked on his door and entered the study. 'I was beginning to think that you weren't going to turn up.'

'I'm sorry, Ian. I had to deal with one of the boys.'

'No problems, I hope?'

'Nothing too big for me to handle. He was becoming a little concerned about something. All I had to do was talk to him, show him how to get a grip on himself.'

'You're doing exceedingly well. Oh, there's your coffee,' he said, pointing to a tray. 'Help yourself to sugar.'

'Thanks.'

'I've been thinking, Christina. The college needs people like you. People who are able to take control. I realize that you're fresh out of training college and have little or no experience, but—'

'I'm gaining experience every day, Ian,' she broke in, the taste of sperm lingering on her full lips.

'Yes, yes, of course. Although this is only your second week at Spadger Heath College, you've made remarkable progress, achieved amazing results with your class. What I was going to suggest is that you help one or two of the other teachers.'

'Help them? How do you mean?' Christina asked, sipping her coffee.

'Let them into your little secret,' he chuckled. 'Only this morning, Mr Carter was saying that he can't understand why you're still here. As he pointed out, the turnover of staff at Spadger Heath is very high. Not only are you still here, but you're in complete control of your class. Mr Carter, for one, would love to know how you do it.'

'It's not a secret, Ian. It's just . . . I don't know what it is. I do my best to come across as authoritative and yet, at the same time, friendly and approachable.'

'But the likes of Doogan and one or two others . . . How on earth have you got *them* under control?'

'I talk to them, try to get to know them and understand their problems. It's not that I take their side against anything they're whingeing about but I do show them that I'm aware that there are two sides to any issue or problem. I'm not a great deal older than the students, Ian. I'm virtually of the same generation, so I'm able to relate.'

'Yes, I see what you mean. So, talking to Mr Carter wouldn't really help. He's in his fifties and is obviously seen by the students as an old fuddy-duddy. That aside, are you busy this evening?'

'This evening?' she echoed, finishing her coffee. 'Er . . . I'm not sure what I'm doing yet.'

'I thought we might go out for a drink.'

'I'll let you know before I leave this afternoon. I don't want to arrange to meet you and then let you down. Oh, there's the bell. I'd better be getting back. Thanks for the coffee.'

'You're more than welcome, Christina. Don't forget to let me know about this evening.'

'I won't.'

Leaving the study, Christina returned to her empty classroom and sat at her desk. The students had a geography lesson, giving her some time to sort through their essays. But she couldn't keep her mind on her work. Things were going very well, but she realized that problems could easily rear up. Particularly if the staff continually questioned her methods of controlling the students. But her explanation to the headmaster had sounded plausible, she reflected, trying not to worry about it.

Turning her thoughts to Alison, she wondered where the girl had got to. Having last seen her flatmate when she had left for the pub, Christina began to wonder whether she was moving out. She might have heard from the hotel, Christina mused, sifting through the pile of essays. Wondering again how Bryony was getting on at the massage parlour, Christina decided to go for a walk. Unable to concentrate on her work and with her next lesson not until after lunch, she grabbed her bag and left the college. There were too many things playing on her mind. Bryony, Alison, Ponting . . . Beginning to wonder how she'd become so deeply involved in other people's lives, she realized that it had been her own doing. She should never have grabbed Ponting's cock and wanked him, she mused, walking down the street towards the common. Had she kept herself to herself . . . But she'd not been allowed to, she reflected. Ponting had approached her – uninvited, to say the least – for sex. And Alison had made the first move, as had Bryony.

'Christina,' Alison called, dashing across the street.

'Hi,' Christina said, smiling at the girl. 'How are you doing? I've not seen you since—'

'God, I've been running around doing this and that. I've got the job at the hotel.'

'Oh, that's great.'

'I've been moving my things out of the flat this morning. I've left a cheque on the kitchen table for half the rent.'

'Are you going to walk with me?' Christina asked. 'I'm going to the common to get some air.'

'Yes, I will. I could do with a break. I didn't realize how much stuff I had. Oh, I've left my key on the table.'

'Right. So, what's your room like at the hotel?'

'Huge. It's right at the top of the building and I can see out over London. I know I'm going to be happy there. Has Bryony . . . I went into your room to get that skirt you borrowed and noticed some things.'

'Yes, she's moved in. I couldn't talk to you about it since you weren't around.'

'Well, it makes no difference now. Do you often come here?' Alison asked as they walked towards the pond. 'I could meet you for a chat during your breaks.'

'Yes, I like it here. When I get a free period, I come and sit by the pond.'

'I don't want to lose contact with you, Christina. We'll still go to the pub now and then. Oh, by the way – a woman called at the flat this morning.'

'Oh?'

'She asked for the name and phone number of our landlord.'

'Did you tell her?'

'No, I didn't. She said that she was from . . . What was it? The rented-accommodation something or other. I was suspicious, so I told her that I was just visiting and knew nothing about the landlord.'

'What did she look like?'

'Forties, darkish hair, shortish skirt, quite well dressed.'

'Perhaps she's genuine,' Christina sighed, picturing Ponting's wife.

'She said that she'd call back.'

'What are they doing here?' Christina murmured,

noticing Doogan and Brown wandering across the common.

'Who?' Alison asked.

'Two of my students. They're supposed to be at a lesson.'

'Skiving off, I suppose. Well, I'll leave you to do your authoritative bit. I have to get back to the hotel and sort a few things out.'

'Right. I'll see you around, then. Either here or in the pub. Call round at the flat whenever you want to.'

'I will. You take care. And take those lads in hand for skipping lessons.'

'OK,' Christina giggled. 'I'll take them both in hand.'

As Alison walked away, Christina watched Doogan and Brown approaching. She realized that there was another lad trailing along behind them. Wondering what the pair were up to as they laughed and joked, she focused on their friend. She didn't recognize him, and wondered whether he was from another class at the college. With his dark hair swept back, he appeared to be clean and tidy, she observed. And pretty good-looking. Trying to turn her thoughts away from sex as the threesome approached, she felt her clitoris stir within the moist valley of her pussy.

'We followed you,' Doogan said unashamedly.

'Why aren't you in class?' Christina asked.

'This is Greg,' the lad said. 'He wanted to meet you.'

'Hi,' the boy murmured. 'I've heard a lot about you.'

'I'll bet you have,' Christina replied, frowning at Doogan. 'So, why did you follow me? What are you up to?'

'It's a nice day, the sun's shining, college is boring . . . We thought you might like a walk in the woods.'

'Doogan, I . . .'

'Come on,' Brown laughed. 'Come into the woods.'

As they walked towards the trees, Christina was about to join them. But she hesitated. It was pretty obvious what they had in mind, and she did her best to fight her inner desires. It wasn't that she didn't want sex. In fact, sex with three teenage lads would no doubt prove most satisfying. Imagining three solid cocks, three pairs of hands groping her naked body, she felt a quiver run through her contracting womb. This was the middle of the working day, she thought, wishing she'd not gone to the common. Sex was ruling her life, she knew as the boys disappeared into the woods. Three solid cocks? Three beautifully swollen knobs? More than enough fresh spunk? Christina sighed and looked around the common before following her young studs.

Her panties filling with her juices of arousal, she walked along the narrow path in the direction of the low voices and chuckles she could hear. Christina found the lads sitting on the short grass in a small clearing surrounded by bushes. They thought that she was a slut, she knew as she they looked up at her with lust reflected in their dark eyes. Maybe she was, she mused, her clitoris now solid in expectation of the ministrations of three wet tongues.

'Well?' she murmured as they gazed longingly at her naked things. 'Now what?'

'Greg wants to get to know you,' Brown said, grinning. 'He'd like to see more of you.'

'You want me to strip, is that it?' Christina asked, her stomach somersaulting, ripples of sex running through her pelvis.

'Yes,' Doogan replied. 'We're doing our bit at college, so . . .'

'You want me to do my bit?'

'That was the deal.'

Kicking her shoes off, Christina unzipped her skirt and allowed the garment to slide down her legs and fall around her ankles. Her audience watching eagerly, she unbuttoned her blouse, opening it and revealing the silk cups of her bra straining to contain her firm breasts. She couldn't fight her inner desires, she knew as she reached behind her back and unhooked her bra. Her young breasts tumbling from the cups, her nipples becoming erect in the relatively cool air of the woods, she knew that her life now revolved around crude sex. The very thought of stripping in front of three teenage lads sent tremors through her young womb. A feeling of great power overwhelming her, she ran her hands over the firm mounds of her mammary globes. Her nipples stiffening, her areolae darkening, she tossed her long blonde hair over her shoulder and flashed a salacious smile at her audience.

'Have I gone far enough?' she asked, running her hands over the gentle swell of her stomach and down to the top of her tight panties.

'Not quite,' Doogan replied, his tongue almost hanging out as he gazed at the triangular patch of material bulging to contain her full sex lips.

'You want me to pull my wet panties down?' she giggled.

'All the way down.'

'That would be naughty,' Christina murmured. 'I don't know whether I should be naughty.'

'Of course you should.'

Slipping her thumbs between the tight elastic of her panties and the firm flesh of her shapely hips, she slipped the garment down just enough at first to reveal the top of her hairless sex crack. Leaning forward, the boys gazed at Christina's full sex lips as she slipped her panties further down her slender thighs, allowing the flimsy garment to fall down her long legs and tumble around her ankles. The boys' eyes bulging as they gazed at her perfectly formed love lips, the opening valley of her young pussy, Christina felt her clitoris stiffen.

Standing naked in front of three teenage boys and exposing the most intimate part of her young body sent electrifying ripples of sex up Christina's spine. This was her forte, she reflected, wondering whether to peel the fleshy lips of her vagina apart and expose her intricate sex folds nestling within her valley of desire. Deciding to make the lads wait, she pushed the flesh of her outer lips inwards, squeezing out the pinken wings of her inner labia. Her opaque juices of arousal seeping from her sex crack, trickling over her hairless flesh, she cupped her right breast in her hand and lowered her head.

Sucking her ripe nipple into her wet mouth, sinking her teeth into her areola, Christina slipped a finger into the top of her sex valley and massaged the solid protrusion of her expectant clitoris. The boys were loving every minute of the show – she knew that as she eyed the bulging crotches of their trousers. Their beautiful cocks would be solid, their rolling balls full and in desperate need of draining. But they were going to have to wait for the feel of her hot mouth sucking their swollen knobs.

Finally slipping her sensitive nipple out of her wet mouth, Christina peeled her fleshy sex cushions wide apart and exposed the wet funnel of pink flesh surrounding the entrance to her tight cunt. Slipping a finger into her hot lust hole, she massaged the creamy walls of her vagina, gasping as the beautiful sensations permeated deep into the core of her quivering body. Withdrawing her sticky finger, she lapped up her vaginal cream, sucking her finger clean before once more driving it deep into the tight shaft of her young cunt.

'I think it's time you joined in,' Christina said, twisting and bending her finger deep within the tight sheath of her young pussy. 'I've stripped, so you can do the same.'

Hurriedly slipping out of their clothes, the teenagers stood in front of Christina with the bulbous knobs of their granite-hard cocks pointing to the sky. Hungry for the salty taste of their purple glandes, she slipped her finger out of her sex-drenched vagina and knelt on the soft grass. The boys stood close together, their swollen plums only inches apart, their heavy balls rolling. This was sheer sexual bliss, Christina mused, pushing her tongue out and tentatively licking each sperm-slit in turn.

Taking the first plum into her mouth, her full lips engulfing its rim, she sucked on the silky-smooth surface. This was a good deal, she reflected. Sucking three teenage knobs to orgasm in return for a well-behaved class? Until she'd come to Spadger Heath, she could never have envisaged doing such a thing to her students. They hadn't mentioned this at training college, she reflected, wondering whether other young teachers sucked their students' cocks in return for good behaviour. And to think that she had the headmaster eating out of her pussy was incredible.

'Can you suck all three?' Doogan asked.

'I'll certainly try,' Christina giggled, slipping the knob

out of her salty mouth. 'I might be able to get your knob in, but that's about all.'

'You're a dirty bitch,' Greg the newcomer chuckled.

'You think this is dirty?' Christina asked, desperate to shock the lad. 'You wait until I have three cocks fucking my arse.'

'All three?' he gasped. 'All three at once?'

'All three at once.'

Taking the plums into her mouth, her succulent lips stretched tautly around the three helmets, Christina snaked her wet tongue over the swollen globes. She'd choke on their sperm if they filled her mouth simultaneously, she mused, gobbling like a babe at the breast as she tried to imagine three solid cocks shafting the tight duct of her rectum. Wondering whether Bryony was sucking the sperm out of an old man's cock-head, she realized that the girl was getting paid for her sexual efforts. *Prostitution*, she mused: Bryony was taking cash, and Christina was enjoying teaching a well-behaved class.

Wondering whether other women did this sort of thing as she sucked on the gasping lads' purple knobs, she turned her thoughts to her mother. Perhaps the woman had sucked on two or more knobs during her younger years. Knowing her mother, though, Christina thought the notion was ridiculous. But no one would have believed how Christina behaved when she was out of sight of the routine world. A conscientious young teacher, respected, well dressed, attractive . . . No one would ever believe that she enjoyed sucking three knobs to orgasm and swallowing sperm.

Pondering on other women as she kneaded the lad's heaving balls and sucked on their twitching cock-heads,

Christina thought that she might not be alone in her debauchery. She didn't reveal her sexual exploits to all and sundry, and neither did other women. The chances were that many women would grab the opportunity to take more than one knob into their sperm-thirsty mouths. No one knew what went on behind closed doors, she reflected. Or in the wooded countryside of England.

As the lads started trembling, Christina knew that they were about to pump their fresh sperm into her thirsty mouth and drain their brimming balls. Fervently gobbling and licking, she hoped that the beautiful cocks would restiffen quickly after their coming and drive deep into the neglected sheath of her tight cunt. Her hot vagina might be able to accommodate two rock-hard penises, she mused. Possibly three huge cocks, if she could think of a way to physically achieve the crude act. As for her bottom-hole taking three solid sex rods . . .

'Yes,' Doogan breathed, his spunk jetting from his knob-slit and bathing Christina's snaking tongue. The other lads releasing their orgasmic cream, Christina did her best to swallow the salty liquid as her mouth overflowed. This was a first, she thought happily, her clitoris close to orgasm, her juices of desire gushing from the entrance to her cock-hungry cunt. Slipping her hand between her naked thighs, she parted her swollen girl-lips and massaged her solid clitoris as she drank the gushing sperm issuing from the three orgasming knobs.

'Swallow the lot, you dirty bitch,' Greg cried, watching the creamy sperm streaming down Christina's chin and splattering the erect teats of her firm breasts. Repeatedly swallowing hard, Christina drank from the spunking knobs until she'd drained the lads' balls and they began to crumple on their shaking legs. Slipping their spent cocks out of her sperm-flooded mouth, she sucked on each one in turn, swallowing the last remnants of their orgasmic fluid before sitting back on her heels and wiping her mouth on the back of her hand.

Watching the lads sprawled out on the grass, their limp cocks snaking over their hairy scrotums, Christina continued to caress the sensitive tip of her clitoris. Her pleasure building, she massaged her clitoris faster. Eyeing the boys' sperm-glistening penises, their rolling balls, she prayed for them to recover quickly and feed the hungry maw of her cunt with their meaty pleasure shafts. In desperate need of a cock repeatedly ramming into her young cunt, she was about to lie on the grass and take her ripe clitoris to orgasm when she heard voices. Ordering her studs to be quiet, she grabbed her clothes and dressed hurriedly as the voices grew louder.

'This is where she brings her clients,' Ponting said. 'She'll probably bring a couple of her students here for sex after college this afternoon.'

'Right, I'll be waiting for her,' Charles said, to Christina's sheer horror.

'I'm glad that I was able to get in touch with you.'

'So am I. She's a lovely girl, but the way she's going . . . I just can't understand why she's turned to prostitution.'

'It's not that I want to expose her and upset her family, but someone's got to do something to help her,' Ponting sighed. 'This is only her second week at the college and . . . well, she's built up a huge clientele. She even tried to lure *me* here for sex, but I'm happily married.'

'What did she say, exactly?' Charles asked.

'She told me that she was into cocksucking. She said that she wanted to feel my cock spunking up her arse and . . . I'd rather not say any more.'

'I quite understand, Mr Ponting. Since she's at work, I'll go and take a look around her flat.'

'There's something I haven't mentioned,' Ponting said softly. 'Christina . . . because of her I've had to resign.'

'From the college? But why?'

'Christina wouldn't take no for an answer. Foolishly, I agreed to meet her here. I was hoping to talk to her, try to help her. She . . . she'd arranged for the headmaster to come along and . . . she made out that I was trying to force her into having sex with me.'

'My God,' Charles breathed.

'I know it sounds incredible, but it's true. Like an idiot, I'd allowed her to . . . I'd stripped off. She'd unbuttoned my shirt and released my belt and . . . I can't deny that she'd aroused me and I'd stripped off. By the time the headmaster arrived . . . well, you can imagine how the situation must have looked to him.'

'Yes, yes, I can. This is terrible, Mr Ponting. I mean, I don't blame you. Christina is a very attractive young woman. Behaving the way she did, I couldn't blame any man for . . . I'll be here this afternoon. If I can catch her with her students, perhaps threaten to tell her parents unless she gives up her life here and goes home . . .'

'I wish you luck.'

'And you, Mr Ponting. I'm only sorry that Christina has wrecked your life.'

As the two men wandered back to the common, Christina felt her stomach knotting as her anger heightened. Watching the lads dress, she wondered what they were thinking. They'd obviously heard every damning word, she mused, biting her lip as she imagined Charles running to her father with his tales. Wondering what to do, she held her hand to her head. Ponting wasn't going to give up, that was certain. The man was obviously obsessed with bringing about her downfall, and wouldn't stop until . . .

'It's OK,' Doogan said, smiling at Christina. 'You leave this to us. We'll sort it.'

'Sort it?' Christina echoed. 'How on earth can you—'

'You just leaving Ponting and that other bloke to us.'

'What shall I do now?' she sighed. 'I don't feel like going back to the college but . . .'

'You go back and do your job. I'll talk to you this afternoon, tell you about the plan.'

'All right,' Christina conceded, realizing that she had nothing to lose.

'Come on, lads,' Doogan said, bucking his belt. 'We've got plans to make.'

As they left the clearing, Christina sat on the grass and looked up at the sun sparkling through the trees high above. Ponting must have contacted Charles through her mother, she concluded. But what the hell did Charles think he was up to? Why was he going out of his way to cause trouble? There was nothing that Doogan and his gang could do to help, she was sure. Why did people have to interfere? Christina decided to go back to the college. Why couldn't people get on with their lives and leave her alone?

# 14

Somehow managing to get through the afternoon, Christina left the college to find Doogan and his gang waiting for her outside the gates. They were clutching several textbooks and notepads, and she wondered what on earth they were up to as a couple of teenage girls joined them. This was going to look really bad, she reflected as they led her towards the common. Charles was bound to think that she was going to have sex with three lads and two girls.

'It's OK,' Doogan interrupted Christina as she launched into a hundred reasons why she didn't think it a good idea to go to the woods. 'We're on a botany outing.'

'A botany outing?' she laughed. 'What the hell . . .'

'This is the plan. We've all got books about plants and stuff. This bloke finds us in the woods, and we tell him that we often go there looking for plants.'

'I doubt that he'll believe that,' Christina sighed.

'He will,' Brown rejoined. 'We've already told old man Wright that you take us on botany trips after college.'

'Why botany?' Christina asked.

'We could hardly say that we go to the woods looking for seashells,' Doogan laughed. 'OK, so this bloke—'

'Charles,' Christina said. 'He's my ex-boyfriend.'

'OK, so Charles turns up and hides in the bushes, hoping that he'll see you getting fucked.'

'That's one way to put it.'

'We happen to discover him and ask him what he's doing. You see him, talk to him . . . We're studying botany. Innocent, virginal goody-goody students . . . The thing is, he has no idea that we know about his plan. That's why this is going to work.'

'Yes, that's a thought,' Christina said, a smile dawning on her pretty face as she began to feel a little more confident.

Reaching the woods, the students opened their notepads and began studying the plants under the trees. Christina discreetly scanned the common for Charles, but there was no sign of him. He'd be lurking somewhere in the woods, she was sure as she led her eager students along the narrow path in the direction of the clearing. Doogan and his crowd were brilliant, Christina thought as they began making notes and looking up wild flowers in their textbooks.

'Is this the one you were describing in class?' Doogan asked Christina, kneeling and pointing to a weed.

'Er . . . yes, that's right,' she replied, aware of someone lurking in the bushes. She winked at Doogan. 'Hopefully, we'll find some fungi a little deeper in the woods.'

'Hopefully,' Doogan echoed, returning her wink and nodding towards the bushes. 'This is such an interesting subject, Miss,' he added, going rather over the top, Christina thought. 'I'll take a look over here for some fungi.'

As Doogan wandered into the bushes where Charles was hiding, Christina realized how stupid the game was. But that was Charles, she reflected. Stupid, childish, hypocritical . . . But she had to play the game, she knew.

She wasn't going to give Charles the opportunity to go running to her parents with his tales of prostitution. Feigning shock as Charles emerged from the bushes with Doogan, Christina held her hand to her mouth and gasped. Charles stammered something incoherent as Doogan said that he'd discovered a peeping Tom in the bushes.

'It's all right, I know him,' Christina said.

'Oh, right,' Doogan murmured. 'I'll go and join the others, then.'

'What are you doing here?' she asked Charles as Doogan wandered off.

'I . . . I was looking for you,' he replied.

'What? You were looking for me in the bushes?'

'I heard that you often came here with . . . with some students.'

'Yes, I do. I've come with my botany class.'

'I thought you taught English?'

'These students are very interested in botany, Charles. To encourage them to write, I'm taking an interest in *their* interest. Is that all right with you?'

'Yes, yes, of course. They don't look the type to be interested in plants.'

'What type *do* they look like? Bingo players?'

'No, no, I just meant . . . So, how are things?'

'After you fucked young Bryony in my parents' garden, I don't think things are too good at all.'

'I . . . The thing is, that girl . . .'

'Don't blame her, Charles. It's bad enough you fucking an under-age girl, let alone blaming her for your actions. You said that you were looking for me?'

'I had some business in town and thought I'd see how you are.'

'Who told you that I'd be here?'

'Oh, er . . . someone at the college. I went there first and—'

'Who was it? What did they look like?'

'Oh, I don't know.'

'I only asked because, apart from the headmaster, no one knows about our botany studies.'

'Yes, it must have been him.'

'He's away for the day, so . . .'

'Christina, it doesn't matter who it was,' Charles sighed agitatedly.

'As long as it wasn't Ponting.'

'Ponting?'

'He's been sacked for running some kind of prostitution ring involving a few of the girls.'

'Really? That's awful.'

'It's dreadful. The way he carried on was . . . anyway, I'm not interested in Ponting and his lies. Look, I have to go and find the students.'

'I thought we might go out for a drink this evening.'

'I can't, Charles. And even if I could, I'm not sure that I'd want to after your disgusting behaviour with Bryony. If my father knew . . .'

'You won't say anything, will you?'

'That depends.'

'On what?'

'You cause trouble for me, and I'll cause trouble for you.'

'I wouldn't do that, Christina.'

'Wouldn't you? Anyway, I'm busy now.'

'Right, well . . .'

Walking away and joining the students, Christina thought how sad it was that she had to continually play mind games. Wondering what the problem was with Charles, why he was obsessed with where she was and what she was doing, she turned and watched him following the path back to the common. Perhaps, in his own weird way, he was doing his best to get her to go home to her parents. He probably thought that he stood a better chance of getting back with her if she lived at home. But he must have realized that, after the episode with Bryony, he'd lost Christina for good.

'OK, it worked,' Christina said, grinning at Doogan. 'Thanks. Thanks to all of you.'

'Any time,' Doogan replied. 'So, what shall we do now?'

'I don't know. Go home, I suppose.'

'We could go to the pub,' Brown suggested.

'Is that all you ever think about?' Doogan laughed.

'All right,' Christina said, eyeing the two young girls. 'Let's go to the pub and celebrate our victory.'

Leaving the woods with her students in tow, Christina walked across the common. Wondering how Bryony was getting on with her new job, she pictured once more the girl wanking off old men. Charles was like an old man, she reflected, wondering whether he'd managed to get into her flat. Even if he had got in, which she very much doubted, there was nothing incriminating there. He'd probably been hoping to find a list of clients, she mused, walking towards the local pub. He'd failed miserably in his mission. And so had Ponting. Charles might now give up, but would Ponting? Christina thought hard as she entered the pub with her teenage gang.

Sitting at a table as Doogan asked her what she wanted to drink, she decided on vodka and tonic. Christina wasn't surprised to see the lad pull a wad of notes from his pocket as he walked up to the bar. What he got up to outside college, she dreaded to think. He was a survivor, that was obvious. He'd never go short of money, no matter where his life took him. Perhaps that was the way to be, she thought as one of the young girls sat beside her. No cares, no worries – just living life from day to day.

'It's not a bad pub, this,' the girl said, smiling at Christina.

'You've been here before?' Christina asked, wondering how old she was.

'Most nights. I'm Josie, by the way.'

'I'm Christina. I've not seen you at the college.'

'No, I left a few months back.'

'Where do you work?'

'I don't. If I worked, I'd get a miserable wage every week. The way things are, I'm pretty well off.'

'So how do you earn money?' Christina asked, dreading the answer.

'I do this and that,' the girl replied, flicking her long auburn hair away from her pretty face. 'Fifty quid here, fifty quid there. It soon adds up.'

'Yes, of course.'

'I do a bit for the massage parlour. Sort of part-time – on and off.'

'The massage par— Have you been there today?'

'Yes, this morning. A new girl started. It was really funny. This old guy comes in, takes one look at her and—'

'What's her name?'

'Bryony. She's a laugh. I reckon she'll do well there.'

'Yes, I expect she will. So, what goes on in this massage parlour? I mean, I've heard things, but . . .'

'Old men, mostly. They want hand relief. Mind you, I don't think they could do anything else. We get a few young lads in. Virgins who want to become men. Sylvia – she owns the place – she reckons that Bryony will be pretty good with the lads.'

'Yes, I'm sure she will.'

'I was telling her – Bryony, I mean – I was saying that she should come out with me in the evenings. She'll earn far more with me. The parlour's OK, but Sylvia takes most of the dosh.'

'So, where do you go in the evenings?'

'I have one or two haunts. I don't walk the streets or anything like that. There's a small club which is pretty good. Businessmen go there early in the evening. They either want a hand job or a quick blow. The owner hasn't got a clue what goes on. If he had, he'd want a cut. I'm hoping Bryony, the new girl, will meet me there this evening. She said she would.'

Watching Doogan place the drinks on the table, Christina thought about Bryony. She was obviously going to be all right for cash, but the thought of the girl hanging around bars and seedy clubs at night didn't please Christina. Bryony might have been sexually experienced, but she was incredibly naive. She was far too young to be in with the likes of Josie. But there wasn't much that Christina could do about it.

'Where is this club?' she asked Josie as Doogan and Brown chatted about football.

'It's called The Rat's Tail. Just round the corner by—'

'Yes, I've seen the place.'

'Why don't you come along this evening? I mean, it's quite respectable. I usually work at a table in a secluded alcove where no one can see what I'm up to. The club's OK for all types, not just businessmen looking for a blow job.'

'Yes, I might look in later,' Christina replied, eyeing the girl's naked thighs.

'Bryony said that she'd meet me there at six. I have to get there early for the businessmen.'

Knocking back her vodka, Christina made her excuses and left the pub. Walking home, she wondered whether Bryony was going to tell her the truth about going out that evening. Or would the girl make out that she was just visiting a friend? Life in London was far removed from existence in the country, she reflected. Businessmen going to the club for a quick blow job and then home to their loving wives, young girls sucking cocks and swallowing sperm for money . . . Bryony was a city girl, Christina reminded herself as she entered the flat and went into the kitchen. Filling the kettle, she thought about the evening ahead, wondering whether to go along to the club with Bryony.

'Oh, hi,' the young ex-student trilled as she breezed into the kitchen. 'Well, that's my first day over.'

'How was it?' Christina asked.

'Great. Sylvia, that's my boss, she pays us at the end of each day. I earned sixty pounds.'

'That's not bad for one day. What did you have to do?'

'Wank a few guys, that was all. We spent most of the time sitting around, drinking coffee and chatting.'

'Sounds like easy money. What are the other girls like?'

'They're OK. There's one I really like. Her name's Josie. She only works part-time, sort of comes and goes as she pleases.'

'I'm glad you like the job. Although it's not the sort of work . . . Anyway, as long as you like it, that's OK. What are your plans for this evening?'

'I'm going out for a drink with Josie.'
'Oh? Anywhere nice?'
'Er . . . I don't know yet. Shall I make something to eat?'
'Yes, why not? Mind you, I don't think there is much. I'll have to go shopping and stock up the cupboards.'
'I'll knock something up,' Bryony said, smiling. 'This is far better than living with my mum. OK. I'll cook and you go and relax.'
'I'm going to take a shower. I might wander out somewhere this evening, take a look around.'

Washing her long blonde hair in the shower, Christina felt jealousy eating away at her. It was ridiculous, she reflected. Bryony was young, single, free to do as she wished with her life. But Christina couldn't help the way she felt. Perhaps the girl had the right idea. Earning tax-free cash every day, no problems or worries, enjoying her life . . . Christina wasn't sure whether she was jealous because the girl was having sex with other people, or envious of her lifestyle. Wondering whether to leave the college, give up her teaching career and work with Bryony, she towelled her naked body dry and went into her room.

It might be interesting to pleasure a businessman, she mused, dressing in a loose-fitting white blouse and turquoise miniskirt. A quick wank beneath the table, or a blow job . . . Wondering how much Josie charged for her sexual favours, she dried and brushed her hair and joined Bryony at the kitchen table. The girl had done well with the food. The cheese-and-egg salad was perfectly presented and she'd even opened a bottle of white wine. Living with Bryony was going to work out, Christina felt sure as she sipped her wine. She was pretty good with food, earned more than enough to pay her share of the rent . . . This was going to work out very well.

'What sort of day have *you* had?' Bryony asked.

'Oh, the usual,' Christina replied, deciding not to mention her visit to the woods. 'The headmaster asked me out for a drink this evening . . . Shit.'

'What's the matter?'

'I said that I'd let him know before I left the college. Oh, well. Not to worry. When are you going to move into Alison's room?'

'Has she gone?' the girl asked, her eyes widening.

'Didn't you know?'

'Well, I wasn't sure. In that case, I'll move in later this evening. I'm meeting Josie at six, so I'd better get a move on.'

Finishing her meal, Christina watched Bryony clear the table and wash up. The girl left the kitchen in pristine condition before taking a shower and getting ready to go out. Christina finished the wine, realizing that she'd not only found a perfect flatmate but a brilliant housekeeper. Calling out from the bedroom, Bryony said that she'd do the shopping on her way home from the massage parlour the following day. This was getting even better, Christina decided. The girl would be washing and ironing for her before long.

'Right, I'll see you later,' Bryony said as she appeared in the kitchen doorway.

'Yes, OK. Have a good time.'

'I will. I'll try not to be too late. We'll open another bottle of wine when I get back.'

'That'll be nice. OK, off you go. And behave yourself.'

'Certainly not,' the girl laughed, leaving the flat.

Wondering how Alison was getting on at the hotel,

Christina thought it odd that she'd not earned money from sex. There again, not every girl who enjoyed crude sex was necessarily into prostitution. Sighing as the phone rang, Christina left the kitchen and went into the lounge. Flopping onto the sofa, she grabbed the receiver and bit her lips as the headmaster asked her whether they were going out that evening.

'Sorry, Ian,' she sighed. 'I was going to come and see you before I left but I got tied up.'

'I heard about your botany class.'

'Oh, yes. The students are very interested.'

'I can't for the life of me think why the likes of Doogan and Brown are into botany. Bars and girls, yes, but—'

'Ian, about this evening. To be honest, I'm feeling rather tired.'

'Oh, that's a shame. You're sitting alone in your flat, here I am sitting alone in my house . . . Another time, perhaps. By the way, Bryony Philips. Her mother came to see me this afternoon.'

'Oh? Er . . . what about?'

'The girl's left home. Was she in class today?'

'No, no, she wasn't. Actually, she's left the college. I was going to come and talk to you about it but I was so busy today. Did her mother say where the girl was living?'

'She has no idea where she's gone. Bryony just said that she'd found a flat and was moving out.'

'I'm sure she'll be all right.'

'Well, it's nothing to do with us. I just wondered whether you knew anything about it.'

'No, nothing.'

'Her mother was talking about going to the police.'

'The police?'

'I don't know what good that will do. I mean, the girl is of age, so . . . anyway, I'll see you tomorrow. Coffee during break as usual?'

'Yes, that would be nice.'

'You get an early night, OK?'

'OK.'

'Sleep well, Christina.'

'I will. Goodbye.'

There was nothing the police could do, Christina was sure. Bryony had left home, which wasn't surprising. She'd not broken the law or . . . Not as far as the police were aware, at least. Grabbing her bag, Christina left the flat and headed for the club. If she was lucky, she'd be able to find somewhere to sit where she could observe Bryony and not be seen herself. If the girl did see her, then she'd say that she'd just been passing and had decided to take a look at the place.

Walking into the bar, Christina was thankful that the place was littered with alcoves and secluded tables. Ordering a vodka and tonic, she noticed Bryony and Josie sitting at the far end of the bar. They were laughing and joking, chatting with a couple of besuited men in their thirties. They were far too busy to notice Christina as she sat at the bar and sipped her drink. The club was nice, Christina observed, looking about her. As Josie had said, it was respectable, and Christina decided to use the place rather than the local pub.

'All alone?' a man in his early thirties asked.

'I'm waiting for someone,' Christina replied, looking up and smiling. 'I'm rather early, though.'

'In that case, mind if I join you?'

'No, not at all.'

'I'm John – John Baxter.'

'Christina. This is my first time here. I rather like it.'

'I come here most evenings on my way home from work. I only work around the corner. I'm an accountant.'

'Oh, right. I work at the college, teaching English. What's this place like? I've heard one or two rumours.'

'Rumours?' he echoed, frowning at her.

'I was told that this wasn't the sort of place for a young lady.'

'Oh, right. Yes, there are a few girls who work the club.'

'Work the . . . Oh, I see what you mean.'

'Jim McConnor, the owner, knows nothing about it. Don't get me wrong, it's not a big-time haunt for prostitutes. There are a handful of young girls who make a living from . . . well, you know?'

'Yes, of course. Do *you* know any of the girls? I mean, have you met . . . I don't mean . . .'

'It's all right,' Baxter laughed. 'I do know one or two of them, yes. Why do you ask?'

'I'm curious, that's all.'

'McConnor could make a small fortune if he was clued up. All he seems interested in is boozing. Still, each to their own.'

'Is that what you'd do if you owned this place?'

'No . . . well, possibly. I mean, there's nothing wrong with prostitution. It's as old as the hills, as they say. I reckon, in a place like this where the girls muck about beneath the tables, there's no harm in it. There's no decent work in an area like this and the girls have to make a living somehow. The rents are sky-high, there's food, clothes and other stuff they have to buy . . . I'm surprised you can afford to live here on your salary.'

'It's not easy. I share a flat, which halves the rent, but it's still not easy.'

Wondering again about Bryony's new profession, Christina realized that she was becoming increasingly interested in the work. The money was good, the lifestyle relaxed – meeting people, enjoying a few drinks . . . Her heart had been set on a career in teaching. But now? Gazing at the young man as he ordered her another drink, Christina wondered whether he'd ever used the services of the young girls. Was he married? Reckoning that he was single, she was thankful that she hadn't married Charles. That was one nightmare she'd been lucky to avoid.

'I'm rather fortunate,' John said, leaning on the bar. 'I own my flat. It belonged to my grandfather and he left it to me.'

'That must be nice,' Christina murmured. 'No rent, no mortgage . . .'

'It gets better. I also own the shop below the flat. The rent I pull in from the shop more than doubles my salary. It's a pretty big shop.'

'God, that's brilliant. My father was thinking about buying me a flat, but . . . well, I'd be for ever beholden to him.'

'Go for it, Christina. You yourself would have no rent to pay – and you could charge your flatmate rent. You'd be a damned sight better off.'

'I hadn't thought of that. My parents live in Hertfordshire, so they're far enough away not to hassle me.'

'I'd definitely go for it if I were you. Another drink?'

'Er . . . yes, why not?'

Deciding to take her father up on it if he offered to buy a flat, Christina realized that she'd be far better off financially. Bryony could pay the same rent, which would cover the everyday bills, leaving Christina's salary to build up. But the thought of turning to prostitution still haunted her. The money to be made from sex was unbelievable, far more than she'd ever get from teaching, or any other straight job for that matter. Eyeing Bryony at the end of the bar, Christina smiled as she saw the girl going to a secluded table with Josie and the two men. She'd probably earn her half of the rent in one evening, Christina mused. A few wanks or blow jobs, and she'd be laughing. Not to mention free drinks for the evening.

'Are you married, John?' Christina asked.

'Me? No, no. One day, maybe. I'm too busy enjoying life to get myself tied down. Take this evening, for example. I can stay here chatting to you for as long as I like. My life's my own, Christina. That may sound selfish, and I have to admit that I get lonely at times. But I'm free to do what I want when I want.'

'Marriage doesn't suit everyone,' Christina said. 'Still, neither does living alone. Do you have a girlfriend?'

'No one special. Between you and me, I *have* joined the girls over there on the odd occasion. I think there's a new girl with Josie. I noticed her earlier. The young blonde with—'

'I've not been looking,' Christina cut in, wondering whether to tell John the truth about Bryony.

She was also wondering whether to make this her paid-sex debut by taking John to a secluded table and wanking his cock to orgasm. But, having no idea how much the girls charged, and reckoning that John wasn't in the mood, she decided against the idea. But it certainly was easy money, she reflected. Free drinks, getting to wank a man and bring out his sperm, and getting paid for the pleasure? Deciding to play it by ear, she sipped her drink and crossed her long legs. Her naked thighs showing, she wondered whether John fancied her as he looked down at her shapely legs and smiled.

'You said that you were waiting for someone?' he breathed. 'That's a shame.'

'Is it?' she asked, grinning at him.

'I think so. Especially if it's a man friend.'

'No, no. I'm meeting my . . . my sister later. Not for another hour or so.'

'Oh, right. er . . . Would you like to sit a table? I don't like propping up the bar and there are no stools free.'

'OK.'

Slipping off her stool, Christina followed John to a corner table and sat down. He settled next to her, the crotch of his trousers out of sight from the people standing at the bar. This was her opportunity, she knew. But how to start the proceedings? Hoping that he'd make the first move, she toyed with her glass as he talked about his flat. She'd have to let on that she knew Bryony and Josie if she was going to charge him for wanking his cock and allowing his spunk to run over her hand. There again, she could make out that she'd never met the girls and worked alone.

John talked about Josie, saying that the girl wanted to rent one of his spare rooms. Christina sipped her drink as she listened to his plans. He had three bedrooms and was wondering whether to move a couple of girls in so that they could work from his flat and pay him half their earnings. He hadn't come to a decision yet, but he was tempted by the idea. The notion got Christina thinking. By allowing Bryony to work from the flat . . . Biting her lip, she reminded herself that she'd come to London to pursue a career in teaching.

'The only problem would be the law,' John said, downing his pint. 'The girls would only bring back decent clients, of course. But the law ... I wouldn't want to end up in court for running a brothel. Anyway, we'll see.'

'It's certainly an idea,' Christina thought aloud, wishing immediately that she hadn't.

'You reckon?'

'Well ... the girls would have somewhere decent to live, and they wouldn't have to hang around bars looking for clients.'

'And I'd earn a small fortune,' he laughed. 'Of course, there'd be an added bonus.'

'Oh? What's that?'

'Well, you know? I'd be OK with a couple of young girls living in my flat.'

'Oh, yes, I see,' Christina giggled. 'I suppose I should be honest with you.'

'Honest? What do you mean?'

'I work at the college, but I also have part-time evening work.'

'God. You mean ...'

'Yes, I do.'

'Oh, right. Well, why not?'

'Why not, indeed?'

'I'd never have thought that you'd be into that. You don't look the type.'

'Don't I?'

'What do you charge?'

'You want something here, now?'

'That depends on how much. One of the girls charges fifty for a hand job. Needless to say, she gets very little work. The average is twenty.'

'I charge thirty,' Christina said, deciding not to under-price herself. 'Above the average – but then, I am above average.'

'You certainly are,' John murmured, taking thirty pounds from his wallet. 'OK, I'll go for that.'

Unzipping his trousers, Christina looked around the bar as she pulled John's solid penis out and massaged his foreskin over his swollen knob. This was easy, she thought, kneading the warm, fleshy shaft of his huge cock. No one could see what she was up to beneath the table, and she doubted that anyone cared. They were all too busy drinking and laughing to take any notice of her illicit activities. Parting her thighs and exposing the tight material of her panties to John's wide-eyed gaze, she pulled the material to one side and displayed the fleshy swell of her hairless sex lips to add to his pleasure.

'You *are* above average,' he murmured, his eyes rolling as he stared at her wares. 'How much to go down?'

'Not in here,' she said softly. 'People will see. Perhaps another time, if we can find a better table where we won't be seen.'

'I like girls who shave,' he said as she pulled her panties further aside.

'You like my cunt?' she asked impishly as he began gasping in his male pleasure.

'Very much. Show me inside.'

'Like this?' she giggled softly, parting the firm cushions of her love lips and displaying her dripping inner folds. 'You'd like your tongue there, wouldn't you?'

'My tongue, my cock, my fingers . . . God, I'm coming.'

His sperm running over her hand as she wanked his solid cock faster, Christina eyed the money lying on the table. Thirty pounds to wank a man to orgasm? *And* he'd paid for her drinks. This really *was* easy money, she thought as he hung his head, his white liquid streaming over her fingers as she drained his heaving balls. Wanking off two or three men each evening would ... No wonder her young ex-student was so keen on the work, she mused, wondering whether she should not only allow the girl to work from the flat but also join Bryony in her new-found profession. Deciding to give the idea some serious thought, she continued to wank John's twitching cock until he grabbed her hand and stopped her.

'That was great,' he breathed, obviously dizzy in the aftermath of his coming.

'I'm glad you enjoyed it,' Christina replied, gazing at her spermed hand.

'What are you going to do with that?'

'I'll find a tissue. I should have one in my bag.'

'Lap it up,' he whispered, zipping up his trousers. 'Another tenner if you lap it all up like a good girl.' Placing the money on the table, he gazed into her blue eyes. 'Well?' he whispered.

Licking her creamed fingers, making sure that John could see the sperm hanging in long strands from her pink tongue, Christina swallowed the salty liquid. He was loving every minute of her lewd act, she knew as she finished cleansing her fingers before slipping the money into her handbag. Wondering how much Bryony had earned, she sipped her drink, washing down John's salty spunk. She reckoned that, between them, they could earn a fortune.

'Another drink?' John asked, grabbing his empty glass.

'Thanks,' she replied, wondering whether to find another client before leaving the club.

'I'll get you a large one. After all, you deserve it.'
'Yes, I believe I do.'

Watching him walk up to the bar, Christina smiled. Forty pounds better off, and another free drink? This was turning out to be a most pleasant and profitable evening. One of many evenings she'd spend at The Rat's Tail Club, she decided. London wasn't so bad after all, she thought, wondering again how much Bryony had earned. They'd have to compare notes later, chat about their sexual exploits over a bottle of wine. *And over a vibrator*, she thought in her rising wickedness. After wanking and sucking her clients, Bryony was bound to be in a high state of arousal. And Christina was the very person to bring her relief.

# 15

Christina had waited up until midnight for Bryony, and had finally gone to bed when she realized that the girl might not be home until the early hours. Her young ex-student had obviously had a good evening, and had probably earned a fortune. Waking to the sun streaming in through her window, Christina put on her dressing gown and went into the kitchen. Filling the kettle, she wondered what the day would bring. Although her class would be on their best behaviour, she didn't relish the thought of spending the day at the college. Again, she thought about the money she could make by visiting The Rat's Tail two or three evenings each week. Trying to drag her thoughts away from prostitution, she took a quick shower and dressed.

'Morning,' Bryony murmured, wandering into the kitchen.

'What time did you get in?' Christina asked, sipping her coffee and glancing at the wall clock.

'About one, I think.'

'I'd better get going, otherwise I'll be late. I did wait up for you, but . . . We'll talk this evening. Unless you're going out again, that is?'

'I'll be out from about sixish.'

'Ah, The Rat's Tail Club.'

'How do you know about that?' the girl breathed, frowning at Christina.

'I was there, Bryony. For most of the evening, as it happens.'

'You were there? I didn't see you.'

'No, you wouldn't have. Not the way you were carrying on, anyway.'

'How did you know about the club?'

'That's my secret. Right, I'm off to work. I'll see you later.'

Leaving the flat, Christina grinned as she walked down the street. Bryony would spend the day wondering how Christina had discovered the club, and why she'd not seen her there. Reaching the college, Christina looked in on the headmaster before going to her classroom. Knocking on his door and entering the study, she found the man sitting behind his desk, fiddling with a piece of paper. Rubbing his lined forehead, he looked worried. Deciding that she wouldn't want to be head of a college and deal with one hassle after another, Christina sat opposite him and asked what the problem was.

'I'm pleased you called in to see me,' he sighed. 'I've just received a letter from the board of governors.'

'Oh?'

'Mr Ponting has been in touch with them. It seems that he's given them a list of complaints against you.'

'Against *me*?' she gasped. 'But he was the one who lured me into the woods and—'

'The complaints are all fictitious, of course. The point is that the board have to look into such matters. I'll be speaking to them later and, obviously, I'll put them in the picture. I would have thought that Mr Ponting would rather the incident in the woods wasn't mentioned. All he's doing by contacting the board is digging his own grave. Once they hear that I witnessed what was tantamount to imminent rape . . . As I said, Mr Ponting is digging his own grave.'

Watching the headmaster leave his chair to gaze out of the window, Christina realized that Ponting wasn't going to go away. He'd try anything and everything to cause trouble, and he'd trample on anyone who got in his way. But there was nothing the man could do to cause any real harm. Once the board of governors were told of the sordid incident in the woods, Ponting would back off. Wouldn't he? Giving up teaching would solve all her problems, Christina thought. No Ponting, no classes . . . She could quite happily fuck anyone and everyone in the woods, and there'd be nothing Ponting or anyone else could do about it.

'I'd better get to my class,' she said, moving to the door. 'I'll see you at break.'

'Yes, yes,' the head murmured abstractedly. 'I'll get onto the governors.'

'You do that. And don't worry.'

'No, no, I'm not worried. It's just that I don't need these problems. I shall tell the board how pleased I am with you, Christina. You've achieved amazing results in the short time you've been at Spadger Heath College. You have a well-behaved class, you—'

'Talking of my class, I really must go.'

'All right, I'll see you at break.'

Walking down the corridor, Christina entered her classroom to find her students sitting quietly. This really was incredible, she mused as Doogan winked at her. The headmaster was right, she *had* achieved amazing results.

But he had no idea how she'd achieved such great success. Ponting had guessed, but had no proof. Ponting could go to hell. Checking her watch, Christina filled in the register and ordered her class to go to their geography lesson. As they left the room in silence, she again wondered what Doogan and Brown had threatened them with. By the way they were behaving, she reckoned that murder might have been mentioned. Whatever the threat, it was working.

'Excuse me, Miss,' a pretty dark-haired girl said softly as she approached the front of the classroom.

'What is it, Becky?' Christina asked, smiling at the girl.

'I know what you get up to in the stockroom. I know what's been going on.'

'Going on?' Christina echoed, realizing that she had yet another potential problem on her hands. 'I'm not with you, Becky. What do you mean?'

'Doogan has been telling us to behave or else. Now I know why.'

'Doogan told you to behave? I can't believe that. And, if he did, then I'm very pleased with him. Perhaps he's decided that it's worth making an effort to learn something, after all.'

'No, it's not that. He wants us to behave because he gets something in return if we do.'

'I'm sorry, Becky, you've lost me. Doogan wants you to behave because he's getting something in return?'

'That's right. He gets sex in return for keeping us under control.'

'Sex?' Christina laughed. 'Now you *have* lost me. Let me try to understand this. You know what I get up to. Doogan has been telling you to behave. He gets sex in return for your good behaviour . . . Are you saying that he forces you to have sex with him if you misbehave?'

'You know what I'm talking about, Miss.'

'I only wish I did, Becky. I'm sorry, but you're going to have to spell it out for me.'

'In the stockroom . . .'

'Right, let's start in the stockroom.'

Opening the door, Christina led Becky into the stockroom and looked around her as if she was searching for something. The girl wasn't doing a very good job of trying to blackmail Christina, if that was her aim. Tidying some books, Christina asked the girl what it was about the stockroom that was so important. Becky lowered her eyes, obviously wondering how to word her threat as Christina moved about the small room and discreetly closed and locked the door. Mumbling about the mess, Christina asked her again to explain her concern and tell her what was supposed to have happened in the stockroom.

'You bring the boys in here and play about with them,' Becky finally replied.

'Play about with them?' Christina chuckled. 'This is a sixth-form college, not a kindergarten.'

'Play about with them *sexually*.'

'Sexually? This is a pretty serious allegation, Becky. Are you saying that I bring male students in here and have sex with them?'

'Yes, I am.'

'What on earth gave you that idea?'

'It's no good pretending that you don't know what I'm talking about.'

'All right, let's suppose that I *do* bring the lads in here for sex. The notion is ridiculous, of course. But let's assume that I have sex with the lads. What about it?'

'I'm going to report you.'

'Where's your evidence? I mean, what proof do you have to substantiate this ludicrous allegation?'

'Well, I . . . Everyone knows what you get up to.'

Eyeing the girl's partially opened blouse, Christina focused on the shallow cleavage of her small breasts. She could just make out her nipples pressing through the thin material of her blouse, and she imagined sucking the girl's petite tits. With long black hair framing her fresh face, Becky was an attractive little thing, Christina mused, her clitoris stirring in anticipation of lesbian sex. Wondering whether the girl was a virgin, she pictured the full lips of her pussy, the creamy-wet wings of her inner lips protruding alluringly from her tightly closed sex crack. The cheeks of the girl's bottom would be firm in their youth – lickable, biteable. Imagining sinking a finger deep into the hot tube of Becky's rectum, Christina felt a quiver run through her young womb.

'You say that everyone knows what I get up to?' she asked the girl. Christina's juices of lesbian desire started to seep into her tight panties.

'Yes, they do. I've heard people talking about it.'

'That's your evidence, is it? Hearsay is all you have, Becky. You won't get very far—'

'Simpson told me what you did to him.'

'Simpson . . . Bend over, Becky.'

'*What?*'

'You heard me. Bend over and touch your toes.'

'No, I . . .'

Forcing the girl to bend over, Christina held her tightly and lifted her short skirt up over her back.

The girl struggled as Christina yanked her panties down, exposing the beautifully firm cheeks of her pert bottom, but she could do nothing to escape. Raising her arm, Christina brought her hand down across the girl's naked buttocks with a loud slap. Again and again, she spanked Becky's twitching bottom globes, delighting in administering the punishment as the girl cried out and struggled to free herself.

'*This* is what I do to naughty little schoolgirls,' Christina hissed, repeatedly spanking her reddening buttocks. 'How *dare* you accuse me of sexually abusing my students.'

'You can't do this,' the girl whimpered. 'You'll end up in trouble if you—'

'I'll show you what trouble is,' Christina retorted, tearing the girl's panties from her trembling body.

'Please – what are you *doing*?'

'What's this, Becky?' Christina giggled, cupping the swell of the girl's vaginal lips in her hand. 'What's this I've found between your thighs?'

'What are you doing?' she cried again. 'Get off me, you, you . . .'

'You have a sweet little cunt, Becky. I like young girls' pretty little cunts.'

'You're insane. Let me go!'

'Unless you stop struggling, I'll tell the headmaster that you lured me in here and pulled your knickers down.'

'He'll never believe you,' Becky gasped as Christina's finger located the moist entrance to her tight vaginal sheath. 'Stop it! For fuck's sake, stop—'

'Swearing, as well? Oh, dear. You *are* a naughty little schoolgirl, aren't you? Keep *still*, Becky,' she snapped, as if possessed by an inner force, a craving to have her wicked way with the girl. 'Stand with your legs apart and allow me to finger your cunt, or you'll find yourself in the head's study.'

Kneeling behind the girl as she finally stopped struggling, Christina drove a second finger into the tight duct of her teenage pussy and massaged her inner flesh. Eyeing the girl's crimsoned buttocks, Christina couldn't help herself as she leaned forward and ran her tongue up and down her anal crease. Breathing in the heady scent of her anal gully, Christina realized that she had no control over her rampant desires. Breathing in the aphrodisiacal perfume of the girl's bottom-hole, she completely lost control of her senses and sank her teeth into the firm flesh of one naked buttock. The girl's young body went completely still as Christina's tongue circled round and round the tight hole of her anus and Christina wondered whether her young student was actually enjoying her crude lesbian experience.

'You taste heavenly,' Christina breathed, lapping at the girl's most private hole.

'Please, this isn't right,' Becky whimpered.

'Right or wrong, it's beautiful. You taste beautiful, Becky. You like me licking you there, don't you?'

'Yes, no, I . . .'

'God, you have a beautiful little hole. I could tongue you all day.'

Christina knew that word of her illicit escapades was getting round fast. Before long, her entire class would be demanding sexual favours in return for not only their obedience but their silence. But that wasn't so bad, Christina thought, pushing her tongue into the girl's bitter-sweet anal entrance as she continued to finger-fuck the tight sheath of her young cunt. If this is what it took to keep her students under control, then she was only too willing to administer sexual abuse on a regular basis. Wanking, knob gobbling, cunny licking, anal fisting ... Whatever it took, Christina would be only too happy to oblige her young students.

Becky obviously hadn't realized the extent of her teacher's decadence. Thinking that she could put the fear of God into Christina, she might have had the idea of demanding money in return for her silence. Money, falsified exam results, favours ... The girl wouldn't have expected a severe spanking following by debased lesbian sex. Slipping her pussy-wet fingers out of the girl's well-juiced vaginal duct, Christina forced the globes of her firm buttocks wide apart, completely exposing the brown tissue surrounding the entrance to her rectal canal. There again, perhaps Becky *had* hoped that her teacher would sexually abuse her. Having heard the rumours, she might have blurted out her threat knowing that she'd have her panties ripped off and her young cunt pleasured by her nymphomaniacal teacher.

Becky quivered as Christina pushed her wet tongue deep into the girl's anal canal and licked the dank walls of her rectum. Her cries of protest now whimpers of pleasure, she parted her feet wide and projected her rounded bum cheeks, offering Christina the open portal to the very core of her teenage body. Holding her pert buttocks wider apart, painfully stretching her anal hole open, Christina sucked and slurped, delighting in the bitter-sweet taste of her inner core. Christina was hooked on young girls' bottom-holes, she knew as she tongued Becky's anal portal. Licking her sensitive brown tissue, sucking the eye of her hot anus, tonguing her rectal duct, she took the girl to dizzy heights of sexual arousal.

Slipping her hand between Becky's firm thighs, Christina kneaded her full sex lips with her fingers, delighting in the feel of the young girl's hot vulva. Slipping a finger into the valley of her wet pussy, she located the solid protrusion of her clitoris and massaged her there. The girl breathed heavily, her young body shaking fiercely as her pleasure built deep within her young womb and her girl-juice streamed from the gaping entrance to her hot cunt.

Becky too was now hooked on lesbian lust, Christina knew as she tongued the tight sheath of her anal tube. This was another conquest, another young girl who'd want more crude sex. Her mouth locked to Becky's brown anal tissue, Christina sucked hard, savouring the arousing taste of the girl's inner core. Her saliva running down the girl's anal valley as she tongued and slurped at her brown hole, Christina couldn't get enough crude sex. All she wanted now was to spank young girls, tongue their tight bottom-holes, finger-fuck their sweet cunts and take them to massive orgasms. She'd earn money from cocksucking in the club, she mused as the girl's vaginal muscles tightened around her thrusting fingers. And derive immense pleasure from young girls' naked bodies. The best of both worlds, she reflected.

'I'm coming,' Becky breathed as Christina slipped her cunny-dripping fingers out of her pussy sheath and massaged the sensitive tip of her clitoris. Caressing the hot walls of her rectal duct with her wet tongue, Christina knew that her student was about to experience the orgasm of her young life. 'I'm coming. Oh, oh. You . . . you shouldn't . . . God, I'm coming.'

Whimpering as her orgasm exploded within the palpitating nub of her solid clitoris, her juices of desire gushing from her yawning cuntal opening, Becky shook uncontrollably in her lesbian-induced pleasure. Her creamy-white cunt milk streaming down her inner thighs in torrents, her legs sagging, she begged Christina not to stop as she rode the crest of her mind-blowing orgasm. Christina had no intention of halting the pleasure she was both giving and receiving. Slipping her tongue out of the girl's hot rectum, she drove two fingers deep into the burning sheath of her tight arse, delighting in the abuse as whimpers of pure sexual bliss resounded around the stockroom.

'You're a naughty little girl,' Christina breathed, sinking a third finger into the inflamed duct of Becky's anal canal. 'A very naughty little girl. You'll be punished like this every day, do you understand?'

'Yes, yes,' the teenager gasped, rocking her hips to meet each forceful thrust of Christina's pistoning fingers. 'God, yes. Every day.'

'You dare to accuse me of sexually abusing my students again and I'll force a candle up your bottom.'

Her fingers embedded deep within Becky's rectal tube, Christina pushed her head between her thighs and tongued the fleshy petals of her dripping inner cunt lips. Sucking the girl's distended inner lips into her hot mouth, tasting her juices of orgasm, Christina continued to massage her pulsating clitoris, sustaining her incredible girl-pleasure. Managing to push her tongue deep into the fiery heat of Becky's spasming cunt, she lapped up her flowing juices of lesbian desire, drinking from the sexual centre of her young body as she cried out in her complete and utter satisfaction.

On and on Becky's orgasm rolled, shock waves of crude sex reaching every nerve ending, tightening every muscle until she crumpled to the floor in a quivering heap. Christina's fingers sliding out of her bottom-hole, her tongue leaving the wet sheath of her cunt, Becky lay trembling in the aftermath of her lesbian abuse as Christina sat back on her heels and grinned in her triumph.

'Let that be a lesson to you,' she said, slapping the girl's rounded buttocks with the palm of her hand.

'Yes, Miss,' Becky murmured, her limbs convulsing wildly, her milky juices seeping between the swollen lips of her vulva.

'To make sure that you've learned your lesson, I want you to lick my cunt,' Christina breathed, lying on her back and slipping her panties off. 'Suck the cream out of my cunt,' she murmured, lost in her wickedness, her lesbian desire. 'Tongue-fuck my hot cunt and make me come.'

'But . . .'

'Do it.'

Opening her thighs wide, Christina peeled the fleshy cushions of her hairless love lips open and ordered her young pupil to lick her clitoris to orgasm. Settling between her teacher's legs, the girl pressed her mouth hard against Christina's fleshy vaginal lips and pushed her tongue into the hot folds of her dripping pussy slit. Becky was obviously experienced at lesbian licking, Christina mused as the girl expertly teased her ripe clitoris with her wet tongue. She'd obviously done this before, and Christina wondered who her latest lesbian lover was and what she had done. Had she enjoyed sixty-nine with Bryony? Had the girls lain side by side and tongue-fucked each other's hot cunts to orgasm?

The students in Christina's class were of the age where they'd be sexually experimenting almost daily. It wasn't unheard of for teenage girls to masturbate each other during their learning, during their early days of sexual discovery. That hadn't been the case at Christina's village school, but in a run-down area of London, where sex shops and prostitutes were rife, it wasn't at all surprising to find girls experimenting with lesbian sex.

Christina was surprised that the girl had not only come to her with her threat but had seemed to have no hesitation when ordered to indulge in lesbian oral sex. But when she thought about it, she realized that word had obviously got round that Christina was heavily into lesbian sex. The girl herself having tendencies in that direction, she'd thought she'd try her luck with her young teacher. And it had paid off. Becky would be another regular, Christina mused as her clitoris pulsated beneath the girl's sweeping tongue and her young womb rhythmically contracted. Becky would be a regular visitor to the flat, that was certain.

London revolved around sex, Christina concluded as Becky slipped at least three fingers deep into the tightening sheath of her hot cunt. But didn't any large city? She should have expected to be confronted with sex at a sixth-form college, she reflected. Teenage girls with hormones running wild, teenage lads with their cocks perpetually erect, their balls always in need of draining . . . Christina should have known that Spadger Heath College, like any other college, would thrive on sex.

Feeling the girl's tongue snaking around the solid nub of her sensitive clitoris, Christina pushed all thoughts of the college to the back of her mind and concentrated solely on the immense pleasure her young girl student was bringing her. Listening to the beautiful sound of her lapping tongue, her sucking mouth, the squelching of vaginal juices, Christina lost herself in her lesbian debauchery as her womb rhythmically contracted and her copious juices of arousal flowed from the bloated opening of her tight cunt. She was close to her orgasm, she knew as she began to tremble uncontrollably. She was fast nearing her lesbian heaven.

*This is like a dream*, Christina mused in her sex-dizzy thinking. Since starting at Spadger Heath, she had had more debased sex than she'd thought she'd have in a lifetime. Cocksucking, sperm swallowing, cunny tonguing, anal fisting, bondage and whipping . . . Were all colleges really like this? she wondered as her orgasm peaked, taking her ever closer to her lesbian heaven. All teenage boys wanked and most teenage girls masturbated. But the students at Spadger Heath were hooked on crude sex of any and every description. And the staff were no better. Christina had not only wanked Ponting's penis and brought out his orgasmic cream but had allowed the headmaster himself to fuck the tight sheath of her cock-hungry cunt.

Listening to the slurping sounds of Becky's tongue as the girl sustained her incredible pleasure, Christina realized that she'd never be able to leave the college and return to her parents' country home. She couldn't leave behind the crude sex, couldn't live without a continual supply of fresh sperm and hot pussy juice. And she wouldn't be able to survive on the meagre wage of a village schoolteacher. Things were difficult enough on her present salary, but at least she had the opportunity to more than double her income by visiting The Rat's Tail Club. She knew now that she'd never leave London.

'God, no more,' she finally managed to cry out as her pleasure began to fade.

'Did you like that?' Becky asked, her cunny-wet face smiling at Christina.

'Like it?' she gasped, her young body convulsing wildly. 'It was bloody amazing.'

'I like your shaved pussy. It's soft and smooth. It makes you look very young.'

'Yes, it does. You've done this before, haven't you?'

'No, I . . . yes, I have,' the girl confessed.

'Who with?'

'I'd rather not say.'

'Who with, Becky? Who's your lesbian lover?'

'Sally Braithwaite.'

'Sally . . . That pretty little thing who wouldn't say boo to a goose?'

'Yes.'

'I'll have to get to know her a little better,' Christina said, her face grinning as she imagined anal fisting the young girl. 'I'll have to get to know her *intimately*. Where do you meet her?'

'We walk to the back of the old warehouses on Cannon Road. There's a place there, a small room. Come with us, if you like.'

'I think I will. So, what was all this nonsense about? Threatening to me report me and—'

'A couple of the girls put me up to it. Everyone knows that you've been having sex with Doogan and Brown. And with Bryony.'

'Sex with Bryony?' Christina said, lifting her head and frowning at her flushed-faced student.

'You're not going to deny it, are you?'

'What would be the point?' Christina sighed, hauling

her trembling body up from the floor and swaying on her sagging legs. 'You lot seem to know more about my sex life than I do. So, what else do you know?'

'Nothing, really. I'd better go to geography or I'll be in trouble.'

'Just say that you were giving me a hand. After all, you were, weren't you?'

'Yes, but . . .'

'I'll back up your story, don't worry. OK, off you go.'

Unlocking the door, the girl left her torn panties on the stockroom floor and headed off to her next lesson. Grabbing the flimsy garment, Christina pressed the wet crotch to her face and breathed in the heady scent of the girl's teenage cunt. *A souvenir*, she mused, returning to her desk and slipping the garment into her handbag. Wondering whether to start a collection of panties, she grinned as she imagined the girl students donating their wet knickers. Deciding to catch up on some work, Christina sat at her desk and began going through the students' essays.

'Excuse me, Miss,' Sally Braithwaite murmured, walking into the classroom.

'What is it, Sally?' Christina asked, realizing that Becky had spoken to the girl.

'I was wondering whether . . .'

'Yes?' Christina said, wondering how the girl was going to suggest lesbian sex.

'I . . . It doesn't matter.'

'Did you want to show me something in the stockroom?'

'She said you . . . Oh, yes, yes, that's right.'

'Start by slipping your panties off,' Christina told the girl.

'What? Take them off in here?'

'I want to see what you're offering me before I take it, Sally. Take your panties off and give them to me.'

Turning, the girl looked at the open door before slipping her hands up her short skirt and tugging her panties down her slender legs. Slipping the garment off over her feet, she passed it to her teacher. Christina examined the crotch of the red material, smiling as she focused on the white stain. Holding the garment to her face, she breathed in the fresh scent of the young girl's cuntal juices before slipping the panties into her bag.

'Now show me what it is that you're offering me,' she said, her stomach somersaulting as the girl grabbed the hem of her skirt.

'*This* is what I'm offering you,' Sally murmured, lifting the front of her skirt up over her stomach.

'I see,' Christina breathed, gazing wide-eyed at the girl's hairless vulval lips. 'Why do you shave? Do you prefer it that way?'

'Yes, I do. Also . . . Becky prefers me shaved.'

'I must say that I'm rather partial to a hairless pussy. Show me inside, Sally. Part your lips and show me what secrets you have.'

Following Christina's instructions, the girl peeled the firm pads of her outer lips wide apart and exposed the intricate folds of her teenage cunt. Focusing on the globules of white cream clinging to Sally's inner lips, Christina felt her heart racing, her hands trembling. Desperate to lick the girl there, to taste her warm cunt-milk, she left her desk and walked to the stockroom. Sally lowered her skirt and followed, grinning as Christina closed and locked the door behind her.

Unbuttoning the girl's blouse, Christina parted the

white material and gazed longingly at her bra. Lifting the cups up over her mammary spheres, she examined the girl's young breasts. Squeezing each mound in turn, Christina grinned. Topped with chocolate-brown teats, the girl's breasts were small and firm to the touch. Opening her blouse further, Christina gazed at the gentle rise of her stomach and wondered whether one of the lads had spunked her there. Picturing the small indent of her navel flooded with sperm, she kneeled on the floor and tugged the girl's skirt down to her ankles.

'Sit on the table,' Christina ordered the teenager. 'That's it. Now place your feet on the table, either side of your bum.' Taking up her position, Sally looked down at her hairless vulval lips bulging alluringly between her parted thighs. Watching Christina press her mouth hard against her naked vulval flesh, she let out a gasp of lesbian pleasure as her teacher's wet tongue ran up her valley of desire. Tasting the girl's vaginal cream, Christina parted her love lips with her slender fingers and lapped at her open cunt hole.

'You taste wonderful,' she murmured, her tongue snaking over the pink funnel of flesh surrounding Sally's vaginal orifice. 'Tell me what Becky does to you.'

'She licks me,' the girl breathed, her young body trembling. 'She licks my clitoris and pushes a candle into my pussy.'

'A candle?' Christina echoed, looking up at the girl's sex-flushed face. 'I'm afraid I don't have a candle.' Looking around the room, she smiled. 'I could make use of this,' she said, taking a small plastic bottle from a shelf. 'I wonder who left this in here?'

'Someone with the same idea?' Sally proffered.

'Maybe.'

Parting the fleshy lips of the girl's young pussy, Christina eased the flat end of the bottle into the tight duct of her young cunt. Quivering, Sally watched wide-eyed as the bottle slipped deep into the hugging sheath of her wet cunt. Her swollen outer lips stretched tautly around the plastic phallus, the nub of her erect clitoris fully exposed, she let out a rush of breath as Christina slipped a finger into the gully of her bottom and located her anus. The girl whimpered as Christina's finger glided into her rectal duct and massaged the dank walls of her inner core. Her clitoris visibly pulsating, she was about to come, Christina knew.

Licking the sensitive tip of her cumbud, Christina pistoned her student's cuntal sheath with the bottle, delighting in the squelching sounds of her lubricious juices as the girl shook violently in her lesbian pleasure. Slipping a second finger into the girl's tight anal tube, Christina sucked hard on her clitoris and increased the rhythm of her vaginal pistoning. Gasping, Sally leaned back and rested her hands on the table as her pleasure built within her young womb. Double fucking her tight sex holes, Christina fervently licked and sucked on her clitoris as she teetered on the brink of her climax.

'Coming,' Sally finally gasped. Wailing as her orgasm exploded within her pulsating clitoris, she pumped out her cunt-milk. The creamy liquid splattering Christina's face as the girl shook and whimpered in her coming, she screamed in her lesbian ecstasy. Someone would hear her, Christina knew as she mouthed and licked Sally's orgasming clitoris. Praying for her to be quiet, she hoped that her orgasm would soon wane as she repeatedly rammed the bottle deep into the drenched shaft of her tight cunt. Again, Sally screamed out as her orgasm peaked, her wails of pleasure reverberating around the stockroom.

'Who's in there?' a male voice bellowed.

'Only me,' Christina replied, slipping the bottle out of the sex-dizzy girl's inflamed cunt. 'I'm just having a tidy-up.'

'Christina?' the headmaster called. 'Are you all right?'

'Yes, I'm fine. Hang on, I'll open the door.'

'I heard a scream.'

'It was someone outside. I heard it, too.'

Ordering Sally to dress and hide beneath the table, Christina composed herself before unlocking the door. Wiping her sex-wet mouth on the back of her hand, she took a deep breath and opened the door. The head was frowning, his beady eyes trying to peer into the stockroom. Christina wondered if he was suspicious. Smiling at the man as she closed the door behind her, she walked across the classroom and gazed out of the window.

'Just some kids messing around,' she said. 'I heard them shouting and screaming earlier.'

'I came to find you since it's almost break time,' the head said, gazing at the stockroom door. 'Is there someone in the—'

'Coffee,' Christina cut in, taking his hand and leading him out of the classroom. 'Coffee and a chat in your study, OK?'

'Yes, yes, of course.'

Walking along the corridor, Christina realized that she was going to have to be more careful. The stockroom was becoming infamous, she reflected, hoping that Sally had had the sense to get out before anyone else wandered into the classroom. The stockroom, the woods . . . They were fast becoming no-go areas. But the old warehouses Becky had mentioned sounded promising. She'd meet the teenage girls there after college, she decided. After all, she had unfinished business with Sally.

# 16

Sitting at the kitchen table, Christina read through the letter again. 'Dear Miss Shaw,' she breathed. 'You are required to vacate the rented accommodation immediately. The property has been deemed unfit for habitation due to structural defects in the rear wall.' Unable to believe the letter from the local council, Christina bit her lip. This was all she needed, she thought, tossing the letter onto the table and sipping her tea. She'd have to contact the letting agency and see whether they had any other flats for rent.

Recalling that Ponting's wife worked for the council, she wondered whether the woman was behind the letter. It would have been easy enough to take a piece of letter-headed paper, she mused. Deciding to ignore it, she took a shower and prepared to go out to The Rat's Tail Club. She was looking forward to the evening, and hoped to meet John again. If she didn't, there'd be plenty of other men to amuse her and buy her drinks. Hearing the front door close as she finished brushing her hair, she left her room and went into the kitchen where Bryony was filling the kettle.

'Good day?' Christina asked.

'Not bad. Twelve old men,' Bryony giggled. 'Twelve wrinkled old cocks to wank. You look nice. Are you going out?'

'I am,' Christina replied. 'I'm going to The Rat's Tail Club for the evening.'

'How do you know about the place?'

'I happened to pass by and thought it looked interesting. And you?'

'Josie took me there. I'll be there at six, so we'll meet up and I'll introduce you.'

'I've already met Josie,' Christina said mysteriously.

'When? Where?'

'You'll find out later. Right, I'll be going.'

'You're rather early, aren't you? It's only just gone five.'

'I want to get a decent table,' Christina giggled. 'If you get my meaning?'

Leaving the flat as Bryony called down the stairs, Christina strutted along the street in her stilettos. It was a lovely evening, she thought. The sun warming her, she swung her bag as she walked. She felt that all her problems were over as she neared the club. Ponting's trick would get him nowhere. She now had Becky and Sally to amuse herself with, and Charles had obviously given up all hope of rekindling their relationship.

Walking into the club, Christina ordered herself a vodka and tonic and sat at the bar. She *was* rather early, she mused, looking around the deserted bar. But she'd be able to grab a secluded table before the place started filling up. A table where she could wank cocks and lap up spunk from her hand without being seen. Sipping her drink as the barman busied himself, she pondered on her decision to stay in London. It was the right thing to do, she was sure. She'd made new friends, her job couldn't have been better, and she was getting more sex than she could handle.

'It'll pick up later,' the barman said.

'I'm sorry?' Christina breathed.

'The bar. It'll get busy later. Are you waiting for someone?'

'Several people, actually.'

'You were in last night, weren't you?'

'Yes, yes, I was. It's nice place. Have you worked here for long?'

'A couple of months. I came up from Kent where I worked for an insurance company. I was made redundant and thought I'd try my luck in London.'

'Any regrets?'

'No, none at all. Oh, sorry. I'm Doug.'

'Christina. I came here from Hertfordshire. It was quite a culture shock after living in the country. Like you, I have no regrets. I'm surprised you earn enough here to pay your rent.'

'I don't,' he chuckled. 'There's no way I'd earn enough doing bar work. I have a sideline.'

'Oh?'

'I'm into photography. Pretty successfully, even though I say it myself.'

'Then why work here?'

'Ah, that would be telling.'

'Oh, go on,' Christina begged him. 'I'm intrigued.'

'Well . . . I get a lot of my work from the club. There are girls who . . . well, let's just say that they make money from being photographed, and I make money by clicking the shutter.'

'Porn?' Christina asked.

'Yes, porn. You might frown upon it, but we all have to make a living.'

'No, no, I don't frown upon it at all. How much do the girls make?'

'That depends.'

'On?'

'On what they do. They get around fifty quid for your basic open-legs shot.'

'Is that all?'

'They get a couple of hundred for oral stuff. It's entirely up to them how much they earn. Why, are you interested?' he laughed.

'I might be,' Christina replied, wiping the grin off his face.

'Oh, right. Well . . . here's my number,' Doug said, taking a card from his pocket. 'Give me a ring some time.'

'I might just do that,' Christina said as a young couple walked into the bar.

'I also work here because it gives me an identity. Income tax, insurance contributions . . . as far as anyone official is concerned, this is my job. Excuse me for a moment.'

As the barman served the couple, Christina realized that she could earn a fortune in London. She also realized that the college was, for her, the same as the club was for the barman. It was her base, as well as a source of teenagers permanently ready for crude sex. She'd definitely made the right decision, she concluded. Thinking about photographic work, she knew that she'd have to be careful. The last thing she needed was incriminating photographs of her being bandied about the college – or anywhere else, for that matter. As the young couple a few feet away from her mentioned the college, she pricked her ears up.

'The caretaker's always gone by eight,' the young man murmured. 'By nine, the place will be deserted. We won't have any problems.'

'I hope not,' the girl replied. 'How long will it take?'

'Twenty minutes, no more. With the alarms out of action, we'll be in and out inside fifteen minutes and no one will be any the wiser. Another five minutes to load the van, and we'll be away.'

'That's not long to lug eighty-odd computers out of the place.'

'Long enough.'

As they moved to a table, Christina wondered what to do. She reckoned that they were planning to take the computers that evening, giving her little time to do anything. She doubted that the police would be interested in bar talk. But she couldn't just sit there and do nothing. Ordering another vodka, she watched the young couple out of the corner of her eye. They were whispering, obviously planning the robbery, and Christina wondered who else was in on the raid. All she could do would be to call the police and tip them off, she decided. If they weren't interested, that was their problem.

'Hi,' Bryony trilled as she entered the club.

'Hi. Where's Josie?' Christina asked.

'She'll be along soon. How do you know her?'

'It's a long story,' Christina replied. 'What are you drinking?'

'Same as you, please. From what you were saying earlier about getting a table, am I to assume that you come here to earn money?'

'I might,' Christina giggled, ordering the girl a drink.

'I thought so. You are awful, keeping secrets from me like that.'

'Bryony, do you happen to know Doogan's phone number?'

'No, I don't. Why?'

'I need to speak to him.'
'He'll be in later. I saw him on my way here.'
'Good.'
'What's it about?'
'I'll tell you later.'

Deciding to get Doogan and his mates to deal with the young couple, Christina smiled as Bryony said that she was going to nab her favourite table before someone else sat there. She sat and thought for a while. What was Doogan up to, coming to the club? He'd never mentioned the place. It might have been his regular haunt, she mused. This particular area of London was very much like a village, she reflected. Everyone seemed to know everyone else, and she wondered whether Doogan knew the young couple. Perhaps he was in on the scam? The man had said that the alarms were out of action, so they must have had someone on the inside.

As the barman refilled her glass without charging her, Christine reckoned that he wanted her to model for him. Again pondering on the idea, she wondered whether he took gynaecological-type shots, leaving her face out of frame. She wouldn't mind that, she thought, imagining the camera lens focusing on the sex-dripping entrance to her cuntal shaft. Her stomach somersaulting as she let out a giggle, she wondered whether to take her own snaps of her open pussy and sell them to lonely old men.

'Hi,' a middle-aged man said as he approached the bar and stood next Christina.

'Oh, er . . . hi,' she replied, watching him pull a note from his pocket and order a pint.

'You OK for a drink?'
'I'm fine, thanks.'
'A friend of mine suggested I come here.'

'Really?'

'He reckons that I'll get what I want.'

'Well, you've got a drink.'

'I was looking for more than a drink.'

'I don't think they do food,' Christina said, knowing full well what he was after.

'I'm hungry, but not for food,' he riposted. 'Anything else on offer?'

'I don't know. You'll have to ask the barman.'

'Shall we stop playing games?' he murmured. 'How much?'

'For what?'

'A blow job.'

'Sixty,' she replied softly.

'That's a bit steep, isn't it?'

'You get what you pay for in this world,' she replied, watching the young couple leave the club. 'I'm good, and I charge sixty. Take it or leave it.'

'I'll take it,' he said, walking over to a secluded table.

Joining him, Christina looked down as he unzipped his trousers and pulled his semi-erect cock out. This was her first real client, she mused, grabbing the fleshy shaft of his penis. No chatting up, no free drinks . . . Straight into cold sex in exchange for hard cash. Taking his wallet out, the man slipped sixty pounds into her handbag as she rolled his foreskin back over the bulbous swell of his glans. Well out of view of the bar, Christina leaned over and examined the man's purple globe. This was what prostitution was all about, she thought, opening her mouth wide. Meeting a stranger in a bar, taking cash, giving a quick blow job and then on to the next client. Christina was now a real prostitute.

Sucking her client's ballooning cock-head into her wet

mouth, she ran her tongue around his sperm-slit to the accompaniment of his stifled gasps of pleasure. Savouring the salty taste of his ripe plum, she took his knob to the back of her throat and sank her teeth into the root of his solid cock. Breathing in the scent of his pubes, she raised her head and went down on his cock again. Bobbing her head up and down, his glans repeatedly meeting the back of her throat, she knew that she shouldn't bring out his spunk too quickly. He obviously wanted his money's worth, and wouldn't take too kindly to her swallowing his spunk before he'd enjoyed the full pleasure of her wet mouth. Stilling her head, the helmet of his purple glans between her wet lips, she rolled her tongue slowly around his sex globe.

'You *are* good,' he murmured, clutching her head as the tip of her tongue prodded his sperm-slit. Sucking hard on his twitching knob, Christina could feel his bulb enlarging as the vacuum built within her hot mouth. Slipping her hand into his trousers and fondling his heaving balls, her clitoris swelling as her arousal heightened, she was desperate for the taste of his sperm. Suspecting that she was becoming addicted to male sex fluid, she recalled licking Becky's bottom-hole, the aphrodisiacal taste of her brown tissue. She loved the various tastes of sex, she mused. Salty knobs, sperm, girl-cum, tight anal inlets . . . The tastes of lust.

Humming softly, the vibrations running through the man's bulbous glans, she continued to tease his sperm-slit as he began to tremble in his rising pleasure. 'That's good,' he breathed. 'Ah, yes, yes. Slowly, slowly. I don't want to come yet.'

Allowing her saliva to run down the man's shaft, Christina kneaded his rolling balls and sucked on his purple plum. He'd feel the cooling liquid coursing down his shaft, adding to his debased pleasure, she knew as she licked and teased the small bridge of skin linking his foreskin to the base of his swollen knob. Unable to hold back, he gasped, gripping her head and thrusting his hips as his penis swelled and his glans throbbed. Sucking, slurping, mouthing, she was thirsty for his cream, desperate now to drink from his huge cock-head. He mumbled words of crude sex as his orgasm welled and his sperm began to course along his penile shaft. Ordering her to suck harder and swallow his come, he let out a long low moan of pleasure.

'Drink it,' he breathed as his spunk jetted from his throbbing knob. Her mouth filling with the salty fluid, Christina repeatedly swallowed hard, desperate not to waste one drop as she drank from his orgasming glans. Once more, he mumbled his words of debased sex. Whore, filthy slut, cum-guzzling slag . . . His words only serving to heighten Christina's arousal as she swallowed his gushing spunk, she knew that she was going to have to find sexual relief of her own that evening. She'd order Bryony to climb into her bed, she decided. The girl would run her tongue up and down Christina's wet sex valley, lick her clitoris to several massive orgasms.

Hearing Doogan's voice as she sucked the last remnants of the man's spunk out of his deflating cock-shaft, Christina sat upright and licked her glossed lips. Standing at the bar with Brown and ordering two pints of lager, he'd not seen her. Brushing her long blonde hair away from her flushed face, she watched her client slip his penis back into his trousers and pull his zip up before downing his drink. By the look on his face, he was happy with her efforts, she thought. And so he should have been.

'I'll be seeing you,' he said, leaving the table. 'You here most nights?'

'Yes, I am,' Christina replied, sipping her vodka.

'Good. I might become a regular, if that suits you?'

'It suits me.'

'Good.'

Placing his glass on the bar, he flashed her a knowing smile as he left the club. Opening her bag, Christina gazed at the cash. She'd done well, she reflected. Sixty pounds in a few minutes? Not many jobs paid that sort of money. Looking up as Doogan and Brown approached, she smiled. She was going to have to tell them about the young couple, she thought, checking her watch. There again, if Doogan was involved . . .

'All alone?' Brown asked, sitting down opposite her.

'I'm with Bryony,' Christina replied. 'She's talking to someone at the other end of the bar. So, what are you two doing here?'

'Drinking,' Doogan chuckled, standing by the table. 'We usually come here because they stay open later than the pub. The botany thing worked out OK, didn't it?'

'Yes, yes, it did,' Christina murmured pensively. 'Have you any plans for this evening? Later this evening, I mean.'

'Yes, we're staying here and getting wrecked,' Brown laughed. 'Why?'

Relating her story about the young couple, Christina hoped that the lads would be able to do something. If they hung around the college gates, they might at least deter the couple, prevent them from stealing the computers. Brown didn't want to get involved, saying that he'd probably end up in trouble if the cops turned up. But Doogan was keen. To Christina's surprise, his attitude was that no bastards were going to nick anything from the college and deprive the students.

'There was a robbery last year,' he said. 'All the computers went and the cops reckoned that it was an inside job. No one was nicked for it.'

'I wonder whether it was the same people?' Christina murmured. 'The young man said that the alarms would be out of action, so there might be someone on the inside.'

'I don't like it,' Brown complained. 'What are we supposed to do? Rough them up, or something?'

'Don't be a prick,' Doogan laughed. 'What we do is hang around and see whether we know these people. If we don't, and they break in, we call the cops.'

'I don't want any involvement with the law,' Brown sighed.

'We don't get involved, do we? We call the cops and then come back here.'

'I suppose so.'

'You'll have to wait until they're inside the building,' Christina said.

'I'm not stupid,' Doogan chuckled. 'I know what to do. OK, let's go.'

'It's rather early,' Christina said, checking her watch.

'I want to check the place out, find somewhere we can hide. We'll see you later, OK?'

'OK. And thanks.'

'Any time.'

As the boys finished their drinks and left the club, Christina realized how much she liked Doogan. He was rather rough, somewhat coarse, but a very likeable young man. He was right, he wasn't stupid. If he kept out of trouble and got down to his college work, he'd probably do well in life. Checking her watch for the umpteenth time, Christina wondered what the evening would bring. Bryony had obviously found herself a client and there'd been no sign of Josie. Unless the girl had arrived while Christina had had her head beneath the table.

'Hi,' Alison said, smiling as she walked into the club. 'What are you doing here on your own?'

'Having a drink and relaxing,' Christina replied, pleased that she had some company. 'How's the hotel?'

'Awful,' the girl sighed. 'The manager's a complete wanker, the chef's a fucking idiot, and there's this waitress who thinks she owns the fucking place.'

'Are you going to leave?'

'Yes, but not just yet. Don't worry, I don't want to come back to the flat.'

'No, no, it wasn't that.'

'I've decided to go down to Devon.'

'Devon? There's not much life there,' Christina giggled.

'There will be when I get there. Seriously, there are some smaller hotels there. I like the hotel business. You get to meet different people, have somewhere to live, free food . . . It suits me. And if I get pissed off with it, I'll come back to London. What am I doing sitting here without a drink? I'll be back in a minute.'

Christina didn't reckon that Alison would last for five minutes in Devon. But the girl was free with no ties, so why not move around? Wondering whether to tell Alison about her new profession, Christina realized that she could work anywhere in the country. Even in Devon there must be men who'd pay for her services, she reflected. Alison returned to the table and announced that she'd seen a friend and would be back later. Christina smiled as the girl walked away. Alison was a free spirit, she mused. But wasn't Christina?

The time dragged on with no would-be clients hovering. Growing bored, Christina downed yet another vodka as she wondered what Doogan and Brown were doing. 'Nine-fifteen,' she sighed, checking her watch again. Wishing that she'd arranged to meet Becky and Sally at the old warehouses, she decided to stay until ten and then go home for an early night. Perhaps there wasn't such a demand for call-girls as she'd reckoned, she thought, looking around the bar.

'Good evening,' the headmaster said, grinning as he approached Christina's table with a pint of beer in his hand.

'Oh, er . . . hello, Ian,' she stammered, wondering what he was doing in the club.

'Mind if I join you?'

'No, of course not.'

'I called round at your flat earlier. Then I went for a walk and ran into Doogan and Brown.'

'Oh? Did they say anything?'

'Only that you were here when I asked whether they'd seen you. Oh, you're not with anyone, are you?'

'No, no. I was with my flatmate – my ex-flatmate – but she's gone off somewhere. Ian, I don't know whether to stay on at the college or not.'

'What? You're not thinking of leaving, surely?'

'Oh, I don't know,' she sighed. 'What with Ponting and . . . I feel that I've made rather a mess of things since I've been in London.'

'How can you possibly say that? Good grief, you've done wonders with your class and . . .'

'I know, but . . . Ponting isn't going to go away. He's going to try to cause trouble for me for as long as I'm in London.'

'Yes, I . . . I spoke with the board of governors. Mr Ponting certainly has it in for you, Christina. It seems that he's been trying to associate you with prostitution. The thing is, the board might have to suspend you while they look into it.'

'What? That bloody man . . . I'm sorry, Ian, but I've just about had enough of Ponting.'

'I quite understand. If they do suspend you, obviously I'll be right behind you. Hopefully, it won't come to that.'

'That's it, Ian. I'm leaving the college.'

'Christina, don't be too hasty.'

'Hasty? As I said, Ponting isn't going to give up. All the time I'm here in London, he'll hound me. I'll have to leave, I'm afraid.'

'Well, I . . . Look, I'll get you another drink and we'll talk about this. I need a refill. Don't go away, OK?'

'OK.'

Christina could hardly believe that she might be suspended because of Ponting's lies. She supposed that the board of governors had to look into the allegation, no matter how ridiculous it was. But to suspend her on the word of an idiot . . . At least she had the headmaster on her side, she reflected. And the students. Recalling the letter she'd received, she was sure now that Ponting's wife was behind it. Between them, the evil pair could go on causing problems for ever.

'Well,' Doogan said, his face beaming as he entered the

club and walked over to Christina. 'You'll never guess what happened.'

'We were undercover,' Brown began. 'There were six of them, armed with automatic rifles and—'

'Shut up, Brown, you prick,' Doogan snapped. 'I'll tell you all about it once I've got a beer. Come on, prickhead. It's your round.'

Christina had lost all interest in the robbery. In fact, she'd lost all interest in the college. Watching the lads walk over to the bar, she wondered what the headmaster would say when he found his students hitting the booze. Still, they were of age and it was up to them how they spent their spare time. He'd no doubt be pleased to hear that the boys had stopped the robber, if that was what they'd done. As he returned and sat beside Christina, he told her that he'd be meeting with the board of governors the following morning.

'I'm not really interested,' she sighed. 'I won't be there for them to suspend me.'

'At least hear what they have to say,' the head murmured. 'Don't make a decision until you've heard.'

'I suppose not. But even if this is cleared up, Ponting will start something else.'

'I told the board about the incident in the woods.'

'And?'

'Well, they said that they'll look into it. We should have called the police, Christina. Basically, it's our word against Ponting's. It doesn't look at all good, I'm afraid.'

Hanging her head, Christina reckoned that Ponting had won. The board of governors must have thought it odd that such a sordid incident hadn't been reported to the police. Obviously Ponting had no proof of his allegations but, whether it was true or not, the board couldn't have one of their teachers linked with prostitution. Wondering whether to go to Devon with Alison, Christina was sure that her teaching career was over. It had been mostly her fault, she reflected. Wanking the lads in the stockroom in return for their good behaviour had been a dreadful mistake. And as for becoming sexually involved with teenage girls . . . Still, what was done was done, she concluded. Ponting would never find her in Devon. Or would he?

'Oh, er . . . sorry, sir,' Doogan muttered as he stood by the table with his beer. 'We'll find another seat.'

'No, no. Please join us,' the headmaster said.

'I think the lads have something to tell you,' Christina said.

'Oh? And what would that be?'

'It was like this,' Brown began. 'There was this armed robbery planned and we—'

'I'll tell him,' Doogan cut in irritably. 'Christina . . . I mean, Miss Shaw told us that she'd overheard a couple talking about robbing the college.'

'Really? Is that right, Christina?'

'Yes, it is. They were planning to steal the computers and Doogan and Brown went to intervene.'

'So what happened? When was this? You should have called the police.'

'We did,' Doogan said triumphantly. 'We were in hiding and this van pulled up, driven by a woman. Two blokes got out and unlocked the gates.'

'They had keys?' the head gasped.

'Yes. Anyway, they opened the gates and the woman backed the van in. They broke into the college through the library window.'

'Didn't the alarm go off?' the head asked, shaking his head in disbelief.

'No, it didn't. Once they were in the building we called the cops.'

'A dozen squad cars came racing round the corner and—'

'Shut up, Brown,' Doogan hissed. 'The cops turned up and nabbed the villains as they were loading the van. We stayed in hiding because we didn't want to get involved.'

'They had a key to the gates and the alarm didn't sound?' the head murmured, rubbing his chin. 'That's exactly what happened before.'

'This is the best bit,' Doogan chuckled, gulping his pint and keeping everyone in suspense. 'Ponting was the inside man.'

'*What?*' Christina gasped, choking on her vodka.

'Ponting was loading the computers into the van with the other two men.'

'Good God,' the head breathed. 'Ponting? *Our* Mr Ponting?'

'That solves my little problem,' Christina giggled.

'I'll get the drinks in,' the head chuckled, rising to his feet. 'You've done very well, lads. Two beers?'

'No, it's OK,' Doogan said. 'We'll leave you two to chat. Come on, Brown. Let's take a look round.'

Unable to believe her luck, Christina downed her vodka in one gulp and laughed out loud. The head sat in stunned silence as he pondered on the incident. Neither of them could believe that Ponting was the inside man, and had obviously taken part in the previous year's robbery. Once this came to light, his wife would probably have to resign from the council, Christina mused happily. The police would obviously search his home for stolen goods and discover his sex den. Not that a sex den was illegal, but it still wouldn't look good.

'Oh,' the head sighed. 'I've just thought of another major problem.'

'What's that?' Christina asked, wondering what else there was to worry about.

'Young Simpson.'

'Oh, er . . . has he said anything?'

'He's coming to see me in the morning. He said that he wants to report something. He wouldn't say what it was, but . . .'

'I think I know,' Christina breathed.

'You know?'

'Simpson has been—'

'Oh, I should explain,' the head broke in. 'Simpson is Ponting's son.'

'What?'

'He uses the name so as not to be treated differently in any way by the other students. Of course, now his father has been . . .'

'Do you have any idea what he wanted to report?'

'No, all he said was that one of the teachers would be sacked. Perhaps he was talking about his father. Simpson is a weird lad at the best of times. He doesn't live with his parents, by the way. He lives with an aunt. I've always thought it an odd arrangement.'

'It certainly sounds odd.'

'Christina, now that . . . You will stay at Spadger Heath, won't you?'

'Yes, yes, I will.'

'And us? I mean . . . we haven't been able to see much of each other, have we?'

This was getting better by the minute, Christina mused, placing her hand on the headmaster's knee. Moving up to the crotch of his trousers, she massaged his stiffening penis. He remained silent as she kneaded his balls and rubbed the swollen knob of his cock. Even when she tugged his zip down, he said nothing. He was obviously in desperate need of relief, she thought as she pulled his solid penis out of his trousers. Rolling his foreskin back and forth over the globe of his swollen knob, she kissed his cheek. Ponting was out of the way, and life was looking good, she thought happily as the head breathed deeply in his soaring arousal.

'I'm really thirsty,' Christina murmured.

'Oh, er . . . I'll get you a drink,' the head offered.

'I'll get my own drink, thanks,' she giggled.

Looking around the bar before leaning over and taking the headmaster's glans into her wet mouth, Christina ran her tongue around the salty-tasting helmet of his cock. The head gasped as she took his ripe plum to the back of her throat and bit gently into the fleshy root of his cock. He needed this as much as she did, she mused, slipping her hand into his trousers and cupping his rolling balls in her palm. Breathing in the scent of his pubes, she could hardly wait for his sperm to gush into her mouth and bathe her snaking tongue. Sperm, girl-juice, the anal ring . . . The tastes of sex.

Young Simpson was in line for a naked-buttock thrashing, Christina decided as the headmaster trembled uncontrollably. A bamboo cane might come in useful, she thought. She'd keep it in the stockroom and correct her students' wicked ways when they stepped out of line. Becky would enjoy the cane, she knew as the head let out a gasp of pleasure, his sperm jetting from his throbbing knob and filling her pretty mouth. Repeatedly swallowing hard, she drank from his fountainhead, delighting in her decadent act.

'God,' the man breathed as Christina bobbed her head up and down, mouth-fucking herself with his granite-hard penis. 'God, that's . . .' Wondering whether the head master had ever fucked a girl's mouth before, she slowed her bobbing motion, tonguing his throbbing glans as his sperm flow lessened to a trickle. Bringing out the final ripples of his orgasm, she sucked out the last remnants of his sperm before sitting upright and grinning at him. Gazing at the white liquid dribbling down her chin, the head zipped up his trousers and let out a chuckle.

'I think we're going to get on extremely well together,' he said, downing his pint. 'This calls for a celebration. Er . . . are you still thirsty?'

'No, but I'll have a large vodka and tonic,' Christina giggled, wiping her mouth on the back of her hand.

'OK. Don't go away.'

'Oh, I won't,' she said as he made his way to the bar.

'I see you're with a client,' John said as he sidled up to the table.

'Oh, er . . . yes, that's right.'

'Will you be in tomorrow evening'

'I can book you in,' she replied. 'Seven o'clock?'

'Seven it is.'

'There we are,' the head chortled, returning to the table as John moved away. 'Let's drink to us,' he said, raising his glass.

'To us,' Christina trilled, winking at John as he leaned on the bar.

'Good God, Christina. To think that Ponting was the inside man. And he tried to make out that you were involved in prostitution. What a dreadful thing to say about such a beautiful young lady.'

'Yes, absolutely dreadful. Cheers, Ian.'

# Sexual Revenge

# I

Rod Johnson pulled my skirt up as Julie Wicks and another girl, Sally Brompton, pinned me against the tree. It was my birthday, and I'd wanted to get home quickly for the family party my mother had arranged. Aunts, uncles, cousins, neighbours . . . Everyone was coming. Stupidly, I'd taken the risk of cutting across the common on my way home from school. The short cut saved about fifteen minutes, but I should have known that the Brook Street Gang would be lying in wait for me.

'Look at her little cunt,' Rod laughed, yanking my navy-blue knickers down to my knees. 'Do you frig your little clitty?'

'Finger her dirty cunt,' Sally Brompton giggled. 'Shove your finger up the fat cow's dirty little cunt.'

Squeezing my eyes shut, I felt Rod's finger running up and down the moist crack of my pussy. The whole gang were there, watching the degrading act, laughing, leering, calling me filthy names. I wasn't exactly fat, but I was certainly chubby. In my early teens, I'd been plagued with spots and greasy hair and I wore a brace to straighten my teeth. Some of the other girls were beautiful. Slim, tall, attractive with shining hair and amazing figures . . . I longed to look like them, dreamed of turning from an ugly duckling into a beautiful swan.

'Show her your cock,' Sally Brompton said, grabbing Rod's crotch.

'Yeah, make her touch it,' Julie joined in. 'Go on, Rod. Force the spotty slag to suck the spunk out of your cock.'

Rod dropped his trousers and proudly displayed the erect shaft of his penis as the girls forced me to my knees. Still in my tender years, I'd never seen a penis before. I must have been the only virgin in the school. All the girls had done it, I knew as I gazed at Rod's huge balls. They'd all had sex. The daily chatter in the playground continually centred around boys. The girls would swap stories, and I'd have to listen to who had done what with which boy the previous evening. Brian Rogers had a huge cock. Ian Williams was a good fuck. Robin Hodges shot out more spunk than the other boys put together.

I despised Southmoore School, hated every aspect of it. I was always making out to my mother that I felt ill, just to get a day or two off. I played truant whenever I could get away with it. Falsifying dental appointments, dreaming up funerals . . . I did whatever I could to get away from the school. But the Brook Street Gang were always there, making my life a misery. Even during the holidays, they'd hang around at the end of my street. I became fearful of leaving the house, feeling sick every Monday morning when I had to go to school.

Grabbing my wrist, Julie made me touch Rod's penis. She wrapped my fingers around the warm shaft near the base of his rock-hard organ. His pubic hairs tickling my hand as Julie held my wrist and Rob swung his hips, I knew that I couldn't take his cock into my mouth. The very thought sickened me. Did the girls suck his penis? I couldn't understand why they'd want to do such a thing.

His foreskin rolling back and forth, his purple knob repeatedly appearing and disappearing, Rod began to gasp. Sally grabbed tufts of my blonde hair and yanked my head up. I thought that she was going to force me to take Rod's penis into my mouth, but she just held me there as he rocked his hips and moved his penis back and forth within my clasped hand. They never raped me. Whatever they were, they weren't stupid enough to rape me. Their fun was derived from humiliating me, degrading me, forcing me to expose the most private parts of my young body. *Why me?* I wondered a million times. I'd lie in my bed at night, wondering why they'd chosen to destroy my life.

The white liquid finally jetted from Rod's purple knob, raining over my face as the girls held me tight. Running down my cheeks, dribbling down my chin and splattering my school blouse, his sperm continued to shoot from his penis as the girls giggled and mocked me. *Cumslut, dirty whore, spunk-lover* . . . Sally moved behind me, her hands roving over my body, her fingers unbuttoning my blouse. My bra lifted clear of my small breasts, shrieks of laughter resounded around the common as Rod's sperm rained over my elongated nipples.

My audience gathered round as Rod's sperm splattered the small mounds of my breasts and trickled over the smooth flesh of my stomach. I'd never felt so degraded, so ashamed and embarrassed. Sally suggested that Rod push his penis into my mouth. She called it *throat-fucking*. Grabbing my head, she pinched my nose with her fingers, forcing me to eventually open my mouth and gasp for air. She hissed her vile expletives, called me flea-bag, fuck-face, cumslut, cunt-mouth . . .

Luckily me for, some people were approaching, their voices growing louder – and the gang fled.

Crawling into the bushes like a wounded animal, I hid not only from the passing people but the world at large. I felt dirty, degraded in the extreme. My pleated skirt was covered with white stains. Spunk. I later told my mother that we'd had a cookery class and . . . I don't know whether she believed me or not. As I cupped my small breasts in my bra, the sperm soaking into the silk material, I swore to have my vengeance. But how? I didn't know how or when, but I did know that the day would come when I'd vent my revenge on each and every member of the Brook Street Gang.

'Southmoore,' the mechanical voice bellowed through the Tannoy as I stepped off the train. Working in London, I'd never thought that I'd return to my home town. My family had moved away, I had no friends there, so there was no reason to return. The town harboured dreadful memories – nightmares – for me and I'd sworn never to return. But then the MD of the company I worked for had announced that they were opening new offices in Southmoore and I was to head the project. Walking out of the station, I looked at the familiar shops, the road leading to the common. Memories flooding back, I wondered what Rod Johnson was doing, what he'd turned out to be. Where was Sally Brompton? Was Julie Wicks still around? Perhaps they'd married, moved away and – Perhaps they were still living in Southmoore.

I was twenty-eight and, although I say it myself, had turned from an ugly duckling into a fine swan. Slim, tall, attractive, with long blonde hair . . . The chubby, spotty teenager with the greasy hair and brace had transformed into a stunning young woman. If I did happen to run into Sally or Julie . . . They'd never recognize me. I tried to put all thoughts of the Brook Street Gang behind me as I walked the short distance to the new office complex. Rod Johnson, Julie Wicks, Sally Brompton . . . I'd moved on, and could only hope that they had too.

'Miss Michaels?' a young man asked me as I walked into the building.

'Yes,' I replied. 'You must be Walker.'

'That's right. John Walker, junior assistant to—'

'There's no need for details,' I cut in coldly.

'No, of course not. It's a pleasure to meet you, Miss Michaels. Your office is on the top floor. If you take the lift—'

'Thank you,' I interrupted him again. 'I'm sure that I'm perfectly capable of finding the top floor. Send some coffee up, would you?'

'Certainly, Miss Michaels.'

I didn't like creeps who thought that they could climb the promotional ladder with their pathetic pleasantries. Arse-lickers, Dave called them. Dave Bryant was the managing director. He was a tall, good-looking man in his mid-forties. He was also married but that hadn't stopped him throat-fucking me whenever I was due for promotion. The casting couch? Perhaps I was as bad as Walker? He was an arse-licker, and I was a cocksucker . . .

My office was large and airy with a view of the common. Unfortunately, I could see Southmoore School, kids milling about in the playground. From my top-floor office, they looked like ants. I'd been an ant once. Were the girls talking about fucking the boys? Were they excitedly telling each other how they'd wanked so-and-so's cock and watched the spunk shoot out? Southmoore School. The bain of my early teens. But I'd moved on. I was successful, the deputy managing director of a huge medical supply company. Where was Julie Wicks? Working in a burger bar?

'Your coffee, Miss Michaels,' Walker said, knocking on my office door and entering with a tray. 'The interviews . . .'

'Are they here?' I asked, checking my watch.

'Three of them are.'

'There should be six. Right, if the others turn up, send them packing. If they can't get to the interview on time, they don't deserve the job. Send the first one up.'

'Certainly, Miss Michaels.'

As Walker left, I poured my coffee and pondered on the forthcoming interviews. I didn't want to waste time talking to pathetic women about their previous jobs and wading though references that were more than likely a bunch of lies. I needed a personal secretary, and quickly. There was work to be done. Setting up what was virtually a new company was a daunting task. But hard work was my forte. Since starting with the company when I'd left school, I'd thrown myself into my work. And, step by step, I'd climbed the ladder to success.

As the first girl knocked on the door and entered, I sat down behind my huge desk and invited her to sit opposite me. She was well-dressed, her black hair very long but neat and tidy. She was about my age, which pleased me. I couldn't abide silly teenage girls who wasted time doing their nails and talking about boys . . . Reminiscent of Southmoore School? Silly teenage girls had no place in a successful company.

'You are?' I asked her, taking a file from my briefcase. It was most unusual for me to be disorganized.

'Brompton,' she replied. 'Sally Brompton.'

Frowning, my heart racing, I raised my head and stared hard at her. I could barely believe that this was Sally Brompton. With long dark hair and a pretty face, her full breasts billowing her white blouse . . . When I'd last set eyes on her at school she'd had very short hair and her tits had been virtually non-existent. She'd changed beyond recognition. But so had I. She obviously didn't recognize me as she squeezed her hands together nervously and looked around the office. Memories flooding back again, I recalled her words that afternoon on the common, on my birthday. *Finger her dirty cunt. Shove your finger up the fat cow's dirty little cunt.*

Was this the day I'd been waiting for? I wondered. All those years ago, I'd sworn to have my vengeance. Had my time come? I was about to inform her that she wasn't suitable for the post when I had an idea. I'd derive little satisfaction from turning her down. I'd be better off hiring her and then sacking her a week or two later. Better still, I'd take her on and . . . Sally Brompton would get the job, I decided. And her time at Dagridge Medical Supplies was going to be sheer bloody hell. What goes around comes around.

According to the file, the little tart had done well for herself. She'd climbed the ladder of promotion at an insurance company and had become PA to the MD. Not bad going for a slut. She enjoyed the job, she told me. But she wanted to expand her horizons and thought that Dagridge Medical Supplies was the sort of go-ahead company . . . I'd heard all this crap before. I'd interviewed dozens of people who had expressed a longing to be part of a dynamic team, blah, blah, blah. Bollocks. They'd wanted a job that paid well, that was all. They didn't give a fuck for the company. I fired all the usual questions at Sally Brompton and made notes as appropriate. I then quizzed her about her personal life.

'Married?' I asked, looking searchingly into her dark eyes.

'No,' she replied, somewhat sheepishly.

'Kids?'

'No, no children.'

'What do you do in the evenings?'

'The evenings?' She frowned, obviously wondering what the right answer was. 'I watch TV or perhaps go out with friends,' she finally replied.

'You don't get pissed every night?'

'No, of course not.'

'Good. I can't have you turning up late with a hangover. Do that once, and you're out.'

'You mean, I've got the job?'

'Yes, you have.'

'Oh, thank you,' she trilled.

'Don't get overexcited,' I snapped. 'There's a three-month probation period. If I don't like you . . .' *Shove your finger up the fat cow's dirty little cunt.* 'Should I decide that you're not suitable, you'll be out.'

'Yes, yes, I understand.'

'I'm a bitch,' I said, obviously surprising her. 'You'll find that I'm a hard boss to work for. That's how I got where I am. By treading on toes, using people . . . In fact, the staff call me the bitch from hell. Fill in this form.'

I passed her a form and scrutinized her as I sipped my coffee. She was extremely attractive. Nothing like I would have imagined her to be. Remembering her from school, I would have thought that she . . . She'd been a bitch at school, but she wasn't a patch on the bitch that *I*'d become. I was queen of the bitches, and proud of it. I gazed at her fingernails as she filled in the form. At school, she had bitten her nails, but now they were long and painted red. Her blouse falling away from her chest as she leaned forward to write, I spied the firm mounds of her breasts.

Sally Brompton had forced me to suck her nipples one Friday after netball. We'd been in the changing rooms. She'd waited with her gang until the others had gone, blocking my exit and giggling as she'd unbuttoned her blouse. The gang had forced me to suck the brown buds topping the small bumps of her chest. They'd laughed and called me names as I'd suckled on each nipple in turn. Before allowing me to leave, they'd made me take my knickers off. I'd had to walk home naked beneath my skirt and then explain to my mother . . . But now, the worm was turning. Sally was going to discover soon that I truly *was* the bitch from hell.

Her long black hair veiling her face as she filled in the form, I knew that she'd never discover that I was the Rachael Michaels whom she had taken great delight in sexually abusing all those years ago. My surname hadn't changed, but these days I was known as Fiona Michaels. I'd taken on the name Fiona after my mother had passed away. My father missed her terribly and . . . anyway, I'd become Fiona. Even Dave Bryant didn't know me as Rachael.

'When do I start?' Sally asked, pushing the completed form back across the desk. 'I have to give a month's notice, so—'

'You'll start today,' I interrupted her.

'But . . . I have to hand in my notice and . . . I can't let my boss down like that.'

'Of course you can. You'll get nowhere in this dog-eat-dog world unless you . . .' I grinned at her. 'There are others waiting downstairs,' I said threateningly. 'I'm sure I'll have no trouble finding a suitable applicant to fill the post. You'll start now, or you can forget it.'

She bit her lip and frowned. 'All right,' she conceded with a sigh. 'I'll start now.'

'Good. I think I'm going to like you, Sally,' I lied. 'There are a few ground rules. You'll call me Miss Michaels at all times. You'll do as I ask when I ask without question. And don't go fucking other members of staff.'

She locked her dark-eyed gaze to mine. 'Pardon?' she gasped, frowning at me.

'I don't want you getting fucked by male members of staff. Once you've been fucked, you won't be able to concentrate on the job. Fleeting kisses, knee-tremblers in the lift, a quick blow job in the stationery cupboard . . . Get yourself fucked, and you won't be able to give the one hundred and fifty per cent I expect of you.'

'Yes, I understand,' she murmured.

'Good. OK, your office is through that door. Go and take a look. When you've done that, familiarize yourself with the building. This is also my first day here so I can't help. Not that I'm interested in where the canteen is, of course. Well?'

'I'm sorry?'

'Go on, then.'

'Oh . . . yes, right,' she murmured, smiling as she walked towards her office.

'Er . . . Sally,' I called, feigning a pained expression. 'I see you're wearing trousers.'

'Yes, I thought—'

'You'll wear skirts – *short* skirts – in future. Men should look like men, and women like women. You'd better go home and change. No doubt you'll want to collect your things from the insurance company.'

'Yes, I'll have to empty my desk.'

'OK, do that after you've looked around the building. It's now ten-thirty. Do what you have to do, have some lunch, and be back in my office at two.'

'Yes, Miss Michaels,' she replied obediently.

I was loving every minute of this. But, more, I was looking forward to the future. I couldn't believe that Sally Brompton was, at long last, in my grip. She and her cronies had destroyed my schooldays, ruined my early teenage years . . . But now the tables were about to turn. I'd make sure that she left the office late on the days when she had something planned for the evening. I'd overload her with work, grind her down until she was an exhausted wreck. I'd not only make her time at the company a complete misery, I'd also wreck her private life.

Wondering whether she was still in contact with the other members of the gang, I watched as she emerged from her office and walked towards the door. She mumbled something about looking around the building before leaving and closed the door behind her. Perhaps she'd kept in touch with Rod Johnson, I mused, finishing my coffee. He'd fucked her often enough. They'd always got on well together at school. Two of a kind. Perhaps he was still fucking her?

'What do you want, Walker?' I snapped as he knocked and entered.

He fidgeted with his tie. 'The filing cabinets have arrived, Miss Michaels,' he informed me. 'The men are—'

'And? What the hell has that got to do with me?'

'They want to bring them up to your office.'

'Now?'

'Well, yes.'

'Tell them to come back later. I'm busy now.'

'But Miss Michaels . . . They've come all the way from—'

'I don't give a toss where they've come from, Walker. I'm busy.'

'Yes, of course. I'll tell them.'

I suppose my attitude was a result of what the Brook Street Gang had put me though. After a horrendous time at school, and then my mother passing away . . . I admit that I'd become angry and bitter. But it had been my attitude that had got me where I was. That, and allowing the MD to throat-fuck me, of course. At school I'd been weak, frightened, timid . . . Far removed from the successful bitch I now was. I had the Brook Street Gang to thank for that. And my ability to suck Dave's cock with expertise.

I'd first sucked cock on the common while being pinned to the ground by Sally Brompton and Julie Wicks. This time I hadn't been taking a short cut, but nonetheless I'd been dragged onto the common by the gang after school one afternoon. The boy's name was Brad Masters. He was a thug and a bully, just like the other members of the gang. He'd taken his trousers off and had been waving his cock at me when Sally Brompton had suggested that he fuck my mouth. I remembered the salty taste of his huge knob, my lips rolling back and forth along his veined shaft as he repeatedly drove his purple plum to the back of my throat.

I'd swallowed his sperm, much to the delight of Sally Brompton. I'd had no choice. His knees either side of my body, his weight resting on his hands, he'd mouth-fucked me, throat-fucked me. He'd finally stood up and put his trousers back on as the others had laughed at the white liquid bubbling between my lips. Julie Wicks had repeatedly kicked me as I lay coughing and spluttering on the ground. I'll never forget her shoe swinging into my stomach, my chest, as she'd called me a fucking slut. Sally Brompton had spat on me before leaving. I can still recall her saliva running down my face, mingling with the boy's sperm . . .

'Hi, Fiona,' Dave Bryant said, grinning as he entered my office. 'How's it going?'

'I've hired a secretary,' I told him.

'Any good?'

'Yes, she's fine.'

'OK, I've got the figures you wanted,' he said, sitting opposite me and brushing his dark hair back with his fingers. 'Fuck me, it's hot today,' he complained, tossing a file onto the desk. 'Is there no air conditioning in here?'

'I switched it on when I arrived. Perhaps it's not working.'

'I'll get it sorted. We need another two girls for the sales office.'

'I thought that had been dealt with, Dave.'

'Tim Black fucked up.'

'That doesn't surprise me.'

'We'll have to advertise again, which takes time and—'

'I'll ask Sally whether she knows of anyone,' I interrupted him.

'Sally?'

'Sally Brompton, my new secretary.'

'Ah, right. Yes, yes, that's a good idea. We need two girls as soon as possible.'

'Leave it with me.'

'Thanks, Fiona. OK, I'm going to take a look around. Do the Big Boss routine and frighten the new members of staff. What do you reckon of Southmoore? I know you've not had a chance to see the town yet . . .'

'Southmoore is . . . I think it's going to be OK, Dave.'

'Good. I know you had your reservations. Have you given any more thought to moving here?'

'Yes, I've decided to find a flat. Coming in by train every day won't be much fun. I'll phone a few estate agents this afternoon.'

'OK, keep me posted. I'll be invited to your house-warming, no doubt?'

'No doubt.'

'We might even sidle off and . . .'

'I'm sure we shall, Dave. I'll try to find a place with a garden full of bushes, just for you.'

'We'll slip into the garden when the party is in full swing and you can show me around,' he chuckled. 'What are you doing for lunch?'

'Er . . . I've nothing planned.'

'Great. There's a pub over the road. The Hen and something.'

'Yes, I know it.'

'I'll see you there. About one?'

'I'll be there.'

'Great. See you later.'

I suppose I hadn't sucked Dave off purely to secure my promotion. I was feeling down when I'd first unzipped his trousers and pulled his cock out. My only boyfriend had left me, gone off with some other woman. I was in need of . . . I don't know what I was in need of. A throat-fuck? Dave's marriage had never been exactly stable. What with the hours he worked . . . I suppose we were both in the wrong place and the wrong time and . . . I'd knelt on the floor and sucked his cock. It hadn't become a regular thing, maybe a couple of times a month. He liked it, I enjoyed it . . . And, of course, it's always good to keep the boss happy.

Southmoore was a smallish town and I wasn't really surprised to see Rod Johnson in the pub. For a moment, I wondered whether Sally had arranged to meet him there. But he was with a couple of other men and, thank God, he didn't recognize me. I watched him from the corner of my eye as I ordered a vodka and tonic. He was looking me up and down, obviously wondering whether I fucked. Had he known that I was the spotty teenager he'd spunked all over . . . Sitting on a bar stool, I listened to his conversation while I waited for Dave.

'She's going for an interview today,' he said.

'Have you heard from her?' one of the men asked.

'No, I haven't. We'll find out tonight when we see her.'

'When we fuck her,' the third man laughed.

'Shush, Brad,' Rod whispered. 'We don't want the whole pub to know.'

*Brad*? I thought, eyeing the man. Was this really Brad Masters? Shit, this *was* a small town, I reflected, wondering who the third man was. *When we fuck her*? What the hell did they get up to? My heart racing, I thought of the Brook Street Gang. Sally, Rod, Brad . . . They were too old to play games now, though, weren't they? Surely the gang had fallen apart when they'd left school. Gulping down my drink, I ordered another one and continued to listen to the conversation.

'I don't know where Julie has got to,' Rod murmured, looking across the pub as the door opened. 'She told me that she'd be here.'

'We'll see her tonight,' Rob said, downing his pint. 'She never misses a meeting. Beers all round?'

*A meeting*? This wasn't a meeting of the Brook Street Gang, surely? I was going to have to keep my eye on Sally, try to glean a little information about her nighttime activities. Checking my watch as I downed my second vodka, I wondered whether Dave had been held up. Ordering another drink, I decided that it would be my last. I had work to do and I didn't want to get pissed in the middle of the day. Sitting at a corner table, I watched the three gang members as I sipped my vodka.

The door swung open and I lowered my head as Sally Brompton breezed into the pub. She'd been home and had changed into a short skirt like I'd told her to. Her legs were long and slender. I had to admit that she really did look good. This was going to be interesting, I thought as Rod bought her a drink. If she noticed me . . . I made out that I hadn't seen her as she looked my way. She nudged Rod, obviously telling him that I was her new boss. She was about to walk towards my table when another girl entered the pub and joined the group – the gang.

'Hi, Julie,' Sally trilled. My stomach churning, I stared at the girl. Julie Wicks. The little bitch who had . . . Forgetting the past, I turned my thoughts to the present. Dave had said that we needed a couple of girls for the sales office. How ironic it would be if I employed Julie Wicks. Gazing at her pretty face, the deep cleavage of her breasts revealed by her partially open blouse, I couldn't help but recall the past. Her shoe repeatedly driving into my stomach, my chest, as I'd lain on the ground with sperm bubbling from my mouth . . .

I stared at the girl, remembering, seething with anger, hatred welling from the pit of my stomach . . . This wasn't going to do me any good, I knew. My stomach knotting with anger wasn't going to help. At least I now knew that the gang was still in existence and that they held meetings. Thankfully, none of them had recognized me. Were the other members still around? I wondered. Apart from Sally, Julie, Rob and Brad, there'd been Kathy Higgins and Kenny Smith, Lucy Barlow . . .

'Hello, Miss Michaels,' Sally said as she approached, her face beaming.

'Sally, sit down for a minute,' I said, a wicked plan coming into my mind. 'We need a couple of extra girls for the sales office. I was wondering whether you might know of anyone?'

'Er . . . well, Julie isn't happy where she is. That's the girl I was with over there.'

'Yes, I can see her. Is she computer literate?'

'Oh, yes. She uses a computer all the time.'

'She appears to be presentable. She speaks well, I hope?'

'Yes, yes, she does. Shall I send her over?'

'No, definitely not. I don't conduct interviews in pubs. My office at three o'clock sharp. If she's interested, that is.'

'I'll tell her, Miss Michaels.'

'You do that, Sally,' I said, downing my vodka and standing up. 'And don't be late back.'

'No, no, I won't.'

Leaving the pub, I made my way back to the office and pondered on the Brook Street Gang. I knew that I could easily allow them to take my mind off my work. I was going to have to be strong. My work was the priority, the destruction of the gang came second. Easier said than done. Images of Kathy Higgins sitting on my face looming in my mind, I couldn't help recall the taste of her vagina. Kenny Smith had pinned me to the ground, allowing Kathy to rub her clitoris over my mouth. She'd come, her sex juices streaming over my face as Kenny had sucked on my small tits.

'Julie will be here at three, Miss Michaels,' Sally announced as she entered my office.

'Good. You've done well, Sally. I think we're going to hit it off, don't you?'

'I hope so, Miss Michaels.'

'So, what are your plans for this evening? Are you doing anything interesting?'

'I'm meeting my friends, the people I was with in the pub.'

'That'll be nice. Have you known them long?'

'We were all at school together.'

'Ah, an old school gang.'

'Yes, yes – we did have a gang.'

'I never kept in touch with my school friends,' I said, smiling at her. 'Mind you, I went to school in Scotland. What was your gang for? I mean, was it just a group of friends or something more sinister?'

'We . . . we were just a group of friends,' she murmured.

'Our little gang was called the Highland Babes, of all things,' I laughed. 'What was yours called?'

'We were the Brook Street Gang. We still are.'
'It's still a gang?'
'Yes. We still meet regularly and . . .'
'And what, Sally?'
'We just meet, that's all.'
'I see. Right, we have work to do. Switch your computer on and familiarize yourself with the spreadsheets that we use. The company database . . . Here's a list of people who need updating. Our new address, phone and fax numbers and the like. You'll find the details on the letterhead paper, which should be in your office unless Walker has fucked up again. It's a boring job but it has to be done. You'll find all the names and addresses in the database. E-mail each contact with our new details.'
'Yes, Miss Michaels,' Sally murmured.
'If you have any problems, give me a shout.'
As she went into her office, I sat down behind my desk. I felt smug, a sense of satisfaction welling from the pit of my stomach as I mulled over my plan. Sally would spend the best part of the afternoon working on the computer. The work had to be done properly, and I was sure she could manage. But I might have to insist that she work late into the evening. There would be mistakes that she'd have to correct before leaving the office. She'd have to go through each entry again and change something. I'd dream up some mistake or other later, I thought, wondering where Dave had got to. I was going to enjoy having Sally as my personal secretary. I was going to enjoy taking her to hell and back.

# 2

Walker showed Julie Wicks into my office at three on the dot. Concealing a grin as she sat opposite me, I scrutinized her. Again, I couldn't help recalling her shoe swinging into my stomach as I lay on the ground with Brad's sperm dribbling from my mouth. She'd kicked me in the stomach, the chest . . . *Now it's my turn*, I thought smugly as she tossed her long blonde hair over her shoulder and waited for me to say something. I didn't need to use physical violence. I had a far better way to vent my revenge.

'Are you married?' I asked her.

She looked nervous. 'Yes, I am,' she replied.

'Children?'

'No, not yet.'

'Good. I can't abide women not turning up for work because their snivelling little brats have thrown up. You may have already gathered that political correctness means nothing to me. So, where are you working at the moment?'

'For a manufacturing company. I'm in accounts.'

'I see. And you use a computer?'

'Oh, yes. All the time.'

'What does your husband do?'

'Ian works for a local bakery. Hill's Pies, on the industrial estate.'

Ian Marshal had been a member of the Brook Street Gang. He'd been more of a part-time member, really. He'd come along to the common on the odd occasion more to leer at me than take part in any sexual abuse. I suppose that, if there'd been one gang member I would have had to rate above the rest, it would have had to be Ian. I'd always thought that he was against the bullying, the abuse. I used to think that he was going along with the others only because he was in the gang and it was expected of him. Perhaps I'd been wrong. Maybe he'd been as bad as the others. He'd obviously not done very well for himself. Marrying a slag like Julie, a career in baking . . .

'He's a baker?' I asked, deciding to mock her.

She grimaced as if the question hurt. 'Yes,' she finally replied.

'Not much of a career. I suppose it's rather like sweeping the road or cleaning public toilets. Someone has to do it.'

'He's a *professional* baker,' she answered sharply, taking the bait.

'Yes, I'm sure he is,' I sighed patronizingly. 'We're looking for two girls, actually. Two girls to complete the sales team. Tim Black is head of sales. I'm going to replace him but he doesn't know that yet. I'm a . . . What was your name again?'

'Julie Marshal.'

'Ah, yes. I'm a hard case, Julie. You'll hear the staff refer to me as the bitch from hell. I don't mind that because they're right. I *am* the bitch from hell. OK, fill in this form with all your details and I'll alert Tim about your arrival.'

'I've got the job?' she asked, her blue eyes wide as she gazed at me.

'There's a three-month probation period. You start tomorrow morning. And don't tell me that you have to hand in your notice. The manufacturing company you *worked* for can go to hell as far as I'm concerned. You work for me now. Complete the form and I'll get Sally to take you down to meet Tim Black.' I pushed a blank application form brusquely across the desktop towards her.

Reclining in my swivel chair as Julie took a pen from her handbag, I looked beneath the desk at her shoes. One kick in my stomach, another to my chest, her foot sinking again into my stomach . . . So, Ian Marshal worked for a local bakery. Hill's Pies. I just might have to contact the company, I mused. Better still, it might be an idea to meet Ian. Should I put his fidelity to the test? Perhaps I'd ring Julie at her home and ask for Ian. I'd stammer, plant seeds of doubt in her mind. She'd think that I was seeing him behind her back.

Julie finally finished filling in the form and pushed it back across the desk. I watched her open her bag and drop the pen inside. Hatred welled in my heart, anger knotted my stomach. But I had to keep my cool. My time of vengeance was approaching and I didn't want to spoil my plans. Grabbing the phone, I ordered Sally to take the girl down to the sales department and ask for Tim Black. Sally emerged from her office, her dark eyes sparkling as she led her fellow gang member away. She was obviously pleased to have a friend working in the same company. Waiting until she'd closed the door, I slipped into her office and took a look at the monitor screen of her computer.

She'd done very well, I observed. She was almost halfway though the list. She might have made an excellent secretary for me – had she not sexually abused me at school. Sitting at her desk, I grabbed the computer mouse and decided to make a few alterations to her work. I felt no guilt, only a terrific sense of satisfaction as I closed the database without saving Sally's work and then reopened it. *All that work lost*, I giggled inwardly, returning to my desk. She'd just have to stay on late that evening.

I pretended to be on the phone when Sally returned from taking Julie downstairs. Her long legs strode across the plush carpet and she closed her office door behind her, giving me the opportunity to make a discreet phone call. I remembered that Ian had been pretty keen on another girl at school. Jenny Wilder. Could Jenny tempt him to commit adultery? I wondered. Directory Enquiries gave me the number of Hill's Pies. I punched the buttons on my phone, planning what I was going to say as a badly spoken switchboard girl answered. I asked to be put through to Ian Marshal. She obliged, a click and then a ringing tone sounding in my ear.

'Hello,' a male voice answered.

'Ian?' I asked. I could hear the whir of machinery in the background. Was he making pies? 'Ian Marshal?'

'Yes. Who's this?'

'Jenny Wilder. Remember me?'

'Jenny, yes.' He sounded pleased to hear from me. 'How are you?'

'I'm fine. I'm back in Southmoore and thought we might meet up for a drink.'

'Someone said that you went to Australia.'

'Yes, I did. So, how about a drink? We can chat about old times.'

'Er . . . yes, all right.'

'You sound hesitant, Ian.'

'I'm . . . I'm married,' he confessed.

*Don't I just know it!*

'But it's not a problem.'

'Isn't it?' *It will be, I'll make sure of that.*

'No, no. Look, I'll meet you this evening. Remember the pub we used to call the Pig's Arse?'

'The Hog's Bottom. Yes, I do. It's a dreadful name for a pub.'

'I'll see you there after work. Say, six-thirty?'

'It's rather early, but . . .'

'I married Julie Wicks,' he announced as if by way of an excuse.

*More fool you.* 'Ah, that explains it,' I laughed. 'She was rather . . . How shall I put it?'

'Bloody awkward at times,' he sighed. 'Things aren't easy but . . . I often have to work late so I'll have no problems.'

'Julie Wicks,' I giggled. 'She was in the Brook Street Gang, wasn't she?'

'Yes, so was I. We still are.'

'The gang is still going?'

'More so than ever. There's a meeting this evening but . . . Look, I can't talk now. I'll see you later.'

'I'll look forward to it, Ian,' I breathed huskily before replacing the receiver.

*Step one*, I thought happily. Jenny Wilder had been slim with blonde hair and I was sure that Ian wouldn't question my identity. He certainly wouldn't realize that I was Rachael Michaels. Still, planning the demise of the Brook Street Gang had to take second place to my work and I spent the rest of the afternoon doing what I was supposed to be doing. But my mind repeatedly drifted back to my schooldays. Images of Rod's cock shooting spunk over my tits loomed in my mind. Taking control of my thoughts, I did actually manage to call a couple of estate agents and I arranged to look at some flats the following morning.

At five o'clock, Sally emerged from her office with her bag slung over her shoulder. She looked a little worried as she headed for the door. She probably thought that she'd done something wrong on the computer and had lost all her work. There was no way she could have caught up, let alone finished the job, I knew. I could almost smell the sweet scent of revenge as she opened the door to leave. My stomach somersaulting, I suggested that she show me how she'd got on before going home. She bit her lip and followed me back to her office. She was nervous, almost frightened as she switched her computer on.

'Oh,' I sighed disappointedly, looking at her computer screen. I felt wicked, nasty. 'You're not even halfway through, Sally.'

'I know,' she breathed despondently. 'I was doing so well and then . . .'

'If you're not up to the job . . .'

'The computer must have crashed or something. I took Julie down to meet Tim Black. When I got back, all my work had gone.'

I could feel my stomach churning with excitement. 'Didn't you back it up?' I asked her accusingly.

'I was about to when you asked me to take Julie down to meet Tim Black. When I returned—'

'There's no need to repeat yourself, Sally,' I cut in angrily. 'This had to be completed today. This isn't a very good start, is it? I suggest you finish the job before going home.'

'Finish? But I have to—'

'The database is going on-line in the morning. I don't want clients being given the wrong information. I'm sorry, but this has to be finished today.'

Leaving her office, I closed the door behind me and grabbed my jacket. Stepping out of the lift on the ground floor, I told the security man that Sally was working late. As I left the building, I once more felt a great sense of satisfaction. *She used to wait for me after school, her gang waylaying me and* . . . But now I was in control. She'd have to work for at least two hours to finish the job. I'd been extremely fair to her, really. She'd be away by seven o'clock and still have time to go to her meeting. Of course, coming on too strong on the first day might have sent her packing. I didn't want her to leave the company – yet. The longer she stayed, the longer I could make her life hell. I was going to have to find a balance between making her life a misery and yet keeping her on.

Walking into the pub, I checked my watch. I was more than half an hour early but I was in no rush to catch the train back to London. The sooner I got myself a flat, the better, I thought, ordering a vodka and tonic and sitting at a table by the window. Initially, I'd sworn that I'd never move to Southmoore. I'd imagined walking down the street or wandering around a supermarket and bumping into Sally or Rod. In my early teens, I'd dreaded turning street corners, walking into shops. I'd dreaded leaving the house.

I recalled bumping into Sally and Julie early one Sunday morning. My father had asked me to buy him a Sunday paper. I'd thought I'd be safe at that time of day, and had breezed into the newsagents without a care. But they'd been there, hovering by the magazines.

They'd followed me as I'd left the shop. I remembered how my heart had raced, my hands trembling, as I'd clutched the paper and quickened my step. Passing an alleyway, I'd frozen as Rod had leaped out and grabbed me. Sally and Julie had lifted my T-shirt while Rod had held me tight. Yanking my bra up, they'd laughed at the small mounds of my breasts.

I remembered the tears streaming down my face as Julie had knelt on the ground and pulled my skirt up. Yanking my panties down, exposing the hairless crack of my pussy to the leering audience, she'd pinched my fleshy outer lips. She'd torn my panties in two and tossed the garment to the ground. My mother had bought them for my birthday, a matching set, silk panties and bra. Rod stamped on them, grinding them into the mud as Sally ripped my bra off and threw it to the ground.

I'd dreaded the thought of returning to live in Southmoore. Me, the bitch from hell, frightened? It wasn't so much fear. I knew that setting eyes on any of my abusers would bring horrendous memories flooding back. But now? Now I knew that the gang was still in existence, they didn't recognize me, I had Sally and Julie working for me . . . It wasn't really surprising that Sally had met her gang in the pub at lunchtime. This was a small town, after all. And now I was to pose as Jenny Wilder and meet Ian. Julie's husband? I'd never have guessed that they'd end up married. Julie and Rod, maybe, but . . .

Noticing a man walk into the pub, I checked my watch again. Five to six. He was about my age, wearing jeans and a T-shirt. It was Ian Marshal, I knew as I scrutinized him. *Another early bird*, I mused. He was tall with large hands and dark swept-back hair. Apart from looking a bit older, he hadn't really changed. As he bought a pint of lager and looked my way, I flashed him a smile. He frowned, obviously wondering whether I was Jenny. If he'd thought that Jenny had gone to Australia, he'd not have seen her for some time and probably wouldn't recognize her. As he approached, I introduced myself.

'God,' he breathed, sitting opposite me and dumping his mobile phone and car keys on the table. 'You *have* changed.'

'You look the same,' I said, licking my red lips provocatively. 'You're still extremely good-looking.'

'You've turned out . . . You're a real stunner, Jenny.'

'Thanks,' I murmured, sipping my vodka. 'So, you ended up marrying Julie Wicks?'

'Yes, yes, that's right.' He took a gulp of his beer. 'It just kind of happened, I suppose. One thing led to another.'

'That's a shame,' I sighed. 'I mean, I'm happy for you both but . . .' I unbuttoned the top of my blouse, revealing the roundness of my breasts. 'I was hoping that you'd be free.'

'Jenny, we can still see each other.' He eyed the cleavage of my breasts, obviously hoping for a glimpse of my areolae. 'How long are you here for? Are you going back to Oz?'

'I'm not sure yet. Ian, I'm not a marriage wrecker.'

'No, of course not. My marriage isn't too good,' he lied, obviously dying to get his hand inside my panties.

'In that case, I suppose we could see each other.'

'That'll be Julie,' he breathed as his mobile phone rang. 'Checking up on me, no doubt.'

'Aren't you going to answer it?'

'No. When I'm at work, I can never hear the damned

thing. I'll tell her that I was working late. She's probably realized that by now.'

'You said that the Brook Street Gang was still in existence?' I probed.

'Yes, it is.'

'I was never sure what the gang was about at school. And now you say that it's still going. What do you get up to? What's the gang for?'

'I'm sworn to secrecy, Jenny,' he sighed.

'Secrecy? You can tell me, Ian. After all, we are about to . . . well, you know.'

His dark gaze fell again to the cleavage of my breasts. 'At school . . . I didn't really want to be a part of it. No, I can't say that. To be honest, I liked the sex.'

'Sex? Is that what the gang's about?'

'Not really. We had sex, experimented with sex . . .'

'I remember that fat spotty girl . . . What was her name?'

He grimaced. 'Do you mean Rachael Michaels?' he asked me.

'Yes, that's it. She used to be frightened of your gang. I remember her hiding in school, waiting until everyone had gone before leaving.'

'We used to get her on the common and . . . well, strip her naked and things.'

'God, I didn't realize. No wonder she was frightened. You mean, you raped her?'

'Not exactly.'

'Why? Why make her life hell?'

'I don't know. We were young and . . . I really don't know.'

'So, what about the gang now?'

'We have regular meetings.'

'What for?'

'They're parties really. A few drinks, sex . . .'

'Sex?' I gasped. 'You mean *orgies*?'

'No, not exactly,' he replied hesitantly.

'But your wife—'

'She's all for it. More so than I am, in fact. There's far more to the Brook Street Gang than . . . How do you think we all got top grades at school?'

'I . . . I don't know.'

'I'd better not say too much. So, what's it like to be back in Southmoore?'

'I'm not sure. I've not been back long enough to come to any conclusions. The place hasn't really changed. Mind you, after Australia, it does seem pretty chilly here. I've not been back to the common yet. God, that place holds some memories for me. I remember . . . Well, my first time was on the common.'

'Who with?'

'Ah, that would be telling.' I flashed him a salacious grin. 'It's a lovely evening, Ian. Shall we take a walk on the common?'

'Yes, why not?' he replied, downing his pint. 'I'll just nip to the loo and we'll go.'

As luck would have it, Ian's mobile phone rang as he went into the toilets. Looking about me, I knew that it was Julie trying to contact him again. He obviously hadn't called her to say that he was working late and . . . *Go on, Rod. Force the spotty slag to suck the spunk out of your cock.* Her words were etched in my memory for ever. I could still feel her foot kicking me. Was this an opportunity to have some fun? Wondering whether to answer Ian's phone, I had a wicked idea. If Julie thought that he was in a pub with another girl . . .

'Hello,' I said, pressing the phone to my ear.
'Who's that?' Julie asked. 'Is Ian there?'
'Oh, er . . . Sorry, I've picked up the wrong phone. Mine's the same as Ian's and—'
'Who is that?'
'Er . . . just a friend,' I breathed. *Just the bitch from hell*.
'A friend? Where is Ian?'
'Sorry, I can't hear you very well. It's rather noisy in the pub.'
'You're in a pub? Where is Ian?'
'He's just getting the drinks in. Who shall I say called?'
The phone went dead as she hung up. I grinned. *A pretty good move*, I thought as Ian returned. The first of many moves towards the slag's nemesis. Finishing my vodka as Ian grabbed his phone and keys, I followed him out of the pub and walked the short distance to the common. His phone rang again as we ambled across the grass. Fortunately for me, he ignored it. Wondering whether to seduce him beneath the evening sun, I looked around me. More memories flooding back, I gazed at the clump of bushes I'd been dragged into by the gang. I really didn't want to be here. The pain was too great. But there again . . .
'I do wish she'd quit ringing me,' Ian said, switching his phone off. 'There. That'll put a stop to it.'
'Shall we sit on the grass over there?' I suggested, pointing to the bushes.
'Yes, good idea. I'd better not be too late home. Julie rang me earlier. Apparently she's got another job. She wants us to celebrate so I can't be too late.'
'I thought you said that it wasn't a problem?'
'No, no, it's not. It's just that . . .'

'Go home now, if that's what you want.'

'No, I'll stay.'

'I don't want to rock the boat, Ian. If you're happy with Julie, then—'

'I'm *not* happy with her,' he stated firmly. 'It's just that she asked me not to work late this evening.'

'I think you'd better go,' I sighed. 'I was hoping that we could at least be friends, but if Julie is—'

'We can, Jenny. I want us to be friends.'

Settling on the grass by the bushes, I felt my clitoris stiffen, my vaginal juices seeping into my panties as I thought about sex. I'd been so tied up with work that I'd not had time even to think about sex, let alone have it. I'd not sucked Dave off for a month or so, and I was beginning to feel really horny. Boyfriends? I'd only had one and he'd gone off with some girl or other. Being career minded, I'd not wanted the ties of long-term relationships. Love, lust, arguments, sulks . . . all such things were unwelcome distractions from my work.

Eyeing the crotch of Ian's jeans, I imagined him fucking Julie. A great sense of elation rolling though me, the reality of the situation hit home. I was with her husband on the common with sex looming in my mind. Sex? Or revenge? A heady cocktail of both, as a matter of fact. Julie was at home, waiting to tell him about her new job. She'd be excited, planning to celebrate her success. Little did she know that her boss was about to fuck her husband . . .

'I always wanted you,' I sighed, my nipples becoming erect beneath the tight material of my bra. 'At school, I could never take my eyes off you.'

'That was a long time ago,' he said, gazing at my naked

thighs as I reclined on the soft grass and stretched my limbs.

'Yes, it was. But I still feel the same way, Ian,' I confessed, nonchalantly parting my thighs.

'You really are stunning, Jenny,' he breathed, moving closer. 'It's a shame that we didn't get together years ago.'

'We're together now, aren't we?'

'Yes, yes, we are.'

Feeling his fingertip running up my inner thigh, I let out a rush of breath. Never in a million years would I have thought that I'd be on the common allowing Ian Marshal to stroke the naked flesh of my thigh. My return to Southmoore was turning out to be extremely interesting. I hadn't thought that I'd bump into any of the gang members, let alone be well on the way to bringing about their downfall. I thought again of Julie waiting at home for her husband, wondering where he was, trying his mobile phone again and wondering why it had been switched off. Ian would lie to her, of course. And probably get away with it. This time.

As his fingertip glided up my leg and slipped across the top of my thigh and under my panties, I decided to mention in passing to Sally that I'd seen a young man on the common. He was with a girl, groping her and behaving despicably. She'd opened her blouse and then dragged the young man into the bushes. I'd ask Sally whether the common was a well-known haunt for young lovers. My plan was for Sally to tell Julie that Ian was with another girl. But how would I let her know that it was Ian Marshal?

I'd work something out, I thought as Ian's fingertip pressed into the fleshy cushion of my outer quim lip. His finger delving between the wet flesh of my inner lips, slipping into the tight sheath of my yearning pussy, I gasped loudly. He massaged the creamy walls of my vagina expertly, making my love juices flow, my clitoris swell, as I lay quivering on the grass. Did he finger Julie's cunt? *I*'d fingered her cunt on the common. She'd forced me to, peeling the lips of her cunt open and making me finger her. *Cunt*. I hated the word. I'd heard it too many times on the common. *Finger the dirty little cow's cunt. Shove your fingers up the fat cow's cunt.*

Many times during my early teens I'd been on the common – in this very spot. Either dragged there or waylaid, I'd been subjected to gross humiliation, obscene violation of my young body. Again, I pondered on how the tables were turning as Ian pulled my wet panties aside and gently slid a second finger into the tightening sheath of my vagina. I'd returned to Southmoore to work, and knew that I shouldn't forget that. Planning my revenge on the gang had to take second place to my work.

But that didn't mean to say that I couldn't enjoy myself. As I felt Ian's hot breath on my thigh, his lips kissing me there, I shuddered as my arousal heightened. I knew that, in seeking vengeance, I'd also find great sexual satisfaction. I was enjoying myself now. Lifting my buttocks clear of the ground, I allowed Ian to tug my silk panties down to my knees. Pulling the garment on down over my feet, he grabbed my ankles, gently parting my legs, opening the rubicund valley of my pussy.

'You're beautiful,' he murmured, his dark-eyed gaze locked to my vaginal crack. Beautiful? He was right, I was beautiful. But, in his mind, *I* had nothing to do with beauty. It was the blonde fleece covering my mons, it was the alluring sight of my firm outer lips and my inner lips protruding from the valley of my cunt. That was what he found beautiful. Did he think me stupid? Next, he'd be telling me that he loved me. I *was* beautiful – my cunt was beautiful, my entire body . . . What he didn't know was that I was also extremely dangerous.

Settling between my parted legs, Ian kissed the soft flesh of my inner thighs, sending delightful quivers through my womb. Breathing deeply, I looked up at the evening sun sparkling through the trees high above me. Again, memories engulfed me, haunting images drowned me. Brad Masters with his knees either side of my head, his cock bloating my mouth, his throbbing knob pumping out his spunk as I coughed and spluttered . . .

'I wish . . .' Ian began, his tongue tasting the swollen flesh of my outer lips.

'Wishing is futile,' I breathed. 'Don't wish for things, Ian. Go out and get them.'

'Yes, you're right.' His tongue leaving the valley of my vagina, he looked at me as I raised my head. 'I don't need to wish now. I've got what I want.'

'Have you?' I asked him, my pink tongue licking my lips. 'My cunt? Is that what you wanted?'

'Er . . . no, I meant . . .'

'Don't lie, Ian. You want my cunt. You don't want me as a person. You want my body.'

'Jenny, you're—'

'Don't say *beautiful*, for God's sake. Beauty is skin deep, as they say. In my case, beauty is cunt deep.'

Resting my head on the soft grass, I closed my eyes as Ian resumed his cunny licking. I could feel his wet tongue running up and down the opening valley of my pussy, his saliva wetting me there, mingling with the juices of my cunt and trickling down between the firm cheeks of my naked buttocks. If he discovered who I was . . . What would he do? What would the Brook Street Gang do if they knew that Rachael Michaels was back in Southmoore? I couldn't imagine them trying to abuse me again, humiliate me. They were too old for that, surely.

As Ian peeled the swollen lips of my vagina wide apart, exposing the delicate inner folds of my sex crack, I knew that he was going to suck my solid clitoris into his hot mouth. I desperately needed to come. My lust juices streaming from my tightening cunt as he fingered me, the hard shaft of my clitoris fully exposed, I hoped that he'd engulf my pleasure bud in his wet mouth and suck out my orgasm. I'd only achieved orgasm once before on the common. Rod and Julie had pinned me down and Sally had torn my knickers off and tossed them into the bushes. My legs forced wide apart, she'd settled between my splayed thighs and examined my bared cunt. She hadn't licked me, but had massaged the nub of my exposed clitoris until I could hold back no longer. The gang had laughed as I'd shuddered and cried out. My copious vaginal juices streaming from my rhythmically tightening pussy as she'd masturbated me, I'd felt humiliated, degraded. But I couldn't deny the immense pleasure she was bringing me. I couldn't stop myself from coming.

That had been the only time I'd derived any semblance of pleasure from the abuse. Normally, I'd been subjected to vulgar sexual acts such as being forced to bend over and part the cheeks of my bottom and expose the brown ring of my anus to the gang. One afternoon after school, Julie and Sally had dragged me onto the common and introduced me to the latest member of the gang. Kenny Smith was a rough lad from the housing estate on the edge of town. After that fateful afternoon in the bushes, I'd dreaded Kenny Smith more than the others put together. His so-called girlfriend, Kathy Higgins, was a common slut. So-called girlfriend? Kathy was a lesbian. At least, she was bisexual. She'd joined us in the bushes that afternoon and stripped me naked. Sally and Julie had decided to show the girl my bottom-hole and had forced me to bend over with my feet wide apart. Kathy Higgins had knelt behind me and examined my most secret hole as the others had laughed at me and called me an anal whore.

I'll never forget Kathy's words as she'd violated me there. *The filthy anal whore deserves to have her dirty little arse finger-fucked.* She'd forced her finger deep into my rectum, giggling as I'd squirmed and tried to break free. She'd fingered me, massaged inside my anal canal for several minutes before yanking her fingers out of my inflamed bottom-hole and committing the most vile act I could have imagined at that early age. Holding my buttocks wide apart, she'd locked her wet lips to my anus, pushed her tongue deep into my rectum – and licked me there.

After that horrendous incident, Kathy and Kenny regularly joined the others on the common. I tried everything to avoid the gang. Hiding in the school, hoping that they'd not bother to wait for me, taking other routes home . . . But they always got me. Kathy wasn't interested in my tits, my pussy. She wanted my bottom-hole, the tight sheath of my rectum. Fingering me there, licking me, sucking on my anus . . . If only I could get my hands on Kathy Higgins now. Kathy

Higgins – but not Kenny Smith. If I ever bumped into him . . . The things Kenny Smith had done to my young body . . . They just didn't bear thinking about.

'Jenny,' Ian murmured, his tongue gliding along the wet valley of my vagina. 'Jenny, I'd like to see you again.'

'I'm sure you will,' I sighed. As his tongue snaked around the solid nub of my clitoris, I had an idea. 'You can see me whenever you can get away from your wife. Do you often lie to her?'

'No, no, I don't.'

'I would have thought that you'd be having a string of affairs. I mean, Julie was never exactly attractive, was she?'

'She—'

'I wasn't going to say anything, Ian, but . . . I saw Julie this morning.'

'She got a new job today. She was probably—'

'She was here, on the common.'

'She likes it here. I expect she was—'

'Ian, she was with another man.'

'Ah, that'll be Rod or . . .'

'I suppose it wasn't another man.'

'What do you mean?'

'He was a lad from the school.'

'I'm not with you, Jenny.'

'Ian, she took him into the bushes and . . . well, I was intrigued and followed them. When I peered through the bushes . . . You wouldn't want to know what I saw.'

'Why didn't you say anything before?'

'I didn't think it was my business. And, since you've pulled my panties off . . . What's good for the goose is good for the gander. That's right, isn't it?'

'Well . . .'

'Are you going to fuck me now?'

Pulling his trousers off, Ian proudly displayed the solid shaft of his huge cock. He was worried about Julie, I knew as he positioned himself between my parted thighs. There was a look in his eyes. Concern, jealousy, anger ... I'd made him angry, which I enjoyed. An angry man fucked with a vengeance. Thinking of his two-timing wife, he'd vent his anger on me, fuck me senseless to somehow get even with the slag.

I let out a yelp as he slipped his swollen knob between the wet lips of my pussy and drove his massive cock forcefully into my hungry cunt. My lower stomach inflated, my body became rigid as he impaled me fully on his beautiful organ of pleasure. It had been years since I'd been fucked, too long since I'd had a huge cock driving deep into my wet cunt. Work had taken over, ruling my life. Why? Why hadn't I been fucked in years? I blamed the Brook Street Gang. They'd stripped me of my femininity before I'd flowered. They'd made me use the word *cunt*. They'd ruined my life.

'Christ, you're hot and tight,' Ian gasped. He withdrew his erect penis until the wings of my inner lips hugged his purple globe and then drove his huge shaft deep into my cunt again. My eyes closed, I lay beneath the trees, the adulterous act concealed by the surrounding bushes. Realizing just how much I'd missed sex, I opened my legs wider, taking his beautiful cock deeper into the contracting sheath of my spunk-thirsty cunt. Again and again, he rammed his knob into my trembling body, grunting with each thrust as he fucked me.

The sensitive tip of my solid clitoris massaged by the pussy-wet shaft of his thrusting cock, I knew that

I was nearing my orgasm. My mind had been consumed by work, and I hadn't even masturbated. I couldn't remember the last time I'd come, and I swore to take up masturbation regularly from now on. I'd neglected my body, my cunt. But that was going to change. As I listened to Ian's gasps, his cock swelling deep within the hugging sheath of my vagina, I shuddered as my orgasm exploded simultaneously with his spunking.

Again and again, he drove his spunking knob deep into my contracting cunt, his male cream bathing my cervix, lubricating our illicit fucking. My young body rocking, jolting with every thrust of his beautiful cock, I could feel his orgasmic fluid flooding my cunt, overflowing and streaming down between the rounded cheeks of my naked buttocks. My mind swimming with sex, my head dizzy as my orgasm gripped my shuddering body, I whimpered and squirmed beneath the trees as Julie's husband fucked my cunt and emptied his adulterous balls. The next time he fucked Julie, he'd think of me, he'd picture my face, feel the squeezing sheath of my cunt as he spunked me. The next time I saw Julie, I'd grin.

'Jesus,' Ian gasped, finally collapsing over my trembling body. 'You're a bloody good fuck.'

'You were a little too quick for me,' I complained. 'Still, next time you might . . .'

'There will be a next time, then?' he asked me, resting his weight on his hands and looking down at me.

'I should think so,' I replied, his deflating cock slipping out of my spunk-drenched cunt. 'We'll meet here again. I like it here, in the bushes.'

'Yes, so do I.' Easing himself off me, he grabbed his

trousers and tugged them up his legs. 'I'm sorry to have to rush off,' he began.

'Your little wife will be longing for you,' I said mockingly. 'You mustn't keep her waiting.'

'Jenny . . .' He looked pissed off as I flashed him a grin. 'Jenny, let's not talk about Julie. When we meet, let's not mention her.'

'Feeling guilty?' I giggled. 'You've fucked me, Ian. You've ruined your marriage.'

'Ruined? Julie will never find out, so I can't see that I've—'

'Won't she?'

'Of course not. How could she?'

'This is a small town, Ian. I realized just how small the minute I came back. People talk.'

'Only you and I know about us.'

'And Julie knows.'

'No, she—'

'She'll know that there's someone else, Ian. She won't know who, of course. But she'll know that you've fucked another girl.'

'No, she won't.' He stood up and buckled his belt. 'The same time tomorrow?'

'I'll ring you.'

'At work?'

'If that's OK?'

'Yes, yes, it is. I'd better go.'

'You go home to your little wife, Ian. I'll see you tomorrow.'

As he walked away, I grabbed my panties and pulled them up my long legs. Concealing the sperm-dripping crack of my fucked cunt, I felt good, wicked, evil. The sense of satisfaction, both sexual and vengeful, was overwhelming. Leaving the bushes, I walked across the common and made my way to the railway station. Day One had been immensely successful. Now, I was looking forward to Day Two of my return to Southmoore.

# 3

Sally wasn't at all happy when she arrived at the office the following morning. Apparently, she hadn't finished updating the database until nine o'clock and hadn't got home until twenty-five to ten. I concealed my triumphant grin and praised her for her efforts. This was the equilibrium I'd wanted. Treat her cruelly and yet balance that harsh treatment with praise.

'I went for a walk on the common last night,' I said. 'I thought I'd take a look around Southmoore before catching the train back to London.'

'It's nice on the common,' she replied. 'I like walking there.'

'Is it a well-known haunt for lovers?' I asked her.

'Well . . . yes, I suppose it is.'

'It's just that I saw a young man with a girl. They were messing about, laughing and joking. The girl unbuttoned her blouse before dragging her boyfriend into the bushes.'

'Oh, right,' she murmured, obviously wondering what I was getting at.

'I only mentioned it because the man said something about meeting Sally later. I didn't think he meant you. That would have been too coincidental. But then he mentioned Julie. I just thought it odd because you and Julie started here yesterday.'

'You didn't hear what the man's name was, did you?' she asked me.

'Ian, I think. Yes, that's right. She called him Ian.'

Sally frowned as she gazed at me. 'Do you know the girl's name?' she asked me.

'No, I don't. Are they friends of yours?'

'I think I know them,' she breathed. 'The man, Ian, is married to a friend of mine, so—'

'Oh, dear. Perhaps I shouldn't have said anything.'

'No, no, it's all right.'

'This is such a small town that I thought you might know them. Southmoore is the sort of place where everyone knows everything about everyone else.'

'Yes, it is rather like that. What do you want me to do today?'

Setting out her morning's work, I felt pretty sure that she'd go running to Julie at the first opportunity. Of course, if Ian ever bumped into me outside the office building or happened to see me in the street when he was with Julie . . . I'd cross that bridge when I came to it, I decided as Sally went into her office and closed the door. Although I managed to get through some work, I spent a lot of the morning planning the downfall of each member of the gang. I was becoming bent on their undoing, almost obsessed with their ruin. Again thinking that this wasn't going to do me any good, I looked up as someone knocked on my door.

'Come,' I called.

'I'm sorry to trouble you, Miss Michaels,' Julie said sheepishly.

'It's no trouble,' I replied, smiling as she closed the door. 'What's the problem?'

'Yesterday, you said that you needed two extra girls for the sales office.'

'Yes, that's right.'

'I have a friend . . .'

'Yes?'

'Well, I was wondering whether you'd consider her for the position?'

If she was going to suggest Kathy Higgins . . . 'Who is this friend?' I asked, sure that Lady Luck wasn't still with me.

'Her name's Kathy.'

*My God. Kathy bloody Higgins.*

'I mentioned the job to her last night. She seems very keen and—'

'You'd better send her along to see me,' I cut in, desperate to have the girl working for me. 'You saw her last night?'

'Yes, I did.'

'Is she married?'

'Oh no, not Kathy.'

'Why do you say it like that?'

'I . . . I just don't think she's the marrying type.'

'I see.'

'I have her phone number here,' Julie said, passing me a piece of paper. 'She's at home since she has the day off.'

'OK, I'll ring her now. You go and have a chat with Sally.'

I didn't normally encourage my staff to chat, but I wanted Sally to tell Julie about her husband. Ian was seen on the common with another girl, she opened her blouse and then dragged him into the bushes . . . Lifting the phone, I was beside myself with exhilaration as I suggested to Kathy that she should come and see me straight away. She agreed, saying that she could be in my office within fifteen minutes. Replacing the receiver, I wondered how Julie was feeling as she finally emerged from Sally's office.

'Everything all right?' I asked her. 'You look worried.'

'No, no . . .' she stammered. 'I'm fine.'

'Good. Your friend is on her way to see me. This is going to be quite a little family, isn't it?'

'A family?'

'You, Sally, your friend . . . All working for me.'

'Oh, yes.'

'Sit down, Julie,' I ordered her, offering her what I hoped was a motherly smile. 'Tell me what the problem is.'

'It's my husband,' she sighed, sitting opposite me. 'I think he's seeing another woman.'

'Oh, dear,' I breathed, shaking my head as if extremely concerned for her. 'That's terrible, Julie.'

'Sally said that you saw him on the common with another woman,' she snivelled.

'*Me*? Oh, you mean last night – was that your husband?'

'Yes.'

'Oh, dear. I wish I hadn't said anything to Sally. I'm sorry, but I had no idea that it was your husband. How old is he?'

'Twenty-eight. Why?'

'It's just that the girl he was with . . . She couldn't have been any older than seventeen or eighteen.'

'As young as that?' Julie gasped.

'She had a school blazer on, so she might well have been younger. She was a slut, that was obvious. The way she opened her blouse and showed off her . . . yes, well. A right slut, if you ask me.'

'I thought that he was working late,' she whined. 'We had a bit of a row when he came home. I'd called his mobile and . . . some girl had answered it. She said that she was in a pub with him.'

'What did he say to that?'

'He said that it must have been someone at work messing about. I believed him, but now . . .'

'This is obviously playing on your mind, Julie.'

'Yes, yes – it is. I'll have a talk with him again this evening and—'

'Is this going to affect your work?'

'My work?' she echoed, surprised.

'Yes, your work,' I replied, my tone growing stern. She'd obviously thought that I was going to be sympathetic. 'It's for this very reason that I prefer my girls to be single, Julie. Bringing marital problems into the office . . . You talk to your husband this evening and get it sorted out.'

'Yes, yes, I will.'

'OK, off you go. Oh, and do remember that you're on a three-month probationary period. If your marital problems are going to affect your work, I'll just have to . . . Deal with it by the morning, Julie.'

She was obviously stunned as she left my office. The bitch from hell? I was the bitch from hell, all right. Feeling a wave of satisfaction rolling through me, I was looking forward to meeting Kathy Higgins. Recalling her words, I felt my stomach knotting with anger. *The filthy anal whore deserves to have her dirty little arse fingerfucked.* This was incredible. Sally, Julie, and now Kathy Higgins. *And* I'd fucked Ian Marshal. Better and better.

When Kathy arrived, Walker showed her up to my office. He was a creep, I mused as he introduced the girl. A snivelling, arse-licking little creep. I'd make his life hell too before long, I decided. Kathy was dressed in a short skirt and a white blouse. She didn't look *too* bad for a bisexual slut. That was my initial reaction, at any rate. As she sat opposite me, I recalled her fingering my bottom, delighting in my plight as she'd finger-fucked my arse. Revenge is so sweet. I began by asking her about her present employment. It turned out that she was unemployed, which pleased me no end.

'You're on the dole?' I asked her disappointedly.

'Well, yes,' she replied hesitantly.

'Oh, dear,' I sighed.

'Is that a problem?'

'I never take on down-and-outs, Kathy.'

'Down and . . . I'm not a—'

'No, no. I'm not saying that you're a down-and-out. It's just that, in my opinion, anyone on the dole is nothing but a scrounger. Why haven't you got a job?'

'I did have. I was made redundant and—'

'So, you're expecting me to take on someone who is redundant? Someone another company has no use for?'

'It's not like that,' she replied dolefully.

'I'm not too sure about this. Presumably you can use a computer?'

'Oh, yes.'

'That's something, I suppose. As it is, I think I've made a mistake by employing your friend Julie.'

'A mistake?'

'It seems that she has marital problems,' I sighed dismissively. 'Her husband is fucking some schoolgirl or other and she's come snivelling to me about it. I can't abide . . . You're single, which goes in your favour. You're not pregnant, by any chance?'

'No, I am not.'

'Good. Snotty-nosed brats, marriage problems . . . We're a go-ahead company, Kathy. There's no room for snivelling brats and marital crap here. OK, I think we'll go for it.'

'Really?' she trilled, her face beaming.

'Yes, really. But you'll be out if you fuck up. Start tomorrow morning. Oh, you'd better fill in this form.'

Passing her the form, I gazed at her fingers as she penned her name and address. The very fingers that had violated my young body, driven deep into my rectum. Kathy Higgins was, at long last, in my grip. She hadn't turned out particularly well, I realized now as I looked at her more closely. Her brown hair was lank, her make-up doing little to conceal her blemished skin. She had very little going for her, in fact. The only reason I'd given her the job was so that I could bring her down, push her into the mire and grind her into the filth with my foot.

Ordering Sally to take Kathy downstairs to meet Tim Black, I rubbed my hands together gleefully as they left my office. Things couldn't have turned out better, I reflected. Three gang members working for me, another one fucking me on the common . . . Despite my previous doubts, Lady Luck certainly *was* smiling down upon me. Nipping into Sally's office, I opened her handbag and rummaged through her things. I wasn't looking for anything in particular. I was simply being nosy.

Pulling out a diary, I flicked through the pages. Checking today's date, I grinned. Sally was meeting the gang members in the pub at seven-thirty. I decided not to keep her behind again, but I'd make sure that Ian didn't turn up. Maybe he could be lured to the common by the thought of my cunt, I thought, slipping the diary into Sally's bag. Opening her wallet, I checked her credit cards. 'Oh,' I breathed, taking out two twenty-pound notes. Replacing the wallet, I returned to my desk and slipped the money into my briefcase. Ian wasn't going to the pub, Sally would arrive to find that she had no money . . .

'Ah, Sally,' I said, smiling as she walked into my office. 'Was Kathy all right?'

'Yes, Miss Michaels,' she replied. 'I'm glad that you gave her the job. She's a good worker and—'

'I don't see how you can say that,' I murmured. 'Seeing as she didn't have a job . . . How's Julie getting on?'

'She's doing very well. She enjoys the work.'

'Good, good. We have quite a little gathering of your friends now, don't we?'

'Yes, we do.'

'I had a phone call while you were downstairs. Do you know a Kenny Smith?'

'Kenny? Yes, I know him.'

'Does he live locally?'

'Yes, he does. In fact, I'm meeting him this evening with some other friends. I'm sorry that he rang here to speak to me. I'll tell him not to—'

'He didn't want to speak to *you*, Sally.'

'Oh?'

'He asked me about Kathy. Are they an item?'

'No, no. They used to be together at school, but Kenny's married now.'

'I see. His wife, was she at school with you?'

'Yes. In fact, most of the people I know are from school.'

'What's his wife's name?'

'Lucy Barlow. Well, it's Lucy Smith now. What did Kenny want?'

Lucy Barlow was another gang member. 'He just asked whether I'd employed Kathy. I told him that it was none of his business. OK, that's all.'

As Sally went back into her office, I perched on the edge of my desk and thought about Lucy Barlow. It was amazing how the gang had kept together. Each and every one of them still lived in Southmoore, they met regularly ... What *was* the gang about? I racked my brains for some clue. Ian had declined to say anything, which I'd thought ominous. Sex? Did they hold orgies and fuck each other? If that was the case, then why was Julie so distressed about her husband screwing around? Grabbing the phone, I called him at work.

'Ian?' I asked as he answered.

'Speaking.'

'It's Jenny.'

'Oh, hi. How are you doing?'

'Fine, fine. Was everything OK with your wife last night?'

'No, far from it. She reckoned that she rang my mobile and some girl answered.'

'But you didn't answer it.'

'I know. And no one else would have answered it. I switched it off, if you remember?'

'Yes, I do.'

'She was in a right strop when I got home. To make matters worse, she called me just now and said that I'd been seen on the common last night with a young girl.'

'*Me*? Who would have—'

'No, no – not you. That's what's so odd about it. Her boss told her that she'd seen me in the bushes with a young schoolgirl.'

'Her boss?'

'I don't know what's going on, Jenny. Anyway, I'd better get home on time this evening or . . .'

'Oh, what a shame,' I sighed . . . 'I was hoping to see you.'

'I know, but . . .'

'Perhaps we shouldn't have started this, Ian. Obviously, it's your wife you want. You don't want *me*, do you?'

'Jenny . . . Of course I want you. God, I've done nothing but think about you since last night.'

'Then meet me on the common after work . . .'

'We're going out tonight. We're all meeting up for a drink.'

'What? This silly gang of yours?'

'Yes, that's right. I can't really get out of it. What with some girl supposedly answering my mobile and Julie's boss saying that I was in the bushes with a schoolgirl . . .'

'I think your wife's having you on, Ian.'

'How do you mean?'

'A young schoolgirl? Come on, no one could have thought that I was a young girl. And no one answered your mobile phone. You had it with you all the time, didn't you?'

'Yes, I did.'

'There you are, then. She's suspicious and she's digging for clues. Has her boss ever seen you?'

'No, never.'

'Then how can she say that she saw you on the common?'

'That's a point. She doesn't know me from Adam.'

'Your wife's messing you about, testing you, sniffing for evidence.'

'It seems that way.'

'Surely you can meet me on the common and spend ten minutes or so with me?'

'Yes, yes, all right.'

'Don't sound *too* enthusiastic, Ian.'

'I'm sorry, Jenny. I just wish . . . I'll see you after work, OK?'

'What time?'

'I'll try to get away early. Say, five-thirty?'

'I'll look forward to it.'

'I usually leave at six. Julie won't expect me home until about quarter past six so—'

'I'll see you at five-thirty, Ian.'

'Yes, I'll be there.'

Hanging up, I rubbed my hands together. I was stirring up some real trouble, that was for sure. I stayed at the office until two o'clock and then went to view a couple of flats. One was a shit-hole and the other was bloody expensive. I'd probably go for the expensive one. The company could pay the rent until I found a place to buy. Dave would go along with that, I was sure. Particularly if I opened my hot, wet mouth for him.

Walker came crawling into my office just as I was about to leave at five o'clock. He was whining about Tim Black, saying that Tim had been coming on strong with Kathy. Apparently, the girl had hung about after Tim had shown her around and they'd ended up giggling over coffee in the canteen. I really wasn't interested. I'd just about had enough of Walker and decided to have a go at him when Sally left the office.

'What has this got to do with you?' I asked him as Sally closed the main door behind her.

'Miss Michaels . . . I know you don't like that sort of thing going on between members of staff.'

'That's true. But what has it got to do with you?'

'Well, nothing. I just thought that you should know about it. The girl doesn't even start until tomorrow morning. If that's how Tim Black is going to carry on . . .'

'Are you jealous, Walker?'

'Jealous? No, of course not.'

'You're not gay, are you?'

'Certainly not, Miss Michaels.'

'Girlfriend?'

'Well, not just at the moment.'

'You want to get your hands inside Kathy's knickers, don't you? That's what this is all about.'

'Miss Michaels!' he gasped.

'Walker, there are some very attractive girls working here. I've seen you eyeing them up.'

'I have never—'

'Never thought about them in a sexual way?'

'Well . . .'

'Come on, Walker. You can't tell me that you're not interested in a bit of cunt.'

'Please, Miss Michaels.'

'What's the matter?'

'Your language. I mean . . .'

'I don't have the time to discuss this now. Come and see me in the morning.' *And I'll fire you.*

'Yes, yes, I will. Thank you, Miss Michaels.'

Shaking my head as he scurried out of my office, I thought that I'd better have a word with Tim Black. But not until the morning. I had plans for the evening. Plans to keep Ian on the common until he was late home, until it was too late to meet the gang in the pub. They were meeting at seven-thirty. No doubt Julie would fume until seven-thirty and then go to the pub without her husband. She might even take a trip to the common, I mused as I left the building. That might prove interesting.

Lurking on the common behind some trees, I watched Ian walk across the grass to the bushes and check his watch. I'd make him wait, I decided. The longer he waited for me, the later he'd get home. According to Ian, Julie wouldn't expect him home until six-fifteen. They were meeting the others in the pub at seven-thirty. I was going to have to keep Ian busy for quite some time. Not that I'd find that difficult.

To my horror, I noticed Julie on the far side of the common. I certainly hadn't anticipated that she'd be there this early – if she showed up at all, that was. This was going to fuck everything up, I thought as I rummaged through my briefcase for the form she'd filled in. Grabbing my mobile, I checked her details on the form and punched in her number, praying for her to answer before Ian noticed her. She stopped dead in her tracks and opened her handbag. My gaze darting between her and Ian, I breathed a sigh of relief as he sat on the grass and lay back and she answered her phone.

'Is Ian there?' I asked her.

'Ian?' she echoed. 'Who is this?'

'It's Sandra. Is that Ian's sister?'

'His *sister*?' She hesitated. 'Er . . . yes – yes, it is,' she said softly, obviously deciding to play along with me.

'He said that he lived with his sister so . . . I hope you don't mind me calling?'

'No, not at all.'

'We were supposed to meet but he hasn't turned up.'

'Oh, right. Where are you?'

'In the pub, waiting for him.'

'I see. Look, I'll get a message to him if I can. Which pub is it?'

'The wine bar in the high street. The Blue Monkey.'

'Yes, I know it. Er . . . are you still at school?'

'Yes, I am. It's our secret but I suppose Ian thought it would be all right to tell you. I'm only sixteen, you see.'

'Yes, I understand. OK, I'll try to get hold of Ian and tell him that you're waiting.'

'That's great. Thanks.'

Slipping my phone into my briefcase as Julie walked away, I looked over at Ian. He was still lying on the grass. Checking his watch, he sat upright and looked around the common. I couldn't believe my luck as I walked towards him. I hadn't been going to take my briefcase home, but I'd had some papers to go through. And, had I filed Julie's details, I wouldn't have had her mobile number with me. *Lady Luck?* I mused as Ian noticed me and leaped to his feet. Perhaps Satan was with me?

'Sorry I'm late,' I said, standing in front of him. 'I got held up.'

'I thought you weren't coming,' he sighed, checking his watch again. 'I haven't got very long.'

'Ian, don't start on about going home already. If it's your wife you want to be with . . .'

'No, no. It's just that it's not easy, Jenny. I don't want

to be with her. But I don't want to give her grounds for divorce. You'd be dragged into it and—'

'Shall we go into the bushes?' I suggested. 'I don't think we should stand out in the open. Especially if your wife is on the rampage.'

'Yes, good idea. Actually, that's a thought.'

'What is?'

'She might come here looking for me.'

'Looking for you and a young schoolgirl? I don't think so,' I giggled, sitting on the grass. 'She made all that up, Ian.'

'I'm not so sure.'

'Why? *Have* you been here with a young girl?'

'No, no, of course not.'

'There you are, then. She made it up. You're becoming paranoid, Ian.'

'No, I'm not.'

'So, tell me more about the mysterious Brook Street Gang.'

'There's nothing to tell.'

'Of course there is. Come on, I'm intrigued.'

'We just meet up for a laugh, that's all.'

'And?'

'Years ago, when we were at school . . . You remember we mentioned Rachael Michaels?'

'The spotty girl, yes.'

'Well, after we'd all left school, we missed teasing her. It was fun, taking her into the bushes and stripping her naked.'

'I'm sure it was.'

'We tried to find her but she'd moved away. Anyway, we found another girl. It was someone Julie worked with. I know that it sounds awful but . . . we blackmailed her.'

'You blackmailed her?'

'Nothing bad happened. Well, I suppose it wasn't exactly *good*. She'd been seeing another man behind her husband's back. We blackmailed her and . . . we all had sex with her.'

'God, Ian. This *is* awful. What do you mean, you *all* had sex with her? The girls as well?'

'Yes, I suppose so. We now have three girls we're blackmailing and using for sex.'

'*Three?*'

'Yes. It's all kept within the gang. Julie's fine about me having sex with the girls, but only within the gang.'

'I don't think I like this, Ian. I thought that you and I had something special. But, seeing as you're having sex with . . .'

'No, no. I never wanted to be involved.'

'So, you blackmail girls and fuck them and that's not involving yourself?'

'Look, I didn't come here to be lectured, Jenny.'

'No, you didn't. You came here to fuck me.'

'I—'

'Before we go any further, you'd better tell me what else the gang gets up to.'

'We hunt down adulterers. Female adulterers have sex with us, male adulterers give us money.'

'So you blackmail women, threaten them, and then fuck them?'

'At the end of the day, if people are going to cheat on their partners . . .'

'Then that's their business. That's no reason to blackmail them, Ian.'

Realizing that I was coming on too strong, I smiled. 'Still, it has nothing to do with me,' I said, licking my red lips provocatively. 'I don't mind what you get up to, as long as I can have a share of your cock.'

'Really?' he chuckled, grinning at me.

'You and your gang can do whatever you like. As I said, it has nothing to do with me. But I *am* intrigued. Tell me about these girls. How old are they, where do they work and—'

'I can't say anything,' he interrupted me.

'God, you've told me just about everything as it is. You might as well tell me a little more.'

'I suppose so. One of the girls, she's about eighteen – she works for a travel agent in the high street. We caught her having it off with her husband's brother.'

'God,' I breathed.

'That's not all. She was having it off with her husband's brother at her own wedding reception. She'd only been married for five minutes and she was screwing her brother-in-law in the toilets.'

I could hardly believe what I was hearing. The gang blackmailing adulterers, taking money from the men and using the women for crude sex in return for their silence? This was incredible. It was also pretty dangerous, I reflected. If my trickery was discovered, if my true identity . . . With people such as that thug Kenny Smith involved, I dreaded to think of the consequences. At least I had Ian on my side. Or did I? No matter what his excuses, he was as guilty as the rest of the Brook Street Gang. I was playing with fire, I knew. This changed everything. I might have been the deputy MD, employing three of the girls, but . . . When it came to the crunch, they had far more power than I had.

'I'd better get going,' Ian said, checking his watch yet again.

'Yes, all right,' I sighed. My libido had crashed.

'I'm sorry, Jenny. I'd love to stay but . . .'

'No, no, don't apologize. You have your wife, young girls . . . You don't need me.'

'I *do* need you. My wife, the girls . . . It's just cold sex, Jenny.'

*Oh, God*, I thought. *He's about to proclaim his undying love for me.*

'With you . . . It's different.'

*Yeah, right.* 'Ian, if you need me then stay with me for a while longer.'

'OK,' he sighed, looking at his watch again. 'I'll stay for another ten minutes.'

Finally sitting down next to me, he offered me a meek smile. He was extremely worried, that was obvious. I wasn't sure what to do as I lay back on the grass and spread my limbs. I could contact the girl in the travel agent's and . . . and what? She'd committed adultery, got caught with her knickers down, and was now paying the price. But it wasn't up to the gang to punish her. What did they think they were? Some kind of self-appointed punishers of adultery? Hadn't Ian committed adultery with me? *Let he who is without sin cast the first stone.* But it wasn't about adultery, I mused. It was about having crude sex, taking money . . . Blackmail. Sex. Extortion.

If the gang got to hear about Ian's extramural activities . . . I had the feeling that the gang was a tight-knit group. Everything was done within its confines. I had to learn more, I decided, parting my legs as Ian stared at my naked thighs. Where did the gang meet? Who were they blackmailing? Who was the ringleader? I had to discover a lot more about the gang and their activities before I could make any plans.

'Ian,' I murmured, 'I realize that you're worried about being here with me. But what about Julie and her adultery?'

'What do you mean?'

'Julie, here on the common yesterday morning, with a schoolboy. I told you about it.'

'Oh, that. I asked her about it. She said that she'd bumped into a friend and—'

'And taken him into these very bushes and fucked him?' *Why hadn't she said that she wasn't on the common?* 'That's what happened, Ian,' I lied. 'I saw it with my own eyes, for God's sake. Don't you think it's somewhat hypocritical of her to come on strong to you about adultery when she's—'

'It's not like that,' he sighed. 'Not at all.'

'Isn't it?'

'Julie does the scouting around, she seeks out people to—'

'Blackmail?'

'Yes.'

'She set out to blackmail a schoolboy?'

'He's eighteen, for God's sake.'

'*He doesn't exist! Why did she fabricate this story?*

'Julie reckons that his parents have money, and lots of it. You don't know the story behind it, Jenny.'

'Then tell me.'

'I've said too much as it is. Look, I have to go now.'

'Don't you want me to suck you?'

'Well . . .'

'Come on, Ian. I've been waiting all day to get at your beautiful cock. Just let me suck your knob and drink your spunk and then you can go home to your wife.'

Reclining on the grass, he unzipped his trousers and

tugged them down to his knees. Wondering why Julie had gone along with the schoolboy story that I'd invented, I teased Ian's penis with my fingertip. I reckoned that she might have been putting it around behind Ian's back. Perhaps she *had* been on the common. Perhaps it was purely coincidence that I'd made up the story about the young lad and she'd happened to meet . . . No. There was coincidence and . . . Perhaps she regularly met men on the common? If Ian heard about it, then she'd put it down to her scouting for new victims.

Ian's semi-erect cock snaking over his hairy scrotum, he closed his eyes as I stroked his veined shaft and ran my fingertips over his heaving balls. He obviously couldn't resist fucking my hot mouth, shooting his spunk to the back of my throat before scurrying home to his wife. I was going to have to make sure that he didn't spurt out his cream too soon. The minute he'd come, he'd be dashing off back to Julie. The longer I teased him, held him back from his orgasm, the better.

His warm shaft expanding in my hand as I gripped the broad base of his penis, his full balls rolling, I retracted his foreskin fully. Leaning over and teasing his sperm-slit with the tip of my wet tongue, I breathed in his male scent, savoured the aphrodisiacal taste of his salty glans. He breathed deeply, his body trembling as I toyed with his balls and licked the solid shaft of his twitching cock. As the tip of my tongue ran beneath the rim of his helmet, his glans swelled to an incredible size – his whole knob positively ballooned. I had to ease off, I knew as his body grew rigid.

Julie would be in the wine bar by now, I thought as I ran my tongue up the length of Ian's twitching cock. She'd be looking for Sandra, a sixteen-year-old schoolgirl. I felt quite proud of myself as I kissed the soft sac of Ian's scrotum. Ringing Julie's mobile, pretending to be a young girl, Ian's young girl . . . She'd question him about it, of course. He'd wonder what the hell was going on, make up some story or other and slip even deeper into the pit of confusion I was digging.

'The time,' Ian breathed, again checking his watch. 'I really have to go, Jenny.'

'You can't go before you've come,' I giggled impishly. 'I haven't had my milky drink yet.'

'We'll have to be quick. It's not just Julie. If I turn up late, the others will . . .'

'Will what? What is it, Ian?'

'When the gang meet, we *all* turn up. And on time.'

'And if you're late or don't turn up at all?'

'It's the rule. We have to have rules, Jenny. Any organization—'

'Organization?'

'This isn't just some silly gang, Jenny,' he sighed irritably. 'The Brook Street Gang is . . .'

'Go on.'

'Do you want your milky drink before I go or not?'

Leaning over, I sucked Ian's glistening knob into my mouth and rolled my tongue around the rim. I had the feeling that he was frightened. Not only frightened of his wife, but . . . There was definitely more to the gang than I'd initially thought. Blackmail, sex, extortion . . . Who was the ringleader? I asked myself that crucial question as Ian began gasping. Kenny Smith? He was a thug, a lout . . . Just the right sort of character to lead the gang.

As my gobbling mouth flooded with Ian's sperm, I swallowed hard. He'd come far too soon for my liking.

He'd rush off to his wife, to his meeting, say that he'd been held up at work . . . But Julie would question him about Sandra the young schoolgirl. At least I had the consolation of some trouble ahead for the unhappily married couple. But I was going to have to do far more than make phone calls and spread malicious rumours if I was to succeed in bringing the Brook Street Gang to their knees. Forcing Sally to work late, making Julie's life hell, ruining Kathy's prospects . . . My antics would cause problems, but I was going to have to get my act together and make some serious moves to destroy each and every member of the gang.

'God,' Ian gasped, his body shaking uncontrollably as I bobbed my head up and down, repeatedly taking his orgasming knob to the back of my spunk-flooded throat. Taking his heaving balls in my hand, I squeezed his scrotal sac. I would have like to have squeezed hard, dug my fingernails into the sensitive flesh of his scrotum and brought him pain. But I wanted to pleasure him to ensure that he'd return again and again to the common to commit his acts of adultery. My time would come, I mused, sucking the creamy spunk out of his throbbing sex-globe. All in good time, I'd bring him pain, torture him, use and abuse him.

Swallowing the remnants of his orgasmic fluid, I snaked my tongue around his knob, kneading his drained balls as he convulsed wildly in the aftermath of his throat-fucking. Finally slipping his saliva-glistening helmet out of my wet mouth, I ran my tongue up and down his shaft. Lapping up the spilled sex milk, snaking my tongue over his balls, I savoured the salty taste of his semen, breathed in the heady perfume of his pubic curls.

'I have to go now,' Ian murmured. 'That was incredible, Jenny. But I really must go now.'

'After work tomorrow?' I said, licking my sperm-glossed lips.

'Yes, yes – I think I can make it.'

'I hope so, Ian,' I said with a hint of sternness. 'Don't get me wrong. I love sucking your cock and drinking your spunk. But I'm not getting anything else out of our affair, am I? You haven't touched me this time, Ian. Perhaps you don't really fancy me? Is that it?'

'God, no,' he replied, sitting straight and pulling his trousers up. 'I'd love to stay and . . . Jenny, I'll sort something out. I'll try to spend a good hour or so with you after work. If I tell Julie that I have to work—'

'I'm not interested in the lies that you're going to tell your wife, Ian. I'm interested in us having sex every day after work. Perhaps I should speak to your wife?'

'Speak to . . . What do you mean?'

I felt my nasty streak coming to the fore. 'It's just occurred to me that she's standing in my way.'

'In your way?'

'I want you, I want your cock fucking me. Julie is preventing me—'

'All right, all right. I'll sort it, OK?'

'You'd better, Ian.'

'Tomorrow, same time?'

'I'll be here.'

'So will I.'

'You'd better be, Ian.'

Watching him slip through the bushes and make his escape, I grinned. There was nothing like a threat to get my own way, I reflected. Ian didn't know me, he didn't know what I was like. He might have thought that I'd never go running to his wife. There again, he couldn't be too sure. The taste of spunk lingering on my tongue, I left the bushes and walked across the common. Tomorrow I'd start on Kathy Higgins, I decided. Her life of misery would begin the next morning.

# 4

'You wanted to see me, Miss Michaels?' Tim Black said, standing in my office doorway.

'Yes, Tim,' I replied. 'Come in and close the door. How's that new girl doing? Julie, isn't it?'

'That's right,' he said, standing in front of my desk. 'She's doing very well. And Kathy Higgins starts this morning.'

'Ah, Kathy Higgins. That's what I wanted to talk to you about, Tim.'

'Oh?'

'You had coffee with her in the canteen yesterday?'

'Yes, I did. I was showing her around the building and—'

'And became rather too familiar with her, from what I heard.'

'I like to get on with the staff, Miss Michaels.'

'Get on? Or get off?'

'No, certainly not. I like to be friendly with the staff. We work as a team. I find they're far more productive that way.'

'Do you? You're not married, are you?'

'I was, but . . .'

'Tim, I know you'd like nothing more than to get your grubby little hands up Kathy's skirt.'

'No, I—'

'Please, don't interrupt me. For reasons that are none of your business, I'm planning to take a special interest in Kathy Higgins. I want to know everything about her. I'm particularly interested in her work. Her mistakes, her downfalls, her weaknesses . . . You'll keep me updated about her progress, do you understand?'

'Yes, Miss Michaels.'

'That will be all, Tim.'

'Oh, the shipment to Spain.'

'What about it? There's not a problem, is there?'

'No, no.'

'There'd better not be, Tim.'

'It's just that the hauliers will have to do the run in two loads.'

'And?'

'Well, they priced the job thinking that one lorry would—'

'And now they're saying that they'll need two lorries?'

'Yes.'

'How does that affect us?'

'The cost . . .'

'They quoted for the job and we accepted. I don't care whether they need one or ten lorries. If they fucked up, that's not my problem. Which firm is it?'

'Johnson-Weave.'

'We put a lot of business their way. Tell them that, if they fuck up on this one, they'll not get another job from us.'

'They have done us favours in the past, Miss Michaels.'

'*Favours*? They've done us *favours*? We're in business, Tim. We don't need favours, for fuck's sake. They'll ship the supplies to Spain at the price they quoted. Deal with it – now. That'll be all, Tim.'

Incompetence had no place in my philosophy of business. Johnson-Weave needed us. Without Dagridge Medical Supplies, they'd go out of business. Tim Black was going to have to be replaced, I decided. There was no room in my offices for dirty little men who constantly thought about the girls' panties rather than . . . There again, if he did continue to woo Kathy, I could blame her and . . . Grinning, I looked up from my desk as Sally breezed into the office.

'It's eight-fifty-five,' I said, checking my watch.

'Yes, I know, Miss Michaels,' she murmured, frowning, her blue eyes downcast. 'I start at nine, don't I?'

'Indeed you do, Sally.'

'It's only five to nine.'

'So, it takes less than five minutes to switch your computer on, load the program, log into the system . . . You won't be able to start work at nine, will you?'

'No, Miss Michaels.'

'Do try and make an effort, Sally. I wouldn't want to have to replace you. Eight-thirty from now on, all right?'

'Yes, Miss Michaels. It's just that the bus—'

'The bus?'

'There's one that gets me here at five to nine. The earlier one would get me here at a quarter past eight.'

'Quarter past eight it is, then.'

I was feeling particularly grumpy. Perhaps it was to do with my having been deserted after sucking the sperm out of Ian's cock. My arousal had soared, and he'd neglected my feminine needs. To put it bluntly, crudely, I needed a fuck. Leaving my office, I went down to the sales department to greet Kathy Higgins on her first day with the company. Tim Black was leaning over Kathy's desk. He was laughing, joking with the girl, as he pointed to her computer screen. Catching sight of me, he stood upright and said something to Kathy before walking across the office towards me.

'Where's Julie?' I asked him, scanning the girls sitting at their desks.

'She's not here yet, Miss Michaels,' he replied, checking his watch.

'Oh?'

'She did phone in. She's been held up because—'

'Held up?' I interrupted him angrily. 'Send her to my office the minute she arrives.'

'Yes, Miss Michaels.'

Walking along the corridor, I decided to go down to the main entrance and wait for Julie to arrive. This couldn't have turned out better, I thought as I noticed the girl walking into the canteen. I stood in the doorway, watching as she ordered a cup of coffee and sat at a corner table. She'd no doubt rowed with Ian after he'd got home late, asked him about Sandra and . . . Joining her, my stomach somersaulting, I couldn't think of a better way to begin the working day.

'Tea break already?' I asked sarcastically, sitting down opposite her.

'Oh, er . . . I'm sorry, Miss Michaels,' she responded guiltily. 'I did phone in to say that I'd be late.'

'You phoned in? How does that help? We need you here, Julie. Not—'

'I . . . I had some trouble and . . .' Her voice tailed off.

'Not your husband again?' I sighed.

'Yes, I . . . I'm sorry.'

'For God's sake. I told you to deal with it . . . I *knew* that this would affect your work. What's happened now?'

'A girl rang my mobile last night. Someone called Sandra . . .'

'Sandra? That's odd.' I hesitated and frowned. 'Someone of that name rang me earlier this morning. She wanted to talk to you but I told her that I don't allow the staff to take private calls.'

'She rang *here*?'

'Yes, she did. You'd better tell me what's going on.'

'Ian – my husband – was late home again last night. I had the phone call from this girl and . . .'

'This should be easy enough to deal with, Julie. What time is your husband supposed to be home?'

'About six.'

'Then tell him that if he's any later than six he'll find that he's locked out. End of subject. End of marriage.'

'It's not as easy as that, Miss Michaels.'

'Of course is it. Look at it from my point of view. I've had some girl ringing me, you're late for work and obviously in no state to do your job properly . . . I may be a hard woman, but I'm fair. Deal with this by tomorrow morning or . . . We had this conversation yesterday. Just deal with it, Julie.'

'Yes, Miss Michaels.'

Leaving the canteen, I felt smug. Julie had been waiting at home for Ian to arrive and she'd also been hanging around in the wine bar, looking for Sandra . . . And I'd been on the common sucking spunk out of her husband's cock. This was all very well, I mused again. But I was going to have to do far more than play games with the gang. Returning to my office, I realized that I couldn't drag my thoughts away from sex. Ian had fucked me, I'd sucked spunk out of his throbbing knob . . . My libido was running dangerously high and I was in dire need of a fuck.

Apart from sucking off Dave Bryant – who was my boss, in any case – I'd never had sexual relations with my staff. Looking back, I'd not had ongoing sexual relations with anyone for several years. The thought had often crossed my mind that it would be interesting to jerk off young Walker. But, fun though it would be, the act would change things between us for ever. He was a snivelling arse-licker and I was the cruel boss. Once I'd wanked his cock, watched his spunk shoot across the office . . . Answering the phone, I froze as a male voice called me Rachael.

'I'm sorry, you have the wrong number,' I breathed shakily.

'I don't think so, Rachael,' he murmured. 'Rachael Michaels, Southmoore School . . . I have the right number. I have the right girl.'

'You're mixing me up with someone else,' I said firmly. 'My name is Fiona, and I've never heard of Southmoore School.'

'Let's not start off on the wrong foot, Rachael. You went to Southmoore School, your name is Rachael Michaels—'

'I'm sorry but I don't have time to play games,' I snapped, replacing the receiver.

My hands were trembling and my heart was thumping hard against my chest. I wondered who the hell had discovered my true identity. More to the point, what did they want? If it was one of the gang members, I was in the shit. There was no point in speculating, I decided. I had to be strong and pull myself together. Whoever it was would undoubtedly call again, and I'd have to come across as cool and calm. It was obviously someone who knew me, probably someone from school. Perhaps they'd seen me on the common. Perhaps they'd thought that they'd recognized me and had followed me . . . I was speculating again. Whoever it was, I had to discover their identity, and quickly.

'Excuse me, Miss Michaels,' Sally said as she emerged from her office.

'What is it?' I snapped.

'Would you mind if I popped out for a minute? I have to pick up my watch from the jeweller's around the corner.'

'You're not going . . .' She was already wearing a watch, I noticed. Perhaps she had two, but the nearest jeweller was actually in the centre of town. 'Yes, yes, that's all right,' I replied, smiling at her.

'Thank you. I won't be long.'

What was the urgency? Why did she have to rush off now when she could easily have picked up her watch at lunchtime? As she left the office, I pondered those questions and became increasingly suspicious. The Brook Street Gang had made me paranoid anyway. Anything I overheard at school, if anything even slightly out of the ordinary happened, I became suspicious. If someone mentioned the common, I immediately thought that they were drawing up their plans against me. But this was more than suspicion. I instinctively *knew* that Sally was up to something.

Grabbing my jacket, I followed her, keeping my distance as she left the building and crossed the street. What the hell was I doing? The question nagged at me. I was supposed to be heading the new branch of Dagridge Medical Supplies and here I was, following my secretary. Had I not had the threatening phone call, I wouldn't have bothered to follow the girl. Threatening? The man had made no threats. But he would, I was certain of that.

To my surprise, Sally met Ian outside the nearby Chinese restaurant. I couldn't get close enough to hear what they were saying, but I had the feeling that they were discussing me. My suspicious mind again? Sally finally made her way back to the office and I decided to confront Ian. I reckoned that word about me, my true identity, was spreading. Someone was on to me, and had probably told Ian . . . Word spreads like wildfire in a small town, I knew as Ian noticed me walking towards him. What were the gang planning? What would they do if they discovered that I was the fat, spotty teenager that they used to . . . They weren't children any more. They were adults who blackmailed people, took money and used girls for sex. Waving, Ian greeted me with a smile and called out.

'Oh, hi,' I said. 'What are you doing here? Day off, is it?'

'No, no. I've just nipped out for ten minutes.'

'Who was that girl you were talking to? I recognize her from somewhere.'

'Sally – Sally Brompton.'

'Yes, that's it. I was sure that I knew her from somewhere. Does she work locally?'

'She works at the same place as Julie. At the new medical supply company.'

'Oh, right. I thought I saw Kathy Higgins earlier. God, all the old faces from school coming back and—'

'Jenny,' he murmured, interrupting me as he glanced up and down the street. 'You remember that we talked about Rachael Michaels?'

'The spotty girl? Yes.'

'I think she's back in town.'

'So?'

'I have an idea that she works for the medical company.'

'What if she does? You seem worried, Ian. What's the problem?'

'There is no problem – yet. She's changed her name. Her Christian name, I mean. She's now known as Fiona Michaels. She's the deputy managing director of the medical supply company.'

'She's done well, then. But I still don't see what the problem is.'

'She knows too much about us, about the gang.'

'That was years ago, Ian. I don't suppose she's even given it a thought. Anyway, how do you know that she's back? Who told you?'

'Julie told me. I've just told Sally to check it out. If Rachael Michaels is the boss . . .'

'I really don't see that it matters, Ian.'

'Rachael Michaels must have come back to Southmoore for a reason.'

'To work for the medical company, I suppose.'

'No, no. There's more to it than that. Sally was saying that her boss, Fiona Michaels, likes walking on the common. I'm going to get Kenny Smith to hang around on the common.'

'What for? Is he going to attack her? I think that you're becoming paranoid. Or is it that you're planning to use her for sex again?'

'Jenny, she knows too much about the gang. If she discovers that we're still going . . .'

'If Kenny Smith is going to be hanging around the common . . . I'm meeting you after work, Ian. You hadn't forgotten that, had you?'

'No, no. I'm hoping that Kenny will run into her at lunchtime. Look, I'd better get back to work. I'll see you this evening, OK?'

'OK. As long as Kenny Smith doesn't pester us. I wouldn't worry too much, Ian. I doubt that Rachael—'

'There's one thing that I'm sure she knows about the gang. If she opens her mouth . . . I'll see you later, we'll talk then.'

'I'll look forward to it.'

As he walked away, I felt my stomach churning. One thing that I knew about the gang? What did I know that could cause them real problems? Walking back to the office, I knew that I was going to have to do something. The main problem was that Ian believed that I was Jenny Wilder. It was one thing denying all knowledge of Rachael Michaels, but once Ian discovered that I was deputy boss of the company . . . This was turning into a bloody mess, I thought as I walked into my office and sat at my desk. I had work to do, and didn't have the time to mess around like this. Again wondering who had phoned, I looked up as Sally appeared in my office doorway.

'Miss Michaels,' she said sheepishly. 'I hope you don't mind me asking, but . . . do you have a sister?'

'Er . . . yes,' I replied, seeing a possible way out of my predicament. 'Why do you ask?'

'You look very similar to a girl I knew at school. Her name was Rachael Michaels.'

'Yes, Rachael is my sister. She now lives in America. She has done for the last ten years or so.'

'Did you live here, in Southmoore? Only I don't recall Rachael having a sister.'

'No, I went to a boarding school in Scotland at an early

age. I had very little contact with my younger sister. Nothing's changed, really. I've not spoken to her for about five years. You were friends at school, then?'

'Well, not really. So, were you born here? I mean, you must have been to the infants' school before—'

'I was born in Scotland, Sally. My parents moved up there for a few months . . . If you must know, I was brought up by an aunt. Now, I'm sure that you have some work to be getting on with.'

'Yes, of course.'

I liked the idea of having a sister: it would solve all my problems. Again wishing that I'd not masqueraded as Jenny Wilder, I decided to take a walk on the common at lunchtime. If Kenny Smith approached me . . . I felt that I wasn't in control, and I wasn't used to that. I was the bitch from hell. *I* gave the orders, *I* was the boss. But now I felt the way I had when I was at school. The gang were there, hanging around, lurking, waiting . . . I managed to get down to some work before leaving the office at one o'clock. My work was more important than anything, wasn't it?

The common was deserted, which I thought odd as it was such a lovely day. Perhaps word had got round and people were keeping away . . . I was being ridiculous, I knew as I walked across the grass. Repeatedly looking over my shoulder, I felt my stomach churning again. *I shouldn't be here*, I thought, my hands trembling. What the hell was I doing? Wandering around on the common when I knew that Kenny Smith was lurking somewhere – I must have been mad. But I knew this feeling of old. My schooldays, the cold fear, the sweat . . .

Noticing Kenny Smith ambling along the path towards me, I took a deep breath. Slipping my shoe off and making out that there was something wrong with it, I leaned against a tree. Pretending to shake a stone out of my shoe, I didn't look up as Kenny approached. He looked scruffy in his torn jeans and crumpled T-shirt. His dark hair cascading over his forehead, he hadn't changed. Slipping my shoe on, I checked my watch and was about to walk on when he stopped and asked me whether I was all right.

'A stone,' I said, smiling at him. 'These shoes aren't really suitable for walking.'

'I know you from somewhere,' he murmured, rubbing his chin.

'I doubt it,' I returned. 'I've only just moved here from London.'

'Rachael Michaels, isn't it?'

'Rachael? Oh, no, no. That's my sister. God, I look nothing like her.'

'*I* can see the resemblance. I'm Kenny, Kenny Smith.'

'Fiona,' I said, checking my watch again. 'Well, I'd better be going.'

'Rachael didn't have a sister.' I detected accusation in his tone.

'In that case, I don't exist,' I laughed. 'You're not the first to muddle us up.'

'There's no muddle, Rachael.'

'That's her, all right,' a male voice said from behind.

'Who are you?' I asked, spinning round on my heels and staring at Brad Masters.

'Hello, Rachael,' he chuckled. 'Remember me?'

'No, no, I . . . I don't,' I replied shakily. 'Look, I have to be going.'

Stunned with shock as they grabbed my arms and marched me through the bushes, I couldn't believe what was happening to me. Horrendous memories flooding back as they dragged me into the small clearing, I remembered Brad Masters fucking my mouth, shooting his spunk down my throat. He'd been a bully and a thug, and obviously hadn't changed. Surely they weren't going to . . . My mind spun as Brad ran his hands over the firm mounds of my breasts, kneading my mammary globes. On the common, in broad daylight? This was a nightmare, it had to be. I'd wake up in my bed, sweating, breathing deeply after my dream.

Kenny Smith held my arms behind my back as Brad unbuttoned my blouse. I could say nothing as he opened my blouse and revealed my white lace bra. Words wouldn't fall from my lips – I was speechless. My arms pulled tighter behind my back, my chest projected forward, my breasts heaved within my straining bra. I should never have gone to the common. The idea had been crazy, dangerous . . .

'I'll go straight to the police,' I said as Brad slipped his fingers beneath the cups of my bra. 'I'll—'

'You've not been very nice to Sally,' Brad murmured threateningly, yanking my bra up and exposing the ripe teats of my rounded breasts. 'And you've not been at all nice to Julie.'

'They're my staff, for God's sake. Look, I don't even know you. You're mixing me up with—'

'If we're mixing you up with Rachael, then what of it?' Kenny asked, pulling my head back by my long blonde hair. 'Fiona, Rachael . . . We don't care what you call yourself.'

'I'm not standing for this,' I spat, struggling to break free. 'I shall go straight to the—'

'I wouldn't go running to the police,' Brad cut in,

tweaking my elongated nipples. 'Three of our members work at the medical company. If there's any trouble, you'll find yourself out of a job.'

'*What?*' I gasped. 'Oh, no, no. You've got it all wrong. The first thing I'll do is sack Sally, Julie and—'

'Rachael,' Kenny breathed, his face only inches from mine. 'You remember how it was in the good old days. You didn't go running to anyone back then, did you? And you won't go blabbing your mouth off now. Nothing's changed, Rachael. We're older now but, apart from that, things are still the same. The first thing you'll do is be extremely nice to Sally, Julie and Kathy. If we hear that you've—'

'You can go to hell,' I spat. 'I'll sack all three bitches, like I said.'

'This takes me back,' Kenny laughed. 'Just like old times, isn't it?'

'It is,' Brad agreed. 'Let's take a look at the spotty slag's cunt.'

'It's a shame Sally isn't here. Still, there will be other times.'

'There will not,' I returned angrily. 'If you think that you can—'

As they pulled me to the ground and spread my limbs, I struggled to break free. But I knew that trying to fight them off was futile. I'd been here before, abused, called names, degraded . . . Again, horrific memories flooded my mind. Brad Masters straddling my head as he knelt, his solid cock fucking my mouth, his throbbing knob shooting spunk down my throat . . . As my short skirt was pulled up over my stomach, I bit my lip and closed my eyes. They were scrutinizing my panties, just as they'd done time and time again all those years previously. I'd not fought then, but now . . .

'There's a wet patch on the fat cow's knickers,' Kenny laughed.

'I'm not fat,' I breathed, although I didn't know why.

'Let's take a look at her dirty little cunt,' Brad rejoined.

'Before we go any further,' Kenny began, kneading the firm mounds of my bared breasts. 'I think we should get something straight. The girls can quite easily ruin your business. If not ruin it, they can certainly cause you massive problems. Sack them, and you'll find that – well, let's just say that you'll regret it for the rest of your days, Rachael.'

'And we don't want any talk about the police,' Brad hissed. 'You might think that you're the big boss, but we have far more power than you'll ever know. Test us, if you want to. Sack one of the girls and you'll see what happens.'

'You can't do this,' I breathed as a fingertip slipped between my lower stomach and the tight elastic of my panties.

'The Brook Street Gang *can* and *will* do as they wish. You of all people should know that, Rachael.'

'I am *not* Rachael,' I persisted futilely. 'You obviously had dealings with my sister, and I dread to think what you put her through, but—'

'Shall we stop this sister crap?' Kenny interrupted me. 'You know us, you know the score. So cut the crap.'

'I think we'd better give her a taster,' Brad chuckled, tugging the top of my panties down. 'You like getting fucked, don't you, Rachael? You enjoy having your dirty little cunt fucked.'

'If you dare to—'

'More threats?' he laughed, pulling my panties down further and exposing the crack of my pussy. 'I don't know what you thought you were doing by employing the girls. You knew who they were. Whatever your plan was—'

'Revenge,' Kenny broke in, his wide eyes gazing longingly at my vaginal crack as Brad tore my panties from my trembling body and spread my legs wide. 'Revenge. That's what she had in mind, I'll bet my life on it.'

'I think you've got it,' Brad said, positioning himself between my naked thighs and unzipping his jeans. 'She came back here to—'

'I didn't,' I stated firmly, lifting my head and gazing in awe as he hauled his huge cock out of his jeans. 'I had no idea that Rachael was involved with you at school. She never said anything about—'

'She's talking crap again,' Kenny said. 'You'd better shove your cock up her dirty little cunt and fuck her senseless.'

*Shove your finger up the fat cow's dirty little cunt. Force the spotty slag to suck the spunk out of your cock.* My teenage nightmares returning, I grimaced as I felt the bulbous knob of Brad's penis slip between the moist petals of my inner lips. I could feel the solid shaft of his cock stretching my vaginal canal, his swollen knob journeying along my sex shaft to the creamy ring of my cervix. My inner labia stretched tautly around the thick root of his rock-hard cock as his purple glans pressed hard against my cervix. He withdrew his organ and then rammed his sex globe back deep into my young body.

'God, you've got a hot little cunt,' Brad gasped, his swinging balls battering the smooth spheres of my naked buttocks with every thrust of his massive penis. 'I'm pleased that you're back in town.'

'So am I,' Kenny chortled. 'It's about time we had some fresh cunt.'

'Fresh cunt, fresh arse, fresh mouth – and all belonging to Rachael Michaels.'

Kenny knelt behind me, gazing at the forced penetration of my vagina as he unzipped his jeans and hauled out his own huge cock. His heavy balls resting on my forehead, he began wanking his solid shaft. I gazed wide-eyed at his purple knob as it appeared and disappeared with the back-and-forth rolling of his foreskin. Breathing in his male scent, the hairs covering his fleshy scrotum tickling my face, I couldn't believe that I'd got myself into this situation. Brad's penis repeatedly gliding deep into the tightening sheath of my cunt, inflating my pelvis, I swore to sack the three girls the minute I got back to my office.

Although I was afraid of the gang and what they might do, I couldn't allow them to dictate to me. If the sluts I'd employed thought for one minute that they had any kind of hold over me, I'd be ruined. There was no way I was going to put up with Sally emerging from her office and informing me that she was leaving early or was taking a day off. Once I'd allowed the tables to be turned, I'd be finished. What could I do other than sack them?

Watching Kenny's foreskin rolling back and forth over the purple globe of his penis, I knew that he was going to spunk over my face. His penis had grown since our schooldays. Long, thick . . . Was he going to fuck my cunt once Brad had splattered my cervix with his sperm? *Fresh cunt, fresh arse, fresh mouth . . .* Surely they wouldn't force their hard cocks deep into my tight arse and flood my bowels with their sperm? My semi-naked body rocking as Brad fucked me, repeatedly ramming his cock deep into my tight cunt, I found myself thinking about leaving Southmoore again.

I couldn't leave, I knew as the young men began gasping. If I ran away now, I'd not only lose my job – I'd have to run for ever. Dave Bryant wouldn't keep me on. Certainly not as deputy managing director of the company. Even if he *did* allow me to return to the London office, the gang would know where I was and probably come after me. I wouldn't be safe anywhere, I knew. Now that they'd found me, now that they were sexually abusing me yet again, they wouldn't allow me to hide. I had to fight, there was no other way. Sack the girls, keep away from the common and—

'Here it comes,' Kenny Smith murmured, wanking his cock faster. His white sperm shooting from his engorged knob, raining over my face as I squeezed my eyes shut, I felt Brad's cock swell to an incredible size within the hugging sheath of my vagina. Pinching my nose with his free hand, Kenny forced me to open my mouth and gasp for air. Positioning his knob as he continued to wank, his spunk dripping into my mouth, bathing my tongue, I had no choice but to swallow his semen. I could hear the squelching sound of sperm and girl-juice as Brad's orgasming penis glided deep into my cunt and withdrew, again and again. I hated the sound of the birds singing in the trees, the sounds of the common, the sound of crude sex.

My breasts bared, my mouth filling with sperm, my vagina brimming with spunk, I felt the degradation I'd known only too well as a young teenage schoolgirl. Pinned to the ground, half naked, throat-fucked, cunt-fucked . . . I felt as though I'd never moved on from my schooldays. The same men, the same common, surrounded by the same bushes ... Only the date had changed. I couldn't go back to the office, I thought, listening to the squishing of semen as Brad's cock repeatedly drove deep into my drenched cunt. My clothes were filthy, crumpled ... But it wasn't only the state of my clothes. I couldn't face Sally.

Watching as Kenny brought out the last of his spunk, the white liquid hanging in long threads from his purple knob before falling into my open mouth, I felt my naked breasts bouncing as Brad made his last thrusts into my hot quim. Finally stilling his penis, his knob pressing against my spunked cervix, he leered at me. How the hell had I got myself mixed up again with the Brook Street Gang? Swallowing the remnants of Kenny's orgasmic liquid, I asked myself the question over and over. I should never have employed Sally. I should have pushed all thoughts of vengeance out of my mind. I should never have returned to Southmoore.

'Look at the state of the dirty little slag,' Kenny chuckled, wiping his sperm-dripping knob over my face.

'And just look at her dirty knickers,' Brad rejoined, slipping his deflating cock out of my inflamed cunt and grabbing my panties. 'Oh dear, they're torn,' he chortled, ripping the flimsy material into shreds.

'Let's get out of here,' Kenny said, standing up and zipping his jeans. 'The boss has got to get back to work and be nice to the girls.'

'We'll be informed of your behaviour,' Brad hissed, rising to his feet and concealing his pussy-slimed cock in his jeans. 'One wrong move, and you'll be very sorry.'

'One wrong move or not, you're going to have your arse fucked rotten,' Kenny chuckled.

As they slipped through the bushes and made their

escape, I sat upright and looked around me. The same men, the same bushes . . . Hauling my semi-naked body up, I swayed on my sagging legs as I cupped my firm breasts in my bra and buttoned my blouse. Adjusting my skirt, sperm coursing down my inner thighs, I wiped the spunk from my face with the back of my hand. Used, abused, humiliated, degraded . . . Lowering my head and gazing at my crumpled clothes, I looked like a tramp. I couldn't go back to the office in that state, so I decided to take the train to London and go home. I'd return to the office in the morning and . . . Sack the girls? *One wrong move or not, you're going to have your arse fucked rotten.*

# 5

I hadn't been to work for two days. Unable to face the girls, I'd called Dave Bryant and told him that I was ill. I felt that I'd failed. Not only had I let the company down, but myself. I'd never before taken time off work. In all my years at Dagridge Medical Supplies, I'd not taken one day off. I had to face the girls, I knew as I sat on the train and stared out of the window at the rows of houses passing by. The back gardens were full of junk. Prams, bikes, broken-down sheds, old washing machines . . . My mind too was full of junk.

'Good morning, Miss Michaels,' Walker greeted me as I entered the building. Ignoring him, I took the lift to my office and hesitated outside the door. My hands trembling, I felt . . . I don't know how I felt. Frightened? Anxious? I was the boss, for fuck's sake. Anger welling from the pit of my stomach, I finally opened the door and headed for my desk. Sitting in my swivel chair, I looked up as Sally emerged from her office. This was it, I thought, smiling at her. This was what I'd been hiding from.

'Good morning, Sally,' I said.

'Are you feeling better, Miss Michaels?' she asked me.

'Much better, thank you.' Was there a glint in her eyes? Was she gloating? 'Right, I have some catching-up to do,' I said, sorting through some papers on my desk. 'Would you get me a cup of coffee, please?'

'I thought that you might get *me* a cup of coffee,' the girl replied impishly.

'Has Tim Black mentioned the shipment to Spain?' I asked, deciding not to play into her hands. 'There was a problem with the hauliers and—'

'No sugar,' she murmured, returning to her office and closing the door behind her.

Leaping to my feet, my stomach knotting with anger, I walked across the thick carpet to Sally's door. Hesitating, I took a deep breath. The gang weren't going to dictate to me, they weren't going to rule my life. I had to put a stop to this before it got out of hand. *Shit*, I thought, grabbing the door handle. It *was* out of hand. I wouldn't go as far as sacking Sally, I decided. I'd be firm, let her know who was boss and . . . Opening the door, I walked into her office with my head held high.

'Sally, please got me a cup of coffee,' I said sternly.

'Don't play games, Rachael,' she giggled. 'Things are changing around here. Get your own bloody coffee.'

'Sally, I don't want to have to sack you.'

'You just dare.'

'Look, Kenny and Brad . . . They seem to think that I'm Rachael Michaels. Rachael is my sister. She lives in America with her husband and—'

'Is there a problem?' Julie asked, leaning in the doorway with Kathy Higgins hovering behind her.

'I'm glad you're both here,' I said as they walked into the room and closed the door. 'Let's sort this nonsense out before—'

'She's lost her spots,' Julie said.

'And her fat,' Kathy rejoined.

'I'll bet she's still got a dirty little cunt,' Sally giggled.

'If this is the way you treated Rachael when you were at school . . .' I began.

'I hear that you got yourself fucked on the common the other day,' Kathy laughed.

'I'll give you one more chance,' I said shakily, realizing that I was losing. 'All get back to work or—'

'Show us your dirty little cunt,' Julie hissed. 'Go on. Lift your skirt up and pull your knickers down.'

'Julie, please get back to—'

'Perhaps you'd rather *we* pulled your knickers down?' Sally said, moving towards me.

'My God,' I breathed, shaking my head. 'Do you really think that you can do this and get away with it? All of you get back to work this minute or you'll find yourselves—'

As Kathy Higgins grabbed me from behind, pinning my arms behind my back, Julie yanked my skirt up over my stomach and pulled my panties down to my knees. I'd known what they were like at school, but I'd never thought that they'd do this. They obviously had no fear, no qualms. To do this to me in the office was . . . As Sally knelt in front of me and ran her fingertip up and down my vaginal crack, I struggled to break free. Her finger gliding deep into the creamy sheath of my cunt, she looked up at me and giggled.

'Remember this?' she asked me. 'Do you remember us fingering your dirty little cunt?'

'You're all out of a job,' I hissed, struggling against Kathy's grip.

'Shove this up her dirty little cunt,' Julie said, grabbing a pen from the desk.

'Her dirty little cunt isn't so little now,' Sally laughed, forcing a second finger into my vagina. 'She's become slack in her old age. The pen would get lost. We'll have to get some candles.'

'Get out of here,' I spat as Sally managed to drive a third finger into my violated vagina. 'All of you get out of here and—'

'You listen to me, slut,' Julie hissed, grabbing my hair and yanking my head back. '*We* run things around here now. You play the game, and you'll keep your job. Fuck up, and you'll be out. Got it?'

'I'll keep an eye on the slut,' Sally said, slipping her wet fingers out of my pussy and standing up. 'Suck your cunt juice off my fingers,' she giggled, holding my nose and forcing me to open my mouth. 'Does it taste nice?' she asked, pushing her fingers into my mouth. 'Do you like the taste of your own cunt?'

'Let's go down to the canteen for coffee,' Kathy said, finally releasing my arms.

'I'll see you later,' Sally hissed, following her friends through the door. 'Don't forget what we said, will you?'

As they left, I pulled my panties up and adjusted my skirt. Tears streaming down my face, I returned to my desk and flopped into my swivel chair. I'd failed miserably, just as I had at school. I'd lost, and the Brook Street Gang had won. Sighing, I wiped my streaming eyes and wondered what the hell to do. If I confided in Dave Bryant . . . OK, so he could sack the bitches. But where would that leave me? They'd hang around outside, lurking, waiting, just as they had at school. Thanking God that I hadn't yet found a flat and moved to Southmoore, I looked up as Walker knocked and entered.

'What is it?' I snapped angrily.

'Your new secretary, Sally. She said that you wanted to see me.'

'No, I . . . er . . . yes, that's right. Would you bring me some coffee, please?'

'Certainly, Miss Michaels.'

'And, Walker . . . thanks.'

'It's no trouble, Miss Michaels.'

Shaking my head as he left and closed the door, I was determined to remain strong. No matter what the bitches did to me, I wasn't going to allow them to drag me down. Strong? How the hell could I remain strong when they were pulling my panties down and mocking me? I was supposed to be the bitch from hell. Had I met my match? *Shit*, I thought, banging my fist on the desk. I'd taken time off work, there was no way I was going to get anything done . . . Leaving my chair, I paced the floor and tried to formulate a plan. A plan? What plan? There was nothing I could do.

Realizing that this was only the beginning of the nightmare, I could see that I had no choice other than to move back to the London office. The gang would find me, but at least they wouldn't be living on my doorstep. They'd have to come up to London every time they wanted to abuse me. They'd have to wait outside the office block, follow me and . . . I'd find another flat, I decided. Sell my present flat and rent another one under a different name. The problem was Dave Bryant. We'd worked for months on opening the new office in Southmoore. Planning, recruiting staff . . . To inform him that I was walking out at this stage . . .

As Sally returned from the canteen and went into her office, I clenched my fists and gritted my teeth. The smug little tart thought that she was so clever. I didn't know what I had in mind as I locked my office door. Walking into Sally's office, I stood in front of her desk and grinned at her. Confused and angry as I was, I nonetheless ordered her to stand up. She smirked, leering at me as she told me again to get her a cup of coffee. Grabbing her arm and pulling her to her feet, I dragged her into the centre of the room. She was alone now, without her friends to defend her. Struggling as I forced her to bend over her desk, she spat her expletives and threats.

'You'll pay for this,' Sally said as I yanked her skirt up over her back and pulled her panties down.

'Shut up, you dirty bitch,' I hissed, spanking her naked buttocks with the palm of my hand.

'When the others hear about this . . . Get off me, you dirty slag!'

'*You*'re the dirty slag, Sally,' I snapped, thrashing her tensed bottom as hard as I could.

'I'm warning you, bitch.'

'No one warns me. No one threatens me, warns me, humiliates me, degrades me . . .' Again and again, I brought my hand down across her reddening buttocks. 'You dare to treat me like that,' I hissed, pinning her down with my free hand as I continued the merciless spanking.

'You've done it now, you filthy cow. When the others hear about this . . .'

'Now, get out of here,' I whispered through gritted teeth, throwing her trembling body to the floor.

Kicking Sally's crimsoned buttocks as she crawled through the open door and finally clambered to her feet and pulled her panties up, I watched her run. I was shaking uncontrollably, my fists clenched, my teeth gritted, as I let myself back into my office, sat behind my desk and tried to slow my breathing. *What the hell have I done?* I thought, trying to calm myself. Attacking my secretary, physical violence . . . I couldn't work. My mind flooded with a million thoughts, I could do nothing.

I nearly had a heart attack when Walker knocked on the door and brought in a tray of coffee. Thanking him, my trembling hand pouring the coffee, I waited until he left before opening my desk drawer and taking out a packet of cigarettes. I hadn't smoked for ten years but I'd kept a packet in the drawer as a reminder, hoping that I'd never be forced to open it. Lighting a cigarette, I inhaled deeply, my head spinning as the nicotine quickly took effect. Blowing smoke high into the air, I jumped as the phone rang.

'Hi, Fiona,' Dave said as I pressed the receiver to my ear.

'Hi, how are things?' I asked, trying to come across as calm and collected.

'Fiona, I've just had a phone call,' he said mysteriously.

'Oh?'

'Your new secretary. Did you . . . I know that this is going to sound ridiculous, but did you physically attack her?'

'*What?*' I gasped, laughing. 'Physically attack her? Good God, no. Whatever gave you that idea?'

'She rang me just now. She said that she was working at her desk and you burst in and attacked her. She said that you threw her to the floor and kicked her.'

'Dave, I've just sacked the girl. That's obviously why she's gone running to you with her lies.'

'She said that you'd sacked her for no reason.'

'No reason? Good grief, she's late for work, she fucked up the computer, she's rude—'

'OK, OK. I just thought that I'd better let you know. I'm hoping to get down tomorrow. We'll have lunch, OK?'

'Yes, I'll look forward to it.'

Replacing the receiver, I drew hard on my cigarette. Sally was a fucking bitch. What the hell was she going to do now? It was difficult to predict. She'd been sacked. She'd told the MD that she'd been sacked so she could hardly turn up for work as usual the following morning. The afternoon wearing on, I began to think about leaving the office and walking to the station. They'd be waiting for me, I was sure. They'd be waiting, just as they used to wait for me when I left school.

Pacing the floor, I looked out of the window at the view of Southmoore School. Wishing again that I'd never returned to the stinking town, I decided to leave early and catch a mid-afternoon train. Grabbing my jacket, I left my office and took the stairs to the ground floor rather than risk being seen in the lift. Slipping through the main doors, I walked briskly along the street, constantly turning my head to make sure that I wasn't being followed. The railway station in sight, I stopped and opened my briefcase as my mobile phone rang.

'Jenny?' Ian asked.

'Oh, hi,' I murmured.

'Any chance of meeting up? I've managed to get away early and I thought—'

'I can't, Ian. I'm pretty busy right now.'

'Oh, that's a shame. By the way, Julie rang me.'

'Oh?'

'Her boss, Rachael Michaels, attacked Sally in the office.'

'Attacked her? What for?'

'There's been a load of trouble. Shit, I wish I had nothing to do with that bloody gang.'

'The Brook Street Gang? What's been going on, Ian?'

'I can't tell you over the phone. It's a bloody nightmare. I feel sorry for Rachael. After all she went though at school . . . Anyway, I'd better let you go.'

I checked my watch. 'OK, let's meet. I have a little time so we'll meet and you can tell me about it.'

'Great. On the common?'

'Er . . . well . . .'

'Is there a problem?'

'No, no.' Three-thirty. They wouldn't expect me to be on the common. 'OK, I'll see you there.'

Walking to the common, I hoped that I'd be able to glean some more information from Ian. The girls wouldn't know that I'd left the building, let alone gone to the common, so I reckoned that I had an hour or so. If I could discover more about the gang, their clandestine activities . . . My fingers crossed, I walked around the edge of the common, taking the long way round to the bushes. There was no sign of Ian, so I slipped into the bushes and sat on the soft grass.

This was dangerous, I knew as I looked around for my shredded panties. But I had to speak to Ian and try to discover what the gang intended to do about Rachael Michaels. My panties had gone. Brad had taken them, I was sure. *Fuck my panties*, I thought, my heart racing as I thought I heard someone approaching. A twig cracking underfoot, I realized that I must have been mad to go to the common. Ian was in the gang. If he'd told the others that I'd be there . . .

'Hi, Jenny,' he said, smiling as he slipped through the

bushes into the clearing. 'Are you all right? You look as though you've seen a ghost.'

'No, no. I'm fine,' I replied, breathing a sigh of relief. 'So, what's all this about Sally's boss attacking her?'

'It's a long story. Jenny, I need someone to talk to. This business with the gang . . .'

'Go on,' I coaxed him.

'I never wanted to be in the bloody gang. OK, I'll start at the beginning. This blackmail stuff. Rachael was never aware of it, but the gang used to take photographs of her.'

'Photographs?' I echoed.

'When they had her naked on the common, they took incriminating photographs.'

'Why?'

'It started out as a laugh. Then they thought that they could blackmail her, threaten to show the schoolteachers and her parents unless she allowed them to have sex with her.'

'And *did* they blackmail her?'

'No. She left school and they hoped that she'd get a job locally. They were going to threaten to send copies of the photographs to her boss. Anyway, she left town, disappeared, and that was that.'

'Have you seen the photographs?'

'Yes, I have. The gang were careful not to show their faces in the pictures. All you can see is Rachael with a cock in her mouth and her face clearly depicted as she sucks on a girl's nipple, that sort of thing. Some of them are pretty disgusting. I can tell you.'

'But that was years ago, Ian. No one would recognize her now, surely?'

'You're right. That's why they've taken more photographs.'

'*More?* When?'

'Apparently, she was here the other day with Brad and Kenny. They fucked her and . . . well, Rod was hiding in the bushes with a camera. Need I say more?'

'God,' I breathed. 'And they're going to show them to her boss, is that it?'

'Worse than that. They're going to send copies to all the staff – including those at the London office.'

'Unless she does what? Do they want money?'

'No. Well, not directly. I told you about the married women they're blackmailing, didn't I?'

'Yes.'

'The gang take porn pics of the women and sell them to a Dutch magazine.'

'A dirty mag?'

'Yes, and they do bloody well out of it. Basically, they want to take porn pics of Rachael. If she won't go along with it, then every member of staff at the medical supply company will receive copies of the photographs of Rachael with Kenny's cock spunking into her mouth and Brad's cock up her fanny.'

'Fuck,' I breathed, realizing that this was far worse than I could ever have imagined.

It occurred to me that Ian might be lying. After all, he *was* a member of the gang. If he knew that I was Rachael Michaels and was lying about the photographs . . . Rod could have easily hidden in the bushes, I reflected. With a cock in my mouth and another fucking my cunt, I wouldn't have seen or heard him. I had to trust Ian, I decided. Not as far as revealing my true identity, of course, but at least I had to try to turn him against the gang.

'You'll have to do something, Ian,' I said. 'You can't allow this sort of thing to go on.'

'*Allow* it?' he echoed, frowning at me. 'I hardly *allow* it, Jenny. What the hell can I do about it?'

'There must be something. Your wife is in on it, for God's sake. You can't allow Julie to . . .'

'It's all gone too far. This has been going on since we were at school. The gang are so organized now that . . . There's nothing I can do about it, Jenny.'

'So, Rachael attacked Sally?'

'Yes.'

'What are the gang going to do now?'

'Fucking hell, I dread to think. They don't mess about, I can tell you that. There was a girl a few years back. She'd cheated on her husband and the gang blackmailed her. She was only nineteen and didn't know what to do so she went along with it and allowed the girls to take porn pics of her with Brad and Kenny. She thought that, by telling her husband that she'd had a fling, the gang would have no reason to blackmail her. Her husband forgave her and she told the gang to sod off. But the stupid girl hadn't thought about the porn pics. The gang then threatened to send copies to her husband.'

'What happened?'

'Because she'd caused trouble, the gang continued to take photographs of her. But not ordinary porn pics.'

'What sort of pictures were they?'

'Suffice it to say that the photographs were taken on a farm.'

'On a farm? But what . . . Oh, God. Yes, I'm with you.'

'As I said, they don't mess about. After attacking Sally like that, I think Rachael's fate is sealed.'

'Ian, there must be something we can do to help her.'

'Such as?'

'I don't know. But we can't just sit back knowing that she might end up at a farm . . . There must be something we can do. Is there anything you know about the gang that Rachael could threaten them with?'

'There's plenty. Blackmail, but it can't be proved. Extortion, using girls for crude sex, illegal porn pics . . . But you try to prove it. They're not stupid, Jenny.'

'Maybe not, but I'll find a way of putting a stop to this.'

'Don't get involved. I doubt that they even remember Jenny Wilder, let alone want to . . . Just keep out of it.'

*Don't get involved?* It was rather late for that, I reflected. I was in up to my ears, and there was no way out. Hiding in London, leaving the company . . . Perhaps there was a way out, but to have to run as I'd done the minute I'd left school . . . If I ran now, I'd be running for ever. If I stayed, I'd have to endure the horrors of the Brook Street Gang every day. Ian couldn't escape. Unless he moved abroad, I pondered. Perhaps I should leave the country and settle somewhere near the Mediterranean. Sun, sex . . .

Strangely, my arousal was heightening. The last thing on my mind should have been sex but . . . Perhaps, subconsciously, I thought that sex might somehow comfort me. Gazing at the tight crotch of Ian's jeans, I could make out the shape of his balls. I should have been concerned about the gang, my job, my future. This was no time for sex. Checking my watch, I knew that I could still catch an early train. Sally and her cronies were probably hoping that I'd walk to the station at five o'clock. If I headed for the station now . . .

'The best thing you can do is go back to Australia,' Ian said. 'There's nothing in Southmoore for you.'

'I wonder why the gang never went for me at school,' I murmured, resting my hand on his knee. 'Why did they pick on Rachael Michaels?'

'She was easy, I suppose. Fat and spotty, she had no friends. She was always alone, walked home by herself . . . She was defenceless.'

'Had she been slim and attractive, I don't suppose they'd have bothered her.'

'They did go for Alison Wheeler once.'

'She was very attractive. What happened?'

'What they didn't know was that she had a big brother. They soon backed off once he showed up and threatened them.'

'It's a shame that Rachael didn't have a big brother.'

Reclining on the grass, I parted my legs wide and grinned at Ian. He gazed at my naked thighs, probably wishing that he'd never married Julie. Not only had he married her, he'd married the gang. He couldn't get out of the gang, and I got the impression that he couldn't escape from Julie either. She was the scout, he'd said. She was the one who sniffed around for adultery and built up dossiers on cheating partners with a view to blackmailing them.

'I need to come,' I breathed as Ian stroked the naked flesh of my inner thighs.

'I'm sure that I can oblige,' he replied, his dark eyes sparkling.

'Your tongue, Ian. I want your tongue.'

'Of course.'

'I . . . I might not see you again. I want you to lick me like you've never licked a girl before.'

'You might not see me again? But—'

'Australia. I might be going back there. Lick me, Ian. Lick my cunt.'

Slipping my panties down my long legs as I lifted my buttocks clear of the ground, he pulled them off my feet and spread my thighs. I looked up at the trees towering above me as he positioned himself between my legs and kissed my blonde fleece-covered mons. I could feel his hot breath playing on my vagina, his tongue licking each outer lip in turn. Arching my back, I stretched my limbs and closed my eyes. I needed this, I thought as his wet tongue ran up the length of my sex valley. I needed to relax, both physically and mentally.

Parting the fleshy cushions of my outer labia, exposing the intricate folds of my sex crack, Ian tentatively licked the sensitive tip of my erect clitoris. I could feel my love juices trickling from the opening of my vagina, running down between the cheeks of my buttocks, as he expertly tongued my painfully solid nubbin. I was growing fond of Ian. Not having had a relationship for some years, I realized what I'd been missing. This was only the third of our clandestine meetings in the bushes, but I was already hoping that we'd meet regularly.

How the hell could we meet again? I reflected on the problem, listening to the slurping of Ian's tongue as my thoughts returned to the gang. I doubted that I'd ever come within twenty miles of Southmoore again, so we could hardly carry on with our illicit affair. And, I had to remind myself, whatever I felt about Ian, he *was* part of the gang. An unwilling member, a part-time member . . . Whatever he was, I couldn't change the fact that he was one of the Brook Street Gang.

His tongue delving into the gaping entrance to my well-creamed cunt, I began gasping and writhing. God, did I need this, I thought, digging my fingernails into the soft grass as my body became rigid. His wet tongue again working around the solid shaft of my clitoris, I began whimpering as the birth of my orgasm stirred within my convulsing womb. My pleasure building, my head spinning as I slipped into a state of sexual delirium, I could feel my body tingling, my muscles tightening.

'Yes,' I gasped, my clitoris exploding in orgasm beneath his sweeping tongue. Driving at least three fingers deep into the spasming sheath of my drenched cunt, Ian finger-fucked me as he sustained my amazing pleasure with his wet tongue. My body rocking as he repeatedly thrust his fingers deep into my contracting vaginal duct, he sucked hard on my pulsating clitoris, bringing out wave after wave of orgasmic pleasure. Shuddering tremors of sex rolling through my quivering body, I thought that I'd never come down from my sexual heaven as my clitoris pulsated wildly and my orgasm peaked.

My mind dizzy with sex, I wasn't aware of Ian unzipping his jeans. Crying out as he thrust the entire length of his solid cock deep into my hot pussy, I could feel my lower stomach bloating as his bulbous knob pressed hard against the creamy ring of my ripe cervix. Repeatedly rocking his hips, his penis withdrawing and thrusting into my tightening cunt, his swollen glans battering my cervix, he fucked me with a vengeance. Again realizing how much I'd missed sex, I looked up at the sun sparkling through the foliage of the trees high above me.

All thoughts of the gang were leaving my mind, drowning in a sea of sex as Ian fucked me. The squelching sound of my vaginal juices filling my ears, the birds singing, I brought my knees up to my chest and parted my thighs to the extreme. With better access to the inner core of my young body, Ian's cock thrust deeper into my cunt, my lower abdomen rising and falling as he thrust and withdrew, thrust and withdrew. My sex juices streaming down between the firm cheeks of my naked bottom, my clitoris swelling against the wet shaft of his massaging shaft, I knew that I was going to reach another mind-blowing climax.

My cunt flooding with spunk as my clitoris erupted in yet another shuddering orgasm, I grabbed my ankles and pulled my feet either side of my head. My cunt lips bulging between my thighs, rolling back and forth along Ian's pistoning shaft, I knew that I'd found my sexual soulmate. Feeling as though I was at one with Ian, our bodies entwined in lust, I imagined running away with him and starting a new life. I'd forget my job, sell my flat, and run off to some faraway country where the sun shone and the sky was blue.

But they were dreams, I knew as my orgasm began to recede and Ian slowed his fucking motions. His cock finally stilling deep within my spunked vagina, he rested his weight on his hands as he looked down at my sex-flushed face. Our starry-eyed gazes locked and no words fell from our lips as we trembled in the aftermath of our loving. *Run away?* I mused. *No*. There were too many problems to run from. Ian was married, he thought that I was Jenny Wilder . . .

Hearing voices, Ian slipped his dripping cock out of my appeased cunt and leaped to his feet. Peering over the top of the bushes as he zipped his jeans and I grabbed my panties, he turned and frowned at me. It was the gang, heading our way. Ordering me to slip though the bushes and make my escape in the opposite direction, he said that he'd keep them talking until I was well away from the common. Tugging my panties up and grabbing my briefcase, I didn't hesitate. Was there no escaping reality? I thought about that weighty matter while smiling at Ian before creeping through the bushes. Running like the wind to the wooded area on the far side of the common, the tight crotch of my panties filling with a blend of sperm and girl-juice, I finally took cover.

'Shit,' I panted, resting on the grass beneath the trees. I'd had a lucky escape, but what was I to do now? The woods backed onto a canal so there was no way off the common without passing the bushes where Ian and the gang were now. I'd have to wait until they'd gone, I knew as I checked my watch. Wishing that I'd caught the early train instead of meeting Ian, I supposed that I'd learned something about the gang. More than something – I'd learned more about the horrors that they put young girls through.

I could never go back to the office, I knew that much. Still, with my track record, I'd have no trouble getting an executive position at some other company. Besides, I had a good deal of cash saved up for a rainy day. I wondered: was this the rainy day I'd been saving for? I peered through the trees at the clump of bushes. I couldn't see anyone and supposed that they were talking – or fucking. Why Ian stayed married to a slut like Julie . . . There again, it seemed that he had no choice. The gang would probably turn against him if he tried to get out of his marriage.

Hearing twigs cracking somewhere in the woods, I kept my head down. Someone walking a dog? Kids messing about? I couldn't be sure as I listened intently to the distant sound of bushes rustling. Hiding my briefcase beneath a bush as I heard someone mention my name, I knew that they were after me. It sounded like Kenny's voice telling the others to spread out. Crawling through the undergrowth, I looked for a ditch or a hole to hide in as I heard the girls whispering loudly.

Snagging my blouse on a branch, my hands covered in leaf mould, I managed to crawl into a shallow ditch beneath a thick bush and hide. I recalled hiding in the bushes all those years ago, feeling like an animal. Now I still felt like a hunted animal. The gang were getting closer, I knew as the whispers grew louder. My heart banging hard against my chest, I did my best to breathe quietly. One sneeze, one cough, the slightest movement . . . and I'd be fucked. Literally.

# 6

I was trembling like a leaf as I huddled in the ditch, trying to make myself smaller by pressing my face into the ground. Breathing in the scent of the decaying foliage, I opened one eye as I heard someone approaching. I could see a shoe, a man's shoe. He was only a yard or so away, searching for me, hunting me down. A girl joined him, her red shoes facing him. They were talking about me, about Rachael Michaels.

'She won't escape,' the man said. I immediately recognized Brad's voice. 'We'll find her and—'

'And I'll kill her for what she did to me,' Sally hissed.

'There'll be no killing,' Brad chuckled. 'Rod's brought his camera. We're after photographs of the slut's naked body, photographs of two cocks spunking in her mouth and—'

'And *then* I'll kill the fucking bitch. She kicked me as I crawled across my office floor. She beat me and then threw me to the ground and fucking kicked me. I'll kill her.'

Sally meant it, I was sure as I cowered in the ditch beneath the bushes. Again wishing that I'd never returned to Southmoore, let alone employed her, I prayed for them to give up the search and leave the woods. Had Ian told them where I was? The worrying possibility occurred to me. If they knew that I was somewhere in the woods, they wouldn't give up. This was the perfect opportunity to get me. After what had happened in the office, they were out for my blood, and they wouldn't give up. Ian wouldn't have told them, would he?

'We'll wait,' Brad said. 'She'll have to come out of hiding eventually.'

'There's only one way out of the woods,' Sally murmured. 'And Rod's covering the path with Kenny.'

'Rachael,' Brad called, his voice echoing throughout the trees. 'Rachael, we know that you're in here. Come out now and make it easy on yourself.'

'She won't come out,' Sally said. 'We'll just have to wait.'

She was right – there was no way that I'd show myself. They'd wait, and I'd wait. Who would give up first? Certainly not me. Once dusk fell, they'd leave, I was sure as I tried to ease myself gently into a more comfortable position. The decaying leaves I was lying on were damp, the moisture soaking into my blouse. Sperm was also soaking into my panties. I felt dirty. Once I was safely home, I'd take a shower and put on some clean clothes. Feeling hungry, I wondered whether Brad was about to leave as he walked towards the bushes. Had he spotted me?

Looking up, I gazed in horror through the foliage as he pulled out his flaccid penis. *God, no!* I thought as his sparkling liquid sprayed over the bush and splashed down onto me. My blouse soaked, my blonde hair drenched, I tried not to splutter as his golden rain splashed my face. On and on his flow of urine cascaded, gushing down on me as I huddled into a ball and squeezed my eyes shut. This was the ultimate degradation. My clothes had been clean, my hair shining, my make-up impeccable, my image smart . . . now I was filthy. I looked like a stinking tramp. But at least Brad hadn't noticed me.

His flow of golden liquid finally stopping, I opened my stinging eyes and gazed at him through the foliage of the bush. I recalled my schooldays when I'd wondered time and time again why I'd been singled out by the gang. No one deserved this, I thought: my clothes were soaked, my hair was wet and matted with urine. As Brad zipped his jeans, he gazed down at the bush. Had he seen me after all? Holding my breath, I froze, keeping perfectly still as he reached out and moved a branch aside. His dark eyes focusing on my huddled body, his narrow lips furling into a grin, he winked at me. Was there a hint of compassion reflected in the black pools of his eyes? Would he tell the gang that he'd found me? Offering him a slight smile, I prayed for him to walk away from the bush and call off the hunt.

'Hey, Sally,' he chuckled. 'Look what I've just pissed all over.'

'What?' Sally asked, standing by his side. 'Fuck me. It's the slut,' she laughed, staring at me. 'You've pissed all over my boss.'

'Where?' Rod asked, joining Sally. 'Oh, dear. You *have* pissed all over her.'

'I'd like to shit all over her,' Sally murmured.

'Hey, you lot,' Brad called. 'We've found the slag.'

'You'd better get out of there, Miss Michaels,' Sally ordered me. 'Unless you want the others to piss all over you as well.'

Clambering out of the ditch, my clothes sopping wet, my hair dripping, I cowered on the ground and curled up into a ball as Sally tried to roll me onto my back with her foot. The rest of the gang surrounding me, I wondered where Ian had got to. He'd obviously made some excuse or other and . . . Julie wasn't there either, I noticed as Sally again tried to roll me over. Had Ian gone to get her? Then I could hear Julie's voice calling as she ran towards the clearing. So where was Ian?

'Well, well, well,' Julie giggled as she joined the others and gazed at my filthy clothes. 'If it isn't the bitch from hell. Why is she soaking wet?'

'I pissed over her,' Brad laughed. 'Where's Ian?'

'Gone back to work, more than likely,' Julie replied. 'Fuck Ian, what are we going to do with the slut?'

'I know what *I*'m going to do to her,' Sally hissed, swinging her leg and slamming her foot into the small of my back.

'Hey, hey,' Rod breathed, grabbing Sally's arm and pulling her away. 'I don't want her covered in bruises. Get her stripped and we'll take some great pics for the mag.'

'Pics?' Sally echoed. 'But she's filthy. Look at the state of her. You can't take photographs . . .'

'This is perfect,' Rod murmured. 'A wood nymph. Yes, that's it. She lives in the woods with the animals. Her blonde hair is wet, trailing over her dirty blouse, her face is grubby, her skirt's torn . . . A pretty little waif living in the forest, grubbing around for food, sleeping with the animals . . . This is great.'

'If you say so,' Sally murmured.

'I do say so. An innocent little girl discovered at long last by missionaries trekking through the jungle. She believes that she'll be saved, taken back to civilization. But the missionaries fuck her pretty little body.'

'You fantasize too much,' Sally giggled.

'These photographs will be some of the best yet. OK, I'll take a few shots of her in her filthy clothes. Rip her blouse open and ease her tits out of her bra.'

Sally complied eagerly, pulling me to my feet before slapping my face and tearing the front of my blouse open and yanking my bra up. My long blonde hair was matted, hanging in rats' tails over my shoulders, cascading over my bared breasts. As if I didn't already look the part, Rod ordered me to pout as he clicked the camera shutter. Julie was leering at me, poking her tongue out and holding her middle finger up. This was only the beginning, I knew as Sally yanked my skirt up, exposing the sperm-soaked crotch of my panties.

'OK, now strip her,' Rob ordered the gang. The girls tore my clothes from my trembling body as the men watched and Rob checked his camera. Once I was naked, Sally stood in front of me, an evil glint in her blue eyes. All I could do was hope that someone would come along and the gang would flee. Where the hell was Ian? I wondered about his absence again as Sally spun me round and pinned my arms behind my back. If someone was walking their dog or . . . As Sally released my arms and gave me an almighty shove, I took a head-first dive through the rough branches of the bushes and landed with a thud back in the ditch.

'What did you do that for?' Rod snapped.

'Because she's a fucking bitch,' Sally retorted as I gazed at the weals across the pale flesh of my breasts.

'Get her out of there, for fuck's sake,' Rod ordered the girl. 'We're here to take porn pics, not conduct some private vendetta. If you want to make yourself useful, get her out of there and stand her against that tree.'

As the girl grabbed my wrist and hauled my naked

body out of the ditch, I managed to break away from her and stand up. Rod focused the camera on the sore teats of my breasts as Sally stood by his side, scowling at me. Hatred reflected in her blue eyes, she really did have it in for me. This was nothing to do with my spanking her, I reflected as she slipped her blouse off and unhooked her bra. She'd hated me at school, and still did. I had no idea why she felt that way, why any of them felt that way about me. Perhaps it had started because I'd been the spotty teenage girl with the brace and it had developed from there.

'OK,' Rod said, lowering his camera as Sally finished stripping and proudly displayed her naked body to the gang. 'We'll start with some lesbian tonguing. Sally, if you—'

'I know what to do,' Sally murmured, her pretty face grinning as she licked her succulent lips.

'You look great,' Rod chuckled, eyeing the gaping crack of her hairless vulva. 'Shaved and ready for lesbian love.'

'Shaved and ready for the spotty cow's tongue and—'

Grabbing Sally's arm, I flung her into the bush. Grinning as she crashed through the rough branches and fell into the ditch, I leered down at her. Groaning, spitting expletives, she propped herself up on one hand and rubbed her naked body. There were scratches across her breasts, her stomach. I'd pay for this, I knew. But it was worth it. Clambering out of the ditch as Rob again reminded everyone that he wanted to take some photographs, Sally climbed to her feet and stood in front of me. As she reached out to grab my nipple, I knocked her arm to one side. With the gang on her side, I knew that there was no way I'd win a fight. But I'd enjoy trying.

'You fucking bitch,' she hissed, slapping me round the head as hard as she could.

'Slag,' I snapped, spitting in her face.

'Are you just going to stand there, Rod?' she asked.

'I'm getting some great pics,' he replied.

'You're going to have some great pics of a dead slut in a minute,' she said, flinging her arm around my neck and pulling me to the ground.

'Oh, yes,' Rod chortled. 'Wrestling. This is excellent stuff.'

Her naked body on top of mine, Sally repeatedly slapped my face. She was incensed, that was pretty obvious, but I managed to roll over and pin her to the ground in turn. Our breasts pressed together, our legs entwined, we struggled on the ground as Rod took his photographs. The gang laughed and joked, but this was no game, I knew as Sally sank her teeth into my lower arm. Kneeing her inner thigh, I managed to free my arm from her mouth and grab hold of her breast. Sinking my fingernails into the firm mound, I placed my forearm across her throat to stop her struggling.

'You fucking bitch,' she hissed, trying desperately to roll over and turn the tables. 'You stink of piss, you filthy slut.' Managing to grab a length of my hair, she pulled hard. I then felt her fingernails dragging across my back and down to the cheeks of my buttocks. Locating my anus, she forced a finger deep into my rectum. Finally rolling over, we crashed into the ditch as Rod took several more photographs. I could feel the sharpness of her fingernail deep within my anal canal as she grabbed a broken branch from the ground with her other hand and began lashing my back. Trying to escape, I realized that she'd somehow jammed me in the ditch.

Her legs around me, her finger embedded deep within my rectum, I couldn't move.

'I'll teach you a fucking lesson,' she hissed, whipping my naked buttocks with the branch. Again and again the branch swished through the air, lashing the tensed cheeks of my naked buttocks, catching the backs of my thighs. Unable to free myself, I could do nothing to halt the gruelling beating as the gang egged Sally on. The crack of the branch landing across my stinging buttocks was punctuated by the clicking of Rod's camera and I knew that Sally wouldn't stop the thrashing. My bottom stinging like hell, I managed to free one arm and slip my hand between the girl's thighs. Easing several fingers into the hot, wet sheath of her tight cunt, I squeezed her inner flesh.

'Stop or I'll rip your cunt out,' I breathed. Grimacing, Sally halted the beating, trying to manoeuvre her naked body to slip my fingers out of her vagina. 'Tell them to go,' I ordered her.

'Are you all right, Sally?' Julie asked, looking down at her friend.

'I . . . She's grabbed my fanny,' the girl replied. 'I can't—'

'You'd better clear off,' I hissed, tightening my grip. 'Get out of here or I'll—'

'Go,' Sally gasped. 'I'll be all right.'

As the gang wandered off, I saw a glimmer of light at the end of the tunnel. All I needed was a chance to grab my clothes and run, and I'd be out of Southmoore in a flash. The gang would probably hide in the woods, waiting until I emerged. This wasn't much of a chance, but it was worth trying. Finally slipping my wet fingers out of Sally's vagina, I clambered up the bank of the ditch and grabbed my torn clothes.

'You won't escape,' Sally said, clambering out of the ditch. 'If you think—'

'I don't know why you're like this,' I cut in. 'I don't know what I've done to deserve this.'

'You haven't done anything,' she returned. 'You don't *have* to do anything. You're just what we want. Blonde, attractive . . .'

'Right,' Julie said, emerging from the bushes. 'Now the fight is over, we'll get down to taking some more porn pics.'

'You can start by licking my cunt out,' Sally ordered me, her blue eyes sparkling as she lay on the ground with her thighs splayed. 'Come on – we haven't got all day.'

'No,' I breathed as Brad and Kenny forced me to the ground.

'You heard her,' Kenny said, pushing my head close to the girl's yawning sex crack. 'Lick her cunt out.'

My face pressed against Sally's hairless vulval flesh as Rod knelt down and focused his camera, I tentatively pushed my tongue out and tasted the salty inner folds of her cunt. I could hear the camera shutter clicking as I ran my tongue over the tip of her solid clitoris. My chin forced between the rounded cheeks of her buttocks, my tongue working its way up and down the crack of her bared cunt, I gazed wide-eyed at the camera lens as Rod moved in and took several shots.

'Now lick my arsehole,' Sally gasped. 'Push your tongue into my arsehole and lick me out.'

'No!' I protested. 'For God's sake, there are limits . . .'

'There are no limits as far as the members of the Brook Street Gang are concerned,' Julie said, grabbing my head from behind. 'Now, lick her arsehole.'

Pushing my tongue out, I tasted the brown tissue

surrounding Sally's anus. Grimacing as the bitter-sweet taste stung the tip of my tongue, I again watched Rod focus the camera on the lewd act and take several shots. Parting Sally's buttocks wide, Julie instructed me to push my tongue deep into her rectum. Complying, I closed my eyes, breathing in the girl's anal scent as she quivered and gasped. She seemed to be enjoying my humiliation as well as the crude anal licking. She was nothing but a filthy tart, I mused, my tongue delving deeper into her rectal duct.

Once I was back in London, in the safety of my own flat, I knew that I'd never return to Southmoore. My job wasn't worth this, I thought as a hand kneaded the burning cheeks of my naked bottom. Licking another girl's cunt, tasting her sex juices, tonguing her bottom-hole, taking a gruelling thrashing . . . Nothing was worth enduring the horrors of the Brook Street Gang.

'Slide your cock into her arse,' Julie giggled. 'Go on, Kenny, give the slut a good arse-fucking.'

'No,' I yelped, slipping my tongue out of Sally's anus.

'No one asked *you* to comment,' Julie laughed. 'If I say you're having an arse-fucking, then you're having an arse-fucking.'

My naked body trembling, I could feel fingers sinking into my buttocks, parting the stinging globes of my bottom. Then the solid head of a penis was pressing against the tightly-closed ring of my anus. There was no point in protesting, I knew as the swollen glans pressed harder against the delicate tissue surrounding my secret hole. My tongue embedded deep within Sally's rectum, I knew that I was a slave to the gang's every perverted whim.

The bulbous knob trying to gain access to my rectal

duct, pressing harder against my anal hole, I couldn't imagine what it would be like to have a huge penis penetrate my rectum. Still, after the abuse I'd suffered in my early teens, I felt that this was almost normal. The gang stripping me on the common, fondling my naked body, laughing at me, fingering my sex hole . . . All they were doing now was taking the abuse a step further. Nothing had changed.

As the bulbous globe of Kenny's huge cock slipped past my anal ring and slid into my hot rectum, I thought that my anus was going to tear apart while I breathed in the heady scent of Sally's anal gully. This was degradation in the extreme, I reflected, recalling my early days of sexual discovery. When I'd been too young to know what was what, I'd fiddled with my vaginal lips while in my bed at night. My fingers had located the hard spot between the top of my outer lips and rubbed there. Orgasms had come freely, but it was some time before my fingers ventured down past my vaginal entrance to the tightly closed hole of my anus.

My first anal experience had been when I'd tickled the sensitive brown tissue surrounding my private hole. I was in my bed one Saturday morning. My parents had gone out shopping and there was no school so I was in no hurry to get up. My fingertip toying with my anus, I massaged myself there for some time before daring to slip my finger into my tight hole. The sensations were heavenly, my young body quivering wildly as I drove my finger deeper into my hot bum. I'd masturbated with one hand, massaging my clitoris to a massive orgasm as I'd fingered my bottom-hole with the other.

'Yes,' Kenny gasped, breaking my reverie as his solid shaft slammed brutally deep into my tight rectum. My brown tissue stretched to capacity, my tongue snaking deep inside Sally's bottom-hole, I shuddered uncontrollably in my sexual excess. I felt as though my pelvis was inflating and deflating as Kenny fucked me. My anal ring gliding back and forth along the greasy shaft of his cock, the in-and-out gliding of his huge organ rocking my naked body, I swore to get even with the gang. To violate my most secret hole, to force me to tongue Sally's anus . . . If it was the last thing I did, I'd get even with each and every member of the depraved, degenerate gang.

Suddenly, Kenny pulled his raping cock out of my bumhole. I soon found out why.

The branch swished through the air and landed across my weal-lined buttocks with a loud crack. I grimaced, cried out and turned my head. It was Julie, grinning as she raised the branch above her head and brought it down again. Sally ordered me to carry on licking her arse as I yelped with every lash of the branch. When Julie's arm grew tired, the thrashing ceased, only for Kenny's engorged prick to be thrust again into the dark depths of my anus. With Kenny's cock fucking my rectum and my buttocks stinging from the beating, I finally begged my abusers for mercy.

'You said that you were going to replace Tim Black,' Julie said.

'No, no . . . I didn't,' I whimpered.

'Yes, you did. You told me that you were going to replace him. OK, *I*'ll have his job.'

'You won't,' I gasped as Kenny increased his anal fucking rhythm.

'I'll start tomorrow. Get rid of Tim Black and I'll take his place tomorrow morning.'

'We'll take over,' Sally laughed, pulling her rounded

buttocks wide apart and exposing her salivated anus. 'Tongue-fuck my arse, you whore bitch,' she ordered me. 'Go on, keep tonguing my arsehole.'

Resuming my anal tonguing as Kenny began gasping, I knew that this was only the beginning of the nightmare. I had to run. There was no other option. The bitch from hell had lost. Kenny's cock swelling, his throbbing knob pumping my arse full of sperm, I knew that I'd not only lost the battle with the gang but I'd lost my job too. Dave Bryant wouldn't understand. After all the planning, the hard work setting up in Southmoore . . . The new office complex had been running for only a few days, and then I decide that I'm leaving. That was the only way Dave would be able to see it. There was no way he'd allow me to return to the London office. In fact, my leaving Southmoore might result in the new branch falling apart.

'There's nothing better than a tight-arsed whore,' Kenny gasped, repeatedly ramming his orgasming glans deep into my spunk-flooded bowels. I could feel his sperm lubricating his pistoning cock, oozing from the inflamed opening of my anus and trickling down between the gaping lips of my vagina. My arse crudely fucked, my tongue darting in and out of Sally's rectum . . . I was a tramp, a whore.

How the hell was I going to get home? I asked myself this question as the squelching sounds of cock pumping into spunk-lubricated rectum resounded around the trees. My clothes were in shreds, my body filthy . . . Perhaps I'd be able to do something with my clothes, try to piece them together and then wait until darkness fell before leaving the woods. How the hell could I go to the station in rags? I'd have to return to the office and order a taxi to take me to London.

'God, I needed that,' Kenny breathed, finally stilling his spent cock deep within the spunk-drenched sheath of my rectum.

'Suck his cock clean,' Sally said, pushing me away from her anus and sitting upright. 'Go on, Kenny. Make her suck your cock clean.'

'You can rot in hell,' I hissed, moving forward and sliding Kenny's deflating penis out of my aching bottom-hole. 'You can all rot in hell.' I started to get up, wincing with discomfort.

'Now *that* deserves a good thrashing,' Sally replied, her long blonde hair cascading over her pretty face as she grinned at me. 'A fucking good thrashing with the branch. Roll the filthy bitch over and pin her down.'

'You just dare,' I spat as Kenny and Julie forced me to lie back down on my stomach. My limbs spread, my naked buttocks projected, I grimaced as Sally grabbed the branch and knelt beside me.

'Are you ready for this?' she giggled.

'If you—'

The branch swishing through the air and landing squarely again across my already stinging buttocks with a deafening crack, I let out a yelp so loud that the birds fluttered from the trees and fled the woods. Again and again, Sally brought the branch down across the burning globes of my naked buttocks. But there was nothing I could do to halt the horrendous abuse of my young body. I couldn't fight, my threats were futile . . . And there was no point running to the police and crying rape.

My buttocks turning numb as the bitch continued the merciless lashing. I buried my face in the leaf mould covering the ground. My mind filled with thoughts of my schooldays as I listened to the cracking of the branch. I recalled the morning when the gang had cornered me in the classroom and ordered me to pull my knickers down. I'd got to school early, hoping that I'd escape them, but they were waiting. My navy-blue knickers around my knees, Sally knelt down and pushed a small candle deep into the shaft of my vagina. My punishment was to leave the candle in my pussy all day.

Pulling my knickers up, the tight crotch holding the candle in place, the gang had said that they'd take a look at my dirty cunt between each lesson. As I'd walked around the school, I could feel the candle massaging inside my vagina, inducing my pussy milk to flow into my knickers. Consumed by fear as they'd chased me after school and captured me in an alleyway, I'd promised to leave the candle in place overnight. Before I'd gone to bed that night, I'd defied them. Slipping the hot waxen shaft out of my pussy, I'd tossed it in the bin.

The following day, they'd captured me in the locker room and had checked my cunt. I knew that I'd be punished for my defiance, but when they'd pulled my knickers down to my knees and held my skirt up over my stomach, I couldn't believe their crudity. Kenny stood in front of me and pissed into my knickers. The hot liquid soaked into the navy-blue material, streaming down my legs and drenching my socks and shoes. Then they pulled my knickers up and told me to go to the classroom.

I had never felt so humiliated as when the teacher stood by my desk and sniffed the air. Gazing at the wet patch on the front of my skirt, she'd led me out of the classroom and had ordered me to go home and change. She'd obviously believed that I'd pissed myself, and my face had flushed with embarrassment. The gang had used the new form of punishment again and again. Many times I'd had to take my piss-soaked panties off and change my socks. I'd felt dirty, filthy, used and abused.

'We'd better get out of here,' Julie said as the laughter of approaching children grew louder.

'Time for the pub,' Sally giggled, bringing the rough branch down across my crimsoned buttocks one last time. 'I'll see you in the morning, Miss Michaels. And remember that I'll be taking Tim Black's place.'

'There's one more thing,' Kathy laughed, rolling me onto my back with her foot as Sally hurriedly dressed.

Looking up at the glee apparent in her expression as she stood with her feet either side of my naked body, I wondered what she was going to do. Lifting her skirt up and pulling her panties to one side, she parted the swollen lips of her vagina and exposed the pinken inner folds of her cunt. The stream of sparkling liquid splattering me, raining down over my writhing body, the gang laughed uncontrollably as I tried to crawl away.

I wondered what I had done to make them treat me like this, managing to roll over as the golden shower splashed over my filthy body. A thousand thoughts flooded my mind as I crawled across the grass. I should have left Southmoore School the minute the abuse had started. I should have told someone. I should never have returned to Southmoore. The children's laughter resounding through the woods, I breathed a sigh of relief as the Brook Street Gang finally fled.

Hiding in the ditch beneath the bushes until the kids had gone, I emerged from my hide and spread my piss-soaked clothes out on the ground. They were useless. Torn to shreds, there was nothing I could salvage, nothing to conceal my nakedness. Slipping my shoes on, I crept through the trees, retrieved my briefcase and grabbed my mobile phone. Who the hell could I call? I needed a coat, a long coat. Finally ringing the office switchboard, I was thankful to hear Walker's timid voice.

He'd had to stay on late and had happened to be passing the switchboard when I'd called. I ordered him to bring me a coat, any coat he could find. He questioned me, asking why I was in the woods and what I wanted a coat for. Threatening him with the sack, I told him to get to the woods within five minutes. Finally agreeing, he did his *Yes, Miss Michaels* routine. *Certainly, Miss Michaels. Of course, Miss Michaels.*

I knew that it was going to be highly embarrassing when Walker arrived, but decided to sack him regardless. I'd wanted to get rid of the snivelling idiot anyway, so I thought that I might as well do it when he'd brought me a coat. Peering out of the bushes, I could see him heading towards the trees with a coat slung over his shoulder. At least it was a warm summer evening, I reflected as the piss dried on my naked flesh. I had my shoes, my briefcase and a coat. I'd take the train home and, after a shower, I'd make my plans.

'Here,' I called as Walker stopped and looked around. 'Over here, in the bushes.'

'Oh, Miss Michaels,' he gasped, gazing wide-eyed at my naked body.

'Give that to me,' I hissed, reaching out and snatching the coat. 'Now, piss off.'

'But, Miss Michaels . . . what's happened to you?'

'You're fired,' I snapped. 'Don't bother coming in tomorrow, Walker. You're sacked.'

'I think not,' he returned, grabbing the coat back from me and flinging it over a high branch of a tree.

'What the hell do you think you're doing?' I yelled, folding my arms to conceal the erect nipples of my firm breasts. 'Get that bloody coat down or—'

'I'd better explain,' Walker sniggered, his dark-eyed gaze locked to the sperm-dripping crack of my vulva.

'Explain?' I echoed. 'Give me that fucking coat or I'll—'

'I've joined the gang,' he told me. 'I'm now a member of the Brook Street Gang.'

Reeling back, I almost collapsed to the ground as his shocking revelation hit me. Joined the gang? Sally and the others had obviously been busy, I mused, wondering what Walker's game was as he licked his narrow lips. Sex? I doubted it. The man was a wimp, a snivelling arse-licking wimp. Reaching up to grab the coat, I knew that I had to take control as he grabbed my arm.

'You've treated me like shit,' he breathed, pulling me close. 'I've done my best for the company. The work I've put in to get the new office up and running . . . and all you do in return is order me about and snap at me.'

'Walker, let me go and we'll talk about this,' I said as he tightened his grip on my arm.

'It's too late for talking, Miss Michaels. You've treated me like a lump of shit, and now . . .'

'Walker, please release my arm and—'

'If you want the coat, then you'll call me sir,' he chortled, finally releasing me. 'Go on. Call me sir.'

Staring in disbelief as he unzipped his trousers and hauled out his erect cock, I stepped back. This was a nightmare, like something out of a horror film. The gang might take over the entire Southmoore office and . . . I was going to have to talk to Dave Bryant, I knew. I'd have to tell him everything. There was no way I could deal with this alone and, if I wasn't careful, the gang might infiltrate the London office too and eventually run the whole company. Was that their intention?

'Kneel in front of your master and suck this,' Walker ordered me, pulling his fleshy foreskin back and exposing the ripe plum of his cock. 'Kneel and beg to suck my cock.'

'You can go to hell,' I hissed, reaching up for the coat.

'You can't get the coat,' he chuckled. 'It's too high, Miss Michaels. I suggest that you call me sir and beg to suck my knob if you want the coat.'

'Walker, if you want to keep your job—'

'You sacked me, remember?'

'Look, I'll keep you on if you stop this nonsense and pass me the coat.'

'Oh, by the way, Sally asked me for your address. She said that the gang would like to visit you, take a look at your London flat. I gave her your address and home phone number. I hope you don't mind.'

'Walker . . .'

'Kneel and suck my cock, you filthy slut,' he yelled, grabbing a tuft of my blonde hair. 'Suck out my spunk or you'll stay here all night.'

Kneeling, I opened my mouth and took his salty glans inside. Breathing heavily, Walker clutched my head as I rolled my wet tongue around the rim of his helmet and sucked gently. Never in a million years would I have dreamed that I'd suck Walker's cock. My naked body stinking of stale piss and spunk, my clothes in shreds . . . What the hell had happened to me? Kneeling in front of Walker in the woods with his knob in my mouth, I knew that I'd not only fallen prey to the gang and lost control, but I'd lost my dignity, my femininity.

Walker came quickly, his sperm flooding my gobbling mouth, bathing my snaking tongue, as I drank from his orgasming cockhead. Rocking his hips, gasping as he mouth-fucked me, he gripped my head hard. I thought that he'd never stop coming as his semen overflowed my mouth and dribbled down my chin. His sperm splattering my piss-drenched tits, bathing the ripe teats of my nipples, his finally withdrew and staggered back. Informing me that he'd mouth-fuck me every morning in my office, he zipped his trousers and reached up for the coat.

'Thank me for allowing you to suck my cock,' he chuckled, tossing the coat at me.

'Walker . . .' I began, licking my spunk-glossed lips as I donned the coat.

'Thank me, slut.'

'Thank you,' I breathed.

'Thank you, what?'

'Thank you, sir,' I snapped, buttoning the coat and grabbing my briefcase.

'Say it properly, Miss Michaels.'

'Thank you for allowing me to suck your cock, sir.'

'That's more like it. OK, you can suck out my spunk first thing in the morning. I'll come to your office at nine every morning and fuck your dirty mouth. Have a nice journey home.'

As he left the woods and headed across the common, I spat out the remnants of his sperm and brushed my piss-matted hair away from my dirty face. I felt like a tramp, looked like a whore . . . I was a filthy slut, just as I had been at school. Fucked, spunked, pissed on . . . There was no way I could return to the office, I knew as I made my way to the station. My job, my career, my whole way of life . . . The end had come, I knew.

# 7

'I can't go into the office,' I told Dave Bryant the following morning on the phone.

'Why not?' he asked irritably. 'Are you ill again?'

'No, it's not that. Dave, I want you to come over to my place. I need to talk to you.'

'Christ, I can't come over now, Fiona,' he sighed. 'I've got an important meeting and . . . What is it? What's wrong?'

'I don't want to talk about it over the phone.'

'This is most unlike you, Fiona.'

'Which should indicate that it's important.'

'OK, I'll cancel the meeting. This had better be good.'

'It is good. Or, I should say, it's bad.'

'Is it the Spanish lot?'

'No, no – it has nothing to do with the company.'

'Thank God for that. All right. Er . . . give me half an hour.'

'Half an hour, OK.'

Pacing the lounge floor, I found myself biting my nails as I waited anxiously for Dave. I'd not bitten my nails since I'd left school, for fuck's sake. What the hell was happening to me? School. Southmoore bloody School. I'd have to tell Dave everything, start at the beginning. The Brook Street Gang, the things they did to me at school, on the common . . . He'd think that I was crazy to allow Sally and the others to control me like this, I was sure. And now Walker was in the gang. . . . Shit, I dared not tell the MD about Walker the wanker. The doorbell ringing, I took a deep breath.

'Come in, Dave,' I said, opening the door. 'I'm glad you could make it.'

'What the hell is this all about?' he snapped, walking into the lounge and flopping onto the sofa. 'I've had to cancel—'

'Dave, listen to me,' I cut in. 'This is important.'

'Yes, and so was my meeting. You've got five minutes, Fiona.'

'It'll take a damned sight longer than five minutes,' I sighed, sitting in the armchair opposite him.

'Just get on with it.'

I told him about my schooldays, the Brook Street Gang and the sexual abuse. It was pretty obvious that he wasn't really listening as he repeatedly checked his watch and looked around the room. I was blabbing about the gang, the common, the school. I wasn't making sense, I knew. When I mentioned Sally and the others I'd employed, he shook his head and sighed. This wasn't the right time to talk, that was for sure. A cancelled meeting, my not going into the office . . . I should have waited until the evening. We should have met in a quiet bar where we could have talked. Where Dave could have listened.

'Sack the bitch,' he said. 'You hired her, so sack her if she's playing you up.'

'Dave, she's not simply playing me up. And she's not alone. As I said, there's Julie and Kathy.'

'Fiona, this is all—'

'Dave, they're planning to take over the Southmoore office.'

'Take over?' he chuckled. 'Fiona, this isn't a James Bond film. OK, what they put you through at school wasn't very nice. But it happens. Kids get bullied at times. Why the hell did you employ these girls, knowing full well who they were?'

'Because . . . because I thought that I might be able to get back at them for what they'd done to me.'

'Revenge? You employed staff simply to—'

'No, I mean . . .'

'Fiona, this is so unlike you. You're brilliant, you're the best. Why the fuck did you employ these girls? There's nothing I can do. Apart from sack the lot of them.'

'No, that wouldn't do any good,' I sighed, feeling stupid. 'They'll come after me. They know where I live, for fuck's sake.'

'Look, I have the company to think about. This mess in your private life . . . Don't get me wrong, Fiona. But the company has to come first.'

'Yes, yes, I understand. OK, so I'll resign.'

'Resign? Fuck me. We've just opened the new office and you're resigning?'

'What bloody choice do I have?'

'You're not leaving me now, Fiona. The fucking work we've done to . . . There's no one else, for shit's sake. Who the hell would I put in your place?'

'I . . . I don't know.'

'Get to the office now and sack the bitches. If you have a problem, then call me. I'll sort them out.'

'All right,' I conceded as Dave leaped to his feet.

'How about a drink this evening?'

'Yes, yes, I'd like that.'

'OK, I'll ring you later.'

Seeing Dave out, I realized that I should have known how he'd react. I suppose I had known, really, but had still thought it was worth trying to explain the situation. One thing was for sure, I thought, grabbing my jacket and briefcase. Sally wouldn't expect to see me walk into the office with my head held high. Dave was right, the company came first. Sally, Julie, Kathy . . . and Walker. They were out. Having an idea as I walked to the railway station, I grinned. The company came first, but there was one thing I had to do before sacking Sally. I felt that she was the ringleader, the cause of my troubles. I'd deal with her most severely before – and after – dismissing her.

'Oh,' Sally gasped from behind me as I walked into my office and dumped my briefcase by my desk. 'I didn't think—'

'Didn't think what, Sally?' I snapped.

'Er . . . nothing.'

'Right, we have things to do.'

'You can start by bringing me a coffee,' she ordered me, grinning as she headed back to her own office.

'Certainly,' I replied.

Closing the door behind me, I went down to the sales department and confronted Julie and Kathy. It was if I'd found some inner strength, I thought as I almost dragged them into Tim Black's office. I was the bitch from hell again. I told them that I was about to call the police and report their thieving. They were obviously stunned when I said that I'd discovered that they'd been stealing money from other members of staff. But they soon broke their silence.

'Bitch,' Julie hissed.

'Tim Black will back me up on this,' I said. 'And Dave Bryant, the managing director. Apart from stealing from the staff, you've taken money from petty cash and falsified sales figures.'

'We've done nothing of the sort,' Kathy cut in angrily. 'I know your game.'

'Yes, I'm sure you do. And you know that I'll win the game. The police—'

'I'm warning you,' Julie whispered through gritted teeth. 'We'll get you on the common and—'

'From a prison cell? I doubt it. Now, both of you get out of here. Leave the building now, unless you want to face the police.'

I was quite surprised as they left the office and grabbed their jackets. I must admit that I'd thought that they would stand their ground. Perhaps the prospect of the police was just too much for them. Maybe they were already known to the police, I mused, walking along the corridor to the lift. As luck would have it, I met Walker in the lift. The insolent bastard unzipped his trousers and, as the door closed, ordered me to suck his cock. There was only one thing for it, I decided, kneeing him in the bollocks.

'Sorry,' I said, smiling at him. 'I hope I didn't hurt you.'

'Fucking hell!' he groaned, doubling up in pain. 'You fucking cow. You'll pay for that. When I tell the others . . .'

'Get out, Walker,' I hissed. 'I've sacked the girls, and now it's your turn. You're a pathetic little wimp. You'll leave the building now, if you know what's good for you.'

Staggering out of the lift as the door opened, Walker made his escape. I felt good, just like my old self as I returned to my office. The bitch from hell was back, and she was staying. I could hear Sally talking on the phone in her office. Now it was my turn to dish out the humiliation, the degradation. Waiting until she'd finished, I perched on the edge of my desk and called her. She emerged from her office frowning, her blue eyes darting this way and that – she must have wondered where her coffee was.

'I have some good news for you,' I said, grinning at her.

'Oh?' She frowned. 'And what would that be?'

'I've just sacked your friends.'

'You've . . . I don't believe you.'

'I don't care what you believe. The point is—'

'You must have enjoyed yourself in the woods last night,' she sniggered. 'At least I hope you did because that's where you'll be going if you've—'

'Sally, don't threaten me,' I interrupted her with a laugh. 'You're a fucking little slut who's nothing more than a frightened cow without your friends to protect you. Now you have no friends to protect you. Not here, anyway.'

'You really don't understand, you do? The gang—'

'Fuck your pathetic little gang. It's just you and me now, Sally. Just the two of us. Shall we sit down and have a chat?'

'You can go to hell. In fact, that's where you'll be going once the others get hold of you. We've already recruited one of your staff and we intend to—'

'If you're referring to that wimp Walker, I've sacked him. Did you honestly believe that you could take on Dagridge Medical Supplies? This is a massive company with offices—'

'Don't forget that we have photographs of you,' she sneered triumphantly. 'Unless you want every member of staff to receive several rather revealing pictures of you . . .'

'So what? I'm sure they'll bring a smile to people's faces. They certainly aren't worth worrying about.'

'I have to go out,' she snapped, grabbing her jacket from her office. 'I'll be back. And I won't be alone.'

'Don't bother to come back,' I murmured nonchalantly. 'There's no place for a filthy slag like you here.'

As Sally stormed out of my office, I reckoned that she'd head for the common in the hope that she'd find her friends there. I'd been pretty bold, I reflected. Bold or stupid? Whatever I'd been, at least I'd made a stand. She had actually been right about the photographs, of course. I'd never be able to face the staff . . . Deciding to cross that bridge if and when I came to it, I left the building and made my way to the common. Sally was bound to have gone there, I was sure as I headed across the grass to the bushes. There was no sign of her or the others, so I walked to the woods. I was taking a huge risk, I knew. I wasn't even sure what I was doing. If I did find Sally . . .

Hearing movements in the woods, I crept through the trees, my ears pinned back. Sally called out for Julie and Kathy, and I grinned. My stomach somersaulting, I made my way towards her, sure that she was alone in the woods. This might be my chance, I thought, spotting her following a path. My chance to do what? Attack her? Closing in on her, I grabbed her from behind and pulled her to the ground.

'You fucking bitch,' she spat, struggling to break free

as I tore her clean white blouse from her young body. 'The others will be here in a minute and—'

'They won't come here,' I retorted, ripping her skirt off.

During the struggle, I managed to tear her bra and panties off. Now that she was naked, I knew that she couldn't escape me. There was only one way out of the woods, and that was across the common. Sally finally broke free and ran, but had nowhere to go. She could hardly run across the common to the busy street in her naked glory. I had her trapped. Ripping her clothes to shreds, I stuffed a few strips of cloth into my pocket and walked deeper into the woods, searching for her, hunting her down. A twig cracking, I turned to my right and followed a narrow path. I could almost smell her as I heard the bushes rustling. I could smell revenge.

Cowering on the ground by a high fence, she looked up at me with fear mirrored in her blue eyes. She was huddled up, her knees to her chest, her hands clasped close to her face. The hairless lips of her young cunt bulging between her shapely thighs, she was completely defenceless. *Cunt*. They'd forced me to repeat that word again and again at school. Cunt, fuck, cock, spunk . . . They'd destroyed my schooldays.

Julie and Kathy had probably found a coffee shop somewhere and were discussing their next move. They wouldn't tramp deep into the woods looking for Sally. For all they knew, the girl was working in her office. Sally was mine. After years of waiting to vent my revenge, I had her cowering like a frightened animal in the woods. Glimpsing one of her nipples, the dark disc of her areola, I felt my stomach somersault with excitement.

'What are you going to do?' Sally asked me shakily.

'When I gave you the job, I told you that I was the bitch from hell,' I replied coolly. 'I'm not sure that you believed me. You probably thought that I was hard, but not a bitch from hell. So I'm just going to have to prove it.'

'The gang will get you,' she breathed. 'If you dare to touch me, they'll put you though hell. You'll be the bitch *in* hell if you do anything to me.'

'Maybe,' I said, grabbing the end of a length of rope hanging loosely from a tree. 'Kids must use it to swing on,' I murmured, tossing her the end of the rope. 'Here, tie this around your ankle.'

'No, I won't,' she replied defiantly.

'Sally, tie the rope around your ankle or I'll thrash you,' I returned, snapping a branch off a nearby bush. 'What's it to be?'

'Look, I—'

'All I want to do is make sure that you don't run off. I want to talk to you, Sally. Let's see whether we can come to some arrangement. Now, tie the rope around your ankle.'

Watching as she fixed the rope around her ankle, I could feel wickedness swirling deep within the pit of my stomach. Wickedness, evil . . . I'd been waiting for this moment for a long time. Not just since Sally had come to the office, but for many, many years before then. Reaching up and grabbing the free end of the rope as she finished tying the knot, I pulled hard. Her leg rising, her foot about three feet off the ground, she fell onto her back as I continued to pull.

'Please . . .' she whimpered, her vaginal crack gaping wide open as I gave a final pull on the rope and secured the end to a tree branch. 'Please, let me go.'

'Let you go?' I giggled. 'I've waited years for this, Sally. When I was at school, I swore to get even with you. But I never thought that I'd see you again, let alone have an opportunity like this.'

'What are you going to do?'

'I'm not sure,' I replied, slapping the palm of my hand with the branch. 'I suppose I could begin by thrashing you.'

'Rachael, please . . .'

'Did you show *me* any mercy when you caught me after school and dragged me into the bushes? No, you didn't. When you pulled my knickers down and Kenny pissed in them, did you show any compassion? No, you didn't.'

Looking around me, I noticed another length of rope lying on the ground. Tying one end to Sally's other ankle, I slung the free end over a low branch of another tree and pulled hard. Her foot rising, her legs parting wide, I gazed at the inner folds of her pink cunt as her crack opened. Propping herself up on her elbows, she watched in horror as I again pulled at the rope. Protesting futilely as her naked buttocks lifted clear of the ground, she spat her threats at me as I secured the end of the rope. Managing to pull her hands behind her head, I bound her wrists with a length of the cloth I'd torn from her clothes earlier and completed the job of bondage.

She was going to have to be silenced, I decided, slipping my panties off. The crotch was wet, stained with my pussy juices. An ideal gag. Stuffing the silk garment into her gasping mouth, I pinched the ripe teats of her nipples. Grimacing as I pulled and twisted the elongated protrusions, she squirmed and writhed. This was what I'd been waiting for, I thought, grabbing the branch in readiness to thrash her bared bottom. Revenge at long last.

'Right,' I breathed, smirking at her. 'I think the time has come to vent my revenge. By the way, I forgot to mention that I'll be leaving you here after I've dealt with you. I'm sure that someone will eventually discover you and release you. There again, it might be several days before anyone ventures this deep into the woods. OK, I'm going to start by shoving something up your dirty little cunt. Do you remember those words, Sally? Dirty little cunt. Filthy spotty slag. Fat cow. Piss slut. I remember those words. Thanks to you, they're etched in my memory.'

Looking around, I noticed a length of wood lying on the ground. About two inches in diameter and with a rounded end, I decided that it would make a perfect dildo. Sally's eyes widened as I knelt on the ground and slipped the end of the makeshift phallus between the wet inner lips of her vaginal crack. She was trembling like a leaf, which pleased me no end. Easing the wooden dildo deep into the tight duct of her vagina, I felt a great sense of satisfaction roll through me. She wriggled and squirmed, moaned loudly through her nose and stared at me with terror reflected in her wide eyes as I eased the shaft deeper into her dirty little cunt.

'No compassion,' I said, grabbing the branch. 'I'll show you no compassion. I remember the time when you and the others took a ruler and spanked my pussy lips. That really hurt, you know. My pussy was stinging for hours afterwards. How about a cunt-whipping with this branch?' I giggled. 'You'd like that, wouldn't you? You're obviously into pain. *Inflicting* pain, anyway. Do you remember the time when Julie held my arms behind my back and you clipped clothes-pegs to my nipples? That really hurt, Sally. And now the time has come for you to have a taste of your own medicine.'

Slipping the wooden phallus out of the creamy sheath of her cunt, I pressed the rounded end hard against the brown tissue surrounding her arsehole. Grimacing as I drove the juice-glistening shaft into the tight tube of her rectum, she could do nothing to halt the abuse of her young body. The tables had turned, I mused, pushing the dildo deeper into her anal canal, the brown ring of her anus stretched tautly around the gnarled shaft. The phallus emerging between the firm cheeks of her buttocks, sticking out of her stretched bottom-hole, I raised the branch above my head in readiness for the vulval thrashing.

Struggling fiercely as I brought the rough branch down across the naked flesh of her pussy, the sharp-edged leaves biting into her vaginal lips, Sally moaned loudly through her nose. The wings of her protruding inner lips turning red, I continued with the thrashing, wallowing in my revenge as her naked body convulsed wildly. I didn't think about possible reprisals from the gang. My thoughts were centred on getting my own back for everything that the bitch had put me through at school – and more recently.

Recalling the clothes-pegs biting into the sensitive teats of my nipples, I remembered the horrendous em-barrassment I'd felt when Sally had yanked my bra clear of my developing breasts. The boys had ogled the small mounds adorning my chest and had made lewd comments about the brown protrusions of my milk teats. The pain had been bad enough, but the humiliation and degradation had been far worse. At that tender age when my body had been developing, I'd been acutely aware of my young breasts, the hairless lips of my pussy. When Kenny and the others had first pulled my knickers down and stared at my sex crack, I'd almost died with embarrassment.

'You'll never know what you did to me,' I hissed, thrashing the girl's swollen vaginal labia with the branch. 'You'll never know what I went through.' Again and again, I lashed her crimsoned outer lips, relishing her pained expression, her grimacing face, her squirming body. This was revenge indeed, I mused, recalling the time when the gang had forced me to bend over in the locker room. They'd made me pull my knickers down and display the rounded cheeks of my naked buttocks to several jeering boys. Sally had stood with my head squeezed between her thighs and yanked my buttocks wide apart, exposing the brown ring of my anus to the delighted audience. One boy had pushed his finger into the hot sheath of my bottom, sending the others into raptures of laughter.

'Bitch,' I spat, bringing the branch down again as I recalled the boy's finger pistoning the once-private sheath of my tight rectum. Another boy had knelt down, parted the soft lips of my pussy and examined my secret inner folds. There must have been half a dozen young lads there, all gaping at me, laughing and joking about my little pink cunt. The episode had been extremely humiliating and degrading, and Sally had laughed hysterically.

'Why did you do it?' I asked Sally, halting the vulval thrashing. She moaned through her nose, shaking her head from side to side as I knelt down and drove a finger deep into the wet heat of her tight cunt. 'You ruined my schooldays, fucked my life. Why the hell did you do it?' Staring at me with her eyes wide, she squeezed her muscles, obviously trying to eject the wooden stick from her rectum. Focusing on the creamy liquid oozing from her gaping sex hole and running down my hand, I drove another two fingers deep into her vaginal cavern. Pistoning her rectum with the stick, I finger-fucked her young pussy simultaneously and gazed at her swelling clitoris emerging from beneath its pink hood. She was obviously aroused by the sexual abuse, and I decided to allow her a little pleasure before beginning the *real* torture.

Massaging the inner flesh of her hot vagina, I realized that I, too, was deriving pleasure from the decadent act. Never in my life had I had lesbian tendencies, but now . . . No, I wasn't a lesbian. Pleasurable as it was, fingering another girl's pussy wasn't my forte. I'd enjoyed toying with my own vagina during my younger years, I recalled, listening to the squelching of Sally's sex juices. Fingering my vagina, massaging my clitoris to orgasm . . . I'd derived immense pleasure from my young body. But that had been different, hadn't it? Of course it had. There was a world of difference between masturbating and committing crude sexual acts with another girl.

Listening to Sally moaning through her nose as I watched her inner lips dragging back and forth along my pistoning fingers, I felt my own clitoris swell and my juices of lust seeping between the fleshy lips of my yearning cunt. At school, I'd been forced to finger the female members of the gang. I'd felt no arousal, no pleasure, only fear and distress. But I was in control now – and this was very different. To watch Sally's clitoris swelling, her inner lips engorging as her pleasure heightened and her sex juices flowed . . . This was supposed to have been revenge, I reminded myself, fingering her pussy harder and repeatedly thrusting the wooden dildo deep into her tightening arse. I was supposed to have been bringing her pain, not lesbian pleasure.

Leaning forward, I tentatively planted a kiss on the weal-lined mound of her mons. Pushing my tongue out and tasting her there, I moved down to the top of her gaping sex crack and licked the sensitive tip of her clitoris. This was the girl I hated, I thought as she shuddered and let out a low moan through her nose. Kissing her, licking her . . . But I couldn't help myself. I supposed that it was the opportunity. Never before had I licked another girl's clitoris voluntarily. Never before had I brought another girl sexual pleasure in that way of my own free will. The enforced tonguing of Sally's cunt and bumhole that the gang had put me through so recently didn't count, I reckoned. No one would know what I'd done, I consoled myself as I ran my wet tongue around the solid budling of her sensitive clitoris. I could do what I liked to the girl, and no one would know.

Managing to drive all four fingers into the contracting cavern of her hot vagina, I watched my knuckles slip past her taut inner lips. With half my fist embedded in her drenched cunt, I wondered whether it would be possible to impale her completely on my hand. She shook violently as I pushed and twisted my hand until her inner lips were stretched tautly around my wrist. I couldn't believe that I'd managed to embed my whole fist in her vaginal cavern. Her outer lips forced wide apart, her clitoris ballooning, I gazed at the alluring sight of her abused cunt in awe. Her lower stomach bulging as I twisted my fist within the hugging cavern of her vagina, I wondered whether she was deriving pain or pleasure from the crude act.

Staring at Sally's stretched outer lips reminded me of the times I used to sit on the end of my bed and hold a small hand-mirror between my thighs. I used to part the soft swell of my outer labia and examine the intricate inner folds of my pink crack. I'd often examined myself, scrutinized the complex fleshy creases nestling within my sex slit. I'd push objects into the sheath of my pussy and tremble as amazing sensations rolled through my young body. But to force an entire fist into a vagina?

Finally withdrawing my hand, my fist leaving Sally's cunt with a loud squelch, I decided that she'd had her pleasure. The time had come to get on with the job of torturing the girl in retaliation for destroying my life. I felt wicked, evil, as I pondered on tightening the ropes and forcing her legs apart to the extreme. I might have been the bitch from hell, but it wasn't in my nature to inflict physical – as distinct from mental – pain. But everything that Sally and the gang had forced me to endure had brought out a sadistic streak in me. No pain, no gain. And my gain was to be revenge.

Easing the wooden phallus out of Sally's tight rectum, I gazed at the yawning hole of her anus. The temptation to try to sink my fist deep into her arse was overwhelming. After all she'd done to me, the humiliation and degradation . . . Driving two fingers into the dank heat of her anal canal, I decided that she thrived on cruelty, and that was what she was going to get. Managing to drive four fingers into the tight tube of her rectum, I watched the delicate brown tissue of her anal ring stretching tautly around my knuckles. Her rectum was hot, slimy, and very tight. She quivered and writhed as I pushed my fingers deeper into her tight arse, and I had no doubt that she was enjoying the experience.

My fist sucked deep into her bloated rectum, the brown ring of her anal inlet hugging my wrist, I couldn't believe what I'd done. Her eyes wide, Sally moaned loudly through her nose as I twisted my fist within the hot cavern of her bowels. This was incredible, I thought, amazed by the elasticity of her anus. I'd heard about anal fisting, but had never believed it possible. My clitoris swelling and my lust juices flowing as I imagined having my own arse fisted I leaned forward and sucked the solid nubble of Sally's exposed clitoris into my wet mouth.

Letting out another moan through her nose, her tethered body shaking wildly, she pumped out her juices of desire as I sucked and mouthed on her swollen clitoris. She was going to come, I knew as I snaked my tongue around the sensitive tip of her pleasure bud. Breathing in the intoxicating scent of Sally's genitalia, tasting the salt of her erect clitoris, I realized that I was taking the opportunity to experiment with lesbianism. I'd never dreamed about having a sexual relationship with someone of my own gender but the intrigue had always been there. What would it be like to suck and lick another girl's clitoris to orgasm? Would I enjoy fingering another girl's wet cunt? Now, in the privacy of the woods, I was able to experiment with a young victim.

Victim? *I*'d always been the victim, I reflected, twisting my fist within the hot depths of Sally's bowels. The tables had turned. For the time being, I was in control, using and abusing Sally the way she'd used and abused me. For the time being. I felt that I had to keep reminding myself of that. What did the future hold? I wondered about that, mouthing and sucking on the trembling girl's pulsating clitoris. What was going to happen by way of reprisals? The gang had pornographic photographs of me performing crude sexual acts in the bushes. Would they send them to every member of staff? That, after all, was what they'd threatened.

Sally's clitoris exploding in orgasm, her juices of lust spewing from the gaping entrance to her tight cunt, her anal muscles gripping my fist, she squealed through her nose as her naked body shook uncontrollably. Driving three fingers of my free hand deep into her spasming vaginal duct, bloating both her sex holes, I continued to suck and lick her orgasming clitoris. Never had I known that such pleasure could be had from pleasuring another girl. My own juices of lesbian desire oozing between the swollen lips of my vulva, drenching my inner thighs, I thought that I was going to come too as Sally shuddered violently in the grip of her climax.

Her orgasm finally receding, she breathed heavily through her nose as I slipped my sex-wet fingers out of the tight sheath of her cunt and eased my fist out of her rectum. Her sex holes left gaping wide open, her vaginal juices gushing from her quivering body, she was going to take some time to recover from what was obviously a massive climax. Brushing my long blonde hair away from my face, I could smell sex on my hand. I needed to come, I knew as my clitoris pulsated, sending delightful quivers through my contracting womb. I needed Sally's tongue snaking around the solid bulb of my clitoris, her fingers pistoning the drenched sheath of my cunt. Deciding to remove the gag from her mouth, I leaped to my feet and was about to move to her side when I heard twigs cracking in the woods.

'Shit,' I breathed as someone approached. There was no time to release Sally. Her clothes were somewhere in the woods, ripped to shreds . . . Creeping through the bushes, I made my escape. I shouldn't have left her, I knew as I finally emerged from the woods onto the common. If a pervert had been wandering through the woods and discovered Sally's naked body bound with rope and a strip of torn clothing . . . After all she'd done to me, though, I really didn't care what happened to the little slut. She'd brought this on herself.

Noticing Julie and Kathy heading towards the woods, I slipped behind a bush and watched them. Julie was calling out for Kenny. Reckoning that he must have gone on ahead and discovered Sally, I made my getaway once they were in the woods. I headed for the office. Repercussions were on the cards, that was for sure. They wouldn't come to the office to get me. But they might try to nab me when I left to catch the train home. Once they'd learned what had happened to Sally . . . *Shit*.

# 8

When one of the young men from the accounts department walked into my office with a large brown envelope in his hand, I instinctively knew that something was wrong. He stood in front of my desk with a strange look in his eyes, as if he was about to pass on some horrendously bad news. Inviting him to sit down as he introduced himself as Rogers and stammered something about not wanting to worry me, I asked him what was in the envelope.

'This,' he replied, taking out a large photograph.

'Oh,' I sighed, gazing at a crystal-clear photograph of my face with a huge purple knob between my wet lips. 'Where did you get this from?'

'It was left at reception, addressed to me. Miss Michaels, I—'

'I can't explain,' I cut in. 'There's no point denying that it's me. But I can't explain why it was sent to you. Were there any other photographs?'

'No, just this one. Has this got something to do with Julie and Kathy?'

'Why do you ask? What makes you think that they have anything to do with this?'

'I overheard them talking yesterday. They mentioned the common, and said something about pornographic photographs. I suppose, seeing this photograph of you, I put two and two together.'

'Yes, this *has* got something to do with them. I fear that this is only the beginning. All I can do is ask that, should you receive any more photographs, then bring them straight to me.'

'Yes, yes, of course. Er . . .'

'I can't tell you anything else.'

'I was only wondering whether you need some help.'

'Help?'

'You're obviously in some kind of trouble. Again, putting two and two together, I'd say that you're being blackmailed.'

'I . . .'

'Before you say anything . . . A friend of mine is being blackmailed. He saw another woman behind his wife's back. It was a silly fling that only lasted a few days. He now has to pay money each week and—'

'How much does he pay?'

'Fifty pounds. It's not a great deal of money but . . . I was wondering whether you might be having problems with the same people.'

'Yes, I am,' I sighed.

'I don't know what it is you've done. I mean, you're not married, so . . . This friend of mine. Would you like to meet him?'

'What for?'

'I just thought that it might help to talk about it, perhaps work something out. He's pretty worried about this, as you obviously are. He works locally and drops into a bar near here on his way home.'

'I suppose I could meet him.'

'If it's all right with you, I'll ring him and tell him to meet you there.'

'Yes, do that,' I said checking my watch.

'It's a small bar called The Shell.'

'Yes, I know it. OK, I'll be there at five.'

'Right, I'll go back to my office and give him a call. His name's Ted. I'll describe you to him.'

'Right. And thanks.'

'No problem. You'd better destroy that,' Rogers said, pointing to the photograph as he left the office.

Sure that this man Ted was being blackmailed by the Brook Street Gang, I grabbed my jacket and left the office. It was only four-thirty, but I wanted to get out of the building early to avoid the gang. Apart from that, I was in need of a stiff drink or two. Repeatedly looking over my shoulder as I walked down the street, I thought it odd that at least one of the gang members wasn't around. Perhaps they were still in the woods, I thought. Maybe they were on the railway station. There again, they could hardly grab me on the platform in front of other passengers. But they were bound to be planning something, I was certain.

The small bar was deserted apart from a young couple standing in a corner, arguing. Relationships were a waste of time, I mused, ordering myself a vodka and tonic as the girl informed her young man that she had never been unfaithful. Suspicion, jealousy . . . If they didn't trust each other now, they probably never would. Thinking myself lucky to have avoided marriage, I sat at a corner table and waited for Ted.

Watching a good-looking man in his mid-thirties wander into the bar, I smiled as he turned and looked at me. Hoping that he was Ted, I thought how attractive he was. With dark, swept-back hair and a suntanned face, an open-neck white shirt and smart trousers, he really was . . . What was I thinking? I scolded myself silently, hoping that he was the man I was waiting for. He was already being blackmailed for his infidelity and I doubted that he'd want to go down that road again.

'Fiona?' he asked, placing his pint of beer on the table.

'Yes. And you must be Ted.'

'That's right. Brian Rogers didn't go into detail, but I gather that you might be in a similar situation to me,' he said, sitting down opposite me.

'Yes, I am. The Brook Street Gang. Does that mean anything to you?'

'Does it mean anything?' he echoed mockingly. 'It means that they are destroying my life.'

'Do you know who they are?'

'I have no idea who they are,' he sighed. 'They have a few photographs of me with a young lady. I made a mistake and . . . Briefly, they're blackmailing me. I don't suppose you have any idea who these people are?'

'I know each and every one of them,' I replied, sipping my drink. 'But I'm not going to reveal their identities.'

'Why not? If I knew who they were, where they live and—'

'Then you'd get yourself even deeper in the shit. These photographs they have of you – are they incriminating?'

'Yes, they are. I was with . . . her name's Alison. We met at my place of work and went for a walk across the common.'

'The common seems to be the gang's hunting ground. Sorry, carry on.'

'We got on really well and ended up . . . well, you know. What I didn't realize was that there was someone lurking in the bushes, taking photographs. Anyway, I pay them fifty pounds a week to keep them quiet.'

'Where do you take the money?'

'I leave it beneath a bush on the common. Before you ask – yes, I have hidden and watched but I've never seen anyone collect the cash.'

'No, you wouldn't. They're not stupid, Ted. They probably collect the money the following day. Or even several days later. No one would find it hidden beneath a bush so they wouldn't be in any hurry to pick it up.'

'What have they got on you? What have *you* done to deserve blackmail?'

'I . . . It would take me all night to explain. I'm not married and I haven't cheated on anyone. I was in the wrong place at the wrong time, I suppose. OK, so we've got to get these photographs back.'

'Get them back? But how?'

'As yet, I have no idea. How long can you stay? I mean, when's your wife expecting you home?'

'She's gone to see her mother and won't be back for a few days. Don't get me wrong, we haven't argued. It's just that her mother hasn't been well and needs someone to look after her. To be honest, it's been nice having a few days to myself. She knows that something's wrong but . . .'

'But you can't talk about it.'

'That's right. Another drink?'

'Mmm, thanks. Vodka and tonic, please.'

As he went up to the bar, I thought about seducing him. His wife was away and I didn't relish the idea of walking to the railway station, especially not by myself . . . Imagining staying at his place for a few days, I knew that I needed a break. I felt like getting pissed with Ted. He was feeling down and I wasn't exactly on top of the world. Perhaps we should get pissed together and then spend the night fucking. Not a very ladylike way of thinking, I mused. But I needed someone. I needed someone to hold me, love me.

'There you are,' Ted said, placing the drinks on the table. 'So, tell me about yourself. Do you live locally?'

'In London,' I replied, thinking that this might be my chance. 'I really don't like commuting. By the time I get home, it's too late to do anything, and then I have to catch an early train to be back here for nine o'clock in the morning. I might look for somewhere to stay for the night.'

'I suppose you could . . . No, it doesn't matter.'

'What were you about to say?'

'I was going to suggest that you stay at my place. But, seeing as I'm already being blackmailed . . .'

'I'd like that,' I interrupted him, putting on an angelic smile. 'No one would know about it, Ted.'

'I suppose not,' he sighed. 'As long as my place isn't being watched.'

'I doubt that they'd do that. They're already getting fifty pounds a week from you, so I don't think they'd hang around watching your place just on the off chance.'

'All right,' he conceded. 'We can have a talk, make our plans.'

'Plans?'

'About this gang, the Brook Street Gang or whatever they call themselves. I can't go on paying them every week like this. Two hundred pounds each month . . . I just can't afford it. How much are you paying them?'

That was a good question. They weren't demanding cash yet. But I was paying them in kind. They were taking my body, using my cunt . . . Downing my drink, I didn't want to hang around in the pub for too long and suggested that we leave. Ted was good company, I thought as he finished his drink and joked about his wife arriving home to find another woman in the house. As we walked along the street, he talked about his work as an accountant. Looking over my shoulder every minute or so in case we were being followed, I wasn't really listening. I just wanted to get to his house before I was spotted.

'Here we are,' he said, opening the front door to a small cottage. 'Home sweet home.'

'This is a nice place,' I remarked, following him into a cosy lounge.

'We've been here for five years. When we moved in, it was in a right state. It was a lot of work but we got there in the end. Take a look round and I'll get you a drink. You can have the back bedroom. Up the stairs and straight in front of you.'

'OK, I'll take a look.'

'If you want to have a shower, there are towels in the airing cupboard. Just help yourself to anything you need.'

'Yes, I think I will have a shower,' I said, running my fingers through my long blonde hair.

'When you come down, we'll have a drink and a chat.'

Climbing the stairs, I thought it was a shame that Ted was married. The cottage was perfect, he was good-looking . . . I was dreaming, I knew as I imagined living there. Walking into the luxurious bathroom, I reminded myself that relationships didn't work as I slipped my clothes off and stepped into the shower. I was happy enough in my London flat, I decided as I shampooed my hair. Commuting wasn't much fun, but there was no way I was going to move to Southmoore.

Taking a towel from the cupboard, I grabbed my clothes and walked across the landing to the back bedroom. Opening the door, I wandered in and stared in disbelief at the whips and chains adorning the walls and a leather-topped table with handcuffs hanging from each corner in the centre of the room. I knew then that I'd walked straight into a trap. Hurriedly drying my naked body, I was about to slip into my clothes and get out of the cottage when the 'bedroom' door closed and the key turned in the lock.

'Let me out,' I called, hammering on the door with my fist. 'Ted, please . . .'

'All in good time,' Sally called. 'Perhaps, after a few days . . .'

'You bitch,' I spat. 'I should have finished you off when I had the chance.'

'Finished me off?' she giggled. 'Don't be ridiculous, Rachael. You'll find a letter on the table in the corner of the room. Sign it and slip it under the door.'

'A letter?'

'When you've signed it, I'll let you go.'

Walking to the small table, I picked up the typewritten letter. Addressed to Dave Bryant, it was my resignation. There was no way I was going to sign it. Screwing the paper up and tossing it to the floor, I slipped my clothes on and checked the window. There was no escape. Apart from being locked, the window had iron bars on the outside. Still, I knew that Sally couldn't keep me shut in the room for ever. She'd have to let me go and . . . Tapping on the door, she asked me whether I'd signed the letter.

'No, I haven't,' I replied. 'I've scrunched it up.'

'I have plenty of copies,' she said, slipping one beneath

the door. 'If you want your freedom, then I suggest you sign it.'

'If I sign it, Dave Bryant won't accept it. Besides, I'll withdraw it once I—'

'No, no,' she cut in. 'You don't understand, Rachael. The letter will go to the MD and he'll accept your resignation.'

'Of course he won't.'

'Once he sees the porn pics . . .'

'He'll laugh when he sees the photographs. Dave and I are—'

'He won't think it at all funny when he discovers that copies have been sent to your customers. I have a printout listing every customer. I suggest you sign the letter and get this over with.'

'Why do you want me to resign?' I asked her. 'What would you gain from—'

'All will be revealed once you've signed the letter.'

Sitting on the leather-topped table, I gazed at the letter lying on the floor. I couldn't for the life of me think why Sally would want me to resign. There was no way that Dave would promote Sally herself to deputy managing director, so what was she after? After half an hour or so, I was beginning to think that it would be best to sign the damned letter. There again, Sally wouldn't allow me to leave before she'd used and abused me. The rest of the gang were probably lurking downstairs, waiting to fuck me, to handcuff and whip me.

Finally taking the pen from the table, I signed the letter and slid it beneath the door. If I was going to be used for crude sex, then signing the letter would at least speed things up and I'd be released sooner rather than later. I could hear movements outside the room, the sound of someone picking up the letter. All I had to do now was wait for the gang to enter and strip me naked. Eyeing the handcuffs hanging from the four corners of the leather-topped table, the whips and chains on the walls, I knew exactly what I was going to have to endure.

'I'm pleased that you saw sense and signed the letter,' Sally called through the door. 'Now, please remove all your clothes.'

'Remove my clothes?' I laughed. 'You must be joking. You open this door now or—'

'OK, have it your way,' she said. 'When it gets dark later, you'll find that the light doesn't work. There's a second switch out here on the landing. If you want light, then take all your clothes off.'

'I'm not bothered about the dark,' I retorted.

'Maybe not. But what will you do when you need the loo? And I'm sure that you must be getting hungry by now. Take your clothes off and you'll not only have light but I'll bring some food up.'

'Go to hell,' I hissed, thumping on the door with my clenched fist. 'And I hope you rot there.'

Pacing the floor, I knew that I was going to have to strip off at some stage. Wondering why they didn't burst in and tear my clothes off, I gazed through the window at the back garden. Even if I managed to smash the double glazing there were no houses overlooking the garden so no one outside the cottage would see or hear me trying to attract attention. Not only was I trapped, but no one knew where I was. Living alone in my flat, I wouldn't be missed until the following day when I didn't turn up for work. Even then, it might be several days before Dave Bryant thought it odd that I hadn't contacted him and decided to look for me.

As darkness fell, I sat on the leather-topped table and wondered what to do. If I stripped naked and allowed them to fuck me . . . *Allowed* them? I couldn't understand why they'd locked me in the room, why Sally had called through the door. And who the hell was Ted? Was this really his cottage? Sighing as the room grew darker, I doubted that his story about his wife was true. I hadn't seen any photographs of a woman in the lounge. Wondering which member of the gang lived in the house, I slipped off the table and paced the floor again. This was ridiculous, I thought, hearing laughter coming from downstairs. What on earth were the gang waiting for?

'Are you naked yet?' Sally called, tapping on the door.

'No,' I replied.

'OK, there's no hurry. We have all the time in the world.'

'You can't keep me here for ever.'

'Why not? No one will miss you. You live alone, you've resigned from your job . . .'

'I *do* have friends in London, Sally. I was supposed to be meeting some of them this evening.'

'If that's true, they'll probably think that you had to work late.'

'What do you want with me?' I asked her. 'Apart from the obvious.'

'We have clients, Rachael. Clients who are prepared to pay good money for an attractive girl like you. Why don't you just take your clothes off and get onto the table? You'll be saving yourself a lot of time and trouble if you cooperate.'

'You want to sell me for sex?' I gasped. 'You going to take money from perverts and—'

'They're *clients*, Rachael. You really don't have any choice. You're stuck here, so why not make it easy on yourself?'

She meant it, I knew as I imagined dirty old men fingering my cunt, fucking my mouth and shooting their spunk down my throat. Unbuttoning my blouse, I supposed that they did have all the time in the world. Dave Bryant would receive my resignation, he wouldn't be able to contact me and he'd believe that I'd gone away for a while or . . . I had to go along with Sally, I knew as I unhooked my bra and slipped my skirt off. The light came on as I tugged my panties down and kicked my shoes off so I reckoned that she was spying on me. Lying on the leather-topped table, I thought about fighting her once she opened the door, but there was no point. The others were downstairs, so I'd never be able to get past them and flee the cottage.

'That's better,' Sally said as she walked into the room and gazed at my naked body. 'I'll get you ready and then show the first client in.'

'You won't get away with this,' I breathed, watching her spread my limbs and cuff my wrists and ankles.

'Of course we will,' she replied. 'No one knows where you are, no one will miss you . . . Besides, you're a willing participant in our games.'

'A willing—'

'There's a video camera up there,' she said, pointing to the ceiling. 'You stripped off and got onto the table of your own accord. You didn't struggle or fight when I handcuffed you. It's all on videotape, Rachael. No one watching the video would think for a minute that you'd been forced to strip and lie on the table. You see, we're old hands at this sort of thing. As you well know, we started when we were at school. We have quite a few years' experience, Rachael.'

'When I get out of here—'

'By the way, there are some more letters and papers that I need you to sign later.'

'More? I'm not signing anything else.'

'We took a look around your London flat. It's a lovely place and—'

'You broke into my flat?'

'Of course not,' she giggled. 'I had copies made of your keys. You've done very well for yourself, Rachael. No mortgage, all your bills up to date . . . You'll be signing the property over to me later.'

'You're fucking mad,' I spat.

'The papers are being drawn up and they should be ready for you to sign tomorrow. Julie's moved into your flat. She's in the process of selling your furniture and—'

'Moved in?' I gasped. 'This is . . . You can't just . . .'

'Rachael, it's all in motion. The papers are being drawn up, your furniture is being sold – and there's nothing you can do to stop it.'

'Why make me jobless and homeless?'

'You're not homeless. You'll live here. This is a beautiful cottage and, as far as work is concerned . . . well, you'll be working for *us*, Rachael. You'll have all you need here.'

'You won't get away with it.'

'So you keep saying,' Sally sighed, running her fingertips over my fleece-covered mons.

'To have the flat signed over to someone else . . . I'd need a solicitor, for a start.'

'One of our clients is an eminent solicitor. He'll act for you, Rachael. In your best interests, of course.'

'There's more to giving a flat away than signing a piece of paper. Don't you think it will look suspicious if I simply *give* the flat to you? When I get out of here—'

'Oh, no, no. I'll be buying the flat. I should have explained it properly. With our funds, I'll buy the flat. Then, once the transaction is complete, I'll take the money back from your bank.'

'*Take* it back?'

'Don't worry about it, Rachael. We've got it all worked out. After all, it's easy enough to transfer money from one account to another. Right, I'll gag you and then bring in our client.'

Placing a rubber ball in my mouth, Sally secured it by placing an elasticated band around my head before leaving the room. Reckoning that her plan to get her hands on my flat would work, I didn't know what to do to stop her. The furniture sold, the flat empty, the sale would go ahead. With a bent solicitor working for her, I really couldn't see that she'd fail. It was all so easy, I reflected. Take my keys from my bag and have copies made, move into the flat and sell the furniture . . . And there was nothing I could do.

'Oh, yes,' a man in his sixties breathed as he walked into the room and gazed longingly at my naked body. Barely glancing at my face, he ran his fingers up and down my sex crack before taking something from a shelf. He was going to shave me, I knew as he massaged cooling foam into my vulval flesh. Gazing at his grinning face as he worked between my splayed thighs, I knew that this was only the beginning of the nightmare. Unable to speak, unable to move, I could do nothing as he dragged a safety razor over my mons.

Finally wiping away the foam, he stood upright and

admired his handiwork. I lifted my head and gazed at my hairless pussy, my naked sex-lips. Shaving my pubic hairs had stripped years off my naked body, reminding me of my schooldays. As he parted the fleshy cushions of my outer labia and examined the intricate folds within my bared sex-valley, I rested my head back on the table and closed my eyes. To have a complete stranger scrutinizing the most private part of my naked body brought memories flooding back. The boys at school laughing and jeering as the gang had forced me to expose my bottom-hole, Kenny pissing in my knickers . . .

'I only have one hour with you,' the ageing pervert said, lowering his trousers and exposing his rampant erection. 'One hour to pleasure myself,' he chuckled, turning a handle beneath the table.

My legs parting, I lifted my head and watched the table top opening like a pair of scissors. Turning another handle once my thighs were wide apart, he laughed as the two sections of the table lifted, taking my legs high into the air. My hairless sex crack gaping wide open, he stood facing my naked buttocks and ran the purple knob of his cock up and down my bared vulval crack. I tensed my muscles as his glans slipped between the petals of my inner lips and glided into my vagina. He was big, his solid shaft opening the sheath of my vagina wide as he drove his cockhead deep into my tight cunt.

'I'll bet you've had a few cocks up you,' he sniggered, peeling the outer lips of my pussy apart with his thumbs. 'How many men have fucked you? Hundreds, I would imagine. I'll bet your cunt has swallowed gallons of spunk over the years. Like a good mouthful of spunk too, do you? Enjoy a good knob-sucking, do you?'

As he rambled on, he began his fucking motions. My

tethered body rocking back and forth as he repeatedly propelled his swollen knob deep into my vagina, I tried to eject the rubber ball from my mouth. I had to speak to the man, get him to send help or . . . *But why should he help me?* I reflected. He was a client, paying good money to fuck me. He probably thought that I was only too willing to have my naked body tethered and my cunt fucked by strangers. No doubt Sally had said that I was a new girl, the latest recruit.

The man's gasps and moans of satisfaction filling my ears, I thought about my flat. From what Sally had said, I couldn't see how she could fail to rob me of my home. I wondered, was it really that easy? The squelching of my vaginal juices resounded around the room. Sign a few documents, the money changes hands . . . yes, it *was* that easy. Who was to know that my flat was being stolen? And, when the transaction was complete, who would believe that I'd been forced into selling?

I wasn't too worried about my job since I could talk to Dave Bryant and explain what had happened. But my flat was a different matter. Sally couldn't keep me imprisoned for very long, I was sure. And if I didn't sign any letters or papers . . . *They might forge my signature*, I thought as the elderly man briefly massaged the exposed nub of my solid clitoris as he temporarily slowed the pace of his thrusts. I had to concentrate on escaping. Once the flat had been sold, there'd be little or nothing I could do. I had to stop the gang now, before it was too late. The oldster began his fucking motions again, ramming his stiff cock deep into my abused quim.

'Yes,' the man gasped, his cock swelling to an incredible size, his spunk gushing deep into my inflamed cunt and bathing my cervix. Again and again, he slammed his throbbing glans deep into my contracting cunt, his swinging balls battering the rounded cheeks of my naked buttocks as he fucked me. I could feel the hairless cushions of my outer lips rolling along his solid shaft, my inner labia stretched tautly around his thrusting cock, my erect clitoris once more forced out from beneath its protective hood. His sperm running down between my naked buttocks, trickling over my anal hole, he continued fucking me until he'd drained his swinging balls.

Wondering whether there were other clients waiting downstairs, I was sure that the old man would leave once he'd satisfied his lust for my naked body. If there were no others waiting, then I might be released and allowed to wash and eat. The gang might keep me prisoner in the room, but surely not permanently chained to the table. They'd have to feed me, allow me to go to the bathroom and . . . and I'd find an opportunity to escape. One mistake on their part – such as the bathroom door left unguarded – and I'd flee the house and run like the wind.

'Worth every penny,' the old man breathed, standing by my side and tweaking the sensitive teats of my nipples. 'You're a very attractive girl. I don't know why you have to do this to make money. Still, that's none of my business.'

Trying again to push the rubber ball out of my mouth with my tongue, I was desperate to talk to him, to explain that I was being held prisoner. Moving behind me, he wiped his spunk-dripping cock on my blonde hair. Hoping that he'd decide to fuck my mouth and remove the gag, I closed my eyes as he ran the sperm-glistening bulb of his penis over my face. His heavy balls resting on my forehead, his cunny-wet shaft stiffening, he finally stepped back and pulled his trousers up.

'I'll be seeing you again,' he said, turning the handle beneath the table and lowering my legs. 'Sally's given me special rates since I'll be calling in every evening to fuck your sweet little cunt. For some reason, I'm not allowed to remove your gag.' He noticed my wide eyes and smiled. 'Still, she won't know if I slip my cock into your mouth and have you suck out my spunk.'

As he moved to the door, I moaned loudly through my nose, shaking my head from side to side in the hope that he'd remove the gag and allow me to speak. Watching him open the door and leave the room, I felt despondency setting in. He'd gone, and had taken my chance of escape with him. I could hear voices downstairs, and then the sound of the front door closing. That was it, I thought as sperm trickled over the shaved lips of my inflamed cunt. I'd endured client number one. I wondered again, were there more waiting downstairs? I could hear movements, someone climbing the stairs. Was another old man going to drive his huge cock deep into my sperm-drenched cunt and fuck me?

'He's going to be a regular,' Sally announced as she breezed into the room and slipped the ball-gag out of my mouth. 'He'll call in every evening to fuck you.'

'I don't think so,' I retorted, licking my dry lips.

'I don't care what you think,' she giggled. 'He'll be here every evening to—'

'He will return,' I cut in, smiling at the girl. 'But, now he knows the situation, he'll bring help with him. Help in the form of the police.'

'The police?' she echoed, anxiety reflected in the blue pools of her eyes.

'He took the gag out of my mouth and I told him everything.'

'Don't be ridiculous,' she murmured. 'Besides, it's all on videotape, so—'

'In that case, you'll see for yourself,' I said, hoping that she was lying. 'Go on, take a look at the tape. You haven't got long, Sally. He'll be back this evening with—'

'Julie!' she called, standing in the doorway. 'Julie, get up here!'

Sally was worried, I knew as Julie bounded up the stairs and joined us in the torture room. They whispered loudly, discussing me, the old man, the police. Had the Brook Street Gang made a fatal mistake? I pondered the possibility as Julie grabbed a long bamboo cane from a shelf. She stood by the table, glaring at me as she raised the cane above her head. Perhaps I'd made a mistake, I reflected, the cane swishing through the air and landing across the mounds of my firm breasts.

'Tell me what happened,' she hissed, bringing the cane down again. 'Did you talk to him?'

'Yes,' I gasped, my nipples rising proud from the dark discs of my areolae as the cane repeatedly cracked across my breasts. 'I told him everything and—'

'You lying bitch,' Julie spat, thrashing my breasts harder. 'Sally, I told you that we shouldn't have—'

'I know, I know,' the other girl broke in. 'I'll go and check the videotape.'

'I don't think it was running,' Julie sighed, halting the thrashing.

'I'll take a look.'

'Now you're in trouble,' I said as Julie raised the cane high above her head. 'And the more you cane me, the more evidence there'll be. The weals across my breasts will be evidence enough of—'

'Shut up,' she whispered through gritted teeth, forcing the rubber ball back into my mouth. 'I'll tell you this. If you've spoken to that man, you'll never see the light of day again. If you haven't, then you'll be severely punished for lying. Either way, you've made things very nasty for yourself.'

Watching Julie leave the room, I lifted my head and gazed at the pink weals fanning out across the rounded mounds of my young breasts. I could stand the pain, endure the stinging sensations. Still, this was only the beginning, I could hear people shouting as they argued downstairs. I'd at least provoked some upset in the enemy camp. But I had the dreadful feeling that the only trouble I'd caused had been for myself.

# 9

I woke to the sun shining in through the window. The shadows of the bars fell across the quilt covering my naked body. A pillow beneath my head, I realized that must have slept all night. Brushing my sperm-matted hair away from my face, I gazed at my hand and frowned. I was free. Moving my other hand, my feet, I sat upright and tossed the quilt to the floor. Slipping off the table, I looked for my clothes but they'd gone. This was a trick, I was sure as I discovered that the door was unlocked. I peered out onto the landing.

Slipping into the bathroom, I took a shower, washing the spunk from my hair and my inner thighs. Had they made a mistake? I wondered. Had they inadvertently left the door unlocked and gone out? Grabbing a large towel from the cupboard, I wrapped it around my naked body, crept out onto the landing and listened for movements downstairs. The house was silent and, I prayed, deserted. The towel concealing my young body, I made my way downstairs and tried the front door. It was locked.

'Shit,' I breathed, dashing into the kitchen to find that the back door was locked too. Noticing that all the windows were barred, I was nonetheless sure that I could find a way out as I gazed through the window at the back garden. Freedom was so close, I thought, wondering what to do. Walking into the lounge, I hoped that I could attract someone's attention by banging on the window, but it was useless. The high hedge between the garden and the street effectively concealed the cottage, so no one would take any notice. Bashing the glass with a chair leg in the vain hope that someone might investigate, I proved this to myself and finally gave up.

Hearing a voice upstairs, I rushed up to the torture room and looked around. There was food on a tray on the table. Toast, coffee, orange juice . . . Someone was in the house, that was obvious. Munching on the toast and sipping the coffee, I knew that I had to eat before doing anything else. Gazing out of the window at the garden as I finished my breakfast, I spun round on my heels as the door slammed shut.

'Who are you?' I asked a young, naked girl as she walked towards me.

'My name's Angel,' she replied.

'Angel? Do you live here?'

'I work here,' she said, her long blonde hair cascading over the small mounds of her breasts.

'You *work* here? What sort of work? Surely, you're too young to . . .'

'Anything and everything,' she giggled. 'Housework, cooking, entertaining clients . . .'

'God,' I breathed, focusing on the hairless lips of her young vulva. 'How long have you been here? Where are your parents?'

'I've been here for years. My parents moved abroad and Sally and the others took me in.'

'They certainly did take you in,' I sighed. 'You entertain clients?'

'Of course. It's all part of my work. You're new, aren't you?'

'Yes, I suppose I am. How can I get out of here? I need to get out of the house and—'

'Get out? You can't get out.'

'You must leave the house sometimes.'

'I never leave. I live and work here. Why should I leave?'

'Because . . . Never mind. Is Angel your real name?'

'I think so.'

'You *think* so? Who owns this house?'

'We all do. Why all these questions, Rachael?'

'They've told you my name, then. What else have they told you about me?'

'Just that you've come here to live and work. They told me to look after you and give you anything you need. Would you like me to pleasure you?'

'Pleasure me? For God's sake, you're far too young to—'

'I'm old enough to do anything,' she cut in, her full lips pouting as she hung her head. 'No one's ever complained about me.'

'I'm sure they haven't. Look, Angel, this place is . . . We're being kept here as prisoners.'

'Prisoners?' she giggled, pulling the towel from my naked body. 'Don't be silly. Of course we're not prisoners,' she said, kneeling in front of me and kissing the hairless lips of my pussy.

'Angel, you shouldn't . . .'

'I'm here to pleasure you,' she breathed, slipping her wet tongue into my sex valley and licking my inner folds.

'Angel . . . For God's sake . . .'

Looking down at her blonde hair as she expertly teased my stiffening clitoris, I knew that I should push her away. Her fingernails sinking into the firm flesh of my buttocks, she locked her full lips to the wet flesh surrounding my clitoris and sucked hard. This was very wrong, I knew as incredible sensations of sex rippled through my naked body. She was too young, this was a lesbian act ... But I couldn't push her away. Whether it was her age, her sex, her expert tonguing ... She was taking me to heights of sexual ecstasy I'd never known before. I couldn't push her away.

'You taste nice,' Angel murmured, slipping a finger deep into the creamy sheath of my tightening cunt.

'How old are you?' I asked as she slipped a second finger into the contracting duct of my vagina.

'Eighteen,' she replied.

'You're never eighteen,' I said, clutching her head as she tongued the sensitive tip of my erect clitoris and massaged the inner flesh of my cunt.

'Yes, I am. They said that I was eighteen.'

'They *said* ... Angel, I really don't think—'

'I'm your personal maid,' she interrupted me, her sparkling blue eyes looking up as I frowned at her. 'I'm here to look after you, to wash you and pleasure you. I'll do anything you want, all you have to do is ask. And you can do what you like to me. They said that I belong to you and I must do exactly what you want, no matter what you ask of me.'

'All I ask is that you get me out of this house.'

'I can't do that, Rachael. Why do you want to leave? I belong to you and—'

'You don't *belong* to anyone, Angel. You shouldn't be here. You should be ...'

'Are you going to come?' she asked me, her wet tongue snaking over the sensitive tip of my clitoris.

'I . . . I don't know,' I gasped as she pressed a fingertip against the delicate tissue of my anus. 'Angel, I . . .'

'Don't talk any more. Just allow me to pleasure you.'

Sally and her confederates weren't simply playing games, I mused as my young attendant drove her finger deep into my rectal canal. Blackmail, imprisoning me, sexually abusing me . . . and they'd incarcerated a young girl whom they'd obviously indoctrinated with their perverted ideas. Looking down at her tongue as she licked my naked vulval flesh and fingered my sex holes, I couldn't believe how arousing I found her. Blonde, fresh-faced, angelic . . . But this was wrong, I told myself repeatedly.

As my solid clitoris was sucked into her hot mouth, I let out a gasp of sexual pleasure. She really did know what she was doing, and I wondered how many women she'd pleasured during her time in the torture room. And worse, how many *men* had used and abused her? She really did believe that her role in life was to give sexual pleasure and wait on people. She should have been out with friends, enjoying her life, not . . . The gang had done to her what they'd intended to do to me during my younger years, I was sure.

My naked body shuddering as Angel mouthed and licked my pulsating clitoris, I wondered whether I'd have ended up in the gang's cottage had I not left Southmoore to work in London. Perhaps what the abuse at school had been leading up to was my eventual abduction and imprisonment. But they'd been kids at school. Had they *really* planned their lives of sex and crime in their early teens? There was far more to the Brook Street Gang than met the eye, I thought.

'God,' I breathed, my clitoris about to erupt in orgasm

beneath the nymph's sweeping tongue. 'God, I'm . . . I'm coming.' My juices of lust streaming from my fingered cunt, my rectal sheath rhythmically contracting, I swayed on my sagging legs as the young girl sucked my orgasm from my pulsating clitoris. Again and again, waves of pure sexual bliss rolled through my shaking body as she double-fingered my sex holes and tongued my swollen clitoris. Clutching her head and forcing my orgasming clitoris further into her mouth, I felt that I was going to faint with pleasure as my climax peaked and gripped my trembling body. My mind swimming with thoughts of illicit lesbian sex, I finally began to come down from my girl-induced orgasm.

'No more,' I gasped as Angel's fingers pistoned my sex holes and she sucked hard on my painfully solid clitoris. 'God, no more.'

'Was that all right?' she asked, looking up at me, her cunny-wet face grinning.

'Yes, yes,' I breathed. 'That was . . . that was certainly all right.'

'Would you like to lick *me* now?' she asked, rising to her feet and lying on the leather-topped table with her young thighs spread wide.

'Angel, I . . . This is wrong,' I murmured, gazing at the tightly closed crack of her young pussy.

'Wrong?' she echoed, lifting her head and frowning at me. 'What do you mean?'

'I mean that this isn't right. Licking each other and . . . Apart from that fact that we're the same sex, you're too young to—'

'The same sex? What has that got to do with it? You liked me licking your pussy, didn't you?'

'Yes, yes, I did. But—'

'Then lick mine.'

Stroking the firm hillocks of Angel's outer labia, I felt my clitoris swell, my juices of desire oozing between the inner wings of my vaginal slit. She was beautiful, angelic, fresh ... Succumbing to a waking inner desire, I ran my fingertip up and down her creamy-wet crack and squeezed the small mound of one young breast as she closed her eyes and breathed deeply. Parting her legs further, her vaginal crack opened as she dropped her feet down at either side of the table. Examining the intricate folds nestling within her bared sex valley, I focused on the ripe nodule of her clitoris. As she parted the fleshy outer lips of her youthful pussy with her slender fingers, I couldn't resist massaging the solid nub of her clittie.

'That's nice,' she murmured, stretching her vulval lips wider apart. My fascination with her young body was interest rather than sex, I mused. Or was it? The temptation to slip a finger deep into the tight sheath of her cunt was overwhelming. Again trying to convince myself that I should leave the girl alone, I did my best to refrain from leaning over and tasting the flowing cream of her vagina. Gasping, Angel parted her outer lips further, the pinken flesh of her naked sex valley glistening in the light, the juice-oozing entrance to her young cunt beckoning my finger, my inquisitive tongue.

I should have been trying to escape, I knew as I looked up at the open door. Apart from Angel, the house was deserted, and I doubted that I'd get another such opportunity to escape. Focusing on the young girl's inner folds, I licked my lips. Her vaginal cream was flowing in torrents from the entrance to her sweet little cunt, her clitoris pulsating beneath my massaging fingertip. I was torn, I had to admit as I focused on the small milk teats adorning her petite breasts. This was wrong, I told myself again.

Finally leaning over, I tentatively licked each outer lip in turn, breathing in the heady scent of Angel's vulva as she writhed on the table. I didn't know why I was doing this, let alone why I was getting such immense pleasure from the illicit act. I'd never had lesbian tendencies. I'd been forced to finger the bitches at school, but had never dreamed that I'd enjoy licking the hairless labia of a young girl's naked body. I wondered, was there something wrong with me? My fingertip massaged the pinken funnel of flesh surrounding the tight entrance to her cunt. Dangerously close to penetrating her vaginal shaft, an inner battle raging in my mind, I stood up and clasped my hands behind my back.

'What's the matter?' she asked me, opening her eyes and frowning.

'Everything,' I sighed. 'Angel, I know that you've been brainwashed by the gang. But you have to understand that this isn't normal behaviour.'

'What isn't?'

'You licking me and allowing me to touch you. You should be out with boys, experimenting with sex, not imprisoned here and used by people.'

'Experimenting with sex?' she echoed, propping herself up on her elbows. 'Why would I want to experiment with sex?'

'How many men have . . . How many men . . .' I could scarcely bring myself to ask her the question.

'Have fucked me?' she asked, with a frightening air of innocence.

'Yes.'

'I've never counted them,' she giggled. 'Why would I count the men? That's what my cunt is for, isn't it?'

'Yes . . . I mean, no.'

'But that's what men want, Rachael. You should know that. After all, you are older than I am.'

'You've been indoctrinated by those evil people, Angel. Your cunt isn't . . . You don't offer your body to anyone and everyone for sex.'

'But that's what it's *for*, Rachael,' she persisted. 'Men love my body, they love fucking me. And there are a few women who like to finger me and make me come. The men love watching me masturbate with a vibrator. You can't say that all these people are wrong.'

'I can and I do, Angel. They're using you, can't you see that? No, obviously not.'

'You *want* to lick me, don't you?' she asked, resting her head back on the table again. 'Go on – you know that you want to push your tongue into my cunt. Everyone else loves tonguing my little cunt, so why don't you?'

'It's not that I don't . . . I mean . . .'

As Angel closed her eyes and peeled the fleshy pads of her outer labia wide apart, I leaned forward and licked the solid tip of her pink clitoris. I'd lost control of myself, lost all perception of right and wrong. She had a beautiful young body, and I couldn't help myself as I slipped a finger into the hot, hugging sheath of her pussy. She was so tight, the walls of her cunt gripping my massaging finger like a velvet-jawed vice as she writhed and squirmed on the table. Sucking the swollen nub of her clitoris into my mouth, I swept my tongue over the sensitive tip and eased a second finger into the wet heat of her cunt.

Tweaking the sensitive buds of her nipples as I sucked

and mouthed her ripe clitoris, I forced a third finger into the tight duct of her hot cunt. Finger-fucking her, I listened to the squelching sounds of her vaginal juices as she let out whimpers of pleasure. She was going to come, I knew as her clitoris swelled beneath my snaking tongue. Her young body shaking wildly, her whimpers becoming loud moans, she arched her back and let out a scream.

'Suck it,' Angel cried, stretching her legs out at either side of the table. 'Finger my cunt hard and suck me off.' Unable to believe the crude words tumbling from her pretty lips, I pistoned her spasming cunt and sucked her pleasure out of her orgasming clitoris. Her juices of arousal streaming down my fingers and running over my hand, I stretched her vaginal lips wide apart with my free hand until I thought the delicate tissue of her inner folds would tear. The full length of her orgasming clitoris sucked into my hot mouth, my fingers repeatedly thrusting deep into her tight little cunt, I mouthed and gobbled until she began to float down from her sexual heaven.

'Finger my bottom,' she breathed as I stood upright and licked my cunny-wet lips. Bending her legs up and back and pressing her knees against the small mounds of her young breasts as I slipped my creamed fingers out of her tight vagina, she again asked me to finger her bottom-hole. The brown ring of her anus fully exposed, the outer lips of her vulva bulging between her slender thighs, she reached behind her naked body and yanked the firm cheeks of her buttocks wide apart.

'Please, finger both my holes,' Angel begged me. The taste of her sex juices lingering on my tongue, I tentatively drove a finger into the hot duct of her rectum. Gazing at the delicate tissue of her anal ring hugging my knuckle, I pushed my finger fully home and massaged her inner flesh. She was so tight, her anal sphincter muscles rhythmically contracting, lovingly gripping my finger as I slowly withdrew and thrust into her again. She writhed and gasped, begging me again to finger-fuck both her sex ducts as I twisted and bent my finger deep within her bottom-hole.

I'd given up telling myself that this was wrong as I slipped a finger into the juice-dripping sheath of Angel's tight vagina. Wrong or not, she was young, fresh, tight – and only too willing to give me her naked body in the name of sex. Lesbian sex? Was that really what I wanted? Repeatedly thrusting my sex-slimed fingers deep into the core of her young body, her hot holes spasming as she let out whimpers of pleasure, I massaged the solid bulb of her expectant clitoris with my free hand. She shook violently, her naked body convulsing wildly as her pleasure built. She was going to reach another massive orgasm, I knew as her clitoris swelled to an incredible size and hardness beneath my vibrating fingertip. Her juices of desire gushing from her gaping cunt-hole, streaming down my thrusting finger, she arched her back and grimaced.

'Coming,' Angel announced, gasping, her sex sheaths contracting, squeezing my pistoning fingers. Lifting her legs, she grabbed her ankles and held her feet wide apart as I worked between her splayed thighs. The very centre of her young body laid wide open, I had better access to her two holes, my fingers driving deep into the very core of her quivering young body. Wondering whether she'd shaved, I focused on the smooth outer lips of her vulva and became aware of my own clitoris swelling between the hairless cushions of my outer labia. I desperately needed to come again. My juices filling my naked sex valley, I needed to feel the girl's tongue there, lapping up my cream, licking my hot cunt, teasing my love spot to orgasm.

Angel finally came down from her sexual heaven, her naked body twitching, her love holes spasming as I withdrew my fingers from her sated body. She was incredibly beautiful, I thought as she lowered her slender legs. Her head lolling from side to side, her long blonde hair veiling her sex-flushed face, she licked her succulent lips and breathed heavily in the aftermath of her orgasm. Hearing a noise on the landing, I looked up as a young man appeared in the doorway. He was in his teens, good-looking with a fresh face, blue eyes and curly blond hair. His naked body looked firm, hard and youthfully unblemished. Lowering my eyes, I focused on the purple globe of his cock pointing to the ceiling. He'd shaved his pubic curls, I observed. The skin around the base of his cock was smooth and his balls were completely devoid of hair.

'John,' Angel said, lifting her head and smiling at the boy. 'Come and play with us.'

'Who are you?' I asked him as he walked into the room and ran his fingertips around the elongated teats of the girl's breasts. 'Where did you come from?'

'This is John,' Angel said. 'He lives here.'

'And I suppose you too work here?' I asked him, unable to drag my eyes away from the smooth shaft of his beautiful penis.

'Yes, I do,' he replied. 'We both work here.'

'What is your job, exactly?'

'He—' Angel began.

'Let him answer,' I interrupted her. 'Well, John? What *is* your job here?'

'I look after the female clients.'

'And that man,' Angel added. 'You look after him, don't you?'

'I have to leave this house,' I said, licking my lips as I imagined sucking the boy's penile globe into my wet mouth. 'I have to get out of this house. Can you help me?'

'Get out?' John echoed, frowning. 'Why do you want to leave?'

'God, not you as well,' I sighed, realizing that he'd been indoctrinated by the gang. 'Is there a way out? Why I want to leave isn't important. Just help me to get out.'

'Of course there's a way out,' he said, moving to the door. 'Follow me.'

Grabbing the towel as Angel leaped off the table, I followed them downstairs to the kitchen. To my surprise, and delight, John took a key from the top of a cupboard and opened the back door. Taking Angel's hand and leading her out into the garden, his penis now flaccid, he turned and waited for me to join them. The feel of fresh air against my body was invigorating. The grass soft beneath my naked feet, I looked around the garden for a gate or low fence. The perimeter wall was at least ten feet high, and I had the awful feeling that there was no way out. To climb the wall would be impossible, and I doubted that the gang had conveniently left a ladder lying about.

'Do you like the garden?' John asked me.

'Yes, but how do I get out?'

'Out of the garden?'

'Yes, John, out of the garden. I have to go and see some people. I have to go home to my flat in London and—'

'London?' he laughed. 'It's beautiful here. Why do you want to go to London?'

'Because . . . It doesn't matter,' I murmured, realizing that I was getting nowhere.

Watching Angel drop to her knees and take John's cock into her pretty mouth, I realized the extent of their indoctrination. There was no way I could make them see sense, I knew as the girl bobbed her head back and forth, mouth-fucking herself with the lad's solid penis. This was like a dream, I mused. An extremely attractive couple, fair-skinned and with fair hair, young and beautiful . . . They were like cherubs. Watching Angel cup John's heavy balls in her small hand, I knew that she was going to suck the spunk out of his cock as he began gasping. Was this all they did? I wondered about their lives in this place. Suck and fuck and . . .

'Do you want his sperm?' Angel asked me, slipping John's deep-purple glans out of her mouth.

'No, I . . . I have to get out of here,' I replied hesitantly, eyeing the saliva-glistening surface of his beautiful knob.

'Go on,' John breathed. 'Drink my sperm.'

Kneeling in front of him as Angel moved aside, I knew that I'd lost all control as I gazed at the fresh shaft of his erect penis. Running my fingertips over his hairless scrotum, stroking the soft skin of his mons, I thought how young he looked without his pubic curls. Caressing his shaft, running my fingertip around the rim of his purple helmet, I cupped his balls in my palm and tentatively licked his sperm-slit. Taking his penis by the root, I sucked his swollen glans into my hot mouth and breathed heavily through my nose as he swayed on his trembling legs.

'All the girls love sucking his knob,' Angel said, settling beside me. 'I milk him at least twice every day to make him produce fresh sperm for the clients. Sally says that he needs to come twice a day to make him last longer when he's with a client. Now that you're living here, you can help me. I usually milk him first thing in the morning and then again late in the afternoon.'

I couldn't believe what she was saying as she rambled on about 'milking' the boy. And I didn't know why I was sucking his cock when I was out in the garden and should have been looking for a means of escape. Although the garden wall was high, I reckoned after all that I'd be able to climb it with some help from John. He was a tall lad and, if I could climb onto his shoulders, I'd be able to clamber to the top of the wall and over it to freedom.

'Here it comes,' he breathed, clutching my head as his glans swelled within my hot mouth and his shaft twitched.

'Drink it all,' Angel said, her face only inches from my gobbling mouth as she watched the crude act. 'Swallow every drop and then he'll last a lot longer when he fucks you.'

His sperm jetting from his throbbing knob, bathing my tongue and filling my cheeks, John let out a long low moan of pleasure as I swallowed hard. Angel grabbed his solid shaft and wanked him, bringing out his spunk as I drank from his fountainhead. He was so young, I mused, the salty taste of his orgasmic cream driving me wild. They were both so young. To spend their time sucking and fucking . . . But I had problems of my own, I reflected. They were both happy, so it was best not to interfere. At least, not until I'd made my escape from the den of sex.

'He enjoys bottom-fucking,' Angel said, running her fingers up John's shaft and squeezing the last of his sperm out of his knob-slit. 'We're pretty good together during the shows.'

'Shows?' I echoed, slipping his glistening plum out of my spunk-drenched mouth. 'What do you mean, *shows*?'

'You'll enjoy doing the shows with us. Usually, there are five or six people in the audience.'

'What do you do during these shows?'

'My favourite is Little Girl Lost,' John said. 'Angel is dressed in a school uniform and she rests in the woods on her way home. I'm an evil man who stumbles across her and—'

'And he rapes me,' Angel giggled. 'The audience like to see my knickers torn off and my little pink pussy . . .'

'Bizarre,' I breathed. 'John, I want you to stand by the wall over there. Give me a lift up and I might be able to clamber to the top and escape.'

'We have work to do,' he said, taking Angel's hand and leading her back into the house.

'But . . .' I murmured, realizing that I was wasting my time.

Looking up at the high wall, I determined to scale it and make my escape. The gang might have returned at any time, I thought, noticing a shed in the corner of the garden. Finding its door locked, I slipped between the shed and the wall. Climbing onto a pile of old bricks, I managed to clamber onto the shed's roof. The top of the wall was now only a couple of feet above me so I leaped to the top and peered at the ground far below me on the other side. Whether or not it was someone's garden I jumped and landed with a thud.

'Yes,' I breathed, punching the air with my fist. Escaping had been so easy after all, I reflected, wishing that I'd brought the towel with me as I looked down at my naked body, the hairless lips of my pussy. Perhaps it was a trick? No, they wouldn't bother to play games. I doubted that they'd even thought that I might climb onto the shed roof and leap to the top of the wall. Angel and John had no desire to escape, so—

'You'll be punished for this.' Sally's voice came from over the wall. 'For God's sake, Angel. Why the hell did you allow her out in the garden?'

'I opened the door,' John said. 'I thought—'

'Search the garden. Look behind the shed and in the bushes. If she has got out, then God only knows how.'

Hiding in the bushes, I sat on the ground and rested my chin on my knees. Wishing again that I'd brought the towel with me, I tried to work out where I was. The cottage backed onto woodland, but I couldn't recall what lay beyond the woods. My sense of direction wasn't too good at the best of times, but I reckoned that the railway station would be at the far side of the forested area. In my early teens, I'd never ventured into the woods for fear of the gang waylaying me.

Listening to Sally shouting at John and Angel, I recalled the time when she'd cornered me in the toilets at school. As usual, she'd forced me to take my knickers off and show her my sex crack. We were alone, and I'd decided that I'd take the opportunity to fight back for a change. Grabbing her wrists, I'd pinned her up against the wall. It had been a fatal mistake. Julie and Kathy had come into the toilets and stripped me naked. Bending me over, they'd spanked my naked buttocks, only halting the gruelling punishment when my screams became so loud that they'd been afraid that one of the teachers would come to investigate. If they caught me now . . . I dreaded to think what they'd do to me.

'She must have gone over the fucking wall,' Julie shouted. 'Search the woods.'

'She'll be miles away by now,' Sally said.

'She can't go far without any clothes. Take Rod and Kenny and search the fucking woods until you find the bitch.'

Creeping through the undergrowth, I realized that I was in the wooded area behind the church. *Sanctuary?* I thought, my naked feet hurting as I trod over the rough ground. I didn't have much time, I knew as I headed for the church. Now that Sally and the others had realized that I wasn't in the garden, they'd hunt me down like a wild animal. This was worse than a nightmare, I thought, sneaking around the side of the church. How the hell had I got myself into this situation? I should have known better than to return to Southmoore, let alone employ three members of the Brook Street Gang. My quest for revenge had brought me nothing but trouble, nothing but danger.

Slipping through the main doors of the church, I looked around the cold stone building. A cassock, a robe . . . Anything would do to conceal my naked body. Once I was decent, I'd try to get home and . . . Home? Returning to my flat would be as dangerous as returning to the cottage. Looking up at the crucifix, I wondered whether praying would do any good. It was only a matter of time before the gang burst into the church and . . . A question popped into my whirling brain: was there a God?

# 10

Slipping into the vicar's office, I grinned as I noticed a circular tray of money on his desk – the Sunday collection, no doubt. That was my train fare to . . . to where, I had no idea. Eyeing a cassock hanging on a hook behind the door, I thought that Lady Luck – or God Himself – must have been smiling down at me. Deciding to go to Devon where my uncle lived, I grabbed the cassock and was about to pull it off its hook when I heard movements in the church.

'Shit,' I whispered, standing behind the office door and praying that I wouldn't be discovered. Listening to someone banging about, I wondered whether it was one of the gang. Once they'd discovered that I wasn't in the woods, they might have realized that the church was a convenient place to hide. Another bang resounding around the old building, I cowered down further behind the door. My heart racing, my hands trembling . . . If they caught me, they'd have a job to drag me back to the cottage in broad daylight, I tried to console myself. There again, they might just frogmarch me through the woods and bundle me back over the wall into the garden.

'Oh,' the vicar gasped as he entered his office and stared at me. 'Er . . . who are you?' Unable to speak as he looked down at the weal-lined mounds of my firm breasts, the hairless lips of my vaginal crack, I watched him close the door. 'Well?' he asked sternly. 'What are you doing in here? And why are you naked?'

'It's a . . . it's a long story,' I finally spluttered, folding my arms to conceal the elongated teats of my rounded breasts.

'Then I suggest you start at the beginning.' He looked angry, threatening. 'I've just about had enough of you evil lot using my church for your devil worship.'

'Devil worship?' I echoed, shaking my head. 'No, no, it's nothing to do with—'

'Don't lie to me, young lady. Your state of undress tells me everything. You were here last night with your evil sect, weren't you?'

'No, I . . .'

'You broke in and used my altar for your vile sexual acts.' Switching the light on, he opened his desk drawer. 'This is what you came back for, isn't it?' he asked, holding up a huge vibrator. 'You disgust me. As I said, I've had enough of this. And I'm not prepared to put up with it any more.'

As the vicar locked the door and lifted the telephone, I knew that he was calling the police as he punched the buttons. At least I'd be able to explain what had happened once they arrived. Eyeing his balding head, his angry face, I reckoned that he was in his mid-sixties. I also reckoned that the gang weren't far behind me. But I'd be safe enough in the vicar's office until the police arrived. I'd tell them everything. Tell them about the gang, Sally, Julie . . .

'I've caught one of the sect,' the cleric said, almost triumphantly, flashing me a glance as he pressed the receiver to his ear. As he rambled on, explaining how he'd discovered me in his office with no clothes on, I felt at ease. The police might take a little convincing but, once they'd checked my identity, and my story, they'd not only release me but go after the Brook Street Gang. Perhaps I'd move to Southmoore after all, I mused. Once I'd spoken to Dave Bryant, and Sally and her cronies were behind bars . . . This was going to be a new start.

'Right, I'll keep her here until you arrive,' the vicar said.

'I'm not a devil worshipper,' I murmured as he replaced the receiver. 'I can explain everything.'

'There's nothing to explain,' he returned. 'You're one of the sect, all right. The state of your body sums it up perfectly. You've been shaved, whipped . . . Leave that,' he yelled as I reached up to take the cassock from the hook. 'You'll stay exactly as you are.'

'You're mistaken,' I said, offering him a smile. 'I came here because . . . I suppose I came here for sanctuary.'

'Sanctuary?' he retorted mockingly. 'You came here for that vibrator. Where are the others?'

'Others?'

'Are they waiting for you outside? Where are your clothes?'

'I don't have any clothes. I came here through the woods and . . .'

'What's your name?'

'Fiona. I mean, Rachael.'

'Fiona, Rachael . . . Lies tumble from your lips with frightening ease, don't they? Stay there,' he ordered me, grabbing the cassock and opening the door. 'You won't have to wait long.'

As the vicar left the room and locked the door behind him, I knew that I wasn't too late to save my flat. Once the police were involved and Julie was discovered to have been living in the flat, everything would be all right. I might have lost some furniture, but that was nothing in comparison to losing my home. I felt rather proud of myself for managing to escape from the gang. They were dealing with the bitch from hell, I reflected. And no one messed with the bitch from hell.

'She's in here,' the priest said, opening the door. 'She's one of the sect, I know it.'

'Is that right?' a middle-aged man in a suit asked, following the vicar into the room. 'You say that you found her nosing about in here?'

'She was rummaging about, looking for something. Probably that vibrator. It was left here by the sect. She obviously came back for it.'

'I can explain everything,' I began, folding my arms across my breasts. 'I was captured by—'

'Save it,' the besuited man snapped. 'I'm not interested in your lies. I want the names of the others.'

'I'll give you their names,' I agreed readily. 'There's Rod—'

'She'll pull names out of a hat,' the vicar cut in. 'We'll get nowhere like this.'

'You're right,' the other man said, grabbing my wrist. 'This church has been broken into, used by devil worshippers and . . .'

'And I've had enough,' the cleric hissed. 'Using the altar for your crude sexual acts, group fucking, devil worshipping . . .'

'What have you got to say for yourself?' the besuited man asked me. 'You've been caught naked in the church and—'

'I'll make a full statement,' I interrupted him, trying to

pull away as he tightened his grip. 'Take me to the station and I'll . . .'

'The station? You want to catch a train?' he laughed.

'No, no. The police station.'

'I'm not a copper,' he chuckled.

'But I thought . . .'

'Bring her to the altar,' the vicar instructed the man. 'We'll get the truth out of her if it's the last thing we do. I'll go and lock the doors.'

Screaming and protesting as I was dragged through the church to the altar, I heard the sound of the main door closing and a heavy bolt sliding across. This couldn't be happening to me, I thought fearfully as the man lifted me off the floor and laid me on my back over the altar. My hopes had been raised by the thought of explaining everything to the police, but now . . . Who was this other man? I asked myself that question as he bound ropes around my ankles. Pulling my feet down either side of the altar, he secured the ropes. My naked body completely defenceless as the vicar pulled my arms behind my head and bound my wrists, I again protested, asserting my innocence. They weren't listening. Talking about the evil sect, they genuinely believed that I was one of the culprits.

The gaping crack of my vagina blatantly exposed, I watched the two men as they examined my inner flesh. I was becoming used to strangers using and abusing me, but that didn't lessen my fear. The chances were that the vicar and his accomplice were members of the Brook Street Gang. Perhaps they'd recruited dozens of members over the years, I thought anxiously. Shopkeepers, people in the street . . . I'd never know who was watching me, waiting to pounce. I could trust no one.

'We'll drive the devil out of her,' the vicar breathed, running his fingertips around the dark discs of my areolae. 'Drive the demons from her and bring her back into the fold. You're the exorcist,' he said, turning to his accomplice. 'She's in your hands.'

'Indeed, she is,' the other man replied, his dark eyes focusing on the naked flesh of my sex crack. 'I've dealt with many a young girl possessed by demons and, although I say it myself, I've had great success. Would you pass me my bag? It's on that pew.'

'Of course,' the priest replied, dumping a leather bag on the altar. 'I have one or two things to attend to in my office. Just shout, should you need me.'

Opening the bag, the man pulled out a handkerchief and pushed it into my mouth. I'd not said anything for fear of being gagged, but I might as well have screamed and shouted. Tying the handkerchief around the back of my head, he delved into his bag again and pulled out what appeared to be a vaginal speculum. He was no exorcist, I knew as he flashed me a wicked grin. Bound and gagged on the altar, a speculum . . . Hardly the sort of props a man of God would use. Was he a member of the gang? I wondered about that again as he pinched and twisted the ripe teats of my young breasts. Surely he'd have taken me back to the cottage if he was . . .

'Punishment causing pain is a form of redemption,' he said, breaking my reverie as he parted the soft lips of my vulva. 'The ransom of sinners from the bondage of sin and the penalties of God's violated law . . . You have been possessed by evil spirits, my child. Your womb is riddled with evil. You'll thank me once I've driven out the demons.'

He was wicked, I knew as he slipped the cold steel

wings of the speculum between the splayed lips of my vagina and drove it deep into my tight cunt. This had nothing to do with exorcism. This was blatant sexual abuse of my naked body, gross violation of my feminine form. But I could do nothing to stop the wretched man as he squeezed the speculum levers, stretching open the tight sheath of my cunt. My clitoris forced out from beneath its pink hood, I grimaced as the speculum opened me further, baring the walls of my vagina, exposing the creamy ring of my cervix to his wide eyes.

'You have sinned,' he said, pushing a finger into my gaping vaginal duct and massaging the taut walls. 'You have desecrated this church with your vile sexual acts. You have polluted the sanctity of this altar by performing evil acts of forbidden sex upon it. You have denounced the Almighty by lying upon this altar and spreading your naked body to satisfy the perverted sexual appetites of men.'

The man was mad, I knew as he slipped his finger out of my gaping vagina and delved again into his bag. Pulling my nipple up, stretching my breast into a cone of taut flesh, he fixed a metal clamp to my elongated teat and tightened the screw. Fixing the second clamp to my other milk teat, he let out a wicked chuckle as I lifted my head and gazed at the brown flesh of my aching nipples as they were forced to inflate. This was crude sexual torture. It had nothing to do with exorcism, and I wondered what other horrors the sadist had in store for me.

'Demons reside in the womb,' he informed me. 'They enter the womb via the vaginal canal, usually as a result of vulgar and illicit sexual acts. The speculum has opened the entrance to your womb, thus allowing any demons within you an escape route. But, sadly, they will not leave of their own accord. To drive them from your young body, I shall have to inflict pain. When the pain becomes unbearable, the fiends will flee.'

Mad? He was completely insane. The vicar must have known that he was a sex-crazed pervert, I thought, wondering if and when I'd be released. Unbearable pain? Thinking it odd that the gang hadn't tried to get into the church, I wasn't sure which was the lesser of two evils. The madman abusing my naked body on the altar, or the degenerate Brook Street Gang? Trying to turn my thoughts to what I'd do once I was allowed my freedom, I knew that I'd just have to endure whatever the so-called exorcist put me through and pray for the abuse to end quickly.

'You have a beautiful young body,' the man-monster said, slipping a finger between the firm cheeks of my naked bottom. 'And such a tight little anus. I wonder whether you've ever had a penis enter you there?' Pushing his finger into the tightening sheath of my rectum, he grinned at me. 'Demons reside there, too,' he chuckled. 'I think I'd better open your bottom-hole and drive them out of your bowels.'

Yanking his finger out of my bottom and taking another speculum from the leather bag, he slipped the two metal paddles into my anal gully. Easing the rounded ends into my anal portal, he chuckled again as he parted the smooth cheeks of my bottom and forced the device past the tight brown ring of my arsehole. I felt that I was going to split open as the cold paddles drove deep into the heat of my rectum. As he squeezed the levers, the delicate tissue of my anus stretched to its limits. The pain increasing, I moaned loudly through my nose.

'Ah, yes,' the vicar's accomplice breathed, leaning over

and gazing at his handiwork. 'Such a sweet little bottom-hole. Tight, hot, fuckable, lickable . . . You've probably gathered by now that I'm not connected with the church. The vicar and I . . . let's just say that we have an arrangement. This sect of yours has been bugging him for some time now. He feels that his clandestine exploits might come to light unless the sect is dealt with. After all, a group of people using the church for sexual rituals is bound to attract attention. The last thing the vicar wants is to be somehow associated with your sect. He called me because . . . because I have a way with girls. After I've finished with you, you'll never return to this church. And neither will your friends, once they hear about your visit. Enough talk. Let's get on with the punishment.'

Taking a huge candle from his bag, the fake exorcist slipped the rounded end into my gaping bottom-hole. The speculum held my rectum wide open and he managed to push the waxen shaft deep into my bowels, bloating my pelvic cavity to the extreme. I couldn't believe that I'd escaped the torture room in the cottage only to be captured by a perverted vicar and sexually abused on the altar by his evil friend. Where the hell had I gone wrong? I pondered on that problem as he took another massive candle from his bag. I'd have thought that a church would have been a safe place, but . . . There again, the vicar *had* caught me naked in his office. And he'd been having problems from some sect or other. I wondered: what was his arrangement with the besuited man? Did the vicar lure young girls to his church and—

'I'll just slip this into your tight little cunt,' the evil man said, pushing the rounded end of the second candle into the yawning entrance of my vagina. I could feel my sex sheath opening, stretching, as he drove the wax phallus deep into my cunt. The end finally pressing against my cervix, he stood upright and gazed at the creamy-white dildos emerging from both my inflamed sex holes. I could endure the abuse – so far. But what other sexual horrors had he planned for me?

Deciding that, no matter what the priest's henchman did to me, he'd eventually have to allow me my freedom, I realized that there was nothing I'd not experienced. The gang had already forced me to endure a host of crude sexual acts. There was nothing that this man could do to me that I'd not been forced to suffer in the past. Standing by my side, he tightened the nipple-clamp screws, a wicked glint in his eyes as he grinned at me.

'I love women's breasts,' he said. 'Full, firm, topped with extremely sensitive nipples . . . They're ideal for torturing. I don't think that you'll be returning to *this* church with your friends after I've finished with you,' he laughed, taking two steel rings from his bag. 'These are designed to bring pain and pleasure,' he said, slipping the rings over my breasts. 'Tightening the screws, like this, forces your breasts to balloon out. The result is that your nipples will inflate and become acutely sensitive.'

Closing my eyes as the pervert continued to tighten the screws, the steel rings closing around the base of each breast, I could feel my nipples swelling within the metal clamps. My sex sheaths bloated by the speculums and candles, my breasts like two balloons, my nipples puffed up, I felt that my entire body was tingling with a strange blend of pain and pleasure. My clitoris was erect, I knew as the evil man massaged its sensitive tip, sending ripples of sex through my contracting womb.

'I might give Rod a call,' the vicar said as he approached. 'I reckon that this little beauty will be an ideal candidate for . . . for certain things.'

*Rod?* I thought, opening my eyes and staring at the vicar. *Rod Johnson?*

'Good idea,' the man replied. 'But I think we should question the girl first. Find out a few things about her.'

'Take the gag off and we'll see what she has to say.'

'I have nothing to say,' I retorted as the gag was removed. 'Apart from the fact that—'

'Shut the bitch up, for fuck's sake,' the vicar snapped.

'Unless you want me to tighten the nipple clamps even further, I suggest you be quiet,' the other man said.

'Where do you work?' the vicar asked me.

'I don't,' I replied.

'Where do you live?'

'In Spain. I'm here on holiday.'

'She's lying,' the man breathed. 'If you're here on holiday, then how come you're involved with the sect?'

'I'm not involved with any sect. I'm here on holiday and . . . I came to the church because a man tried to rape me in the woods. He tore my clothes off and . . . and I managed to get away.'

'Are you here alone?' the vicar asked, his expression one of concern.

'No, I'm with my father and brother,' I lied. 'I was supposed to meet them in a local café but—'

'If she's telling the truth . . .' the besuited man murmured pensively.

'Then we're in the shit.'

'Who's Rod?' I asked.

'Never you mind,' the vicar replied. 'We'll have to . . . well, you know,' he said, checking his watch.

'What?' I gasped, tugging on the ropes binding my wrists.

'Have some fun with you,' the besuited man said, dropping his trousers.

'That's right,' the vicar confirmed, tugging his cassock over his head. 'There's no rush to get you out of here. We have plenty of time to enjoy your naked body. You'll enjoy a double-fucking. After all, you've been fucked on this very altar before.'

'I haven't,' I whimpered. 'I've never even been to this church before.'

'I can see that I'm going to have to shut you up by ramming my knob down your throat,' the cleric chortled. 'You'll enjoy a throat-spunking.'

*A throat-spunking.* My thoughts again returning to my early teens, I recalled Sally and Julie capturing me and dragging me into the bushes on the common. They'd hung an old blanket between two bushes, and I'd wondered what it was for as they forced me to kneel on the ground. A solid penis emerging through a hole in the blanket, I'd gazed at the massive shaft in awe. The purple knob had been huge, the foreskin fully retracted, the sperm-slit 'eye' seeming to peer at me.

I'd been forced to take the swollen glans deep into my mouth and suck it. The girls had giggled as they'd held my head, bobbing me back and forth, the solid cock mouth-fucking me. I'd realized that it wasn't Rod's penis, or Kenny's. I'd been forced to kneel in front of the blanket and suck the unidentified cock several times after that fateful day. Swallowing the spunk as it had gushed from the slit and filled my hot mouth, I'd been forced to drink from the cockhead. It was always the same cock, but I'd never discovered who its owner was.

Watching as the vicar and his accomplice stripped naked, I eyed their erect cocks as they clambered onto the altar. The vicar kneeling astride my head as his sidekick slipped the candle and speculum out of my vagina, I knew what I was in for. Ordering me to suck his knob, the vicar pressed his purple glans against my pursed lips and let out a wicked chuckle. What was to become of me, I dreaded to think as I took his salty knob into my wet mouth and rolled my tongue around the rim. The other man's knob gliding deep into the inflamed sheath of my cunt, all I could do was pray that they'd release me once they'd satisfied their hunger for crude sex.

The vicar's heavy balls battering my chin as he repeatedly drove his swollen knob to the back of my throat, my lower stomach inflating as the other man thrust his cock deep into the constricted sheath of my wet cunt, I wondered again who Rod was. If they'd been talking about Rod Johnson, then I was pretty sure that the gang would have come to the church and searched for me. They'd have asked the vicar whether he'd seen me, I was sure. It was odd that the cottage was so close to the church, I reflected. The vicar and his accomplice must have been in with the gang, I was certain.

'There's nothing I like more than fucking a filthy slut's mouth,' the priest gasped, my full lips rolling back and forth along his veined shaft as his knob battered the back of my throat.

'I rather like this little slag,' the man fucking my cunt breathed. 'It's a shame that we're going to have to—'

'Don't talk about that now. Just enjoy the bitch while you can.'

They had something evil planned for me, I knew as I

gobbled on the vicar's solid knob. They wouldn't do away with me, would they? There were too many unanswered questions. Who was the young girl in the cottage? How long had she and the boy been there? Were the vicar and his disciple involved with the Brook Street Gang? I didn't know what to think as the two massive cocks repeatedly drove into each end of my tethered body, fucking my mouth and my cunt. It was probably best not to try to work things out.

'I'll do her arse later,' the man shafting my vagina breathed. 'Do her tight little arse and fill her bum with spunk.'

'Ever had your arse fucked?' the vicar asked me, grabbing a tuft of my long blonde hair and ramming his knob to the back of my throat. 'How about two cocks together fucking your arse? I'm sure you'd love a double arse-fucking.'

Trying to block out his crude words, I thought about my career, the new office complex, the plans Dave Bryant and I had made. It was all over – for me, at least. I couldn't help but recall my thought and feelings from my schooldays. I'd felt the same then. Despondent, worthless, useless, defeated . . . The gang had stripped me of my confidence, my virginity, and destroyed my life. I'd thought that I'd bounced back. Deputy managing director, the hard bitch, the ever-confident leader, a beautiful flat in London . . . But the gang were far more powerful, and successful, than I was. No one could smash them. Exactly how big was their operation? I thought about that.

My gobbling mouth filling with the vicar's sperm, I looked up at his grimacing face as I repeatedly swallowed his orgasmic cream. Perhaps the gang had alerted him about my escape and he'd been lying in wait in the church. It must have been pretty obvious that I would head for the church after scaling the garden wall. After all, there was nowhere else to hide. My thoughts were running away with me, I reflected as my mouth overflowed and the evil priest's spunk trickled down my cheeks.

Deciding that the vicar really had been plagued by some sect or other, I realized again that he might well believe that I was involved. Discovering me naked in his church, skulking in his office, what else would he think? Wondering whether I should admit to being a member of the sect, I thought that I might be able to a deal with the vicar. No, he wasn't the sort to do deals. But he might be interested if I offered to bring young girls to the church, supply him with fresh young cunt to satisfy his lust for perverted sex.

The sheath of my contracting vagina flooding with spunk, I hoped that the abuse would be over now that the two perverted men had drained their balls. I needed to talk to them, to tell them about my plan to supply them with teenage girls. *If you can't beat them, join them*, I thought. Or at least seem to be joining them. Feeling a little more confident as I swallowed the last of the cleric's sperm, I mulled over my plan. If I made out that the sect was a pretty big organization, and that I was its ringleader, I might be able to convince the vicar . . . An idea suddenly coming to mind, I grinned as the vicar slipped his spunk-dripping knob out of my mouth and clambered off the altar.

'You obviously enjoyed that,' he chuckled as I smiled at him.

'Very much,' I replied, my vaginal lips closing as the

other man withdrew his deflating cock from my cunt. 'I'll be honest with you. I *am* a member of the sect.'

'I thought as much,' he muttered. 'How many are there in your pathetic little circle? Four? Five?'

'I am the Grand Goddess,' I announced, opening my eyes wide and staring hard at him. 'There are fifty-odd members of the sect in Southmoore alone.'

'*Fifty*?' The vicar flashed his accomplice a frown before looking down at me again. 'So what were you doing here in the middle of the day? Why were you naked in my office?'

'I was—'

'You wouldn't come here in broad daylight,' the other man cut in. 'You wouldn't come here alone and—'

'Who said that I was alone?' I asked him.

'She's bluffing,' he said, looking at the vicar. 'There are only four or five of them. They come here at night and have sex on the altar. All this crap about a Grand Goddess . . .'

'We won't be in Southmoore for long,' I interrupted him. 'Once we've done our job here, we'll be returning to London.'

'Job? What job?'

'There's a group of people . . . I can't say too much but we're here to deal with a gang of people.'

'A gang?' the priest echoed. 'This is all bollocks,' he chuckled. 'Torture the truth out of the whore,' he instructed his friend. 'Tighten the rings until her tits burst.'

'My pleasure,' the evil man replied, his dark eyes grinning as he moved to my side. 'I have several other wonderful instruments in my bag. I'm sure that she'll be blurting out the truth before too long.'

'I'm going to make a phone call,' the vicar murmured, walking back to his office.

My plan had failed. I realized that my story had come across as pathetic. At least I'd tried, I consoled myself, watching the vicar's henchman delve into his bag. Taking a small metal device from the bag, he parted the sperm-wet lips of my pussy and pressed on the soft flesh surrounding my clitoris. As I felt the cold metal against my clitoris, I reckoned that it was some kind of clamp. I was right. Lifting my head, I watched him turn a small screw, the clamp tightening around the base of my clitoris, forcing the pink protrusion to inflate painfully.

Resting my head back on the altar, I closed my eyes and tried to take my mind off my abused body. All I needed now was for the gang to turn up and drag me back to the cottage, I thought, wondering whether I'd ever escape the nightmares of Southmoore. Who the hell was the vicar phoning? What plans did he and his accomplice have for me? My clitoris painfully inflated, I grimaced as the man tightened the screw a little more. I couldn't take much more, I knew as he rammed one of the huge candles back deep into the sperm-flooded sheath of my vaginal canal.

I hadn't thought that the crudities, the sexual abuse of my naked body, had been particularly dreadful so far. Sure, the men had fucked me, spunked my cervix and my throat, clamped my nipples, inflated my firm breasts . . . but even the clitoris clamp, though painful, was not unbearably so. The candle bloating my rectum wasn't unpleasant, and I was beginning to think that the evil pair meant me no real harm. They were simply living out their perverted fantasies, using and abusing my tethered body for crude sex with a mind to letting me go once they'd satisfied their rampant cocks. I reckoned that they'd release me, probably with some threat or other to ensure that I returned, and that they planned to enjoy my naked body many times in the future. Even vicars were capable of sexually perverted acts and blackmail, weren't they?

'Release her,' the cleric said, leaving his office and walking towards the altar.

'Release her? What the hell for?' his henchman asked, somewhat perplexed.

'I've just been talking to one of our friends on the phone. We've been offered a considerable amount of money to hand her over.'

'Hand me over to whom?' I laughed, fearing that the gang had offered cash for my capture. 'What are you talking about? Are you completely mad?'

'Get the clamps off her and tie her up. We'll keep her in the basement until she's picked up.'

As the men removed the clamps and candles, I was sure that the gang had offered cash for my return to the cottage, to the torture room. This was ridiculous, I thought, watching the vicar clear the altar and replace the instruments of torture in the leather bag. My furniture had probably been sold, my flat was on the market ... and now I was being sold to the gang. Slavery? Thinking that this was worse than a horror movie, I realized how easy it was to abduct someone. There'd be no trace of me, I reflected. My resignation handed in, my flat sold ... People would believe that I'd moved away to make a fresh start or had gone on holiday abroad. Why should anyone worry about me?

Lifting me off the altar, the vicar's sadistic sidekick left my wrists bound with rope and marched me across the church to a small side door. Ordering me to descend the steps behind it to the basement, he switched the light on and closed the door behind me. The cellar room was extremely small, about six feet square with only a small vent high up in the wall. I heard a heavy bolt slide across as I looked around me. The stone floor was wet, and a familiar odour filled my nostrils. I wondered what this place was, looking up at the vent to see a flaccid penis poking through a hole.

Shining liquid raining down over my naked body, splashing over my head and coursing down over my young breasts, I realized all too soon what they used the small room for. There was no escaping the golden rain. Moving to a corner, the liquid still splashing over my naked body, all I could do was squeeze my eyes shut and hold my breath. The shower stopped – but only briefly: I looked up to see another penis slip through the hole. Soaked with urine again, I thought that I'd gone to the depths of hell. This was a church, for Christ's sake. No – it was the Devil's lair.

No windows, no way out . . . I was trapped.

# 11

I'd been locked in the basement for well over an hour when the door opened. Staring at Ian as he stood there clutching a coat and a pair of shoes, I wasn't sure whether to smile or glare at him. Had he been told that I wasn't Jenny Wilder? Had he been told that I'd conned him, tricked him? He was a member of the gang – but whose side was he on?

'Put this on,' he ordered me, untying my wrists and passing me the coat.

'Ian . . .' I began, slipping into the coat.

'Don't say anything. Put the shoes on and follow me.'

Climbing the stone steps, I half expected to be confronted by Sally and Julie. But, to my surprise, the church was deserted. Following Ian through the main doors, the sun warming me as I breathed in the fresh air, I knew that I'd found freedom. There was no way the gang would pounce in broad daylight, was there? Leading me to a car, Ian ordered me to get in.

'Where are we going?' I asked, brushing my urine-matted hair away from my face as he started the engine.

'You lied to me,' he murmured. 'You said that you were Jenny Wilder.'

'I couldn't tell you the truth, Ian,' I said as he drove down the road. 'You're in the gang and—'

'The gang,' he breathed. 'The fucking Brook Street

Gang. Yes, I am in the gang and I've been sent to pick you up. I'm supposed to make out that I'm double-crossing the gang and letting you go.'

'So, what are you going to do?'

'They believe that I'm taking you to meet them at a house on the outskirts of town. The idea of leading you to believe that I'm rescuing you is—'

'So that I won't try to escape. Yes, I see that, but . . .'

'Rachael, the gang is far bigger than you realize. This isn't like it was at school where a group of kids would form a gang and terrorize other kids. The kids have grown up and so has the gang. The vicar and his mates have formed their own gang. Actually, I don't like the word *gang*. It sounds childish. They've formed a *group* – a group of perverts. The vicar abuses his position in the church to lure young girls into his den.'

'How long has this been going on?'

'A year or so. A girl went to confession and spilled the beans about Sally and her friends. The vicar thought the idea was brilliant and decided to set up on his own, threatening young girls unless they . . . Look, we don't have much time.'

'Where are we going?'

'I was going to get you as far away from here as possible. Whatever you do, don't turn round. We're being followed.'

'Shit.'

'Exactly. I think it's Rod and Kenny. OK, when I turn the next corner, I'm going to drive into a lamp-post. The minute we stop, get out of the car and head down the alleyway towards—'

'The park, yes I know.'

'They'll obviously follow you and think that you're

hiding in the bushes or behind the cricket pavilion. But you won't be in the park. When you're in the alley, climb over the fence into a garden. Wait there until they pass and then come back into the street and run for it.'

'OK, I've got it. I'll go into the supermarket at the end of the road until the dust settles. Ian, when will I see you again?'

'I'll meet you this evening at seven o'clock. You know the place we used to call Miller's Corner by the canal?'

'Yes, I know it. I used to like it there, sitting and watching the rippling water.'

'I'll meet you there at seven.'

'I'll be there.'

'OK, here's the corner. They're pretty close behind us so you're going to have to be quick. I'm going for that lamp-post by the alley. Are you ready?'

'Yes – go for it.'

As the car crashed into the lamp-post, I opened the door and ran like the wind. Halfway down the alley, I leaped over a garden fence and hid behind a shed, cowering like a hunted animal. This had to work; I thought, hearing Kenny's voice as he raced through the alley to the park. My heart racing, my hands trembling, I slipped back into the alley once they were in the park and sprinted down the road to the supermarket. Ian was going to have some explaining to do, but at least his plan had worked.

I loitered in the supermarket for half an hour before one of the security guards became suspicious. I couldn't hang around for much longer, I knew. Leaving before he could question me, I began the long walk to the canal. Turning and looking over my shoulder every few minutes, I finally took a short cut across open country. The chances of anyone spotting me were pretty remote. Rod and Kenny were probably looking for me in town, hanging around the railway station thinking that I might try to get to London. For the first time in days, I felt safe.

I was pleased with myself as I sat by the canal and gazed at the play of light on the water. Although I had to admit to myself that without Ian I might never have tasted freedom again. He'd taken quite a risk, I reflected, wondering what he'd said to Rod and Kenny. Crashing the car into a lamp-post was a believable ploy, I thought. If he'd said that I'd struggled or that a dog had run out in front of the car, the others might not question it. And they certainly wouldn't have thought it odd that I'd done a runner. But, I wondered, what now? Slipping the coat off as the sun beat down on me, I thought that I would be safe by the canal. Miles from anywhere, hidden by trees, there wasn't even a towpath. No one would discover me.

Lying naked on the soft grass, I felt such a failure. From a confident, successful young woman to a homeless, hunted fugitive, it seemed that I'd failed miserably. For one thing, where was I going to live? I recalled my early teens, the times I'd been desperate to leave home. I'd run and hid from the gang then, and now I was doing exactly the same. Used and abused, humiliated, degraded, frightened . . . Nothing had changed, other than the date. I was in Ian's hands now. All I could do was enjoy the summer sun and wait for him.

When he arrived, I looked around for the others. I should have trusted him but . . . I was beginning to trust no one. He looked down at my nude body, his eyes smiling as he focused on the hairless lips of my pussy. Grabbing the coat, I slipped it on and concealed my femininity as he sat beside me. Fortunately, Rod and

Kenny had believed his story about swerving to miss a cat. They'd searched the park and had eventually given up. To my surprise, far from blaming Ian, they'd felt sorry for him.

'I was pretty convincing,' he said proudly. 'I made out that I'd hurt my leg and they believed me.'

'So, what are we going to do now?' I asked. 'More to the point, what are *they* going to do now?'

'They'll keep searching for you. That's where they think I am, out looking for you. It's all right, no one followed me here.'

'I wish I'd never come back to Southmoore,' I sighed.

'They were expecting you, Rachael.'

'*Expecting* me? What do you mean?'

'They'd been planning to infiltrate a large company for a year or so. When news broke that a new office was opening here, they did their homework and made their plans. They followed you home from your London office. They knew that you were the deputy managing director and learned all they could about you. Of course, when they discovered that you were Rachael Michaels, they couldn't believe their luck. You must have thought it odd that no one else turned up for the interview when you took Sally on?'

'Yes, yes – I did.'

'Sally had warned the other applicants off. Anyway, you took her on, and Julie and Kathy, and they were well on their way to achieving their goal.'

'What *was* their goal?'

'To milk money from the company. Lots of money. They've since realized that they shouldn't have let on that they knew who you were. It's just that you were such a bitch to Sally . . . Anyway, that's another issue. As you know, this all started at school. There was a girl . . . I forget her name. She had a new coat for her birthday. It was suede, and pretty expensive. Sally wanted it. She waylaid the girl one Saturday afternoon in town and simply took the coat from her. It was that easy, Rachael.'

'She stole it?'

'Yes. The gang took pocket money from the other kids at school, took their belongings . . . It was easy, too easy. When we left school, the idea of carrying on stealing seemed quite natural. After all, it had become a way of life. Threatening people, blackmailing them, even using them for sex . . . It grew and grew until none of us had to work for a living. We were running a racket, and still are. A very successful racket, at that.'

'So, what did they plan to do with me? I mean, I must have presented a massive problem to them – I suppose I still do.'

'You can say that again. They didn't really have any plans as far as you were concerned. They thought that, once you were out of the company and had no home, you'd fade away into oblivion. Don't forget that they have the porn pics as reserve ammunition. Sally reckoned that you'd go away, find a job and rent a flat somewhere, and that would be that.'

'So that perverted vicar knows all about the gang?'

'Well, he doesn't know *everything*. He does know that it's best to keep out of their way. After they stole his cottage—'

'The one close to the church?'

'Yes, that's the one. He sold it to Sally. And then she took the money back. Just as they plan to do with your flat.'

'But how—'

'He sold it to her, Rachael. It was a perfectly legitimate sale. How she got her money back is another matter. The point is that you're not dealing with a bunch of kids any more. They have friends in high places, to use that awful expression.'

'Who's Ted? I thought he owned the cottage?'

'Ted is a pawn in the game. No doubt your next question will be about Angel and John?'

'Yes.'

'They're nowhere near as young as they look. And they're not in the gang, as such.'

'But they live in the cottage, don't they?'

'They don't even live in Southmoore, let alone the cottage. They do some work for Sally from time to time, that's all. You've probably gathered by now that Sally is the ringleader. She always was.'

'So why do you work at the bakery?'

'That's another story. It was Julie's idea, my ever-loving wife. Sally had her eyes on the bakery and I had to take a job there. I was to be the insider. Of course, when Sally heard about the new office complex, she thought that would be far more lucrative. I just stayed on at the bakery to keep out of the way. I could sit here all night talking, and you wouldn't even know the half of it. We'd better get going.'

'Yes, I'm looking forward to getting home.'

'Home?' he gasped surprisedly. 'Julie's at your flat, for fuck's sake. You can't—'

'Can't I?' I said firmly. 'If you think I'm moving out of my flat . . .'

'You haven't been listening to anything I've said, have you? The gang . . .'

'Ian, are you going to drive me to London or not?'

'Yes, yes, all right. But I know that you're making a big mistake.'

Following him to his car, I was determined not to be swayed. There was no way I was going to allow anyone to steal my home from me. Or my job, for that matter. Sally Brompton, Julie, Rod . . . they weren't going to wreck my life again. They'd ruined my early teens, and there was no way that they were going to manage a repeat performance.

Ian didn't say a great deal as we travelled to London. I reckoned that he was frightened of his wife; which was understandable. But he wouldn't have to face her. All I wanted from him was a lift home. I had a spare key hidden in the gardens, so I'd be able to let myself in and . . . and confront the bitch. The rest of the gang would still be tearing Southmoore apart in an effort to track me down, leaving Julie alone in the flat. She wasn't a big girl, I reflected as Ian pulled up a few yards from the entrance. She'd never been particularly big or strong, and I was sure that I could overpower her. Especially as I aimed to take her by surprise. Unless she'd been warned to expect me after my escape.

'I'll wait here,' Ian said as I climbed out of the car.

'Thanks,' I replied, smiling at him. He looked worried, as if he'd let me down. 'It's all right, I do understand,' I said.

'I'll wait here for you. If—'

'If things go wrong, you can't get involved, Ian. If the others are there . . . I'll see you soon.'

Taking the spare key from its hiding place in the gardens, I crept up the stairs to my front door. I could hear movements in the flat, the rattling of cups and saucers. Reckoning that Julie was packing up my belongings, I slipped the key into the front door and turned it slowly. Feeling like a thief in the night, I opened the door and peered into the hall. There was a light on in the kitchen, someone moving about. It seemed strange having to sneak into my own flat, into my home. At least it was still my flat. Passing the lounge, I glanced through the doorway at an empty room. The bitch had sold all my furniture – she'd stripped the flat of everything I owned.

Julie didn't see me as I peered around the kitchen door. She was packing my cutlery into boxes, obviously removing every trace of me and my belongings. At least she was alone in the flat, I reflected, wondering what to do. Creeping along the hall as I had an idea, I took the key from the inside of the bedroom door. Switching the light on, I hammered on the door and slipped into the bathroom. Julie did exactly as I'd hoped. Wandering along the hall, she went into the bedroom to investigate. I moved quickly, closing and locking the door before she realized what was going on. The flat was on the third floor with no balcony, so there was no way out of the room. She tried the door, banging with her fists and shouting. What I was going to do with her, I had no idea.

'Who's there?' Julie called, banging again on the door.

'The owner of this flat,' I returned. 'You're my prisoner now.'

'Rachael?' she murmured. 'What the hell . . . You'd better let me out before the others get back. They'll be here in a few minutes.'

'It'll take more than a few minutes to get here from Southmoore,' I laughed. 'By the way, Ian has left you.' I didn't know why I'd said that. Spite?

'Ian . . . What are you talking about?'

'He's left you, Julie. He's been seeing me behind your back.'

'You're lying.'

'Am I? He's been helping me all along. He's told me everything about the vicar and his friends, the cottage, Angel and John . . .'

'You were taken to the cottage, that's how you know about that. Angel and John live there and—'

'They don't even live in Southmoore, let alone the cottage. And they're nowhere near as young as they make out.'

'Don't forget that we have the porn pics, Rachael,' she said threateningly.

'I no longer work for the medical supply company, so it doesn't matter whether you send them to the staff or not.'

'Maybe not. But it would matter if we were to send them to your family. Why don't you open the door and we'll talk about this?'

Unlocking the door, I flung it open and stared at the girl. She was in her bra and panties, her pretty face frowning as I grinned at her. She was unsure of me, I knew as I walked into the room and closed the door. Backing away, she sat on the bed and looked up at me as I stood towering over her. She'd obviously hung onto the bed because she was living in the flat. Noticing that my dressing table and wardrobe were still there too, I was thankful that I had at least *some* furniture.

'What are you going to do?' Julie asked me as I opened the wardrobe.

'You suggested that we talk,' I replied, taking three leather belts from the wardrobe. 'We'll talk once I've secured you to the bed.'

'You're not going to . . .'

'Julie, we can do this one of two ways. Either you allow me to tie you to the bed, or I force you. Which is it to be?' She glanced at the door as if thinking about making a dash for freedom. 'You can't go out in your bra and panties,' I reminded her. 'And you certainly can't leave the flat with your tits on show,' I added, tearing her bra from her young body.

'You fucking bitch,' she screamed. 'If you think that I'm going to allow you to tie me down and—'

Flinging my coat across the room, I pushed Julie back onto the bed and pinned her down. The sensitive teats of our naked breasts pressed together as I tried to hold her arms above her head and secure her wrists with one of the leather belts. I felt a pang of arousal quiver through my womb. Breathing in the scent of her long blonde hair as we fought on the bed, I recalled her repeatedly kicking me as I lay on the ground while coughing and spluttering on Brad's sperm. She'd swung her foot into my stomach, my chest . . . But the tables were turning, I knew as I finally managed to bind her wrists and secure the free end of the belt to the bedstead.

'You'll fucking pay for this,' she hissed as I grabbed her left foot and bound her ankle with another belt. Fixing the end to a bed leg, I grabbed her right foot and forced her legs wide apart. She squirmed and spat her expletives at me as I managed to secure her other ankle to the other bed leg. Her struggle was futile, I thought happily, standing up and brushing my hair away from my flushed face. She was completely defenceless, her young body tethered. Revenge would be sweet.

'Fucking cow,' Julie breathed, pulling at the leather belts.

'Do you remember kicking me when I was on the ground?' I asked her. She stopped struggling – she obviously did recall the cruel event. 'I was almost choking on Brad's spunk, and you repeatedly kicked me. Sally spat at me, you kicked me . . .'

'That was years ago,' she said.

'Yes, it was. And now, all these years later, it's my turn to be cruel.'

'Rachael, I . . .'

'You what?'

'Let's talk about this. I know, why don't you join us? Why not become a member of the gang?'

'Why would I want to do that?'

'You'd have money and—'

'No, thank you. Besides, I already have money. And I have a lovely flat, Julie. You've sold my furniture, haven't you?'

'Yes, but—'

'There are no buts about it. You've stolen my furniture, moved into my flat, used and abused me . . . No more talk, it's boring. I've been waiting for years to get my hands on you.'

'Rachael, listen to me.'

'I've done enough listening. What I want now is vengeance.'

Tearing Julie's panties from her trembling body, I focused on the hairless crack of her vagina, the petals of her inner lips protruding invitingly from her sex valley. She was still swearing at me, calling me every name under the sun. I didn't want the neighbours to hear her screams, her pleas for mercy as I sexually tortured her, so I rolled her panties up into a ball and stuffed them into her pretty mouth to shut her up. Taking another belt from the wardrobe, I ran the soft leather through my hands as she stared at me with fear mirrored in her wide eyes.

'I've waited years for this,' I murmured. 'I used to get home from school and go to my bedroom and hide from the world. I dreaded walking to school, and was terrified of walking home. You did that to me, Julie. And now you're going to pay for it.'

Raising the leather strap above my head, I brought it down across the mounds of her pale breasts with a deafening crack. Her tethered body convulsed, twitching wildly as I brought the belt down again across her breasts, her ripe nipples. Moaning loudly through her nose as I repeatedly lashed the sensitive teats of her reddening breasts, her eyes rolling, her head tossing from side to side, Julie writhed on the bed like a snake. I was enjoying my revenge, but I'd only just begun. Halting the thrashing, I gazed at the puffy lips of her vulva. She looked so young without her pubic hair, I thought, eyeing the fleshy protrusions of her inner labia. Her naked sex crack reminding me of my schooldays when she'd forced me to finger her pussy, I raised the belt above my head and brought it down across the swollen cushions of her outer lips.

Julie's naked body jolted as the belt struck home with a loud crack. Her vulval flesh turning red as I brought the leather belt down again, I watched her vaginal juices seeping between the petals of her inner labia. We had the whole night ahead of us. Perhaps not enough time to vent entirely my revenge for years of sexual abuse, but certainly time enough to teach the slut a lesson or two. Bringing the leather belt down again across the swelling lips of her sex crack, I felt my own juices of arousal seeping between my engorged inner lips.

Wondering what Ian was going to do, I shifted the focus of chastisement up my victim's writhing body and thrashed the firm mounds of her crimsoned breasts. I realized that Julie would question him about our illicit affair. If she told the gang that he'd been helping me . . . I dreaded to think what would happen to him. If I could get Julie on my side . . . No, that wasn't possible. What options did I have? I couldn't keep her imprisoned in my flat for ever. There again, I couldn't let her go.

Hearing movements in the hall as I raised the leather belt above my head, I moved to the door and listened. Someone was out there, I knew as I heard a muffled noise. Tossing the belt onto the bed, I grabbed my coat and covered my naked body before inching the door open. Whoever it was had gone into the lounge. Sally? I left the bedroom and closed the door quietly. Creeping along the hall, my heart banging hard against my chest, I breathed a sigh of relief as I peered around the door and saw Ian.

'What's happening?' he asked.

'Julie is tied to the bed,' I replied softly. 'I've been enjoying myself by whipping her.'

'God,' he breathed. 'When the others find out . . .'

'They mustn't find out. I don't know what to do, Ian. But they mustn't . . . I told Julie about us.'

'Us?' he gasped. 'Shit. Now you've dropped me in it!'

'I'm sorry. I realize that I shouldn't have said anything but . . . well, it's too late now. I'm glad you're here.'

'You left the front door open.'

'God, that was stupid. Anyone could have come in.'

'Rachael, we're going to have to think of something. And fast. They'll come here looking for you, that's definite.'

'I know, I know,' I sighed.
'I'll go and speak to her.'
'You can't do that, Ian.'
'I'll say that you were lying and . . . Shit, I don't know what to say. I'll have to speak to her.'

Following Ian through the hall, I waited outside the bedroom door and listened. The minute he'd taken the panties out of his wife's mouth, she spat her expletives and demanded that he release her. This was a mistake, I was sure as Ian tried to calm her down. He said that he'd locked me in the lounge and was planning to call the others. She made her threats, saying that I'd be dead meat once she got her hands on me. She demanded again that he release her. If he did, then we were both in serious trouble.

'I can't let you go,' Ian said.
'What?' she gasped. 'You fucking bastard. You'll fucking well release me or—'
'Julie, calm down. Just listen to me, for a change.'
'Listen to *you*? You've been shagging that slut behind my back, you come here and refuse to release me . . . She's not locked in the lounge, is she? You *are* on her side, I know it.'
'I never wanted to be on anyone's side.'
'Look what that bitch has done to me.'
'Yes, and look what you did to her at school. I never wanted any part of your stupid gang. You're nothing but a slut, a thief, a blackmailing little—'
'When Sally and the others hear about this . . .'
'They won't hear about it, Julie. I can't allow that to happen.'
'So, what do you intend to do? You can't keep me here for ever.'

'Who said anything about keeping you here?'

'You're serious, aren't you? For fuck's sake, Ian, I'm your wife.'

'Wife? You're nothing but a filthy slut. You've been fucking around behind my back all along.'

'Working for the gang, I've had to—'

'Track down people to blackmail – yeah, I know. You fuck married men, take incriminating photographs, and then threaten to expose their infidelity unless they pay up. You blackmail people, Julie. You sneak around digging up the dirt on young married women and then take porn pics of them and sell them to that magazine. You're nothing but a filthy lump of shit.'

'I assume from your abusive comments that you want a divorce?'

'I want more than a divorce,' Ian returned. 'I want you and the gang out of my life, for good.'

'You can divorce me, Ian. But you'll never be able to divorce yourself from the gang. We're far too big, can't you see that? Look at the pies we have our fingers in. Look at the money we rake in from the porn pics. Look at the contacts we have in high places – contacts like solicitors, councillors, even MPs.'

'Yes, and look at your lifestyle. Threats, blackmail, treating people like animals . . .'

'Life stinks at the best of times. All we're doing is taking what we can. Listen to me, Ian. Stay with me, and the gang, and we'll . . . Please, untie me so that I can go to the loo.'

'I can't do that, Julie. I've made my mind up about you and the gang.'

'OK, so what are you going to do with me?'

'I don't know yet.'

'They'll be here before long, you know that as well as I do.'

'They won't get in,' I said, walking into the room and grinning at Julie. 'This is my flat and if anyone tried to break in I'll call the police.'

'What a great idea,' she laughed. 'So, the police arrive and ask you why you have a naked girl tied to the bed. What will you say to them?'

'They won't find you, Julie,' Ian said.

'The attic,' I breathed, grabbing Ian's arm. 'This is the top floor. There's a hatch in the hallway ceiling that gives access to the attic.'

'Another great idea,' Julie laughed. 'How long do you think you can keep me in the attic?'

'She's right,' Ian sighed. 'We'll have to get her out of here.'

'You'll have to kill me to shut me up,' she said.

'We might just do that,' he replied. 'I can't see that your death would be a great loss to anyone.'

Stuffing the panties back into Julie's mouth, I led Ian into the kitchen and filled the kettle. We needed to talk, to relax and chat over a cup of coffee. All this talk about killing frightened me, although I knew that Ian wouldn't dream of doing such a thing. There had to be a way out of this mess, I was sure. But, in reality, I knew that the gang would have to be disbanded to put an end to the nightmare. Passing Ian a cup of coffee, we sat at the kitchen table and gazed at each other.

'I wish I'd never got involved with the bitch,' he sighed.

'It's no good looking back,' I said, smiling at him. 'We have to look to the future, decide what we're going to do next.'

'Yes, you're right. OK, so these are the problems. Basically, as I see it we only have two problems. Julie and the gang.'

'Two *massive* problems, I reckon. We'll have to let Julie go, there's no question about that.'

'All right, we'll let her go in the morning, I can't see that they'll come all the way up to London this evening.'

'This might be interesting,' I said as the phone rang.

'You're not going to answer it, surely?' Ian breathed as I left the table.

'Hello,' I said, grabbing the receiver.

'I thought you'd be there, you fucking whore,' Sally hissed. 'Where's Julie?'

'Tied up,' I replied. 'We're waiting for the police to arrive.'

'We'll be visiting you, Rachael. You'd better release Julie before—'

'I don't think so,' I laughed.

'Right, we're on our way.'

Replacing the receiver, I gazed at Ian. He looked nervous, and I thought it would be best if he left. There was a small hotel across the street, and I reckoned that he'd be better off staying there for the night. I doubted that Sally and her cronies would do anything stupid like breaking down my front door, but I couldn't be certain. If they did manage to get into the flat, the last thing I wanted was for them to find Ian there. He argued, insisting that he should stay with me for the night. But I finally managed to persuade him to leave and saw him to the front door.

'I'll see you first thing in the morning,' he said. 'Whatever you do, don't answer the door to anyone.'

'I'm not likely to answer the door,' I laughed. 'To be

honest, I don't think they'll turn up. I told Sally that the police were on their way so I really don't think that she'll come here. Not tonight, anyway. The front door has a pretty good lock, Ian. And there's no way they could climb up to a window. These flats are built like Fort Knox.'

'OK, I'll see you in the morning.'

Once Ian had gone, I locked the door and went back to the kitchen. The phone rang as I sat at the table finishing my coffee, but I ignored it. Looking around the kitchen, I knew that I should have felt pleased to be home at last. But the nightmare was far from over. If the Brook Street Gang didn't turn up that night, then they'd be there the next day. Turning all the lights off, I returned to the kitchen and sat down at the table. It was going to be a long night.

# 12

Drinking coffee and pacing the lounge floor all night, I hadn't slept at all. Even if I'd wanted to sleep, there was no sofa and Julie was tied to my bed. At least I had some clothes, I thought, deciding to take a shower. Wondering what the day ahead would bring as I shampooed my long blonde hair, I also wondered what the hell to do about Julie. I'd have been better off throwing her out of the flat, I reflected. To keep her prisoner was a crazy idea.

Walking into the bedroom wrapped in a towel, I stared at the girl. She'd managed to push the gag out of her mouth and immediately began spitting out expletives and threatening me. Opening the wardrobe and choosing a short red dress, I ignored her as I grabbed a pair of panties and a bra from my dressing-table drawer. I'd have to release her, I knew as she warned me that her friends would come and get me.

'I need the loo,' the bitch complained as I dressed.

'Really?' I chuckled. 'What a shame.' I eyed my quilt, praying that she wasn't going to piss all over it.

'Rachael, you can't keep me tied to the bed like this,' she sighed, obviously deciding to calm down. 'I'm hungry, I need the loo . . .'

'There were times when I couldn't eat. Many times, when I got home from school, I was too riddled with fear and anxiety to eat anything.'

'OK, so what we did was wrong.'

'*Wrong*?' I laughed. 'It was *evil*. I'll bet you enjoyed your weekends. I'll bet you went out with your friends in the evenings. I was stuck at home, hiding, trembling, cowering. When I did my homework, I deliberately made mistakes, put the wrong answers. I did that because I thought that you might attack me if I was top of the class. You'll never know what you put me through.'

'I didn't realize, Rachael.'

'Maybe not, but you realize now. And you're still forcing me into crude sexual acts, still terrorizing me and—'

'OK, OK, I'm sorry.'

'Sorry?'

'We'll stop. I'll speak to the others. From now on, we'll leave you alone, OK?'

'No, it's not OK. In fact, it's *far* from OK.'

'So what are you going to do with me? Be realistic, Rachael. You can't imprison me for ever.'

'I know I can't. That's why I've made plans for you.'

'Plans? What plans?'

'The first thing I'm going to do is earn some money. I know a lot of people who would pay to fuck you. I might as well make some money from you before dealing with you.'

'Dealing with me? Rachael, please . . .'

'I've lived in London for a long time. I've got to know many people, some of whom are most undesirable types.'

'What will you do when Sally and the others get here?'

'They're not coming here, Julie.'

'Of course they are.'

'I spoke to Sally on the phone last night. We have a deal.'

'Sally wouldn't . . . What sort of deal?'

'We had quite a long chat. She decided that you're no longer needed. Ian was never really involved with the gang and Sally reckons that it would be best if you both left and went your own ways.'

'You're bluffing.'

'I have no need to bluff, Julie. The truth speaks for itself. Where are your confederates? Why aren't they here? Why haven't they come to rescue you?'

'They will, you can be sure of that.'

'No, they won't. Look at it from Sally's point of view. She no longer has me in captivity so the sale of the flat can't go ahead. If she caught me again, what would she do with me? Bear in mind that Ian is now on my side. If she caught me, she'd also have to deal with him. She reckons that it's just not worth the trouble. Sally and Kathy work for the medical company, which was their aim. So why bother with me and my flat? As Sally said, she wants to concentrate on the company, working out fiddles, getting her hands on money.'

'But . . . she wouldn't desert me.'

'She *has* deserted you, Julie. Do you really believe that Sally and the others are going to come all the way up to London, break into the flat, rescue you, capture me and drag me back to Southmoore . . . As Sally said, it's just not worth the trouble. The deal is that I keep out of her way, and she'll keep out of mine.'

Leaving the room as the phone rang, I knew that I'd worried Julie. My story sounded feasible – it made sense. It was just a shame that it wasn't true. Still, if Sally left me alone, then I'd certainly keep out of her way. Lifting the phone, I wondered whether Ian had my number as I listened to background noises. Sally finally asked whether it was me, and I felt my stomach churn. A thousand thoughts flooding my mind, I plucked up the courage to speak.

'Of course it's me,' I replied shakily. 'What do you want?'

'I want to speak to Julie.'

'You can't.'

'Rachael, I'm not going to play games.'

'Neither am I. Julie's cooking breakfast, and she doesn't want to speak to you.'

'Cooking . . . You lying bitch,' she hissed. 'We'll be visiting you very soon.'

'Ian's also here. We've been up all night, compiling a dossier on the Brook Street Gang. It's all there, Sally. Names and addresses, events, threats, blackmail, the cottage, the torture room, the vicar . . .'

'What good will that do you? We have porn pics of you and—'

'And it's all in the dossier, sealed in an envelope – ready to be posted to the police.'

'You've got nothing on us.'

'Haven't I? Ian and Julie have revealed everything about you and your escapades. If you think that I'm bluffing, then go ahead with your plan and come to my flat.'

As Sally hung up, I knew that I'd shaken her. She wouldn't know what to believe, I reflected. Was I bluffing, playing for time? Had Ian and Julie really defected? Sally was going to have to make a decision. She either left me in peace, or . . . Or what? It would be pretty risky coming to my flat and attacking me. I might have friends round or . . . Jumping as the doorbell rang, I hoped that it was Ian as I walked through the hall.

'It's me,' Ian called, tapping on the door.

'Thank God for that,' I sighed in relief, opening the door and letting him in. 'Was the hotel all right?'

'Yes, fine. But I wish that I'd stayed here with you. So, is there any news?'

'Sally rang,' I said, leading him into the kitchen and filling the kettle. 'I told her that you and Julie had defected, left the gang and—'

'She called me just now on my mobile.'

'Oh? What did she say?'

'She threatened me. She said that I'd find my flat burned down if I spilled the beans.'

'She wouldn't . . .'

'She would, Rachael. Do you remember Mr Collins, the geography teacher?'

'Yes, I do. I liked him. He was young and—'

'He left the school, didn't he?'

'So? What has that got to do with anything?'

'He left because of Sally. She stayed on after school to talk to him about her homework. They were alone in the classroom and she opened her blouse and lifted her bra up. She was very attractive, and pretty well developed. He resisted temptation, told her to behave herself and go home. She then lifted her skirt up and pulled her knickers down.'

'God. What did he do?'

'He made the fatal mistake of kneeling down and touching her. As you said, he was young and . . . What he didn't realize was that Kathy was hiding behind the book cabinet, taking photographs of him. When Sally showed him a couple of photographs and threatened to expose him unless he gave her money, he resigned.'

'She ruined his career?'

'OK, so he shouldn't have touched her. But, she came on really strong and—'

'She's a bitch, she really is.'

'She'll stop at nothing, Rachael. You don't know the half of it.'

Passing him a cup of coffee at he sat at the table, I remembered the geography teacher. He was a nice man, young and good-looking. It was his first teaching job and . . . and Sally had ruined his career. She was an evil bitch, I reflected, sitting down opposite Ian. She had to be stopped – but how? As Ian brushed his dark hair back with his fingers, I thought how tired he looked. Sally had ruined his life, too. She was ruining everyone's lives.

'Is there anything that you know about Sally that I could use?' I asked Ian.

'To threaten her with?'

'Yes.'

'There's no proof, Rachael. She covers her tracks well. She has friends everywhere and . . .'

'Come on, Ian,' I sighed. 'You've been in the gang for years. And so has your wife. There must be things that you know about Sally and the others.'

'She got into some trouble a couple of years ago. You may have wondered why you've not seen Lucy around.'

'Lucy Barlow?'

'She's Lucy Smith now, Kenny's wife. She was the gang leader at one time. Sally wanted her out and thought that the best way to do it was to split her and Kenny up. Sally caused no end of trouble. She screwed Kenny at every opportunity, and made sure that Lucy found out.'

'What happened? Where's Lucy now?'

'Sally became leader and Lucy . . . She's still with Kenny, but she's not in the gang.'

'But—'

'When I say that she's not in the gang, what I mean is . . . Lucy is running a pretty lucrative little sideline, but Sally doesn't realize it. Lucy was the brains behind the operation. All Sally did was sexually abuse people, fight, threaten, blackmail, steal . . . Lucy was subtle. She let Sally carry on, let her believe that she was in charge waits, biding her time while Sally and the others do the dirty work. And then she moves in for the kill.'

'The kill? What do you mean?'

'There was a young man a few months back. He was newly married and was building a future with his young wife. Sally set him up, flashed her bedroom eyes, her fanny, and lured him into her bed. Photographs were taken, threats were made . . . and he had to pay the gang fifty pounds a month to keep them quiet.'

'So where does Lucy come into it?'

'She got hold of the photographs and the negatives and went to see the man. For a payment of one thousand pounds, she gave him the lot.'

'But Sally must have realized that—'

'Sally hasn't got the photographs nor the means to reproduce them so she has nothing on the man. Kenny looks after all the incriminating photographs, including the negatives. For obvious reasons, no one wants evidence like that in their homes. Kenny keeps them somewhere safe, and Lucy knows where.'

'What did Kenny say when Sally asked him where the photographs were?'

'He told her that the rain had got in and ruined a couple of dozen photographs and their negatives. He knew that Lucy had taken them, but . . . There's a hell of a lot more to it but we don't have time to talk about it now. We'd better make some plans. First of all, what the hell are we going to do with Julie?'

'Leave her where she is. Ian, have you got Lucy's phone number?'

'Yes,' he replied, taking a small address book from his pocket. 'What are you going to do?'

'Does Lucy know about me?'

'She knows that you're back in Southmoore and that you're deputy MD of the medical supply company. She's been keeping her eye on things, as usual.'

'How do you know about her? I mean, how do you know that she went to see the man and—'

'I slip her information, keep her posted about what's going on. We always got on well. We still do.'

'OK, I want you to phone her and arrange to meet her somewhere. Tell her that things are getting out of hand and that you need to talk to her.'

'And what are you going to do?'

'Go to her house and get the photographs.'

'You'll never find them, Rachael. Only Kenny knows where they are. And Lucy, of course.'

'I'll find them. Ring her now.'

As Ian lifted the phone and dialled Lucy's number, I felt positive for the first time in days. Lucy had always been the clever one at school. Passing every exam, coming top in all subjects . . . She wasn't simply taking photographs and using them to threaten the blackmail victims. There was far more to it than that, I was sure. And I reckoned that Kenny was working with her. He had the photographs, and probably a load of other incriminating evidence. Between them, I reckoned that they were earning a small fortune on the side.

Ian arranged to meet Lucy on the common at midday. I gagged Julie before we left. Again complaining that she needed the loo, I told her that I might be some time and she'd just have to piss herself. If my hunch was right, then I'd soon have more than enough money to buy a new quilt, and more than enough evidence on the gang to . . . to take over? Was that what I wanted? I wondered about my own motives as I left the flat and followed Ian to his car. I wasn't sure that I'd want to go back to the medical supply company. Running the gang seemed far more . . . Reminding myself that the gang's activities were actually highly illegal, I turned my thoughts to Lucy. It was no wonder she'd not been involved in my abuse, I reflected. Subtle. Clever.

'Does Lucy have a garden?' I asked Ian as we neared Southmoore.

'A garden? Yes, why?'

'I just wondered. Is there a back way in?'

'Yes. There's an alleyway running behind her house.'

'OK, drop me by the alley.'

'It's only half-eleven. She's not meeting me until twelve so she's probably still in the house.'

'Let me worry about that,' I said as he pulled up by the entrance to the alley. 'Which house is hers?'

'You can't miss it. It's the one with a half-built extension out the back.'

'OK. I'll meet you behind the library. I can get there though the back streets without being seen. Keep Lucy talking for as long as possible.'

'Right. Good luck.'

'Thanks.'

Sneaking along the alleyway, I peered over the fences at the houses until I came to Lucy's. The back door was open and a radio was pumping out music. I could see Lucy in the kitchen, but I was in no hurry. She'd be leaving for the common soon. All I had to do was wait, and pray that Kenny wasn't there. After ten minutes, she locked the back door and left the kitchen. She wouldn't have bothered locking the door if Kenny was there, and I was sure that I was safe as I clambered over the fence and slipped into the garden. The photographs and negatives weren't in the house, I was sure. Kenny had said that the rain had destroyed some photographs. OK, so it was a lie. But I reckoned that there was a reason for him mentioning the rain. The photographs were outside.

I searched beneath bushes, looked under the shed, checked the flower borders . . . But found nothing. I was looking for a box, a waterproof box. Shaking my head as I looked around the garden, I began to feel despondent. But I then noticed a paving slab by the shed door. The grass hadn't grown over the edges of the slab, as I would have expected. In fact, there was a small gap between its sides and the earth surrounding it.

This was it, I was sure as I grabbed a spade resting up against the half-built extension and prised the slab up. Grinning, I lifted out a large plastic box from the hole beneath the slab. I'd done it, I thought, my heart racing as I replaced the flat stone. Clutching my spoils, I slipped over the fence into the alleyway and ran like the wind. I didn't want to be seen in the street so I made my way as quickly as I could to the waste ground behind the library. Once there, I sat on an old oil drum and got my breath back before opening the box.

It was all there. The photographs of me with a cock in

my mouth, pictures of a young girl sucking two purple knobs . . . There were dozens of incriminating photographs. God only knew how many people these bastards were blackmailing. Looking through the photographs, I knew that it was going to take a long time to track down the victims. I'd return the evidence, I decided, closing the box. As Ian approached, I began to wonder whether I should trust him. He'd helped me so far, but . . . Then again, if he was going to double-cross me, he'd have had the gang lying in wait at Lucy's house. I *could* trust him, couldn't I? Discreetly dropping the box onto the ground behind the oil drum, I smiled as he stood in front of me.

'Well?' he said. 'Any luck?'

'Yes,' I replied. 'I found the photographs.'

'Really? Where are they?'

'I've hidden them.'

'Hidden them? But I thought—'

'I can't trust anyone, Ian,' I sighed.

'Oh, thanks a *lot*.'

'Please try to understand. What did Lucy have to say?'

'I don't know whether I should tell you, Rachael. Seeing as you don't trust me . . .'

'I *do* trust you. It's just that—'

'Lucy reckons that Sally and the others are going to your flat today. They're after me, as well as you.'

'Shit.'

'You can say that again. They mean business, Rachael. Lucy also reckons that Sally has it in for you.'

'I know that, for fuck's sake.'

'No, I mean in a personal way. She has some private vendetta, and she won't stop until she's destroyed you.'

'Destroyed me? Ian, may I borrow your car?'

'My car? Er . . . yes, I suppose so. Where are you going?'

'I have a few things to do. I'll meet you back here later. Say, seven o'clock this evening?'

'All right,' he said, passing me the keys. 'It's parked in front of the library. But I really do think that—'

'I'll see you later.'

'OK, as you wish,' he sighed, walking away. 'I'm going home to wash and change.'

Once Ian had gone, I grabbed the box and headed for his car. Driving through Southmoore, I made my way out to Miller's Corner by the canal. I held on to one photograph before hiding the box in some thick bushes. Slipping the picture down the front of my panties, and with the rest of the evidence safely stored, I knew that I'd be safe. The photographs were my insurance, I reflected, driving back to London. Hoping that I'd get to my flat ahead of Sally and her cronies, I decided to release Julie. There was no point in hanging onto her. If anything, she was now a liability.

Reaching my flat, I knew that Sally would turn up at some stage. But, once she realized that I had the photographs, it would be me who called the shots. The day had been very successful so far, I thought, edging the front door open and listening for movements in the flat. Silence. Julie had probably fallen asleep, I mused, hoping that she hadn't pissed my bed. I had the evidence, I had Ian on my side . . . Hearing a noise in the bedroom, I opened the door and grinned at Julie.

'Oh dear,' I sighed, pulling the wet panties out of her mouth. 'You've pissed yourself.'

'You fucking bitch,' she spat. 'When Sally gets here—'

'I've told you, Julie. Sally isn't going to come here.'

'Aren't I?' Sally said, standing in the doorway. Wearing a black leather catsuit, she was wielding a leather whip. 'We're *all* here, Rachael. We've been waiting for you.'

'I have the box of photographs,' I told her, keeping an eye on the whip. 'I've been to Kenny's house and I have the photographs.'

'Liar,' she returned, running the leather tails of the whip across her palm. 'You've caused us more than enough trouble. We have the papers for you to sign. Our solicitor is here with the papers, so release Julie and then we'll get down to business.'

'Go fuck yourself,' I hissed. 'I'm signing nothing. Now that I have the photographs . . .'

'Rachael, you don't have any photographs.'

'How's this for starters?' I asked her, pulling the photograph out of my panties. 'It's a picture of a man spunking over your face.'

'That . . . that doesn't prove anything,' she said shakily, gazing at the photograph.

'Where would I have got this from?'

'Anywhere. It doesn't prove anything.'

'*Anywhere*? You mean, I might have found it in the street? Don't be fucking stupid, Sally. This proves that I found the photographs.'

As Rod and Kenny appeared in the doorway, I could see by their expressions that they were worried. Saying nothing, they grabbed my arms and marched me into the lounge. Kathy was there, standing beside Brad Masters and several other men. There was a table set up in the centre of the room, handcuffs and chains lying beside it on the floor. As Sally walked into the room with Julie, I reminded her again that I had the box of photographs.

'Where do you keep the photographs?' she asked Kenny.

'In a plastic box beneath—'

'Wait,' Sally cut in. 'Let her answer. Beneath what?' she asked me.

'Beneath a paving slab by the shed door,' I replied. 'Proof enough that I have them, Kenny?'

'Proof enough that you know where they are, but—'

'But what? I've been into your back garden and taken the box. Which is now hidden. And, unless I return to Southmoore this afternoon, the box will be given to the police along with the dossier.'

'You fool, Kenny,' Sally breathed. 'You said that no one would ever find the porn pics.'

'She *can't* have found them,' he replied, shaking his head and frowning. 'There's no *way* she could have—'

'She *did* find them. You just said that it was proof enough that she knew where they were. Get her onto the table,' Sally snapped. 'We have to get the photographs back, and I don't care how we do it.'

As my clothes were ripped from my trembling body and I was dumped on the table, I realized that I should have told Ian where I was going to hide the photographs. I should have trusted him. What could I have been thinking of, returning to my flat and knowing that the bastards were going there too? I'd wanted to release Julie but . . . I'd fucked up big time, I knew as several men stood around the table gazing at my naked body, the shaved lips of my vagina.

'Where is the box?' Sally asked me as my limbs were stretched out and my wrists and ankles tied with rope to the four table legs. 'You'll tell me where it is, Rachael. You'll tell me sooner or later.'

'It's already too late,' I said. 'If I'm not back in Southmoore by—'

'Then you'd better tell me now.'

'Go to hell,' I hissed, spitting at her.

'OK, get the truth out of her,' Sally ordered the men. 'I don't care what you do or how you do it. Just make her talk.'

One of the men was in his sixties. He was balding, with narrow lips and an evil look in his dark eyes. He moved in first, tweaking my elongated nipples and pinching the hairless outer labia of my pussy as the others gathered round and watched. Leaving my breasts, he moved down and concentrated on my naked vulva. Yanking the soft cushions of my sex lips wide apart, he thrust several fingers deep into my vagina and pressed my inner flesh hard against my pubic bone.

'I'm a doctor,' he informed me. 'I carry out experiments on young girls. Pain threshold, intensity and duration of orgasms, vaginal capacity tests, clitoral enlargement experiments . . . I enjoy my work very much. You're a fine specimen. What I intend to do is carry out an experiment to determine the capacity of your anal canal. I begin with the dilation of your anus.' Grinning, he looked up at the other men. 'Release her legs and take her feet up either side of her head,' he ordered them.

As the men complied, my knees pressing hard against my breasts as they held my feet either side of my head, I knew that my bottom-hole was blatantly exposed. The 'doctor' stroked me there, running his fingertip over the delicate tissue of my anus as the audience looked on. Ordering someone to pass him a candle, he massaged cooling oil into my anus before pushing the end of the huge candle past my anal sphincter muscles. I hadn't realized until now that he had a bag with him, and I dreaded to think what instruments of sexual torture he had in it.

Easing the massive candle deep into my rectum as the two men held my feet, he chuckled wickedly. Someone passed him another candle: he mumbled something about the diameter of my anal entrance as he pushed this second waxy phallus alongside the first, deep into my quivering body.

'I have managed six in the past,' he said, taking a third candle. 'The walls of the rectal duct have surprising elasticity.'

'I wonder how many candles it'll take before she talks,' Sally chuckled.

'I have a dozen or so in my bag,' the evil man informed her.

'We ought to take bets,' Julie said. 'I reckon she'll talk once you've stuffed five candles up her arse.'

'I'll go for seven,' Sally breathed.

'We'll see,' the 'doctor' chortled, pushing the third candle deep into my bloated rectum.

Taking yet another candle from his bag, I realized that I could play for time by telling Sally that the photos were hidden behind the church. She'd have to go to Southmoore and check it out. There again, she'd probably ring someone and get them to search for the evidence. Either way, I'd gain a little time. Again wishing that I'd told Ian where I'd hidden the box, I grimaced as the fourth candle drove into my inflamed anal canal.

'Take a look,' Sally said, holding a hand-mirror behind my bottom. Lifting my head, I gazed in horror at the reflection of my anus, the brown tissue stretched almost to tearing point around the four candles. I was going to have to give in, I was sure as the man took another huge candle from his bag. Trying to force the waxen shaft past my anal ring, he ordered one of the men to pull my buttocks wide apart. As he managed to ease the end of the candle into my painfully bloated rectum, I finally cried out.

'All right, all right,' I gasped as Rod took several photographs of my abused anus. 'I'll tell you where the box is.'

'So soon?' Sally sighed. 'I was rather hoping that you'd be able to take seven candles up your tight arse. Oh well, not to worry. So, where are the photographs?'

'Behind the church,' I breathed, grimacing as my anal sphincter muscles twitched. 'Beneath a bush behind Southmoore Church.'

'Take the candles out,' she ordered the so-called doctor. 'I want each man to fuck her arse. Fill her with spunk while I go and make a phone call.'

The candles sliding out of my bloated rectum, my wrists untied, I was dragged down the table until my rounded buttocks were just over the edge. My feet held behind my head again, I watched as the first man stood at the foot of the table and pressed the swollen knob of his huge cock hard against my gaping anal ring. His solid shaft gliding deep into my inflamed rectum with ease, I counted the men standing around the table. There were six. Six cocks, six pairs of full balls, six loads of spunk . . .

My naked body rocking as the anal fucking began, I could feel the man's rounded glans repeatedly thrusting deep into the heat of my bowels. His swinging balls slapping the firm cheeks of my bottom as he arse-fucked me, he grabbed my hips and increased his fucking rhythm as the audience watched the lewd coupling. As Julie parted the swollen lips of my vulva and drove a huge candle deep into my hot cunt, I listened to the obscene comments coming from the chuckling men. I was nothing but a lump of female flesh to be abused, fucked and spunked. The sheath of my rectum burning, stretching with every savagely thrusting entry of the man's massive cock, I felt like a whore, a slut, a filthy tramp. Wondering what was to become of me as the man neared his orgasm. I knew that Sally would go mad when she discovered that the box wasn't hidden behind the church after all. I'd have to endure more candles, the whip, more crude fuckings . . .

'Here it comes,' the man gasped, the shaft of his penis swelling, his throbbing knob inflating. I could feel his spunk gushing deep into my arse, lubricating the forbidden union, filling my bowels. The others chuckled, remarking on my naked body, my fucked arse, my tight cunt. This was degradation beyond belief, humiliation to the point of inhumane cruelty. But I had to endure the repeated fuckings. The gang's degenerates weren't going to break me now.

'I hope for your sake that you weren't lying about the photographs,' Julie said, ramming the candle deep into my contracting cunt as I lay gasping on the table. 'If you were, then you'll have six cocks fucking your arsehole.' Ignoring her as the sound of squelching spunk echoed around the room, the candle fucking my cunt in time with the man's thrusting cock, I knew what to expect once they discovered that I'd lied. Fucking, spunking, whipping, sexual torture . . .

My two holes painfully stretched, the cock still pumping spunk into my arse, the candle battering my cervix, I felt as if my insides were being sucked out as the man eventually withdrew his spent organ. My sperm-drenched anus gaping wide open, I let out a gasp as a fresh cockhead drove deep into the very core of my abused body. As the second anal fucking began and the candle was repeatedly rammed into the tightening sheath of my drenched cunt, I wondered how much more I could take. Julie ordered the men to keep holding my feet wide apart.

'Further,' she said as they complied. 'I want her legs as wide apart as possible.' Grimacing as my thighs parted, my candle-fucked cunt bared, I watched a man clamber onto the table and kneel with his erect cock quivering and throbbing above my flushed face. Thrusting the candle into my cunt with one hand, Julie grabbed his cock with the other and began wanking him. He was going to spunk over my face, I knew, watching his purple knob appear and disappear as she rolled his fleshy foreskin back and forth.

'Do her dirty little cunt with the candle,' she ordered one of the men. Taking a vibrator from the bag of the 'doctor', she switched it on and pressed the buzzing tip against the man's swollen knob. Letting out gasps of pleasure as his glans visibly swelled, he looked down at my face and moved back slightly. The candle once more fucking my burning cunt, my rectum contracting, gripping the thrusting cock like a velvet-jawed vice, I waited for the sperm to rain over my face as the vibrator buzzed and the man looming above me let out low moans of debauched pleasure.

He came quickly, his spunk jetting from his throbbing knob, his shaft rhythmically twitching in time with his sperm pump. The white liquid splattering my face, I felt my rectum fill with spunk as the man shagging my arse gasped. My eyes closed, my naked body rocking with the double fucking, I felt the spunk landing on my nose, my cheeks, my mouth. The orgasmic liquid running down my neck, my temples, I wondered again how much more I could take.

Finally opening my eyes, I watched a long thread of sperm hanging from the man's purple knob. The vibrator still buzzing against his glans, the strand of spunk stretched and finally landed on my lips. Julie laughed as she switched the vibrator off and squeezed the last of the man's milk from his deflating cock-shaft. My face drenched with jism, I locked my gaze to hers as she stared at me.

'I told you that Sally would come here,' she said. 'I warned you, didn't I?'

'I have the photographs,' I replied triumphantly as the spent cock slipped out of my spunk-soaked rectum. 'I have the photographs, and your husband. What have *you* got?'

'You filthy slag,' she hissed, slapping my sperm-wet face as another solid penis drove deep into the inflamed duct of my arse. 'If you've lied, if we don't get the photographs back . . .'

'You can do what you like to me. You'll never—'

'Don't worry, we *will* do what we like,' she snapped, clambering onto the table and positioning the yawning crack of her pussy over my face.

As she lowered her naked body and pressed her vaginal flesh hard against my spermed mouth, she ordered me to tongue-fuck her cunt. Pushing my tongue out, I tasted her inner folds, licked around the wet entrance to her vaginal sheath. I could take this, I mused as she rocked her hips, massaging the solid nub of her clitoris against my lips. The men taking turns to fuck me, Julie rubbing her dripping cunt over my face . . . I was strong.

'She lied,' Sally yelled, bursting into the room. 'I rang

Ted and he's searched everywhere behind the church. He's just phoned back and . . . The fucking bitch lied to us.'

'Oh dear,' Julie sighed. 'Now we're going to have to torture the truth out of her.'

'I found these,' Sally said. Even with Julie's cunt smothering my face, I could still see what it was.

'They're Ian's car keys,' Julie breathed. 'If she came here with his keys, then—'

'Then she's borrowed his car.'

'Perhaps the photographs are in the car,' Rod said.

'No, she's not that stupid,' Sally murmured pensively. 'Where would she hide the box? Not on the common, that's for sure. She hasn't been back to the office. Somewhere safe, where no one would go searching. Maybe in the woods or . . . Do you remember that place by the canal where some of the girls used to go? This slag often went there. I remember lying in wait for her but—'

'But she didn't turn up,' Kenny broke in. 'We followed her there once but . . . Miller's Corner. That's what we called it.'

'And *that*'s where she's hidden the box,' Sally announced triumphantly.

I wished again that I'd told Ian where I was going to hide the evidence. As Sally ordered the men to dress, I watched Julie lift the dripping crack of her cunt off my face and clamber off the table. They were all leaving, I knew as they tied my wrists and ankles to the table legs. If I was left alone, then I might be able to escape, I reflected as the gang dressed and moved towards the door.

Finally alone in my flat, I pulled against my bonds. There was no way I could escape, despite my previous brief burst of optimism. I knew that as I struggled again to free myself. Sally would be back within a couple of hours, I thought as I prayed for Ian to come to my rescue. But he wouldn't come. I had his car, and we'd arranged to meet behind the library at seven o'clock. Why would he travel up to London on the train? Once Sally got her hands on the evidence . . . My fate was sealed.

# 13

Within minutes of the gang leaving, I heard the front door open. Initially, I thought one of them had come back for something. Watching the lounge doorway as I heard movements in the hall, my hopes began to rise. Was it Ian? My heart in my mouth, I lifted my head off the table. Someone was moving about in the hall, creeping, lurking. Sally wouldn't have done that, I thought. She'd have walked straight in and—

'There was no room for me in the car,' the 'doctor' said, grinning as he walked up to the table and gazed at my naked body. 'So I decided to stay and keep you company.'

'Please let me go,' I said, knowing full well that he'd never release me. 'If you untie me, I'll—'

'Why would I untie you?' he asked, delving into his bag. 'If you escaped, then I'd be to blame. I wouldn't want Sally and the others to blame me.'

'I have money,' I said. 'I'll give you money if you let me go.'

'I don't want money,' he chuckled, licking his thin lips. 'I want *you*.'

'Yes, yes . . . you can have me. Let's get out of here and go to your place. We can have sex and—'

'I can have sex here,' he interrupted me. 'We have at least two hours before the others return.'

'We'll have more than two hours if we go to your place. I'll give you sex, all the sex you want.'

'Maybe,' he said, smiling at me. 'I wouldn't mind having someone like you around the house.'

'Let's do it,' I urged him. 'I'll come and live with you and . . .'

'I like the sound of that. But first, there are one or two experiments I'd like to carry out.'

I must have been mad to think that he'd release me. But it was worth a try, I reflected as he pulled a rubber hose from his leather bag. I felt more vulnerable than ever as he parted the firm cheeks of my buttocks and pushed the end of the hose into the inflamed eye of my anus. What he intended to do to me, I dreaded to think. He was evil, completely mad, there was no doubt about it. Chuckling wickedly, he delved into his bag again and pulled out two metal clamps. Spending some time fixing the clamps to the outer lips of my vagina, he attached a thin chain to each clamp and dropped them down at either side of the table. Hanging two heavy weights from the chains, he laughed as I felt the valley of my pussy stretching wide open.

'There's nothing better than a gaping cunt hole,' he said, peering into my yawning vaginal entrance. Taking a metal device from his bag, he placed it over the exposed nub of my clitoris and tightened the screw. 'And a bulging clitty,' he chuckled as the bulb of my clitoris ballooned. The clamp fully tightened, my clitoris painfully inflated, he slipped his trousers off and displayed the huge shaft of his erect penis to my wide eyes. He was big, the shaft of his cock at least ten inches long and as thick as my wrist.

Removing his shirt, he knelt on the table with his knees

either side of my head and the huge sac of his scrotum brushing against my nose. Ordering me to lick and suck his balls, he lowered his body, pressing the fleshy bag of his scrotum against my lips. Opening my mouth, I tentatively licked his balls, the taste stinging my tongue as I breathed in his heady male scent. Again ordering me to suck his balls, he lowered his body further until I managed to take one of his huge sperm-eggs into my mouth. My clitoris aching, my outer labia painfully stretched, I wondered what the rubber hose was for as my anal sphincter muscles spasmed. I had no doubt that I was soon to find out as the man began wanking the massive shaft of his cock.

'Now lick my anus,' he instructed me, moving forward slightly and aligning his anal hole with my mouth. Tasting him there, running the tip of my tongue over the brown tissue surrounding his rectal hole, I gasped as he pinched and pulled my nipples. 'Push your tongue into my arse,' he ordered me. Unable to comply with his obscene request, I continued to lick around his anal hole, the taste biting into my tongue as he gasped in his debased pleasure.

'Tongue-fuck my arse or I'll pull on your nipples until you scream,' he said, yanking my milk teats away from the discs of my areolae. Finally pushing my tongue into his anus, I licked the dank walls of his rectum. Releasing my painfully sore nipples, and reaching beneath his body, he yanked his buttocks wide apart, opening his rectal inlet to allow my tongue deeper penetration of his arse.

I had to endure at least two hours of torture by the evil pervert, I reflected. But what worried me more was what I was going to have to endure when Sally and her cronies returned. Becoming used to the taste of the man's rectal duct as he parted his rounded buttocks further, I continued to tongue him there. This was nothing in comparison to what I was going to have to endure, I knew as he gasped and let out long low moans of pleasure.

'Like it?' he asked me, holding his buttocks wide apart. 'I'll bet you just love tongue-fucking men,' he chuckled. 'Push your tongue further into my arse. Go on, tongue me properly, otherwise I'll show you just how sensitive your nipples are to pain. And your clitoris. The last girl I experimented on ended up with a huge clitty. After several days of vacuum pumping her clit . . . I won't spoil the surprise,' he sniggered. 'But you'd better tongue my arse properly if you value your nipples and your sweet little clitty.'

Doing my best to push my tongue deeper into the shaft of the pervert's rectum, my nose pressed hard between the splayed cheeks of his bottom, I could barely breathe. Was he going to wank his huge cock and spunk over my face? I wondered as he writhed and moaned in the grip of his anal pleasure. I'd rather he spunked over my face than suffocated me with his arse, I thought as he finally raised his body. My tongue slipping out of his anal hole, I breathed heavily as he turned round and offered the purple knob of his massive penis to my gasping mouth.

'Now suck my knob,' he ordered me, holding his rock-hard shaft by the base. 'Roll your wet tongue over my knob, around the rim and in the slit.' Complying as he slipped his swollen glans into my hot mouth, I snaked my tongue over its silky-smooth surface, tasting his salt as he gazed at my full lips encompassing his glans. Was he going to come in my mouth? I wondered, my clitoris aching, my outer cunt lips swelling as the weights swung.

Placing his hand behind my neck, he lifted my head, forcing me to take his bulbous knob to the back of my throat as he repeatedly thrust his cock into my bloated mouth. Rocking his hips, he clutched my head with both hands as he mouth-fucked me. My lips rolling back and forth along his veined shaft, his heavy balls battering my chin, I breathed heavily through my nose as I waited for the inevitable gushing of his spunk.

My thoughts drifting back to my schooldays as the vile man mouth-fucked me, I was reminded of the time when Sally and Julie had trapped me in the changing room after PE one afternoon. They'd brought a young lad in and ordered him to pull his trousers down as they'd forced me to sit on a chair. Holding my nose, Sally had ordered the lad to pull back his foreskin and fuck my mouth. He'd complied readily, slipping his salty glans into my mouth as the girls had giggled.

I'd been forced to swallow his spunk as he'd gasped and rocked his hips. I recalled the salty taste of his male liquid as the 'doctor' began gasping in the onset of his orgasm. The young lad had pumped my mouth full of spunk and the girls had forced me to swallow hard. That had been my first mouth-fucking, I mused, the man's knob swelling within my bloated mouth. My first enforced mouth-fucking – but not my last.

'Swallow it, you dirty little whore,' the pervert breathed, holding my head tight as he rocked his hips and pumped out his creamy sperm. My cheeks filling with his orgasmic fluid, I finally gulped it down. My mouth filling again as his spunk continued to gush, I swallowed repeatedly, drinking from his throbbing knob as his balls drained. I could feel his cream overflowing, dribbling down my chin and trickling down my neck.

Praying for my ordeal to come to an end, I gasped for breath as he finally withdrew his deflating penis from my sperm-flooded mouth.

'I needed that,' he breathed, his evil face grinning at me as I licked my spunk-glossed lips. 'Give me a few minutes to recover, and I'll fuck your sweet little cunt.'

'You won't get away with this,' I said stupidly.

'But I *am* getting away with it,' he chortled, clambering off the table. Wondering where he was going as he left the room, I heard him moving about in the kitchen. The fridge door opening and closing, I imagined him forcing the huge shaft of a cucumber deep into my cunt. He was capable of any perversion, I mused as he rummaged about in the cupboards.

As I waited for him to return, I looked around the empty lounge. My sofa, coffee table, TV and hi-fi equipment . . . everything had gone. I supposed that it was easy enough to get a house-clearance firm in. But it would also be easy enough to replace my furniture, if I ever escaped the gang. The taste of sperm lingering on my tongue, my face splattered with the pervert's male liquid, I wondered whether I'd be allowed to take a shower when the others got back. I hadn't allowed Julie to go to the loo, so I really didn't think that she'd—

'Here we are,' the 'doctor' said as he entered the room with a bunch of bananas. 'I don't know about you, but I'm feeling rather peckish. Would you like a banana?'

'Go to hell,' I murmured as he peeled a banana.

'I think I'll eat it out of your cunt,' he chuckled, standing at the end of the table and pushing the soft fruit deep into the wet sheath of my vagina. 'I like a little cream with my bananas, don't you?'

Ignoring him as he rambled on about my cunt, I

watched him peel a second banana and force it deep into my vaginal sheath. He was a sad individual, I reflected as he managed to ram a third banana into my already bloated cunt. Leaning forward, he pressed his lips to the gaping entrance of my vagina and sucked hard. I could feel the fruit leaving my naked body, hear the sound of his slurping on the creamy pulp. But, again, I knew that I could endure this. Mouth-fucking, arse-licking, the bananas . . . I could take this, all right. But what was the rubber hose for?

'Mmm, nice and hot,' he breathed, lapping at my vaginal hole. 'Oh, there's the telephone,' he said, wiping his mouth and walking into the kitchen. Wondering whether it was Sally, I reckoned that she could have arrived at the canal by now. She'd have found the box, I was sure as I tried to hear what the 'doctor' was saying. His voice was low, and I couldn't make out whether he was pleased or annoyed. Shaking my head as I imagined Sally clutching the box, I blamed myself for my miserable failure. To have had the evidence in my hand and then . . .

'Oh dear,' the man sighed as he returned. 'Young Sally isn't at all pleased.'

'Good,' I murmured, wondering what he was getting at.

'Unfortunately, the box wasn't there.'

'I never said that it was,' I returned, unable to understand why she'd not found it. '*She* was the one who decided that it was by the canal. *I* didn't say anything about it.'

'You'd better tell me where it is. By the sound of it, Sally is in no mood to play games.'

'Ian has it,' I said, wondering what his reaction would be. 'I gave it to Ian to look after.'

'Right, I'll ring Sally's mobile and—'

'She won't find Ian or the box,' I cut in, wishing I hadn't incriminated Ian. 'He's . . . he's moved away from Southmoore. And I don't know where to.'

'A nice try,' the pervert chuckled, leaving the room.

Thinking again about the box, I couldn't understand why the gang hadn't found it. There were enough of them to search the place thoroughly, I reflected, wondering whether someone else had found it. Stuffed in the bushes, I doubted that anyone passing by would have seen it, so . . . All I could hope for was that Sally had simply missed it. I couldn't for the life of me see how, but the notion gave me something to cling to. As the 'doctor' talked on the phone, I reckoned that Julie would go home in the hope of finding Ian with the box. He wouldn't have it, so I had no worries there. But I was nonetheless concerned for him.

Lifting my head as I thought I heard the front door open, I strained my ears. I'd definitely heard a click as the pervert had been talking. It wasn't Sally, and no one else had a key, so . . . Hearing my tormentor go into the loo and lock the door, I once more strained my ears. Someone was in the hall, I knew. My face beaming as Ian peered round the door, I remained silent as he held his finger to his lips. Thanking God that he'd arrived as I watched him hide behind the lounge door, I heard the pervert coming back.

'Well,' he said as he walked up to the table, his flaccid cock snaking over his hairy balls. 'They're going to find Ian and he'll give them the box.'

'I don't think so,' I retorted, concealing a grin. 'As I said, Ian has left Southmoore. He's left his slag of a wife and that bloody town.'

'We'll see,' he chuckled. 'Now, where was I? Oh, yes. I was in the middle of eating bananas out of your dirty little cunt.'

'Tell me something,' I said as he leaned over the end of the table. 'Are you from Southmoore?'

'No, no. My surgery is . . . I'd better not say anything.'

'Why not? I mean, once Sally gets the photographs from Ian . . .'

'Yes, you're right. Well then, my surgery is just outside Southmoore. When I say *my surgery* . . . You've probably gathered that I'm not a real doctor. I – how shall I put it? – I pay Sally to bring me young girls.'

'So your house isn't in Southmoore Town?'

'As I said, it's just outside. On the road to Farmingly.'

'Yes, I know it,' Ian said, emerging from the shadows.

'Oh,' the man gasped, spinning round on his heels. 'Who are you?'

'It's all right,' Ian laughed. 'I'm a member of the Brook Street Gang.'

'Are you? I must admit that I've not met all the members.'

'I'm Dave, Dave Charlton. I was on my way here when Sally rang me. She said that we're to take the girl to your place.'

'What, now?'

'Yes, so you'd better get dressed.'

'Oh, er . . . yes, yes – of course. Has Sally got the photographs?'

'Yes, Ian had them. She didn't want to travel all the way up to London again so she suggested that we all meet at your place. She also thought that you might like to experiment with the girl in your surgery rather than here.'

'Oh, indeed I would.'

'OK, I'll take her into the bedroom and get her ready.'

As Ian released me and led me to my bedroom, I began to wonder whether this was a trick. But when he smiled and kissed me, I knew that I was safe. Whispering in my ear as I dressed, he explained that he'd guessed where I'd hidden the photographs and had gone to Miller's Corner and found them. He'd taken the box to the allotments behind Southmoore Football Club and had buried it beneath the holly tree where I used to collect berries for the Christmas decorations. Thankfully, the evidence was safe. Once I was ready, he tied my wrists together and we finally left the flat and climbed into his car. The pervert sat in the back with me, his hands wandering over my young body as Ian drove to Southmoore. I couldn't believe my luck as I watched the countryside flashing by. Sally would go back to my flat and believe that the 'doctor' had taken me somewhere. She'd no doubt go straight to his house and . . . and what?

'Left here,' the pervert said as Ian rounded a corner.

'Nice place,' Ian remarked, turning onto a long drive and finally pulling up outside a huge house surrounded by trees. '*Very* nice.'

'It *is* rather handy,' the man said, leaving the car and pulling me out. 'Hidden away like this with no neighbours, I can do what I like.'

'You must show me your surgery,' Ian said, taking my arm and leading me to the front door. 'We'll lock the girl in the surgery until the others arrive.'

'Yes, yes, of course.'

Opening the door, the man led us across a huge hall

and through a large dining room. Moving a heavy curtain aside and opening a small oak door, he went down some steps. Following, we found ourselves in his basement surgery. It was a large room packed with whips, handcuffs, other even more horrific-looking instruments of torture and an examination table. On a trolley beside the table, I noticed several vaginal speculums and a large vibrator. Wondering how many victims he'd dragged into his chamber of horrors, I rubbed my aching wrists as Ian released me.

'I'll prepare the girl,' Ian said, leading me to the examination table. 'Any chance of a cup of coffee before we have some fun with her?'

'Yes, of course,' the pervert replied. 'Coming up.'

'OK,' Ian whispered as the man left the room. 'Obviously, Sally and the others will come here at some stage. We can't stay here, we can't go to my place and we certainly can't go back to your flat.'

'So where *do* we go?' I asked him. 'And why did we have to come here?'

'I've heard Julie talking about the so-called doctor. I'd never met him before today, which is fortunate, but I know quite a lot about him.'

'Ian, he'll be back in a minute,' I whispered anxiously. 'I still don't understand why we had to come here.'

'Apparently, he's stinking rich.'

'So?'

'Apart from that, he looks after the gang's money. He keeps the cash in the house. And I'm not talking about a few thousand pounds.'

'You mean we're going to take his money?'

'No. We're going to take the gang's money. And then we can leave the country and—'

'God, I can't keep up with this. Take one step at a time, Ian.'

'It's simple. We take the cash and—'

'I don't like the idea of stealing.'

'The money's already been stolen from the gang's victims. Either that or it's dirty in some other way – prostitution, the sale of porn pics . . . We can't talk about it now. OK, we'll hide behind the door. When he comes back, we'll slip out of the room and lock him in. I've already taken the key out of the lock.'

As the 'doctor' wandered back into the room carrying a tray of coffee, we crept out of the door and Ian turned the key in the lock. *So far, so good*, I thought as the man started yelling. *But now what?* I didn't want to have to spend hours searching for the cash. The house was massive, and the money could have been stashed anywhere. Once Sally discovered that I'd escaped, she was bound to head straight for the man's house and if we were still there fucking about searching for money . . . Shaking my head, I followed Ian up the steps to the dining room as the man hammered on the door. I didn't want money. All I wanted was to get out of the place.

Lingering in the hall as Ian dashed up the huge staircase, I heard a loud click coming from the front door. Becoming increasingly frightened, I walked to the door and turned the handle. It was locked. Realizing that the pervert might have some sort of security system, I began to panic. Turning the door handle again, I feared the worst. We were locked in the house of sadistic sex. We'd be dragged down to the surgery, experimented on . . . Chasing after Ian, I found myself on a huge landing with a dozen or more closed doors surrounding me. Something was very wrong, I knew instinctively as I tried each locked door in turn.

'Ian,' I called. 'Ian, where are you?'

'In here,' he replied, hammering on one of the doors. 'It's locked itself. I can't get out.'

'*All* the doors are locked,' I said. 'It's some kind of automatic system.'

'Stand back,' he called. 'I'll smash it down.'

This was all we needed, I thought fearfully as I stepped away from the door. The eccentric 'doctor' might have a way out of the surgery and come looking for us. With Ian locked in the room, I'd be unable to defend myself and the pervert would sexually torture me and... Trying to calm myself, I cowered in a corner as Ian began bashing at the door with something. I knew that the heavy oak wouldn't split. The house was built like a castle, and it was going to take a battering ram to break the door down. Leaving Ian to get on with it, I went back down the stairs and looked around the hall.

'There's no way out,' a voice said, seemingly coming from all directions. 'I have the young man trapped, and you'll be next.'

'Where are you?' I called, my hands trembling.

'In the surgery, waiting for you. I can see you on my video monitor. The house is wired with video cameras, microphones, security systems... You'll never escape, so why don't you come down to the surgery?'

'Never,' I retorted.

'Then I shall just have to come and get you.'

I wasn't sure whether the pervert could get out of the surgery or not as I ran back up the stairs. And I wasn't going to hang around to find out. Ian was still bashing at the door. The wood hadn't split, and I doubted that he'd ever break out. Running along the landing to a far door that was ajar, I peered into a large room. It was a trap, I knew. Once I walked into the room, the door would close and lock. And I'd be trapped. This was a bloody nightmare, I reflected, wondering what to do.

'I can see you.' The pervert's voice echoed around the old house. 'Come down to the surgery and I'll examine you.'

'Go to hell,' I said, walking along the landing to the top of the stairs. 'You can't get out, can you?'

'I'm waiting for you. Come down to the surgery before the others get here. You have such a sweet little pussy. Fresh, hairless, with full lips, hot, tight, wet . . . I'd just love to try out my vaginal expander. Come down here and we'll have some fun.'

'Rachael,' Ian called, hammering on the door. 'It's no good, I can't break out.'

'I'll find a way out and get help,' I said.

'There *is* no way out,' the 'doctor' chuckled as I bounded down the stairs. 'There's no escape.'

He was right, I knew as I hammered on a window with my fist. The glass was incredibly thick, probably bulletproof. I could hear Ian battering the door again as I walked through the dining room. If he kept at it, the door would have to break eventually. Unless it was steel-lined, I thought anxiously as I descended the steps to the surgery. My heart banging hard against my chest, I froze as I reached the bottom step and gazed at the open door. How the hell had the pervert escaped? More to the point, where the fuck was he?

I didn't know what I was doing or why as I walked into the surgery. This was the very room that I should have kept away from and yet . . . I seemed to be drawn there. I recalled the many times I'd stood on a railway platform, gazing at the live rail. The rail was like a magnet, attracting me, pulling me towards it. The temptation to reach out and touch it had been almost overwhelming at times. Why were people attracted to danger like that? I pondered on the question as I stood by the examination table.

'Welcome,' the pervert said, closing and locking the door.

'No,' I breathed, spinning round and gazing at his grinning face. 'Please . . .'

'Please? You're begging for it, are you?'

'I'm begging you to release me. Please, let me go and . . .'

'Now that your young male friend is safely locked up, we have all the time in the world to get to know each other intimately. Sally and her gang won't be here for a while, so why don't you slip out of your clothes and lie on the—'

'You can rot in hell, you fucking pervert,' I hissed as he walked towards me.

'That's not very nice. By the way, I know who your friend is. I now have Ian Marshal and Rachael Michaels under lock and key. Quite an achievement, don't you agree?'

'Go fuck yourself.'

'There'll be plenty of fucking before long, don't you worry. Oh, how remiss of me. I haven't introduced myself. I am Dave Shrimpton. You may have heard of me.'

'No, I haven't.'

'You know me intimately,' he chuckled. 'Or, I should say, you know my cock intimately.'

'I've never seen you before,' I murmured.

'No, you haven't. But you've sucked the spunk out of my cock many times. Remember the common; the blanket hung between two bushes? That was my cock, my knob. That was my spunk you swallowed. I've been watching you, Rachael. From the day you stepped off the train at Southmoore station, I've been watching you. You probably think that Sally leads the Brook Street Gang. In fact, *I* am the leader. I've been involved with the gang for a long time. When you were at school and Rod took photographs of your naked body, your sweet little pussy and petite breasts . . . Those photographs were for me. I have quite a collection of photographs. Not only of you, but of other schoolgirls.'

'You're a sad pervert,' I murmured, recalling a man who used to meet Sally after school on the odd occasion. 'To think that, when I was in my early teens, I'd sucked the spunk out of a dirty old man's cock . . .'

'Not only do I run the Brook Street Gang, but I'm the treasurer. I deal with the money, I plan . . . but I won't bore you with the details. Now then, Rachael. I don't want to have to force you onto the table. I don't like forcing girls to strip and lie on the examination table. I feel far happier if they cooperate and willingly allow me to—'

'*Willingly*? No girls would *willingly* allow you to sexually torture them.'

'Torture? I don't like that word. I *experiment* on young girls. I had a girl here only last week. She was a beautiful little specimen with long blonde hair, petite breasts, ripening nipples and a hairless pussy. I spent many hours examining her, experimenting on her little pink pussy.'

'You should be locked up,' I breathed, looking around the room for something to attack him with.

'I *am* locked up,' he chuckled. 'We're *both* locked up – in my surgery. Of course, if you were to join me . . .'

'Join you? What do you mean?'

'Work for me. No, work *with* me. There's a young girl being delivered tomorrow. If you worked with me, we could—'

'All right,' I cut in, rather too eagerly. 'I'll work with you. I'd like that. Experimenting on young girls, shaving their little pussies and . . .'

'Sit down and we'll talk about it,' he said, pointing to an old leather armchair in the corner of the room. 'I reckon that we'd work well together.'

'So do I,' I said, sitting in the chair. 'I know several young girls. I could bring them here and . . .'

'Do you? Now, that *is* interesting.'

'They're quite young,' I said, going for broke. 'They have the cutest little titties and beautiful hairless pussies . . .'

'Yes, you could bring them here and we could experiment on them, work together and . . .'

'No,' I cried as he pressed a button on the wall and a steel bar slid across my lap.

'It's all right,' he chuckled as I grabbed the bar and pulled at it. 'I like a captive audience.'

'You bastard,' I hissed, realizing what a fucking idiot I'd been.

Moving behind me, the 'doctor' pulled my hands behind the chair and cuffed my wrists. There was no way I could escape, I knew as he unbuttoned my blouse and lifted my bra clear of my firm breasts. Totally defenceless, completely vulnerable to his every perverted whim, all I could do was watch as he took a pair of scissors from a shelf and made a cut up the front of my skirt. Tugging the garment away, he then carefully cut through the flimsy material of my panties before cutting my bra and blouse.

'There,' he said, standing up and admiring his handiwork. 'You look far better without your clothes. I'm really looking forward to working with you. I didn't really have a chance to get to know your body properly when we were in London. But, now that you're in my surgery, I can get to know every inch of you intimately. One of my experiments involves my dog. He's an Alsatian, a beautiful beast. He'll certainly enjoy getting to know you intimately. He loves licking . . .'

His words tailing off as a buzzer sounded, he left the room and closed the door behind him. It was obviously some sort of warning device – but warning him of what? Was someone at the front door? Perhaps Sally had arrived, I thought anxiously. Unless Ian had managed to break out of the room. The silence was almost deafening as I waited. *An Alsatian?* I thought, horrific pictures filling my mind. *He loves licking? Licking what?* As if I couldn't guess.

This was the worst situation I'd been in so far, I reflected. Locked in a house in the middle of the countryside with no one having a clue about where I was . . . My only hope was that Ian might manage to escape. He was young and fit, and could easily overpower the pervert. If he had a chance to, that was. *Dave Shrimpton*, I mused. I'd heard the name somewhere. But where? He was definitely the man who'd met Sally after school sometimes. I wondered: had he started the gang? Had he got his grubby hands on Sally and Julie and suggested that they start a gang?

Hearing a dog barking somewhere upstairs, I cringed

and squeezed my naked thighs together. Was the pervert bringing the animal down to the surgery? *He loves licking*. The nightmare was far from over. It had barely begun.

# 14

I'd been in the surgery for what seemed like hours when. I finally heard movements outside the door. The key turning in the lock, I waited with bated breath as the handle rotated. I'd lost all hope of Ian escaping and coming to my rescue. The pervert had probably got his hands on him. Either that or the room was so well secured that it was impossible to break out. The door inching open, I reckoned that it was Sally and her confederates. They'd been to my flat, found the place deserted . . . and had come to the pervert's house to hunt me down.

'What are you doing here?' I asked as Becky Phillips, a girl from my class at school, peered around the door.

She'd hardly changed, and I recognized her instantly. She was dressed in a red miniskirt and white T-shirt. Her auburn hair cascading down over the mounds of her breasts, she was extremely attractive. But what was she doing in the pervert's house? I wondered as she looked around. And how had she got in? Had the evil man sent her down to the surgery to torture me?

'I've come to get you out,' she whispered, walking into the room.

'You've come to . . . How did you get in?'

'I came here earlier. I've been hiding, waiting until—'

'This is a trick,' I breathed as she gazed at the steel bar running across my lap.

'It's not a trick, Rachael. I've been working on exposing the gang for years. I've built up evidence and . . . I'll tell you about it later. We have to get out of here.'

'That button on the wall,' I said. 'Try pressing it.'

As she walked across the room and pressed the button, I watched the steel bar retract. Leaping to my feet, I looked around for something with which to cover my naked body. There was nothing. I would just have to leave as I was. Had she brought a coat or . . . Thinking again that this was a trick as she walked across the surgery to the far wall, I watched her pull a heavy curtain aside, revealing a small door.

'Come on,' she said, opening the door. 'This is the way out.'

'How do you know that?' I asked her. I was becoming increasingly suspicious as she told me to go first.

'Come on,' she urged me again. 'We don't have much time.'

'No, you go first,' I said, gazing into what appeared to be a dimly lit tunnel.

'Rachael . . . look, I know about this place because I've been here before. You have nothing to lose by trusting me, have you?'

'What do you mean?'

'You're trapped here. I can hardly lead you into a trap when you're already imprisoned here, can I?'

'I suppose not,' I finally conceded, lowering my head and walking through the low doorway.

Going along the tunnel with Becky close behind, I finally came to another door which led us out into the woods. Fortunately, it was a very warm night. Although I didn't relish walking through the woods naked, at least I wouldn't be cold. And, hopefully, I'd be heading for freedom. Closing the dor behind her, Becky took my arm and said that she'd lead the way. We tramped through the woods to her car, which was parked in the lane. This was all too easy, I thought, repeatedly turning and looking over my shoulder as she unlocked the car. The pervert must have known about the secret tunnel, so . . .

'Get in, for goodness' sake,' she said, flinging the passenger door open and starting the engine as I waited outside the car.

'Where are we going?' I asked her.

'To my place. Come on, we haven't got all night.'

'All right,' I breathed, climbing into the car and closing the door. 'How did you know that I was there?'

'I didn't,' she replied, driving off. 'I'd been watching the place. When I realized that the doctor was out, I went into the house to gather evidence. When he came back, I didn't have a chance to escape through the tunnel so I hid.'

'Where did he go? I heard a buzzer and he went upstairs.'

'That's an alarm. I don't know what set it off. Me moving about, more than likely. Anyway, he went upstairs so I came out of hiding and went down to the surgery to escape. And I found you.'

'You said that you were there to gather evidence.'

'I was abused by the gang at school. And I've spent years compiling evidence against them.'

Remaining silent as Becky drove the short distance to a small cottage, I thought that her story was believable. But, what with the elaborate security system protecting the house, I couldn't understand why the pervert would leave the tunnel wide open like that. Anyone could come and go as and when they pleased. It just didn't make sense. Unless he and Becky had set me up. But, as she'd said, why lead me into a trap when I was already imprisoned?

'This is it,' she said, parking the car outside the front door. 'Home sweet home.'

'This is lovely,' I breathed, folding my arms to conceal my breasts as I left the car and followed her into the cottage. 'Do you live here alone?'

'Yes, I do. This was my aunt's place. She left it to me. Grab some clothes from my bedroom. Up the stairs and first on the left. I'll put the kettle on.'

Grabbing a dress from her wardrobe and stepping into a pair of Becky's shoes, I was thankful that I no longer had to walk around showing off my naked body. I was also thankful to be out of the pervert's clutches. But I still didn't trust Becky. It seemed rather odd that she'd known about the surgery and the secret tunnel. It was also odd to think that she'd been abused at school by the gang. Becky had hung around with a group of girls who'd had nothing to do with Sally or the others. As far as I knew, she'd never been troubled by the gang. There again, *I* certainly hadn't broadcast the fact that I was being used for sex by Sally and her cronies.

Descending the stairs, I thought about Ian. Was he still locked in that room? Had the pervert got him? Where *was* the pervert? Where the hell had he disappeared to? At least I could now get help, I reflected. Ian wouldn't come to any harm locked in the room. All he had to do was hang on until I was able to send help. Then I wondered: was he in on the scam? If he was working with the pervert and Becky . . .

'There you are,' Becky said, leading me into the lounge

and placing a cup of coffee on the small table. 'Sit down and make yourself comfortable,' she invited me, sitting in an armchair and brushing her long auburn hair away from her pretty face. 'So, you're free.'

'Yes, I am,' I replied, flopping onto the sofa. 'Thanks to you.'

'It was purely luck that I happened to be there. I hadn't expected to find anyone in the surgery. All I was doing was making my escape.'

'Had you not come to my rescue . . . I dread to think what that bastard had planned for me. This is a lovely cottage, Becky. You're really lucky.'

'I like it,' she replied. 'What was all that banging in the house? It sounded as if someone was trying to break in.'

'Someone was trying to break out. My friend Ian is still in that pervert's house. He got himself locked in one of the upstairs rooms and—'

'Ian Marshal?'

'Yes. We have to get help, Becky.'

'He'll be all right,' she said as I sipped my coffee. 'Old Shrimpton won't harm him. If anything, it'll be the other way round.'

'I hope you're right.'

'We will send help, of course. I have one or two friends who might be able to get him out. OK, so I've been collecting evidence over the years. I suggest we work together to expose the gang.'

'That sounds good to me,' I replied, still unsure of the girl. 'What evidence have you got?'

'Dates, times, names and addresses of victims who are willing to testify . . . and a few photographs of the gang on the common. I don't keep them here, of course. But I have a few pictures of Sally and the others dragging girls into the bushes.'

'That's brilliant,' I said, beaming. 'You've done well.'

'Not well enough, I'm afraid. Obviously, I know about Shrimpton and his surgery. I know about the cottage by the church . . . But I need more evidence before I can go to the police.'

'The more the better,' I murmured, wondering about the box of photographs that Ian had buried. *Should I tell her?* I wondered.

'The gang made my life hell at school,' she sighed. 'I was raped, whipped . . . It was *worse* than hell.'

'I didn't realize,' I said. 'I thought that I was the only one.'

'No, no. There were several girls who were sexually abused, threatened and blackmailed. I'm in touch with most of them. We're working together to put an end to the gang. There are a lot of photographs that the gang have. They use them for blackmailing people. If I could get hold of them . . . then I'd have more than enough evidence.'

'It's the ringleaders we have to nail. Ian said that Lucy runs things.'

'Yes. But she has nothing to do with the gang. I don't know why Ian said that.'

'Neither do I. He was pretty sure that she was running things. He said that—'

'Lucy has nothing to do with the gang, Rachael. She doesn't even live with Kenny now.'

'But I saw her in her kitchen . . .'

'She moved out. What were you doing at Kenny's house?'

'I . . . I was looking for Ian. You say that she moved out?'

'All they did was argue. From what I've heard, Kenny

screwed anything and everything in a skirt and she got fed up with it. Lucy was never into the sexual side of things. She wanted to run a proper operation, a tight ship. She wanted to make money and—'

'Where does she live now?'

'She lives in an old farmhouse just off the Southmoore Road. But she—'

'Royston Farm? That huge place?'

'Yes. Look, we have to get our hands on some real evidence. Photographs . . .'

'I . . . I might be able to help you,' I breathed.

'Oh?'

'I know where the photographs are.'

'You do?' she trilled. 'Rachael, that's fantastic. Where? Where are they?'

'I . . . I'm not sure whether I should . . .'

'For God's sake, Rachael, you *have* to tell me.'

'And *you* have to understand that I'm not sure who I can trust. This might be a trick, for all I know.'

'Hardly,' Becky replied, forcing a laugh. 'If you believe that I'm working with Sally and . . . God, I can't believe it. I rescue you, bring you here . . . Go, if you want to. You're free to leave.'

'No, no. OK, the photographs are in a plastic box. Ian buried it beneath a holly tree on the allotments behind the football club. If we go there now—'

'In the morning,' she broke in. 'It's dark now – we'll go in the morning. Would you like something to eat? I can easily cook us a meal.'

'Yes, that would be nice,' I replied. 'And, if it's OK, I'd like to take a shower.'

'Help yourself. You'll find all you need in the bathroom.'

'Thanks.'

Finishing my coffee, I climbed the stairs and went into the bathroom. I felt a lot easier as I slipped out of the dress and stepped into the shower. Although the gang were undoubtedly after me, at least I now had some time to think and plan. As Becky had said, Ian would be all right. The 'doctor' might be a sad pervert, but I doubted that he was capable of physically attacking anyone. Lathering shampoo into my long blonde hair, I turned my thoughts to the box of photographs. What with Becky's evidence and the incriminating porn pics, we'd be home and dry.

Becky had said that she had the names and addresses of the blackmail victims. If they were willing to testify against Sally and Co . . . There again, they probably wouldn't like the idea of their partners discovering their adultery. At the very least, though, we'd be able to stop the blackmail threats. Finally stepping out of the shower, I dried my naked body with a towel and slipped into the dress. Feeling fresh and clean, I left the bathroom, went into Becky's bedroom and brushed my hair before going down to the lounge.

'All right?' Becky asked as I entered the room.

'Yes, much better,' I replied, sitting down opposite her. 'Thanks for all you've done.'

'No problem. I'm only too pleased to be able to help a fellow victim of the Brook Street Gang. The meal won't be long. I hope you're hungry?'

'I'm famished. So, what do you do for a living?'

'Nothing,' she laughed. 'When my aunt left me the cottage, she also left me a small fortune.'

'What about your parents? Didn't they want . . .'

'They live abroad. They have enough money of their own. They moved to Canada several years ago.'

My mind drifting, I noticed Becky's white panties as she sat with her thighs apart. I felt my stomach somersault, my womb contract as she talked about her parents. I wasn't a lesbian, and yet . . . Becky was very attractive, extremely sensual-looking. Feeling guilty about Ian as I gazed at the bulging material of her panties, I tried to drag my thoughts away from her full sex lips.

'So I moved into the cottage,' she said.

'Yes, right. Well, it certainly is a nice place. It's quiet, too.'

'I couldn't live in town,' she murmured, her thighs parting a little further. 'What with the traffic and the noise . . . I've always loved the countryside. Would you like a drink?'

'Thanks.'

'I have vodka, gin . . .'

'Vodka, please.'

'And tonic?'

'Thanks.'

'Being in a position where I don't have to work, I've been able to concentrate on the gang,' she said, opening a drinks cabinet.

'They must know that you live close to Southmoore. Surely, one of them must have seen you around.'

'If they have, then they've left me alone,' she said, passing me a drink. 'I've often wondered why they haven't found out where I live. I used to worry about it but—'

'That pervert has video cameras in his house,' I interrupted her as she sat down again, holding her drink. 'I'm surprised that he hasn't seen you creeping about.'

'I really don't know,' Becky sighed nonchalantly.

This was rather odd, I reflected, spying the bulging

material of her tight panties again. If she'd been to the house several times, the man must have caught her on videotape. And living so close to Southmoore . . . My suspicions roused again, I wished I hadn't told her where the photographs were buried. Had she phoned Sally or one of the others and told them? Was that why she'd suggested we wait until the morning before retrieving the porn pics?

Sipping my drink as I gazed at her sex-bulged panties, I wondered whether Becky was deliberately parting her thighs. She seemed unaware that she was showing off her panties, but I couldn't be sure. Recalling my schooldays, it occurred to me that I'd never seen Becky with a boy. In fact, she only hung around with other girls. Was I reading something into that? Perhaps – the thought suddenly struck me – I hoped that she was a lesbian.

'You didn't marry, then?' I asked her.

'No, no,' she giggled, leaping to her feet and refilling our glasses. 'I was never one for the men. How about you?'

'No, I didn't marry,' I murmured pensively. *Never one for the men*? 'I prefer female company,' I added stupidly, wondering what I was trying to say.

'You and me both,' she giggled, knocking back her drink and refilling her glass. 'Are you . . . well, you know?'

'What?' I asked, smiling at her. Was there a glint in my eyes?

'A lesbian, silly.'

'Oh, er . . . yes, yes, I am.'

'I reckon that we're going to get on really well together,' Becky laughed, raising her glass. 'To us. And the night ahead.'

'Yes, to us.'

I didn't know what I was trying to achieve as I sipped my drink. Did I need love? I pondered the question, gazing at the swell of Becky's petite breasts beneath her tight T-shirt as she stood in front of me. I'd experienced so much cold sex that I wasn't sure what loving sex was. Thinking back, I realized that I'd never been loved. Perhaps I'd been too much of a bitch, I mused. The experiences of my early teens had obviously moulded me, turning me into a cold, hard bitch who couldn't show love.

Lifting her short skirt up over her stomach, Becky moved closer and yanked her panties down her shapely thighs. I gazed in awe at the pouting lips of her hairless vulva, the creamy crack of her young pussy. Her outer labia were ballooning, puffy and very swollen. I'd never seen such large sex lips, and I placed my glass on the floor to lean forward to examine her femininity. Opening her love crack, she exposed the inner folds of her vagina to my wide eyes and suggested that I kiss her there. *I need this*, I thought, eyeing the intricate folds nestling within her gaping valley of desire. *I need to unwind, stop thinking about the gang and relax*. Again suggesting that I kiss her pussy, Becky allowed her panties to fall around her ankles. Kicking the garment aside, she stood with her feet parted, offering me the most intimate part of her young body.

Breathing in her female scent as I pressed my lips into her yawning vaginal crack, I pushed my tongue out and tasted her there. Becky quivered, letting out a gasp as my tongue snaked over the erect bud of her clitoris. She tasted heavenly – salty, creamy – and I pressed my mouth harder against the intimate inner flesh of her beautiful cunt. Trying to convince myself that I wasn't a lesbian as she released her sex cushions and clutched my head, whimpering as her pleasure heightened, I moved down her gaping sex valley and lapped up her vaginal cream.

'Yes,' she breathed as my tongue repeatedly swept over the pink funnel of flesh surrounding her pussy hole. 'God, don't stop.' Her pouting love lips pressing against my cheeks, I thought again what exquisite labia she had. Moving back, I gazed at her slit, the ballooning hillocks of her outer lips rising either side of her valley of lust. Her plump vulva reminded me of a bottom, the deep gully nestling between the firm buttocks.

Licking her there, sweeping my tongue up and down the beautiful crevice of her cunt, I dug my fingernails into the firm cheeks of Becky's naked buttocks and pulled her closer to me. My face buried between the soft hillocks of her outer lips, I drove my tongue deep into the sex-wet sheath of her tight vagina and licked its creamed walls. Again, she let out whimpers of pleasure, her young body trembling as her juices of desire flowed from her sex duct in torrents.

'You're good,' Becky breathed, stepping back and smiling at me. 'I'll sit on the sofa and then you can lick me properly.'

'Your pussy lips are amazing,' I said, my eyes transfixed on the puffy outer labia of her vulva. 'I've never seen such—'

'I have a machine,' she broke in. 'Wait there and I'll go and get it.' She left the room.

Slipping out of the dress she'd lent me, I looked down at the shaved flesh of my pussy and smiled. Becky would lick me there, I mused, my clitoris swelling in expectation, the juices of my vagina flowing, trickling down my inner thighs. She'd love me there and . . . Love? Again wondering what love was as I ran my hands over the firm mounds of my breasts, I sat on the sofa and parted my thighs wide. My fingertip toying with the solid protrusion of my ripe clitoris, I was desperate to come.

'You're beautiful,' Becky said as she returned with a length of rubber hose and a black box trailing a length of electrical flex. Plugging the box in, she settled between my feet and pushed my thighs wide apart. 'This is a vacuum pump,' she enlightened me, the black box humming as she placed a transparent plastic cup over the swell of my pussy lips. 'There, now watch your pussy lips swell.'

Focusing on my outer labia inflating within the cup, I began to breathe deeply in my soaring arousal. My outer labia ballooning, my clitoris sucked out from beneath its protective hood, I lay back and closed my eyes. The incredible sensations running throughout my naked body as Becky knelt in front of me and sucked on each elongated nipple in turn, I felt the erect nipples of her own young breasts pressing into my stomach.

She was so sensual, I reflected, breathing in the scent of her long auburn hair as she suckled like a babe at my breast. Her dark hair cascading over my naked body as I listened to the humming sound of the vacuum pump, my outer cunt lips swelling, my clitoris pulsating gently, I could feel my juices of lust being sucked out of my quim. Becky's machine was incredible, I mused as she sucked and mouthed on my erect nipples.

'Kneel on the floor and rest your head on the sofa,' Becky ordered me, sitting back on her heels. 'It's all right, the suction cup won't fall off,' she giggled as I took my position. 'God, you have a beautiful bottom,' she complimented me, running her fingertips over the firm moons of my naked buttocks. 'Now, just relax and allow the pump to suck on your lips while I love your bottom.'

Parting the firm cheeks of my bottom, she ran her wet tongue up my anal gully. My face buried in the sofa cushion, I trembled as she repeatedly licked the brown ring of my anus, moaning softly through her nose as she lost herself in her arousal. Ordering me to part my knees further, she yanked my buttocks apart and pressed her thumbs into the tight hole of my anus. Opening the entrance to my rectal duct, she pushed her tongue deep into my trembling body and licked the inner walls of my most private place as I breathed heavily and began to drift away on clouds of arousal.

Never had I known such immense pleasure, I thought as Becky tongued my rectum. My body shaking uncontrollably, my outer labia inflating like balloons, I knew that my pulsating clitoris was about to erupt in orgasm. I could hear the slurping of Becky's tongue, feel the pulsating of my rock-hard clitoris, as she expertly attended my bottom-hole. Again and again waves of pure sexual bliss rolled through my contracting womb. My anal sphincter muscles spasming, my clitoris painfully hard, I jumped as my lesbian lover drove two fingers deep into the tight sheath of my arse.

'God, you're hot,' she breathed, nibbling on the firm flesh of my buttocks as she bent and twisted her fingers. 'You have the most beautiful bottom, Rachael. So hot and tight and—'

'I think I'm going to come,' I murmured, my lust juices gushing from my spasming cunt and filling the plastic cup. 'Finger me,' I gasped. 'Finger my arse hard.'

'I'll make you come,' Becky whispered, forcing

another finger into the bloated sheath of my rectum. 'Come now,' she urged me. 'Come for me.'

My clitoris exploding in orgasm at long last, my entire body shaking violently, rocking with the anal pistoning, I felt as if I was drifting high in the sky, floating with the clouds. I wondered: had I found love? I relished the feel of the girl's wet tongue snaking around her thrusting fingers as she massaged the inner flesh of my bottom. Was this love? Or was this cold lust? Lesbian lust, sex for the sake of sex . . .

'God,' I cried, my orgasm peaking, the plastic cup full of my juices of pleasure. Driving a fourth finger into the rhythmically contracting sheath of my rectum. Becky sustained my climax with her inner massaging as the vacuum pump sucked my orgasm out of my pulsating clitoris and drained my lust juices. On and on my orgasm rolled, tremors of sex transmitting deep into my convulsing womb, reaching every nerve ending of my young body, tightening every muscle. Whimpering in my sexual heaven, drifting, my mind blown away on the tempest of female lust, I finally lost consciousness.

Hearing movements behind me, the vacuum pump still humming, I finally drifted back into my sated body and lay breathing deeply into the sofa cushion. Becky was saying something, her soft words echoing around my mind as I felt her fingertips running over the firm globes of my naked buttocks. Was she going to love me? I asked myself the question as she lifted my arms. Still drifting in the aftermath of my massive multiple orgasm, my naked body at last beginning to calm, I hoped that she'd allow me to drink from her tight cunt, suck an orgasm from the swollen nub of her clitoris. We were going to enjoy a night of lesbian love, I mused as I felt the slight swell of her lower stomach pressing against the warm cheeks of my bottom. Finally moving away, she murmured something. Words of love? Words of—

Came the sound of something swishing through the air and landing with a deafening crack across the tensed cheeks of my buttocks. I let out a scream. Lifting and turning my head, my eyes wide, I watched as Sally raised a branch of a bush above her head and brought it down across my glowing bottom. I couldn't move. A strap across my back, beneath my arms. I was pinned down. Again, the branch swished through the air, lashing my burning buttocks, the rough leaves catching the backs of my thighs. I could see Julie lurking by the sofa, grinning as Sally continued the gruelling lashing of my fiery buttocks.

Wondering where Becky was, I imagined that the gang had sneaked up from behind, covered her mouth and dragged her out of the room. Was she locked in her bedroom? Were the men raping her? My tethered body convulsing wildly with every lash of the rough branch, I was determined not to tell Sally where the photographs were. No matter what she forced me to endure . . . Had they got Ian? I contemplated the possibility fearfully.

'Right, then,' Sally gasped as she halted the beating. 'I have some good news for you.'

'I'll tell you nothing,' I retorted, lifting my head and glaring at her.

'You don't have to,' Julie laughed. 'Rod and the other lads are on their way to get the photographs, thanks to Becky.'

'Becky?' I gasped, turning my head further. She was sitting in the armchair, a smile on her pretty face. 'Becky, I thought . . .'

'I'm sorry,' she murmured. 'But we had to get the photographs back. We couldn't allow you to expose us, Rachael. I rang Sally and told her where the box was buried.'

'And Rod will be digging it up as we speak,' Sally added triumphantly. 'You'll never beat us, Rachael. You'll never beat the Brook Street Gang.'

'Where's Ian?' I asked, fearing the worst.

'Don't you worry your pretty head about Ian,' Sally said, kneeling behind me and removing the plastic cup from my ballooning outer sex lips. Sitting beside me, she lifted my head by my hair. 'Drink this,' she instructed me, holding the cream-brimming cup to my mouth. 'Go on, drink your own come-juice.'

Forced to drink my own vaginal juices, repeatedly swallowing the lubricious cream, I knew that the gang had finally won. Sally was right, I'd never beat them. It had been futile to try to beat the Brook Street Gang. I should have learned that from my schooldays. I could trust no one: I had no idea whether Ian was safe, Becky had betrayed me . . . I doubted that Dave Bryant had even bothered to report me missing. After receiving my written resignation, why would he bother to come looking for me? He must have tried ringing my flat and . . .

'We were hoping that you'd give up your fight,' Sally said as I finished drinking my own orgasmic liquid. 'We thought that you'd accept that you couldn't beat us and that you'd then do as you were told. You could have lived in Southmoore, worked for us, had enough money to—'

'Then you thought wrong,' I hissed.

'Yes, we did. We've had to make other plans for you now. You'll still work for us, Rachael. You'll earn money for us by using your body and—'

'Never.'

'Please let me finish. We own a small property not far from here. You'll live and work there. You'll never be allowed to leave, of course. But you should settle in to your new way of life, eventually.'

'I'll never stop fighting,' I spat. 'The day will come when—'

'The day will come when you'll grow old. You'll be of no use to us when you're old, Rachael. No man wants to pay to have sex with an old hag. When that day comes . . . Still, don't worry about that now. The boys will be here before long There's Rod, Brad, Kenny . . . They're just dying to fuck your tight little arse, Rachael. You'd like that, wouldn't you?'

'Go fuck yourself,' I spat.

'You're the one who's going to get fucked,' Sally giggled, leaping off the sofa and kneeling behind me. 'Mmm, your arse tastes lovely,' she breathed, her wet tongue snaking around my anal eye. 'We'll give you a good arse-licking to prepare you for the boys' massive cocks.'

As Becky, Julie and Kathy settled behind me, their wet tongues sweeping over the rounded cheeks of my stinging buttocks, I couldn't believe that I'd fallen into their hands yet again. Several fingers driving into the drenched sheath of my inflamed cunt, a tongue delving deep into the dank tube of my rectum, I shuddered. Desperately trying to deny my soaring arousal, I could hear the juices of my vagina squelching as the fingers repeatedly thrust deep into my abused cunt.

Raising my head as Becky moved behind the sofa, I watched in amazement as she lowered its back to the floor, turning the piece of lounge furniture into a large bed. Sitting with the gaping crack of her sex-dripping cunt only inches from my face, she yanked my head up by my hair and moved forward. Forcing the swollen inner folds of her hot sex-slit hard against my mouth, she ordered me to lick the juices out of her tight cunt. Complying, I pushed my tongue into her sex hole, tasting the lubricious juices of her vaginal duct as tongues snaked within my anal gully.

When the men arrived, I knew that they'd waste no time in pumping my bowels full of spunk. Cocks fucking my arse, my cunt, my mouth, my young body would be awash with sperm . . . This was to be my life now, I knew as Becky ground her cuntal flesh hard against my wet mouth. Swivelling her hips and aligning the solid nub of her clitoris, its solid protrusion pulsating beneath my sweeping tongue, I knew that she was about to reach her climax as her juices of desire gushed out of her hot cunt and flooded over my chin.

I'd thought that I'd found love, I reflected, sucking on the pink bulb of her ballooning clitoris. Soft, warm, sensual . . . I'd thought that Becky was different. She and the gang had obviously planned my escape from the pervert's house. I should have realized what they were up to. I hadn't even thought about the photographs. Recalling Becky's words when she'd met me in the surgery, I couldn't think why I'd been so stupid. *I can hardly lead you into a trap when you're already imprisoned here, can I?* Why the hell hadn't I realized that they were after the photographs?

'Coming,' Becky wailed, her juices of desire streaming down my chin as I gobbled and sucked on her orgasming clitoris. My own clitoris nearing its climax as one of the girls massaged the sensitive tip, my naked body shaking violently, I sustained Becky's pleasure as I reached my own orgasm. I could feel my cuntal fluid gushing between the pouting lips of my vagina, coursing down my inner thighs as a tongue repeatedly thrust into my contracting rectal sheath. When the tongue was replaced by several fingers, I thought that I was going to split wide open as someone tried to force her entire fist deep into my tight arse.

'Fist-fuck the slag,' Sally trilled, obviously delighting in the crude abuse of my tethered body. 'Go on, push your fist deep into the slag's arsehole.'

It was Julie, I was sure as my anal ring expanded to capacity. I could feel her knuckles driving past my anus, her fingers slipping deeper into the very core of my naked body as Becky continued to pump out her juices of orgasm. As Julie's fist was finally sucked deep into my bowels, the delicate tissue of my anus gripping the girl's wrist, I gasped through a mouthful of vaginal flesh. I couldn't take it. I was going to tear open, I—

'Here it comes,' Becky giggled. I didn't know what she meant, what she was talking about. Until golden liquid squirted from her urethral opening and splashed all over my face. A fist up my arse, fingers deep in my cunt, piss raining down on my face . . . This was degradation beyond all comprehension. This was also the beginning of my new life, I was sure as the girls' giggles echoed around the room.

They finally left my naked body drenched in urine, vaginal juice streaming down my thighs. They went into in the kitchen and made sandwiches, laughing and joking about me, what they intended to do to my cunt, my arse. Where was Ian? Had the gang got him? I asked myself the questions fearfully, obsessively. I couldn't believe that, having at last got my hands on the photographs, the gang had then found the box. Ian should never have told me where he'd buried it, I reflected. There again, they'd only have dragged him down to the 'surgery' and tortured the truth out of him. All was lost, I knew as I listened to Sally talking about the boys, the way they were going to fuck my tight arse and pump their sperm deep into my bowels. All was lost.

# 15

Rod and his friends finally arrived. I could hear them laughing in the kitchen, talking about the box they'd dug up from beneath the holly tree on the allotments. That was it, I thought dolefully. I'd lost the evidence I'd needed to destroy the gang. Now what? I contemplated various possibilities as I waited for the arse-fuckings. No news of Ian, no evidence . . . only several cocks fucking my rectal canal to look forward to.

Watching as the naked men filed into the room, their huge cocks fully erect, their purple knobs pointing at the ceiling, I closed my eyes and prayed for someone to rescue me. There was no way out this time, I knew as Rod knelt behind me and scooped up a handful of sex-cream from between the pouting lips of my hot cunt. Massaging my vaginal juices into my anal ring, he pressed his bulbous knob hard against my rectal inlet and breathed heavily as he tried to force his glans past my tightening anal sphincter muscles.

'We'll be using the vacuum pump on your pussy lips every day,' Julie said as Rod's purple plum finally slipped into the tight tube of my hot rectum. 'Men just love hairless pussies. And they crave huge, swollen cunt lips. We'll have your fanny looking like a small bottom,' she giggled as she watched Rod's solid penile shaft driving deep into my arse.

'We'll vacuum pump your tits as well,' Sally rejoined as Rod pushed his cock fully home, his knob absorbing the inner heat of my bowels, his heavy balls pressing against the painfully inflated lips of my vagina. 'We're going to earn a fortune from your body, Rachael. Porn pics, prostitution . . . I don't think that things could have turned out better.'

'Kathy will be here soon,' Julie told me. 'She's a terror when it comes to torturing girls. Oh, and Angel and John will also be joining us in our night of lust.'

'And Ted will be here with the doctor,' Sally giggled. 'God, are you going to get fucked tonight! And tomorrow and the next day.'

As Rod began his fucking motions, my tethered body rocking back and forth, I watched Kenny sit with his rolling balls inches from my wide eyes – and from my mouth. His veined shaft was solid, the purple knob glistening in the light as he retracted his foreskin fully. I was going to have to suck out his spunk, I knew as he grabbed his penis by its base and offered his bulbous glans to my gasping mouth. Taking him inside, the tangy salt waking my taste buds, I closed my full lips around the rim of his knob and sucked hard.

He was big, his glans swelling, ballooning within my gobbling mouth as he gripped my head and gasped in his debauched pleasure. Rocking his hips, Kenny fucked my mouth, his knob repeatedly gliding over my wet tongue in time with Rod's anal fucking. Two cocks driving into each end of my tethered body, the girls laughing as they watched the sexual abuse, I wondered how many men would fuck and spunk my tight orifices before I grew old and the gang discarded me. The anal fucking halting as I pictured dozens of men queueing to fuck my mouth, I suddenly realized what was happening.

'She can take it,' Julie giggled as a second swollen knob pressed against my already stretched anal ring. 'Go on, Brad, force your cock in alongside Rod's and double-fuck the slut's tight arsehole.'

'It's going in,' Sally trilled excitedly as the delicate tissue surrounding my anal inlet expanded. 'Oh, yes. It's going right up her dirty little arse.'

Squeezing my eyes shut as the two cocks drove fully home, stretching my anal canal to the limit, I felt several fingers delve into the restricted sheath of my hot cunt. My sex holes bloated, I jumped as someone slapped my buttocks with the palm of their hand. More hands reaching beneath my naked body and painfully squeezing and pulling on the sensitive protrusions of my milk teats, the girls' laughter reverberating around the room, I realized again that this was what my life now consisted of. Crude sex, forbidden sex, fucking, spunking, bondage, whipping, cruel abuse . . .

'Oh, it looks like I'm just in time,' a male voice said as its owner entered the room. I couldn't take any more cocks.

'John!' Sally trilled. 'Where's Angel?'

'She's on her way. Looks like you've all started without me.'

'We couldn't wait,' Kenny gasped, his cockhead swelling within my hot mouth as he neared his orgasm. 'And I don't think I can wait any longer. Christ, here it comes.'

Gobbling for all I was worth as his glans throbbed and his spunk gushed from his knob-slit, I repeatedly swallowed his orgasmic liquid. The two cocks ramming deep into my arse suddenly erupting in orgasm, I could feel my bowels flooding with spunk as the men behind me gasped and let out long moans of debased pleasure. The sperm-squelching sound of my abused rectum filling my ears as I slurped and swallowed, fingers squishing my vaginal juices, I shuddered as my own orgasm erupted within the pulsating bulb of my clitoris.

Again and again, waves of pure sexual pleasure rolled through my tethered body as I drank the spunk from Kenny's throbbing knob and my anal throat swallowed its double load of creamy semen. I felt as if my entire body was awash with sperm, as if I was drowning in a sea of spunk, as my orifices bubbled and overflowed with the products of three male orgasms. Two cocks thrusting deep into my burning rectal duct, another driving its throbbing knob to the back of my throat, my clitoris pumping shock waves of sex throughout my trembling body, I thought that I was going to pass out as my orgasm peaked.

Finally pulling his spent knob out of my sperm-flooded mouth, Kenny moved to one side to make way for John. Spunk dribbling down my chin, I took the next cock into my mouth and sucked hard. John gasped and writhed as I snaked my wet tongue over the velvety surface of his fresh knob. He was young, I thought, eyeing the hairless flesh of his mons as I sucked and gobbled on his bulbous glans. But not as young as he'd made out at the cottage.

'Suck it hard, bitch,' he murmured, clutching my head and driving his swollen knob to the back of my throat. 'Bite it, suck it, take it right down your throat and swallow my spunk.'

'Do it,' Sally giggled. 'Force your knob down her throat.'

I couldn't believe what was happening to me as John's glans slipped down my throat with ease. Breathing through my nose, I could feel the solid globe of his purple glans inside my throat, the root of his huge shaft stretching my lips to capacity. Withdrawing until my lips encompassed the rim of his helmet, he glided into me again until his knob bloated my throat. As he repeatedly withdrew his cock and drove his glans down my throat, I could feel the lump of his knob inside my neck, bulging like an Adam's apple as he throat-fucked me.

'People will pay well for this,' Julie murmured, watching his knob plunge down my throat. 'I thought *I* was good, but she's incredible.'

'You're right,' Sally said. 'Men will pay very well for a genuine deep-throat-fucking.'

'She's going to be a real asset,' John gasped, his balls battering my chin with every thrust of his penile shaft. 'Does she eat cunt as well as she sucks cock?'

'Oh, yes,' Becky rejoined. 'She eats cunt and sucks clit *extremely* well.'

They were talking about me as if I wasn't there, as if I was a lump of female meat to be fucked and spunked. I realized that was all I was to them as John let out a gasp and I felt his spunk pumping down my throat. His spunk shooting down into my stomach, I'd no need to swallow as he repeatedly drove his throbbing knob down my throat. The two cocks finally slipping out of the fiery sheath of my rectum, sperm bubbling from my inflamed anal eye, I shuddered as my clitoris transmitted ripples of sex deep into my contracting womb.

I was done, I mused as John withdrew his knob from my throat. I was done, fucked, spunked, used, abused

... The 'doctor' was joining us, I reflected. And Ted and Angel and ... How many more were calling round to pump my arse full of spunk, to flood my mouth with vaginal juice? Again wondering where Ian was as Sally released the strap running across my back, I managed to haul my aching body up from the sofa. Kneeling in front of the girl, I looked up at her as she laughed.

'How could you ever have thought that you'd beat us?' she said mockingly. 'A filthy little slut like you, how could you beat the Brook Street Gang?'

'She needs another good thrashing,' Julie hissed.

'And I think it's my turn to do it,' Kathy chortled, grabbing the branch and holding it above her head. 'Stand the bitch up, bend her over and I'll thrash her arse until it glows fucking red.'

'Our pleasure,' Rod replied.

As Rod and Kenny dragged me to my feet and forced me to bend over and touch my toes, I felt spunk gushing from the gaping ring of my anus and running down between the pouting lips of my vagina. I couldn't take another thrashing, I knew as Kathy stood by my side and brushed the rough branch over my projected buttocks. Forcing my feet wide apart, Sally flashed me a wicked grin as I gazed at her between my parted legs.

'I told you,' she said as Kathy raised the branch above her head. 'I told you that you'd never win. By the way, I was talking to Dave Bryant today. I'm stepping in as your replacement until he can find someone else. I'm hoping that, by the time I've got my hands on his cock and got to know him a little better, he'll promote me to deputy managing director.'

'He wouldn't do that,' I returned. 'A filthy, pigshitignorant slut like you run the Southmoore office complex? You must be joking.'

'You want to watch your mouth, bitch,' Sally hissed. 'OK, Kathy, do your worst. When you've finished, I'll give the whore-slut the thrashing of her fucking life.'

The branch swishing through the air and landing across my naked buttocks with a loud crack, I let out a scream. Again, the bitch brought the branch down, obviously delighting in my plight as my screamed protests resounded around the room. The rough leaves catching the back of my legs, I tried to stand upright but Julie held me in the degrading position. My naked body doubled over, the lips of my cunt bulging, the branch repeatedly lashed the sensitive cushions of my vulva. Again and again, the branch whipped my burning buttocks, the backs of my stinging thighs, the swollen pads of my outer labia. I could feel my clitoris retreating beneath its protective hood as I tensed my muscles. The juice of my pussy streaming down, a gush of urine joined it to splatter my inner thighs as the rough branch bit into the soft cushions of my pussy lips.

'Please, no more,' I begged Kathy as she giggled wickedly. Ignoring me, she continued with the gruelling thrashing as my urine splashed over the carpet between my feet and the audience laughed uncontrollably. This was far worse than anything the gang had forced me to endure at school, I reflected, the sound of the swishing branch seeming actually to hurt my mind. Again and again, she beat me. On and on went the merciless thrashing until my naked body crumpled to the floor.

'There's a problem,' Becky said, returning from the kitchen with the box of photographs.

'What's wrong?' Sally asked the girl.

'The photographs . . .'
'What about them?'
'Most of them are missing.'
'*What?*' Sally gasped, snatching the box. 'Fucking hell. Apart from a few photos, the box is full of screwed-up newspaper.' Looking down at me as I cowered on the floor, she swung her foot and kicked my naked buttocks. 'Where are they?' she asked me. 'Where the fuck are they?'

'I . . . I don't know,' I stammered.

'She said that Ian had buried the box,' Becky said. 'He must have taken them out and—'

'Shit,' Sally spat. 'He's *your* husband, Julie. Where do you reckon he is?'

'God knows,' Julie sighed. 'After breaking out of Dave's house, he could have gone anywhere.'

*Breaking out?* I mused. That was the best news I'd heard. If Ian was free, then . . . But did he know about Becky? Did he know where she lived? It seemed that the gang kept things from Ian. Probably because they didn't trust him. He had never been a real member of the gang, I reflected. At school, he'd been more of an unwilling hanger-on than an active member. Where had he hidden the photographs? As Sally paced the floor, spitting expletives, I pondered this crucial question. And where was Ian hiding?

'It's no good asking her,' Sally said, kicking my buttocks again. 'It's Ian we need to get our hands on. Does he know about this place?'

'I don't think so,' Julie replied.

'You don't think so? Does he or doesn't he? He's *your* husband, for fuck's sake.' Sally was upset enough to be repeating herself.

'Yes, and I had no idea that he was screwing that slag. I don't *own* him, Sally.'

'That's true,' I murmured.

'Shut the fuck up,' Julie hissed, spitting at me. 'You'll pay for this, you fucking whore.' Turning to Sally, she placed her clenched fists on her hips. 'We've had nothing but trouble since that little slut arrived. She escaped from Ted's cottage, she's been fucking my husband . . .'

'And sucking his cock,' I said. 'We've been fucking behind your back all along. Before I came back to Southmore, he was fucking Sally behind your back.'

'He was . . . Is that true, Sally?'

'No, of course it's not. The fucking cow's lying.'

'Am I?' I muttered, grinning. I knew that planting seeds of doubt might cause a rift between the two gang leaders as I looked up at Sally. 'Ian said that you'd been after him for years. Sucking his cock, offering him your cunt . . . You wanted Julie out of the gang.'

'I did *not*,' Sally retorted. 'She's trying to cause trouble.'

'I never did trust you, Sally,' Julie said. 'The times Ian used to go out and . . . He was meeting you, wasn't he?'

'Don't be ridiculous. Ian's the last man I'd want.'

'You've always wanted me out of the way. You like to run things, be in charge and—'

'Fuck off, Julie. Just because you ended up marrying a prat—'

'There's no point in arguing,' Kathy broke in. 'Whatever Ian did or didn't do is beside the point. We have to get the photographs back.'

'She's right,' Rod said, walking into the room. He'd put his clothes back on. 'We have to find Ian. We'll go and look for him. You girls stay here and keep an eye on her.'

Once the men had left the cottage, I crawled across the floor and sat in the armchair. Without the photographs, Sally was fucked, I reflected. Wondering again where Ian had got to, I concealed a grin as Sally left the room. Julie followed, shouting and hurling accusations at the other girl as they went into the kitchen. Kathy and Becky joined the others, doing their best to calm them down. They were so busy arguing that they seemed to have forgotten about me. Leaving the chair, I grabbed the dress I'd been wearing earlier and slipped it over my head. The chances of my creeping out of the cottage without being noticed were slim, but it was worth trying.

Stepping into my shoes, I peered around the door into the hall. The girls were in the kitchen, the argument in full swing. Eyeing the front door, I moved slowly along the hall and turned the handle. To my surprise, the door opened, the cool night air filling my nostrils as I slipped out of the cottage and closed the door behind me. I could still hear the girls shouting as I hurried into the lane. Running like the wind towards Southmoore, I had no idea where I was going or what I was going to do when I got there. All that mattered was that I was free, at long last.

Heading for the common, I knew that the girls would go mad once they discovered that I'd escaped. Unless . . . Was this a trick? I became suspicious, noticing a car pulling up a hundred yards or so away. Were they hoping that I'd lead them to Ian? If Rod and the others had been in hiding and had then followed me . . . I couldn't lead them to Ian, I reflected. But they might grab me again and . . . I couldn't allow myself to fall into their hands again. Walking across the common, I had the crazy notion of hiding in the woods. I should have gone into the middle of town, I thought. I'd probably have been safer among people.

'Fiona?' a man called as I neared the woods. 'Fiona, that is you?'

'Dave,' I breathed as he approached. 'Dave, am I pleased to see you!'

'What the fuck are you up to? Look at the state of you.'

'I know, I know. Let's go to your car and . . . Just get me away from here.'

'All right,' he sighed. 'I received your resignation, Fiona. What the fuck is this all about?'

'I'll tell you everything once we're in the car. What are you doing here?' I asked him as we walked across the common.

'I've been at the office, your office. Things are in a right mess. Without you . . . I take it that you *are* coming back?'

'Yes, yes, I am. I didn't resign, Dave. I was forced to . . . I'll tell you when we're safely in the car.'

As we drove out of Southmoore, I explained everything to Dave. His initial reaction was to suggest that we go to Becky's cottage and sort the girls out. And then he wanted to go to the pervert's house and deal with the man. Once he'd calmed down, he parked the car outside a country pub and asked me what I thought we should do. I couldn't go into the pub looking like a tramp. And I couldn't go home . . . I didn't know what to do.

'We'll have to get this sorted out,' he sighed. 'This Ian bloke. Where do you reckon he might have gone?'

'I have no idea,' I murmured.

'Shit, I could do with a drink. You don't look too bad. Shall we—'

'Dave, I stink of piss. I'm not going into a pub like this.'

'I suppose you do pong a bit. What the fuck are we going to do? It seems to me that the answer is to get hold of these photographs. No photographs, no blackmail . . . Where does Ian live?'

'He lives . . . He wouldn't have gone home, surely? If his wife . . . OK, turn the car round and head back to Southmoore. I reckon that it's worth a try.'

As Dave drove back to town, I became even more sure that Ian wouldn't have gone home. That would have been the first place that Rod and the others would have checked. Ian probably had a friend somewhere, I mused. This was going to be like searching for a needle in a haystack. Feeling despondent, I tried to look on the bright side. I was safe, I still had my flat and my job . . . My job? I could hardly go back to the office knowing that I was a hunted woman. I was a fucking fugitive, I thought anxiously as I directed Dave to Ian's house. Pulling up a few yards from the front gate, he asked me what I was going to do.

'You'd better not ring the bell,' he said. 'This street gang or whatever they call themselves might be there.'

'The place is in darkness,' I sighed. 'We're wasting time. I'm wasting *your* time, Dave. I'm sorry.'

'No problem,' he chuckled. 'I only have my wife to go home to and that's not something I'm looking forward to. OK, so where to now?'

'I don't know. Until I speak to Ian and get hold of the photographs . . . Lucy,' I breathed pensively. 'Lucy Barlow.'

'Who?'

'Dave, drive out of the town back towards that pub we stopped at.'

'I thought you said that you didn't want to go into the pub looking like that?'

'We're not going to the pub.'

'That's a shame. I really do need a drink.'

'If I'm right, we'll have a drink later. After I've seen Lucy.'

'Sounds good to me. Right, let's go.'

*Royston Farm*, I mused, recalling Becky's words. Why had she said that Lucy had nothing to do with the gang? Ian had said that he got on well with Lucy. *I slip her information, keep her posted about what's going on.* He'd hardly get it wrong. He'd said that Lucy was running things so . . . I'd seen her in the kitchen, I reflected. She must have been planning to move out, so why hadn't she taken the photographs with her? If she was running the show, if she knew where the box was hidden . . . It was no good trying to guess, I decided, directing Dave to the farmhouse. Asking Dave to wait in the car as he pulled up at the end of the drive to Royston Farm, I opened the door and climbed out.

'Are you sure that you want me to wait here?' he asked me. 'It's fucking dark out there.'

'I'm not bothered about the dark,' I giggled nervously. 'Well, I suppose I am but . . . I'll be all right, Dave. Wait there and, if I don't come back within—'

'OK, don't worry. If you don't come back, I'll . . . Shit, I don't know what I'll do. I could do with a drink, I know that.'

'So could I, for fuck's sake. I won't be long, I hope.'

'Any chance of a blow job when you get back?'

'Dave, I've had more than enough spunk pumped into my body for one day. Later, maybe.'

'Great. I could really do with—'

'I know, I know,' I said, closing the door.

Walking towards the large house, I noticed a light on in what appeared to be the lounge. Hoping that Lucy was in, I prayed for Ian to be there too. Peering through the lounge window, I couldn't see anyone. The television was on, so someone must have been in the house, I mused. Moving to the front door, I reckoned that the house was worth a fortune. Lucy had done well, very well. At other people's expense, of course. Finally plucking up the courage to ring the bell, I stepped back and waited.

Lucy opened the door and flashed me a knowing smile as if she'd been expecting me. She was wearing a short dress . . . silk, turquoise, expensive. Her long auburn hair cascading over her shoulders, her make-up impeccable, she looked absolutely stunning. Inviting me in, she led me through the huge hall to the lounge. Surrounded by antique furniture, I looked around the room in awe. She'd done extremely well, I thought, wondering whether I'd walked straight into a trap. At least I had Dave waiting outside, which made me feel a little easier.

'Rachael Michaels,' she murmured, pouring me a glass of wine. 'You look . . . you look nothing like you did at school.'

'I'm a mess,' I sighed as Lucy passed me a drink. 'I don't usually go around looking like this.'

'I'm sure you don't. Sit down. I think we need to talk.'

'Yes, we do,' I said, losing myself in a huge leather armchair. 'Is Ian here?'

'Ian's all right, you have no need to worry. I hear that you've been causing trouble.'

'*Me*? Well, I . . .'

'Ian told you that I'm the gang leader. He also said that Sally and the others don't know what I get up to.'

'Yes, that's right. He told me that you run things but the others—'

'He was partially right,' Lucy interrupted me, her blue eyes sparkling. 'Sally is nothing but a slut, and so is Julie. All they're interested in is sex and drinking too much.'

'And you're not?' I asked her. 'Into sex, I mean.'

'Not the way those sluts are into crude sex. And the money they've had over the years . . . They spend, spend, spend. Drink, holidays abroad, going out and wasting money . . . As you might have gathered, I've been prudent with my cash. Sally and the others are stony-broke. They live from hand to mouth, which is something I've never done and never will. I've invested my money in property, Rachael.'

'*Your* money? Don't you mean the money you've screwed out of your blackmail victims?'

'I don't blackmail people,' she laughed. 'Sally and the others are into that, not me.'

'But Ian said . . .'

'Ian doesn't know everything, Rachael. Sally has fucked up time and time again. She gets pissed, puts the others at risk with her antics . . . She's a nightmare. I don't interfere. I just let her get on with it.'

'So you have nothing to do with the gang?'

'No, I don't. I keep my eye on them, of course. Ian updates me, tells me what they're up to, what their plans are. I run my own business, Rachael.'

'Oh?'

'I work here, from home. I'm not going to tell you what I do because it's none of your business.'

'I heard that you left Kenny.'

'Kenny!' Lucy laughed mockingly. 'He's a fool. They're all fools. Kenny's only interest is sex. Sex with young girls, sex with anyone and everyone. I stayed with him because it suited me. I no longer have any use for him, so I left him. I don't think he's even noticed that I've gone. But that's another matter. The point is, what do *you* want to do?'

'I . . . I don't know. I mean, I can't stay in Southmoore.'

'You came back to Southmoore to run the new office,' she said, refilling my glass. 'Isn't that what you want do?'

'It *was*. I was planning to move down here and . . . well, things have obviously changed. I daren't even go out, let alone go back to the company. Too many people know me now. Too many people are after me. Apart from Sally and the gang, there's a pervert living in a huge house . . .'

'The doctor?'

'You obviously know him.'

'I know him, all right. He's my father.'

'*What?*'

'The others don't know who he is. As far as they're concerned, he's nothing more than an extremely well-off eccentric pervert. I own the house he lives in.'

'You *own* it? But . . . I don't understand.'

'No, you don't.'

'Does Ian know that the "doctor" is your father?'

'No one knows, apart from you. You're very attractive, Rachael. Would you consider working with me?'

'I don't know what it is you do.'

'I'm a prostitute. A high-class prostitute.'

'God, I . . . I had no idea.'

'No one has any idea. The choice is yours. You can either work with me, or . . .'

'Or what? Is this a threat?'

'No, of course it's not. Ian likes you very much. Do you feel the same about him?'

I wondered: did I feel the same? I wasn't sure what I felt. My life had been turned upside down, ripped apart, since I'd returned to Southmoore. I didn't know what – or whom – I wanted any more. But why was Lucy taking such an interest in me? She obviously had no intention of handing me over to Sally. Far from it, in fact. *A prostitute?* I thought, gazing at her breasts swelling the tight material of her dress. She had good legs, long and . . . *A prostitute?*

I didn't know what was going on. Dave was sitting outside, waiting for me, the gang were hunting me, Ian . . . Where the hell was Ian? The pervert was Lucy's father? And she owned the huge house he lived in? All along, I'd thought that Sally was the clever one, the one who'd made money, bought property and . . . But she had a solicitor. The papers had been drawn up for the sale of my flat. I was confused.

'Well?' Lucy said. 'Do you feel the same about Ian?'

'I . . . Yes, I think so.'

'What is it that you want, Rachael? Given the opportunity, would you like to carry on working at the medical supply company and live here, in Southmoore?'

'Well, yes but . . .'

'But you're worried about the Brook Street Gang?'

'Of course I'm worried about them. For Christ's sake, they—'

'Take a look over there, on the table.'
'What is it?' I asked her, leaving the armchair and walking to the huge table. 'God, it's . . .'
'The photographs.'
'Lucy . . . Where the hell did you get them from?'
'Ian gave them to me for safe keeping.'
'He's here?'
'Before we go any further, I think that you'd better tell Dave Bryant that you're staying here for the night.'
'How do you know . . . I suppose you know everything.'
'Not quite. You can't leave him sitting out there all night.'
'No, I can't. OK, I'll go and talk to him.'
'And, when you come back, I think you'd better take a shower.'
'Yes, I will.'
'You don't want to work with me, do you?'
'Work as a . . . No, no, I don't.'
'OK, the choice is yours. Go and see your boss. Oh, and tell him that you'll be in the office tomorrow morning as usual.'
'But . . .'
'That *is* what you want, isn't it?'
'Yes, of course, but—'
'Just do it, Rachael.'
Dave was understanding, but very concerned for my safety. He didn't like the idea of leaving me there with Lucy. But we finally agreed that he'd pick me up in the morning and drive me to the Southmoore office. If something happened to me, if I wasn't at Lucy's house the following morning, then he'd call in the police. He was also a little disappointed because he wasn't going to

get a blow job. He'd done a lot for me, gone out of his way to . . . Unzipping his trousers, I hauled his cock out and leaned over.

Taking his purple plum into my wet mouth, I ran my tongue around its rim and sucked gently. He breathed deeply, clutching my head as I gobbled on his knob and kneaded his heavy balls. Could I be faithful to Ian? I thought hard, bobbing my head up and down and mouth-fucking myself. Ian and I weren't an item, I reflected. We were . . . I didn't know what we were. Dave let out a long, low moan of satisfaction and pumped my mouth full of sperm. Whatever Ian and I were, I had to keep the boss happy.

'I'll see you in the morning,' I said, licking my sperm-glossed lips.

'God, I needed that,' Dave breathed, zipping his trousers. 'No matter what happens, we'll still . . . well, you know.'

'I don't see why not,' I replied. 'You're the boss, so I have to do as you tell me.'

'You're great, Fiona. We're a team, don't you reckon?'

'We like oral sex, Dave.'

'Talking of which, how about me giving you a good licking-out?' he chuckled. 'We've never . . . Isn't it about time we fucked?'

'I'll see you in the morning,' I said, climbing out of the car. 'You're the boss, so I have to do as you say,' I added, closing the door.

As Dave drove off, I walked back to Lucy's house with a smile on my spermed lips. I liked Dave, and he obviously liked me. Or, I should say, he liked my mouth. At least he knew where I was, I reflected, closing the front door and making my way to the lounge. Was I walking into another trap? Dave knew where I was, he knew all there was to know about the gang . . . I was safe enough. But how the hell could I be safe with the Brook Street Gang searching for me?

After a shower and a meal, Lucy and I sat in the lounge, talking about the gang. I still had no idea where Ian was, but Lucy assured me that I'd see him before long. We chatted about our schooldays, our lives, as we sipped wine and relaxed. Lucy had never been in the gang, she told me. She'd hung around, getting ideas, and then started her own moneymaking schemes. Namely, selling her young body to men for sex.

'When I realized how much men loved schoolgirls, I went for it,' she said. 'I used to make out that I was far younger than I was and dress up in little-girlie clothes. I shaved, of course, and the old men lapped it up. Literally.' She giggled as the wine took effect. 'I soon realized that there was a hell of a lot of money to be earned, but I didn't like the idea of hanging around street corners. So, as the years passed, I saved and saved until I had enough to put down on a house. At eighteen years old, I was living in my own property.'

She'd done well, I reflected. But, no matter how much money was involved, prostitution wasn't for me. By the time Lucy was twenty-one, she'd paid off her mortgage and was buying her second house. I have to admit that I was envious. I'd slaved to get where I was. Working all hours for a mere pittance . . . Still, prostitution wasn't for me, I repeated to myself.

'I made a couple of phone calls while you were in the shower,' Lucy said, a grin on her pretty face.

'Oh?' I breathed, wondering whether Sally and Co. were on their way to get me.

'As I told you, I own this house and my father's place. I also own Becky's cottage.'

'God,' I gasped. 'You *have* done well. So, how come Becky's living there?'

'She rents it. Where are you thinking of living now that you're back?'

'I don't know. Lucy, if I go to the office in the morning . . .'

'As I said, I made a couple of phone calls. You have nothing to worry about now.'

'You rang Sally?'

'Yes, I did. I threatened her. In fact, I did more than threaten her. I told her that I'm taking over.'

'Running the gang?'

'Yes.'

'And she accepted that?'

'Seeing as she too is living in one of my properties, she doesn't have any choice. I've thrown Becky out, by the way. I'll see all of them thrown out of town if they don't do as I say. It's getting late, Rachael. I think I'll go to bed.'

'And me. I have to go to work tomorrow. It'll seem strange, going back.'

'You'll be all right. After all, you're the boss.'

'Yes, yes, I am.'

Following Lucy up the stairs and into a large bedroom, I was surprised to find that she'd laid out some clean clothes for me. She'd taken me under her wing, I mused as she said good night and closed the door. Did she feel sorry for me? Perhaps she'd just had enough of Sally and her antics. Naked beneath the quilt, I closed my eyes and thought about the office. Walker would have to go, I reflected. The bastard had double-crossed me. He'd come to the woods when I needed help and had forced me to suck his cock. The first thing I'd do was sack the bastard, I decided. Unless I kept him on as a plaything, I mused. I could make his life hell, I thought happily. Tomorrow was going to be an interesting day.

# 16

'Good morning, Miss Michaels,' the man at reception said as I breezed into the building. Ignoring him, I took the lift to the top floor. It was strange being back after what seemed like a lifetime away, and I wondered what the staff knew, where they thought I'd been. I didn't care what they thought, I decided. Dressed in a short skirt and blouse, I looked good. Ready to face anyone, anything.

Opening my office door, I walked into the room and looked around me. I hadn't thought that I'd ever see the place again, let alone work there. I had Lucy to thank, I mused, sitting at my desk and grabbing the phone. Ordering a cup of coffee, I wondered again whether I could trust her. She might have wanted me back in my office so that she could control me and, eventually, control the company. Perhaps she had some long-term plan where . . . No, the idea was crazy. My imagination was working overtime. Wasn't it?

'Oh,' Walker gasped in surprise as he entered with a tray. 'I . . . er . . .'

'Put it on the desk, Walker,' I told him.

'I thought Sally was—'

'You thought Sally was what, Walker?' I asked, glaring at him. 'Did you expect to find her here, sitting at my desk?'

'Well, I . . . I'll clear my desk and leave.'

'Leave? I don't want you to leave, Walker. I want you to stay here and work for me.'

'But after . . .'

'Ma'am. You'll call me ma'am, Walker.'

'Yes, ma'am.'

'You're a fucking little shit, Walker. I asked you to come to the woods to help me and you . . . You're a fucking little shit. Pour my coffee.'

'Yes, ma'am.'

Watching his trembling hand as he poured the coffee, I knew that I was back in my domain. *The bitch from hell*, I reflected. But I was more of a bitch now than ever. Sack Walker? Oh, no. He wasn't going to get off that lightly. He was going to be my slave. Recalling his solid cock as he'd mouth-fucked me in the woods, I felt my clitoris stir, my juices of arousal seep between the knickerless lips of my vagina. I didn't like wearing panties at the best of times, particularly in the summer. As Walker placed a cup of coffee in front of me, I pondered on his massive cock. The bastard might come in useful in more ways than one, I mused.

'Get on the floor,' I ordered him. 'On all fours.'

'On the floor?' he said, his expression one of puzzlement. 'But, ma'am . . .'

'Just do it, Walker,' I snapped, moving my chair back from the desk. 'That's it. Now crawl beneath my desk like a dog,' I ordered. There was a so-called modesty board fitted to the desk, so anyone entering my office wouldn't see him. 'Go on, Walker. Crawl beneath my desk like the fucking dog you are.'

Complying, he crawled beneath my desk and looked up at me. He must have thought me crazy, wondering what the hell I was up to. Moving my chair forward, I lifted my short skirt up and exposed my hairless sex slit to his dark-eyed gaze. My thighs parted wide, I could feel my clitoris swelling expectantly as I moved forward on my chair, offering him the gaping crack of my vagina. His tongue hanging out, his eyes bulging, he stared in disbelief at my blatantly exposed femininity. I could see that he was totally confused. And he was obviously wondering why I hadn't sacked him.

'Now lick me, Walker,' I ordered him, reclining in my swivel chair. 'You're a fucking lump of stenching shit. You're a fucking dog. And I shall treat you like a dog. Now, lick my cunt out.'

His breath hot against my pouting pussy lips, he pushed his tongue out and repeatedly lapped at my wetting vaginal crack. I was enjoying my first day back, I mused, closing my eyes as he expertly licked the swelling nubbin of my clitoris and lapped up my flowing juices of lust. This wasn't what I was supposed to be doing, I thought, eyeing a pile of papers on my desk as I listened to the soft slurping sounds of my dog's wet tongue. But there was plenty of time to work, I mused, my breathing fast and shallow as my juices flowed.

'Oh, you're here,' Tim Black said as he knocked and entered.

'Yes, yes, I am,' I replied, doing my best to conceal my satisfaction as he stood in front of my desk.

'Did you enjoy your break?'

'Break? Oh, yes, yes, I did. What is it that you want?'

'Sally asked me to—'

'Sally is no longer here,' I snapped. 'I don't even want to hear her name.'

'Oh, right. Er . . . here are the papers she asked . . . the papers concerning the Spanish deal. I thought you might want to check them.'

'Yes, I do. That will be all, Tim.'

'Yes, of course. By the way, I'm short of two girls now that Julie and—'

'And I need a personal secretary,' I sighed as my dog's tongue snaked into the drenched sheath of my spasming cunt. 'Don't worry, I'll deal with it.'

'Right, thanks. We're pretty busy and without staff—'

'I said, I'll deal with it.'

'Thanks.'

As Tim Black left and closed the door behind him, I lay back in my chair and opened my thighs wide as Walker slipped two fingers into the tightening sheath of my wet cunt and licked the sensitive tip of my clitoris. He was good, I mused as he sucked and mouthed on the solid nubble of my clitoral bulb. *My personal lap dog.* I laughed inwardly as the birth of my orgasm stirred deep within my rhythmically contracting womb. I'd use him to satisfy my feminine needs. I'd also use him when I needed a mouthful of spunk. He'd obviously derive pleasure from pleasuring me, I reflected. He'd be only too happy to fuck my mouth when I needed to taste and swallow sperm. He'd enjoy coming to my office and performing. But I'd still make his life hell.

My clitoris pulsating as I teetered on the brink of my climax, I massaged the swell of my breasts through my blouse as I gasped and writhed in my chair. My juices squelching as the bastard finger-fucked my contracting cunt, my clitoris suddenly erupted in a massive orgasm. Letting out stifled whimpers of pleasure as my entire body shook uncontrollably, I could feel my orgasmic fluid gushing from my inflamed cunt, splattering my naked inner thighs as my 'dog' licked and fingered my sex-hungry cunt.

Walker would have to lick my thighs clean, I decided, my pleasure rolling through my trembling body as he sustained my orgasm with his pistoning fingers and lapping tongue. He was useless as far as the company was concerned, but pretty good at attending my intimate needs. What I needed was a personal secretary who . . . *A lesbian*, I thought as my orgasm peaked, transmitting shock waves of pure sexual bliss deep into my pelvis. A beautiful young girl who could type and use a computer. And eat pussy.

'Enough,' I finally gasped as I shuddered my last orgasmic shudder. Walker's fingers slipped out of my sex-drenched cunt with a loud sucking sound as I pushed my chair back. I kicked him. 'Clean me,' I ordered him, kicking him again. 'Lick the cream off my cunt lips and my thighs.' He lapped at the swell of my wet outer lips like a trained dog, running his tongue over the naked flesh of my thighs until I ordered him to stop. He looked up at me, obediently awaiting my next instruction.

'Now get out of my office,' I hissed. Walker crawled out from beneath the desk and leaped to his feet as I pulled my skirt down and sat upright. 'Get out,' I ordered again. He looked puzzled, confused. 'I'll call you when I need you.'

'Yes, ma'am,' he said, licking his cunny-wet lips.

Once he'd gone, I grabbed the phone and rang Tim Black. There was a girl I'd seen in his department, a young girl with big blue eyes and long blonde hair. Not wanting to waste time advertising for a secretary, I decided to steal one of Tim's girls. The qualities required in a personal secretary were few and simple. Beautiful, sensual, young, lesbian . . . and able to type, of course. Tim wasn't at all happy as I described the girl to him and ordered him to send her to my office.

'I'm already short of staff,' he complained.

'And now you'll be even shorter,' I snapped. 'This girl. What's her name?'

'Angela,' he replied. 'I can't do without her. She's excellent at her job and—'

'Is she married?'

'Married? Er . . . no. No, she's not.'

'Boyfriend?'

'I don't think so.'

'There was a rumour about her.'

'Oh, that,' he sighed. 'I don't know whether it's true or not.'

'Not married, no boyfriend . . . She might be a lesbian.'

'It's just a silly rumour, Miss Michaels,' he sighed. 'What has that got to do with it?'

'Everything. Nothing. It's just that I like to know my staff. OK, send her up.'

'But . . .'

'I'll replace her, and the others.'

'Soon, I hope.'

'I'll get onto it straight away. Send the girl up.'

When Angela knocked at the door and entered my office, I ordered her to close the door behind her and stand by my side. She was extremely attractive. Her long blonde hair cascading like a curtain of silk over the mounds of her petite breasts, her blue eyes sparkling, her succulent lips curled in a smile as I scrutinized her. She was wearing a white blouse and a very short red skirt. Her legs were long and slender, her naked thighs were beautifully . . . Focusing on her slender fingers, I wondered whether she masturbated, frigged her clitty to orgasm, and pistoned the tight sheath of her sweet cunt with her long fingers. Angela would be my personal secretary, I decided, breathing in the aphrodisiacal scent of her perfume.

'Do you have a boyfriend?' I asked her.

'No, Miss Michaels,' she replied softly.

'Good. I'm looking for a personal secretary, Angela. A presentable girl with no ties, no snivelling brats at home, no marital or relationship problems . . . Do you fit the bill so far?'

'Well, yes. I'm single, no children . . . and I like to think that I'm presentable.'

'I'm looking for a personal secretary who will devote her life to the company. And to me.'

'Are you offering me the job?' she asked, a smile on her pretty face.

'I might be,' I replied, eyeing her ripe nipples pressing through her blouse. 'Are you a lesbian?' I asked her bluntly.

'No, Miss Michaels,' she gasped, obviously shocked by my question.

'You've never experimented sexually with another girl?'

'No, Miss Michaels.'

'That's not what I've heard, Angela. I make it my business to listen to rumours. I like to know what's going on in the company.'

'The rumours aren't true,' she murmured, hanging her head.

'Have you ever been with another girl?'

'No, never.'

'Have you ever thought about another girl? Sexually, I mean?'

'Well, no . . . I mean . . .'

'Tell me the truth, Angela.'

'Yes, when I was at school, I . . . I *did* experiment. It was just—'

'Just what?'

'I was growing up, that's all. I was interested in other girls. Learning, experimenting . . .'

'I'll be blunt, Angela. If your salary was trebled, would you be happy to perform other duties for me?'

'Other duties?' she echoed, her blue eyes reflecting puzzlement.

'Attending my needs – my *feminine* needs.'

'Oh, I see. Well . . . yes, I suppose so.'

'I realize that this is unusual, Angela. But I need more than a personal secretary. Discretion, needless to say, is of paramount importance.'

'Yes, of course.'

'So, do you want the job?'

'Yes, Miss Michaels.'

'Lock the door, please.'

As Angela walked across the room and turned the key in the lock, I focused on the backs of her long legs. She really was a little beauty, I mused, my stomach somersaulting as she stood by my side again. People would do anything for money, I reflected. Everyone had their price and Angela obviously couldn't turn down the prospect of having her salary trebled. Hoping that she'd be discreet, and that she'd enjoy her clandestine duties, I asked her to lift her skirt and pull her panties down.

'Pull my panties down?' she murmured, frowning at me.

'I want to take a look at you,' I said, smiling at her. 'Your other duties, Angela . . .'

'I didn't realize that you meant . . .'

'What's the matter? I thought that you wanted the job?'

'I do, but . . . When you said that I'd be attending your feminine needs, I thought you meant doing your hair and—'

'No, Angela, that's *not* what I meant. Perhaps I can persuade you to take the job,' I murmured, grinning at her as I felt my nasty side surfacing. 'Unless you take the job, you won't have a job at all.'

'You mean, unless I do as you ask, you'll sack me?'

'That sums it up nicely, Angela.'

'But that's blackmail!'

'You have no idea what real blackmail is,' I chuckled. 'I could tell you things about blackmail that would . . . Of course, if I sacked you, you wouldn't get another job in Southmoore. I have influence, Angela. Don't make me use it. Now, lift your skirt up and pull your panties down. In fact, take them off.'

Watching as the girl tentatively lifted her short skirt up over her stomach, I focused on the bulging material of her tight red panties. Hesitating, she slipped her thumbs between the elastic of her panties and her hips and began to pull the red silk down. Reminding her that she wouldn't find another job anywhere – let alone in Southmoore – as she hesitated again, I also told her that the rumours about me were true. I was, indeed, the bitch from hell.

Angela at last tugged her panties right down past her thighs and the flimsy garment finally fell around her ankles. I gazed longingly at the soft swelling of her full sex lips. She was beautiful. Her sparse blonde pubes barely covered her mons, doing little to conceal the sweet crack of her vulva. She stepped away from her panties where they lay on the floor of my office and obediently awaited my next instruction. Ordering her to part the soft lips of her vagina and push her finger deep into her cunt, I moved forward in my chair. Complying with my commands, she opened her vulval crack, exposing the intricate inner folds of her valley of desire to my wide eyes. Her finger slipping between the pink petals of her inner lips and gliding deep into the creamy duct of her cunt, she quivered.

'Are you all right?' I asked her.

'Yes, Miss Michaels,' she breathed.

'Pull your finger out and put it in my mouth,' I said, licking my lips. 'I want to taste you, Angela.'

Slipping her finger out of her wet cunt, Angela held it to my lips. Sucking her juices of arousal from her slender finger, tasting her lubricious cream, I felt my clitoris swelling between my swollen cunny lips. It wasn't only the prospect of lesbian sex that drove me on and sent my arousal soaring. The idea of blackmailing this girl turned me on. Threatening her, coercing her, using and abusing her against her will . . . If she played her cards right, then she'd do well in my employ, I mused. Young, fresh, beautiful, sensual . . . She'd do *very* well. And so would I.

Ordering her to place one foot on my desk, I watched her vaginal crack open as she positioned herself. Leaning forward, I licked her gaping sex crack, lapping up her warm cream as she let out soft whimpers of pleasure. Concentrating on her ripening clitoris, I tongued and sucked the sensitive protrusion of female pleasure as she trembled in her obvious arousal. She tasted heavenly.

Creamy, lubricious, warm . . . I couldn't get enough of her cunt-milk. Ramming two fingers into the hugging sheath of her young cunt, I massaged her inner vaginal flesh as I sucked and mouthed on her solid clitoris. Losing myself in my lesbian arousal, I breathed in the heady scent of her vulva as I continued to massage the inner walls of her tightening vagina.

'I'm coming,' Angela gasped, clutching my head and pushing her hips forward. Her whimpers were now soft and stifled cries of pure sexual ecstasy and as her orgasmic juices flooded over my pistoning fingers, her clitoris exploded in orgasm beneath my snaking tongue. I rammed my fingers again and again into the dripping duct of her beautiful cunt and sucked on her pulsating clitoris until her beautiful young body finally drooped in sexual exhaustion. Slipping her foot off my desk, she swayed on her sagging legs as I slipped my fingers out of her teenage cunt and sucked them clean.

'Well?' I said, my cunny-wet lips curving in a smile. 'Do you want the job?'

'Yes,' Angela breathed softly, clinging to my desk to steady her trembling body.

'I'll keep these,' I said, taking her panties from the floor and slipping them into my desk drawer. 'You are *not* to wear panties in the office – do you understand?'

'Yes, Miss Michaels.'

'And no bra. Do you masturbate?'

'Well, I . . .'

'I'll take that as a yes. Good. I like watching young girls bring themselves off. Right, you have one last test before I give you the job. Unlock the door, and then crawl beneath my desk.'

'Beneath your desk?' she echoed.

'Just do it, Angela.'

As she unlocked the door, I moved my chair back, giving her room to crawl beneath the desk. She knew what was expected of her as she took her position beneath my desk, her sparkling blue eyes looking up at me. Reclining, I pulled my skirt pulled up and parted thighs wide. She was hesitating, I knew as I looked down at her. Gazing at the yawning valley of my cunt, my blatantly bared sex hole, she again looked up at me. Smiling, I nodded my head as I parted the fleshy outer lips of my vulva, offering my sexual centre to her pretty mouth. Leaning forward, she licked my inner flesh, tasting me there, lapping up my sex-milk as I let out a gasp of lesbian pleasure.

'I think you're going to be very happy working for me,' I breathed as she repeatedly swept her wet tongue over the solid nub of my sensitive clitoris. 'Push your fingers into my cunt, Angela. Pleasure me well, and the job's yours.' Following my order, she pushed two fingers into the tight sheath of my cunt and massaged my G-spot. Writhing and gasping, my clitoris rock-hard beneath her snaking tongue, I gripped the arms of my swivel chair as my orgasm exploded and my juices of lust streamed from my finger-fucked cunt.

I was in my element, my domain, I mused, my mind blowing away on clouds of lesbian lust. My body shaking uncontrollably as the teenage girl expertly attended my feminine needs – my *cuntal* needs – I whimpered and gasped as she sustained my incredible pleasure. Shock waves of ecstatic bliss rolled on and on through my young body. My cunt muscles gripping Angela's pistoning fingers, my clitoris pulsating wildly, I gazed at her shiny blonde hair as she tongued, sucked and fingered my insatiable cunt. She was my girl-slave.

Finally drifting down from my sexual heaven, I lay gasping in the chair as Angela sucked the last ripples of sex out of my sated clitoris. Ordering her to lick me gently, to suck out my juices and drink from my burning cunt, I smiled as the phone rang. Instructing Angela to continue her licking, I grabbed the receiver as the girl's tongue lapped up my cunt-milk. To my surprise, I heard Lucky's soft voice. Wondering what she wanted as she asked me whether I was all right, I thought that she might try to threaten or blackmail me.

'Are you all right?' she asked me for the second time.

'Yes, yes – I'm fine,' I replied, listening to the sound of my girl-slave's slurping tongue.

'Becky's moved out of the cottage. I thought you might want to live there.'

'Yes,' I said eagerly. 'That would be great. How much rent do you want?'

'Nothing.'

'You mean I can live there for free?'

'No, no. The place is yours. I'll sign it over to you.'

'*What?*' I gasped. 'Lucy, why are you doing all this for me?'

'Because I like you. I don't like Sally, I don't like what they've done to you . . . You don't have to take the cottage. It's up to you.'

'No, no. I'll take it. But . . .' Was this a trick? 'What do you want in return?'

'Nothing. Don't worry, there are no strings attached. Would you like to come over for dinner this evening? I'll give you the keys to the cottage and—'

'Definitely,' I trilled as Angela thrust two fingers deep into my yearning cunt. 'I'll be there after work.'

'OK, I'll see you this evening.'

'Right, I'll look forward to it.'

Replacing the receiver, I lay back in my chair with my thighs spread wide as Angela's mouth sucked at my ripening clitoris. A huge grin on my face, I couldn't believe that I was going to live in the cottage. But what did Lucy want from me? Was she a lesbian? Was she after my naked body, my wet cunt? No one gave anything away without wanting something in return. Or was I being too cynical?

I was going to come again, I knew as I felt Angela's wet tongue snaking around the solid bud of my clitoris. Her fingers thrusting, her mouth sucking, she was obviously experienced at pleasuring girls, whatever she might have said earlier. 'Never been with another girl,' indeed! The rumours were probably right, I reflected, my lust juices squelching, my clitoris painfully hard. My girl-slave was a lesbian. And that suited me perfectly. My orgasm exploding, my cunt gripping the girl's pistoning fingers, I almost passed out as my mind again blew away on clouds of lesbian lust.

'You're good,' I complimented my new secretary as she sustained my lesbian pleasure. 'Very good.'

'I pleased that you're happy with me,' Angela replied, lapping at my clitoris.

'Excuse me, ma'am,' Walker mumbled as he knocked and entered. 'I thought you might . . .'

'Kneel on the desk,' I breathed. 'Kneel on the desk and get your cock out.'

'On the desk?' he gasped, his dark eyes reflecting his confusion.

'Just *do* it, Walker.'

Following my instructions, he knelt on the desktop in front of me and unzipped his trousers. Hauling his penis out, he retracted his foreskin fully and offered his purple plum to my mouth. I gazed longingly at his sperm-slit as my girl-slave continued her cunny-fingering, her clitoral sucking. Taking his beautiful glans deep into my mouth as Angela brought me to yet another orgasm, I sucked and licked his knob as he looked down and gasped. His rock-hard cockhead bloating my mouth, my lips stretched tautly around his broad shaft, Walker certainly was huge. Gripping his massive organ by its base, I gobbled and sucked for all I was worth as my secret lover lapped at my beautiful clitoris. I was desperate for Walker's spunk to fill my mouth, desperate to drink from his fountainhead.

'Quickly,' I said, slipping his knob out of my mouth and licking his huge ball sac. 'Spunk down my throat, you fucking bastard.' Breathing heavily as I again engulfed his glans within my wet mouth, Walker clutched my head and rocked his hips. I could feel his bulbous knob gliding back and forth over my tongue, his hairy balls tickling my chin, as he mouth-fucked me. Sucking and licking his glans, I wanked his massive cock-shaft to bring out his spunk as Angela expertly finger-fucked my tight young cunt and licked my swollen clitoris.

The tables had turned, I thought happily. *Shove your finger up the fat cow's dirty little cunt. Force the spotty slag to suck the spunk out of your cock. Cumslut, dirty whore, spunk-lover. Greasy-haired tart. Look at her dirty little arsehole. Do you stick your finger up your arse and then suck it clean?* My loathsome schooldays were long gone, I reflected as Walker's sperm jetted from his orgasming knob and filled my cheeks. Had the gang now dispersed? I wondered about that possibility as Angela sucked another massive orgasm from my aching clitoris. Southmoore School, the Brook Street Gang . . . The tables had turned. The bitch from hell was back.

'Now get out of my office, you slimy creep,' I hissed, slipping Walker's spent cock out of my mouth. He clambered off the desk and zipped his trousers as I ordered him again to get out. Waiting until he'd scurried off, I looked down at Angela's cunt-wet face. 'And you can get yourself to your new office,' I ordered her, pushing my chair back. 'Through that door there,' I said, pointing across the room as she crawled out from beneath my desk. 'You're a filthy fucking slut, Angela. When I need your little pink cunt, I'll call you.'

'I thought . . .' she murmured sheepishly. 'Have I done something wrong?'

'On the contrary, you've done everything perfectly. You'll get used to my ways,' I said, giving her a slight smile. 'You'll get used to working for me. Now, take your dirty little cunt to your office and sit on it until I need it.'

Wandering dazedly across the room, Angela disappeared into her office as I pulled my skirt down and licked my sperm-glistening lips. I felt good as I looked around the office, around my domain. Dinner with Lucy that evening, Walker and Angela at my beck and call . . . Grabbing the ringing phone, I was pleased to hear Ian's low voice. Pleased and yet . . . I couldn't be faithful to one man, I knew.

'Lucy's told me everything,' he said.

'Ian, I . . . Thanks for all you've done for me.'

'Any time. How about meeting me this evening for a drink?'

'I'm having dinner with Lucy. Tomorrow, maybe.'

'Maybe? Do I detect a note of—'

'No, no. It's just that I've been through so much lately. I need some time to relax.'

'I'll relax you,' he chuckled. 'I know just where to massage you to relax you.'

'The last thing I want at the moment is sex, Ian,' I sighed, the taste of Walker's sperm lingering on my tongue, the feel of Angela's saliva cooling my outer love lips. 'But we will get together, I promise.'

'I hope so. Sally and her lot have disbanded.'

'Really? Tell me more.'

'The Brook Street Gang no longer exists. Mind you, I reckon that Lucy has a few ideas up her sleeve.'

'That's what worries me. Where are you going to live? I mean, now that Julie . . .'

'I've thrown her out of the house.'

'That's great, Ian.'

'She's gone off with Kenny, of all people. Anyway, I'll call you tomorrow.'

'Ian, I'll . . . I'll meet you on the common at lunchtime, OK?'

'Yes, great.'

'Say, ten past one?'

'I'll be there. Rachael, I . . . I really do like you.'

'I'll see you later,' I said, replacing the receiver.

I didn't know what I felt about Ian, I thought as I rested my chin on my clasped hands. Thinking again that I could never be faithful to one man, I wondered how he'd escaped from the pervert's house. Lucy must have called the 'doctor,' I assumed. She wouldn't hesitate to threaten to throw him out of the house, even though he was her father. There were many unanswered questions, I mused, sifting through the pile of papers on my desk. I'd talk to Lucy over dinner, find out more about . . .

There again, perhaps it was best not to know. The war was over.

'Excuse me, Miss Michaels,' Rogers from the accounts department said as he knocked on the door and entered my office. He was the young man who'd been sent a pornographic photograph of me. It was a shame that he'd seen the evidence of my enforced debauchery. He was good-looking, well-dressed, and good at his job from what I'd heard. I didn't want to have to sack him, but I instinctively knew that he was after something as I locked my gaze to his. I could see blackmail lurking in the dark pools of his eyes. I could smell threats.

'What is it, Rogers?' I asked him.

'I'm hoping for promotion,' he said.

'Oh? And what makes you think that you *deserve* promotion?'

'I'll come straight to the point,' he breathed, looking over his shoulder. 'The photograph . . . I have a copy and—'

'And what, Rogers?'

'Obviously, you don't want people seeing it, discovering your sordid secret.'

'Of course I don't. You hang on to it, Rogers. You can gaze at my naked body as you wank yourself off.'

'*What?*' he breathed, obviously stunned by my remark.

'As you said, I wouldn't want other people to see the photograph. So take good care of it, OK?'

'No, no . . . you don't understand,' he said, forcing a laugh. 'What I'm trying to say is . . . I wouldn't want to have to show people. Of course, if my promotion—'

'Do you know anything about blackmail?' I interrupted him.

'I wouldn't call it blackmail, Miss Michaels. All I want is promotion in return for giving you the photograph.'

'But I don't want the photograph.'

'*You* might not, but I'm sure others would love a copy.'

'How long have you worked for the company?'

'Four years.'

'You don't have a criminal record, do you?'

'No, certainly not,' he replied angrily.

'And you don't want me to sack you?'

'No, I . . . Look, I have a photograph of you—'

'I've been checking up on the company's accounts, Rogers. You've been fiddling the books for years, drawing money and—'

'I have *not*,' he cried indignantly.

'You know that and I know that. But when the police see the figures . . .'

'You can't—'

'Rogers, I *can* and *will* do anything. Now get back to work.'

'You'll be sorry . . .'

'No, Rogers. *You*'ll be sorry if that photograph comes to light. I have a friend who lives in a huge house. He's a doctor, and I'm sure he'd love to experiment on an attractive young man like . . . Don't make me do it, Rogers.'

'Do what?'

'You don't want to know. Keep the photograph. Gaze at my cunt while you wank and shoot your spunk all over your stomach. I hope we don't have to talk about this again. The doctor . . . You may go now.'

As Rogers left, I felt good, even smug. I'd chat to Lucy about her father, I decided. The old pervert might come in very useful. I was sure that he'd be only too happy to experiment on Rogers. Or anyone else who tried to cross me. I'd be forever indebted to Lucy, I knew as I lifted the phone and ordered another cup of coffee. That didn't bother me. If Lucy wanted lesbian sex, then I'd be only too happy to oblige. But I was still feeling anxious about the gang. They might have disbanded, but . . . Answering the phone, I was shocked to hear Sally's voice. My heart racing, my hands trembling, I asked her what she wanted.

'I'd like to work for you,' she murmured.

'Work for me?' I laughed. 'If you think that I'd take you back as my secretary . . .'

'No, I don't mean work for the medical supply company.'

'What, then?'

'Now that you're running the Brook Street Gang . . .'

'Who told you that?'

'Lucy told me. She said that you lead the gang now. She said that you have all the photographs and—'

'I see.'

'The others have dispersed. Kenny and Julie have gone off to Scotland, Rod is setting up as a photographer in London, Becky's going to Canada . . . I'm the only one left.'

*All alone, completely defenceless* . . . 'Really?' I breathed, a grin spreading across my face. 'We'll have to talk about this, Sally. There's a lot of unfinished business . . . Look, ring me this afternoon and we'll arrange to meet.'

'Yes, I'd like that. I have no income now that the gang . . . Anyway, I'll ring you later.'

Life was good, I mused as I hung up. Rachael

Michaels, running the Brook Street Gang? The tables hadn't just turned. They'd been turned upside down. I'd won, I mused as Walker brought in my coffee. Southmoore Town had better look out. The fucking bitch from hell was back – with a vengeance!

# Order These Selected Blue Moon Titles

| | |
|---|---|
| My Secret Life | $15.95 |
| The Altar of Venus | $7.95 |
| Caning Able | $7.95 |
| The Blue Moon Erotic Reader IV | $15.95 |
| The Best of the Erotic Reader | $15.95 |
| Confessions D'Amour | $14.95 |
| A Maid for All Seasons I, II | $15.95 |
| Color of Pain, Shade of Pleasure | $14.95 |
| The Governess | $7.95 |
| Claire's Uptown Girls | $7.95 |
| The Intimate Memoirs of an Edwardian Dandy I, II, III | $15.95 |
| Jennifer and Nikki | $7.95 |
| Burn | $7.95 |
| Don Winslow's Victorian Erotica | $14.95 |
| The Garden of Love | $14.95 |
| The ABZ of Pain and Pleasure | $7.95 |
| "Frank" and I | $7.95 |
| Hot Sheets | $7.95 |
| Tea and Spices | $7.95 |
| Naughty Message | $7.95 |
| The Sleeping Palace | $7.95 |
| Venus in Paris | $7.95 |
| The Lawyer | $7.95 |
| Tropic of Lust | $7.95 |
| Folies D'Amour | $7.95 |
| The Best of Ironwood | $14.95 |
| The Uninhibited | $7.95 |
| Disciplining Jane | $7.95 |
| 66 Chapters About 33 Women | $7.95 |
| The Man of Her Dream | $7.95 |
| S-M: The Last Taboo | $14.95 |
| Cybersex | $14.95 |
| Depravicus | $7.95 |
| Sacred Exchange | $14.95 |
| The Rooms | $7.95 |
| The Memoirs of Josephine | $7.95 |
| The Pearl | $14.95 |
| Mistress of Instruction | $7.95 |
| Neptune and Surf | $7.95 |
| House of Dreams: Aurochs & Angels | $7.95 |
| Dark Star | $7.95 |
| The Intimate Memoir of Dame Jenny Everleigh: Erotic Adventures | $7.95 |
| Shadow Lane VI | $7.95 |
| Shadow Lane VII | $7.95 |
| Shadow Lane VIII | $7.95 |
| Best of Shadow Lane | $14.95 |
| The Captive I, II | $14.95 |
| The Captive III, IV, V | $15.95 |
| The Captive's Journey | $7.95 |
| Road Babe | $7.95 |
| The Story of O | $7.95 |
| The New Story of O | $7.95 |

Visit our website at www.bluemoonbooks.com

## ORDER FORM
**Attach a separate sheet for additional titles.**

Title                                                               Quantity    Price

_____     _____    _____
_____     _____    _____
_____     _____    _____
_____     _____    _____

                          Shipping and Handling (see charges below)  _____
                                       Sales tax (in CA and NY)      _____
                                                         Total       _____

Name _____
Address _____
City _____ State _____ Zip _____
Daytime telephone number _____

❏ Check            ❏ Money Order         (US dollars only. No COD orders accepted.)

Credit Card # _____ Exp. Date _____

❏ MC                        ❏ VISA                              ❏ AMEX

Signature _____
               (if paying with a credit card you must sign this form.)

### Shipping and Handling charges:*
Domestic: $4 for 1st book, $.75 each additional book. International: $5 for 1st book, $1 each additional book
*rates in effect at time of publication. Subject to Change.

Mail order to Publishers Group West, Attention: Order Dept., 1700 Fourth St., Berkeley, CA 94710, or fax to (510) 528-3444.

**PLEASE ALLOW 4-6 WEEKS FOR DELIVERY. ALL ORDERS SHIP VIA 4TH CLASS MAIL.**

**Look for Blue Moon Books at your favorite local bookseller
or from your favorite online bookseller.**